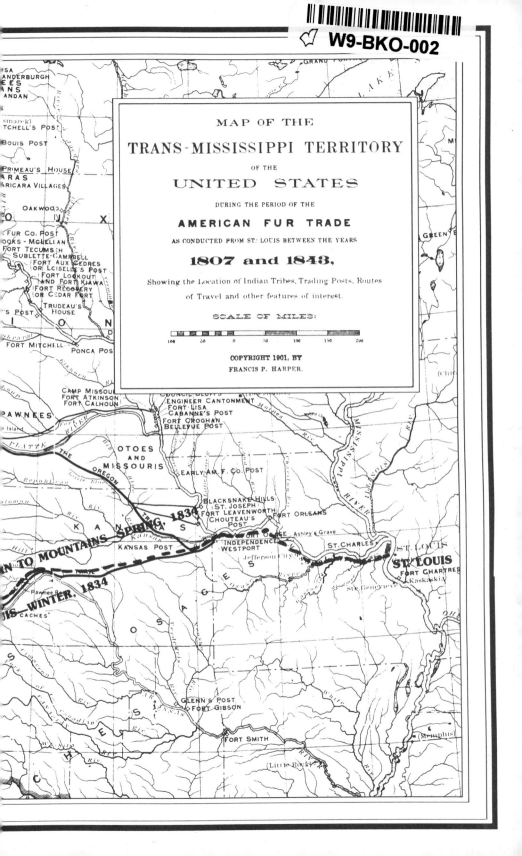

MAP OF THE

TRANS-MISSISSIPPI TERRITORY

OF THE

UNITED STATES

DURING THE PERIOD OF THE

AMERICAN FUR TRADE

AS CONDUCTED FROM ST. LOUIS BETWEEN THE YEARS

1807 and 1843,

Showing the Location of Indian Tribes, Trading Posts, Routes

of Travel and other features of interest.

SCALE OF MILES:

100   50   0   50   100   150   200

COPYRIGHT 1901, BY

FRANCIS P. HARPER.

One-Eyed Dream

THE FRONTIER LIBRARY

One-Eyed Dream (*1988*)
TERRY C. JOHNSTON

Borderlords (*1985*)
TERRY C. JOHNSTON

Carry the Wind (*1982*)
TERRY C. JOHNSTON

The Woodsman (*1984*)
DON WRIGHT

The Misadventures of Silk & Shakespeare (*1985*)
WINFRED BLEVINS

Charbonneau (*1985*)
WINFRED BLEVINS

Across the Shining Mountains (*1986*)
CHRISTIAN McCORD

Buckskin Brigades (*1987*)
L. RON HUBBARD

Yellowstone Kelly: Gentleman & Scout (*1988*)
PETER BOWEN

Farewell Cantuckee (*1988*)
STANFORD SIMMONS

The Stick Floats West (*1989*)
STANFORD SIMMONS

TERRY C. JOHNSTON

One-Eyed

Dream

JAMESON BOOKS, INC.
Ottawa, Illinois

Jameson books are available at special discounts for bulk purchases for sales promotions, premiums, fund-raising, or educational use. Special editions, of book excerpts, can also be created to specification.

ONE-EYED DREAM is the final volume in a trilogy. The two previous novels are CARRY THE WIND and BORDERLORDS.

For information and catalog requests contact:
The Frontier Library
Jameson Books, Inc.
P.O. Box 738
Ottawa, IL., 61350
815 434-7905

10 9 8 7 6 5 4 3 2 1   88 89 90 91

ISBN: 0-915463-38-5

Printed in the United States of America

Distributed by Kampmann & Co., New York City

Librarty of Congress Cataloging in Publication Data

Johnston, Terry C., 1947–
One-eyed dream.

I. Title
PS3560.0392054   1988   813.54   87-37842
ISBN 0-915463-38-5

For a little span
Their life-fires flared like torches in the van
Of westward progress, ere the great wind 'woke
To snuff them. Many vanished like a smoke
The blue air drinks; and e'en of those who burned
Down to the socket, scarce a tithe returned
To share at last the ways of quiet men,
Or see the hearth-reek drifting once again
Across the roofs of old St. Louis town.

—JOHN G. NEIHARDT
The Mountain Men
"The Song of Three Friends"
("Ashley's Hundred")

The spawning Earth
Is fat with graves; and what is one man worth
That fiddles should be muted at his fall?
He should have died and did not—that was all.

—JOHN G. NEIHARDT
The Mountain Men
"The Song of Hugh Glass"
("The Return of the Ghost")

One-Eyed Dream

1 IT CAME, THAT wind, one night, like a living thing, came sneaking in on padded feet, and it was part of the night, like the night creatures, padding about, muzzling in the grasses, slinking over the land, prowling restlessly, prowling in the night.

The wind tormented loose things outside the shelter—the way a little pup would find something to toy with, something to wrestle. The night wind sniffed like a circling wolf, nosing around and slipping over motionless, jutting obstacles, moved along the surface of flat planes, and sought out those cracks it could find in the bedding.

It grew suddenly chill.

Titus Bass sat up at the same instant he heard one of the ponies whicker down on the good grass near the stands of old cottonwoods. He held his breath and shivered as the wind moved along the shelter and buckled, then billowed, the blankets overhead.

Maybe it was his imagination. The wind just woke him up, that's all. Maybe one of the ponies tangled up in its picket rope. He lay back down to listen to the sounds of the night.

After the wind sighed and inhaled to take another breath, the night filled the void with a burst of what was left. The sounds of crickets and tree frogs, small insects in the grasses, sang out, thrummed, buzzed, chirped, perhaps to seal off tiny territories, to attract mates in the web of romance.

Bass turned his head toward the darker recesses of the shelter and heard the young woman snoring softly with a rhythm that almost matched that of his night-nervous heart. After all these years, night sounds still made him skittish. Maybe because Scratch could not put a picture with the noise. Or perhaps because the picture his mind envisioned created even more primeval horrors. But now the wind picked up again and concealed all other sounds from his ears. Bass rolled over and draped an arm across Waits-by-the-Water, inhaling deeply of her fire-smoke and wild musk perfumes.

Why did he let anything intrude upon his being with this woman, his thoughts of her, his loving her? Scratch did not know the answer to that. Finally he let his eyelids droop once more, giving in to fatigue from the previous day's labors. Not even the wind blustering outside would take him from her.

There is a singular place halfway back in a man's mind, along the trail his mind takes on its way to sleep—a place of time when it seems many things happen to yank him up from the deeper recesses of that journey. Bass was there. Warm, content once again. Accustomed finally to the quiet crying of the wind as it made other things noisy.

And suddenly his limbs went tense. The wind slowly subsided, no longer able to conceal the night sounds. Yet, he felt the night around him, felt what it warned him of rather than hearing any distinct sound.

Quickly, as if with years of practice at this, he slid his arm off the woman and rolled to his left. There his hand found the rifles—both of them. His flesh quickened and shivered at the chilly air as the blankets slid off his shoulders. An unfringed shirt was yanked over his head. Bass slipped the tacked knife sheath beneath the belt, over his right kidney. Then his hand found a pistol laid out in the dark.

Good, he thought. Right where it was supposed to be. A finger sought out the lock and found the frizzen snapped down over the pan. That meant the pistol was loaded. Ready. He was, too.

Scratch rolled silently beneath the stretched blanket at the side of their improvised shelter. Then he lay there, letting his eyes and ears adjust to the cool darkness. The old trapper lay flat on his belly, straining his eyes to pick up something that was out of the ordinary, something that didn't belong out there, as he peered through the tall grass and sage toward the trees where the horses were picketed.

A pony whickered again. Sounded just like the buffalo runner to him. Spooky critter, Bass thought. A lot like himself, he smiled. The smile dripped off his lips quickly as another dark shape streaked across the dark blue night horizon to join the pony's legs. It was an arm, reaching up to grasp the picket rope as the pony shied away from the intruder. Now Bass was sure. All the rest had been a warning.

With his rifle held against him, Bass rolled to his left two more times and came to a stop at the edge of Josiah Paddock's shelter. The old trapper reached out to pick up the bottom edge of the blanket, lifting it so he could stick his head inside the shelter.

The cold, metallic, circular shape pressed against the flesh of his brow. It could be nothing else. There was no mistaking the feel of it. The muzzle of a pistol. Then he heard Josiah sigh quietly.

"Damn . . ." Josiah cursed, almost too silently to be heard. "Could have killed you!"

"You 'wake, eh?" Bass had to smile. Almost like a proud parent. All the while he had expected the young trapper to need awakening.

"Just about blew out what you got left for brains—and you ask if I'm awake?"

"C'mon . . ."

"I know," Paddock answered before Bass went on. "I heard it, too."

"I seen 'em, son," Bass said as he began to slither backwards from the shelter. "We got vis'tors payin' us a call."

"Then let's go pay them our respects." Paddock followed Scratch out from beneath the edge of the thick woolen blanket.

They lay beside one another as if it had been planned that way—in concert.

4

Each man, alone in his own thoughts as he sought to control his breathing, strained his eyes into the darkness of the moonless sky. Each fought back that ball of sudden fear, sudden uncertainty, that rose in the throat, choking a man on its distinctive bile. Once the fight started, once the killing began, then it was different. Things had a way of sweeping a man up into them and he took part resolutely. But now—just on the edge of that yawning chasm that was a descent into hell for a man—he had time, however brief, to reflect. And that reflection often made a man ask, Why the killing? Why did it come down to him or me?

The wind came up again. Against the deep blue of the horizon, just above the earth's stage, the two trappers caught the movement and the slash of black forms inked against the sky's canvas. Two were in the ponies. But now a third, then a fourth appeared, riding up atop the mounts they had chosen from the herd. The shifting wind lifted the loose hair that hung over the thieves' shoulders. Not a one among them wore feathers; no decorations could be seen hanging from the long, dancing tresses.

Pony raid, Bass thought. No foofaraw, like they'd wear if they were out after blood and hair. Out for horseflesh only. Been a scalp raid, he mused, why, I just might be pounding sand for the Devil himself right now.

The buffalo runner whinnied loudly and brought Bass up on his knees. A second horse thief came up to help the first control and quiet the Nez Perce pony. As the first brave leapt atop the animal, the second man slashed at the picket rope.

"That do it." Scratch rose to his full height suddenly.

Paddock rose beside him and looked over at the older trapper. "Time to dance?"

"Let's doe-see-doe, son," Bass answered, then brought two fingers to his lips and whistled to the pony.

Responding to the whistle, the buffalo runner suddenly wheeled and trotted toward the trappers' camp. The Indian on the animal's back yanked and sawed at the hackamore, yet none of his cruel, brutal efforts had any effect on the Nez Perce pony as it continued toward the shelters.

The horse thief whacked the side of the pony's head. The horse reared and danced in a crude circle and even though the Indian tried both to hang on and to control the unruly animal at the same time, he fell off anyway.

Bass whistled again for the pony as he saw more dark movement along the blue horizon. Other riders were coming. Two of them came up to trap the pony with the spotted rump, while a third came from behind, pulling a long string of the trappers' ponies with him. Barked orders slashed in the chilly summer night air and Bass felt something familiar slide along his spine. He thought he knew a few of those words spoken. A man might even fool himself into thinking he knew the one who had spoken them.

The older trapper brought the rifle to his shoulder and aimed as best he could at a rider out in the darkness. It was like shooting at shadows: lucky if you hit something, and even if you did, the ball went right on through without hitting anything of substance. A shadow only.

5

A bright meteor of light burst free of the muzzle after a smaller flash spit out of the pan on the rifle's lock. His eyes instantly burned with the sudden, intense light and he shut them reflexively. Bass heard Paddock's rifle bark at the dark forms as he opened his eyes. The next moment he tore off on a dead run toward the intruders.

Scratch realized he was yelling at the horse thieves as he pitched headlong through the darkness. Just like a death song, he thought. Makes a man a little less jumpy, a little less scared when he can make some noise at the enemy.

One of the riders was hit. The Indian slid to the ground like thick honey. Maybe Scratch had hit him, maybe the younger trapper had—didn't matter now. One was down, but there were several more to go. A rider skidded up to help the fallen horse thief. As the rider reached down for his companion, Bass fired the pistol. Another blinding explosion of light erupted as the older trapper stuffed the pistol into his belt.

The riders yelled garbled commands at each other, shouting their death songs at the white men. Scratch bolted off again at the group of horse thieves and milling ponies. The warrior who had come to help that rider bucked from the buffalo runner, weaved from side to side. The thief pulling along a string of ponies was the first to see Bass coming. He gave heels to his own horse and rode off with the entire packstring clattering obediently behind him.

"By God's teeth!" Bass shouted as he watched his animals disappear into the darkness. To his left, Paddock skidded to a running stop, aimed his newly-reloaded rifle, and fired.

"You hit one of them niggers!" the older trapper responded to a yelp of pain from one of the retreating riders over the rumble of Paddock's gunfire. "Let's be sure we got them other two down for good."

He ambled over to the two Indians on the ground while muttering vile curses about horse thieves and lazy Injuns with nothing better to do than steal an honest white man's ponies. Titus kicked the first body that loomed out of the darkness among the sage. The Indian lay stretched on the ground almost as if he had fallen there to go to sleep—legs curled up slightly, one arm tucked under the head for a pillow. The trapper kicked the corpse a second time before kneeling to peer closely at the face and features.

"He dead?" Paddock inquired quietly.

" 'Bout as dead as the bear grease slicked on his hair." Then he rose and vaulted over to the second body.

Grasping the Indian's shirt by the collar, he raised the limp upper body off the ground. Bass studied the features, the hair, and then the clothing. He could not be certain, but he was pretty damned sure.

"You act like you knew him," Paddock commented. He stood over Bass and the horse thief, his wrists crossed over the muzzle of his rifle.

"Not 'sactly, son." Again Bass rose to his feet. "But they look to be Snakes."

"Snakes?" Josiah wheezed. "Why they taking our horses? Thought they was friends to white men."

"Thought so, too." Scratch tromped away into the darkness a moment, then returned with his hand at the neck of a nervous pony where he held onto what was left of the slashed picket rope. "Here, Josiah." He handed the short length of rough, rawhide rope to the young trapper. "Get this'un saddled up an' ready to ride."

Bass whistled into the darkness twice before he heard the hoofs stomping the ground and heading his way.

"We going after 'em, huh?"

"That's right, son," Titus answered. "Gotta."

"These only two left?"

" 'Pears to be."

"Then you and me gotta get our ponies back, old man. Seems we can't do without the rest of 'em."

"They makin' ground on us with you jawin' away." Bass caught the hackamore of the buffalo runner. "Be ready when you are." Paddock disappeared into the blackness with the other pony.

They rode through the early morning hours of darkness, following the thieves by instinct. The trappers sure couldn't see a trail, much less the Indians and horses. From time to time Bass led them onto a grassy knoll or bench where he could survey the ground before them. From atop this high point he could reason how the thieves were moving across the landscape and set the next part of the chase in his head. So it was into the first gray light of dawn when they caught sight of a cloud of dust, made red by the newborn sun.

It would be good. Bass knew that in the early hours of daylight the sun would be at their backs. Perhaps it would even blind the Indians so they couldn't see their pursuers coming along behind them. But less than an hour later, the old trapper did not feel as good as he had at dawn. The race was not going the way he wanted it to go. The gap had not narrowed. Still ahead, the Indians only rarely looked back. Once, while on the run, the three thieves had changed over to fresh mounts without stopping.

The old trapper finally understood. He yanked back on the rawhide and brought the buffalo runner to a halt. Josiah shot on past before he realized the old man had stopped. Paddock rode back to Titus, both ponies blowing from exhaustion.

"Ain't gonna catch 'em this a-way," Bass snorted sourly and blew his nose, snorting a stream of moisture onto the ground. He never took his eyes off the retreating horse thieves and their small herd of trappers' ponies.

"You got something else in mind, don't you?" Josiah turned to look off in the distance at the silhouettes trotting west at an easy lope.

"You're learnin' 'bout me, Josiah Paddock."

"Oughta, you ol' buzzard," he smiled as Bass finally turned to gaze in his direction. "Been with you over a year now."

"That long, hmmm? You're right, ain't you, young'un?"

"What can we do now?"

"It be a long wager, boy. A long chalk at that. Them red niggers stayin' to the creek bed, runnin' for the Green, I 'spect."

"That where they're heading?" Paddock nodded toward the riders.

" 'Pears to be—goin' to the Seeds-ke-dee." He spit quickly after pushing his new chaw to the side of his cheek with his tongue. "We just gotta be there afore 'em."

"How far?"

"Two, maybe three miles—I reckon on that track. End of that ridge anyway."

"We take the ridge, ride high while they ride low." Josiah smiled over at the older trapper, sure of himself.

"Like I said, you're learnin' 'bout me, Josiah Paddock."

As the older trapper gave heels to his pony and sawed right to head off for the ridge, he was thankful for what those brief moments on the hill had given their horses. Not much of a rest—more of a brief respite, a chance to blow for the lathered mounts. The pony's steamy scent, fragrant and sweet in a familiar, earthy way, rose to his nostrils once more as they set off. If he were correct, the horses they rode would not need a lot more energy. The ground they had to cover was not much now. The ponies could last until they dropped off this ridge. Then their work would be over and the time come for more killing. If he was wrong—well, they'd have to come by more ponies some other way.

Paddock wondered how the old man could be so damned sure of the ridges leading to the river, and that river being right where he was so damned sure it would be. How did Bass know that? If Scratch were right about it all, they'd be up against three warriors, maybe just kids out to steal ponies. Just get the horses back, then turn around for camp. Looks Far and Joshua. Damn!

Maybe he was a fool after all, traipsing off after some damned horses when his wife and boy were back at camp. Bass's woman, too. No one to watch out for the three of them. Were the horses worth all that much to leave the women and child behind? After all, couldn't they just find some tribe and trade for some more ponies—just like he and Bass had done for the Nez Perce ones back in Pierre's Hole? That seemed logical to him. This chasing after Indians through the night on into dawn—this seemed crazy thrown up against the simplicity of trading for horses. But Bass wouldn't let it go, he knew. He wouldn't sit there and let those Injuns steal something from him. It just wasn't in the old man's blood.

So Josiah rode along beside the older trapper, through the gray, glistening air. Scratch did have his own way of looking at things. Yet, Josiah followed the old man. It was too late to turn back now. They were almost at the bottom of the ridge. He could see the cottonwood and willow thick by the river. He could even smell the water—the way a horse did when it was thirsty, needing water badly.

Scratch pulled up a moment in the new, brightening air of this late-summer morning. They had come down to the river near a ford used for countless years, first by buffalo, later by Indian and white men alike. Wide and shallow. This was where the thieves were heading with the stolen horses.

He nodded for Paddock to follow and kneed his pony right, heading upstream. After some forty yards he pushed the buffalo runner off the steep, sandy bank into the slow-running water. The high, fast water had already gone on its late summer way south and west by now.

Bass reined back downstream toward the shallow ford, swimming the horses. He kept glancing at the muddy water the horse's hoofs were kicking up, stirring the murky river bottom. The old trapper looked about, finally focusing on a spot downstream, a short distance away.

"There." He pointed for Josiah and took off for the stand of trees surrounded by willow. "You stay here." He clipped the words hard. Then he saw Josiah coming off his horse. "No. You gotta stay forked for this. My plan don't work an' all hell be breakin' outta the pen. Best be in your saddle to cut 'em off. Only way. Be sure you wrap your critter's nose tight. He can't make a sound."

Bass glanced back up the valley, then continued. "Now—I come out shootin', you take number three of 'em. I'm goin' for the second one."

"What about the first one across?"

"Way I figure, they're gonna be strung out 'long that line of our ponies—the way they been ridin'. I'll take the second nigger when he steps up onto solid ground. That means the third one's gonna be yours. He's gonna be in the water."

"That still don't tell me what the hell happens to the first damned Injun who comes across on us—the one leading the whole damned parade."

"Maybe he's gotta go on by us to make this shitterree work. Maybeso I can plug him in the ass from behind after I drop the second boy. But, we don't rightly know, do we, son? Now, we best get lined up an' ready for 'em. Them niggers is fixin' to sashay down on us real quick."

Titus gently heeled his pony and turned out of the willows. Having found a place to hide himself, he brought his left leg over the pony and dropped to the ground with a quiet thud. It was good he made it to cover, he thought. Here come them thieving brownskins now.

The leader of the group was well in advance of the other two Indians and the ponies. Back from the willows on the east bank, he checked the crossing. He studied not only the vegetation on his side of the river, the sandy soil for tracks, and the water itself, but also the opposite shore.

Bass could hear his own heart drumming—certain the horse thief leader could hear it, too. He clamped his hand tightly near the top of his runner's nose, just behind the nostrils. If he kept a locked grip, chances were his pony would not be able to whinney when it saw or heard the approaching horses.

From where he had concealed himself, the old trapper looked and studied, watched and measured. Something about that redskin, something about that old boy, the trapper contemplated. The way that Injun sits his pony, moves up and down the bank. Something.

Then it was too late to make sense out of what he felt was a dim nagging familiarity, perhaps recognition, with the Indian. The other two thieves had arrived with the small band of horses. Too late to worry a sweat onto your brow now—the fat was fast dripping into the fire.

The first rider turned at the sound of those many pounding hoofs, waited until he saw the ponies come through the trees at a lope, then headed his animal into that shallow water of the wide ford ahead of the others. High stepping, the pony he rode splashed its way across the river, soaking the Indian's leggins up to mid-thigh.

The Indian carried a rifle, held it cocked in the air, its butt resting against the warrior's right hip. In addition, a bow and quiver of arrows hung bouncing at his back, swinging pendulously from side to side with each of the pony's steps. The thieves had been traveling light. None of the Indians wore an outer garment in late summer. They had tied blankets around their lower torsos, leaving their arms completely free.

By the time the leader splashed up on the western bank to quickly survey the soil for tracks, the others had already pushed the ponies into the ford. The head man turned, saw his companions on the way, then reined around and set his dripping pony off to the west once more at a lope.

Just as he had figured. Bass eyed the leader, then looked back to the left and the oncoming riders. He quickly calculated timing and distance. The leader would be out of range very quickly now—but the second man at the head of the pony string wasn't yet where the old trapper wanted him to be before he opened fire. One of the thieves had already been hit. The last one favored a wound in the arm that had a dark-stained bandage covering it. And the two stragglers were taking their own sweet time with the crossing, yelling back and forth at one another, laughing—the way youngsters tease and chide playmates. These two were young. Bass could see that well enough.

Old enough to go stealing my ponies, they old enough to know better. And old enough for some serious thumping.

The trapper pulled his pistol out of the belt, snapped the hammer back to full cock, and set it on the ground where he could quickly scoop it up when the time came. Then he brought the rifle to his shoulder. Bass held on the second Indian's chest, studying the young man. Seventeen. Maybe eighteen summers. Just a kid. But he had been playing for heavy stakes. And they were Shoshone. Snakes. Almost no doubt about that now. The hair, and the way they dressed—they were Snakes, all right. Scratch had always thought Snakes knew better than to steal a white man's horses.

Maybe them Injuns just getting cocky after all these years of trappers in the mountains. Think now they can get away with that shit—taking my ponies. Gonna teach these red niggers a hard lesson to chew. You don't steal nothing from Titus S. Bass. Nothing.

The rifle shoved back into his shoulder. He smiled inwardly knowing the front blade had been held plumb center on the Indian's chest. It surprised the trapper when the weapon exploded. Just the way it was supposed to—squeeze and be surprised when it goes off. Above the cloud at the muzzle he saw the young Snake driven backwards as he was yanked off his pony, his whole body seeming to explode into the air as the lead ball smashed through his torso.

As Scratch tossed the rifle to his left hand so that he could scoop up the pistol in his right, he began his turn to the side. Even before his head turned, his eyes were already searching for the thieves' leader. In the middle of his turn, Bass caught a glimpse of the second brave being driven sideways off his pony at the same time the muzzle blast of Paddock's rifle reached his ears.

The leader turned at the sound of the first explosion. Yet the second explosion made him savagely saw the rein to command his pony on up the trail. Two shots, two men down. He pulled hard on the rawhide rein, leaning in the direction he commanded of the pony beneath him. And that singular movement in twisting to his right saved his life.

Suddenly there was a burning sensation across his upper left arm. The blood flowered out of the hole and petalled around the wound. If he had been sitting up straight when he was hit, he would have taken the ball in mid-chest.

Again he kicked the horse beneath him, slapping the rein against its neck to emphasize the command. His pony shot off as the leader looked behind him to see but one companion, that solitary Indian lying on the bank with the muddied water lapping over his upper body. He couldn't see the second horse thief at all. Both of them youngsters, he thought. Seems no one else ever came with the older warrior anymore when he proposed a scalp or horse raid. Only youngsters anxious to count coup or who wished to become wealthy in ponies.

"Goddamn!" Bass cursed as he saw the bullet hit the thief's arm, instead of square in the lights. He saw the warrior shudder, then right himself atop his pony and kick the animal once more, slapping its neck.

The old trapper turned to see Paddock stride out of the willows. He looked back at the river. Bobbing lazily on the gentle waves, the third horse thief's body floated away slowly to their right.

"You hit him," Josiah stated calmly as he came up to stare after the escaping Indian.

"Not near good 'nough, son." Bass suddenly wheeled and began to reload the rifle while Paddock took the pistol from him to recharge.

"Why don't you just let it be, Scratch?" Then the young trapper fell silent as he burned from the fire in Bass'ss glare. Finally the older man's gaze dropped back to the loading process.

"Long time ago, son," he said as he glanced up quickly at the young man, his eyes smarting with a salty moisture, "I learned to finish what I started."

"But we got our horses now," Paddock protested strongly. "Let's just get our asses back to the women. I don't like leaving them alone so long. You remember what happened at rendezvous with them St. Louis fellas?"

"Ain't no white man near 'bouts." Bass snapped. He shoved the ball home against powder with a solid clunk and yanked the ramrod out of the barrel. "Only Injuns. Injuns wantin' our ponies. Women'll be safe. Now—we finish what we started, son."

Scratch scooped up the buffalo runner's reins, stuffed the offered pistol into his belt, then swung up onto leather. "You comin', ain't you?" he said as his pony danced.

"I killed one. Two today," he said as he nodded back at the river behind them. "Suppose I let you finish what you started." Paddock stepped back out of the prancing pony's way.

"If'n that's the way the tune's gonna be played, only me gonna dance—so be it." Scratch walked the pony out of the willows and cottonwood, then heeled it into a lope. Once out onto the flats leading away from the river, he quickly set the pony into a ground-eating gallop and took after the escaping horse thief.

Josiah would probably never understand, he thought. Out here, in the mountains, stealing from a man was damned close to killing him. Take a man's beaver, his horses, his weapons. All the same—you were maybe putting an end to that man's life. There wasn't a man could get away with that. No man stole from Titus Bass.

Around a thick stand of cottonwood he finally pulled into sight of the Indian ahead of him. The warrior was veering off to the right toward some low bluffs. Bass wondered if he should shoot the man. Take the chance of missing him on the run and then have to chase him down all over again. A man going full speed on horseback could be a tough target, with him bobbing and me moving, too, he thought. Easier job would be to take out the horse he'd stolen. Put the man on the ground, then finish him off pretty as you please.

Scratch leaned low along the neck of his buffalo runner, holding the rein in his left hand, the rifle low along the pony's body in his right. This close to his animal, its sweaty-sweet musk filled his nostrils. It was good. Let the pony go full-out now. Give him his head. Cool air burned across his chapped cheeks, making them feel like burnished rawhide as the tears were wind-whipped from the corners of his eyes. Tight, drawn skin above the whiskers, stinging below the watery eyes, he squinted against the wind and the glare of a new sun.

At last he was close enough. Bass pulled the rifle up and years'-long instinct told him when he was ready. The sights were placed just ahead of the Indian's right leg. Squeeze. The rifle barked, its sound lost behind him quickly at this speed.

As the warrior rode away from the white men, his whole arm was growing numb. But he would not think about it and the pain would eventually go away. Only a loud ringing in his ears that buried beneath it the thumping of his heart, the thudding of the pony's hoofs, as he drove the animal to more and more speed. No sound. No pain to bear. Only the wind in his face.

He had been a respected warrior among his people. He had counted many coups. He had owned many ponies. Then things began to turn sour summer before last, in the valley the white traders called Pierre's Hole, when the American trappers had penned some Blackfeet in the timber. It was after the battle that his medicine had begun to clabber—when this Shoshone warrior had found that the Blackfeet had escaped in the night. The fleeing enemy had left few dead to mark the path of their retreat, but this warrior had come upon a dead Blackfoot brave, cradled in the arms of his squaw who would rather die than leave her man behind to fall into the hands of their enemies. A crowd had quickly gathered around the couple, the woman wounded herself and unable to walk, her leg still bleeding from a bullet that had shattered the bone. At the center of the crowd was an old friend, a white trapper this Snake warrior had known for some years. He had often sold the old trapper pemmican in exchange for trade goods.

But in the valley of Pierre's Hole there were insults hurled that the trapper was not brave enough to kill a squaw. The trapper had answered that there was no glory in killing a woman. The Snake warrior had promptly laughed with contempt for the stupid white man, then suddenly plunged his tomahawk completely down through the top of the woman's head. The warrior had known ever since that this nagging wound to the broken circle was not yet settled with that white man. And that sense of incompleteness, that rip in the great circle of all things had caused this warrior's medicine to turn bad.

In an effort to make his medicine powerful once more, he had taken to raiding trappers' camps, running off with the white man's stock, stealing what weapons he could, killing the white men if it came down to that. Vengeance on that white cause of his own bad medicine. He did these things to right the wrong done to him that day in the valley west of the Tetons. But now, with a badly wounded arm, he would return to his people's camp alone. A very bad sign that his fading power was almost gone when no warriors returned with a raid leader. No longer would anyone follow him on the trail for ponies and scalps.

Then suddenly the shock of it coursed through the warrior as he was brutally yanked out of his bitter reverie. He sailed through the air over the pony's neck and slammed to the ground. The impact sent thick shards of cold pain cascading through his body. Consciousness began to slide away from him. The warrior tumbled in a crumpled ball across the warming, dust-covered sage. He rolled to a stop, then came to fully. Slowly he rose to his feet and shakily turned to face his attacker, vision clearing only gradually. The hoofs beat closer and closer. Tears of pain, tears of defeat and frustration smeared his cheeks as he awaited his enemy.

Bass saw the warrior's pony pitch forward, flipping, its hind quarters flying over its head. Landing in a loose heap, the horse thief tumbled over and over through the dry, dust-smeared sagebrush. Scratch bolted on by as he yanked back on the rein and tortured the pony's head hard to the left to come around. By the time he got close to the Indian, the Snake was standing, half-crouched, rubbing the top of his bleeding left arm. Bass swung the empty rifle as the horse thief turned toward him to meet the challenge.

At the same time the trapper felt the rifle jolted away from its target, Scratch saw the face clearly. How did this fit? All too much to understand.

Scratch's legs pushed hard against the stirrups as he pulled the pony up short, turned him. The Indian circled with the trapper. Bass allowed the pony to prance back toward the warrior. Then he slid a left leg over the animal's back and thumped to the ground. The warrior straightened and turned full face at last.

Slays in the Night.

Last time I seen this Injun was in the valley of Pierre's Hole. Killed a squaw with a busted leg. She had stayed with her man till the end. This nigger called me a coward 'cause I wouldn't kill her. And I considered him less than that 'cause he would kill a woman.

In a small way, ever since that day, Bass had known there would always be a score to settle with this proud warrior. But this was different. Killing a squaw in cold blood was one thing. Having to kill a white man on equal terms, another.

Did this nigger know them was my horses? Come to run them off 'cause of the tally to even up on account of Pierre's Hole? Nawww. Nigger proud as Slays in the Night ain't gonna be one to just run off with my ponies, knowing they was mine. He'd be one to stay back and settle things before taking off with the horseflesh. Always had him his pride. Bad thing for a fella—that pride. Gets a child in a pot, in the stew, many a time.

Bass studied the Indian's eyes for a moment. He knew the Snake recognized him, too. Slays in the Night still gripped that ugly, bleeding arm where the bullet had ripped through the flesh. His left hand closed into a fist, then loosened, closed into a fist and loosened again. Over and over as if to test its strength, to see if the arm was useful.

"You are the one the Sparrowhawk people call Coyote," the Indian signed with his good hand, using a formal salutation that seemed foreign to the trapper. It was as if they had never been friends at all.

"You know me, Slays in the Night," Bass answered quickly, the rifle laid in the crook of his left arm, out of the way of his talking hands.

"Yes," the Indian nodded.

They were twenty feet apart when Bass stopped. He noticed the Indian shiver slightly in the cool morning breeze. "You are cold, my friend?"

"I will be very warm in stealing your horses."

"You knew they were my ponies?"

"I know now. And so they become my horses."

"Shame." Bass shook his head, almost mockingly. "I have the ponies back." He gestured toward the river far behind them. "The others who rode with you, they are dead. Two at my camp. Two at the river. Gone." He rubbed one palm over the other, letting the top hand eventually fly off the bottom palm to signify the soul's direction of the men who had been rubbed out. "You are now alone."

"I am not alone."

Bass didn't understand at first. Then he sighed and nodded as his gaze rose from the dust at his feet. "Yes. You have your medicine."

"That is the power with me."

Those two words, medicine and power, were signed in much the same way. It was only with the latter word that the warrior drew himself up to full height and swelled out his chest like a proud cock strutting the sage to impress the hens. Power.

"Your power brings you here, with boys, to take my horses from me?"

"They are—they were—old enough to know the way of a Shoshone warrior." The last two words were shown as a wriggling symbol for a crawling snake and two fingers brought to the side of the head, held upright to represent coup feathers a man wore when he had performed two deeds befitting a warrior.

"They are dead because of you," Bass said, shaking his head in disagreement.

"They are dead because their power was not as strong as mine."

"You do not mourn them?"

"A warrior killed while taking scalps or ponies is not to be cried over—only by squaws."

"Like the squaw in the valley west of the Big Breasts?"

The Snake's eyes hardened at the speaking of what had been on each man's mind for long moments. "Yes. Squaws do not fight like warriors. They are left to cry over a fallen warrior."

"It does not take much of a warrior to kill a squaw."

The Indian stiffened at the insulting slur. "Squaw make many warriors. War-

14

riors plant the seeds in the squaw. She carry the seeds of those to come in her body. I see that she never again carries warriors in her belly to kill my people."

"You should have made her prisoner of your people," Bass argued fervently. "Should have made her bear the seeds of Shoshone warriors."

"Blackfoot dog-woman!" The Shoshone spit after he had signed the words, as if he'd been forced to say something distasteful. "She would give birth only to slugs defecating under the rocks."

"You took her scalp that day?"

Slays in the Night pulled at the wide thong that held the woolen blanket around his waist. It crumpled to the ground at his feet. Stepping out of the heap of the dark blue blanket, the Snake pulled up the bottom of his hunting shirt. From his belt hung the long, black hair attached to the scalp along with the tops of the woman's ears.

"You were proud to take her scalp." Bass moved his hands to sign-talk once more. "Proud to kill a woman."

"A mother of more Blackfoot vermin," the Shoshone answered immediately. "Not human as we are—you and me."

"I, too, hate Blackfeet. But, I do not kill women." Bass shook his head. "There is no courage shown in killing a woman waiting to die with her brave man."

The warrior jerked, again hit with the insult. He took a long, deep breath and let it out slowly. Then pulled his knife from its sheath at his belt. "I think you are not human as I am. Perhaps I have to kill you after all this time you have fooled me—thinking you are human."

Bass watched the fingers of both hands come to rest, the left ones by the Snake's side, gripping and releasing a fist in the warming, late-summer air that nevertheless always foreboded an early fall and long winter. The right fingers clutched the knife that shuddered only slightly with the short, labored breathing of a man struck with pain, a man left to fight off his own adrenalin, perhaps his own devils.

Finally the trapper let his own shoulders sag a little, dropping the muzzle of the pistol from its target. "I have my ponies back now."

"You go?"

"Yes." Bass merely nodded, then started to turn away from the warrior.

For the first time, Slays in the Night spoke aloud, not using his hands and that universal sign language of plains and mountains. "*BAAASSSSS.*" He drew the word out and waited until the old trapper turned his head back over his shoulder. "I kiilll you."

"You kill me," Bass spoke softly in English at last. The words seemed frozen in the cool, early morning air. Hung in their own mist, it seemed like hours since last he'd spoken at the river. "You kill me, or I have to kill you," he said and sighed with a shake of his head. "No. This is where it stops, old friend." As he turned back toward the buffalo runner with its head hung in exhaustion from the chase, he saw a slash of movement on his right.

The trapper jerked back toward the Indian as Slays in the Night rushed across the final few yards between the two of them. The knife was held out from his body, held low. Bass jerked sideways when the Snake collided with him, twisting the Indian over a hip and flipping him into the sage and dust. Slays in the Night rose to one knee, looking around frantically for his weapon. The knife had disappeared in the dirt among the clumps of sage.

"You will not make me kill you." Scratch gritted, stuffing the pistol back into his sash. "That is my power. And that power is stronger than yours." He signed the last two concepts besides speaking them aloud in English.

"I will kill you—someday." The Snake rose as he pulled the broken bow from its place in the wolf-hide quiver at his back, busted in the fall from the horse he had stolen. He tossed the bow aside where it skidded across the dirt, spinning into the sparse vegetation.

"Not today." Bass sighed and glanced at the red orb pushing up from the horizon. "This is not a good day for either of us to die. Not a good day, old friend."

"I am not your friend!"

"You were once." Bass nodded for simple emphasis. "I will remember you that way—before you killed a squaw, before you stole a white man's ponies."

"You must kill me now," Slays in the Night shouted, his eyes begging the white man. "I cannot go back to my people without the other warriors, without the ponies. It is without honor what you send me to do."

"You did that to yourself," Bass said as he caught up the rawhide rein and turned to look across the sage at the Indian before he signed his reply. "You did that to yourself long ago. Made yourself a man without honor when you killed a squaw. Your people believe such a thing to be strength—then your people are wrong." He put his right foot in the stirrup and swung aboard the pony, adjusting the rifle across his thighs.

Titus studied the Indian for a long moment. The bleeding had stopped in the Shoshone's wound. The Snake had a blanket. He would not freeze at night on his long walk back to his village, wherever that was. Maybe such a long journey would make the Indian think. Maybe it was good for a man to walk a long time so he would have to think on big things.

Yet there was a sad nagging that told him he should have killed the warrior this morning. He should have finished it, be done with the Shoshone. But it was finished for the old trapper. He'd finally said what he wished he'd said back in Pierre's Hole more than a year before. It was like spitting up a foul-tasting stone that had lain in his belly for all this time. But, it was good to be rid of it. Perhaps they would meet again some day, as Slays in the Night had promised. But it would not be like this. Bass knew he would have to kill him then, or be killed by the Shoshone. It would come down to that once more. Always a common denominator—death. What equality it gave to all living things, he thought.

"I curse your children," Slays in the Night spit in Shoshone toward the trapper.

Bass turned the pony's head to the right and nudged it into a slow walk across the sage. Ain't got me any children, you stupid nigger.

"I curse your children," the Shoshone repeated, shouting now into the chill air, words hung frosty on each breath. "May they be without medicine."

Bass turned his back fully on the Indian now, allowing the pony to tramp away from the warrior slowly, keeping his broad back to the Snake, feeling the dark eyes searing a spot between his shoulder blades.

"Kill me!" the warrior yelled. He leaned down, picked up a ball-sized stone and hurled it at the retreating white man. "You must kill me or your medicine is weak," he taunted.

Trying to goad me into killing him. Bass could not smile. There was a genuine sadness to the Indian's life now. There was indeed no honor in how he would return to his village. If he went back home. Perhaps he would choose not to suffer the humiliation, choosing instead to remain outside the tribe, alone and on his own. Like a lone wolf. Perhaps like a mad wolf. Always the wolves. They come to steal life. Always the wolf.

"You and your wife and your children will eat the dung of proud people all your days. They are fit only to eat the dung of warriors."

But I ain't gonna eat your shit, you stupid nigger.

"They will be poisoned and die a thousand deaths before they are allowed to pass on!"

"Cowards and fools, my old friend. Cowards and fools," Bass mumbled softly to himself. A thousand deaths maybe. But yours won't be on my hands today, or forever. No. Not on my hands.

The young trapper raced around the treeline. When he saw Bass slowly walking his pony away from the solitary Indian, Josiah reined up his own horse quickly. He brought his animal prancing up to where Bass had stopped to await him.

"What the hell's going on now?" Josiah asked, his mouth and tongue dry from the ride. "Decided to come help out after all." His head nodded in question toward the warrior.

Bass looked back at the Indian who gestured animatedly and shouted in his foreign tongue before the white man gazed over at his young partner. "Just had me a talk with him. Slays in the Night."

Paddock stared intently across the distance in the new, shimmering light of morning. "The Snake fella? Down to Pierre's Hole last summer?"

"Same."

"That why you ain't gonna kill him?" Josiah asked, puzzled. " 'Cause you knowed him once a time?"

"Nope." Bass shook his head and twisted in his saddle to stare back at the Indian.

Finally, he caught Josiah's eyes once more. "Just decided not to spill no more blood on this. Ain't no need. Enough niggers dead already. Let this one go. Just another Snake, one more or one less. Don't make no matter."

He softly tapped the ribs of his buffalo runner and started out as he caught sight of Paddock's movement out of the corner of his eye. The young trapper was muttering almost under his breath.

"You tell me this big speech—no one steals from you, huh?" Josiah stuck his hand into the folds of his coat. "Tell me you always gotta finish what you start— huh, old man? Well, now, we ain't gonna leave no stragglers around at all."

He yanked the pistol out of his belt and brought it down on the Snake just as

Bass bolted back up on his animal and slashed across Paddock's arm with his quirt, driving the young trapper's gun hand down and sending the ball smashing into the sage.

"W-what the b-blue—" Paddock sputtered in rage. "I was gonna clean up what you said needed cleaning up. Finish what you started."

"I dad-blamed well didn't start it." Bass was angry now. "But I sure as hell gonna be the one to put an end to it. Nigger out there wanted me to kill him. He would purely love for you to kill him, young'un. Worst thing I could do to him now is not do what he wants me to. It'd give him honor for you to kill him. 'Sides," he said as he paused to watch it all sink in. " 'Sides, Josiah, comes a time when there's been enough killin'. Comes a time when you gotta shut it down. Just us leave it be for now."

Paddock studied the old man's face, then looked across the dust and shimmering waves of early-day heat toward the Snake warrior. Finally he turned back to see Bass heel his pony around and take off at a crisp lope. Paddock shook his head and stuffed the pistol in his belt. He started to turn after Bass. But first, he tossed a farewell salute to the Indian before he pushed his pony into heading after the older trapper.

Bass heard the hoofs crushing the sage and cured grass as the other pony raced up behind him. It took a far braver man to walk away when it was not a good day to die. A far braver man to decide not to kill. This was Bass's courage, this was his medicine now. More strength it took to turn the pony away from the warrior and leave him to the wilderness. Knowing he himself had stripped the Shoshone of honor, Titus still figured the Indian had long been without honor, by killing the Gros Ventre squaw in the first set. Didn't really matter what he did to the warrior now anyway. It simply was not a good day to die. For either one of them.

Bass sucked in the crisp air just warming with the climbing sun. The air's tingle felt good to him as it charged into his lungs with a shocking alertness. A tingle that pulsed through him. To be alive, and to choose to leave others be. That was good.

Maybe I've learned something, he thought. A lot to be said for letting others be.

2 LAZILY.

Only lazily did he pull the small party out of the narrow valley. Bass directed his course down the Little Snake until it spilled into the Little Bear River which would lead them almost directly toward the seductive shadows on the west side of the Rocky Mountains. Ever closer, the foothills loomed in purple, their cool offerings of shade being welcomed by the summer-baked travelers. Then Bass drew to a halt along the Bear River and swung out of the saddle.

"What we stopping here for?" Josiah inquired. "You thirsty?"

Instead of answering immediately, Scratch toe-dug his way along the sandy bank which had been left exposed after the spring flood runoff. He searched out his spot before plopping down on the damp sand and then let go an audible sigh. Happy as a toad in the sun.

"Why we pick this place to stop and sit?" Josiah spoke softly as he came up behind the older trapper with the two women and his child in tow.

Scratch merely turned around and motioned for the others to join him on the bank. Josiah plopped to Scratch's right, and the two Indian women sat in the shaded green grass, a respectful distance behind the older man. Looks Far held little Joshua on her lap.

"You gonna tell me what we're doing here?" Paddock watched Bass working at the greasy knot holding the blue bandanna on his head.

Bass removed the floppy, sweat-stained, horsehair-banded, brown felt hat and set it on the sand at his left knee. Then he tugged again at the loosened knot before grasping the back of his hair and the bandanna. Slowly, almost reverently in a way all his own, Bass slid the stolen scalplock off the back of his head. Very rarely was the bone of his skull exposed to the sun, to family, to friends. After he spread the greasy, smelly, sweat-soaked blue bandanna on the ground immediately in front of his crossed legs, Scratch took the long, black scalplock he kept greased with bear lard out of his lap and laid it out atop the faded bandanna.

"This's got something to do with your hair, huh?" Josiah quickly waggled his head as if he could find an answer by rattling something loose up there. "With you losing your hair?"

Paddock gazed up and down the river that flowed closely by their feet. Then he glanced behind him toward the two women and shrugged his shoulders in resignation. After all, this was a cool spot for a short break in their hot travel of

19

the day. Here in the shade of willow and cottonwood. Made no matter the old man wouldn't tell him what they had stopped for. The air smelled cooler, almost sweet, with an elixir that syruped over the heat of the afternoon. Water larruping at the bank in gentle wavelets worked in quiet concert with droning insects.

"Lost my hair, you're right." Bass finally glanced over at the younger man. "Right here—where we sittin'."

He watched Josiah owl at the ground, quickly, at either side of where he sat. Behind him, Bass heard Waits-by-the-Water speaking in a soft whisper to Looks Far. Some of the words were in Crow, some he figured in Flathead, more still in their own private tongue.

Titus turned slightly, and out of the corner of his eye, he saw them both bow their heads suddenly, reverently. There was medicine on this ground. There was great power here about them. They were in the presence of a great mystery.

"What the hell're they doing?" Josiah nodded back toward the two women behind him. "They know you lost your hair here, on this spot?"

"I suppose they do, now anyway," Scratch answered. "Seems they know now."

"Know there's medicine here—where we are," Josiah remarked. "Why don't we have a smoke?" he said as he nodded at the clay pipe and tobacco pouch that hung from the older man's neck alongside his personal medicine bag.

"Say, that do sound like a right smart notion." Scratch nodded and pulled the small clay stem free from the loops on the tobacco pouch. "Good notion, son."

He filled the bowl with fingertip pinches of brown leaf, then pulled a small German silver container from his shooting bag. From it he removed charred cloth, a piece of flint, and his firesteel. With the stem of the fragile clay pipe clamped firmly, yet gently, between his teeth, the older trapper struck the flint and charred cloth with the steel until a spark glowed in the blackened cotton material. He blew on the bright coal until it burned on its own and then set the ember atop the tobacco in the bowl.

Drawing deeply several times against the strong tobacco leaf and willow bark mixture, Bass stoked the pipe to a smoky, heady glow. He pulled the stem from his lips and passed it to Paddock. Josiah put his hand up suddenly.

"Nawwww—you first, old friend," he said. "Your hair. You go first on this one."

Bass nodded in reply. "S'pose you're right, son."

Scratch presented the short stem of the clay pipe to the four directions, once to the earth and one last salute to the sky.

"Grandfather, we ain't got us much 'baccy here to do a lot of prayin', but I'm one to think you already know the words in my heart anyways." With six quick puffs he let smoke follow the four cardinal directions, one small puff to blanket itself across Mother Earth, and a last long puff let free toward the heavens. Bass handed the pipe to Josiah.

The younger trapper held it for a brief moment across his two flat palms until the warmth of the super-heated clay pipebowl told him it was time to grasp the stem. He completed the prescribed address of all directions and puffed six times on the stem. When he was finished, Paddock held the pipe at the end of his outstretched arms, pointing it to the white-dappled sky.

"He will always know the thoughts in our hearts."

"Wagh!" Scratch commented with a grunt—the sound of approval, that roar of a grizzly bear in battle.

Titus took the pipe back from the young man and saw there was still some yet unburnt tobacco in the bowl. Bass sucked on the stem until a rich, gray plume streamed from his nostrils and lips. With a cupped left hand he brought the smoke over his bowed head four times, symbolically rubbing the smoke onto the bald spot at the crown of his head. It was there the scalp had been taken from him. Four clouds of smoke wreathed his head as four times he rubbed the sacred, prayerful smoke onto the years-old wound.

He was finished. The pipe went out. The prayer was complete. After a few long moments, Bass finally raised his head and smiled first at Josiah, then turned to his left and smiled over at the two women, letting them know his ceremony was finished. They returned his smile with grins of their own.

"This why we come by this way?" Paddock started to rise but stayed in a kneeling position beside the older man.

"One of the reasons, I s'pose," Bass said as he gradually climbed to his feet. "Memories always got 'em a way of tuggin' hard at you. Makin' a feller wanna come back. Sometimes even if the memory ain't all that good." His voice fell off as he gazed downstream, back in the direction they had come along this river. He looked upstream, toward the hills and those peaks before them. "Bad memories ain't all that bad, son. 'Specially when you got lots of good memories to go along with 'em."

He wheeled and gestured for the women to go ahead toward the ponies. The animals drank at the bouncing water as the river lapped gently against the bank. Josiah stepped ahead of him as the group skirted along the willow to their horses. Scratch stopped after he had put one foot in the left stirrup, ready to push himself off the ground.

"I just now thought of that, you know, Josiah," he said, looking over the saddle at Paddock. "Old, bad memories ain't all that awful to think about when a fella's got him good memories to go along with 'em. Ain't a bad taste to it a'tall."

He slowly swung onto leather and pulled his pony around, tugging at the pack string to get them into motion. He twisted to face the three others coming along behind him.

"We got a few more hours of light, and use it all up we will. Get on up toward the hills I'm sorely needin' to see. That's where we make our camp tonight. Get away from all them pesky skeeters an' flies. Damn them critters! Damn 'em to hell! It'll be cool, too cool for 'em when we get on up into the hills a bit. Away from this bottom land."

"Skeeters?" Looks Far, holding her young son's hand, turned to Josiah to inquire of the new word.

Josiah smiled and pantomimed for her, slapping the side of his cheek first, then peering into the empty palm. Suddenly he slapped the back of his neck and stared once more into the empty hand.

Looks Far grinned widely, with flashing white teeth, and nodded, almost like a young child would do in sudden recognition. Releasing Joshua's hand, she slapped at her own cheek and giggled merrily. Then the Flathead girl opened her hand and peered into the make-believe of it. From her palm she pulled an imaginary mosquito and threw it aside. Another quick slap on her forehead and she brought that hand up to her mouth. The young comedienne slowly opened her fingers until the palm was flat, then puffed on the imaginary insect and blew it on its way.

Little Joshua covered his mouth and giggled. Paddock laughed out loud, along with Bass and Waits-by-the-Water. Good to laugh. Memories they were making together. Not all that bad. Most of them good.

The young trapper reached over and clamped a hand around his young wife's neck, pulling her into him as he leaned toward her. He planted a loud, joyful smack on her lips. A happy, contented, exuberant kiss that surprised her, causing her eyes to open wide and stare at her husband.

Josiah straightened and laughed loudly once again. It felt good. It all felt so damned good.

UP into the cool recesses of the pines, where the summer air already possessed a tingle of autumn. Over the long, flat and winding pass, and three days later, they were greeted with a rock formation jutting up off the mountain peak, a formation that reminded Bass of the two ears on a rabbit. The group dropped slowly, winding their way through the forests until the valley lay before them.

Scratch drew the party to a halt. "Middle Park, son." He nodded forward, indicating the valley stretching south away from them.

"We don't have much more to go, do we?" Josiah nodded himself.

"Down there, you mean?"

"No. On to South Park. Must not be all that much more a ride now. Right?"

"We're purty nigh on to bein' close, Josiah," Bass answered and raised his eyes toward the peaks banked against the southern end of the valley, each pyramid piled against the others it joined. "We move direct on south through Middle Park. Gotta climb up and outta the bottom. Not all that bad a trip. A good pass it is this time of year. Then we got only some few miles to put under our hoofs before we finally lay eyes on it."

"Lay eyes on what?"

"Bayou Salade, boy!" he exclaimed. "What we've been talkin' about. South Park, Josiah Paddock. South Park."

"If it's all that special, like you been saying it was, then we best be getting. Can't let it be waiting for us. Not polite to make it wait too long."

They nudged their animals into a lope to catch up with the two women and the pack animals. With clattering saddle gear clarunking-tharumping beneath them, they steered the ponies around the sage and scrubby oak brush, through the cured, summer-burnt grass. Their final boyish whooping caused the two women and Joshua to turn and look back up the hill. The shouts caused the pack animals to prance sideways in alarm. The ponies calmed and settled when they recognized the familiar smell of the two men, along with the familiar odors of the trappers' mounts.

A man could always drink deeply of the fragrances of the high country to muscle away the summer-long-day's saddle stench. Dust could cake inside a man's nostrils, make it hard for him to breathe ofttimes, much less smell the sweetness, that peculiar lightness to the thin air of the high country. Yet a man could always resort to snorting, blowing like the animals he lived among. And with the bellowing came the freedom to smell the lure once more. There was something powerfully narcotic about the high altitudes for such men, something powerfully addicting.

No matter the nature of the hold it had on him, Bass gladly followed the lure, panted after the siren's song.

EIGHT more days of travel, climbing out of the long, narrow mountain valley they called Middle Park, lying between Park Kyack to the north and their destination to the south. Across the high, dried grasses of the small meadows dotting the valleys, into the richness of the aspen and blue spruce and lodgepole forests. The small party climbed south into the higher reaches still. Already a hint of the autumn to come, the frozen water slicked with a film of ice in the iron kettles each morning. Just the merest suggestion each new day as they scrambled the horses, packed the loads, stomped their small fire out and slid atop leather for another day's ride to the Bayou. Beautiful country, all.

"Ain't never been here, in these mountains," Paddock commented almost wistfully early one afternoon not long after they'd passed over the huge hump of timberline where they had nooned high among the treeless meadows, joining the squeaking marmots in the sun-drenched middle of the day. Land that touched the sky.

"I know you ain't." Bass turned and smiled, the crooked line of his grin pushing one side of his beard farther into his cheek than the other. "Glad I'm the one to show you."

Paddock twisted slowly from side to side, gazing about at the forested hillsides and open, yawning meadows of golden-cured grass. "Injuns?"

"Nawww, not really none to speak of, son," the older one answered. "Might'n be some Yutas, maybe. Mostly 'Rapahos down hereabouts. Knowed of Crow to make it all the way into South Park. Yessir, I have. Some years back a band of Blackfoot got all the way down 'long the front range, but on north of here. They run onto a bunch of wanderin' Crow—each bunch of 'em lookin' for buffler. T'were a bad year for buffler, you see. Tribes had to wander far, wander wide outta their own lands. Crow penned them Blackfoot up in some big rocks juttin' right up outta the prairie. Blackfoot had a good spot to fight safe from for awhile, they did. Then them Crow saw they wasn't gettin' nowhere doin' what they was doin'. Took the fight right into them rocks and the Blackfoot."

"They wipe the Blackfeet out?"

"Almost, they did," he answered. "Some few got away. Crow didn't figure on chasin' 'em down."

"Arapaho mostly, huh?" Josiah inquired.

"Mostly," Bass said. "Some Cheyenne been known to wander on into South Park. It's country where there's no tellin' who you might'n run onto. Good country sometimes that way, Josiah. Lotta folks always lay claim to good country. Like the Bayou."

"Many white men?"

"Yep," Bass answered thoughtfully. " 'Sides myself, there's likely to be lotta fellas workin' outta Taos an' Santa Fee gone up to see what this Bayou Salade is all about. Word can pass from one man's lips to 'nother man's ears pretty fast— especial' when they're gabbin' 'bout prime beaver country."

"Know any of 'em?"

"Know most of 'em—anyways," he answered. "But there's always new blood comin' into Taos. Just like you, Josiah Paddock. You'll be new to them sun-grinner diggins this winter. That's certain."

"Friends?" Josiah asked. "Or just some fellas you know of?"

"Bit of both," came the reply. "Seems a man's life is often that way, don't it? He's got him a handful he really can call his friends. The rest're just people he knows—people who know him. Friend be somethin' special, someone—some-one you count on when the goin' grows thin on you. When times is lean, you got a person sticks with you—now, that's a friend."

"Like you." Paddock smiled beneath the shade of his hat.

"Like both of us, son." Bass returned the grin, cracking the side of his graying whiskers in early afternoon light.

"Chances be we run onto someone you might know down to this South Park?"

"Not very likely we run on to someone. Not really," Titus said thoughtfully. "More likely we run onto someone I know on down to Taos when we get there for the winter. More likely we bump into Injuns than white men down to the Bayou, son."

"Know of any trappers will be down there?"

"You lonesome for other company?" Bass chided with a broad grin. "My palaver runnin' a little on the thin side, boy?"

"Nawww," Josiah quickly confessed. "Not anything like that, Scratch. Just wondering, is all. I suppose I'm just curious and that made you think I was getting tired of hearing your voice."

"Why, me? I t'wouldn't think no such a thing." Bass slapped a palm against his chest in mock anguish.

"C'mon now, wouldn't do nothing to hurt you—"

"An' I'm funnin' with you, Josiah."

Paddock was instantly relieved. For a moment he thought he really had hurt the older man's feelings. Once, with a misunderstanding over a woman, he had unwittingly scarred Bass. And Paddock would never do that again.

"There's one ol' coon—" Bass turned to Paddock to see if the younger man was paying attention. "Josiah? You listenin'?"

"Huh?" Paddock jerked his head around. "Oh—you say something?"

" 'Bout one ol' coon you an' me might run onto down to the Bayou Salade."

"What else?"

"What you mean, 'what else?' " Scratch shook his head, trying to keep from becoming frustrated. "Nothin' else. I gotta go on with the story."

"Then—go on with it, Scratch."

"I swear on me own heart! Sometimes you're just a real onery nigger, ain't you? Devilin' me all the time with this or with that. Swear I don't know when you mean it—when you don't."

"Sorry—" Josiah muttered.

" 'Pology accepted." Bass straightened a little and peered at the high, hot sun before continuing. "Williams. Bill Williams. Come to believe just what animal his God-fearin' soul gonna pass on to when he goes under. Bull elk—he says it'll be."

Bass nodded for emphasis when he saw the wondering look on Paddock's face. A look of disbelief. "That's right. He's gonna come back as a bull elk. Make you no mistake 'bout that, son. Bill believes that. He's gonna come back with his soul in a big, heavy-horned fella."

Scratch lapped the reins around his saddle horn once, balanced the long rifle across the tops of his thighs and brought both arms up alongside his head. "Tells all us who come and go down in the Bayou just what he's gonna look like that day come when he's gone on to bein' a bull elk. Big horns—nice rack on the boy, he says he'll have."

"How you know you won't shoot him by mistake?"

"That's why he's tellin' all of us what come into the Park, Josiah. So we know it's him!"

"Ohhh—"

" 'Bout time you catch on," Bass grumbled.

"Sure, sure. About time I caught on," Josiah muttered under his breath, not sure if Bass believed it all or not.

"Got him one good set of horn." Scratch waved his left arm. "But, the right side got broken, like this—"

Titus suddenly bent his right arm at the elbow to represent a broken antler. The left arm was outstretched along the side of his head, fingers spread to make-believe antlers. Then the right arm dangled from the elbow loosely.

"That be his sign for us. 'Don't shoot me now, boys,' Ol' Bill always one to say.".

"He's dead then?"

"Not by the last hair I heard tell of him, he ain't," Bass replied.

"Someday, most likely," Paddock commented dryly.

"Ever'body, Josiah. Sure that'll be. We all die sooner or later. Cain't just sit around waitin' for it to happen, can we now?"

"Nope. I suppose you're right there," Paddock answered. "How this Williams think he's gonna be rubbed out? Injuns? Freeze to death? Grizzly? Die of the clap!"

"Whoaaa! That's a good one!" Bass slapped a knee automatically and nearly dropped his rifle. He juggled it back in balance. "That's a prime one, son. Ol' Bill ain't been back to St. Louie in some time now, I don't imagine. How in hell's blue balls he gonna get the clap?"

"Bedding them Meskin ladies down in Taos, I figure."

"Wrong there, my friend." Bass shook his head emphatically. "Ain't gonna pick up nothin' nasty like that down there."

"How you so sure?"

"Why?" Bass winked at the younger man. "Looks Far ain't enough for the likes of a young bull like you?"

"Hell!" He snapped his head over at the older man.

"A lil' too heavy in the horn, eh, Josiah?"

"Stop it," Josiah roared. "Why're you thinking I'd do that woman wrong? Where you get off thinking that?"

"I was just askin'—"

"Quit your asking. And your thinking about such things, too. Ain't no way I'd do any wrong to that woman up yonder. No way. Shit!" Josiah said, feeling exasperated himself. "Just asking a question and there you go to put words in a feller's mouth for him."

" 'Pears to be it's my turn to 'pologize to you, Josiah Paddock."

"I accept."

"No harm intended."

"Well—ain't none taken."

They rode silently for a few minutes, the heat billowing down upon them in waves at this higher altitude. Fortunately, the cool breezes danced through the meadows and forested hillsides with a wandering softness, caressing the skin to wash away the heat of the high-mountain summer sun.

"Injuns."

"What's that?" Paddock asked after Bass had muttered the single word.

"Said, Injuns," Bass answered. "You asked how Ol' Bill figured he would be rubbed out. I told you Injuns, Josiah."

"How's he figure so strong on that?" Josiah twisted back and forth, working at some of the knots in his muscles that had come from the long ride.

"Had him a dream," Scratch replied. "Dream that told him a bear ever laid a paw on him—why, then a Injun's gonna raise his hair."

"A bear, huh?"

"Yep."

" 'Bout like McAfferty and you telling me that a bear means bad tidings for a fella. Running onto that bear—" Josiah let his voice drop.

"Yeah?" Scratch asked almost too quietly, knowing that Josiah had suddenly remembered.

"Running onto that bear like we did. I see it now."

"McAfferty. Havin' to go after him, hunt him down," Bass said as he shook his head. "It did come true, son. The spoiled meat of it. All the bad medicine. Right?"

"Right." Paddock nodded and stared ahead at the two women steering the packtrain into the trees along the southern slope. "I suppose it ain't all that wrong for a fella to think one thing just might mean something else."

"He figures a bear lays a paw on him, means for certain sure a Injun gonna rub him out."

"What about you?" Paddock turned toward the older trapper. "How you figure you gonna get rubbed out? Bear? Maybe Injun?"

"Most likely," Bass replied. "Ain't likely to be no white man, Josiah."

"Say—we come close, back at rendezvous."

"Nawww." Bass grinned widely and shook his head. "I ain't gonna go that a-way. Most likely a Injun."

"How?"

"Prob'ly a arrow, son. Maybeso, take it in the back."

"Injun. Sure?"

"Injun."

Bass remembered the huge bear in his nightmares, those private visions visited upon him. The huge bear with one eye scarred shut. The dream grizzly that reared on its hind legs and snarled at him from deep in the dark forest of his dreams. The monster's snout had been scarred from many battles, one eye sealed shut with the scar that ran down the forehead, across the mangled eyelid and onto the wounded snout. He would never forget that one eye scarred shut. Never forget that bear which always beckoned him deeper and deeper into the forest. Never forget Emile Sharpe. Assassin hired to kill Paddock. With his one eye scarred shut. A bear hug was a bad omen for a man. Plenty bad medicine.

"A fella doesn't count on just dying in his sleep when he comes out to the mountains, does he?" Paddock turned to look sidelong at his older partner.

"You got you two winters under your belt—an' you're askin' me that question? C'mon, now," Bass declared as his face cracked with a grin. "You know better'n that, son. Chances are, you won't die a old man out here. Gone under afore old age comes 'round. Not many an old man out here in these mountains." His arm swept a grand arc from south to northwest.

"You old for the mountains?"

"Well, now. There's some say that I am that, Josiah. There're some say Titus Bass is an old man out here."

" 'Cause most fellers are younger—"

"That's right," Titus replied. "Most fellers out here be strappin' young pups like you, Mr. Paddock. Green as spring an' wet behin't the ears."

"Now wait just a minute here—"

"An' most of 'em never make it two winters, like you have, Josiah," Bass piped, interrupting Paddock's protest. "You come a long way, son. Long way, indeed."

"You keep saying that, Scratch."

" 'Cause I mean it. There's been a lotta growin' inside you, down where the man of you comes from—down inside the gut. That's where the growin's been."

The younger man cranked his head over to look the older trapper in the eyes. "There been times, I admit to, when I told myself I was ready to head back east somewhere. Get away from here with my hair while I still got it."

"Yeah?"

"But I don't belong back there anymore," Josiah blurted out. "I know it's only been two winters I've been out here, but I still don't belong in what's left for me back there."

"Most of us don't belong back there, neither. Cain't go back for one reason or 'nother. A few, sure—they're runnin' from the law. Knowin' the law ain't gonna come after 'em out here. Most of 'em, howsomever, most of 'em come out here lookin' for somethin' these mountains can give 'em. Somethin' they ain't found yet—leastways not back there." He threw a thumb east.

"What is it they come looking for?" Josiah asked.

"You don't know? You come runnin' out here your own self."

"I come running is right," Josiah agreed. "I was running *away* from something—not trying to run *toward* something."

"You may think that to be true, son, but there you're lyin' to yourself," Bass began, then spit a brown jet of tobacco juice into the grass at their feet. "Lotta fellas think the same way as you. You all believe that you're runnin' away from somethin'. Let me tell you a certain now. All the time a fella runs away from somethin' back there, an' that fella ain't lookin' back—he's really runnin' toward somethin'. If'n you ain't lookin' back at what you left behin't, you ain't runnin' away from it, Josiah. You're runnin' toward somethin'. Somethin' you may not even know what yet. Even though you got them two winters hiver'nin' in these high hills."

Paddock chewed over the words for some time before he finally responded. "Since I didn't ever look back when I left St. Louis, back at what little was left me there when I pulled away—you're saying that I ain't running away?"

"Right."

"I think I see it, see what you're saying, Scratch." He nodded once for emphasis. "I see what you mean. I was looking for something more than just a place to hide out here. Something much more."

"An' you found it. Wife—"

"And a strapping son up there with that good woman. Good friends." Josiah flashed a toothy smile Bass's way.

"Good friends always help matters, don't they?"

"Yessir! I see just what it is now. Been looking at things wrong for the past couple of years. Feeling guilty, too. Guilty 'cause I thought I was running."

"You was wrong for it," Titus injected. "Let it be. You're out here where you belong, in these mountains. Where you come to, an' where your kind belongs."

"Never thought of it that way," Josiah replied softly. "My kind. Feels strange to count myself into all this. My kind." He shook his head. "I just don't know."

"If you don't know by now, son," Bass said, then spit again for added emphasis, "you may never know if you're with your own kind."

He looked up ahead and noticed that the two women had halted the pack string where the trees ended on the rise. They awaited the arrival of the two white men. The partners drew up alongside the Indian women to look down into the valley before them. Waits-by-the-Water turned toward Bass with a question in her eyes, gesturing with her arm toward the beautiful mountain park stretching itself below at their feet.

He nodded. "Yes, lil' lady. This is it. South Park. The Bayou Salade. Whoooeeeee! We made it with our hair!"

"This really where we spend the fall trapping?" Paddock asked. "We finally made it?"

"This is the genuwine place, son," Bass smiled broadly, the deep lines around his nose crinkling.

"No more travel for awhile then?"

"You're right there again, Josiah Paddock." Bass nodded once then leaned over to kiss his woman lightly on the cheek. "The women set up a camp an' we don't have to move 'til winter wants to come settin' in on us. More beaver—prime beaver down there—why, we'll be as busy as we wanna be. Fill out our packs afore we head down to Taos to trade for the winter. Geegaws for the winter! An' some lightnin' for our dry throats ever'day. What say you?"

"It all sounds all right to me," Paddock roared back enthusiastically.

"*All right?* You crazy pup. We've made it! To the Bayou Salade an' all you can say is it's *all right?*" The crow's feet at the corners of his eyes danced electrically. "This is prime doin's! Ain't no other place like this'un in the whole of the mountains—ain't likely the rest of the whole world."

"Jeeezuz! All right! Enough already!" Josiah waved his hand at the older trapper. "I believe you. This place is sure enough pretty, gotta be one of the prettiest I've seen in my two years. I'm a true believer, Scratch. I'm a believer!"

"If you agreed with me all along, why the hell we sittin' here arguin'?"

Josiah shook his head in wonder. "I don't have the slightest notion, old man."

"Let's be gone down there an' set us up a fall camp. Got good light for several more hours. We get us a lot done while these gals cook us up a roast, somethin' such. Jumpin' Jehoshaphat! I'm back! Back to South Park! The Bayou Salade!" His voice trailed off after him through the stands of pine as Bass roared down the mountain side.

Paddock looked at the two bewildered women, and grinned. He nodded to let them know it was time to pull the packstring off the slope. "We better follow him," he said as he watched the older man whooping and yelling, galloping full tilt, waving his hat in the air and singing out at the top of his lungs. Scratch rode high, standing tall in the stirrups.

"Looks like he needs someone to look after him," Josiah smiled. "That old man's lucky he's got me, and you ladies. Crazy loon's lucky he's got us to look after him."

3 THE RAIN THREW itself against the wooden siding of the house with a staccato rage. Wind wallowing its way through the huge old trees surrounding the house sped the raindrops on their way toward a noisy attack on the thick windowpanes. Wind and rain rose and fell, rose and fell, whining their wet way around his little world.

Eventually he turned away from the cold at the window and hobbled slowly toward the iron stove standing alone in the corner of this small, private study. After opening the tiny door and stirring at the fallow coals, chilled and aching hands threw more kindling on the feeble, unsure flames. Surely the heat from the rekindled fire would warm all the aching joints throughout his body.

He turned at the sound of a gust of wind battering hard against the house, against that very window, the only one in the small room. It was almost as if the wind itself were trying to force entry to his refuge, this lonely sanctuary he had sought. For many, many days now he had not emerged from his small study on the attic floor of this huge old house. Up and away from things—exactly why he had run here. Taking his meals as the servants brought them. Whisking them away as they came to remove the chamberpot. He cared little for their ministering to his diminishing needs. He was getting too old to care. Yet, he mused, ultimately an old man should be concerned if there would be someone to care for him when he was not able to care for himself.

The wind pressing against the clapboards, seeking a way in at him, made him shiver and draw the heavy, woolen cloak about his shoulders all the more tightly. Yet the cloak and a shawl were still not enough. He was cold from the inside out. Perhaps only the fire would help. Outside fell a rain that spoke of autumn and the coming, gray winter. From now on, the days would get much colder. But he could not warm himself as it was. Finally the kindling caught fire and he threw some small pieces of wood atop the new flames. He kicked the door to the stove; it clurunked shut and latched.

Back to the window where he stood staring out a moment before leaning his head against the cold windowpane. Then closed his eyes. The glass cool against the scrimshawed skin of his forehead. Perhaps not even his stove's fire would help this coming winter. The snow would blanket deep and wet and heavy. The wind would come to seek him out once more, this time with a vengeance. Winter, and cold—and vengeance.

He slowly opened his eyes, staring through the pane and the water raging against the window. With a sigh he forced the aching joints in his hips and knees to carry the rest of him toward the small bed the servants had thrown together at his urging. Brought up from the servants' quarters, it was made with wooden slats barely two feet off the walnut plank floor. The down mattress lay suspended in a brown web of rope. He needed not the comfort of the huge bed below him on the main floor. He felt he did not deserve it. Not like before. Perhaps never again.

The cold pain seared through him as he gradually leaned back and stretched the arthritic joints out across the narrow bed. Like shards of hot ice piercing his weakened body. He tugged at the thick, woolen coverlet so that it draped over most of his thinning frame. Finally, the gray head resigned itself to rest and thrumped back against the thick pillow he allowed himself during his solitary cloister. Such simple joys he bestowed upon himself.

It had always been that way. Starting out as a clerk and making his own fortune in the early days of the fur trade along the rivers. Seeing that the company crews pushed their hazardous way ever farther into the lands of fur-bearing animals and those Indians who dwelled there. Stingy, folks had called him back then. While he had been amassing his considerable fortune, the old man had rarely spent any of that young man's money on himself. So it was that naturally he had come to gather a tidy bit of wealth while other, lesser, men would always be found wanting at his advanced age. Yet, never had his wife, nor any of his sons gone wanting for a thing. Not through all the years.

He shivered with the thought. She had left him on such a day. So damp, so cold. His wife of but few years, wasting away under the strain of two stillborn sons before they finally had two healthy sons, and then young Henri, their pride. His wife finally died in a third stillbirth. All so fitting, he agonized many times over. So bitterly fitting that she should waste away giving him sons.

The old man had buried his wife and sought not another. Putting efforts and time and energies into the young infant Henri who grew into a handsome boy, then a young man and finally the young fellow who had joined his brothers at their father's side in the family business. Furs from the upper rivers. Far up the rivers—

Would he ever come? It had been so long already. It was fall, wasn't it? Yes, autumn of the leaves afire, their colors lighting up the frosty mornings. Autumn already and the man had not returned with—with—

He would not think on it any more today. Just shut his eyes and dream. Slip back into sleep and move his mind away from the pain of waiting. Ever since it had been that month, that week, and that day when the one he had hired should have returned. Ever since that singular hour he had taken to this small study and not emerged.

Here he would wait. From his attic window he could watch the docks and wharfs down by the huge warehouses hunkered at the water's edge. From the single, small window by his tiny bed, the frail, thinning old man would be able to see anyone approach the gates in the great stone wall surrounding his house. He would be able to see the guards admit the tall hired one. He would watch the long, loping strides as the hired one made his way up the stone walk toward the portico and the main door. Through those great oak doors he would easily shove himself, push past the frightened house servants, bound heavily up the great flight of walnut stairs. Then suddenly the hired one would thrust himself into the small attic study where the old man had secreted himself. The hired one would know where to find the old man. He would know the small one was hidden up here, awaiting the hunter's return. He would know—just as the hunter had known everything else.

The frail man's breathing rattled against the fluid in his chest. Just a touch of some fever, he thought. Nothing but a bit of a fever. He'll find me up here. He'll have to find me here, or he does not receive the rest of his own small fortune. And he will want what is coming to him.

His eyes fluttered open a moment, like tiny, dark wrens taking flight. He gazed quickly at the small sack of gold specie nestled on that tiny table which stood opposite the window. Near the door. The rest of the giant's pay. What he would return for. That—and to gloat, most likely.

The tired eyes closed after staring at the object next to the velvet sack bulging with coins. Even in the dimming light of the cloudy, blackened afternoon, the beauty of its patterned metal still vividly carved a place in his mind. Over and over the past countless days he had stared at the barrel of the pistol. Again and again he almost willed himself his own chance at his son's murderer. So sweet! He swallowed against the imagined taste in his mouth. How sweet revenge could be to a man who had lost close to everything he had ever cared for. He suddenly willed himself a place in the wilderness alongside the hired one.

There, at the giant's side—to pull the trigger himself. To watch the murderer fall, his blood spilling across the grass and dust. To watch the young, black-hearted American's life slipping away. Ahhhh, so sweet it would be. He had willed himself a place along with the savage, monstrous messenger of death. Himself a lord of the borderlands. That borderland somewhere between justice and retribution. Along the border between civilization and the wildness that was the far west. Out there where few survived, he had sent the best. The hired one, a *borderlord.*

A frail smile wrinkled the old man's lips. He was amused that he too was a borderlord. Was it not *his* money, *his* wealth, *his* power that ruled a goodly portion of that far western wilderness? Was it not that he too was a borderlord? Let no man mistake that. Just as worthy, all the more powerful if need be, the old man knew he had long ago earned himself that distinction. He, too, was a borderlord.

When would he return?

The smile faded from the gray, ghostlike skin.

When will he finally bring me, bring to me—the proof he had done what he was hired to do? When—oh, when?

The small, thinning, wasting body suddenly twisted to the side and was racked with pained sobbing. It would be soon. To finally know death had come to his son's murderer. To hear the words from the lips of the giant himself. Only then would the old man feel strong enough to leave this small room. Only then

32

could he venture forth from sanctuary. Only after he was told the job was finished would he leave this prison he had locked himself into—his own jailer.

The thin, weakened body quaked with the crackled sobbing. A hard taskmaster he had made of himself. A cruel jailer he had become. No one else would ever know what toll he had exacted upon himself. No one.

Except God. And the giant. Borderlords both.

SO quickly the season began to turn. Already the first days in the *Moon of Black Calves*. Back east they would have called it September. But out here in the mountain west, things were kept simpler, in a more natural order. A man did not have to remember where a certain named month fell within that order which he had learned to recite the twelve months of the year. Out here a man remembered instead the rotation of the moons with what happened between the earth and the sky in the natural order of living things. A great turning. A great turning within that greater circle of his universe. The *Moon of Black Calves*, when the young spring buffalo calves shed their birthcoats of light red wool for the more mature dark browns and blacks of coming adulthood. The seasons turned and the circle came back on itself.

So it was, another turning in the great circle. Titus Bass had come back home to his beloved valley. It was here that so many treasured memories lay, here that so many important chapters of his life had been written. The old trapper had led his little party down the mountainside into the wide, peak-locked valley. At the lower elevations the air still whispered of coming autumn. Already some of the aspen back up there, high in the early-snow-dusted passes, having stood silent for all those circles of years, were now briefly smitten with gold once more. Their bright colors began to glitter and sparkle across the shimmering hillside among the dark green of pine and spruce.

It took them the better part of the afternoon, but Bass finally led the group of humans and sweated animals into a bowl large enough for grazing the stock through many weeks, yet small enough for their security. It was off the beaten track of things, he had told them. Not anywhere near the usual tramping grounds over which the various tribes who haunted South Park would roam. Finally, Scratch had dropped to the ground and motioned for the others to do likewise. Nodding several times with satisfaction, he darted here and there over the site.

"You have been here?" Waits-by-the-Water asked him in Crow.

"Years ago," Scratch answered in English. "Right here—a—a few years back."

"This where you want to do it?" Josiah asked as he strode up to the older man's side.

Scratch turned and smiled. "This is the place. Not much the worse for wear, neither." He sighed openly. "This is where we put down stakes for the fall hunt."

"Won't go hungry, that's for sure," Paddock added. "With all the buffalo we come by. All them humps moving, why the valley floor looked like the hills themselves were alive, slowly rolling up and down."

Scratch grinned widely. "Told you it was some, didn't I? Ain't no other such place like this. Critters come down outta the mountains all 'round this valley, come to the valley floor for special. The grass is loaded up with natural salts, natural licks. Four-legged critters get drawed here—just like this ol' two-legged runagate hisself."

"Suppose we get busy taking the loads off the animals we got with us." Josiah turned toward the pack horses.

"You an' the women get it all dropped." Bass started off, then turned back toward Josiah. "I got to lay out our territory."

Josiah watched him turn away, headed into the trees where he paced uphill some twenty yards and turned his back to the campsight. From where he stood, he could only see what looked like the old man pulling aside his breechclout. Intrigued, Paddock braced uphill toward the older man.

"What the hell are you doin'?" he asked as Bass went off to skitter farther along the side of the hill some twenty more feet.

Bass wheeled, startled, then pulled his penis out of his breechclout once more. "I'm waterin' the place, son. Lettin' the critters know this is my place. Our place. You can help, too, if you've a mind to. I been holdin' this water for a few hours now, knowin' I was gonna have to have me some to mark the spot for our camp."

"Y-you—you what?" Josiah shook his head, incredulous. "You're peeing on the ground?" He suddenly had to take off after the older man as Bass relocated another thirty feet away and sprinkled the grass, trees and bushes with his urine.

"That's plumb center! First whack, boy."

"L-like—like a dog?" Josiah squeaked in amazement. "Just like a dog would stand on his three legs and mark a spot for his own?"

"Sounds to me like you're learnin'."

"I'll be go to—" he whispered.

"Better you be goin' pee," Scratch said. "Better you be goin' pee down the hill for us." He motioned in a large arc with a free arm. "Sprinkle your water here an' there. Give us lots of room. Mark the outside of that meadow down over there, son. Give the horses lots of room."

Josiah stood riveted to the spot when Bass lumbered off the next time. He waggled his head as if something might come loose. "Just what critter you expect to scare off with your pee?"

Scratch turned toward the younger man. "You still don't get it, eh? I ain't about to scare off no critter with my pee. But, if'n you wanna know—wolves, coyotes an' such. They come in an' chew up saddle gear, tack an'—"

"Damn! If that don't take first prize an' the kitty to boot," Josiah roared in merriment. "Peeing like that. No wolf I know of gonna tuck his tail between his legs just 'cause of some lil' bit of your piss. No, sir. Damn. This is a good one you're trying to pull my leg on, and you're doing it with a straight face, too—like you want me to really believe you."

Scratch watched the younger trapper laugh all the harder, deciding not to let himself get angry over the insult because, after all, the boy knew no better. He had never had to set up a fall or winter camp on his own. The young man simply knew no better.

"Hhhrrruummppp," Bass grumbled as he moved to a new spot and began wetting it down.

"You remember that wolf I killed last fall?" Josiah asked as he slapped his thigh in mirth. "The one I killed with my knife?"

Josiah waited for Bass to answer, waited for the old man to recall the huge, black animal which had slunk into their campsight, dangerously close to the men and their fire. But all Bass did now was to glare back over his shoulder a brief moment, then continue on to select another new watering location.

"That one." Paddock finally slowed down the chuckling. "That big son of a bitch would walk right on by your little tinkle-pee on the bushes." That set him to guffawing again.

Scratch wheeled and marched purposefully downhill a few yards to where the young man crouched half-bent over, laughing merrily to himself. Titus yanked his breechclout aside and quickly sprayed Paddock's lower leggings and moccasins. Josiah immediately shut up and jumped back out of the warm stream's way.

"What the hell you do that for?" Paddock bellowed.

"Maybe, just maybe, you shut up for once an' really listen what I'm sayin' to you," Bass said before he set off to water another spot back up the hillside. "This is the way of the wolf, Josiah Paddock. An' the sooner you learn of it, the better we both be. Better off, son. The way of the wolf. This is 'sactly the same way he marks his ground. So, it's 'sactly the way I always mark mine. Much as I hate wolves, much as a wolf don't trust me—we can get along for a time."

"Just what—"

Bass saw the younger trapper waggle his head from side to side again. "The wolf wants his sign, his pee, to be respected by all other critters. So, he's one to respect the sign of them other critters. He'll stay away."

"Now how you so dad-blamed sure of that?" Josiah stared down at his soaked leggings and moccasins.

"Wolves them ownselves taught it to me, son," Bass answered.

"How'd they show you? By peeing?" Josiah grinned.

"You shut your mouth long enough, your ears can hear so you can learn somethin', young'un," Bass snapped and began to spray a new location. "I learned all 'bout the wolf 'cause I watched him. Then I tried what he did. An' it worked. Nary a wolf come into my camp after I started sprayin' a little pee here, layin' a little pee there."

"Well—why—why you have to—"

"Have to what, Josiah?" Bass cocked his head back to gaze at the young trapper. "Have to spray you?"

"Yeah. Why you have to go and piss on me?"

"Shit. Don't you see, boy?"

"See what? I don't see at all why you had to go and get my leggings wet with your piss. You paying me back for getting your pisser sunburned, ain't you?"

35

"Nothin' such, Josiah. Just want you to be safe, is all." Bass turned and sprinkled the base of some aspen trunks.

"W-what? You want me to be safe? Safe from what?"

"Wolves," Bass answered.

"Yeah?"

"Ain't a wolf about to touch you now, son," Bass grinned.

"Why? 'Cause Titus Bass marked me as part of his ground—like he's marking our camp?"

"Nope," Bass answered simply. " 'Cause you smell so bad with that pee on your ownself." He pinched his nose dramatically. "Whoooooeeee! You smell devilsome."

This time the old one had to laugh. And a good chuckle it was, especially when Paddock finally joined in. Josiah stomped up beside the older trapper and slapped him on the back. Then Josiah theatrically yanked aside his breechclout and began to sprinkle the leaves of bushes and trunks of trees with his urine. He hopped away, clamping down hard on his penis and sprayed another area. Chuckling all the while, both of them sprinkled. Paddock began humming as he hopped around the meadow, spraying the bushes and the grass. Humming happily, contented, his leggings and moccasins beginning to dry already.

This was their spot, their place in the world. And he would help the older man claim it from the forest for their use. Stake out their part of the wilderness the same way the wild things would claim theirs. This was his ground. It was here that his family would live for the short fall season. It was here that he would set down roots, here as much as any other place he had ever been.

Paddock drew back and sighed. Across the small meadow, Bass had evidently finished his claiming of that territory. The old trapper was picketing the first of the pack animals, having drawn off its load from the horse's back. The small Indian mustang immediately proceeded to plop to the ground, roll from its side onto its back, legs waving, flagging the air like a huge ungainly coon dog. By twisting and rolling, the small pony was able to scratch its back tortured by the trappers' load it had carried over the mountains from rendezvous. Too, a good roll and dusting helped protect against the biting of both flies and troublesome mosquitoes. A good romp in the grass before teeth-tugging, grass-chewing happiness. First the bliss of a good hide-scouring wallow on the ground.

Scratch finished driving the picket pin into the rocky soil, then stared at the gyrating pony a moment. He bent down and yanked up a huge handful of the tufted grasses. Bass tossed the weathered grass at the pony. Almost playfully—like a young boy teasing his pet. Then the older man plodded back toward the campsite itself, where he would free another of the ponies from its trail burden.

Several magpies darted overhead and swept low past Josiah. He was startled by the jagged shadows as they flitted across the ground. Then he laughed at himself for getting boogered at the flitting shadows—being scared of something so familiar and not a thing to be the least bit skittish of. His chuckle ended, yet the smile remained as he watched his family and friends across the small meadow. Soft sounds on the light breeze lifting the leaves and needles of the trees about him. The gurgling murmur of the small creek that ran through the middle of this open bowl. Plenty of water. Bass never made a mistake in choosing a site. Always had good water where he bedded down.

Josiah turned slowly, gazing about him at the little valley they had chosen for a home, a valley that ran down toward the larger park, the Bayou Salade. Here they would be sheltered by the hills and rock outcroppings. Double purpose, double use from those rocky hillsides. The stony faces would reflect the heat of their warm cooking fires on those nippy, frosty fall mornings and evenings to come. Additionally, these rocky outcrops served to better hide the entrance to this small valley from those who would casually stroll through the larger valley below them. And among the trees, plenty of deadfall and squaw-wood galore. If they had to, they could last the winter here. Yes, he thought. Enough to last the winter right here. But still the young trapper was anxious for the fall hunt to pass quickly so they could get on south to the Mexican lands. Perhaps like a sailor giddy for a new port, novel experiences, some new adventure, meeting foreign peoples. Yes, already he yearned for that time to come when they would push on south toward this famous Taos town.

"Want some help?" Josiah had wandered back across the grassy side of the meadow to approach the older trapper.

"Sure," Bass nodded after looking up from freeing the coarse packsaddle cinch off another pony. "Here, son, you finish with these here pack animules. I'll be helpin' the women get the gear sorted out, and all the truck put away proper. Help 'em get the shelters pulled up. You go 'head an' finish this here."

Bass skittered over to shove himself between the two Indian women, almost like a fussy, nosy, busybody. "Here, here, ladies. Lemme help you two. Like this," he said as he tore at the rawhide knots, freeing the buffalo-hide panniers so the women could get to the camp goods packed inside.

"Just like that." Bass stood back to let the two women worry over the gear. "Purty slick, if I don't say. I always pack me a mean mule—an' you gotta be able to get to your truck quick. That's right, just lay that over there."

As Paddock dropped each animal's packs, Bass was there to work at the tight rawhide knots, to pull free the thick rawhide lashings. Scratch finally pulled loose the large half-dome structure that had been his winter home for those freeze-ups gone by spent with the Sparrowhawk people. A multitude of memories flooded over him until he looked up to find Waits-by-the-Water staring softly, doe-eyed at him.

"We let the young'uns use this," he muttered, his hands flapping uselessly, self-consciously.

"How will you stay warm?" she asked of him in Crow.

"I have you, lil' darlin'," he answered in English, continually prodding her to use more and more of his tongue.

"That will not fight off the chill that tells of Winter Man's coming," she continued in Sparrowhawk, refusing to use the more difficult English. "I am not fat enough to keep you warm under the robes come wintertime."

"Ah! That's where you are soooo wrong. You make this ol' buzzard's blood boil, you li'l she-cat."

He quickly reached out for her and pulled the Crow woman to him in a tight embrace. Bass drank deeply of her scented hair—slicked shiny with bear grease, made fragrant with crushed leaves, flower blossoms and sage. The smell of this very wilderness. Fragrances that sank deep into his lungs and rose headily to his brain.

"I have you for all time to keep me warm, my woman," Bass pushed himself to arms' length away from her, his hands still resting gently on the top of her shoulders. It was her tongue now that he spoke, though less and less frequently he reverted to Crow. He only used her language whenever there were concepts he could not adequately express in English, when there were things to be said between them he could not find words for in his own language.

"I am fat enough to keep my husband warm?" she asked as she turned her face slightly away from his, knowing just how much of a coquette, just how much of a tease she could be with this man.

"Yes, you are fat enough," Bass smiled as he kissed her forehead.

Damn but this copper-skinned woman was the most seductive animal on two feet he had ever met. He patted both sides of her hips, feeling their maturing roundness before he let his gnarled, rough hands wander on back so that each palm cupped a globe of her rear end. He suddenly tugged her against him fiercely.

"My husband wants me now?" Waits-by-the-Water inquired, wide-eyed after catching her breath.

"Soon," he answered hoarsely in her ear. "Maybe tonight. We celebrate coming to this valley. I want to give you a child."

She pulled her head out of his shoulder and beamed up at his grizzled, gray-bearded face. "I, too, wish to give my husband a child."

"Then all we gotta do is keep tryin'," he smiled widely, showing his teeth before he gave her a gentle peck on the cheek and dropped to his knees.

Together they stretched out the buffalo-hide structure, then dragged it over by the site chosen for the shelters. Bass handed his wife a camp axe and waved for her to follow him into the trees. There they attacked a grove of tall, stately lodgepole pine. He cut the narrow trees down and set Waits-by-the-Water to skinning the branches and knots off the trunks. Soon he had himself an armload to drag back into camp where he dropped them by the shelter site. After two more loads pulled back to camp, Scratch called a halt for a breather.

"This ol' feller ain't young as he used to be," he wheezed, a little short of breath. "Ain't near as young as you." He sank to the ground beside the hide shelter and the lodgepole pine, leaning back to relax.

Looks Far came over to the couple, quickly joined by Paddock who had finished his own chores with the pack animals and had staked the riding horses out close to camp. The Flathead woman had just laid Joshua out on a buffalo robe where the child was sleeping with a full tummy of warm milk. Now she was ready to pitch in once more.

"Looks to be all of you're ready to put this ol' man back to work, eh?"

"That's about the shape of it, Scratch," the younger man answered. "Let's get some shelter up before it gets too dark to see any longer."

Scratch considered the fading sunlight as the bright orb fell upon those tree tops stretching up toward the western peaks. "Think you're right, son." He stood up slowly, the kinks from the day's ride having knotted in the muscles and settled in his joints during the short rest. "Best get it finished afore dark."

The four set up the old buffalo-hide shelter. With that secure, they pitched a frame of the lodgepole over which was draped the old mackinaw blankets Bass had carried for countless seasons, then topped off with some limbs the Crow woman had whacked off the lodgepole pine. Bass eventually stepped back to appraise the results of their labor.

"Looks good enough," he said. "Let's call it home. We need us a fire goin'—right about—here."

His moccasined toe made a circle on the ground, showing Josiah where to make the firepit in the center of their little compound. While Josiah built the fire and Looks Far began slicing some meat to roast over the flames, the other couple set about roping together another framework of that lodgepole still not used. They wove the extra pine boughs together before they stored away their trade goods and supplies in the bower lean-to. Camp was complete.

"Looks to be we're finished," Scratch commented with a breathy sigh.

"And just about time," Paddock chimed in merrily. He pointed first to the waning light turning purple on the western skyline, then he held up the tip of his knife. From the glinting point hung a thin strip of venison that had been barely kissed with flame to bring out its juicy, savory pinkness. "Supper's on, all."

Both women ate more delicately than did their husbands. The two trappers were doubly ravenous after the long trail-riding, mountain-climbing day, the exertions of unpacking and setting up camp. Quickly they wolfed down strip after strip of the lean, juicy meat, every bite dripping grease into their shaggy, unkempt beards.

"Don't think it can get much better'n this, can it?" Bass inquired, punctuating his question with an elbow jabbed into Paddock's ribs.

"You glad to be here? To be back here, huh?"

"Yup," Scratch mouthed around the bite he had just torn off. He gulped and swallowed the fire-roasted flesh, then licked his fingers clean of the dripping grease.

Finally, he looked about the group and sighed. "Home," the old trapper said quietly. Each of the others answered with a smile. Titus sighed contentedly and listened to the sounds of the coming evening.

Insects buzzed before the paling daylight, rushing in flight against the stretching darkness. The calling of birds now and again answered the howling of coyotes and wolves out among the surrounding hills. And finally there rose those songs played by the breezes through those trees near camp. Joshua snored gently from the robe at his mother's side.

Then Paddock suddenly belched loudly from the hearty meal he was wolfing down and both the women let go with their gentle, musical, tinkling laughter. All the sounds of this wild place made comfortable for him and his friends. Family all.

"Damn!" Scratch exclaimed loudly. "It's some punkins!" he roared. "Good to be back home!"

4 "JUST WHAT YOU fixin' to do with that?" Bass halted in the shade beneath a canopy of pines.

"This?" Paddock turned toward the older man, finished with his rummaging around in their equipment and plunder.

"Yep. That's what I asked, you young whelp."

Josiah rose with the bow and the arrow-filled quiver that had once belonged to Asa McAfferty. "Fixing to learn how to shoot it—if it's so all-fired important for you to know exactly what I'm gonna do with it."

"You just been full of all kinds of surprises, ain't you?" Scratch commented.

"Same as you, old man."

"You been actin' some strange here lately, boy." Bass sat down on the large stone near the wisps of a dying fire. "Ever since we pulled outta that valley down to the Green—where we got the ponies stole. Weeks ago. Somethin' not quite the same with you. Leastways, I had to say it, son."

"Not quite the same, huh?"

"Nope." Bass spit into the ashes, causing a small eruption of gray feather-ash to explode into the air.

Bass waited for a moment while the young trapper continued to strap on his belt and knives, next pulling over his shoulders the shooting pouch and powder horn. Finally Paddock slipped the coyote-hide quiver over his shoulder before Scratch continued.

"You ain't gonna admit you're up to somethin'?"

"Ain't up to nothin' at all now," Josiah answered as he tugged to straighten out his shirt.

"Not a thing?"

"Nope."

Scratch shook his head, feeling the incompleteness of it. "I just cain't rightly put my finger on it. Somethin' just ain't the same here. Between us. Maybeso just with you. I ain't changed, leastways as I can savvy I ain't."

"Dammit, you're just a fussy old woman sometimes," Josiah sputtered defensively at the old trapper. "Ain't a thing wrong with me. Ain't a thing wrong between us neither. All this over me wanting to learn how to shoot this damned thing?" He stuffed the bow down into the quiver along with the rosewood-shafted arrows.

"Fussy old woman, am I?"

"That's right." Josiah smiled generously.

"Nothin' eatin' at your craw, is it?"

"Not that I know of," Paddock answered with a wide grin.

Bass turned at the sound of hoofs crunching across the dry needles. Looks Far was leading two horses into camp. She handed one rawhide rein to Paddock, then climbed aboard her own small pony.

"What you two doin' with Joshua?" Titus asked, turning his head from side to side, searching the camp.

"He is sleeping—shhh!" came the loud whisper from the shelters where Waits-by-the-Water motioned for the jabbering adults to be quieter.

"You takin' care of the boy while these two young'uns go galavantin' off across the damned countryside?" Bass asked, surprised.

The Crow woman merely nodded in the affirmative and went back to repairing one of Bass's many worn moccasins.

"I figure it's good training for her," Josiah said as he eased himself down onto leather. "It'll be good practice for you, too." He tapped knees along the pony's sides.

"W-what you mean, practice for me?" Bass hollered after him.

"When you finally start a family of your own, old man!" Paddock yelled back as he and the Flathead woman trotted into the trees, heading down into the bottom of the broad valley.

"Hhrrrmmppph!" Bass said as he spit again into the firepit. He trudged over to sit down beside the Crow woman and stared after the younger couple as they disappeared into the dappling of light and shadow draped across the aspen-covered hillside.

The couple rode for more than an hour, that whole time without a word spoken to one another. From time to time, their only communication was but a look, a glance at the other and smiles that spread quickly across their faces. Theirs to enjoy, this moment alone with one another. A time not cluttered with words. Feelings only, perhaps. Letting things pour over them in this private time together. Sharing this ride, sharing the country.

Paddock brought his hand up slightly to signal the young woman to stop. Then he brought his arm forward to point down into the meadow below them. There in the grassy bottom of the bowl flowed a small stream, for the most part dammed up by industrious beaver. Around the still, glassy water gathered several deer, buck and doe both. Looks Far nodded, and tapped on the quiver at Paddock's back.

He nodded once in answer, then handed her the rifle he had been carrying across his thighs while on horseback. The Flathead woman signed that she wanted no horn—that she did not want him to kill a buck. He agreed. A doe would be tastier, more tender for dinner this night. Kicking his right leg over the top of his saddle, Josiah slipped to the ground before handing the woman his rein.

The young trapper slipped the wood and sinew-reinforced bow out of the coyote-skin quiver, then removed one of the arrows, to be held in his left hand with the bow. With his right hand he caressed his woman's bare calf. She smiled down at him before he turned away, strode into a stand of trees that ran down the hillside toward the open meadow.

Looks Far waited a moment, then slid down from her pad saddle. As she stretched to tie the two ponies to a young aspen, the buckskin of her dress drew tight across her swollen breasts. They were already full of milk again, and Joshua would not be able to nurse from her until they returned to camp later in the afternoon. Then she would feed the infant, now six months old, while her man was out setting traps and rebaiting the old sets. With a juicy venison roast spitted over the flames, it would indeed be a good dinner for them all. She and Waits-by-the-Water had located a harvest of wild mushrooms and wild onions and turnips, too. With these, every dinner had become a feast. They would laugh and giggle with one another, watching as the two white trappers devoured the wild plants the women had cooked to a savory softness.

Looking down now at her skin dress beneath the elkhide cape over her shoulders, Looks Far saw the damp stain radiating out around her nipples, stains that bespoke each breast's fullness. Yes, again she would enjoy having the little one's lips suck and draw on her nipples this night. With his nursing, she felt the growing closeness to that little life she had carried within her belly for so long—through the difficult labor that had caused others to think both mother and child should be taken away to the Other Side. Until, with the help of Dreams-of-Horses, a mystical crone old beyond years, the young Flathead finally delivered the newborn life amidst the heavy, wet snows of a late March storm.

A smile grew on her lips as she sat down in the grass to await her husband's return from hunting. True, she enjoyed the feel of the infant's gentle pull at her nipples, the suckling of his little, toothless mouth at her breast. There was something almost sexual, warmly sensual in the pleasure. So sensual, Looks Far was not so sure it was right to feel this way when her son suckled at her breast. There was really no one she could ask, not even the Crow woman. Waits-by-the-Water had not yet had a child, so she wouldn't know. Perhaps, after all, there was nothing wrong in this pleasure it brought her to feel the lips tight on her breasts, the pulling and suckling at her nipples.

Suddenly, the doe below her dropped as she watched, barely an instant after it had raised its head from drinking. The animal twisted in the grass by the pond's edge, thrashing slightly and causing the other nearby animals to bolt away into the trees, altered by something unknown, unseen and almost unheard.

Escape.

The word crystallized in the woman's mind. But it was too late for the doe. The animal flailed wildly, unable to rise on her legs. Escape from death. Too late, Looks Far thought as she saw Josiah emerge from the quaking, golden-touched aspens, another arrow ready and partly drawn against the taut bowstring.

For an instant, Looks Far was amazed that her husband looked so much like a Flathead warrior, perhaps even one of the young men she had grown up with in her village. Then he finally stepped out from the shadows of the sun-smitten aspens. Her husband again became a white man. He was tall against the trees, in a way almost stunting the short bow he was just now letting drop to his side, assured of his kill—assured that the doe would not leap up and bound away.

Yes, he was ultimately a white man, she thought. Yet for all the difficulties that fact caused for the two of them, she still loved this young trapper. Completely. At times he was totally unable to understand her life—her past growing up in the wilderness, wandering season after season in search of buffalo. Each day strung like beads on a longer and longer thong. Much of the time he failed to grasp her reverence for each and every day, worshipping its pains as much as she exalted in its joys. Her man tried so hard, she thought. True, he tried to understand her special reverence. At times he sat beside her in silence, watching the sunset along with her, gazing down at his son suckling at the young mother's breast. He did try.

That thought warmed her all the more from within. The sun dripped down over her, now causing Looks Far to take off her cape and drape it across her pad saddle. Then she tugged gently at their two ponies and led them down toward her husband and the deer he was dressing out.

"She is a fine one, this little doe," Josiah said as he rose from the carcass, his fingers bloodied by the long slice he had just made from neck to haunch.

Looks Far Woman tethered the ponies to a clump of willow and let them browse before she stepped over to her husband's side.

"My husband shot well," she said in Flathead.

Many times when they were alone, and Josiah had the patience, the couple would converse in her native tongue. At other times, perhaps when he was out of sorts with her, angry at almost anything and perhaps blaming her, Paddock despised speaking in her language. Yet, some of their most private moments were reserved for the soft, trilling sounds of her tongue.

Josiah sighed. "I am glad you did not tell the old one that I have been practicing with the bow." He smiled gently at her.

"We all have secrets, those we hold dear." She knelt beside the warm carcass and placed a hand on one of the hind quarters. "She was fattening herself for the coming winter. Perhaps to have a young one come the *Moon When Ice is Breaking.*"

"The doe will be fine eating for us—for us all," Josiah responded and knelt beside his wife. His mouth watered at the thought.

With their knives working in unison, Paddock and his woman set to work skinning the deer beside the small beaver pond where a few curious animals occasionally wrinkled the surface. From time to time the dark noses broke that flat plane of the water and struck out across the shimmering surface, causing a vee to erupt across that glasslike plane in gentle wavelets. The voyeurs eventually stopped trying to warn neighbors and ceased the loud slapping of their tails on the water. It seemed the animals finally recognized that the two humans at the edge of the pond warranted them no harm. These humans were busy in a world of their own, and posed no trouble for the beaver population in this meadow.

After the warm, sticky hide was pulled off and laid out close by, the couple began to work at the choicer cuts of the young doe. The heart and liver were quickly set upon the green hide. They cut several steaks from the back haunches. Finally four large roasts joined the other select parts. Looks Far quickly trimmed two thongs from the sticky hide, then knelt over the chosen portions. One at a time, the four corners of the hide were gathered up so that the meat could be carried inside the furry container. With the first of the two thongs she made a loop that hung from the gathered portion of the hide, and with the second she secured that loop and the four corners of the green hide all in one process. With the loop, the whole of their meat package could be lashed back of Josiah's saddle.

Looks Far now turned back to the carcass where her husband was pulling at thin strips of soft, lean meat and sucking at them between his bloody fingers. Looking down at him, squatted on the ground beside the ravaged carcass, he reminded her somewhat of a little, starved beggar hunkered down over the remains of a feast.

"What's so funny?" he asked, looking up at her when she began to giggle.

"You cannot wait until dinner?"

"No," he said as he pulled another long slice of meat out through his lips, sucking up the juices and blood as the flesh came out pressed between his teeth.

"You like the warm juices?" She knelt beside him. "And the warm blood?"

"Yes, little one." He smiled at her and smacked his lips.

"You are messy, my husband," she said, pointing at the blood and juices dripping off his lips onto his brown whiskers, then down the front of his leather shirt.

"It makes no difference, my little one." He offered her a slice, but she declined. "I can get as bloody as I want. There is all the water I need right here to clean myself up."

"You do not mind getting bloody?" she asked, with the giggle bouncing around her words.

"Nope," he answered in English, pulling another slice from along the ribs with his knife. Then he shook his head from side to side before he tilted his chin back and let the strip of soft, red meat slither down into his mouth.

He let the warm flesh glide slowly past his lips, clear to the back of his throat. Warm, thick juices to be drawn sensually from the red meat. She felt a tingle race quickly across her belly. But she pushed the feeling away, feeling playful and happy and warm in the afternoon sun, on this day with the burnished fall colors glittering in the meadow about them.

You are one to like the blood." She let her fingers fall almost carelessly into the empty cavern of the doe's abdomen, the organs having been removed and tossed into a gut pile several yards away.

"Told you," he repeated in English. Then he spoke again quickly in Flathead. "Told you I do like the juice and the blood. They make me strong."

"It also makes you a mess." She looked into his face to catch his eyes before she moved.

"It makes me what?"

It was then that she put her plan in motion. The hand that had been carelessly placed out of sight within the empty abdomen now suddenly shot up at him before he could get out of the way. Half-congealed blood spattered across his face. Her hand smeared the thick, dark juices across the cheeks, painted it

44

down his beard and onto his chest before Paddock could react. He fell backwards, sprawled across the drying grass, unable to escape her onslaught. She was on him with a second bloody handful before he could roll away from her attack.

Again and again she slapped at his face with the thick, warm liquid. Josiah pushed her away once, but she was quickly on him again, smearing with her fingers and the heels of her hands. He shoved her again and knocked her off balance, this time sending the Flathead woman backwards. Now he leapt to his feet and charged after her. He wiped some of the blood from his own face and chest, smearing it right across her own look of surprise. He painted her face and neck with the warm liquid. Then his hands dropped, wandering on down to spread the liquid across her breasts as she had done to him.

With the touch of his palms brushing across her nipples, Looks Far suddenly stopped smearing her husband's face. His touch at this most sensitve part of her body halted everything else for her but the complete enjoyment of that touch. A fiery tingle raced once more across her groin.

Josiah suddenly realized where he had placed his hands. Staring down at them, each hand on one of her milk-swollen breasts, the young trapper stopped almost simultaneously with Looks Far. His gaze slowly rose from his hands on her firm breasts to stare into her dark eyes.

The Flathead woman now held his cheeks cupped between her hands, her husband's whiskers still dripping with the red fluid. Her smoky eyes answered the question in his. Paddock reached out, pulled up the bottom of her dress, brought it over her head. As he yanked his belt loose and ripped his bloodied shirt off, his woman slipped her feet out of her moccasins, stood before him naked.

Paddock gulped as he gazed at the wild beauty of her young, tiny body. The coppery breasts were not large nor heavy as many white men liked them. Josiah took another deep breath and held it while she yanked at the thong holding his leggings and breechclout around his waist. There was a suden gush of air from his lungs as the rest of his garments slid down his legs into a cluttered pile at his feet.

A slight searing shiver of anticipation gripped him as he stood transfixed, staring at his wife. Her belly was flattening once more following the pregnancy. His eyes raced over her form. After all this time, he thought, she was only now becoming a woman. My woman.

Paddock knelt and quickly scooped at the empty carcass, his left hand coming away filled with the thick, warm blood slowly collecting in the abdomen. With both hands he began to paint her body, in broad, slow strokes. He smeared the thick, dark liquid across her breasts and up across her neck and shoulders as she sighed with a growing intensity. His hands gently traced lines down from the curve of her neck, across the rigid mounds of her swollen breasts where the nipples hardened beneath his touch. Josiah painted down across the tightening flesh of her belly, then felt her thighs quiver as he brushed the warm liquid across their copper softness. Looks Far moaned from deep in her throat.

45

Almost a whimper. Something so close to immediate ecstasy she was not sure she would be able to remain standing much longer. Her legs shuddered as he continued to rub more insistently against her thighs. The blood was soft, and thick, and sensual. His fingers moved up toward her private self. Looks Far reached out for him.

Paddock was ready for her. Rigid and warm. She moaned audibly at the heat of him in her hand. They both glowed with anticipation.

Looks Far Woman slowly dropped to the grass. Paddock was beside her before another heartbeat coursed its blood through his fiery body. He bent his head down to suck at her breast, easily bringing forth the rich, warm milk which fed their infant son. Now he would draw life from her body. As surely as he drew life from her love. Her love an answer to so many of his prayers.

He rolled over on top of her as she licked at the thick, drying fluid across his shoulder. And he moved inside her, dancing to a rhythm of eons, pulsing to the beat of millennia of animal life. Two animals brought together as one in that glowing, climbing crescendo. Looks Far fought back at him in her own passion. The intensity of their love making almost threw him off but still he rode on. Climbing with her. They had both been more than ready for this moment. They each realized that now. The blood, coupled with the warmth of the sun and the smell of the autumn-touched grass. It all came pouring over them as they coupled beside the still water—their only visitors the curious beaver which worried the calm surface of the pond near the wrestling couple.

Suddenly she screamed and the sound erupted back at them from the hillsides surrounding the quiet meadow. And almost as quickly the roar broke free from his throat. They had risen together, and reached that glorious pinnacle with one another. At the top of that mountain the air is always thin. At the top one's heart is racing as if to pump itself free of the lover's body.

Paddock, sated, rolled to the side and gently drew his woman against him. The sun radiated down on them as their breathing slowly became more regular, as their joyful hearts finally calmed from their mutual racing. How long they lay there, he had no idea. It was only when he awoke that Josiah knew he had been sleeping. Without moving his head, the young man tried to look down over his body. They were both smeared with the dried blood. Weird, crazy, primitive paintings they each had created on the canvas of each other's body. Paddock chuckled quietly.

Looks Far stirred, then finally raised her head. She smiled at her husband before propping herself up on one elbow. The dark brown doe eyes ran up and back the length of his frame before she nuzzled down into the curve of his shoulder.

"You are still a mess," she whispered with a soft giggle.

"And no thanks to you, little one." He started to move out from under her.

"Where are you going?" she asked as he stood and reached out a hand toward her.

"Where *we* are going," he corrected.

Looks Far placed her hand in his and stepped through the grasses and spreading creepers toward the edge of the water. As the cool liquid lapped there at the bank of the pond, Paddock tested its temperature. He took a deep breath with eyes closed, feeling the warm, afternoon sun's light mantling over his body like a wool cape. Then he suddenly dove away from her.

The young trapper broke the surface, coming up near the middle of the pond. His long, curly brown hair dripped down his bearded face as he sputtered and turned toward the naked woman sitting on the bank.

"Are you going to clean me?" he suggested in Flathead.

Looks Far smiled broadly and dove into the water. A fraction of a second was all he caught of the sight of her two swollen breasts suspended in the air before she cracked the surface of the water. He turned, waiting for her to emerge. He turned again, worried now. Where was she? Had she struck her head on something?

A frighening surprise and a slight pain gripped him. She held his penis captive in her small hand as she broke the surface of the pond to stand before him. Black, shimmering hair was smeared carelessly across her face by the water, dripping across and down the burnished skin of her breasts that met the wavelets of the pond's surface like two arrow points. Again and again she stroked him into readiness.

"Yes," she whispered hoarse and deep. "I will clean you."

Looks Far placed him inside her once more, the passion of their last coupling only bringing forth a deep need to satiate this new desire. "But first," she rasped, "You will wash away this burning I have for you."

Their love making finished, both man and woman slowly swam to the bank with leaden arms and legs. The couple fell exhausted onto the damp grass, laughing and rolling with one another until they dozed off once again.

The sun was impaled on the treetops when next they awoke and dressed in the cooling, early-autumn air of the mountains. Josiah strapped the green hide satchel to his pony.

Paddock hoisted his woman aboard her animal before she tugged at his sleeve. With her fingers beneath his chin, Looks Far raised her man's face to her own and bent over to kiss Josiah's lips. Her tongue darted into his mouth, then out just as quickly.

"A third time?" he asked, almost breathless as he finally pulled away from the teasing moistness of her mouth.

"Would you, my husband?" she giggled.

"I could not," he finally admitted.

"Then I will not do this thing you call a *kiss* to you." She straightened up on her pony.

Paddock climbed reluctantly into his saddle and rode up beside her, studying her wide grin, the full-lipped mouth. His gaze wandered down the soft curve of the neck and across the fullness of the breasts straining with their milk load against the skin of her dress.

"No, you better not kiss me again like that, with your tongue. Until tonight," he smiled.

Paddock reached out to squeeze her hand before letting it go, then tapped his pony's sides with his heels. They prodded their animals around the small pond, their pond, and up across the meadow. At the edge of the golden aspens just before the top of the hill, Josiah halted the pony and turned toward his woman. Together they twisted in their saddles to gaze back down the hill, back across the meadow at their pond. He felt her eyes caressing him and turned.

Looks Far leaned toward him once again, her mouth open slightly, inviting him. Their kiss was soft, moist and warm. Paddock pulled away almost reluctantly from her musk and swallowed hard. It had never been this good between them. And their life was only beginning. Josiah knew a dramatic chapter had been written back there, as he stared at the pond for a last time.

Eventually he turned back to the woman and smiled warmly. They pushed on over the top of the hill, toward the setting sun, toward their camp where waited their son and two friends. More than that, they forged toward the rest of their lives shared together.

EACH time his mother bent over, young Joshua would gurgle and babble. The constant cooing that came with her every movement pleased Looks Far Woman as she knelt to pick mushrooms and dig for the bulbs of wild onions she often used in her stews and broths. The soil in this valley where she had never been before this fall was so rich in minerals, so vital with a life all its own—she was amazed at the abundance of herbs and wild vegetables which grew here. And the animal life.

She raised her head at the soft sound and caught sight of the doe bounding into the edge of the small meadow where the Indian woman had wandered in search of her wild fare. The doe stopped abruptly to stare at the human. In turn, the young mother gazed back at the animal for their long, shared instant in time. Then the doe suddenly took flight once more, bounding away as if pushed airborne and leapt over the deadfall strewn across the forest floor.

Looks Far smiled and knelt again, once more slipping into her own most private of thoughts. Listening to the quiet, reassuring sounds of her son at her back, here working among the plants of the forest to prepare a meal for her man and their friends, there came an all-encompassing sense of completeness in things. A sense of order. That dream of the great circle drawing close around her made the Flathead woman glow with a sunlit warmth. The young mother began to hum softly as she stepped past the sunlight into the fringes of shadow, here and there the forest floor remained dappled with patches of smoky mist rising from the warming, rich soil.

The sounds of hoofs faintly caught her ear. She smiled once more as she turned. The sound of yet another deer came from the same general direction where she had spotted the first doe. Almost as close as the last one had been— her mind told her as she turned toward those quiet steps crunching across the forest floor needles. Another animal, not a deer. Four legs, as her eyes slowly climbed up the body of the tall animal. Medicine dog. The horse of the white man. Bearer of burdens. And this one carried another animal on its back.

The solitary rider was quickly joined by six other warriors who nudged their ponies out of the dim, smokey forest shadows when they at last determined the woman was alone. The leader of this small band turned once to either side in greeting his fellow warriors with a slow nod of his head. And a smile. They had come upon a solitary woman—and after so long out from their camp, on this hunt for ponies and scalps. This hunting party had been far from successful, finding no camps with fine pony herds to raid, locating no small numbers of enemy to kill. But now, at least, they would take their pleasure from this young woman standing before them. And in that way, these young braves would release some of the foul venom that had built up over their lack of ponies, scalps, honor.

Looks Far straightened, never taking her eyes off the seven warriors. Joshua began to babble once more as the warriors' ponies began a slow walk toward her. The ends of their ragged crescent closed around her more quickly than did the center, like the two licking ends of a snake's tongue, tasting the air, hypnotizing its victim before striking with the fangs at the center, at the heart.

She took a step backwards, then another. The horsemen were in no real hurry. They continued to advance. She stumbled over a large, dead limb, rolling to the side to protect the infant strapped on her back. Quickly she rose to her feet and stumbled backwards again—hoping against hope, always, that she could find some safety, some shelter, protection from what she feared was going to happen to her.

On they came, slowly, like the dark mist that creeps up a river on bitter cold winter nights. Only this dark mist was filled with hideous smiles and twisted grins. A couple of the warriors began to make lewd, suggestive gestures toward her. And as yet no one had said a word. Not the seven wandering warriors. Not Looks Far Woman.

Suddenly her back slammed against a tree. Joshua cried out in that instant of pained surprise. There was little room to run—the forest was so thick, so well carpeted with deadfall. She would not make it very far if she chose to run. It would have to be here. Slowly she began to slip one arm from the cradleboard straps. Then the second arm. As she lowered the cradleboard to the ground, the Flathead woman caught a fleeting glimpse of her son's face. His eyelids were drooping. It was all the better, she thought, as she laid the cradleboard behind a downed tree trunk. There he would be protected somewhat from what was to happen to his mother. There he would not have to see with his young eyes what these men were going to violently wrench from her body.

As the young mother straightened, her left hand barely brushed the handle of that big pistol her man had given her to take along on this food gathering trip. The mountains could hold big surprises, he had always told her with his ready grin. Maybe a wandering grizzly, out to eat his fill here in the late months of an old autumn. Filling a belly that must get him through the long months of a winter's slumber. Surprises—and he did not want his woman surprised by such a monstrous animal. So he had taught her to use the heavy rifle, and this big pistol with the pretty metal pattern on the barrel. He had taught her to reload for him. And he had shown her how to pull the hammer back, to hold on the target without jerking. To squeeze at the trigger. Like giving their little son a hug. Just a gentle squeeze. Yet she still preferred her knife.

Suddenly the leader spoke, with words she could not altogether understand, a foreign language—yet his intent was very clear.

"This one is no stranger to men, my friends. She knows what it is to have a man push himself inside her. Now she will know what it is for all of us to have her."

"I—I am Looks Far Woman, daughter of a Flathead warrior chief," she croaked back courageously in her native tongue, with a mouth suddenly as dry as a dusty August prairie.

"See. She tries to speak to us, my friends." The leader turned to his fellow warriors. "We do not know of her words—her tongue. She must be from far away." He cautiously glanced about, at the forest around him. "From far, far away," he repeated.

The sound of her language was indeed very strange to him, yet struck something of a responsive chord from his past. As a child, he remembered the prisoner who had been captured wandering, lost this far to the south. He was captured and tied to a tall, peeled stake near the chief warrior's lodge. From there the prisoner had taunted his captors, cursing and jeering at them in a language none of them understood. His words were a bold challenge from a brave man who had accepted his impending death. And from that dim childhood recollection, from the recesses of that faint memory, now came the unsettling strangeness of her tongue.

"Looks Fawwwrrr Wooo-man," she said, rolling the words out as she had been taught.

"This one, now she tries to speak the white man's words," the warrior said, laughing loudly. The sound of his bellow rang out into the forest around them. "Perhaps she thinks we are really white men. That is funny, my friends."

They all laughed loudly and gestured lewdly toward the woman again. At last the leader slipped from the back of his pony. He opened his capote and tugged at the front of his breechclout, exposing himself to the young Indian woman.

"Look at this," he said as he held himself out to show her. "We are not white men. White men do not have a real part like I do. They are not really men like us."

The others about him hooted and guffawed, as a few more of them slipped to the ground and dropped their ponies' reins. This was fast becoming real fun now. All the pent-up frustrations of being gone so long from their homes, being gone so long without victory—all of the common despair came flooding over the seven as they continued to step ever closer toward the solitary young woman.

"I am wife of a trapper," she squeaked in Flathead, trying to control the sound of her voice. She must be brave. Barely sixteen summers now, in the full blossom of womanhood, Looks Far had met her husband the summer before last in that valley of the Trois Tetons, a place the white men called Pierre's Hole. There at the great annual trading fair between the hairyfaces and some merchants from the East, she had met her man. And the young girl's heart had spoken to her of love for the first time in her life.

The memories flooded over her in that instant as she choked down the hot coal in her throat and swiped at the tears scorching her eyes. They had lain together—the young trapper and the Flathead girl—beneath the wondrous

50

summer moon for one night. Her initiation into the world of white men, into the world of man. The next morning she had reluctantly returned to her village, not allowing this young white man to enter the encampment with her. In a way, she was already shamed, already scorned by her people—already her man's *woman*.

Through the rest of that summer, the fall and into the deep throes of winter she had carried the growing seed of his life within her belly. And after a painful, agonizingly long labor, his son had been born to her. Forever a piece of her man would remain with her, and not be taken from her. Their son.

Late spring and the young woman finally had been accepted once more by her people, the Flatheads. Her little life would grow to become a Flathead warrior. He would know of his father only from those words his mother chose to describe the young white trapper she had loved.

Then the older white man had stumbled onto the Flathead village accidentally early one late-spring evening. And all things in her world had changed once more. Now she again gloried in the hope of finding her man. Of being held in his arms again. And the hope of showing him their son for the first time. A son with no name as yet, for among her people, the fathers gave names to their children.

That older white man rode the girl away from the village of her childhood, took her with him to find Josiah Paddock and Waits-by-the-Water. Things were mixed up in those days of early summer—the old trapper with Looks Far Woman. Josiah wandering with Waits-by-the-Water in search of Bass. Until at last they found each other. And the heart of each was filled in that great reuniting. Now the young trapper had his woman and new son with him. And the old trapper was brought together with his Crow woman once more.

All the memories, some bittersweet to be sure, yet fully a part of her, they all rushed in upon her now as she swiped the back of a hand across her eyes a second time to wrench away the burning liquid still scorching them. They must not see her cry. These enemies must not know I am scared. I must fight.

"I am wife of Jo-si-ahh Pawww-dock." She slowly pulled at the knife handle, slipping the first of two knives from their sheaths. "You will have to kill me." The Flathead words accompanied the left hand pulling a second knife from her belt. "I will not give myself up to you."

The warrior stopped his slow advance and let go of himself. The breechclout flap fell back over his groin. He no longer grinned as his eyes focused on the two knives held by the young woman.

"This one," he said in a louder voice, "this one will have to feel the sting of my special dagger, I am thinking."

There was an edge to the laughter that brought its cutting sound to her ears. The warrior leader dropped his capote to the ground after removing his arrow quiver and a pouch that had been draped over his shoulder. The other braves hooted after him, urging him on toward the challenge of the young girl with the two knives. A good fight, then they would spread her legs and each one force his own pleasure upon her. They might yet let her live. Yes. They would leave her alive, they laughed among one another. That way she could go tell her man, go tell her people of what real men were about. They would know of what real warriors were made.

51

A leering grin crawled its way across the leader's face as he started to advance for the last time. Looks Far brought the two knives up, having learned how to slash and cut, jab and tear, and always twist with a flick of her wrist. That way she would draw the most blood, do the most damage to her enemy. She would exact a heavy toll this day before they forced themselves into her. With her knives, her fists, her knees, and finally with her teeth if need be. Their victory would not be total. Her loss would not be without some small kernel of victory over the seven of them.

He crouched lower as he drew up to the woman. He carried no weapon in his hand. The only defense against the knives she jabbed toward him was his speed, his agility, his strength and that horrifying grin smeared across his face. The leader caught one of the young woman's wrists and she cried out in surprise as he yanked her to him. He tried to grab the other wrist but she was already stabbing with the knife. The blade ripped across his chest and down at a jagged angle across his belly. Stunned, the warrior looked down at the tear across his leather warshirt, fascinated at the spread of the dark fluid that pumped from the long wound. He still had his right hand crushing her small wrist.

He yanked and pulled hard with the bruising grip he had on her, sending the young woman sprawling backwards. She rolled twice before he caught up to her. Quickly, each of his moccasins clamped down on her arms as he stood over her. The pain of his wound only aggravated his lust. Already he knew it would be a long time healing from the course her knife had taken down his body. But he would take what he had meant to take from her anyway.

As his hands pulled aside the breechclout to again expose his rigid member, the blood from the chest and abdominal wound dripped across his hands and down onto his penis. He stroked the hardened flesh before her eyes.

"My blood will soon be smeared inside you!" he roared. "This blood you caused to flow from me—it will be shoved inside you and you will have a real warrior for a son! My blood into your body!"

Horrified, Looks Far Woman knew her short, valiant battle was over. Already she was on the ground. Already she had been defeated. The only weapon this enemy would use on her for the time being was to be his manhood. Unspeakable enough. Then the death they would bring her when they finally slit her throat would be merciful.

Now! Please do it now! The words roared in her head with all the consuming flame of a raging prairie wildfire. Kill me now!

In that instant the tip of the arrow ripped itself through the warrior's chest. The iron-tipped arrow protruded half a foot out of the body and began to drip with more of the Indian's blood, just as did the penis he held in his hand. The warrior was stunned. Slowly his eyes dropped to stare at the arrow. Hypnotized, the young woman's eyes were transfixed by the sudden emergence of the iron-tipped rosewood shaft from the man's chest. The man continued to look down at the arrow in disbelief, then began to raise his hand toward it. Just as the fingers touched the bloody iron point, Looks Far Woman was blinded, splattered with gore and gray matter.

The warrior's face seemed to explode above her as a second arrow ripped through the back of his skull, on through his brain, and was driven out through his nose, splattering blood and bone before it. The Indian stumbled backwards, his heart pierced by the first arrow. He was already dead even as it had struck. But a second arrow penetrated him now, as his mouth began to work up and down with no sound except the frothy, agonized gurgling at the back of his throat. He fell backwards two more steps toward his fellow warriors and crumpled to the ground. The body quivered violently twice, then lay still, bowels voiding.

The six others were stunned with this silent mystery. In that instant they stared at their fallen leader, caught up in the suddenness of his death, an almost silent, whistling death. Then one warrior and another began to howl their hideous war cries. One of the warriors stepped over toward the prostrate woman in a crouch, cautiously jerking his head from side to side to search the forest about him for the enemy who had fired the arrows. They would not take their pleasure from this woman this day. But they would take her scalp.

The knife flashed out in a smoky streamer of misty sunlight as the blade flashed down toward the woman's head. But he jerked up, a bloody tip suddenly protruding from his groin. The pain seared through his bowels like a narrow river of fire. The arrow had caught him in the buttocks and had come ripping out from his groin. He could not straighten himself without tearing flesh against the willow shaft. Bent over, he began to hobble away toward his companions who had dropped behind trees and deadfall, their eyes frantically searching, scanning the misty forest for their unseen attacker.

This second wounded warrior howled in pain for help as he stumbled toward a friend. A third warrior got up to help his wounded companion as the roar of a rifle bit through the morning silence of the forest meadow. The wounded second warrior watched in horror as his friend was thrown to the ground several yards away by the force of the ball's impact. The four other warriors pointed toward the trees where the gray smoke sifted slowly out among the branches.

There! The enemy!

Two of the Indians fired their smoothbores toward the dense foliage where the gray-white veil still clung among the green branches. The sounds of their barking weapons rolled away across the hillsides as the meadow fell into silence. The Indians quickly looked at one another nervously. Two of the warriors cautiously studied the treeline while the two who had fired now frantically reloaded. The forest fell quiet around them until all that could be heard was a magpie screeching out somewhere below them, on down the wooded hillside. Then the wounded second warrior's raspy, pain-laden breathing punctuated the stillness. At times, the Indians would turn around to glance at Looks Far Woman, who had climbed over behind some deadfall. She grasped the cradleboard, clutching her infant son to her breast and whimpering softly.

The sudden impact of a lead ball spun another warrior around and spread him backwards over the downed tree he had hidden behind after the first rifle blast from the trees. The arrow-pierced second warrior cried out again in fear and pain. The three who were now left to fight stared dumbfounded, before their glances finally tracked into the forest on the other side of the clearing, opposite from where the first shot had come. Two of them began to crawl away on their bellies, seeking better shelter from the new rifle fire. The third warrior taunted the two, berating them loudly for their cowardice. He rose and took off sprinting toward the new drifting smoke in the trees. This warrior was certain he would make it to the attacker before that mysterious rifleman could reload.

The lead projectile entered his back and exploded out the Indian's chest, causing the body to be flung suddenly forward with the force of the impact on bone and muscle. Now the two remaining Indians burst to their feet and dashed toward the ponies. They flung themselves aboard the saddleless animals and frantically spurred them into action, scattering the remaining riderless ponies ahead of them. The horses clattered noisily down through the trees toward the valley floor.

The forest gradually fell quiet once more beyond the fading shouts of the frightened warriors as they sped from the scene. A pall of gray-white smoke hung heavy on either side of the small clearing, in answer to that dark gray veil of pain suffered by the wounded warrior curled on the ground between four of his companions. His gaze feverishly darted from body to body for signs of life, signs of someone to help him from his predicament. To remove the arrow so he could stand, so that he could run—but there was no one to help him.

The shadow crawled up behind the warrior. Twisting, with a pain-wracked grimace crossing his face, the Indian looked up into the eyes filled with loathing and hate.

"Gonna let you die real slow right here, you bastard," Paddock said hoarsely as he stepped over the Indian's body on his way toward his wife and son.

The warrior turned, reached out toward his knife. Now it lay just out of reach. Slowly he began to inch toward the long dagger.

She cried out for her man, quickly laying the cradleboard aside as she jumped to her feet. They met in a tangled embrace of damp flesh and frantic grappling. So desperately close to death moments before, now alive and rejoined. The tears poured from their eyes as each gazed into the face of their loved one. Finally, Josiah bent down to scoop up the cradleboard.

"It's all over now, son," he cooed softly. "All gone away now." The infant's eyes flickered back and forth between his parents' faces. They both turned suddenly at the sound of a muffled voice from behind them.

"Nigger fixin' to gut somebody." Bass stood over the wounded warrior. His foot pressed down on the Indian's arm that held the dagger. "Looks to be he was countin' on makin' it you, boy." He clucked as he bent down to knock the sharp weapon from the warrior's grasp.

"What are they?" Josiah let his eyes drop from the old trapper to the wounded man. "What tribe?"

"My guess be 'Rapaho," Bass answered. "Way they dressed—the hair, too."

"What'll we do with him?" Paddock stopped beside his partner to stare down at the skewered Indian.

"Say we kill him," the old trapper grumbled sourly.

"He's gonna die anyway, ain't he?"

Bass looked into Paddock's eyes with surprise for a moment before he responded. "S'pose—I s'pose he is now. He will, that is. Certain as sunset."

"Looks like he can't move too well—can't get out of here." Josiah continued to stare at the warrior.

"You thinkin' of leavin' him here? Just like this?" Scratch inquired.

"Yes." The answer came quiet, almost too quiet.

"This nigger here almost scalped your woman!" Scratch bellowed. "They was fixin' to—rape—make their way with your wife."

"I know that, Scratch. I know that." Josiah looked over at the Flathead woman cradling the infant in her arms once again. "He's gonna die anyway. Can't get up and get outta here. Probably some wolf'll get him. Die of hunger—maybe of thirst. Leave him be—for his medicine."

Bass whistled low and shook his head. Finally he spoke again as he let the butt of his rifle clunk to the ground next to the warrior's head.

"By the beard of Holy Mary, the Lord's Mother! Ain't that some now. Sure do beat all, it does. You goin' an' robbin' this nigger of his place on the Other Side, ain't you?"

He watched Paddock nod and then stare off into the trees in the direction the other warriors had taken in their flight. "Ain't even gonna take his hair, are you?"

"Nawww, don't think I will," said Josiah.

"Some things you grab onto right quick, son. Yessir, some things you're learnin' real smart."

The younger trapper's shoulders quaked with a sudden spasm before he answered. "Had me a good teacher, old man. A damned good teacher."

Paddock knelt to pick up the Indian's wide-bladed dagger. Josiah turned so that he was crouched right over the warrior who lay on his side, curled up almost fetally. He was unable to straighten himself out with the arrow skewering him from rump to groin. Paddock slowly gathered up the warrior's greased, rancid-smelling hair into the fingers of his left hand, pulled it skyward as the tip of the blade came toward the forehead. The warrior's eyes widened perceptibly, but no sound burst from his throat.

Josiah's face suddenly creased with a widening slash of a grin, and he let the hair tumble from his fingers. Finally he brought the knife away from the flesh and stuffed the weapon into the back of his belt. He rose and walked over to Looks Far and their son. He started to guide her back down the hill toward their ponies and camp.

Bass looked after them for long moments, at last letting his gaze come back to rest on the lone warrior. "Sometimes, this child learns himself a thing or two from a young'un. Sometimes—"

Scratch tapped at the fletching on the arrow with his toe, causing the Indian to swing a fist at the trapper's foot.

"You'll do just fine here. Kinda like a stuck pig, nigger." Bass looked down into the young Indian's painted face. A face he'd seen so many times in all those warriors, in all those battles, over all those years. "Seems like we got you spitted for the fire." He gazed downhill once again to see the man and woman disappearing into the gold-leafed trees. "Yepper. Sometimes I'm the one what learns hisself somethin'."

Scratch rambled away toward that line of bright light and quaking aspen, his own head shaking from side to side as he chuckled to himself.

"Ain't that some now. Purely some."

Finally the chuckle became a loud, joyful roar that rang back at him from the hillsides as he fully reveled in that joke on himself.

5 EVER SINCE THE attack on Looks Far Woman, time had begun to pulse more quickly. No longer did the days crawl by at a slug's pace across the earth. No longer did the days go on forever with brief interludes of darkness thrown between the glorious hours of sunlight. Summer was over in so many, many ways.

There came the heady smell of autumn to fill the air. It was like nothing else. The smell of summer done and gone away. The smell of things dying.

Autumn was advancing with an amazing swiftness above them on the mountainsides. Each new day seemed to bring with it the racing line of gold-smitten aspens tumbling down the hillsides toward the beautiful park of Bayou Salade. Every morning it would seem as if autumn had sped down the slope in their direction overnight. Ever since the attack on the Flathead woman, things had changed. Things done and dying.

The wildflowers were swept away from the meadows, joining the summer-cured grasses in parched oblivion. The tall grasses ripened, dried and fracturing in cooling brittleness. Each succeeding day brought the deer and elk farther down the forested hillsides toward the security and winter pastures of the Bayou. These shorter days were filled with the background noise of bugling elk and snapping, cracking bucks' antlers locking in battle. Each morning the sharp whack of the sparring antlers echoed earlier and earlier from the hillsides surrounding their camp. Every day the bugling of bull elk challenges rang clearer and clearer, ever closer from the slopes of dark pine-green and gold-splotched aspen.

Farther below, the cottonwood and willow would be the last to give way before the mysterious forces of nature and time and season. Their leaves finally began to shrivel with age, marked with the passing of time and the invisible hands of nature's clock. Those leaves that hung on did so in stubbornness before the harsh winds that took most of the shrivelled brown tendrils and gustily whirled them away down the valley.

Then suddenly the Bayou burst with frantic activity for several days. Swarms of migratory birds blackened the skies. Over the lower peaks and passes, formation after formation of the spear-headed migration paraded across the crystal autumn blue. Each formation transformed itself from black specks far in the sky to a low-swooping V of geese or ducks, sweeping in to settle across the ponds and still water of the valley with thunderous splashes. The longnecks craned, searching for a landing spot, making a long, graceful figure-eight loop across a spread of marsh. Then the geese slanted, banked and hit the green water, kicking up sprays as they emitted their wild squawks. There were so many of them there seemed no room for more out on the huge marshes—there seemed no room, yet still they came. And always there was space for the new arrivals in the grand expanse that was the Bayou Salade. The trappers took their share of the rich, dark, fat meat. And it lay good in their bellies.

Other smaller birds feasted before the onslaught of winter on those insects, locusts, beetles clinging cooled and torpid on those grasses dried by the slash of autumn winds. Time hung in the balance, and fall was a time when it was decided just what creatures survived and what creatures would not. Each was making ready for the change in its own ages-old dance of the seasons, each life form readying itself for the time of cold and death that was winter in the high country. Winter Man would decide just what lived, what would not.

There was a rhythm across the land, set so long ago that years were still in the womb of time.

Much had changed in the days following the attack on Looks Far Woman. Things were not the same in so many imperceptible ways. Things would not be the same and time moved on at its quicksilver pace. The very air itself about them had in it a sensation of quickening, of change, of things never returning to the way they had been. As if too much had already transpired, too much had gone before. And never to be the same again.

The blackness of night was now reluctant to retreat from the east, but morning light ripped a pink purple laceration along the ragged peaks. Bass left camp quietly in the pre-dawn darkness, having lain awake most of the night—fitful, restless, unable to sleep. Scratch felt the tingle of something unknown, unseen, unexplained and forbidding all about him. Perhaps in his own camp. So he must purify himself and seek an answer—the answer to his being at this water's edge here at dawn. Dawn, its pink giving way to red, turned orange and finally the brightening yellow that would ultimately spread glistening golden light over the valley of South Park.

He shivered through the long hours of waiting in the cold darkness, chilled and damp, listening to the pre-dawn breezes carry their whispers of things past seen and done, whispers carried by him, around him, never for him—murmuring sounds in gray light before the coming of an ever-shorter day. The secrets of the night; he knew nothing of them. But now the edge of the orange ball forced itself up through the jagged cuts of raw mountain architecture, dripping through the spear-like treetops of fir and lodgepole. And with the re-birth of the day, with the coming of the life-giving sun, he was ready to give thanks.

Bass threw back the heavy, dew-laden, four-point wool blanket he had brought to the water's edge. Then he stood to remove his shirt against the goosepimpling, cold breezes that stabbed at him—eager to send him running from this place, escaping from this place by the water.

He stood naked before the sun as it reached the top of the peaks, a bloodlike orb resting on the spires of treetops above him. He spread out his arms, almost in supplication, in a readiness to receive, to know. The silence about him in the forest was almost soul-crushing. Much would have to come before he would be allowed to have that knowledge.

Bass hung his head, the grizzled gray beard brushing the graying hairs of his chest. Saddened that he could not know immediately what his heart sought. Saddened that time would take its own course in this matter of great mystery, and man would have to wait. Again.

Scratch knelt and yanked at the sage leaves from the plants around his feet. When he had two full hands, the old trapper rubbed the gray-bellied green leaves over his arms, scouring and scourging his belly and loins, down his thighs, across his shoulders, briskly rubbing his calves. The process was repeated with three subsequent handsful, four in all. Each time the rubbing grew harder, more savage, as if in punishment of oneself, as if to purge something unclean from his body, perhaps from his soul.

The four handsful, the four scouring purges, the full tingling of the silver-bellied sage leaves, and the trapper smelled of the forest once more. For the moment all his manness was gone. Bass waddled into the freezing stream like a grizzly. And plopped down among the licks of thin ice dancing against the sunlit bank. Soon enough the warmth of an autumn day would cause the night's ice to disappear. But for now the soul-bruising cold washed up to his armpits, brutalizing his sage-scoured body. This was necessary. He poured handsful of the ice-laden water over his head, then on his shoulders, more on his head—back and forth—quaking in the water, shuddering with each splash down his spine. Yet nothing so cold as his sense of something having changed around him, something gone away, fleeing from him. Never would it be the same again. And he shivered violently with that black thought.

Quaking uncontrollably, Bass stumbled onto the bank. Frost on the brittle grass lay like a pink wound in the new, red light. He rose from his hands and knees to face the sun and spread his arms in offering. Finished, he returned to his pile of clothing and sat atop the blanket. Still naked, the old trapper ripped at bunches of the old grass until he had a crude circle cleared of vegetation. In the dirt he laid four stones he had found in the cured grass. Each small stone was set on a cardinal point.

The trapper did not know what Old Man Coyote looked like, nor had he ever really thought about it. Besides, Scratch mulled, he wasn't much of a picture painter anyway. Bass grinned as he leaned forward to claw out a huge X in the middle of the circle. Each arm of the X rested between two of the four stones. Yes, a lot of people used this same mark to signify themselves. It only made sense to the old trapper that if he did not know how to draw, didn't even know what the old Crow trickster looked like, the X was suitable enough to represent Old Man Coyote.

Digging through his rumpled, hastily dropped clothing, Bass found his belt. His fingers traced along the wide leather band to locate the first knife sheath. He pulled free a sharp skinning blade, then settled once more before the simple medicine wheel he'd created on the ground.

59

Carefully, with a light touch, he drew the razor edge across his left palm, opening up a tiny hairline of rosy flesh. Intently, he watched the line begin to bubble and bead with the swelling of capillary blood. When the fluid finally had welled up enough, the old trapper turned his hand over and allowed drops of the dark fluid to fall to the ground along the lines of the circle. The blood coagulated and began to stop its beaded flow by the time he had completed bloodying the medicine wheel. It was good, he thought. Enough of an offering. And accepted in this way by the spirits of the mountains. They had approved of his blood, his body offering, and asked for nothing more. They had stayed his bleeding.

He smiled down at the creation. The four stones and the X for the Old Man Coyote spirit. And finally the large, dark circles of moist dirt where his blood had soaked into the soil around the greater circle. He had made medicine here. It was good. The answers he sought would come to him in their own time. He had probably known that all along, even through the dreadful night of restless sleep and agonized, fitful nightmares. He had known it when he had decided to come down here in those coldest, blackest hours just before dawn.

Bass stared down at his left palm with its thin line of sundered flesh darkened now with the coagulated blood to form a blackened thread across the lighter, wrinkled skin. He smiled again. It would come to him in its own time, what was to be. It always had.

Strange now, the feeling pouring down him like that icy water he'd bathed himself within, colder still now in the quiet breeze dancing along the bank. That dark feeling which mumbled something at his ear, then moved away. Mumbled incoherent words, barely understood—all about something having changed forever, never to be the same again. And he was at the center of it. Bass had asked to hear the words more clearly, and he had been told to wait. The old trapper accepted. He always had. His heart would eventually hear the words, know the words—when it came his time at last.

Dressing quickly in the still-damp, chill air, Bass drew in a breath as he draped the wool blanket about his shoulders. He slowly turned and looked about himself at this holy place created for him alone, this holy place that had beckoned to him out of the darkness.

Scratch turned and looked back down at that consecrated spot from farther up the hillside. He sighed and wheeled slowly to gaze back up the rising corduroy of tree line to the white-shouldered peaks.

On a tree nearby he noticed the red nodules of hard, sticky gum clinging to the gnarled bark. It made him smile. So very long it had been since he had last chewed the gum. Titus bent around the trunk, then glanced at a nearby tree. Yes, there was the light tan gum on that tree trunk: a gummier, softer substance almost the color of rainwater left standing in lowland puddles. He quickly gathered what he could of the hard red nodules and scraped off an equal amount of the soft, tan gum into a flap of his breechclout. Mixed together, the two kinds of tree gum would be very pleasant to chew. The red was too hard and brittle by itself. Alone, the red tended to crumble in his mouth and he found he was soon spitting it out. Almost like a pemmican that didn't have enough fat in it.

But, when he had learned to add the second, softer, fleshier gum to the red nodules, Bass not only had a lively, tart taste, but he had created a chewy substance that kept its flavor, held its consistency, and delighted him as much as a child sucking on a sugar cane.

Scratch smiled and smacked loudly as he entered camp. Waits-by-the-Water was just rising, coming out of their blanket and pine-bough shelter. Josiah and Looks Far sat up in their hide shelter to stare curiously at the older trapper. Scratch stood between the two shelters and smacked as loudly as he could for them. Grinning all the time just like a little boy who had been given the wealth of a penny and had just returned from the sweet shop with his purchases.

"All right," Josiah said as he rubbed at his crusty, sleep-laden eyes. "What is it you're eating?"

"Ain't eatin' a thing, young'un." His breath made bubbles around the gum as he grinned wide.

"So—what you chewing on?"

"Gum."

"G-gum? Whakindagum?" Josiah yawned and scratched his head.

Looks Far bent over to scoop up their son, who was crawling past his father, seeking to scoot out of the shelter and play in those morning sunbeams dancing into camp.

"What is his *gum*?" she articulated very slowly.

"I figure he's about to tell us." Paddock nodded toward the older trapper who knelt before them with his breechclout held out.

Bass slowly pulled back the flap to show the clumps of tree sap like so many clods of red and brown mud.

"Go 'head," he prodded. "Try some."

Paddock glanced quickly at the older man's face and only then reached for some of the red gum, deciding it looked more delicious. He was about to plop it between his lips when Scratch clasped the young man's wrist.

"No, son," he ordered. "You gotta mix it with some of this first." He held up a specimen of the flesh-colored gum. "Makes it so you can chew it without it all fallin' apart on you. Tastier, too, if you're askin' me."

"Well, I wasn't," Josiah said as he obligingly plopped the second clump into his mouth. He let his tongue run over and around the two masses, mixing them together through the process, swallowing hard, choking with the tangy, strong wood-turpentine taste.

"What you think?" Bass leaned forward a little to examine Paddock's face more closely.

Josiah looked first at his Flathead woman. Then down at his infant son, crawling at his knee. At times the pungent fragrance of the wood chemicals rose high in his nostrils and seared at the back of his throat. It was an exhilarating sort of taste—different from anything he'd known before. Light-headed at times, he had to breathe deeply through his nostrils from time to time to lessen the sting of the sharp taste as it bit its way back through his head.

"It ain't—" He stopped to swallow the turpentine at the back of his throat. "It ain't half bad. Not half bad at all, old man."

Bass rocked back on his heels. He beamed broadly at each of the adults about him. "See?" he said joyfully. "I told you." He presented his breechclout to Looks Far. "Here. You have some, too, lil' lady."

Then over to Waits-by-the-Water. "Here, darlin'."

Soon they were all chewing, smacking happily. At times the pungent taste and strong fragrance rising at the backs of their throats caused them each to wince or screw their faces up. Before he knew it, Bass caught from the corner of his eye a glimpse of Joshua moving his tiny hand from the breechclout to his mouth. Darting quick, like a hummingbird wing, the little paw stuffed its treasure into the tiny mouth.

"Why, you lil' beggar," Bass chuckled. Then each of the adults stared into the infant's face for a moment, watching, studying that twisted, contorted grimace Joshua made as he bit down on the clumps of tree sap. In the next breath, the child spit his wad out, hurling the mass across the buffalo robe and Bass too.

"I suppose he'd tell you he don't like it," Paddock said as he fell backward, guffawing.

"There's one in every crowd, I'm thinkin'," the older man clucked.

"You mean someone in every crowd who won't like the gum, huh?"

"Nawww," Bass said as he looked down at Joshua. "I mean every crowd got a expert who'll find fault with anythin'. Looks like he's the one in this crowd."

Josiah and Scratch laughed gently at first. Then the two women joined in, sure they were meant to laugh along with their men. And that made the two trappers roar all the more merrily.

"Got us two of a kind. Yessir! Two of a kind there, Josiah!" Bass squeaked out the words. "These here are real eager to please, it seems. An' this here lil' pup of your'n—why, he's real eager to show just what he thinks of his ol' uncle-man. Goin' an' spittin' on a man. Why—I do declare! WAGH!"

He swiped at the front of his shirt where the child had sprayed his half-chewed clumps of tree sap. "See if I ever give him such a fine treat again."

"Y-you're the one should've known better!" Paddock chimed.

"Don't understand all that much 'bout pups, you know." Scratch looked wounded for all to see.

"Neither do I," Paddock admitted. "Till the woman here began to teach me. But I'm thinking I come on it as natural as any woman can. And that means you can too."

"Need me a pup first, don't I?"

"I think everybody needs a child—or two, maybe three!"

"Whoa! Hold on now! One at a time!" he protested with a beaming grin. "We ain't even got started yet, near as I know." He stole a quick glance at the Crow woman's belly. "One at a time, son."

"Least one, Bass."

"Some folks better at being a pappy than others, too. Seems like you been doin' purty fair in that part of the woods."

Paddock shook his head a moment. "You know what, ol' man. You sure can get things all catty-whompused real quick if I'd let you."

"What'r you talkin' 'bout now?"

"You!" he chuckled. "You, Scratch! You're the one who'd make a fine pappy for a whole passel of children. You'd make the finest pappy I'd know of."

"Nawww." He tried to dismiss the compliment, embarrassed.

"I'm serious now, old man." Josiah scoffed at Scratch's dismissal. "It ain't always like we was brothers. No, sir. Ain't always like we was friends. Maybe not even like you was my uncle. Shit—sometimes I feel like you're more a pappy than I ever had from all them fellas who helped my ma over all the years."

"Never really had you a pap, did you now, son?"

"That's a fact," Josiah smiled with a gentle, inner glow. "It just may be that I run onto you a-purpose. Every kid needs his pappy to help him finish growing up. It was you helped me do that. Maybe you was picked."

"Picked a-purpose to be your half-pappy?"

"Maybe not so much that, as a step-pappy," he answered thoughtfully. "Mostly to help me finish the growing up, Scratch."

"Fair enough, son." He rose with Josiah. "I helped you finish your growin' up."

"And, you'd still make one fine, fine pappy for a young'un. You would." Josiah reached out to embrace the older man. He crushed Titus within his large arms, eager to show Scratch some of what he had so long felt inside.

"Thank you, son." Bass withdrew to arms' length. "Need me a child now, a young'un, I s'pose."

"You're working on it, ain't you?" Josiah nodded toward Waits-by-the-Water and winked at the old man.

"W-we been—been practicin', yes," he stuttered, feeling the heat rise up his neck.

"It'll happen," Paddock confided. "Just matter of time, I'd wager."

Bass studied his Crow wife for a long moment before turning back to look at Josiah. "That surely would make this ol' man feel like his circle was whole. Like the whole of it all was healed up again. Havin' me a lil' pup—a real young'un."

Quickly the old trapper scooped up little Joshua and sat the youngster on his right shoulder. "It sure is a bee-you-tee-full mornin'! Full of vinegar an' rum! A great mornin' for a man to be alive!"

"Ain't much better than this, is it, old man?"

"You said it all!" Bass cranked his head around to stare into the infant's smiling, gurgling face. "It really don't get much better'n this!"

THE early snow was wet enough that he made no sound tromping through it. His wet moccasins slogged through those white furrows he plowed, every step creating a damp suction on the foot.

Bass stopped and listened. Quiet enough to hear the heavy, sloughing flakes landing on the thick, wide, green branches. A lot of weight building up quickly, he thought as he shot measured glances at the pine and spruce thrust up like ordered sentinels about him. Yet, he knew the snow would be gone in less than four or five suns. Too warm still for the hard, dry, crunching freeze of a winter storm. This was merely a foretelling of those snows yet to come.

It was enough for him that this snow would bring most of the game down from the higher valleys. Too, it looked as if the buffalo were finally scattering. The valley-smothering herd was breaking itself into smaller groups that would find their way into the many bowls and valleys and meadows radiating from the floor of the Bayou Salade.

He was after buffalo this time out. He followed the tromped, muddied ruts and plowed snow furrows created by a small band of black shaggy beasts. The defiled, sundered mud and snow coaxed him around the side of the hill and into the trees, back up the slope at a gentle angle before the trail dropped into the meadow. There they were at last. Huge, out of focus, dark blots without defined edges. Black and brown, misted and mantled with swirling strokes of white, all barely visible through the sifting snowfall. The curtain of mist and snow shifted constantly, dancing with the gray wind, swirling the heavy, fat flakes of early winter straight at him.

Scratch plowed on through the gauze curtain. His eyes strained against the whirling flakes to search out a young cow among all the dark blotches. The buffalo would raise their heavy, shaggy heads, each attempting to catch wind of the two-legged in their midst. Then each dark animal would slowly turn and slough away from the hunter's path, unhurried, and continue feeding. Time crawled with his every step. Time—plenty of that, he chuckled inwardly. Then time quickly ground to a halt.

He saw her. What looked to be a yearling cow—young, tender—the most tasty. His mouth watered as he studied the animal, snow whirling its dance over them both. Hunter and hunted. Ghosts in the storm.

His eyes measured the spastic breezes that ordered white flakes to pirouette about him, measured their erratic direction. He stood still, silent in the midst of the storm. He smelled the wet, woolly beasts. He breathed deep of the earthy, organic odor of wet animal and fresh dung steaming in the white swells of snow. He was all the more of them for it.

Bass heard them pawing, scraping against the soggy, thick blanket covering their hoped-for breakfast. And they snorted from time to time to each other—about him, the two-legged among them.

Soon enough it would be too late for her. Scratch smiled as he inched closer through the curtains draped one upon the other, closer through the swirling mist of snow and wind. Each step brought him closer to the cow.

The old trapper leaned over the rifle he cradled protectively in his arms, sheltering it from the wet flakes. Only then did he pull the greased leather sock from the flintlock mechanism. The small glove-sock protected the dry powder in the lock's pan from becoming soggy and useless on wet days such as this. The sock bounced, suspended from its thin leather cord tied at the trigger guard. All was set.

He eased the rifle to his shoulder, then shoved back into it, the thickness of his wool shirt and elkhide coat compressed so he could reach the trigger more easily. Scratch's right eye peered down the length of the wide, octagonal barrel, glanced over the front blade as he brought it in line with the rear buckhorn sight. The right eye searched beyond the end of the barrel for his cow. Through the mist the front blade locked on her. At this close range, one killing shot could be made through the lungs and heart.

Then his left eye sparkled. More frequently it was happening. Flaming, shooting stars radiated out like a bright corona from its hot core. Bass squeezed hard against the sudden brightness, such a contrast against the storm's dull, gray light—unexpected, and it affected the vision in the right eye now. That eye quickly compensated for this bright meteor shower occurring in the other. He clamped both shut angrily, and muttered a curse in silence. Rifle locked on its target. The only things moving were the buffalo cow leisurely pulling at the season-cured grass beneath the snow and the swirling snow that drifted between her and the hunter. His lips tightened in quiet, angry frustration at the magical lights pouring from his left eye. The meteors weren't real, Scratch told himself. He ordered them away.

Slowly he opened the right eye. Gradually its wet, fogged vision cleared. The cow had moved a little after he had shut his eyes to the blinding, shooting stars. She had moved and now the front blade followed her. Behind the front leg, hold, breathe, release the air and squeeze before there came another episode of shooting stars from the eye.

The blast sounded dull, muffled, in the soggy, snow-laden air. The echo bounded back at him again and again and again from the sides of this bowl. Quickly he dropped the rifle away from his shoulder and cranked his head to look all around him. Find out just what the other beasts were doing, if they were unsettled, skittish at the blast, had suddenly become afraid of the hunter in their midst. Most of the black shaggy ghost animals sniffed in the air and, finding nothing at all disturbing, returned to eating their breakfast. Others, closer to the cow's carcass, pawed at the ground. No blood smell yet. But as soon as there was such an odor on the wind, those critters would be long gone with a high-tail from here. As he approached the downed cow, the others easily ambled out of his path.

A few steps from the animal he stopped and waited, calculating in those long moments if she were truly dead. Blood oozed from her nostrils, dribbled between her lips, over the lolling tongue to stain the thick, white sugar icing on the ground. Suddenly he felt cold. Not until this moment had he realized just how wet this snow truly was. Its dampness made his old joints and each old wound ache with its own torment. Each old memory screamed for attention in the wet snowfall.

Carefully he leaned the rifle into the crook of his left arm and set to reloading. First powder, then bear-greased patch and finally the huge .54 caliber round ball slogged home against the black grains of powder. Scratch snapped the frizzen on the lock open, dusted out the pan and reprimed the lock before setting the greased sock over the mechanism. Only then did he step forward and use the rifle's muzzle to tap at the cow's bloodied nostrils. Urgently he prodded the animal to be sure she was dead, to be sure that the cow would not come roaring to her feet, horn and hoof slashing at the hunter. Only the huge, shaggy head moved, and it moved only at his insistence.

Relieved, Bass dropped the rifle into the crook at the beast's shoulder in front of her foreleg. At his back he pulled the knife free of its sheath. His blade made a quick plunge just beneath her jaw in the thick flesh of the neck. With effort and tiring muscles, the old trapper ripped the razored weapon through the tough hide and thick matted curls. When he would make this same incision in other, warmer seasons, Bass could expect his hands to be crawling with fleas, watching the blood-gorged ticks roll fat and turgid out of his knife's way through the thick hair, to escape across the hide—away from the hunter's invasion of their domain. The job finished in that warm weather, both hands would be bloodied, gore-drenched and mottled with fleas and ticks, the incessant drone of bottle-green flies accompanying his handiwork. But now, here in winter, it was just too damned cold for any of them.

"Almost too damned cold for me," he exclaimed quietly.

Bass knew better. He knew it wasn't all that frigid yet. Such winter chill was yet to come. He hated himself for feeling this damp cold more and more with each advancing winter. The heavy wet snows that shut down the high country warned him more and more strongly each autumn. His season was advancing in concert with theirs, and one winter would be his last. Some winter to come, it would be his last in the mountains.

"Not yet, it ain't," he protested quietly, finally at the hind end and the last few inches to cut through to the tail. He quickly jabbed the knife into the meat of the rear leg and left it. Gnarled fingers tore at the bloody incision he had created, strong fingers ripping at the hide, pulling it slightly apart so that those fingers could worm their way down into the warmth of the beast.

He sighed. "Better'n 'em freezin'," he muttered to himself.

His fingers speared beneath the flesh, down into the fat she had been put-ting on for the coming winter. There his fingers could escape the wet, cold, movement-robbing storm. He could warm himself a few moments, then proceed with the butchering. Go fetch the ponies which had plodded along behind him as far as the trees back across the slope. He figured they must be grateful to have a chance to browse through the wet, white blanket also.

"All critters alike in a storm, ain't they?" he said to no one at all. "All critters alike—gettin' food for their bellies come a storm like this'un."

His fingertips began to tingle with renewed warmth. The still-warm blood and flesh imparted a need for the trapper to finish the job at hand. "We get this done right off, then we can skeedaddle back to camp an' the other folk. Make us up a mess of fine vittles."

He worked the knife, pulled hide away from flesh down the length of the deep, mid-line incision. Steam rose lazily into the heavy mist, clouding his work, yet welcomed by the old trapper. The cold, sloughing flakes danced in the air down through the warm, misting steam. And those fat snowflakes landing on the newly-exposed flesh disappeared instantly in the animal heat rising from the cooling carcass.

From time to time Bass warmed his aching hands in the flesh, around an organ. Now and again he dipped his head close to the misting, steaming flesh so that his raw face could be warmed once more. Finally the butchering was over.

Reluctantly he pulled his bloodied paws from the plundered carcass and quickly scrubbed at his flesh with wet snow to cleanse some of the gore from his hands. The cold shot through him again with a sudden, agonizing shock. But Titus laid his hands over the gaping carcass to rub his aching fingers together within the milky mist lazily hanging over the cooling flesh. At last he was ready to retrieve the ponies.

By the time he got back to the trees the snowfall had begun to taper off. He looked into the sky. Here and there across the expanse of gray white sparkled several small, reluctant patches of promised blue. The early snowstorm was breaking up, having at last spent itself across the Bayou and thrown its wet fury upon the peaks surrounding the valley. Perhaps its late-autumn rage would gather itself farther east out on the plains. Perhaps all that was left now would be cold, blustering winds. By afternoon the skies could be clear and blue and true as a crystal over the Park. Clean and bitter cold tonight.

He yanked the four animals behind him, pushing his own mount through the snow, scattering the small herd of black shaggy beasts before him. On his knees again, Bass broke bones and tore at joints, until each of the four pack animals was loaded with its prized meat. He stepped back to view the scene of his morning's efforts. The bloodied hide would be left for the wolves to fight over. It was of little use to him or his woman. Much too hard to stretch and cure such a thick hide in this damnable weather. Besides, the cow had only begun to put on her best coat, her winter hide. Better to leave this hairy offering to other creatures of the forest winter. The hocks of the legs lay scattered in the muddied snow, the trampled white brown snow reddened here and there in small, frozen splotches. And the gut piles, stacked here and there, as if posted as sentries for the torn hide itself, all offerings to the wild creatures of this land.

Bass drew in a long, deep breath, feeling the warming air seeking out his lungs. Already the sun would begin to wipe the traces of this storm from the mountainsides. He felt better already. Not quite as chilled. The bones still ached but with a dull pain. No sharp misery knifing through him now. His chilled fingers fought their way into the woolen mittens tied at the cuffs of his huge coat. The coyote cap was pulled down snugly into the coat's collar and yanked to his eyebrows in front.

Sucking in the air as it warmed against what few white flakes still persisted from the clouds overhead, Scratch decided to head home to his camp along a path different from the one which brought him here. As he watched, the heavy, thick soup of flakes and mist rose from the trees, partially freeing the meadows and forested hillsides of their blankets. This thick quilting of milky steam persisted enough to hang in the trees a few feet over his head. At least the ground was clear, he smiled. There'd be full bellies for days to come.

The old trapper snapped at the thick, braided rawhide rein muzzled around his buffalo runner to set the animal in motion. His prize pony had the first pack horse tied to its saddle. The first had the second pack animal lashed to it, and so on. Each had its place in the string, trained for that position, trained for its specific job. When their rawhide ropes were tugged, they followed.

Bass snorted with the sudden thought.

Strange. He was the same way much of the time. As free as he had always thought himself to be, he got his rope tugged and he had followed right along. A woman could do that to you real easy. Real easy to get tied up with a gal, let her get where she can crawl in and outta your skin. Then all she has to do is yank a little on your rope, and you come running right along like you was a trained animal in a medicine show.

Wait a minute now. It ain't all that awful bad, is it? Waits-by-the-Water never treated him that a-way. For certain she was under his skin, tight and true. And for certain, if she yanked on his lead rope, Titus Bass would be one to follow. But, considering it for real now, that woman was just about the best thing ever happened to him. Glad he was that she come along when she did. It was nigh onto getting too late for you, wasn't it, old man?

He laughed quietly and stared at the heavy hanging mist clinging in the trees and draped across the meadows. It would take a while, but the sun would eventually burn away the waning strength of the mist. Eventually blue sky would prevail and the cold dampness would retreat from the face of the land. Bass turned his face toward the faint golden globe hidden behind the gauze of gray mist above him. He was feeling better already—some of the chill and cold really retreating from his body. Already the outer pair of moccasins, those made of buffalo with the hair turned inside, were getting soaked from the heavy, wet snow. But the two inner pair were still dry, and they kept his feet warm.

Man learns to live out here in the wintertime. That—or he don't live at all.

Seasons call the tune. Not just women. Seasons tell a man what he's gotta do, what he can't do. Any season. A man gotta dance to the tune the seasons play, or he don't dance at all. Why, just last year—

Yes—just last year—his memory snagged on the thought and hung on like a tenacious wolverine. It would not shake loose of him. He had followed right along back then, too. Make no mistake about that, you crazy ol' loon. You done it back then, back that time, too. Had your rope picked up and yanked but good. You rode right along with McAfferty smack into Blackfoot country, coming along like a good lil' pup would. Thought you'd get it all figured out soon enough. But—you didn't solve it until there were two people dead and you were on a cold, dead-of-winter trail, tracking an old friend down. Yet, you followed right along, just like you should, didn't you? Less than a year ago. Had there been really much choice to it? Never really any deciding to be done. The choice was already made, the answer already given to you.

Women and Injuns. Always getting a fella in trouble, it seemed so anyway. Womenfolk yank on your line and you get yourself pulled right along with them. And those Injuns—why when they ain't after your scalp, they at least after your ponies and plunder. Make no mistake about that. And then, to top it all off, when those scalps, ponies or plunder ain't enough for them, they want you to go off after an old friend who murdered the chief's wife. They want you to kill that old friend. Sure, you know all the time it's gotta be done. And sure, you finally admit you figured it would come down to something like this for so long a time now anyway.

But none of that helped the feelings boiling inside, the ones you carry deep and let only a couple of folks see from time to time. Down deep inside where you can get yourself hurt—down deep inside, far enough to keep it pretty safe. Where you keep your friends.

Yep. Women, Injuns—and friends. Friends can hurt you bad, too. They tug on your rope, get you to come right along. McAfferty weren't the first time. Nawww, the first time for you making a damned fool of yourself it weren't. Bud, Silas and Billy took you for the fool back then. Hell, you was a fool! Gave them three all your furs to head out to parts unknown. Supposed to trade them in for another year's supplies for you. Fool! Never saw them three again, have you? Ain't never gonna, neither. Fool!

Ain't but one man get away with calling me a fool—and that's me. Only one who can do that. You may feel like a damned idiot—hell, you may even be one. But, I'll be damned if I'm gonna let any man call me a fool.

Someday he'd find out where the three disappeared to, where they left their bones. Till then, he'd have to put up with calling himself a damned old fool. Until then.

THE easy way around the side of the hill led him and the horses away from the buffalo herd, through the thick stands of aspen and clumps of spruce, then down into another meadow. Bass pulled up. The feeling washed over him like cold water down his spine. The air smelled strange now, here. Something out of place. Some odor that just didn't quite fit right. Then something else tugged at him. He remembered this place. He had been here. Back a moon or so. Enough of it tugged at him. Bass had to find out.

The old trapper worried the lead rope and set the ponies into motion behind him. Bass followed his curious nose. Perhaps he should ride—get up and out of the snow. But he really did not mind the walking. For a lot of trappers, winter was a time when their ponies weren't ridden all that much. So, come spring, the animals would be rangey, feisty, almost back to being wild mustangs once again. A man would have to break his pony to saddle all over again. Scratch would never let that happen to his animals. They'd be ridden every now and then—keep them broken in. Keep reminding them of the touch, the smell of a man. Especially a white man.

Surprised, his head jerked around at the sudden shrill screech of the gray hawk darting through the shaft of sunlight blazing its own way into the meadow. "Keee-er—rr! Keee-er-rr!" The bird's shadow raced across the snow, then disappeared down the hill in the mist and the trees. Bass relaxed again. The tenseness caused by the bird's sudden flight overhead slowly seeped from his muscles.

You're acting like a young pup now, he chided himself. Ain't nothing spooky about a bird taking to the wind over you. Maybe, could be you're on edge because you know you've been here before. And you know something ain't right. Maybeso, that's why your guts are all tied in knots.

His breathing slowed along with his heartbeat as he kept talking to himself. At last Scratch studied the sunbeam plastering patches of yellow on the new snow.

Over at the edge of the meadow, there in the play of sunlight and mist, where the deadfall lay heaviest—there was something new. Bass drew in a long breath and tramped soggily, reluctantly toward the play of sunlight on snow.

He tied off the buffalo pony to a stout branch of a fallen spruce, then stepped over the downed tree to inspect the scene. Kneeling beside the scattered snow and dirt, he found what remained of bones and decaying flesh held pitifully to those bones. Finally he put his fingers around the straight shaft of that spear which had been driven into the ground at his side. A burial site. He could find only one skull, the flesh ripped and torn, the face unrecognizeable. Yet there were still far too many bones for only one body. There had been four—maybe even five bodies cramped together in this shallow grave.

The wolves had been busy here, even during the recent storm. They knew meat was meat. Ripe, too. Even if it had gotten a little rancid over the past weeks. Five of them, Arapahos. Four for sure, and a fifth left to die. Abandoned to the forest and the wild things.

Scratch stood and yanked the spear out of the ground. He fought down the urge to break the slim shaft over his knee and stepped between the other four spears driven into the snow-blanketed soil. If it hadn't been so cold, this place would smell rank in a man's nostrils, even a man used to smelling dead and dying things. He gathered the five spears and tied them together with whangs made from his legging fringe.

He was resolved to it. He had been since that day when the warriors came to dally with Josiah's woman. The trappers had killed four and wounded a fifth. Bass had resolved himself to the fact that when the rest of that raiding party took off, got away—there'd be more to come back.

He hobbled back to his pony.

The newcomers had made medicine here over the bones of their fallen comrades. Silly, stupid youngsters. They didn't know any better than to attack a woman. Didn't know any better—that she would belong to someone. And that someone wasn't about to let them get away with—no, not that. And suddenly, they were caught up in it with you and there was no escape but fight or run. He and Josiah, they had let the rest go when five lay on the ground. Enough was enough, Paddock had told him. The fifth warrior would die anyway. And his spirit would walk the earth forever, unable to make it over to the Other Side. Enough done, and no more. But them Arapaho wouldn't know any better.

Bass gradually pushed himself onto leather and reached out for the rawhide rein. The spears were balanced across the crook of his left arm with his old rifle. Then his heels nudged the pony forward again.

There was no denying the sickening, gnawing lump in his belly. This was not finished. More to deal with come the next time. To have to live with that grave-like uncertainty once more. Not knowing when, or even where, they would strike. One thing and one thing only was certain. The warriors had returned to bury their dead, at least what remained of the bodies after the animals of the forest had torn the carcasses apart. Warriors had returned to this meadow and now they were out there searching. They were looking for the camp where lived their companions' killers. And they would go on looking until they found that camp.

Bass looked around nervously, automatically, as the pony finally led him into the pines heading down the slope. Uncertain, yes. Scared, maybe a little. But he was glad something had brought him along this ridge, up from the bowls and valleys, back to this place. Something had drawn him along to discover that the warriors had returned. That much was still strong within him. His peculiar sort of power still worked. Perhaps it was medicine after all. Something powerful enough to pull him here, to give him warning.

He would show the others the spears he had collected. He would tell them of the return of the dead warriors' companions. And they would have to move. Farther south, much farther along the eastern flank of the great park. Move out in that gray, early light before the next rising of the sun. Then again another short distance each evening during twilight, after the sun had gone to rest and before the sky dressed itself with star-sparkled blackness. The new snow would give them enough reflected light to travel some early each morning and a little more late each evening. They could do it. They'd have to. He and Josiah could see to it they were not caught out in the open.

He was not looking forward to dragging poles and plunder and ponies away from the cozy camp they had already established. Bass had hoped it would have been his home for the entire fall. Sometimes, things had a way of changing your mind for you. Sometimes things just come up and a man has to flow with the course of things. Sure, he could try to fight the tide, pitch himself against the current, and what might he get for all his efforts? Tired arms would be the least of his problems then. Scratch wasn't about to see any of his friends lose hair if he could help it.

No, sir. They'd all be ready. He'd see to it they moved their camp. And he'd see to it they were ready. Come what may, they'd all be ready.

6 HER FLESH AGONIZED with the memory of his touch. Hour after hour she would scratch at the inside of her thighs, clawing away the scabs and coagulated blood. She scraped up bleeding, oozing sores each time she sought to remove the tortured discomfort he had left on her most private flesh.

The milky skin now raked and ravaged by her own claws, the insides of her thighs seemed to bubble with a constant, irritated torment, almost as if there were some animal worming just below her skin, fighting to release itself, scratching, and cutting, and biting from within. But still she raked at her flesh until exhaustion finally overtook her.

The young woman brought her bloodied fingers to her face and began to weep softly. If only someone would come to cradle her once more. If only someone came to speak in soft, soothing words—any words. She did not care. She could not understand.

She was cold again. The biting ammonia smell of her own urine began to seep into her consciousness. A hand went between her legs. From where did this moist, foul dampness come? Several times a day it happened. At times she became smeared with her own feces, not able to control her functions when the private terror seized her mind.

It was then the young woman left and moved to a quieter place. Somewhere safe, where he could not reach her. Some safe place where the big man could not force himself against her flesh after ripping the clothing from her body. She felt the meal that fed her this morning begin to twist and heave within her belly. Then that first, foul taste of bile crept to the back of her throat.

She thanked her own God that it was coming up. They always forced her to eat. They held her down and made her eat. And this was just the manner in which she sought revenge against them for that insult to her body. She could force it back up by willfully bringing to mind the thought of him rubbing cruelly against her flesh. By rubbing his scaly body against her soft, smooth thighs now butchered and scabbed from her perpetual raking of her own flesh. The only way she could fight back at them, the ones who invaded her body as he had done. She could throw back up the food they forced down her.

And her fear rose in a crescendo with the first waves of vomiting, a fear that she would never be allowed to throw up what he had done to her. That it would grow inside her, fester there and become a grotesque thing sucking life from inside her bowels. The young woman hammered again and again at her stomach, hoping to kill what it was that was growing within her. To expel it with her every heave from that infected belly.

Fear gripped her that she could never throw up enough, never vomit from deep down enough to rid herself of what he had left inside her. The fatal seed left deep where no man had touched before.

The young woman's dark head shuddered after the final, racking spasm of vomiting. It felt warm against her cheek as she lay down in the acid-foul, bile-reeking pool she herself had made. She could never be truly warm again. He had left her so cold inside. Dying from the inside out. His poison would fester and grow within her, until it rotted away everything she had left. Then she would simply not be.

Desperately her two beings fought with one another as the young woman's eyes closed in weariness. One being battled to convince her that death was the only way out. The other being was full of black rage and sickened gall that would simply not let her die. She would fight what he had left behind inside her. She would fight the others when they tried to hold her down to clean her body. To put medicine on the cuts and ravaged flesh she had caused herself. She would continue to fling herself at the doorway when she heard them coming down the hall toward her room.

Now she crawled over toward the small oak door. With her cheek smearing the noxious vomit against the wall, the dark-haired woman let her eyelids fall shut. She would wait here until they came to feed her, to clean her up, to medicate her self-inflicted wounds. Then she would escape down the hall, down the stairs, down the lawn to the streets and be lost among the crowds. From there she would somehow know where to seek the monster. Or—she would seek someone who could find the monster—to take this thing from her.

It would not be her young fiancé. He was dead now. Murdered. How long had it been? About two and a half years ago now since she had tossed dirt in the grave. Then others had come to court her after the polite period of mourning had dutifully passed. They would not help—not against such a monster as had outraged her. No, there perhaps would be only one. The American. The young, tall one from the shop. He truly loved her, the fool that he was. He had professed his love for her—a poor American boy. Then he killed her French fiancé, and set this wheel in motion. He was the one who caused the monster to possess her. He was the one who could remove the haunting from her being now.

He was the only one. The American.

"THEY'RE HERE." Paddock slid from his pony at the center of camp.

The older man turned immediately, his eyes narrowing. "You seen 'em?"

"Back at the foot of the ridge a ways." Josiah threw a thumb in that direction. "They're still looking. It'll take 'em some time to come on us here. But—the niggers are getting a might warm, Scratch."

"I was 'fraid of that," the old trapper mumbled.

"We both were hoping it could have been different." Josiah handed his reins to

73

Looks Far Woman. "Sometimes, things have a way of making up a man's mind for him."

"That they do." Bass surveyed Paddock's eyes, satisfied with the young trapper's conclusion. "That be a fact, son."

Bass's weary gaze crawled east, studying the entrance to the rock formation they had chosen as their new camp, looking at nothing at all. He felt very tired once more. Perhaps he wasn't up to this task, making the decisions. Damn! But there were so many more lives at stake now. Not just his mangy old hide anymore.

Scratch spit out the stream of thick, browned juice and ruminated on their communal problem. Arapaho warriors had returned to the valley of the Bayou Salade, to avenge the death of their comrades more than a month before in the *Moon of Black Calves*. Traders called it September. In the high country it could be early winter. It could be late fall. Either way, it was a time of transition. Both earth and sky seemed unsure of themselves. One day was summerlike, the next whipped frothy with a grand fury and full of wintry bluster. Perhaps because in the high lonesome it was said the mountains made their own weather. And right now was the time the mountains were the most restless as they prepared for their winter's troubled sleep. Almost like a child, energy spent, tossing and turning itself into relaxation before it would finally drift off, sleep assured.

Soon would come those first days of the *Moon of Deer Rutting*. And Bass always smiled at that one. Why the Indians down below on the great expanse of plains called this the *Moon of Deer Rutting* he'd never know. Up here in the high country the season closed in much quicker. The animals up here went into the rhythmic cycle of the rut sometimes as much as six or eight weeks earlier. They were long done with the ages-old dance of romance and challenge, fighting and fornicating by now. The clocks of their bodies telling them there were other things to worry about with the coming cold of the winter. The clocks ticking off with shorter and shorter time to prepare. Some things were more important than sex.

Scratch spit once more. Then his face half-wrinkled with a grin. Damn, but a man could be the same way. Seems like when a man gets heavy in horn, that's all he can think about—getting his stinger dipped in some sweet honey. Then, that fella finally gets himself laid with a lady, why—he's satisfied for a while and can move on to other things. He gets sex off his mind, visions of soft, willing flesh—then he can think of something else. He wasn't all so damned different from other critters, was he now?

All of that was going to be so much spilled milk in a day or so. Those warriors had been getting closer and closer ever since he had found sign they had tried to bury the remains of their dead in some proper way. Didn't put the bodies up in trees like he'd thought they would. Instead the soil was scratched a bit. Then what was left of the bodies dumped in the crude hole. Maybe a few words said over the final resting place. Wouldn't be no one to say some final words over his folks unless he got started handling the problem.

"You figuring on what to do?"

Bass turned toward Josiah to answer the question. "S'pose we gotta do somethin'. Don't look like we're gonna be able to sit it out here any longer. We been havin' to hide hunkered down in this damned place." His arm swept the rock fortress he had found for the small party of humans and horses. "And you an' me been makin' do with runnin' trap lines like we was smack-dab in Blackfoot country. Wagh! Ain't no way for a man to have to act down here to the Bayou Salade, it ain't. Yeah, it's come time for us to make a stand, son."

Josiah toed the snow-dusted ground at his feet before he eventually gazed up at the older trapper. "I don't see no other way really. What do you figure to do?"

"How many of them brownskins you see?"

"I make it ten, maybe a dozen at the most."

"Shit." Bass leaned back and swelled out his chest, a little relieved and anxious for the others to shed their anxiety, too. "This be cub's play. Only a dozen of them poor niggers? We take care of that come this evenin'. Use the fallin' light for ourselves. You an' me gotta set this up just right, there bein' only the two of us, Josiah."

"Is not just two," Waits-by-the-Water said as she stepped into their midst.

"I cain't take that chance, Waits-by-the-Water." Bass wheeled and grasped her shoulders. He studied her eyes for a long, long moment, measuring what he saw in their black cherry depths, weighing what she was telling him. Still, he refused her offer. "No, I cain't. You women will stay here," Scratch directed in Crow.

"Is it not true you have taught me of your rifle?" the Indian woman asked in Sparrowhawk.

"And I, too." Looks Far slid up, having understood enough of the Crow words spoken between the couple.

Titus looked in exasperation over at Paddock. "We cain't—" His gnarled hands flew like worried doves with no place to land.

"Can't what?" the younger trapper inquired. "I don't know a damned thing what you've been talking about."

"The gals here wanna come along with us—"

"By the blood of—" Paddock snapped his head toward his young wife. "What about our boy?"

"There is no sense in leaving me here," she began to explain.

"I didn't ask you about *you*," Paddock stammered in English. "I was asking what you planned to do with the boy."

"I was telling you," Looks Far explained politely. "If you do not return, there is no need for me to go on in this life." She watched Josiah's eyes squint quickly in recognition of her words. Then the Flathead woman continued. "So it is that should I go away, who will be left to care for Joshua anyway?"

Paddock turned to Bass, befuddled. At the same time he was struck with the simplicity, yet the complexity of her argument. He shook his head twice and looked down at her rounded face.

"No one said you could not go on without me," he said, choosing his Flathead words as best he could. "The odds weigh against our old friend and me. If we do not return, you must go on—for our son. He is life and breath for you."

"He can live, he can die," she finally whispered quietly. "Perhaps Man Above will not look kindly upon me in telling this. But Man Above is the one who answers who lives and who does not live. It is not my choice to make. It is not yours either, my husband. I want you to see it is not my life I am concerned with. It is yours. Should you go on to another resting place, I wish to be with you there, as I am here." She dropped her head for a moment. "Man Above will guard over our son should we be together in death."

Josiah stared first at Scratch, then at Waits-by-the-Water, then back at the older man. He read nothing in his friends' faces.

"Don't ask me, son," Bass said, half his face carved with a crooked grin. "Looks like you're the only one to understand Flathead."

"But she's asking me to understand more than just Flathead," Josiah sputtered. "She's telling me she's going with us because it ain't worth living without me. I can't understand it."

"It ain't yours to understand," Bass said, shaking his head. "Ain't yours to understand her mind, the way it works. She's been brought up thinkin' a whole differ'nt way in all things. 'Specially 'bout life—'bout life an' death. She's been taught not to fear this thing called dyin'. She's been taught that she will be watched over in death, too. That she will be led somewhere for a purpose in it. All her young life, she's been taught that each and every day might just be a good day to die. There be no pain in passin' on. Her Man Above will see to that. See to it that there be a time an' a reason for her goin'."

"A good day to die, huh?"

"Looks to be the shape of it."

"Ain't for me." Josiah shook his head vigorously. "Ain't a good day for me to die at all. No matter what she believes, it ain't for me to think the same way. My God don't allow me to go off wasting life —"

"Wastin'?" Scratch interrupted. "You call the deer you kill—the buffalo I bring in to this camp *wastin' life?*"

He paused a moment until he saw Paddock's brow knit up in contemplation. Finally Bass continued. "Them critters give up their ghost so we could go on. Looks Far is just tellin' you it's the same thing with all livin' beings, son. She believes some livin' things pass on so other livin' things can go on."

"Not my way of thinking," Josiah muttered, already sensing the odds mounting against him.

"No one," Bass began, then waited a moment. "I s'pose no one's forcin' you to think that way. I'm only tellin' you it's the way her mind works."

"*Axace.*" Waits-by-the-Water declared the word as introduction, then studied the trappers' faces to determine if she had permission to continue. "Axace is the One Above for not just Sparrowhawk people. All people. He watches over white men too."

"The Sun," Bass said, when his wife was finished speaking. "The One Above's power is the Sun an' He guards over us all."

"You're all standing against me on this?"

"Nope," Bass smiled engagingly. "I s'pose the way it is, Josiah—you an' me is outnumbered by these gals here. Them two against us just ain't fair odds at all!"

Paddock listened to Bass chuckle a moment. Then the young trapper remarked with a smile all his own, "I suppose there are times when a man feels outnumbered one on one with his woman!"

"Don't look like she give you much of a choice," Bass sighed, serious once more.

"No. It don't look that way," Paddock agreed, not taking his eyes from Looks Far's face.

Titus turned toward the entrance to the little valley, their refuge for the past few days. He exhaled deeply. After he spit the rest of his tobacco wad into the fire pit, the older trapper spoke again.

"Ain't no time like now to get this done."

Josiah glanced quickly at the two women. "I think we were all waiting on you, old man."

Bass cleared his throat. "Thanks for tellin' me I was the one holdin' you up," he snorted with a chuckle. "Let's be gettin' on with this lil' shindig."

Scratch wheeled to his shelter and retrieved his pistol and shooting pouch, then shook his powder horn to see if there was a good measure left in it for the job at hand. Waits-by-the-Water was at his side momentarily, handing up to him their rifles. Two of the pistols taken from those St. Louis assassins hired to kill Josiah last summer were carefully loaded from her own pouch, then securely tucked into her wide woolen sash.

In a moment the older man stepped up to join Paddock and Looks Far, who were likewise strapping on equipment. The Flathead woman had stuffed Emile Sharpe's huge horse pistol into a fold of her wide waist sash. And now she was quickly rolling up a small section of buffalo hide and a tiny rawhide harness, all to be strapped behind her grass pad saddle.

Josiah nodded to Bass. "We're ready to roll."

"No sense wastin' any more words, any more time. Let's go settle this fandango, son."

The white trappers helped their women board their small ponies, then each handed his wife a rifle. Scratch slung an extra one behind his right leg in a scabbard lashed against his saddle. He slipped his right foot into a stirrup and swung atop his Spanish saddle. He felt loose, ready. The muscles were not taut, strung as if tense or anxious. Maybe it was good, Bass decided as he tapped heels to his runner's ribcage.

Scratch smiled back at the three young people plying their way along behind him in single file through the snowy stands of pine and spruce, climbing into the aspen. He would take them up higher along that ridge extending for several miles before opening into the Bayou itself. Not so much a rock formation, the ridge divided the huge park from several smaller bowls and valleys that were dispersed from the main valley.

Occasionally one of the party coughed or stifled a sneeze. But no words were spoken. Each knew well enough not to speak. For the time being, the only sound was the hawing breath of the four animals as they took their riders farther and farther up along the side of the ridge. Between the snow and the cold, most of the trees had little of their golden display left. Beneath the ponies' hoofs lay a brilliant assortment of eye-aching white along with yellow and gold and sun littering the bright hillside. Bright patches of color caught the afternoon sunlight to make the stands of aspen explode in shimmering brilliance. What gold tinsel still hung on their branches glittered and danced with lightbeams. Frosty breezes snaked through the trees.

A silent wind made other things speak for it. In this case the rustling of dry autumn leaves, the fringe on his leggings and the loose wisps of graying, autumn-of-his-life hair dancing at his cheek. His left eye smarted in the cooling, late-afternoon light. Couple of hours is all they had. If they didn't find the warriors, the small trapper party would cold-camp the night until first light, then begin the search once more. Seek until they found the scalp warriors. Turn the hunters into the hunted. And the quarry back-trailed on the warriors until—

The thought suddenly cracked his cold, raw face with a dim smile. Turning the game around once more. It was what he enjoyed doing most. Exchanging places unexpectedly with his hunter. Strike first while the hunter was mired down in the chase. Cast the first, sudden, shocking blow while the scalp party had its mind on other things, before it could rally itself. Decide to throw yourself into the mire of blood and gore while it is of your own choosing, on your own ground, when and where you decide.

It seemed the breeze was insistent there at Scratch's left cheek. The left eye watered more in the nagging, cold dryness of the wind. Scratch finally succumbed and turned to his left as he rubbed the moisture from the offending eye. He saw the warriors below them.

Bass pulled on the rein and threw up his left arm, signaling to halt. He turned in the saddle as he drew up on the pony's rawhide rein, then motioned for the others to remain quiet. With an affirmative nod from Josiah, the older man brought down the left hand from his lips and pointed down the side of the ridge littered with deadfall.

The war party's shadows were long in the late sun. Most likely they would be giving up the hunt for the day and soon enough seeking a campsite for the coming frosty night. Their dark, snaking shadows crept out of the pines and skirted along the edge of the meadow, tracing the dark line of trees. Most of the warriors wore buffalo robes or elkhides wrapped about them, a few preferring the use of a warm, woolen capote. Perhaps they would eat a cold supper before dozing off as the night turned black. That way they could be up with the first crack of light along the east slipping over the mountains.

Another day of looking for us, Bass thought.

Titus turned toward his young partner, then threw his left arm up the side of the ridge toward a grand outcropping of granite and sentinel pines beneath the rock face. Paddock understood and nodded. He motioned for the two women to follow him.

Josiah led the party into the thick pines and deadfall beneath the outcropping. Bass was the last into the trees. He pulled up beside the younger man.

"I got struck by a idea," Bass said, keeping his voice low, almost a husky whisper crackling in the cold, dry air.

"Yeah? I'm listening."

Bass nodded at the lengthening shadows just beyond them at the edge of the pines. "We ain't got time to set us up an ambush proper, what with the light goin' soon."

"Yeah. Go on."

"Well, now. Seems to be them brownskins down there was maybe lookin' to find them some trappers nappin'." He licked his dry, cracked lips, feeling some temporary relief as he reached into his shooting pouch. "An' that's the way this ol' child is gonna catch them. What say?"

Paddock watched the older man pull a bear-greased patch from his pouch, using it to swab his dry lips. Josiah waited for Scratch to rub his lips together before responding.

"You thinking we ought to surprise them the way they was gonna surprise us? Right?"

"That's the way I calc'late it." Titus offered the greased patch to his Crow woman, who took it to medicate her own cracked lips.

"Tonight, then?"

"Mornin'd be all the better, son. Too much darkness soon for doin' it at night. An' their fire ain't gonna be much at all. Injun fire never is a big one anyway. Not much light, not enough to count on. Nawww, I reckon we all're better off if we get some sleep up here. Go to sleep purty-nigh soon. Come time when the moon is high, we leave the ponies here an' lightfoot it down to get all set up for first light."

"Take the women with us, huh?"

"That's why they come along, son."

"I suppose—"

"I don't reckon you could turn 'em back around now anyways."

"You've probably got that one right." Josiah finally let slip with a grin for his old friend.

"We set them gals upwind of them ponies. We may live out here in these mountains just like them cussed runagate Injuns down there, just like them women—but we are still white men. What we want is for the red niggers' ponies to smell them women of ours. Injun women. You see?"

Bass waited for Josiah to nod in agreement, finally in understanding. "Awright, son. Them women we set up there, upwind of them ponies, upwind of camp. Maybe one of them niggers has got him a good nose. He'll smell nothin' else but Injun. Maybe you an' me take out two of them. Right where they lay on the ground by the fire. I figger the women can take a couple more as the others come rollin' outta their sleepin' robes. Hmmm—that would put four of 'em down an' leave us with just our four to their eight. Nice round numbers."

"And twice what we have," Paddock whispered at the old man, his gaze returned from looking at the two women. "Still don't like them odds."

"Neither do I."

"Even with the pistols, still means we gotta reload, Scratch." Josiah shook his head grimly. "That—or we gotta take the fight right on into 'em."

"I'd try most anything before I'd sashay into that camp filled with a bunch of half-sleepy, crazed-up red niggers all wantin' my ha'r."

"You got any better idea?"

"Maybeso we can have time to reload an' fire on them that's left. But I don't count on them women gettin' done with that in time. Let's give 'em each a pistol to use after the rifles are empty."

"Looks like that'll leave half a dozen. Three for each of us on the second go 'round, old man."

Bass shook his head gravely. "We gotta do somethin' to even up the odds better'n this, son. I guess I'm no differ'nt than them red niggers—I don't like wadin' into a fracas less'n I know I got a good chance to come out on top of it."

"They'll put one sonuvabitch down by the horses, won't they?"

"Most likely they will, son." Bass ground his teeth pensively.

"I'll take him out." Josiah tapped a palm against the handle of his huge knife.

"That takes us down to only five of 'em." Bass pursed his lips and twisted them into his beard in contemplation. After a few long moments he nodded slightly. "I s'pose we just gonna have to see what comes up. See how the cards get—"

"Dammit, Scratch!" Josiah interrupted hoarsely. "Why the hell didn't I think of it before?"

"What're you jabberin' about now?"

"Shit! My friend, we do have a way to cut the odds down a bit." Josiah turned back to his pony and hooked a foot in a stirrup.

"Where you headin'?" Bass put a hand out to stay the younger trapper from rising to his saddle.

"I'm gonna go back to camp. Get my bow." Josiah turned toward his woman. "You watch my family while I'm gone. I'll be back after dark, most likely."

Scratch watched Looks Far quickly rise and scamper in their direction. "Best tell her what you're doin', son. Tell her goodbye."

Looks Far slid into Josiah's arms. "I'm coming right back," he explained to her in Flathead.

"Where do you go now?" she asked.

"Back to our camp. I go for my bow." He pulled away to arms' length and held her shoulders in his large hands. "The bow will help us in the fight with the war party."

"You need the bow?"

"Yes, I have said. For the coming fight."

A whimsical smile washed across Look Far's face. "My husband is sometimes very fast in the loving, to get started. But he is slower in the thinking."

"A fine time for you to speak to me of loving," Josiah grinned.

"I speak to you of thinking," she corrected. "I speak to you of planning."

"I do not understand." Josiah shook his head as he watched his woman turn away to her own pony.

Looks Far tore away the thongs holding the buffalo robe behind her pad saddle. She gave the end of the robe a snap to unfurl it between them. Within the folds of the dark, curly mat of hair lay the skin quiver and the short, powerful bow.

Bass whistled his approval, low and long. He looked up at Waits-by-the-Water. "You catch any of what she told him?"

"Not all of it," was her reply in Sparrowhawk. "Enough to know she told him there comes times when a woman has to take care of her man. Not always a man caring for his woman."

"It is this way many times with us," Scratch replied in Crow. "Many times with us, little one."

Paddock embraced Looks Far, then released her. "Looks like we're all set for morning now, Scratch." He turned to beam at the older trapper.

"Looks to be we're all set," Bass agreed. "We finish us some of the jerky the gals brought along. Curl up in the trees an' grab us little siesta 'til it's high-moon time."

Josiah gave his woman another squeeze with one arm, then motioned for her to take Joshua back under the overhang of a spruce's lower branches. Back beneath the canopy was a patch of ground cleared of snow, not yet reached by the early snowfalls regularly dusting these higher slopes. The white mantle hung in here although on a southern exposure. Sunlight found it difficult to penetrate the thick stands of spruce and pine and aspen. But they would have some dry, clear ground on which to sleep until the moon reached the middle of the sky. They could burrow down into the pine needles like ground squirrels and try to sleep until it was time to begin their stalk down the ridge toward the Indian camp.

Bass watched the women settle back beneath the low boughs. Looks Far opened her capote and pulled aside the sleeve of her woolen dress. Joshua took to the offered nipple hungrily, making little "ngh-ngh-ngh" sounds as he ate his late supper.

Josiah smiled and turned away to stare down the hill. Somewhere down there were the warriors sent to kill them. Down in that camp were a dozen Indians ready to kill or be killed. It was just him and the older trapper, really. He thought he would have known better than to bring his wife and child along on this fool's errand. But he'd let himself get talked into this. Damn! but things always had a way of sweeping him up and carrying him along. He wanted to change that. He wanted to take control. To do more than merely react.

A dozen of them against him and the old man. Not the kind of odds to feel all that good about. But he was here, and it had to be done. The cold air did a lot to dry out the moisture gathering at the back of his neck beneath the brown, curly locks. The frosty breeze took away the dampness of his brow. Paddock swallowed hard against the jerky he chewed.

He didn't know for positive, but it sure felt like he was praying. He had never done all that much of it, but still, it sure felt like he was praying.

THE silver orb rode near mid-sky when Bass stirred the three others out of their cold, restless sleep. That nibbled moon gave a luminous, metallic luster to the fresh layer of dry snow covering everything. This new dusting lay fluffy in their tracks of yesterday. A man could even tell the blue spruce from other pines with such a moon only a few days shy of fullness.

Looks Far asked for a few minutes to nurse little Joshua. The infant at first complained of being awakened in the cold, frost-laden air. He didn't like being disturbed in the middle of his night. But as soon as the warm, rigid nipple was presented to his tiny mouth, the youngster sucked greedily at the warm milk offered him. The adults had to settle for the dry jerky brought along and a small gourd of water—privations that made each of them wish this ordeal was over, for better or worse.

Within moments after he was strapped in the leather sling at his mother's back, Joshua was snoring lightly. A full tummy of warm milk, wrapped in wool and fur, his tiny head burrowed down inside the curly darkness of his sling cocoon, the infant had it best of all. He would not remember this cold night journey through the snowy, silvery forest in anticipation of death.

Bass led the small party down the ridge in the jewellike light. He had allowed himself the time to pick and choose his route for the benefit of the women. A path that would be easier going for them although it would take an hour or more longer. The snow was not deep enough at this altitude, at this time of early winter, to make their going tough. In places the drifts had built up above their knees, but by and large they traveled in snow that climbed up to mid-calf only. It muffled the noise of their steps and reflected the gem-light available from both moon and stars.

Bass's heart pounded steadily. Mouth and nose became dry from time to time in the thin air. He would stop the party and scoop up some snow in his mittens to show them to suck on some of the glistening silver flakes. It soothed the dry, tortured membranes, temporarily. At each of their momentary rest stops through the cold, strenuous hours, Scratch continually surveyed each of the women and their weapons, continually assessing how they were holding up to the journey on foot. Neither of the two seemed to be breathing hard with the exertion, neither one seemed to have trouble with her particular load.

Looks Far was giving Joshua back and forth to Waits-by-the-Water so that each could carry the two rifles from time to time. In that way, they had decided between themselves, they would share all responsibilities. In their own private vocabulary, which neither man spoke, the two women had again sworn to each other their friendship and their love. Waits-by-the-Water had given her grave oath when asked by Looks Far—should the Flathead woman be killed in the coming fight, her Crow friend would raise the child as if he were her own son. That much settled in whispered fragments of conversation, the group set off into the blue shadows and silver light once more.

At last the old trapper halted the party and pointed for them to crouch beneath the low, snow-sagging branches of a huge pine.

"You stay here," Bass rasped quietly, the dryness causing an unfamiliar wheeze to his words. "We are close. I will be back after sizing up their camp."

Scratch repeated his Sparrowhawk words in English to Josiah who turned and quickly explained to Looks Far. The Flathead woman nodded and turned to her cradled infant. Any time now he would awaken and be hungry, demanding more milk unless she was ready for him.

Scratch crabbed out from under the white flocked branches and was gone into the blue shadows.

It was almost an hour before he returned. The old trapper was almost upon their tree before Paddock could hear his partner's footsteps slogging through the snow. Titus slid back under the heavy branches on hands and knees. He accepted a relieved embrace from Waits-by-the-Water.

"I take it you found them?" Paddock asked as the Crow woman pulled her head away from Scratch's shoulder.

"Yep. On north of where we spotted 'em last evenin'," he rasped hoarsely, then ran his dry tongue around his mouth with a mitten full of snow. " 'Bout where I was figgerin' 'em to bed down." He nodded, then grew pensive.

"What is it?" Paddock asked, sensing something was wrong.

"Just thinkin', like I been doin' all the way back," Bass said, then sucked more of the moisture-giving snow. "Sure glad we left them ponies where we did. They give their animals graze all apart. Out on four sides."

"And their ponies would have smelled ours, huh?"

"Right," Bass answered. "Probably sniggered an' started up the whole camp."

"Sounds like our long walk was worth it," Paddock admitted.

"Things go right, we'll be ridin' back 'stead of walkin'."

Paddock waited a moment, again allowing Bass time in his own thoughts. "Go ahead. You got it figured out?"

"Hopin' so." Bass fished through the pine needles until he found some small pine cones and piled them in front of his knees where he crouched. From his pile he selected one. "This is where them red niggers is sleepin'." He took four more cones and put them on the cardinal points. "They got three ponies out at each point, here—here, there—and here."

"Sounds like we're dealing with some smart Injuns," Josiah ventured.

Scratch looked up at his young partner in the silver light. "Like I said, they'd know from the ponies if'n their animals smelled 'nother horse."

Josiah watched the older man bow his head to stare at the diagram on the ground between their knees. "But you and me both know them ponies likely to smell us, too. You and me."

"Yes." Bass drew the word out with a hiss, reluctantly. "I really figured we'd have to deal with that."

"You gonna take the chance of you and me sneaking up between two bunches of them ponies?" The young man motioned with two fingers on each hand walking between the groups of horses so that the sleeping warriors would be caught in a deadly crossfire.

"I don't see no other way," Scratch said. "We got to take us that chance. Less'n—you got a better idea?"

Paddock stared at the cones and his fingers for long moments, trying to come up with something until his head ached in desperation. Finally he admitted, "I ain't got idea one."

Suddenly Bass scooped up one of the pine cones, and another. "This is Looks Far." He set a cone down to his left, between two groups of the Arapaho horses.

"Yeah, so. Go ahead," Josiah prompted.

"Now this is Waits-by-the-Water." Bass picked up a cone and showed it to his wife, to be certain she understood what he was explaining. Her role in this would be crucial. "If you do not wish to take this chance, you must tell me now," he said to his woman in Absaroka. "We will choose another way."

"You must explain it to me," she answered as she slid up closer to his diagram on the ground.

"You have your knife?" Bass asked. When she indicated that she did by tapping her sheath, Bass continued. "There is but one night guard. He is making the circle: from here, to here, and so on." He pointed with an index finger. "I will find out where he is when we get closer to their fire. Your part is to go to this group of horses first." He showed the southern three cones. "And there you will slit one animal's throat."

Scratch watched his wife's eyes as he spoke the Sparrowhawk words slowly, painfully, deliberately. She likewise bore into his eyes and read the concern therein. Finally she nodded and smiled.

The older man smiled back at her. "Then you move here," he said as he gestured in a semicircle toward another graze of ponies at the northern end of the compass, "to select another pony to die. Do you understand what is asked of you?"

Again she nodded.

"You will do this?"

"I will die if I must," she answered.

"You do this, my woman," he said, selecting his words carefully, "so that—so none of us will die. Your part is very important for our safety in setting up this kill."

"We all will live," the Crow woman answered.

Paddock had watched the exchange between his two friends. From what he still fragmentally remembered of the Absaroka tongue, from the gestures across the diagram and from Bass slicing a finger-knife across his own throat in pantomime, the young man knew this had something to do with the ponies. Not only did they need to worry about the warrior making the guard rounds, but the horses had been staked out to graze as sentinels. He understood why slitting the throats of two ponies might help.

Scratch looked through the white and silver branches. The light was growing into a paler blue black along the east. They could wait no longer. He began to scoot on hands and knees like a crab across the snow. "We best be goin'."

"Hold up a minute," Paddock ordered in a husky whisper. Bass stopped before the young man continued. "Where you and me gonna be through this?"

Scratch again settled before the diagram and picked up two final cones. "This is my young, knot-head partner," he said as he set one cone down on the left side of the camp. "This be the smart ol' man who ain't ready to lose no more ha'r to a pack of mangy 'Rapaho niggers." Bass placed the second cone near the right side of the warrior camp.

"That's where you're gonna fire the first shot into 'em?"

"Nawww." Bass shook his gray head. "Remember your bow?"

Paddock nodded.

"You gotta take out as many of them as you can." Bass motioned like he was drawing back and firing arrows, three of them, before he spoke again. "Take your time with your shots. Make 'em count, son. Make damn sure they count. You snuff as many of them niggers you can afore one of 'em wakes the others. Then the whole shebang comes loose. I don't fire afore then. Things break loose on their own, you drop the bow an' fill your hands with that rifle of your'n. The womenfolk know to make their shots count when it comes down to it. You gotta do what you can to even up the odds some afore the rowdy noise starts."

"So, what're you gonna do in all this 'til the fun starts?" Josiah grinned up at Scratch. "What pleasure have you reserved for yourself, my friend?"

The silver in the older man's beard crinkled and danced as his smile grew wider. Even his tobacco-yellowed teeth shone bright in the jeweled light. "Son, I save the best of it for myself. I got me the night guard to rub out."

The old man tore off his right mitten and pretended his index finger was a knife he now drew out of the sheath at his left side. With it placed beneath his left ear, Scratch slowly drew the weapon under the jaw and across the windpipe until the tip of the finger-knife made its way to the right earlobe. He snapped his head forward to indicate death.

Paddock shivered slightly as he watched the bloody pantomime. He suddenly felt cold. But not from the temperature of the air.

"Always save the most fun of it for myself, Josiah," Bass finally whispered, having caught the almost imperceptible tremble of Paddock's shoulders. "No one else gonna take this away from me."

It was settled.

Scratch crawled through the branches feeling the others close at his heels. No one would yank the pleasure of it from his grasp. It was his alone—and he would see it through.

7

SCRATCH KNEW THE man was cold. He could hear the warrior's teeth rattle from time to time.

The trapper inched forward a few more steps toward the horse guard as the Arapaho stomped his feet to stay warm. That noise and the diversion from the Indian's concentration allowed the white man to snake closer to the guard. Within half an hour the sky would be light enough to allow a man to see features on another's face. He hoped by daybreak they would all be on the way back to their camp.

It did not matter that Bass had killed many men. It was also of no consequence that most of those men were killed close up, within an arm's length, their faces visible. Where you could see their eyes. None of that made this kill any easier. None of what had gone before made this something routine, mechanical. Titus was still scared right down to his cold feet. That never changed. The only thing that mattered to him right now was how he handled the fear. Would he bungle this, letting his fear take over? Then have to straighten things out as best he could? Or, would he again be able to wrestle down fear, conquer it as he would any enemy? He swallowed hard. A man had to do what he had to do. Nothing more than that. No foofaraw. Just do it.

Scratch was glad the warrior actually stood apart from the horses. Those animals dozed heaviest here just before dawn. The guard preferred to spend his watch in among the trees rather than among the three horses staked here on the east side of the Arapaho night camp. He probably thinks it's warmer in them trees, too.

Bass crinkled his frost-laden mustache with a grin. Hell, it'd be lots warmer standing in amongst them ponies and their body heat. Besides, standing in with the horses would make a man a harder target. And that's what Bass had waited for. He had patiently lingered in the frigid air until the guard decided to move away from the horses. Far enough away that the Indians' ponies might not smell him, even in their sleep.

The next time the guard would stomp his feet and slap his arms to work up warmth and stimulate circulation, Bass would make his move. Two quick steps and he would be at the warrior's side. Two quick steps and it would be a test of surprise versus youth, muscle against older sinew, one man's fear against another man's dread.

The Indian stomped his feet in the ankle-deep, silver white snow. Bass barely cast a shadow in the gem-light left before dawn, and he was behind the guard.

With the second step that brought him next to the Indian, Scratch had his left arm ready. It lashed around the warrior's neck. The hand locked back over the right shoulder. Stiffening, the guard attempted to turn into his attacker. He was strong. Titus knew he would not last long wrestling this one. In the next instant the knife was already on its way. The tip slid past the warrior's hair, breaking the skin just beneath the skullcap at the base of the brain. Just to the side of the first knuckle on the spine.

One jab. The warrior stiffened and tried to jerk away from his attacker. Bass quickly drove the knife in hard. Up into the back of the brain. The wriggling, squirming guard made this second plunge something less than smooth, fighting against the left arm that held him locked against the trapper. Just as the Arapaho lashed out with his leg and began to pull the locking arm away with his own two mighty arms, the trapper's knife finished its work. Scratch felt the blade rip past the resistance of muscle and sinew, finally plunging into the softer tissue. There was a gush and flow of fluid hot across his cold flesh as it billowed down the handle of the knife and over his fingers.

Scratch twisted the blade, back and forth, back and forth. Within the weakening grip of his left arm the warrior stiffened spastically, then went as limp as a new moccasin, his bowels releasing in death. Bass swallowed hard against the hot lump searing his throat, a lump that twisted and stuck like a knot in a rope. He shook slightly, not knowing if he quaked from the cold, or the final relaxation of his own muscles.

He waited to see if there were other sounds coming from the nearby fire, from the guard's companions. None of the sleeping warriors seemed to stir. Bass himself waited to breathe. The air finally rushed out of his lungs in a torrent. Bass pulled the cold air back in just as greedily.

Then he held his breath and listened to the night. Somewhere across the fire a horse snorted softly. The forest grew quiet once more. It was almost as if the only sound a man could hear was the silvery light itself slinking across the snow. The metallic glow crept and snaked against the blue black shadows near the trees.

At last he let the body slip out of his grasp. It crumpled to the snow in a bloody heap. Impact with the ground was muffled, softened, like a man plunging into a featherbed. Then the silence radiated about him once again.

Scratch straightened. He swallowed once, gulping the strong, heady air. It was cold. The hot lump was gone. Then he backed into the trees, back within the shadows once again. He took the long way back to that place where he'd left his wife. She was to wait near the northern group of ponies. It would be there she would kill her first of two horses.

Perhaps he should not have put such a burden upon her. A young woman barely out of her teens, being dragged into this life-and-death struggle. And to top it off, she was the only one who could drop a pony, to cover the odor of the white men. A lot to put on her. The singular task of killing a tethered, hobbled Indian pony. To do it quickly, efficiently enough that the animal made no noise, did not struggle, did not harm her.

Bass almost regretted his decision now.

He did not see the woman where she was supposed to be waiting. His heart took a leap and waited such a long time to fall. The cold air hung at the back of his throat. Was this the right place? Here in the inky darkness, without much light, he could only hope his memory served him right. Was this where he had left her, for sure? The panic rose in him like a foul-tasting bile. Either he was not in the right place, where he had told her to await his return, or—

He didn't want to think about her being gone, captured, dead, or worse.

A sound so quiet it was like the moaning of a heart slipping up a man's throat, she moved out of the trees and stopped. The Sparrowhawk woman stood close enough to the shadows that a man would not see her unless he was looking specifically for the woman. She planted herself out from the trees just enough for him to pick her out from the indigo darkness. Titus took in a rush of air, relieved to see her there at last, where he had left her, where she was to have stayed.

As he slid beside her in the silver light, the trapper hungered for her instantly. There was a painful gnawing need and fiery desire in his relief to find her safe. A part of his being had returned, completing him.

Waits-by-the-Water turned at his last step toward her, half-crouching as she wheeled around. The knife in her hand slid up between them, then fell jerkily when she had determined it was her husband who crept up on her in the darkness. The Crow woman fell against him in relief. The white man cradled her gently quaking shoulders and rested his chin against the top of her head.

Finally she pulled back and looked up into the dark coals that were his eyes beneath the moon's light. Waits-by-the-Water raised her knife and held it up for him to see. The blade did not glitter in the silvery light. He reached up to feel the blade and the hand that held the knife. They both were wet, drenched with a sticky, thick fluid.

Blood.

He put a finger to her lips, then his, to signal silence between them. Next the finger moved to his throat and slashed across it. She nodded. He quaked for what she had already done. The woman had disobeyed his instructions. She had not waited for his return before killing the first pony. Instantly he was angry and proud, both. Finally the growing light relieved him of the inner struggle. The silvery air of pre-dawn was becoming the blooming gray of dawn.

Just as quickly he was glad for what she had taken upon herself. They might have time, just enough minutes left, to skirt the camp and reach the ponies staked to the south of the warrior's fire. Scratch gently moved her knife aside and pulled her into him. A kiss on her forehead and he turned to lead her away.

The growing, gray light sliding into the valley gave the snow a lustre of ash. No longer a brilliant silver blue, the dull ash gray and charcoal lay brightening before the onslaught of pale yellow at the horizon. The air was always coldest now, just before the sky awakened for the day. Weaving in and out through the tangle of pine, spruce and aspen, Bass felt the warmth of her nearness. That radiance gave him strength. He hoped his being with her would now give his wife the resolve to complete her bloody task. Halfway there and only the Crow woman could complete the circle.

To his right through the deep blue mist laced in the timber he could make out that small, smokey fire at the center of the warriors' sleeping camp. Around the tendrils of tired, gray smoke lifting into the heavy dawn air were the scalp hunters themselves. Radiating from their fire like the spokes of a carriage wheel, the eleven lifeless forms were like so many cocoons under the new blanket of white snow. He cut to his left immediately to put more distance between himself and the warriors. The eastern group of horses should be close by, so the trapper pushed farther into the timber, farther away from their sleepy noses.

He stopped to look about him at the forest for a few moments. The trapper needed bearings. Yet there was no sun, and he could not be sure at this moment where the eastern horizon lay. With the dense mist, he could not be guided by the morning stars lying low along the western horizon.

She sensed his consternation. The Crow woman touched his arm, pointed to his right. He gazed down at her for a long moment, then understood what she had told him. There was no good reason to trust her in this matter, yet he followed her direction. Scratch set off again, bearing more and more to the right. Finally, he heard a pony nicker through the dark timber. Out there in the growing, gray light, he thought he could make out the gauzy forms moving as if in slow motion. The southern grazers.

The trapper turned to smile at his woman before she left his side. He stopped her, cupped her chin within a palm and bent to brush her lips. A gentle smile blossomed at the corners of her lips. Stretching on toes, she reached up and brushed his lips with another kiss.

He watched her move away through the trees, slowly, one cautious step after another. Always toward the ghostlike, misty animals out there in the dark timber. Then the swirl of thick soup swept into the trees like an avalanche rolling down the side of a slope. The ponies were gone. Waits-by-the-Water disappeared with them.

The Sparrowhawk woman ground to a halt as the mist rolled in around her. Only another twenty feet and she would have been among the animals. The fear rose within her like a fever. Her skin prickled with its heat. Yet, like a wave of warmth washing over the skin, it was quickly gone to leave her shivering in the damp fog. Ahead was the heavy tussing of hoofs. Waits-by-the-Water heard a pony blow somewhere out there in the mist. She was relieved. The fear washed off her. Then she stepped on through the soup once more.

It made the Crow woman feel a little better holding the knife out in front of her. Ready to protect herself should something leap out of this mystery cloud. A few more steps and two ponies materialized out of the mist. They seemed like ghosts to her—undefined, not quite real. She moved a few steps toward them, eyes alert and burning to find the third pony staked here. Finally the third animal loomed dimly out of the fog.

The animals all appeared to be clean-boned. A little slack from the long ride to this mountain valley, but all surely would be quick as sin and long-winded. Each stood some fourteen hands, spare in build and set on good, stout legs with a short back. For a moment in the frost the woman admired their full barrels, sharp, nervous, peaked ears quaking over large, bright, owling eyes. The first pony was asleep, enjoying its deepest sleep just before dawn. The second closed its eyes to the two-legged stepping out of the mist. It would pay her no mind.

The third horse was awake, wide awake. Its nose raised in the air, testing the breezes, trying to scent her. Waits-by-the-Water stopped, forced her thoughts to bore into the pony's mind.

Little brother, it is not you I wish. I will be quiet. You must not speak. It is not you I wish to take with me. You may live long. You have nothing to fear from me, Little Brother.

The animal's nervous ears twitched. Then it shivered once and dropped its head to resume pawing at the snow. Its sides rippled in another cold shudder and the pony blew.

In the cold, sparkling air the other two ponies exhaled breaths as big as shovel heads. She could see the tiny icicles frozen at their chins, hanging like frosty tinsel in the damp mist. From the two she selected the larger, the older of the horses. The younger had longer to live perhaps, more to experience on this great circular walk through life. This older one had been down many trails before, had probably seen much of what was meant for the medicine dog to see with its eyes through a lifetime of sweetgrass and willow shoots. She would allow him to cross to the Other Side now.

The chant rose in her heart, echoing through her mind with a soft whisper returning again and again and again. Almost at the back of her throat, the words were trapped, unspoken, yet as vivid as if they had been screamed aloud to crack the morning mist.

> *Little Brother!*
> *It is time for us.*
> *Little Brother, come!*
> *Your nights are past*
> *And the hills are never more.*
> *Little Brother, come!*

Her arm slipped over his neck and she caressed his withers. Slowly she put her lips near the pony's ear and again she spoke to him.

> *Sweet water and grass await you,*
> *Old friends of yours, Little Brother.*

Waits-by-the-Water patted and caressed, stroked his neck, currying his mane between her fingers like a breeder's brush.

> *Darkness is no longer for you.*
> *The day comes to take you home.*
> *Little Brother, come!*

She brought her left arm up with the skinning blade, tightening her caress of the pony's neck.

> *Little Brother!*
> *It is time for us.*

The woman laid the edge of the knife against the animal's muscular neck, feeling the blade throb with the pulsing rhythm beneath the steel.

Little Brother!
Your nights are past.
Old friends await you.

The words drifted into the animal's ears as would a needle sliding through silk. The pony's head flexed once as the edge of the blade slid across the veins and the huge windpipe. She imprisoned his neck, fingers buried in the mane.

Little Brother, come!
The day is here to take you home!

The horse collapsed to his forelegs, then the rear legs slowly gave way. Waits-by-the-Water felt the rushing, pulsing waves of blood flooding over her left arm. The animal flexed, a stronger, more desperate lunge now, but still she held on as he fought to rise. There was an ugly, futile wheezing as the pony fought for air, fought for its legs, fought the woman holding him.

Little Brother,
I thank you for your life.

The huge head grew very heavy and began to collapse from her grasp. Waits-by-the-Water eased it down into the red, mushy snow. The ground was slick with the blood broth where she stepped. Already her arm was chilled where the fluid had bloomed over her.

She turned and slipped back toward the dark timber where Titus waited for her. The other two horses wandered out of the mist to investigate this new odor on the breeze. Nostrils flexing, the animals nuzzled at the heavy gray air. Their eyes wide with fear, inquiry, mystery, they watched her until the Sparrowhawk woman disappeared into the trees.

He stood before her. Bass stepped suddenly from behind a tree, right out of the morning's ashen mist. Waits-by-the-Water stifled a scream of surprise. He touched her lips with two gnarled fingers, the woolen blanket mitten dangling from the cuff at the end of his elkhide coat. Then he gently pried the knife from her fingers and put it back in her sheath after he wiped the pony's blood from it. Slowly, Scratch pulled the pistol from her belt and put it in her left hand. After he had given her the rifle she was to use, the trapper led her into the gray light timber.

It did not take many steps before they were about halfway between the southern group of ponies where she had slit one's throat and the western group of browsing animals. Right to the edge of the trees which gathered around the warriors' camp in the forest he led her. Bass set his own weapons against a spruce and helped the woman settle in behind some deadfall. He showed her that here she would not only have protection from Arapaho arrows and lead balls, but she would also have a rest to use for her first, well-aimed shot.

When he was sure she understood not to fire the rifle until she had first heard his rifle blast into the warrior camp, Bass left his woman and melted back into the forest mist.

Scratch pushed north from her post, finding the Flathead woman and Josiah between the westerly and northern stakes of horses. He took Josiah on with him as they circled those northern ponies still investigating the smell of blood from their fallen companion. He and the younger man waited a few moments to watch if the first part of their plan was working. Both were relieved to find the horses were dividing their time between sniffing at the sacrificed pony and pawing in the snow for browse. The men moved on.

Scratch left Paddock near the edge of the trees. After a few steps, Bass turned and caught the last glimpse of the young man having set his rifle against a tree in readiness, then pulling the bow and a handful of arrows from the quiver at his shoulder. The old trapper slid into the milky melding of morning fog and snow-laden pine.

He shivered through those minutes of waiting, certain it was only the cold. Bass checked his pistol again and again, being sure it was on half cock there in his belt. He would reach for the rifle first, assessing the amount of priming in the pan. Then he fussed with the .64 caliber smoothbore which stood at the rifle's side. Three shots he would get before having to reload.

Paddock had been mentally clicking off the minutes since Bass had stepped away. Surely it must be time. Surely he had waited long enough on Bass.

Selecting one of the arrows he had lightly stuck into the snow at his side, Josiah nocked it on the bowstring. He drew the rawhide string back to his cheekbone, placing the arrowhead at the middle of the warrior's chest. He wasn't sure if the Arapaho was on his back or belly. The only thing he knew was which end was which. The black hair spilled out of the robe at the end farthest from the fire. Injuns always sleep with their feet to the fire, Josiah reminded himself as the arrow leapt from the bow with a quiet *thwuuuunggghh*.

He was close enough to the fire to hear the air explode from the victim's lungs, the sound of death as the warrior grunted. He was already dead. The first one did not move.

Next to the first warrior another stirred fitfully. He rolled in his sleep as Paddock hurriedly nocked a second arrow. The second arrow slashed through the mist toward the dark form. The form twitched spasmodically with the impact, then went limp.

Across the fire toward the Crow woman's side, one of the warriors unexpectedly sat up and rubbed at his eyes. He shivered from the damp cold as the buffalo robe slipped away from his shoulders. He looked about him, studying his sleeping companions.

Paddock wrenched the arrow out of the snow and slapped it against the rawhide bowstring.

The solitary warrior's hand hung in the air like a bird surprised in flight. Not another muscle moved. Only his eyes. They climbed from the feathered shaft sticking out of his companion across the fire. They leapt to the second shaft in the body beside the first. The dark eyes suddenly burned into the mist around the camp, puckering wildly in cold scrutiny, willing that the mist would lift magically so his dreaded, hated enemy would be exposed.

His cold fingers sought the knife at his side while he drew the huge pistol from his belt.

Paddock slapped the arrow onto the rawhide string and began pulling it back to his cheek.

The robe slid off the warrior like water running off his back in a spring shower. Rising in his throat, the scream burst from the warrior's lips to pierce the stifling gray light.

Bass was ready. The huge ball from the smoothbore ripped through the Indian's chest, driving him violently sideways to land on top of the warrior beside him who was just beginning to rise. Bone and lead tore through the brown body as the second warrior started to scramble to his feet.

All about the fire, the other Indians twisted in their robes and blankets, bolted upright, crouching on their knees or lying on their stomachs. On the north side of the fire, a warrior rose to one knee and placed his aged smoothbore against a shoulder, aiming at the puff of smoke in the trees that gave away Scratch's position. Just as the warrior fired into the trees, Looks Far Woman's ball smashed through his body, sending him sprawling face down into the smoking firepit.

Pandemonium broke loose about the fire as frantic warriors jerked here and there, seeking protection and cover from the rifle fire hailing down on them from both sides of the clearing. Two of the warriors pushed themselves flat against the wet snow behind their fallen companions.

Paddock fired at an Indian scooting away from the firepit. The ball sent the Arapaho tumbling, with a wound high in his shoulder. He bellowed in pain as Paddock cursed his shot for not killing the warrior.

On the far side of the fire, a warrior stood bravely, chanting the protection of his war song, crying out the promise of his death song. He wrenched up his bow to fire toward the white smoke hung back in the trees which told of Looks Far Woman's shot. The arrow flew on its way and thwacked into the pine beside her head. Terrified, she fell back into the snow, her heart clutched high in her throat.

Josiah could not see her through the mist and the trees. He could not know if she were alive or dead from the Arapaho's bowshot. It did not matter. There was blood in his eye. Paddock pulled his pistol free and advanced from the treeline into the clearing. Warriors kneeling and those standing to meet the challenge suddenly wheeled to see the lone white man advancing with the pistol held out and ready before him. The moment hung while no one but the young trapper moved. Suddenly bows and guns swung toward the tall, bearded intruder.

Paddock fired at the bowman, catapulting the warrior backwards into the new snow. The trapper dropped to his knees and searched his belt for the huge knife he carried.

Bass leapt out of the cover of the trees and fired his second shot at a warrior taking a bead on Paddock. Both weapons roared simultaneously. Through the gray smoke puffing up from the pan, Scratch watched his partner roll over through the snow. At the same time the Arapaho was thrown into the fire by the rifle's blast. The old trapper was concerned that he had heard no sound from his wife's positition as he drew the pistol out of his belt and pulled the hammer back to full cock.

To the old man's right, with a flash of movement at the corner of his good eye, there came a rush of color and light against the pale gray fog. The roar of the warrior's battle song reached his ears as the trapper began to turn. He had one ball left. The pistol arm swung up as straight as a pendulum through the smoke and mist.

The Arapaho came on in a leaping rush.

No aiming—no time. Just instinct. The will to survive.

Scratch snapped the trigger. He watched the warrior's face disappear in a blazing corona of blood. The Arapaho slid to a stop and dropped his rifle. He began to topple backwards as both hands came up to clutch at his missing face, drenched with blood and gore. He crumpled backwards in a heap, his life fluid flooding over him.

Looks Far appeared at the edge of the trees. Fearing her husband was seriously wounded, she ran across the snow toward him. Josiah rose to his knees, clutching his left arm in a bloodied right hand.

Paddock's screamed for his woman to turn back. The tall, skinny warrior was rushing toward the short woman, a large dagger in his hand. His face was hideous: sparsely painted, some of the red and black greasepaint over his cheeks smeared after his cold night sleep in the robe. In one motion Paddock exploded to his feet, a shoulder crashing into his wife to throw her to the side. He rolled on over her through the soggy snow. Tumbling up onto his feet his bloodied right hand slipped his knife free from his belt and in one underarmed motion sent the huge blade on its way.

The tall warrior skidded to a stop and stared at the center of his chest. Crumpling to his knees, his own knife still held out before him, the Indian stared down at the thick handle of the weapon which had just gored him. Blood gushed out of his warshirt over the knife blade. The smeared red and black paint pushed itself into a gritty smile as the Arapaho pitched forward. The smile froze in death.

Looks Far and Josiah rose almost as one. She adjusted the harness that carried their son and immediately tried to inspect her husband's left arm. The young trapper pushed her behind him roughly. He stood between her and the fire. At his feet the ground was already muddy in the growing, pink light, already slickening with blood.

Bass was about halfway between the fire and the meadow's edge of lodgepole pine when he realized he was finally out of firepower. Both rifles had been used, and now the pistol was empty. He glanced down at the muzzle on the six-inch barrel. Gray smoke still curled from the huge hole. In the next instant the pistol flew from his grasp.

The old trapper's lungs exploded with the impact. The warrior had knocked the wind out of him. Together they sailed through the air toward the pines. He tried to gasp for air as the warrior rode down on him. Then the pain washed over

Scratch in gigantic waves once more as they struck the ground together. The Arapaho had the advantage. He had landed on top of the white man.

Back near the circle of smoke and ash, one of the younger warriors had crouched watching the short-lived battle. As the lead balls and arrows had sped around him, the Arapaho had seen one after another of his companions in the scalp party rubbed out. His eyes flicked down to the torn snow reddened with their blood. He knew it was time to leave. Better to fight another day. The old white man was walking toward the younger one, the one who pushed the woman behind him.

That tall, young warrior watched one of his painted party leap at a dead run and strike the older white man, both of them sprawling into the slippery snow. The young Arapaho jerked at the rustle of movement near the edge of the trees behind him.

It was another woman. She clutched a rifle in her hand. She was banging on the weapon's lock, trying to make it fire. Again and again she would pull the trigger, then tap the pan with her palm.

She would be his escape. A weapon and a hostage. The horses awaited him.

The young warrior shoved aside the muzzle of the rifle as the woman's head snapped up in surprise. The scream of horror caught in her throat and barely squeaked past her lips. He was suddenly behind her, a knife tip pushed into her ribs, pricking the flesh beneath her dress and capote, an arm locked tight about her throat. He picked her off the ground. Her feet dangled, her neck stretched.

Waits-by-the-Water watched with eyes of fear as the other warrior tumbled over her husband. He lay motionless for a long moment beneath the Arapaho, trying to catch his breath. One arm was pinned beneath the large warrior. Suddenly the old trapper twisted to the side, attempting to free the other arm. The Indian smashed a huge fist across the white man's cheek. The blow pounded Scratch's head back onto the ground underneath the snow and left him dazed. The impact of the blow echoed in his head like an axe on wood, resounding again and again.

Bass finally realized the Indian was beating him with his fists. Using his hands like huge, hardwood clubs. This one could use his hands well. Back and forth the old trapper's head rolled with each and every blow.

The older trapper rolled back and forth with the pummelling, putting his mind on one arm, one hand, one set of fingers. They found the knife at the side of his belt. Slowly the weapon worked free as Bass's body twisted and squirmed beneath the Arapaho on top of him. Like a piece of light in a mirror, the blade flashed up into the sunlight.

The razored edge caught the warrior squarely below the right side of the jaw. The Arapaho jerked backwards as if to escape the knife. But the weapon's work had already been done. The blood exploded from the wound as the flesh tore apart. Blood billowed down on Bass as the Indian wavered over him. The white man was blinded as the crimson gore rained down on him.

The Indian tumbled off to the side, vainly clutching at his torn neck, blood and frothy fluid spilling over his hands. His mouth moved mechanically, trying to speak. Only pink, bubbling fluid came out. His legs jerked. Finally his whole body twitched twice more and lay quiet, his legs still tangled with the trapper's.

Scratch pushed himself up on first one elbow, then the second. His breathing slowed eventually. His mind cleared. The old trapper snapped his head to that spot in the meadow where his woman had been standing. Josiah and Looks Far Woman looked across the battle site toward the tall warrior.

The Arapaho was joined now by the companion wounded high in his shoulder. This second warrior clutched at the ragged hole with a bloodied hand. He looked weak from the loss of fluid. Wavering, he stood close to the tall warrior and his Crow captive.

Bass pulled his legs free and rose to his knees, never taking his eyes off the tall warrior. It was as if he were studying the Indian, calculating just what the Arapaho would do under one circumstance or another. What to risk? What could he not afford to risk?

As the old trapper got to his feet he saw that Paddock had scooped up a knife from the snow. The younger trapper was easing around the other side of the fire, ambling closer and closer to the tall warrior. Then Bass stood to full height, aching in all those places that weren't frozen. The tall warrior grumbled to his wounded companion. The shorter, slower man stumbled off toward a group of their horses.

Silently, Paddock crept out of the tall warrior's line of sight. He melted into the trees and that mist reluctant to leave the shadows. Scratch's eyes returned to the tall warrior. The Indian seemed nervous, anxious. He was not ready to die, and the old trapper knew it.

Still, he held that knife pressed beneath the Sparrowhawk woman's breast. He sucked air in huge, frantic gulps. His left arm clenched and loosened, clenched and loosened around the woman's neck.

Then they all heard the scream.

Its unearthly sound rolled out of the mist still hanging in the blue shadows. The tall warrior jerked his arm tighter about the woman, momentarily lifting her off the ground. The cry of horror rolled away in echo. Nervously the Indian sidled back a few steps. He put more distance between him and the old trapper who worked at slowly closing the gap.

Paddock appeared in the clearing. He held aloft the full scalp of the wounded warrior who had been sent after the horses. Step by step, the young trapper began his walk toward the tall warrior. Josiah held the scalp out before him, the reddened knife in his right hand. The grisly trophy dripped blood across the snow as he approached the Indian.

"Easy, easy, son," Bass snapped. "Don't get this nigger too riled up. His feathers get mussed up, he's just liable to slip that blade on into her. Take your time."

Paddock stopped, realizing just what he was doing. Goading the warrior. Outnumbered, the Indian would probably do something rash, something stupid, something deadly. Josiah watched the dark eyes flit back and forth from trapper to trapper, from Bass to Paddock.

"That's it, that's it," Scratch's voice soothed. "Just keep him on the edge. Don't wanna push him over it, son."

Bass took another step. The warrior jerked his knife anxiously. Scratch stopped, waited. Something would come up, he hoped. Something would happen that would present an opening. Meanwhile, he would stand stock still, and reload his pistol. That ought to make the nigger just downright nervous.

Scratch filled the pan with powder from the priming horn he carried slung from his pouch strap. He snapped the frizzen down over it, brought the hammer back to full cock and eased the pistol forward, muzzle yawning in the frosty air.

At first the warrior looked back and forth between the two men. Then his eyes locked on the older man and the pistol pointed at him. The warrior's face slowly broke with a grin. It was not an amused look. Scratch was not sure he could tell why the Indian was smiling at him.

Then the warrior brought the knife blade away from the woman's breast to wave it menacingly at the white man, as if in challenge to the pistol. Bass returned the Indian's smile. As the trapper's bearded face cracked with its grin, the warrior shoved Waits-by-the-Water off to the side—straight into the old trapper's arms.

Bass was totally stunned. He caught the woman as she careened into his outstretched arms. And in doing so he was suddenly afraid he had made a fatal mistake. Immediately the warrior was on top of the staggering couple, shoving them backwards, ripping the pistol away from the old trapper.

Just as quickly the sick smile fled from the warrior's face. Blood bubbled across his lips, spilling over his chin. He turned to the side, his pain-glazed eyes boring into Paddock. The handle of the knife quivered in the Indian's back. It was stuck high in the thorax. The warrior turned, corkscrewed into the snow, dead as he fell.

Waits-by-the-Water collapsed against the old trapper, embracing him frantically, whimpering. She sobbed into the crook of his neck. The Crow woman stifled the next sob and swiped at her eyes, then her nose, with the sleeve of her capote.

Wearily Scratch looked over the battle scene. The ground was slick with muddied snow tromped by horses and men, bloodied and littered with the weapons of those ten dead men scattered around the fire. Two had never known what had killed them. The rest had approached death as bravely as their medicine had allowed. All but one, and Paddock held his scalp. That one had been wounded and tried to escape. Not as brave as his companions. Yet each was as dead as the others.

The Sparrowhawk woman brought him out of his reverie, touching his bleeding lip and the skin that was split open over a cheek, reddening his beard with pink, frosty icicles. He smiled and gazed over the top of her head to Josiah and Looks Far.

The Flathead woman had removed the young child from the warm harness at her back and placed him on one of the Arapaho robes stretched across the snow. She seemed intent upon cleaning him here in the coldest dawn air, as if the battle had never taken place. Paddock was kicking life into the remains of the small, smoky fire at the center of the clearing. The scalp party had gathered enough wood to keep the fire going on through the night plus enough left over with which to cook their morning meal.

Bass brought Waits-by-the-Water under his arm and together they sat silently by the fire. Looks Far took the clean infant and placed him within her warm coat. She offered a nipple to the hungry child. The greedy sounds of his suckling mingled with the crackling pop of dry pine as it caught flame.

It was after the infant had eaten, fallen asleep again, before anyone finally spoke. Until then, each person seemed content to be alone with his thoughts, watching the flames dance in the retreating gray mist, hypnotized by the smoke crawling out of the fire into the heavy dawn sky. Josiah leaned back against a corpse beneath a robe, his hand stretched over his woman's shoulder. Waits-by-the-Water rested her head on Bass's knee, gazing into the whirling, crackling flames.

"I s'pose we ought to be goin' on home now," Scratch said softly.

"You wanna take it all?" Paddock asked.

Bass sighed. "Don't see why not," he said. "But we don't need them robes. Most likely got li'l varmints in 'em anyway. You best just burn the lot of 'em, son."

"Moccasins?"

"Yep, we can always use spares, fast as my hoofs go through 'em."

"Their guns?"

"I reckon. We'll take those with us."

"Never know when you can use an extra rifle or two," Paddock said as he rose to his feet.

"Even them ol' Brown Bess guns might'n just save our wick some day, Josiah."

Paddock stretched his left arm gingerly. The bleeding had stopped. He painfully rotated it several times, testing it.

"You'll be awright?"

"Believe I'll be," Paddock answered the older man.

"You pull together the weapons. Take all the knives an' 'hawks, such as that. But the rest of it, robes an' all, burn it all to hell."

Paddock watched the old man staring into the flames intently, eyes unblinking.

"What are you heading off to do?"

"Horses," Bass looked at Paddock. "Ain't gonna leave good horseflesh around for the likes of wolves, bears an' such. We might be able to use some of the mangy Injun ponies ourselves."

"Them as we don't need?" Josiah inquired.

"Sell—we'll sell 'em, son," Bass answered. "Down to Taos. Turn a coin or two on them Injun ponies. Might as well."

Scratch came to his feet at last, then wheeled to slog off across the wet snow, gummy with blood and death.

Paddock gazed about him, studying the scene for the first time.

He watched the two Indian woman, disbelieving their quiet, numbed countenances amid the carnage, among the bloodied victims of the battle. This was something foreign. These women sitting here around the fire as if they were merely intent on cooking breakfast. They acted as if nothing had happened right there a few moments ago. As if they all had not been staring into the face of death. But here was his wife, not a trace of the toll on her face. And, in looking over at the Crow woman, he could not see any price exacted in her eyes.

Josiah shook his head and knelt to throw some parfleches into the fire he had stoked to a roaring warmth. He would burn just about everything they would not be taking along. Maybe it was all as easy as that. What you didn't take for yourself, you destroyed so that no one else could have it. It seemed the way of things out here in the free mountains.

One moment you were killing and close to being killed. The next you were plundering your enemy's camp. You took what you could carry and destroyed the rest. What's more, you never gave a second thought to it.

Paddock turned to stare at the Crow woman. Then his gaze flicked over to the young Flathead mother. Never a second thought to it.

You took what you could carry and destroyed the rest. "Might as well," he mumbled, throwing a dirty, muddied blanket atop the leaping flames.

"One thing at a time, Scratch. One thing at a time."

The steamy stench of death and dung rose thick about him in the frosty dawn air.

Suddenly, Josiah gagged.

8 EIGHT RAGGED SUNS had risen and set over the Bayou Salade since the trappers' attack on the scalp hunters. The *Moon of Deer Rutting* was little more than a week old. The mornings broke frosty, foretelling of winter to come. Each day would exhaust itself in the high light during this season of change. For most of the hours while the sun rode high, a man could do without a capote for warmth. Especially if he kept himself busy setting his traps, pulling beaver from those traps, along with the other labors of skinning, stretching, pressing all the hides into bales for the trail south.

As evening slid headlong through the valley a man would find himself pulling something around his shoulders for warmth, something to ward off that chill which came sneaking like a damp, hoary thief robbing him of the will to move anywhere far from the fire. At times the lengthening purple shadows would be licked and spittled with huge, dry flakes of snow. Yet no storm had come since the night of stalking the scalp hunters' camp. There came only the occasional reminder that the season was growing old around them, and they with it.

The sun was settling among the craggy spires to the west when Paddock pulled into camp at the head of the small string of ponies. He dropped to the ground and turned as Titus emerged from the trees at the tail end of the packstring. The men had returned from retrieving the beaver pelts they had cached upon leaving their first campsight.

Scratch slid from his saddle to untie those fresh pelts they had skinned from beaver caught in the morning's traps. He tossed the ragged, bloodied hides toward his younger partner.

"You get these," he suggested quietly, his words laden with fatigue. "I'll take care of the rest from here."

Bass nodded down the line at the ponies loaded with their packed beaver bales, the results of their efforts in the fall hunt thus far. He watched Paddock signal that he would grain and stretch the new pelts. Josiah turned away to drag the hides on into camp, one arm held out to enfold Looks Far as she ran to greet him.

The old man decided he would not fuss with the packs all that much this evening, saving that sort of labor for tomorrow, the middle part of the day when a man wasn't busied in setting the traps nor skinning the beaver caught in those sets. He glanced back in the direction of camp, hopeful of seeing Waits-by-the-Water emerge from the purple shadows woven among the trees that ringed the bright firelight in their camp. After a moment, when she did not appear, Titus reluctantly returned to his labors. Scooping up the beaver packs, he carried them over beneath the trees with the bundles of other camp goods. Back and forth he trudged between the trees and the ponies, until the trapper could at last take the pack animals off to be staked with the other horses for the night.

The light was smokey gray by the time he entered the stand of aspen surrounding their campsite and stepped into the bright ring of firelight. Paddock already had his hands full. The young man sat cross-legged on the ground near the fire, weaving a thin strip of rawhide back and forth through a series of holes he had punched in a green beaver hide. On each turn through the hole, the rawhide strip would be wound around a circular hoop of willow as he gradually stretched the hide into that particular round shape that had come to be known as the beaver dollar. Their camp was dotted here and there with the circular trophies, on one side dark and hairy, on the other side red-streaked and bleaching.

Yet it wasn't stretching the hides which tonight required Josiah's full attention. His son crawled back and forth across his father's legs, over the beaver hides and right through the work at hand, wanting his father's awl, tugging at the fringe along his father's sleeve, and darting for the firepit repeatedly. Paddock would lace one hole through a green beaver hide, then stretch over to yank his son back from the fire. Then another hole was laced and the young trapper would retrieve Joshua before the tad could pick up the sharp awl. It all looked to be a game with the boy and much more fun than work for Paddock.

"What are you laughing at now, old man?" Josiah glanced up as Bass strode into the circle of bright light.

"Seems like you're havin' a rougher time with that young'un of your'n than you did with them 'Rapaho scalp hunters."

"He can be a real handful, Scratch." Josiah reached out to grab at his son who was crawling away toward the firepit.

"It ain't no worse'n takin' you to raise, boy," Scratch grinned, teeth flashing vividly in the firelight.

"I think I heard this round before, old man," Josiah said, returning the older trapper's smile. "How about you—" He had to pull the sharp awl out of Joshua's tiny fist. "—you helping out here, instead of just standing there telling me how good you were in raising me?"

Titus knelt down to retrieve the energetic bundle of arms and legs. "C'mere you lil' hell-kitten," he said as he brought the child up to his shoulder. "We'll go find out what that Crow woman of mine has been up to."

As the old trapper approached the two women, Waits-by-the-Water lifted her face to smile happily at him in the light from a larger fire the women were using for cooking. She set aside the leather she was working and sprang to her feet. Looks Far stood and pushed aside a strand of hair that kept falling in her eyes. Her hands were bloody and dirty from pounding stakes through the edges of an elk hide she was stretching on the ground. Around her lay three other hides in various stages of curing: one totally scraped, another free of flesh and hair and soaking in brains, and a third which she had just begun to scrape.

"You gals been stayin' busy." Bass nodded approvingly at the women's joint efforts.

Both females had been raised in a culture that eons ago mandated the warrior male hunt the game and bring the meat home. From there on out most everything became the woman's responsibility. First she would skin and butcher the animal. Next she would bring in water and wood to build a fire over which to cook the meat. In addition, she now had a new hide for either the lodge or clothing, or she could rawhide the skin so that stiff parfleches and storage cases could be made. It was up to her and her alone to keep a meal constantly available by the fire and each member of her family properly clothed.

Both Indian women had grown up knowing nothing else. From their labors they drew their worth as a person, a way in which to return the love and protection of their husbands.

"Ouch!" Bass yelled and snapped a hand up to catch Joshua's tiny paw as it pulled on the long, narrow braid hanging along the old man's cheek. "How you feel if I pulled your hair, eh?"

The youngster howled as the trapper tugged on the boy's short, curly locks. Duly punished, he buried his little head down into the trapper's shoulder, begging pardon for his crime. Bass patted his little buttocks in forgiveness.

"Looks Far?" Scratch said as he stepped over to the Flathead woman. "You best take him now. I punished him 'nough already."

"A man-child needs to know." Looks Far spoke in halting, improving English.

"Know who's boss?" Bass asked.

"His folks. Yes," she answered, cradling the youngster to her shoulder.

Joshua immediately stuck a tiny paw down the neck of her wool dress, attempting to pull the front of the garment aside. He sought a full breast. Looks Far removed his hand from its explorations. The child sniffed angrily and stuffed his hand right back down her dress. He made smacking noises with his lips.

"You see," she said as she shook her head and grinned at the other couple, "my son shows me who is really boss."

"A young'un gets hungry—there ain't no stoppin' him," Bass chuckled. "I s'pose grown folks find out in a hurry just who the real boss is. That's a natural fact."

With the child fed, both women set about serving up an elegant meal. Around their cooking fire arose a delicious corona of mouth-wetting aromas. The women had used their time well this past fall, gathering the onions, wild turnips, elk-cabbage and the huge mushrooms they all favored. All had been sliced thin, then dried to preserve them for the coming winter. In one of the small iron kettles bubbled a rich, spiced soup, the stock for which was buffalo blood, along with bone marrow that melted like butter, and laced with slices of prairie onions, chunks of turnip and huge portions of the wild mushrooms.

Spitted over the two kettles were a couple of sage hens, a bird often called a grouse or fool's hen. Long green branches of willow were used to spit these birds over a low fire, the hens' juices dripping into the kettles beneath them so that the grouse could be repeatedly basted in their own juices. Succulent strips of elk and buffalo hung at the edge of the same fire, juices dripping into the spitting flames.

102

From time to time one of the women would fork bread from a kettle where it had fried to a golden brown in hot animal fat.

For dessert the adults scraped with their fingertips at the marrow inside some bones roasted in the hot ashes at the side of the fire. The bones were cracked open with a knife handle or a handy palm-sized stone. This rich, butterlike treat they devoured greedily. Bass smacked his lips as the marrow melted away in his mouth and ran down his throat like a thick syrup.

What a bounty the wilderness provided for a man, he thought. Nearly everything that walked, crawled, flew, swam or was alive was some form of food. To the Indian. For Titus Bass, too. At first he had been appalled at seeing Indian women stir into their stews and broths those flies, spiders, and hard-shelled beetles that made the mistake of tumbling too close to the main dish. Butterflies, grasshoppers, even a darting moth fell prey if it landed on the surface of a simmering broth.

Scratch chuckled, recalling the humorous memory of watching an old Ute woman fighting one of the family dogs for a piece of meat that the cur had stolen from the family's stew pot. She bludgeoned the dog into releasing the half-chewed piece of venison which the squaw promptly returned to the kettle. It made no matter to her that the dog had been chewing on that meat, dragging it across the ground, mauling the chunk between its dirtied paws. Amusing now to remember how he had later seen the old woman putting a freshly skinned dog's carcass in that same bubbling pot, most likely to replace that meat the offending animal had eaten.

During those early seasons in the mountains, Scratch himself had tired of eating nothing but lean meat and cold creek water. Out of the monotony the trapper soon learned to ferret through the driftwood along the bigger water courses for Jerusalem artichokes that both gophers and ground squirrels had hidden there against the coming winters. He had developed a real taste for the hips he plucked off wild roses, having learned early on they and other vegetables would protect him from the scurvy normally contracted on a meat-only diet. There were always the sarvis berries, chokecherries, or wild raspberries to spice up a meal and startle the tastebuds dulled by the monotony of lean, red meat.

The light had slipped away to indigo while they had eaten. Above their camp, splotches of evening stars appeared. With every moment the sky darkened, bringing out more and more a dusting of spun sugar across the blackening heavens. The coffee boiled and spewed into the fire for an instant before Josiah rescued the battered, fire-blackened veteran pot from the flames. Both trappers leaned back against saddles and apishamores, their feet stretched toward the fire's welcome warmth.

This had to be the highlight of a man's day. Having reluctantly left his warm robe and soft-skinned wife even before the sun had yawned, the trapper began his daily labors. In fall camp there was always something to be done. If not re-staking the ponies or riding them for exercise, there was the scraping and stretching of the hides. If it were not repair of saddles and tack, it was mending a sore hoof or the bloody wound caused when one pony bit another in the cavvyyard. The saddle sores and cinch ulcers of a summer's travel were treated with those herbs and roots known to draw out poisons and heal the flesh of man and beast alike.

The strength in Paddock's wounded arm was returning. For days after the battle he had worn a rawhide sling which kept his left arm all but useless. Yet with the ministrations of both the old trapper and Looks Far, Josiah had begun to heal quickly. With each advancing day a little more of the strength and mobility returned to the youth's arm. Tomorrow would be the third day he had refused to use the rawhide sling. He was satisfied that soon he would once again feel whole.

Bass watched Josiah blow across the top of his tin mug of coffee. The steaming mist enveloped the young trapper's face as he sipped carefully at the hot liquid. Black as a devil's night, hot as the old demon's hell itself and as rich as sin, the coffee these trappers drank was a fitting treat to end a day of hard, cold labor. Each man enjoyed his cup in silence, listening to the crackle and snap of resin-loaded firewood and the gentle snores of the infant asleep on a robe beside his mother. Looks Far sat to Paddock's left, sewing up several pair of new moccasins for her husband.

Bass turned as his wife's shadow swept over him.

"Husband," Waits-by-the-Water addressed him in Crow.

Scratch looked up at his woman bathed in the gentle firelight. "What is that?" He threw a hand toward the soft garment she held up for his inspection.

"It is for the coming winter and its mighty winds," she smiled proudly.

Titus kicked aside the buffalo robe wrapped over his legs and creaked to his feet before the woman. She held out a long shirt that would reach to his knees. The thicker elk hide would prove warmer than buckskin. The neck hole had been trimmed with red trade cloth, no doubt a strip cut from the hem of her wool rendezvous dress. The sides of the shirt were tied together and fringed, as were the sleeves. But the loving touch was ultimately the bright colors glinting in the dancing firelight. Greasy yellow. Oxblood red. Robin's egg blue. Colors she had dyed those quills used to decorate the strips that ran over both shoulders and down both arms. The center of both chest and back was emblazoned with a large quilled rosette.

Scratch was speechless, a rare occasion for him.

For weeks he had watched her using her spare moments in camp at her quillwork, dyeing the plucked quills after they had been sorted and bleached. Then she had flattened each one with a special tool. Yet each quill had received a final flattening between her front teeth before it was sewn on a strip of smoked leather. He had watched her apply those colorful quills back and forth in straight, even rows, tying each wrap down with two separate stitches of animal sinew as thread. In those spare moments she had stolen out of each day before they had had to move camp, Waits-by-the-Water added row after row to her strips and rosettes. But Bass had not seen the quillwork since they had established this new camp. He had supposed his wife was making something for herself, or for the young child of Looks Far Woman.

There were no words for the shirt's beauty. He opened his mouth once, then a second time, and finally a third before he could speak. Across the fire were murmurings of approval from both Looks Far and Josiah. Yet, Titus could find no adequate words. Instead he tossed down his coffee mug and flung his arms around the woman. He hoped this embrace would say all he wanted it to tell her.

"The colors, they are perfect." Bass stepped back so that he could hold the shirt up in the dancing firelight.

"They are the colors for your power, my husband," she declared with pride, beaming in the soft, copper light.

"My god," he whispered, almost like worship. "It's—it's—so damned bee-yu-tee-ful!"

"The blue is for the power of the sky above," she explained in Crow, a finger tracing the path of some blue quills. "This red is for the blood of our Mother, the earth." She ran a fingertip across some dark, oxblood red quills.

"At last comes the greasy yellow, for that power coming from the sun above, source of the greatest medicine."

"*Wagh!*"

Scratch wrenched her and the shirt into the tight circle of his arms, raised her off her feet and swung the woman around in a tight dance for a moment before she squealed for breath. Paddock and Looks Far watched, laughing, clapping their hands in joy and amusement. In such a family, all shared the joy one felt.

Dizzy, the older trapper finally stumbled to a halt and let his wife slide from his grasp. Both were breathless for a moment until she reached up to brush a kiss upon his lips.

"There are leggings, my husband." She turned and knelt beside a painted rawhide box.

"Leggings, too?" He leaned down over her shoulder, like a little boy watching someone fetch a treat for him.

"My man cannot go about with nothing on his legs, can he?"

"I s'pose the woman's got a point." Bass broke back into English when he turned to address Josiah and Looks Far.

Waits-by-the-Water rose from her rawhide box with the two leggings rolled up in her palms. She handed one to Bass, then unfurled the other. The shirt's quillwork pattern ran down the outside length of the legging. He whistled low and long at the quality of her work, at the softness of the smoked elkskin, and finally the care she had given to the fringe being cut very, very thin, then each strand pulled and twisted.

"I'll prance as one fancy nigger!" he exclaimed, holding the shirt across one outstretched arm and a legging dangling from the other.

"Fannn-ceee nigg—gerrr," the Sparrowhawk woman smiled, happy at his exuberant pride over the new clothes she had sewn for him.

"One lucky nigger, too," he roared, wrapping an arm about her.

Again they were a swirl of arms, legs, warshirt and leggings. The fire popped and crackled, sending flares of bright fireflies into the black sky over their heads. Josiah finally tired of clapping and stomping his foot. He reached out to slow down the prancing couple.

"How—how about some of that whiskey—you always keep around?" Josiah was breathless.

Bass and he stood weaving against one another, both exhausted from their revelry.

"Why—now, that do make a nice thought, don't it?" Bass puffed. He wheeled quickly, smacking his lips. In a moment he returned to the fire with a large tin flask, emblazoned with a lion crest on one side.

"Ladies first," he said as he worried the cork out of the neck and bent over Looks Far Woman's cup.

She rarely, if ever, drank coffee, and had only occasionally sipped at whiskey while they had been at rendezvous. Both were a man's drink. Next Bass slipped a few drops into his woman's cup. Then Josiah was at his side, cup in hand. When both men had enough for a toast, Bass raised the flask into the light above the cheery fire.

"To the warmth of liquid cheer!" He brought the flask to his lips, then watched those around him sip at their whiskey.

"To the warmth of a roarin' fire!"

Again he touched lips to the flask neck.

"But, most of all, to the warmth of friends!"

Again he watched over the neck of the flask as the others sipped at their portions of the burning liquid. He dragged the back of his hand across his mouth and sat down when Josiah joined Looks Far near the sleeping infant. Waits-by-the-Water curled her legs up and tucked herself in beside the older trapper.

A star flared as it entered the atmosphere to begin a fiery course across the sky. Bright enough to cause each of them to watch its flaming descent to earth, the star's yellow-blue tail lit up the western night sky. Scratch stood, not quite sure he couldn't hear the meteor falling through the sky with its faint whistle of flaming speed.

In the cavvyyard their ponies were becoming restless. They had heard the meteor, too. Bass plunged through the trees quickly, into the shadows and to the meadow where the horses were staked. Here each animal could paw away the snow to get at the sun-cured grasses. The old trapper watched a few of the animals pitch their heads toward the meteor and roll their eyes in fright. Nostrils flared. Just as the first star disappeared beyond the mountains, a second shooting star began its path across the dark heavens. Now many in the herd were snorting, frightening each other. Some took to loud whinnying, a shrill scream. They yanked and pulled at their picket pins. Those previously docile enough for hobbles now loped about clumsily, bumping into other horses, stirring the others into a frightened, excited frenzy.

Bass was sure he could hear the faint whistle of the second star as its yellow-green tail plummeted toward earth. In the west the sound grew louder.

He ducked into the trees again, groping through the shadows back toward the camp and the firelight. Behind him the trapper left the screams and cries of the horses. Ahead through the pines came the piercing wail of the infant.

Looks Far cradled the child in her arm. She sat on the ground rocking him to and fro. Joshua wailed on and on in differing pitches. His mother cooed at him, spoke to him in her Flathead tongue, anxious to quiet him.

"He got skairt of the bright lights, eh?" Bass strode into the firelight. He cranked his head back up toward the sky, where two more stars began their descent to earth together. "Enough to frighten a lil' pup, it is," he clucked as he looked down at the wailing infant. "Hell, it's enough to scare us grown folks."

Scratch looked around the fire. Paddock stood watching the sky, intent on the falling stars. Looks Far divided her attention between the luminous heavens and her shrieking son. Waits-by-the-Water sat looking up in apprehension, then scooted around the fire to plop down beside Looks Far. Sisters of a sort, they exchanged grim smiles.

The Crow woman scooped up the baby's rattle and shook it in front of the child's face as a diversion to soothe him, to remind him that things had not changed in his little world. The rattle had been made by attaching dew claws from antelope and deer to rawhide-wrapped willow. The green willow had first been shaped into a small hoop with a short, straight handle. The tinkling, clattering dew claws were strung around the inside of that oblong hoop.

Joshua stuck a tiny paw out of his deerhide blanket and shoved the rattle away. Looks Far apologized to the Crow woman with her eyes. Waits-by-the-Water smiled patiently. From the blankets in Paddock's shelter, she retrieved the dried, puffed antelope bladder the young trapper had filled with tiny, round pebbles from the bottom of a high country stream. The bladder had been wrapped with sinew on a peeled willow wand. The Crow woman shook it gently in front of the child's face, hoping this diversion would work to quiet him.

Joshua backhanded the rattle out of his way.

Still patient, Looks Far grabbed up a painted willow hoop about eight inches in diameter. From its circumference hung four little tin cones that tinkled against each other. That did not please Joshua. Instead, he wrinkled up his tiny face and threw some punches at the air to show how disgruntled he had become. Waits-by-the-Water next tried the deerskin doll she had stuffed with the hair from a buffalo's hump. The combination made for a soft, pliable human effigy. Large emerald green pony beads served for eyes, while the mouth was sewn with blood-red seed beads. The doll wore a miniature warshirt and a tiny breechclout was sewn around its waist. Now the Crow woman made the ten-inch high effigy dance and cavort before the enraged little boy. Joshua clamped his eyes shut, refusing to watch the performance.

Looks Far put her hand down into his swaddling stuffed with cottonwood down and moss for absorption. The child was not wet nor had he dirtied himself. All that remained was to see if the boy was hungry.

The Flathead woman parted the folds of her blanket capote, pulled aside the billows of her doeskin dress. She exposed a full, rounded breast beneath the gaping sleeve. Her nipple nudged the wailing infant's lips. He tasted and licked at the warm milk for a brief moment. But it was not what he really wanted.

The infant broke out bawling again. Overhead the sky flared still with the luminescent tails trailing along behind the shooting stars. Josiah was close to the end of his string. The fiery skies overhead made him strangely nervous. He had never before experienced such a vivid, massive phenomenon. And, never before had his son persisted so long in an angry, crying fit. He wondered if the two were not connected in some mysterious way.

"Dammit, woman!" he said as he wheeled on Looks Far. "Can't you get him to quiet down?"

She jerked at the sharpness of his words, hurt, surprised at the same time. Looks Far moved her lips but no sound came out.

"E-easy." Bass stepped to him, placed a hand on Josiah's shoulder. "Just take 'er easy, son. Lookahere. Them ponies out there don't know what the devil's goin' on. They ain't never seen nothin' like this happen in the sky afore. An' lil' Joshua here, he's just like them animals. He's got him a little mind just like them ponies. So, he don't know any better. Them ponies out there cryin' an' wailin' away. Lil' Joshua here don't know why he's scared, why he's mad at the sky."

"I'll take the flat of my hand to his lil' bare ass," Josiah gestured with a huge palm.

"That won't serve no goodly purpose." Scratch shook his head. "Just make him madder, I'd s'pose. 'Sides, man should never go punishin' a boy. Injuns don't punish a boy by strikin' him—cause that makes the young'un have a broken, cowed-down spirit. An' no Injun pappy wants that out of a lil' he-pup of his own. 'Stead of bein' a warrior, the boy'd be called a squaw—an' bein' called that is like bein' cussed at in the worst of ways. Sayin' a man is a squaw is like sayin' he's a coward of the worst color."

Josiah shook his head, exasperated with the crying, exhausted in his patience. "You got any bright, shiny ideas? Something to try to get Joshua back to sleep?"

"First thing," Scratch instructed paternally, "you take the boy from his mother."

Paddock bent over and took up the squawling infant, all legs and arms and a face screwed up in anger. Already his little throat was becoming raw and hoarse from the crying.

"I'll be back shortly." Bass wheeled and headed away from the fire.

"Where the hell you going?" Josiah's gaze followed the old man into the shadows. "Nice time for you to be thinking of taking a piss! Hey, Scratch! You leavin' me here with this bawling kid?"

After a few minutes, the older trapper returned with a gerkin of water sloshing at his side. "Gimme a cup," he requested of the Crow woman as he sat down between the two women.

Josiah had been *sho-o-o-ing* and *shussshhhing* just about as long as he could take it. "Here," he said as he handed the squirming infant to the old man.

"Ooof! What a lil' chunk of it you are," Scratch said as he accepted the squawling, kicking child.

Josiah watched the old trapper dip his tin cup into the bucket of bitter cold water. "You grown patient in your old age, huh, old man?"

"Nothin' of the sort, son. This just be a case of knowin' what to do 'cause I learn't it watchin' the Crow."

Bass slowly began to pour the first cup of the mountain stream water over the child's little head. For a moment the infant was shocked, numbed, surprised. His rage sputtered to a halt. The little mouth o-o-o-ed up in cold shock. Then Joshua wailed even louder than before.

"Why, you lil' hellion." Scratch dipped a second cupful from the bucket and slowly let it trickle over the infant's head.

"Why's he giving us such a fit tonight?" Josiah asked.

"Don't know, son." Scratch glanced up at Paddock a moment before he dipped a third cup from the freezing water. His left arm was full of the sopping, cold, wriggling bundle. "Looks to be sometimes a pup don't really need a good reason to have him a fuss."

"So you give him a reason to bawl?"

"Looks like that's the ticket, Josiah," Scratch answered as he poured another slow, cold cupful over the tiny head. "Joshua cain't decide what he's mad at, I'll give him a reason to be mad. We'll get him all worked outta his lather real quick-like now."

Both women watched the older man dip the cup again and again into the water, pouring the freezing liquid repeatedly over the infant's little head. In turn, Joshua had worked himself into a real tizzy: screaming, hollering, flailing away with his tiny legs and arms at the world, spending every ounce of his puny rage.

Bass gritted his teeth as he struggled with the mighty, tiny bundle slung across his left arm. "There be more damned arms an' legs here on this critter than there be in a hill of red ants." He continued to pour water over the blubbering infant.

"Kid's as grumpy as a sore-tailed bear, Scratch." Josiah smiled as he watched the ancient process of man teaching boy.

"We'll work the peedoodles right out of him yet."

"Looks like he wants right outta your grip."

"Well, he ain't goin' nowhere, son," Scratch responded as he struggled with the cold, wet, miserable infant. "He can climb all over me if'n that's what he wants—but he ain't goin' nowhere."

Josiah looked at both women's faces. Where he thought he might find worry or consternation on Looks Far Woman's face, he found instead amused attention. Waits-by-the-Water likewise seemed tickled to watch the clumsy old trapper battle the yowling bundle of appendages.

"This rumpus'll die down soon now," Scratch said as he looked around at the others. "Son, want you to punch that fire real good now. I want it mighty warm so this lil'un don't catch him the death of a chill—come down with the ague or such."

Paddock worked quickly, adding fuel to the fire, stoking it higher and higher until the camp radiated with a cheery warmth once more. Overhead the sky was thickening with the shooting stars. From this direction and that, the meteors raced across the backdrop of the inky heavens. The ponies continued to whinny and scream in fright, their high-pitched cries an eerie backdrop to the infant's wailing.

At last it began to sound like Joshua was losing steam. Bass kept pouring the icy water over his tiny head, one slow cupful at a time. Paddock noticed the difference in the intensity of these new wails and screams let out by his son.

"You honery ol' bastard," Josiah said as he glanced at Bass. "I wouldn't let you get away with that if I was the kid you was trying to pour water on."

Bass matched Paddock's grin. "I am honery, son. That's a natural fact. Only 'cause my ma raised me on sour milk."

His eyes dropped to look at the little boy cradled within a soaked left arm. The infant was sputtering to a halt. He merely sobbed weakly, his little breath catching pitifully. At last it seemed he was exhausted from his crying, his anger cooled.

Yet Bass did not yet give up the water. He continued to slowly pour two more cups of water over Joshua's head. The infant suffered them in complete silence, his little mouth drawn up in a numbed, puckered O. Beneath the dribbles of icy water, Joshua's little dark eyes owled up at the old trapper.

"I'll be go to—" Paddock leaned in and stared down at his son in the old man's lap. "Looks like you've worked a honest-to-goodness miracle cure here. Seems like you're real handy at settling children down. Done this before, haven't you?"

Bass shook his head slightly, then snorted. He set the tin cup aside, staring down at the little brown eyes below his, staring back full of wonder at his old ones.

"Nawww, Josiah. I ain't never done anything like this before. Just watched them Crow is all I done. Told you. Lordee! To tell the truth, with a young'un around, 'specially in my arms, why—I feel 'bout as clumsy as a eight-hundred pound black bear back-slidin' down a smooth-skinned quakie."

The two women huddled close at Scratch's knees. Looks Far wanted desperately to reach out, to touch her son as he rolled his dark fawn eyes at his mother. Yet, she knew that she must not. Bass cooed at the infant, instructing him never to pull such a fit again or the same punishment would be exacted upon his little head. The old trapper admonished the youngster to mind his mother one more time, then handed the infant to Looks Far.

The Flathead woman readily accepted the soggy bundle. Joshua continued to sob, his little body quaking with the noiseless, stifled cries. His heart had been broken, but not his spirit. Looks Far gazed up at Bass with a wide smile. He answered with a grin that cracked across his leathery face.

"Worked slick as a peeled onion, didn't it?" he beamed. "Slick as a durned peeled onion."

The old trapper rose. Beneath his elkhide coat, his leggings and the left arm and tail of his buckskin shirt were soaked. In the frosty air, the damp leather grew chilly very quickly. Waits-by-the-Water raced around the fire to retrieve his new outfit.

She happily presented him again with the garments, tugging at his wet clothing, squealing in her excitement to see him dressed in her new gift. Scratch obliged quickly. He pulled off the wet legging and the shirt, his naked skin prickling in the freezing air. Finally the dry legging was changed and he stood before them resplendent in his new outfit. Satisfied with everyone's approval, the older trapper once again slipped on the elkhide coat.

Scratch leaned down over the infant. Joshua was asleep already, a warm, dry blanket now wrapping him so that all Titus could see was the contented little face.

Bass smiled over at his woman. "Young'un is as sound asleep as a bark beetle in cottonwood down." He sighed and cranked his head up at the sky. The indigo canopy was coming alive, flaming with long streamers of blue and yellow-green. They were not witnessing isolated shooting stars. This was working itself into a full-blown meteor shower.

"What you think of this?" Paddock said as he came to stand beside the older man.

"Don't know just what to make of it, Josiah," Bass said after a moment of reflection. "There'll be some Injun camps from Wah-to-yah in the south to the Musselshell in the north where folks are sayin' a heap of prayers right now. If it ain't the end of the world—then it be some mighty big, big medicine to 'em."

"Y-you—you ain't worried none about all them falling stars?" Josiah continued. "Nothing serious with it?" He quickly shot a glance at his wife and son across the fire.

"Josiah, in all them seasons I got stuffed under my old belt here," he said as he poked some straight fingers beneath the leather band, "my eyes been privy to a lotta glory sights out here in the free mountains. I been scared enough to shit peach pits at times—in the early days, that is, I want you to know. By now, howsoever, ain't nothin' like this show here to cause me no great concern."

Bass watched the sky fill up with the fire: yellow, green, orange and blue lights. He shook his head. "It 'pears to be a purdee-glory wonderment, that it is. But I ain't worried 'bout it at all." He turned back to Josiah.

Paddock's eyes dropped from the exploding heavens. "There gonna be any stars left up there when this damned show of yours runs out?"

Scratch looked back at the night sky. "Son, them stars ain't like you an' me. There be plenty of them up there. For all the fireworks an' as long as it's been goin' on now, I ain't noticed a damned one of them stars missin' up there. Don't seem to be a empty place in that sky out there."

After a moment of thought, Paddock finally responded. He chuckled lightly and put a hand on Bass's shoulder. "I suppose you are right. Doesn't appear to be a single star missing up there at all. Plenty of them left."

"Those stars are like folks back east, son. There's plenty of them that a few don't get missed," Bass commented with a dry sadness. "Out here, in all of this country, a man would be sorely missed."

Scratch then turned to look up at the tall youth by his side. "Josiah, we're just like them stars up there. Shooting stars. There's so many white folks who'll one day come floodin' over this land, why—folks like you an' me ain't gonna be missed at all. Hell, they won't ever know we was here afore 'em."

He shook his head sadly as he dropped his eyes away from Paddock's face. "We're just like them stars, son. Burn ourselves out, an' ain't a soul what will miss us when we're gone."

"You can't be happy about that at all," Josiah injected.

"Nope," Scratch chopped the word smoothly. "Man wants to leave somethin' behind. Any man does. Even if it only be a son, a child to carry on his name, maybeso carry on his way of life. No other soul gives a damn about him, consarn 'em! Man hopes he might have a boy to carry on. You're a lucky soul, Josiah

Paddock." His eyes climbed to the young trapper's face. "That son of yours back there can be what you leave behind."

Paddock glanced for a moment at the woman and child. Then his eyes returned to the streaking heavens. Beyond the trappers their herd of ponies was still restless. Not an animal was occupied with eating the summer-stunted grasses beneath the snow. Instead, every pony pulled at the picket pin keeping it from bolting into the black-kettle night. Each eye the size of a tin mug, both rolling wildly and full of fear, the horses' nostrils flared. Some cried out, sounding almost like a child in fear. Other ponies whinnied their shrill fright of the heavens.

Bass clucked his tongue against his teeth. "Nawww, son. There ain't a soul back to them settlements what'll know we was even here."

He watched some of the strange lights a moment, streaks of bluish white that continued to light up a trail across the sky for a few minutes after the star itself had ceased to be, after it had completed its race across the dark backdrop.

Bass spoke again. "Save for a few traders maybe, some of the fur company booshways an' fatbacks—ain't a solitary damned soul gonna know we was the first to come out here a'tall."

"That ain't what you're looking for are you, Scratch?" Josiah glanced over at the older trapper. "You looking to have a lotta folks know your name some day? Know who Titus Bass was?"

Scratch chewed on that, his eyes filled in wonder at this winter sky dusted with falling stars. The indigo canopy was so streaked at times it seemed that images were conjured: images that reminded him of many things, images that reminded him of nothing at all. Things recognizable, things he had never before witnessed. Explosions, pulsings, whistlings and screams—the night was alive with its own destruction, perhaps with its own re-creation.

Finally the old man responded. "Nawww, son. I ain't all that fired up 'bout havin' folks know just who Titus Bass was when the time comes for me to pass on. I'd just like to have more of them pilgrims back east know what we done for 'em, just so they could have 'em a fancy hat, them gals have 'em a muffler or beaver collar. Let 'em know just who it was that came out here to wade bare-assed into the ball-freezin' streams to get that beaver without losin' their hair in the bargain."

"And if they did know?" Paddock asked after a moment of reflection.

Bass dug a toe at the frozen crust of snow beneath him. "Most likely them kind wouldn't give a damn. Would they now? Nawww, I doubt it, son. You're prob'ly right on that."

He let his eyes climb back toward the sky and its racing tracks of blue-green, yellow-white streaks. It didn't matter that such a sky demanded of a man that he heed a warning. The Indians knew Old Man Coyote was telling them all something of great importance. So be it that the Old Man was doing this in his prankster fashion, lighting up the sky just like a celebration of the young country's independence from the Britishers. That was exactly his style, the Old Coyote Man. He was a one now! He was a one! That Old Man wanted folks to know he'd been around for sure, wanted them to remember he had talked to them. Put on such a show as this. To hell in a metal trap. Who'd remember Titus Bass had come along? Didn't really matter much after all, did it?

All that really seemed of any importance right now was that the trickster, the Old Man Coyote, was trying to tell Titus Bass something, and Scratch wasn't sure yet just what that something was. It did have something to do with the sky, he supposed. It might have been about the Arapaho if this meteor shower had occurred better than a week ago. No. Not the scalp hunting party. There was some solid reason Bass knew for the sky thickening like a blood soup and coming to a boil. Each star a bubble in that roiling caldron. All blood-red with light, streaked yellow, green and blue, shafts of luminous, exploding nodules falling to earth. Old Man Coyote had really put himself out for some reason. He would not have gone to the effort of such a display as this without a damned good reason.

Scratch did not like the fact that he didn't know that reason. Yet, over time, he had come to accept, and with that acceptance years ago had come a patience. With the patience ultimately had come the peace to let a lot of it slide, run right off his shoulders like water off his bare back. Let it go and move on. He'd find out what the crazy old coot wanted with him soon enough as it was. No sense in worrying about it now.

"Let's get on back to camp—get us some more of that popskull whiskey we brung along." Titus slapped Josiah on the shoulder, then turned toward the trees.

"Damned fine idea you got there, old man."

Bass took out his pipe, sat down to light it. After he had it smoking, he leaned back against his saddle and horse blanket at last and watched the women finish their chores after their grand supper. Soon he would have Waits-by-the-Water bring them some more of his whiskey.

Paddock studied the women bent over their chores, kettles and pots, taken up with their happy squaw chatter. He could see that the women were not listening. Finally he worked up the courage and bent toward Scratch as the older man tossed a burning twig back into the fire after lighting his pipe.

"Scratch?"

"You got somethin' on your mind, eh?"

"J-just wanna know something."

"Go 'head, son," he coaxed the young man patiently. "Get shet of it."

"W-when—" he began, swallowing. "Just when does all the killing end, Scratch?"

The older trapper watched his partner's gaze leave the waltzing flames and meet his. Bass took the pipestem from his lips and blew a gray-white halo about his head. He looked down into the fire before he answered.

"You meanin' the 'Rapahos?"

"The first bunch, then those that come last—ones we had to kill," Josiah started out. "Them two from St. Louis, then Sharpe—just when does it all end?"

Titus swallowed hard and stared down into the blackness of his pipebowl. He did not have anything wise to say to the young man. "Josiah, them that come

113

from St. Louis—Sharpe, too—there was no puttin' a stop to until we killed them or they kilt us. The cloth of it were cut no other way. Weren't no other choice in that."

"And the Injuns? Them Arapaho warriors?"

"They was fixin' to do some evil to your wife!"

"I know that, dammit," Josiah snapped quietly. "I—I was just thinking there must have been a better way."

"Only way to finish it was to kill 'em all." Bass had a little edge to his voice, something cold and honed, something hardened to killing over the years, something pushing down the bile that always rose in him when he did. "First time, we made the mistake of letting them others get on back to their village, tell what happened. Should have kilt 'em all—like we did back on the mornin' —"

"No," Josiah interrupted. "That ain't always the way."

"Why? You got the answer?" the older man quietly wondered. "You got a better answer?"

"No." Paddock's eyes flicked up to Scratch's face. "No, I don't have any answers to any of this, old friend. How the killing keeps on trailing me, dogging me—won't let me be. Ever since St. Louis—"

Bass listened to the voice trail off into silence. "You're soundin' almost ghosty, sayin' them things. Almost like you figure you got the fates after you, son."

Paddock was sick of it riding in his gut. He wanted it out and examined, over with. Ever since that morning they had attacked the scalp hunters' camp he had wondered on it, and in his wonder a bitter distaste for himself had festered.

"I don't think I'm ghosty as you yet, my friend," Paddock gulped. "I'm just trying to figure things out."

"Sometimes you push an' yank at somethin' all too hard," Scratch offered. "Sometimes, Josiah—you gotta just let it go right on by you."

"What if it takes you along with it?"

Scratch chewed lightly on the reed stem of his pipe before answering. "Man's gotta do what he's gotta do, I s'pose. It's up to others to understand, son. If they cain't understand what he's done—leastways they can accept it. You gotta learn to accept things as they come. Life's full of all of it. Some of it's ugly, to be sure. But most of it's purty. Not all of this is ugly, Josiah."

Paddock tossed the twig he had been toying with into the flames. "Would they've gone on, if we'd let them?"

"That pack of blood-guzzlin' runagates?"

"Yes," Paddock answered innocently enough.

"Son, as long as you been out here in these free mountains, as much as you wore the green off already—I'll be hanged to dry if'n you still cain't figure out the color of the cloth. Josiah, them Injuns was out to lift our hair. No two ways about it. They would've gave us no choice—like we give the two of them the first time. We let them go. That was the mistake. Not killin' 'em all was the mistake. We made the mistake of not killin' 'em all the first time."

"But it ain't right, is it?"

114

"To answer your question. Yepper, the stragglers would've gone if'n we'd let 'em. An' they'd be back straightaway with more help. Them brownskins are itchin' to rub us out." One palm moved quickly over the other.

"I—I—I just wanna be left alone, Scratch." Josiah almost begged with the tone of his voice.

"I know, son. What do you think I want sometimes more'n anything else? You get to wonderin' why they just cain't let you be." He watched Paddock nod in agreement before he went on. "An' sometimes it ain't in the cards—not for nothin' you done, not for nothin' you caused. It's them other folks that cause you the devil. An' you got to make a choice again an' again an' again. It might just come down to you or them over an' over an' over."

Scratch watched Paddock's head shake sadly while he gazed into the blue-yellow flames licking at the sky. Then the old trapper continued.

"Choices should come easy when a man's got him folks dependin' on him. Looks Far an' Joshua, they need you to make a lotta the choices for 'em. Makin' a choice gets easy when a man wants to take care of what's his."

"Sounds like you're saying the killing doesn't ever end," Paddock said. "Sounds like you think a man's always gotta make that choice."

"Yes," Bass answered quietly. "That's the simple truth of it. Out here the killin' may go on an' on. It's the way of life to accept. Or you don't. That choice is up to each man."

"Isn't any room for a fella who doesn't want to do the killing?"

"No one can say I wanna do the killin', Josiah. I don't cotton to takin' another man's life away from him—unless he's wronged me, unless there's no other way out of it."

"I'm sorry, Scratch," he apologized. "I know better. I never figured you for lapping up the chance to kill someone."

Paddock held his gaze on the older man, trying to read the eyes merrily dancing with firelight, dark waters brooding beneath that cheery surface. Bass was a puzzle inside a maze. Confusing at best, especially when you believed you had found the answer to his riddle.

"I'll walk away from trouble when I can, Josiah. Howsoever—if a man wants to bring trouble to my doorstep, he best be ready to go the whole hog, right down to the last bristle on that hog's tail."

"Yes," Josiah agreed, watching the two women stand from their chores, drying their hands across their wool dresses.

"Looks Far and the boy are dependin' on you, Josiah."

"I know they are."

"They're lookin' for you to protect 'em, keep 'em safe—best way you know how."

Paddock nodded in agreement. "I know that. It's just—at times I don't know how best to be doing exactly that."

"That's where it comes in—the hard part of bein' a man. Havin' to decide just how to do it for them that you love."

"Every man for himself?"

115

"Every man gotta decide for himself, son. No one else can make that choice for you."

"If it's my choice to make—I'm choosing more whiskey," he said, changing the subject as the two women joined them at the fire.

Paddock held his cup out to the Crow woman who carried the tin flask. He would have to consider all he had discussed with Bass. But for now, with the women close at hand, the conversation had to end. His mind and heart would have to work on it some more. Paddock smiled as Waits-by-the-Water worried the cork back and forth from the neck of the flask. She poured him a little whiskey in his coffee tin.

Scratch held out his cup. After she had poured some into her husband's tin, Waits-by-the-Water sat beside him. The trapper sipped at the strong grain alcohol mixture. The whiskey burned in his gullet, just like the heavens broiled above them. It comforted the old trapper that his woman had returned to the fire and cuddled him by the flames. She warmed the very part of him that had grown cold with the talk of killing.

Waits-by-the-Water so rarely drank, yet he offered her his tin cup. She took it from him, allowed the whiskey to brush her lips, then brought the cup away. The tip of her tongue licked delicately at the whiskey. That sip would do her. She gave the mug back to him and smiled. It was the kind of smile that told him the magic of this sky was casting a spell on her.

Waits-by-the-Water turned now to glance at Looks Far. The Flathead woman turned to meet the gaze. They both shared the same childhood, lived out in those northern mountains. Looks Far silently told the Crow woman she understood what Waits-by-the-Water was remembering. Though a mystery, magical and perhaps a portent of that to come, the Flathead woman was familiar with the light shows in the skies.

She herself could remember the pale, blood-red luminescence in the northern sky that would intensify as her people had watched in wonder. Then brightly-colored streams of blue-green, yellow-orange would burst out of the blood-red until there was a curtain of billowing light pulsating and wriggling, as if it were a glowing, living creature crawling over the horizon. A long, fiery snake that stretched from edge of the earth to edge of the earth, its dancing hood composed of darting nodes of blue or green or yellow explosions. The snake often darkened to bloody crimson as if in warning, then burst forth with the white-blue and orange-green filaments streaking, shifting, worming their way across the sky.

"When this happens," Looks Far said as she turned to Josiah by her side, "it is my people who tell that the Great One Above is dreaming again, as he did when he was getting ready to make our world out of mud and sky. We again see the magic of his dream on the heavens." She gestured toward the massive fireworks exploding above them through the overhanging branches.

"What happens when the Great One Above is dreaming again?" he asked.

Looks Far turned toward her husband. "He is getting ready to change things here on our world, my husband," she whispered softly in Flathead. "Old Coyote Man must not be asleep when the Great One Above dreams like this. If he is asleep, then he will miss the warning that things must change. If Old Coyote Man is awake to see the dream, then he can help the People to change things and make them right again. The circle starts in the north at the Great Dream, and the circle continues around us if it is not broken."

"Is it broken, my wife?" Paddock asked.

"I do not know of such things," Looks Far answered after some thought. "I pray for our son that the circle will be healed and we never have to part in death."

Paddock stared into the dancing fire at their feet. His ears had become adjusted to the noise of the horses, stomping and crying out in the darkness. He had yet to become fully reconciled to his wife's view of life. He recalled how she had talked him into allowing her and their son to join the attack on the scalp-hunters' camp. Life and death seemed so intertwined, inseparable. She believed they were just that, one process. If the great circle of life were to be fully healed, then life would go on for all the forevers that would exist. They would never again part, never again suffer the pain of separation. If the circle were complete.

He watched the night sky, listening to those faint whistlings and screams of the night heavens.

"You listen close enough, son," Scratch said softly, piercing the young trapper's reverie, "you can almost hear a song."

Paddock looked over at the older man and smiled in the bright firelight. He strained against the tussing of the ponies' hoofs, their frightened whinnying, and the crackling of wood in the hypnotic flames. There was something back there, beneath it all, a strange sort of sound. He finally nodded.

"You hear it?" Bass inquired.

"Yeah," Paddock nodded. "I think I do."

"You'll know it if you do hear it," Scratch said. "Up this high, up here where the sky is so clear, where the sky's so damned near—you'll be able to hear angels sing."

"That must be what I'm hearing," Josiah said.

"You'll know it if you hear it."

"What's it saying to you, Scratch?"

Bass cocked an ear like a hound would at a bear's den, straining to catch a hint of a sound foreign to its ear.

"Tellin' me it's time we push on, son. Time to pack up—head out to Taos."

"When?"

"Day, maybe two," Bass sighed, relieved, contented. His eyes were heavy with sleep. "Take time to bundle all them plews up proper for the trip. Not quite as far a jaunt to get down to Taos way as it were to get down here from ronnyvoo." He gazed into the great dome overhead. "Angels tellin' this ol' child he better be gettin' while them passes ain't locked with the early snows. Better make it to the southwind side before it's too late."

"Angels tell you all of that?" Josiah cast a questioning look toward the heavens, grinned.

"Angels," Bass spit into the fire, "maybe my medicine—maybe that night sky up there. All the same, son. They're all the same."

Bass rose slowly to his feet, knees and hips popping painfully after a long sit on

117

the cold ground. "Right now, howsoever, my woman's tellin' me to come to bed with her. Long winter nights mean that much more time for snugglin'."

He reached out to help pull Waits-by-the-Water to her feet, chuckling softly as he led her off toward their shelter. While she crawled in among the blankets and robes, the mountain man draped a threadbare mackinaw over the front of their pine-bough sleeping shelter. The firelight danced through the thin, worn places in the blanket. Bass slid under the robes. The heavy warmth of the animal hides felt good to him. As he warmed, he took off the elkhide coat.

The man heard the woman's gentle breathing as she took his rough hand in hers. Waits-by-the-Water led his fingers to her bare breast, small and full beneath his coarse skin. Like velvet with a rigid center, her breast almost like life itself. She was so soft, yet there was that strength at the core. Bass grew rigid. Soon he took his hand away from her breast, moved her soft fingers to his groin.

"We make a child on this night of magic," she whispered, husky, the sound of overpowering desire strong in her voice.

"It is a night of great mystery, woman," he answered, pulling aside his breechclout so she could touch him. "A night to end some things. A night to begin others."

She moaned, felt his readiness.

"There are many things in this night that are yet to be revealed to us," he said as he rolled atop her naked body. "Many things to know in the time to come. That time will be ours, woman. We take it as ours. It does not belong to anyone else. Ours. It cannot be taken from us."

"Take me with you, my husband, wherever it is you go." There was more urgency to her voice now as she moved beneath him in a growing cadence of pleasure.

"If the spirits choose, you will never leave my side, dear one. If the spirits choose, we will forever be together."

The dance of the dying fire flickered across the blanket doorway. With luminous trails of light overhead, this moment with her was like a prayer. He would ask forgiveness. He hoped his prayer would be granted. Bass hoped he would receive an answer soon, one way or another, to know if he had been forgiven. But for the time being, he would be with this woman, the meeting of their bodies like a prayer—begging forgiveness, asking for time, hoping for healing.

A prayer yet for healing.

9 HE PAINFULLY TURNED away from the little table beside his bed. *Tuesday.* He had already circled the date on that calendar scroll laid out beside his stationery. The night of November 12th, 1833. He would certainly have to remember this cold, damp night. Across the date he had scrawled the words, *star shower.*

The old man returned to the small garret window, with the kitten stretched across his arms. One of the servants had brought him the animal a little more than two months before, hoping it would cheer the master of this tired old house. If the tiny, playful, orange furred ball of energy did not end the isolation of the old man, at least it gave him distraction, and with that distraction came a peace of sorts.

There were times he would sit in the lone, straight-backed oak chair by the window, allowing himself no padding for those hours on end when he would watch either the street below or the wharf not far away and the lazy river just beyond the steamboats lashed securely to St. Louis. Yet for all the time spent motionless gazing out the window, the little kitten would remain on his lap. She purred to him as he ran his bony, gnarled fingers gently along her tiny body. This kitten returned the old man's affection by giving him something close to tranquility at those moments. To stroke the animal, to hear and feel her body throbbing beneath his fingertips with her joyful purr, that all gave the man pause, and in that reflection he began to regain fragments of peace he had known long ago.

Usually the purple evenings made the streets quiet below him. The laborers had left their work at the wharves behind for the day. Most of the city's residents were already home with their families, dining and whiling away the evening in one fashion or another. Occasionally there were folks who would pass by that great stone wall surrounding the house yards, snatch a quick peek through the heavy wrought iron gate and scurry on about their business. The lamps on the corners of each block would be lit, casting a pale corona of light over the snow-muddied, hard rutted streets.

This very evening had begun in much the same manner. Yet, not long after the light had fallen from the sky and the night went lamp-black with its usual dusting of stars, the old man caught a fleeting glimpse of that solitary shooting star racing across the inky heavens. Of itself this was not at all unusual. There were always shooting stars to be seen if one watched the night sky long enough. The old man

119

watched this sky every night. He knew just what stars and constellations were up there beyond his tiny attic window.

Nor had he been concerned with the second, nor the third, but when the meteors began to rain with more and more urgency, his attention became total. Soon enough the kitten was no longer content to lie still across his blanket-shrouded lap while he stroked her. Instead, the animal grew restless, then rose to her feet, arched her back with a feral shriek and tore off out the door he left cracked open for her.

Below him in the night spotted with yellowed rosettes of light, people were gathering along the muddied sidewalks, craning their necks to the sky. Down by the warehouses a crowd had gathered round a doomsayer preaching that this was the coming of that day of judgment—the end of the world. A sure sign the Lord God was raining fire on the world. No more flood. God had said the next time would be fire. Raining destruction on the world He had created, and a world He was now going to end for all its many sins.

Tiny knots of frightened spectators clustered together, feeding on each other's fears and superstitions. Then there were those casual observers, out this evening to follow the unusual phenomenon. Mere spectators were in a minority this night. Most folks were certain this blazing sky of fire-rain was a portent of some great calamity, at least a warning of God's unbridled wrath upon man.

The old man wondered if the priest at the cathedral was lighting candles at this very moment of the star shower. The black-robed man of God saying his pre-scribed prayers, his intercession on behalf of a sinful world, begging God's forgiveness, begging that God not destroy His most noble creation.

He laughed suddenly. Something he had not done for a long, long time. A sound strange to his own ears. And with the laugh came the phlegm webbing at the back of his throat to make him gag and cough. It was always this way. The fluid returned stronger and stronger with every passing day. He would hack up great balls of night phlegm each morning. And through each day he continually spit into the huge brass spittoon the house servants emptied and washed for him several times a day. He had refused their suggestions to call a physician, some-one who could tell them just what ailed the old man, what it was that sucked the very strength from his wasting body, what it was that wracked his frame with the horrendous coughing fits.

He finished this attack, spitting out the last of those balls of thick mucus. Wiping his lips across the back of his sleeve, the gray-head peered from his tiny window once more. The sky lit up with blue-green, orange-yellow, yellow-green and blue-white streakings. The wispy tails of the shooting stars raced across each other, as if to spawn more and more of the blazing meteors. He had been concerned at first, but nothing more than that as he watched the sky giving birth to its explosive offspring.

Down in the yard near the front portico were gathered some of the house servants. More superstitious than most people, the ebony-skinned slaves had served the old man obediently for these many years. Here in St. Louis the Negroes were called Inks. The old man now heard their low, frightened voices clamoring in the yard below his attic window. Here in the darkness of the cloudless, star-rippled night, the servants all but disappeared from view. Occasionally he could pick out their wide rows of teeth as they talked, perhaps their huge oval eyes widening in fear at the celestial streamers. He smiled a moment, feeling safe with such people around him. They knew no better. The Inks had their superstitions and primitive beliefs. In their ignorance came a sort of security, a protection in the face of such a frightening phenomenon. It was the priests, the learned ones, his wealthy associates who really deserved his ridicule. They should know better.

Horses whinnied and cried out from the stable at the rear of the great house. The hounds had set up a great howling by now and the frightened wails of other animals had finally pierced his little world high in the cold attic. If not every man in the city, at least every animal, was driven to believe there was something to be afraid of in this meteor shower.

Down in the street a carriage lumbered past, bouncing and swaying back and forth across the rock-hardened ruts. The driver clung on as best he could, clawing at the reins, attempting to control the fright-crazed horses. Behind him, the cowering passengers jumbled and bounced against each other. The iron-rimmed wheels clattered off through the night, the cries of animal and man alike disappearing into the inky blackness of the cold St. Louis frost.

The clamor rose and ebbed, rose and ebbed with the number of stars plummeting toward earth. On the street some people darted here, others there, rushing to get home, others to find a place safer than home. At the wharf one of the steamers shrieked its whistle, telling all that the engine fires had been stoked and brought to running temperature. The captain must have been superstitious himself, ordering his boat to cast off into the night flow of the Mississippi River rather than risk the destruction of the world while lashed to a St. Louis wharf. The whistle faded off downriver.

Head on to Nachez, perhaps all the way to New Orleans. If it were the end of the world, there would be no escape. No escape at all.

He wondered if others around the world would see this same star-smudged sky. Could they see it and how were they reacting in Quebec? Or New Orleans? Along the Red River of the North? The Souris? The Roche Jaune and out along the Platte? Was the night sky more clear out in that great expanse of western territory? If so, would it be more frightening? Could they see the mystery held in this fiery pageant? Would they view it as the end of their world?

How would the inhabitants of those regions regard this night? Would those primitive peoples gaze upon the sky in numbing fear as did the people here below him on these St. Louis streets? Would their medicine men be whipping the true believers into a religious frenzy around huge bonfires and the hypnotic thumping of animal skins? Not all that different from the priest in the cathedral—except the Black Robe did most of his praying in private.

The night of shooting stars served good purpose to the few who held sway over the many.

He was several ages older now since the meteor shower had begun hours ago. The old man felt the muscles stiffen, complaining in his knotted back and along his cramped buttocks. Still he did not move. The night sky held him fascinated,

121

enthralled, hypnotized. He wondered if he was under its power, wondered if at last its magic held him in its grip.

Perhaps the world was coming to an end in some form or another. The thought flashed over him as surely as the shimmering light bathed his gray head, the starshine flooding through the tiny window where he sat frozen, an observer who had prayed, supplicated his God to participate.

Now at last he realized the world as he had known it was indeed coming to an end. His tiny, sheltered, protected world had cracked some two and a half years before. Through that jagged portal in his protective wall had slipped the young American who had killed his beloved Henri. From that point on the old man's little world had begun to disintegrate. It had taken him this long to realize it. Better than two years and for all that time the old man had refused to accept that things must change—accept that things would change. With, or without him.

The heavens hung heavy, dripping with light, all blue-white and yellow-green like wispy party streamers when the family would ring in a new year. But it was November 13th already. Past midnight by the tiny clock on the table, yet the sky flamed on. He would remember this night. Much more than a mere inked circle on his weather calendar—he would remember. This night in the waning weeks of 1833 when he had finally realized the huge giant, Emile Sharpe, was not returning to St. Louis, to the street below, to this house.

The old gray head bent and fell against the window pane. Below him the screams of frightened humans and the cries of terrified animals continued unabated. The old man did not hear. He was praying.

It was a prayer that nothing more would slip through that ragged, torn portal in his protective wall. He had tried to reach out from St. Louis with the arms of others. And each of them had failed. Three hired to kill that single young American. All had failed to return. The old man's familiar, comfortable world was coming to an end under the spectacle of the meteor shower. No longer could he rely upon others to do what he should have undertaken himself on the first account. He should have acted two and a half years ago while he was stronger. All of this he realized now.

His prayer begged his God to bring the young murderer to him instead. A pitiful prayer, pleading for intercession—bring the young American to him so that his hands alone could kill the murderer of his Henri.

Dear God. Bring him to me so that my tired hands might know of his death at last. Please, dear God—if ever you would grant a man his wish, bring him to me that I might see his blood on my own hands.

His eyes finally raised to the heavens from whence his answer would come. He knew his God personally showed him this sky as a message, a foretelling. He knew his God told him the murderer would be delivered to him. The young American would be brought to St. Louis, to this great house, to this very room. And here he would kill the murderer, with the pistol that had waited by the door for so long now. By his own hand—his own bloodied hand.

The old man's prayer would be answered. This flaming, mystical night sky raining fire and destruction down upon the world told him so. His prayer would soon be given answer. His prayer answered at last.

MOST of the days had broken clear as crystal, ringing cold and cloudless, leaving ice-slicked water crusted in their kettles and waterbags. The pack animals and Indian mustangs slicked the air with frosty halos for most of the morning ride until the high sun finally warmed the air above their mist-shrouded worm snaking along the timbered ridges.

Bass had brought the party through the pass in three miserable, freezing days. They had huddled around fires each long winter's night in the snow, but they had survived their climb out of the Bayou Salade. The snows were not so deep that man nor horse could not push themselves over the pass. The early winter skies had been held in abeyance. No snow had fallen during their trip over the high side. Winter was drawing in rapidly around them, but the old man had been lucky to move when he had. Good weather held until they had dropped away from the pass. Behind them the clouds had tumbled in over the hoary peaks, covering the ragged, torn granite with raging winter storms punctuated with flying ice and wispy streamers of dry, silky snow. It was as if a door had slammed shut behind them, a portal never to be opened again.

The small brigade had dropped into the high mountain valley named for the very same saint blessing that hub of America's fur trade. St. Louis rested along the Mississippi River. And here the San Luis valley rested along the Rio Grande River rolling south toward the vicinity of Taos. The old trapper had crossed and recrossed this valley many times, climbing in and out to the north along the route they had just left.

If he ever entered the valley from the west, the mountain trapper climbed up from the river they called the Blue, long before named the Rio San Xavier by Spanish explorers. It flowed through a black, ruggedly beautiful and darkly yawning canyon that led the trappers into that high country of the west slope. Over the Cochetopa Pass they trailed, that western portal to the San Luis valley at times known to the Spanish as *El Puerto de los Cibollas* or "Buffalo Gate." From that 10,000-foot height the traveler would drop into the high San Luis valley, travel south and eventually pick up the Rio Grande.

Everything was familiar to the old man here. It was like getting close to home after a long trip away from the hearth. Herds of wild mustangs raced across their path daily, requiring the men and women alike to strain at keeping the pack horses and extra ponies from running off. A horse thief's paradise, if a man wanted to make the effort to capture the wild creatures. Much of the land now lay under almost a foot of new snow, this white dusting like spun sugar covering their baggage and sleeping robes each morning. Later in the day the brightness of the high sun at times hurt the eyes, making them smart and water with the dazzling reflection. Yet, the same high sun made the land come alive for the old man. The colors of the hills and animal life and streams and the very sky itself— they all were more vivid than he had remembered. Bass felt his heart beat louder the closer they drew to Taos.

Waits-by-the-Water spent more and more time beside him during these days of cold, early winter travel. They chattered aimlessly, talking together of important matters, talking of things with no importance at all. There was a vitality they

123

shared together, a strength that drew itself from each other. Bass finally realized why the colors danced more vividly for him this trip, why the homecoming to Taos seemed all the sweeter. He had this woman to share it with; he had Waits-by-the-Water at his side. He was bringing his woman to Taos, taking her toward the closest thing to civilization he had seen in more than ten years.

Hell, she'd never even been to a damned fur-trading post—and here I am, taking her down to Taos. It was enough to boil the britches of any man who grew up in those United States back east. To think of bringing someone here who has never seen a town before.

"You are thinking of something tonight?" She had a way of coquettishly half-lidding her eyes whenever she asked the question.

"That may be," he responded in Sparrowhawk. "But what I was thinking of was showing you this wonderful place called *Taos.*"

The last word seemed out of place butted up against the sounds made in the Crow tongue.

"My husband is glad to be coming to this place—Ta-a-a-house?" she asked with wider eyes.

"I am very glad to be coming here," he nodded. "Just like the big valley of the South Park, I am glad to share this with you. I am most happy that you are here to share it with me now." He spread his arm across the rolling country, as if to lay it at her feet, his gift for her.

This mountain southwest was a land of extreme contrasts. While there were rich flowered valleys, so too were there high, snow-capped peaks. The green, rolling meadows ran up against the sun-hardened desert wastes speckled with ocotillo and barrel cactus, mesquite trees and frequent reminders of an even more ancient time in the sharp, black lava that would dot the landscape. Always the land of the lizard, horned toad, prairie dog and rattlesnake, this was also a land where the infrequent streams would be bordered with cottonwood and willow. From such gypsum-tainted streams would come the "gyp" water that would cause many unaccustomed travelers to become sickened, ill with bowel distress. Vast, yawning plains stretched toward the purple bulk of hills, up to brick red mountains timbered with pinon pine and cedar. At sunrise, treeless ridges would stare back at a man like some swollen, puffy, fight-injured eye. When the sun was high the same vista was painted hazy blue, falling away to a deep purple as the sun finally went to rest. In such a land there was always the heat of Hell, or the bitter cold of an unexpected and uncompromising winter storm.

For much of their way through this land of color and contrast they had been approximating the deep course of the Rio Grande as it rolled almost due south. Last evening they had finally dropped into the Taos valley itself. Running mostly north and south, the valley was flanked on the west by that deep gorge, the canyon of the Rio Grande. To the north, south and east erupted the pinon-timbered mountain peaks.

"In the past, I mostly come down along the Front Range from the country north of here," Bass explained at their nightfire. "Fella climbs them hills there," he said, wagging a knife toward the Sangre de Cristos, "comes on over a pass that you can still run in the winter. Then you can follow the Little Fernandez River down here to the valley to find the town you been lookin' for—Taos."

The Rio Fernando de Taos eventually flowed into the Rio Grande, leading the weary traveler scrambling down out of the Sangre de Cristos on to the settlement squatting beneath the early winter sun. Those streams rushing down the western slope of the mountains which did not dump their flow into the Rio Grande drained into a lake some twenty-five miles long by about five miles wide, designated on the earliest of maps as Laguna Grande. The valley seemed to offer refuge and haven to all who entered here. The winter storms could spend their rage on the mountain peaks bordering the valley, giving the weary, frozen traveler pause and warmth here below the fury. From spring until fall, the green fields welcomed the prairie-jaded wanderer who had pushed himself along the dry and dusty course of the Santa Fe Trail. Here that wanderer could find refreshment, cool breezes and clear water in the shade of the Sangre de Cristos.

As early as the 1300's, the Indians had begun building the massive multi-storied Pueblo of Taos, constructing the thick mud walls up against the Taos mountain at the northern end of the valley. Successive pueblos had been added over the centuries. Finally, after the threat of frequent, bloody attacks by the Comanche had diminished, a new Spanish settlement had been given birth. Named after a seventeenth century Spanish pioneer of this valley, the village came to be known as Don Fernando de Taos.

Bass stopped the party on a low rise overlooking the town.

To the south was a scattering of mud houses sprinkled around the largest structure, the church. As the tallest building in the settlement, the church was complete with two bell towers, their height graced with bells. The whitewashed adobe walls glittered in the high winter sunlight.

Bass turned to his woman, enjoying this chance to watch her quiet reaction to these simple mud buildings scattered across the valley floor. While they might seem like hovels or shanties to an American trader bringing costly goods across the prairie from Missouri, the whitewashed adobe huts and houses surrounding the magnificence of the Catholic church left the Crow woman slack-jawed.

Don Fernando de Taos. Some of the Spanish called it Don Fernandez de Taos. Others corrupted it farther to San Fernandez or San Fernando de Taos. Whatever name the Spanish or American travelers hung on it, to the mountain man it was known simply as *Touse.*

Paddock himself had imagined something a bit more on the grand scale, at least from the magnificent description given by the older trapper. Where Josiah had expected to find rich carriages and the teeming, silk-lined boardwalks of a St. Louis fur trade center, what he now saw disappointed him.

"T-this—is Taos?" he turned to ask of Bass.

"What do you think, Josiah?"

"I-it's—just like you told me, Scratch."

"Whooeeeee! C'mon, you folks," Bass cheered happily with a grand sweeping arc of his arm. "Let's get on down there with them pelados—see if we cain't find us a place to put up for the winter."

Mangy hounds and skinny, mixed breed dogs had raced out to bark and yip around the ponies' legs as the group neared the outskirts of town. Few, if any, of the horses were alarmed by those noisy dogs. The ponies had been raised in Indian camps where a man could find almost as many dogs as he could horses.

A few heads lifted from chores to notice the small trapper band entering from the north, then resumed their late afternoon duties. The sight of American trappers arriving in the Mexican settlement was routine by now. There was nothing to distinguish this ragtag band with some two dozen horses loping along behind it.

Taosenos, rich and poor alike, were much accustomed by now to the Americanos entering Mexican territory. The older residents of the village had long ago seen their first Yankee visitor. As it was, most Taos citizens had reached their middle age growing up with a constant ebb and flow of both American traders and trappers. The lighter-skinned gringos had been visiting their village for many years.

Under that bright, high light of early winter, the whitewashed adobe houses radiated a pleasing sight to the eyes of these new arrivals. Bass had returned to the scene of so many fond memories. Down the narrow, unpaved, hard packed streets smeared with snow and dotted with mud puddles, the old trapper led his string of ponies.

It had been a long time since the Mexican residents had seen this many riderless horses. Taosenos glanced from windows or raised their heads from late afternoon labors to gaze at the newcomers. Dusky-skinned, buxom wenches peered at the buckskinned trappers from the shadow of doorways, their eyes challenging and inviting at the same time.

Where Josiah had first thought he had stepped off into a brutally spare land, he now became caught up in the rhythm that was this Mexican village. Where first he had seen nothing but a confused scattering of flat-roofed adobe buildings, Paddock now was greeted with faint strains of happy music and the sing-song of a foreign tongue ringing at his ears. Mexican citizens wandered and sauntered about slowly, as if really having no place to go.

Scratch led the group around the plodding oxen which pulled squeaking, two-wheeled *carretas* that looked more like roofless bird cages than small wagons. No sewer system existed in the Mexican village and the streets proved to be a dumping place for human and animal waste alike. Goats, horses, sheep, oxen and mules moved aside as the trapper and his friends made their way up the crowded, bustling streets toward the main plaza.

The church they'd seen from the hillside faced public buildings and vendors' shops around a treeless square at the center of town. It was here that the frenetic activity of the day's trading would soon wind down for the night. Barking with advertisement of their particular wares, shrill-throated vendors screamed out the virtues of their goods from here and there around the plaza.

Mexican and Indian women alike peered curiously up at the Crow and Flathead women as the new arrivals came to a halt in the milling village square. Studying Looks Far and Waits-by-the-Water from beneath the folds of their black dyed rebozo shawls, the Mexican women fluffed at their bright red and blue skirts. They smiled at the newcomers from behind their tall stacks of soap cubes, their wheels of goats' cheese, eggs, vegetables, hot onions and peppers. Here a customer could purchase a sugar-dusted sweetbread baked in a domed mud oven, or a tamale from bubbling pots simmering over the coals of glowing braziers.

The plaza was like nothing they'd ever seen before. One vendor sold choice cuts of buffalo, another offered pork or lamb. Chickens hung lifeless and naked from their vendor's stall. Selections of liver, intestines and tripe lay beneath a loose netting that was to protect the meat from insects. Stacks of dried hay, bundles of mesquite and pinon firewood, even animals on the hoof were offered for sale.

As the two Indian women were helped down from their mounts by their two buckskinned husbands, they were appraised from beneath the shade of wide-brimmed sombreros. The men in the square were clustered around iron braziers where they talked and warmed themselves and smoked their corn-husked cigarillos.

Two Mexicans walked around the plaza's circumference, lighting the smokey torches with the short, oiled firebrands they carried. When all the torches were lit, the church bells rang out across the square. And when the tolling of the bells faded away, the plaza became silent.

Bass signalled his group to remain quiet as hundreds of whispering voices mumbled their evening vespers. As the prayers were spoken, candles inside the church were lit by a priest. Field hand, peon laborer and slave-owning gentry joined in silent prayer with young caballeros in their black-dyed buckskins. Black rebozos and colorful shawls were pulled over women's bowed heads as they recited their communal prayer.

Suddenly there arose the tinkling of smaller, livelier bells. The muted whispering ceased. Heads lifted and people began chatting noisily again. The people moved about the plaza, securing their purchases before they headed home at this ending of the day. And just about every one of them gave the new gringos a onceover before passing on.

"Ho! Bass!" the voice cried out from within the bustling crowd. "Bass!"

The shaggy head bobbed up above the crowd as a skinny-framed man struggled through the surging Mexicans. Scratch turned at the sound of his name, attempting to place the voice before he could see the face.

"Bass! Is that really you?"

The tall, skinny gringo stood before the old trapper, his balled fists resting on his hips, feet spread shoulder-width, chin cocked in a jaunty pose. Scratch looked him up and down but once.

"Rowland?"

"That it is."

"I'll be—damn—what a sight for sore eyes." Titus lunged out as each man wrapped his arms around the other, flailing away at the other's back with hard pounding exuberance.

"Gawd, but I'm surprised to find you here after all these seasons," Rowland cried as he pulled back from Titus with a wide grin etched across his deep-lined face.

"It's been some time, ain't it?" Bass smiled. He motioned for his young partner to come forward. "This here is my young compañero, Josiah Paddock," Bass declared proudly.

"He's a real chunk of it, I'll say," Rowland said as he shook hands with Paddock.

"This skinny whiffet on a stick goes by the name of John Rowland," Scratch told Paddock. "We go back a long way."

"Winter of '24-'25."

"Up to the Green it were that year, was it not?"

"Yep," Rowland answered. "And a ball-freezing, pizzer of a blue winter that was." His crow-footed eyes traveled to the capote-wrapped women who stood behind their men. "Who might these comely wenches be?"

"The purty one with the young'un is Paddock's wife, Looks Far Woman," Bass explained.

"And my son, Joshua," Paddock added.

"And the other lovely damsel?" Rowland asked.

"Waits-by-the-Water," Bass beamed proudly. "She's my Crow wife. Looks Far is Flathead. Howsoever, they're two of a kind."

"I'll wager that's right on the stick." Rowland turned to stare into the old trapper's face. "What brings you down this way as the cold of winter is fixing to break on over the mountains?"

"Do you know of any finer place to while away a winter, John Rowland?"

"Not me, Titus Bass." He slapped a bony hand on Scratch's shoulder. "Seems to be you found another place to spend your winters," he said with a quick nod toward Waits-by-the-Water.

Bass winked. "How've you fared, old friend?"

"I've—I've been better," Rowland admitted. "Made the mistake of trapping some dry traces of late."

"Got a woman?" Scratch asked.

"There've been several," Rowland said as he toed the snow beneath his feet. "Got a young Yuta gal now. Bought her off a band of Comanches come in to trade this past fall. I ain't never done without a woman."

"Where is it you're layin' over?" Scratch asked.

"Kinkead's place, as a matter of fact."

"Mateo Kinkead?" Bass said with a sudden excitement to his voice. "He's still castin' a shadow across dear ol' mother earth?"

"Too damned good a person for the Good Lord to fetch up yet," Rowland smiled. "Not like you or me, Bass. The man's a known saint in these parts."

"Wagh!" Bass snorted. "You're right there. You s'pose ol' Matt would let some poor wayfarers lay over a night or two whil'st they find themselves some proper diggin's of their own for the comin' winter?"

"Need you ask?" Rowland laughed.

"Let's find the old runagate an' give him a mountain squeeze. If he's not moved since I last was here, I should remember where he's livin'." Bass nodded. "Let's get this brigade movin', Josiah."

Scratch pulled on the reins to yank his buffalo runner along behind him. The women tugged on the rawhide ropes of the long string of some two dozen pack animals, most laden with baggage or beaver packs.

That bright rose light of a late winter afternoon was slipping reluctantly from the sky as Rowland led the procession around the side of the treeless plaza. Nothing could grow where so many feet trod day in and day out. There was no vegetation, yet no one ever seemed to notice. The plaza always seemed alive all of itself. Under the first wet snows of early winter the hard-packed, sun-baked streets had become muddied, rutted remnants of corduroy, ribbed with all the thousands of footprints and wagon or cart wheel tracks. Soon enough the shrill cries of what vendors remained in the square were fading behind them. Some shop owners would stay until the very last customer had retreated for the winter night. The plaza would fall silent under a star-studded sky awaiting its resurrection with the morning's new sun.

Those brays and bleats, whinnies and curses, slipped from the ears as the party wound out of the square along a rutted, snowy street headed south. The closer to the square, the more wealthy the homeowner. The farther out along the narrow, rutted avenues, the poorer you were, it was said. Yet a genteel nose would have appreciated living farther away from the hub of commerce. Bass was able to drink in the fresher air now as they moved down the narrow street. He was glad to be leaving the plaza and its mingling of simmering food spices and fresh animal dung underfoot. The pungent smoke of many fires and the evening's oiled torches mixed with the heavy, wet wool smell of the sheep, not to mention the sweated, hard-worked odor of burros, mules and horses. But now his nose cleared as the air grew sweeter once more.

A *carreta* rolled past, its passengers several children not yet in their teens. They were clearly Indian, driven by a Mexican who was hoping to get home to his master's *hacienda* out in the valley before dark. The huge, well-run *ranchos* were maintained in and out with peon and Indian slave labor. Many of the southwestern tribes stole children from one another and sold them to slave traders who would bring those children to the major villages to sell to the highest bidders. While the Navajos were most adept at stealing the children of other tribes, the poverty stricken Paiutes often were forced to sell their own children into slavery. Boys grew up working with animals or in the fields. There was more of a demand for girls, however, as they became valued house servants around the hacienda of the master.

The blue light dimmed to purple shadow along the narrow streets of low, flat-roofed mud homes. Here and there passed saraped men scurrying home after a day of labor or gracefully stepping women returning from the marketplace. Between the lips of most, man and woman alike, was the ever-present corn-shuck cigarillo, its dull red glow dotting the purple evening light.

Kinkead's place of itself did not look like much at first. It too was a grouping of squat, one-storied, flat-roofed buildings. Three smaller adobe structures of varying sizes sat out from the main house. All was surrounded on three sides by a wall which in this case was not much taller than five feet. As they came down the narrow, muddied road from the rise, the whole of the place had a pleasing, welcoming attitude about it for the weary traveler.

While prosperous citizens of Taos blockaded themselves behind high, protective walls, the poorer inhabitants of the village had only the walls of their homes behind which to retreat. Through those great high walls of the wealthy was usually but one gate, iron-barred, wide enough to permit a carriage egress. While in contrast—in the homes of those poorer citizens was a door so small many times even a short man had to stoop to enter a house. Most of these houses were really little more than mud huts, a single room where a large family eked out their existence. If there were any windows, it was certain they were not covered with glass. That extravagance was reserved for the more wealthy. Instead, the windows, which were no larger than portholes, might be covered with scraped rawhide or translucent mica. While the walls were of sun-baked adobe mud, so were the roofs. During rainy or snowy weather, most of the ceilings leaked muddy water or brown, slimy mud itself. Some water-sodden roofs had even collapsed on unsuspecting, sleeping inhabitants.

While not wealthy, Kinkead was comfortable by most standards of the day. He was not merely scratching out an existence as were the peon laborers who worked the hacienda fields dotting the valley floor. Mateo had long ago decided to remain somewhere in between. To live comfortably without the trappings of wealth, to go without want of a meal when hungry or a dry robe to curl up in with his Mexican wife when sleepy—there was really little more. From time to time Kinkead had been known to head out for months, trapping what he could, then returning with his catch when all pack animals were laden with his efforts. The furs he sold and traded for provided just enough to support his privately held conception of comfort.

While he had become a Mexican citizen, baptized in the Roman Catholic church, and married a Mexican woman, Mateo Kinkead still remained apart from his fellow native born Taosenos. It was not from a want of friendliness on the part of the other Taos residents. It was Kinkead's own choice in the matter. He preferred to spend most of his time either by himself, or immersed in that constant ebb and flow of buckskinned mountaineers visiting the valley, season after season. Always a gracious host, he helped many trappers sell their furs at the right prices, secure staples and trade goods at a fair market, and intervened when trouble with the local officials raised its head. Each and every American mountaineer who found shelter or aid from Mateo Kinkead was sure to share some of his hairy wealth with the old, naturalized Mexican citizen. Here he was the recognized entertainer for all the hunters who entered the Taos valley.

Soft light spilled out in arched rainbows from each mica-paned window—pale, candlelit, welcoming. Across one window barred with stout wooden limbs brushed the shadow of one of the inhabitants. At all the windows' sills were mud and wooden boxes, during the long growing season bedecked with gay blue and red geraniums. At the side of the house stood two small mud ovens that resembled inverted coffee cups. During the days these beehive-shaped structures were used for baking. At night they were shelter for the family's dogs.

The Kinkead dogs had already set up a yipping, howling chorus to announce that someone was coming down their road. Yellow light suddenly poured from the front door, framing a wide man of middling height. The man stepped into the yard where some of the dogs ran to greet him.

"Ho! Kinkead," Rowland called out.

"Rowland?" the gravelled voice answered. "John Rowland? Is that you now?"

"Mateo, it's Rowland for sure," he replied, entering the gateless portico within the adobe wall.

John turned to Scratch, whispering under his breath, "Ol' feller's eyesight ain't all that good these days. Things far off are just a blur he tells us. He's kinda touchy about it."

"Hell, I know just how Mateo feels," Scratch said.

"Who's that with you?" Kinkead called.

"Titus Bass, Mateo," Bass cried out as he approached the Taos resident, his hand now empty of both rein and rifle.

"Titus—Titus Bass?" Mateo sang out. "Scratch?"

"One and the same, old friend," Bass said as he put his hands on the wide, stout shoulders and pulled Kinkead into an embrace.

After much hugging and slapping of backs, Scratch pulled away. "It's been some time, Mateo."

"Too much," Kinkead nodded. "Who are all these folks with you, my friend. Don't they know they are welcome at Kinkead's house?"

Bass motioned for the others.

"One of these women has to be related to you, Scratch," Mateo chimed, after he'd looked over the newcomers.

"This gal," Scratch said as he stepped to his wife's side and put his arm around her waist. "Waits-by-the-Water, my Crow wife."

Kinkead swept low in a graceful bow. "I am pleased to meet you, dear lady." He turned to Bass. "You always were partial to them Crow, wasn't you?"

"I finally found me a keeper," Titus beamed proudly.

"This young lady, and her child?" Mateo said as he stepped to the Flathead woman's side to view the sleeping infant slung from her back.

"Looks Far Woman," Paddock said as he stuck out his paw toward the old mountaineer. "Our boy, Joshua."

"And, you are?" Kinkead asked.

"Josiah Paddock. Two years out of St. Louis and pleased to make your acquaintance, sir."

"This young'un's real civil," Mateo said as he glanced at Bass and Rowland. "He hasn't had time to become ruin't like you two tough old hard-cased hides."

They all laughed as Mateo turned toward the house. A woman stood in the doorway, wiping her hands across her muslin apron.

"If I forget my manners here, Mama will serve my ol' threadbare scalp to you for breakfast," Mateo chuckled, pulling the woman out of the doorway.

131

She came forward with her husband and gave several quick curtsies from the waist.

"This is Rosa," Mateo said. "My Rosalita. Finest cook this side of the Heeley and south of Wah-to-yah." Mateo turned to Bass. "You had supper yet, old friend?"

"Well, no we—" he stammered.

Kinkead started giving directions. "Rosa, you take these women in. Introduce yourselves," he said as he herded them toward the door. "They got a little young'un with 'em. A boy by the name of Joshua."

Rosa beamed and circled to Looks Far Woman's side where she brushed a finger across the infant's cheek. "Joshua," she chimed in imitation English.

"Woman's a sucker for kids," Kinkead said. "Here," he said as he led the men around the corner of the house. "We'll put all these animals of yours back here. Got a pole corral that ain't being used."

Behind the house, Kinkead showed the men the corral, then pointed to the smaller of the two adobe buildings which were some twenty yards from the main house. "Over there. You can put your tack and trappings in that one. Beside the shed, you'll find all the hay your animals can eat. If we need more in the morning, we'll take the wagon out to the field where there's more hay cut and stacked."

"Be glad to help out anytime," Paddock said.

"Right now, you fellas get them horses put up for the night." He turned toward the second adobe building. "Drop your plunder in there. That'll be where you stay. John, best go grab your woman," he said, nodding toward another hut. "She'll be wanting to meet these new ladies. Supper's about ready." Kinkead wheeled around and left the three in the starlit yard.

"We only need to spend a night or two, Kinkead," Scratch hollered after the old man.

"I don't care none if you spend the whole winter with me, you slack-eared redbone," Mateo shouted back. "I'll be sure you earn your keep. Now, *andele!* Hurry up, boys. Rosalita runs this house and she runs me, too. If you want something to eat at Rosa's table, you best be getting washed up and sat down. She won't wait on you none."

Bass and Rowland began pulling the ponies into the corral where they stripped the horses of their loads and packsaddles. Scratch turned when he saw Paddock hadn't joined them.

"You comin', son? Give us a hand here?" Titus called out.

"He must love her an awful lot," Josiah replied as he watched Kinkead until the old mountaineer disappeared into the house and shut the door.

"Why, yes, son," Scratch said. "I'll bet he does. A man can put up with quite a lot, he loves a woman enough. Probably learned to love all her funny little ways."

Josiah turned at last toward the pole corral and tugged at a stiffened rawhide knot as he thought about it. You learned to love someone, you learned to put up with some of their silly, childish ways. He felt good as he looked over at his older partner. They had put up with one another over all this time because they loved each other. Just like Rosa and Mateo. Just like Scratch and Waits-by-the-Water.

He and Looks Far Woman. Now under the illumination of the stars, the old man's beard stood out even more silver than Josiah had remembered. He smiled.

"What you lookin' at?" Scratch demanded when he turned to find Josiah staring at him.

"You, my friend," Josiah answered simply. "Just looking at my best friend."

10

IT SMELLED CLOSE to contentment.

Paddock drew in a deep breath, his eyelids at half mast. The rainbow of fragrances danced around in his nose. Burning pinon and cedar from the fireplace, mingled smokey scents with the faint aroma of red peppers that hung in huge, festive garlands drying on the walls. Those smells blended with the scent of freshly baked bread and heady black coffee just coming to a boil. Paddock greedily drank in his dream aromas and plopped an arm over on the buffalo robe beside him.

"Good morning," she whispered in Flathead.

Looks Far Woman's smile warmed him as the buffalo robe fell away from his chest. She sat at the end of the thick, woven rug, in the fashion of Indian women, her legs tucked in at her side. She had been brushing her long hair with a porcupine comb. Then she nodded down at the robe beside her husband, where their son Joshua was still sleeping.

"You both sleep long this morning." Her voice was as soft as her eyes.

"He is not hungry?"

"He has not asked for his milk yet," she answered. "I am enjoying this time of quiet without him always pulling at me. Joshua acts like it is his nipple. Like it does not belong to me."

Josiah reached out to cup the back of her head and gently pulled her toward him. His fingers slid across the soft skin at the neckline of her dress, then continued on down until he held a milk-firm breast suspended in his palm. He massaged it gently.

"You are both wrong," he murmured. "This belongs to me."

She pulled back and gave her husband a playful slap as he raised his arms to defend himself. They laughed together, tussling on the robe until Paddock felt something tugging at his wrist. He pulled his hands away from his face to discover his son pulling on his arm.

"He is awake now," Looks Far declared.

"That I can see."

"It is your fault that he is awake," she pouted. "Now he will want his milk."

"You are quick to blame that on me," Paddock smiled. He wrapped his wife in one arm, picked Joshua up with his other. "I think we will start something new in our family this morning," he said in Flathead words. "We will allow Joshua to suck on some milk first—then you will let me."

134

Looks Far pushed him away again.

"Decent folks cain't get no sleep," Bass said as he stuck his head out from under one of the thick blankets they had hung as a divider in the small two-roomed hut.

Waits-by-the-Water pulled up the blanket partition and stepped out from their little section of the main room. Bass drew back instantly, pulling at a blanket to cover himself. Looks Far clapped a hand over her mouth when she got a glimpse of the old trapper's naked body.

"What we just saw wasn't decent at all, Scratch," Josiah laughed.

"You see enough?"

"Really saw more than I wanted to see, if the truth be known."

Bass sought something to throw at Paddock. When he couldn't find anything, he squatted there and growled curses at his young partner while he finished getting the second legging and the breechclout on behind the privacy of the blanket.

"What's all the durned racket?" Kinkead said as he shoved open the wooden door to the small hut.

Rosa ducked under his arm and came into the room, carrying a tray covered with dishes, each piled high with sweet biscuits called *biscoches*. A small crock of honey was stuffed in the midst of the hard, porous treats. Paddock pulled a low table to the center of the room and Rosa set the tray down, then stepped out of Mateo's way.

Kinkead balanced another small tray of treats in his right hand. Suspended from his left hand was the bail of a huge coffee pot, pocked and blackened over many years of fire boiling. On the fingers of that same hand hung tin mugs. Mateo set the pot down on the low table and distributed the cups. Waits-by-the-Water poured and soon everyone was biting into the hard, cookielike treats, including Joshua who sucked and gummed his morning sweet.

They sat on the hard-packed floor, amid a profusion of colorful Navajo rugs which would soon be rolled up and placed against the wall, after use in place of chairs or bedding for the night.

Bass turned back to the small group gathered at the table, blowing across his mug of hot coffee, after he'd thrown some cedar and pinon limbs atop the coals of last night's fire. Built into a corner of the front room of the hut was a triangular adobe fireplace which soon filled the whole house with that fragrant warmth peculiar to a winter morning. Sunshine poured like thick honey through the frosted mica windowpanes.

Over the past several days since their arrival in Taos, they had been busy. The first night at Kinkead's place had been grand. Rosa seemed to take a quiet delight in the two women, and continually fussed over the infant. After the extravagant spread placed before them that evening, the men had adjourned to the main room of the house and stoked up the fire in the corner fireplace. Mateo's dwelling surrounded a center patio, an enclosed courtyard. Every room in the house opened onto this small patio where Rosa had another oven.

The four American men had settled down onto the thick woven Navajo rugs and filled their pipes with tobacco brought in from Missouri by Santa Fe Trail

135

traders. Bass had leaned back and relaxed, feeling some of the aches from the long journey melt away from his body.

The walls about him were adobe, covered with gypsum, a substance which rubbed off easily on a person, so most of the walls in Kinkead's house were covered to the height of a person's shoulder with bright calicos. Here in the main room of this home the hard-packed earthen floor was covered with a coarse domestic fabric known as *gerga* which served the purpose of a light carpeting.

Kinkead had asked his old friend what the two partners were going to do for the winter. Bass had described their plan to spend the cold, snowy months in Taos, then retrace their steps back to the Bayou Salade for the spring hunt before rendezvous farther north.

Bass had asked Mateo if he knew where they could find a vacant place in Taos to lay over for the winter. Kinkead had stated that he did know of such a place, but that the cost might be dear, even for as rich a trapper as Titus Bass.

"Just how—dear?" Scratch had asked.

"They'll be expecting you to pitch in and help with the chores," Mateo had answered.

"That's only natural," Bass had replied. "What else are they asking?"

"You should bring in game to add to their larder."

"That ain't nothin' onreasonable," Bass had said. "What else do they want? An' just who the hell are these folks?"

"What they want from you," Kinkead had smiled as he pulled the pipe stem from his lips, "is for the lot of you to enjoy the winter with 'em, Christmas and all, as their guests. Rosa and me are the ones doing the asking."

"Spend the winter—right here?" Bass gulped.

"Right here with you and Rosa?" Paddock had echoed.

"That's what we've decided already this evening. Tell us now, you'll accept?"

Scratch studied Paddock's smiling face, then turned back to Kinkead. "I s'pose it wouldn't do any good to go ask them women 'bout this?"

"You can see well enough for yourself." Rowland swept an arm toward the doorway where silently stood his wife, along with the two other Indian women, between them little Rosa cradling Joshua in her arms. All three faces wore the same rosy smile and bright, expectant sparkle in their eyes.

Bass realized he was outnumbered again. "Ain't no use at times. Looks like you've got vis'tors for the holidays."

There was a general rejoicing as the women shrieked and hugged Rosa and each other, dancing around the rotund woman. Rowland's wife came over and embraced the trapper. Paddock stood and did a little jig right on the spot, soon joined by Mateo before the fireplace. The two men were quite a spectacle, arm in arm, spinning first this way, then whirling that way. John Rowland whistled a tune while Bass clapped his hands in time with their impromptu mountain stomp. Above it all little Joshua squealed and giggled his own approval of all the fun.

Thus began a routine those first few days that started before dawn with a cold, loping walk from the small house to the main dwelling where Rosa always had coffee ready, along with some tortillas and beans. After getting something in

136

their bellies, Bass and Josiah slipped back into the pre-dawn cold to feed the many horses, cut some animals out into the fields where they would be picketed for the day. After the ponies were fed and their pack sores tended, the men would slip back inside for another quick cup of coffee just after the sun came up. Here they would be joined by Mateo and plans for the day's activities were discussed.

Paddock and Bass once again returned to the small building out back where they untied all the bales of beaver so the pelts could air. Each and every plew was checked carefully for insect and vermin damage, dusted, then repacked once more. There was always chopping wood or hunting in the surrounding hills to take up what was left of the afternoons. By the fifth day Mateo had his fellow trappers join him in planning another, larger corral south of the big house. It was there Kinkead told them they would keep their impressive herd of stolen horses.

Bass wrinkled his nose at the suggestion that his horses were stolen. He always shouted that they had come by the ponies fair and square, according to mountain law in the Bayou Salade. He told Mateo they had tried to talk the Arapahos out of the horses for a fair price, but the warriors had wanted nothing more in trade but the white men's scalps.

"It come down to tradin' or fightin'," he told Kinkead with a grin.

"Them Arapahos ain't the kind that'll ever forget," Mateo sighed when he got serious one afternoon. "They can trouble a man across a big chunk of territory. They ain't the kind never to forget, Titus."

Bass studied his old friend's eyes, then reached up to tap the back of his head where the scalp was tied down over the baldspot on his skull. "I ain't the kind what never forgets neither. An' I ain't never give a thought to forgivin'."

"You've set your mind to it?" Kinkead wiped his brow.

"I cain't have no Injuns runnin' me outta the mountains now, can I?" Scratch inquired.

Mateo understood immediately. "Man finds himself a place to make his stand, plant his feet—"

"He'll put up with a lot so folks'll let him be," Titus finished.

Kinkead did understand. He had found his place, he was making his stand here in the autumn of his life. He knew what it meant to finally find that one thing for which Bass was still searching. He only hoped his friend from over the years one day would find that peace and contentment he had found here in the Taos valley.

Scratch was happy enough right now. This morning around the little table in their adobe hut, watching his wife and friends chatter happily about him, Titus found a mellow glow spread within him. It was close enough to contentment for the time. He studied them all, feeling as a stranger here in their midst, not one of them. It was nothing any of them had done. It was something Scratch had to work out on his own. Feeling distant, apart, not belonging here with the life of these people.

"You listening?" Mateo inquired. "Scratch, where'd you wander off to? I've been calling your name."

Scratch snapped his head around. "I—I wasn't listenin'."

137

"I know," Paddock agreed. "We've been trying to get your attention."

Bass shook his head, the cobwebs of reverie still thick. "What was it you was sayin'?"

"We were talking about Christmas, Scratch."

Bass turned to Kinkead. "Christmas?" It had been so long since he'd allowed himself to think about Christmas. There was something childlike and magic about the season that tinkled like a bell inside him, somewhere distant, somewhere long ago. Almost too faint to be heard.

"I haven't had a Christmas celebration in—" Paddock counted off the years on his fingers. " '31—'32—this'll make it three Christmases."

Scratch squinted hard, staring into his coffee mug. "Christmas," he sighed wistfully. "Been so—so long." He looked up to find them all staring his way.

"How long, old friend?" Mateo asked.

"I—I don't remember," he answered slowly, sadness creasing his leathery face.

"You've been in the mountains for—better than ten years, hasn't it been?" Mateo continued.

"Ten years? Ten years. Comin' up on ten years now." His voice sounded distant, like the wail of a river steamboat whistle crying out from somewhere in the night.

"Christmas is such a happy time 'round Taos," Mateo said.

"I ain't had a Christmas in—long before the ten years," Titus mumbled.

"There are native holiday celebrations and all the people in Taos decorate the outside of their homes with pinon branches tied up with red bows. Ahh, it is something to enjoy for long after."

"We'll celebrate Christmas in style, Mateo," Josiah said with a wide smile. "Scratch, how does that sound?"

"Sounds real good, son," Bass finally answered, his mind elsewhere. "When is Christmas? How far off?"

"It's only two weeks away," Mateo smiled.

"Then, New Year's isn't far behind," Scratch said.

"There's a fandango this year on New Year's Eve, old friend," Mateo said. "We'll all go together. Been some time since you stomped away the whole night, ain't it, child?"

"That—that fandango on New Year's Eve—it be my birthday," Scratch said wistfully.

"I didn't know that," Mateo said.

"I didn't either," Josiah declared. "You never said when your birthday was, Scratch."

"So, New Year's Eve is your birthday," Mateo said.

"Nawww, not 'sactly. New Year's Day more proper," Bass answered.

"We'll help the New Year roar in by celebrating your birthday, then."

Titus looked at Kinkead. "What—what year is it—the year it's gonna be?"

"Why—1834, Scratch," Kinkead answered. "Tough, ain't it, to keep track in the mountains?"

"Yeah."

"How old's that make you?" Paddock asked.

"My folks told me I was born in '94," Titus said. "How old's that make me now?"

"You're going to be forty, Scratch," Paddock said with a warm smile.

"Just a pup," Mateo said as he reached out and slapped Scratch on the thigh. "Young'un like you'll always be a kid to me."

"Never thought no one could get as old as you." Scratch nudged Kinkead with the toe of a moccasin.

"You watch yourself, you young long-eared hawg. Gotta be showin' respect for your elders."

"A man starts losing some of his youth in the mountains," Scratch said quietly. "Along with it, he can lose some of what it takes for him to survive in them mountains."

"Yes," Mateo said wistfully. "You still hear all right?"

"Sure do," Bass answered firmly.

"Not all the time," Paddock added.

"What do you mean by that?" Scratch demanded.

"Just what I said, Scratch. You don't hear so good all the time."

"I hear just fine," Bass pouted. "Sometimes—I don't hear so good when folks is sayin' somethin' I don't wanna listen to. That's all."

Mateo glanced over at Paddock. "How's his eyes, Josiah?"

"I suppose they're all right," Paddock said. "I can't say I've seen his eyes fail him."

"An' you ain't never gonna," Scratch said.

"Man needs both out in the mountains," Mateo said. "Eyes and ears working full time. Old friend, I finally had to own up to the fact that I was getting on in years. Had to own up to the fact that things didn't work as well as they used to when I was Josiah's age."

"Josiah ain't got nothin' on me," Scratch smiled. "I can still whip 'im any way he cares to cut the mustard."

"And you can still hear all right?" Mateo asked gently.

"I hear all I wanna hear. Nothin' else."

"And your eyes? They're not giving you any problems?" Mateo asked, leaning forward.

"When I don't strain 'em none," Bass lied. "They get a lil' tired now and again, but they still see clear as a bell and twice as far as Paddock's."

Josiah stood up and slapped Titus on the shoulder. "Don't worry, old man," he laughed. "We'll see your fortieth birthday in together."

"Wagh!" Kinkead agreed. "We'll make it a fandango they'll not soon forget here in Taos."

"We'll make it a real special party for you," Josiah added.

Bass raised his coffee mug in a toast. "Here's to 1834. An' to seein' it in with old, old friends."

"With old friends," Paddock echoed.

"To old friends!" Kinkead agreed.

"Yes—with my old, old friends," Bass repeated, smiling over the lip of his mug.

11 THE DAYS BEGAN to flood past, in an ever-quickening rush toward Christmas and the celebration of the New Year. His sweet, smokey, youthful memories of his childhood days rode high in Scratch's mind when he entered the plaza and felt the gaiety of the shoppers. Watching the preparations for the holidays—the festive decorations the Taosenos hung both inside their homes and out, the colorful pageants on the streets always winding their way to the Cathedral, the bright anticipation registered on everyone's face —meant a lot to Titus Bass.

He enjoyed being swept up in the rush toward this happiest of holidays. He remembered Christmas as a time when his family gathered merrily for a rare day of rest, to bask in the glow of their communal love. They would exchange little gifts, from each family member to the others, and then the feast. What a feast it was, he remembered. Enough now to make his mouth water and pucker in anticipation—over all these miles, across all these years.

With Christmas so close at hand, could his birthday be far behind? It had been a long time since he had allowed himself the luxury of thinking about a birthday. It wasn't so bad growing old after all, when there were others who could help you celebrate that annual event. Such a long time since he had done anything more than wonder if it were getting close to Christmas or his birthday—an empty, cold wondering during those long winter-locked nights, in a cold camp made all the colder without family or friends to cheer a man on a special day. So many years that Titus Bass desperately wanted this coming New Year's to be all the more special for him, for his family, for his friends here in Taos—special enough to make up for all the birthdays slipped by without celebration, without notice, without the warmth of others.

There was a light tensing in the air as the holiday approached. The religious festival was so much a part of life in the Mexican provinces. There was little else to do but live, work and die. When the chance for a celebration, a festival, a fandango or holiday came along, it was joined with fevered gusto. So it was that the music and processions occurred almost every day now as the days of Christmas drew near.

Little children carried their tallow candles, parading through the snowy, muddy streets where the horses and mules joined in song with their own brays and whinnies. Always the village priest headed the processions, behind him others who carried the platforms bearing the crude effigies of the Madonna,

140

Joseph, and the infant Christ child lying in a corn crib. All activity on the streets or in the main plaza would grind to a halt while the procession passed by. The crowd joined in singing their religious appeals for the sacred birth day and its coming. All bowed as the black-robed priest trudged by, carrying the large, wooden cross before him, its effigy of the wounded, dying Christ nailed and sacrificed upon the crossed timbers. After that moment of prayerful reflection upon the true reason for Christ's entry into this world hundreds of years before, the Taosenos were free to clap and sing and revel with that happiness associated with the child's birth.

These simple, happy people had been celebrating life itself longer than any one man could remember. Far back into the gray areas of any memory, back to a time when the first Spanish settlers had come to this valley, an annual tradition itself had been born. In late July or early August the great Taos fair had always been held. Drawn like moths to the flame, the traders of different colors flew into the high valley nestled beneath the chilly, dark peaks of the Sangre de Cristos, that valley of green, verdant meadows watered with icy, snow melt streams. To Taos came the traders and merchants out of those Spanish provinces to the south. Packed aboard the *carretas* piled high were the treasures of Chihuahua. Mexican traders laid out their wares brought all the way from Spain, bright tin objects to dazzle the eye along with the large silver coin pieces so valued as ornaments by those visiting Indians who used the metal currency to bedeck themselves in a grand fashion. Up from the city of the pass, El Paso, came the traders with carts groaning under the earthen jars sloshing full of a rich, heady wine judged to equal any Spanish variety. The richest Pass brandy made the customer all the more warmly willing to part with his own money or trade goods.

From the outlying provinces of New Spain came those hundreds of traders who sought the riches afforded at these annual fairs. While one might bring horses to trade, another would bring edged weapons, knives and short swords, or trinkets and bracelets and rings. Always a colorful marketplace, the economic tension of the annual fair increased as tribe after rival tribe entered the valley to trade.

Here to the land of the Pueblo dwellers came those warring groups—Arapaho, Comanche, Kiowa, Navajo, Apache, Pawnee, Ute and others. Hostilities suspended for a few days of merriment and bartering, the enemies contented themselves with growling and trading, threatening and selling their wares. Each of them held to a temporary truce even during the bloodiest of inter-tribal wars. Each knew they could return to the killing soon enough. After a few days of pleasure—the annual affair came but once a year.

The Indians brought their pelts: huge, black buffalo robes; fine, supple, silk-like chamois; and slaves. Human misery was the primary staple of the Indian trade. Captives stolen, kidnapped during raids on neighboring rival tribes, or from the New Mexicans themselves. The suspicious Indian traders bartered away their human currency for trinkets, blankets, metalware and weapons— always the staple of trade with primitive peoples at any time in history, at any place around the globe. And always there was the strong drink, the water lit with fire that made a man act as if he were a touched-by-the-moon being. They always traded for the brandy and wine, some for the stronger, headier Taos lightning, that pale, mule strong blending of spirits distilled from wheat and corn. *Aguardiente*—the drink favored by Indian and mountain trapper alike.

As the days sped toward Christ's birthday, the weather finally cleared. Each morning burst bright under the high light, saffron spread over the snow-iced valley. While still cold, the welcome sun warmed a person's skin enough that he could venture out to celebrate the coming holiday in comfort. Many men spent much of their winter day sitting propped lazily against the sunny wall of some house or shop in the great plaza. Draped in multicolored Navajo blankets or striped sarapes, the older men would gossip, nap, and gossip some more while consuming one after another of their cornhusk cigarillos. Children who sat long enough with the older ones were recruited to pick lice off the old men. Up and down the narrow streets passed the women returning from springs outside of town, balancing earthen jars on their heads or shoulders with Old Testament grace.

These were days filled with gay, sprightly music performed by the same blending of instruments that served church service and fandango alike. Even at funerals for a small child, the band would play the happy tunes for, after all, the deceased had gone on to eternal grace before he or she had been corrupted by a temporal and most evil world. This was a lazy time of gambling and games of chance, cock fights and horse races.

Dashing young *caballeros* bedecked in their tight, black-dyed leather pants and short waisted jackets dripping with silver ornaments goaded one another into their games of skill and chance. There was always the game of *El Gallo*, the sport wherein a horseman rode at full tilt down the street to scoop up a shrieking, terrified rooster which had been buried up to its neck in the sandy soil. Or, there was a variation called *El Correr el Gallo*, requiring more skill and dexterity. A cock or hen was tied by its feet to some limb of a nearby tree so the bird would hang just within the reach of a man on horseback. The squawking head was then well greased with lard so that it would easily slip from a man's fingers. Then it was up to the challengers to race beneath the shrieking bird and tear it from its noose in the tree. If one of the young *caballeros* was successful, he would tear off with the others in hot pursuit, everyone attempting to capture the cock, during which struggle the bird would be literally torn to pieces. Finally, there was *El Coleo*, a headier game for the more stout of heart. The dashing *vaquero* vied with others to seize a fleeing bull by the tail and bring it to the ground with a quick flip of the beast's tail.

The tempo and religious fervor of these celebrations picked up as the days drew closer and closer to Christmas. In the midst of the great plaza among the many burros and mules, goats and pigs, the native inhabitants of the Pueblos were caught up in excitement of the approaching holiday. Many of the Indians accepted Christianity in grand ceremonies on the Cathedral steps, led by the black-robed priest. The Pueblo dwellers accepted the image of the man nailed to the tree timbers without abandoning their own ancient beliefs, just as surely as they had come to accept the encroachment of the Spanish in their valley while still grinding corn between porous stones as had their ancestors centuries before.

Bass would always enjoy the plaza whenever he journeyed into town. Besides the vivid, colorful sights, there were so many new and foreign sounds for the ear to record. And the smells—oh, those aromas mingling in a rainbow of hunger-producing fragrances. Huge kettles of *chile colorado* simmered over fiery braziers, the aroma of which was enough by itself to burn a man's mouth and make his eyes bubble with tears. Women slapped and swung sticks at the dogs which constantly made forays into the square through the stacks of goat's milk cheese heaped in tall pyramids. There was little fruit to speak of most of the time—few apples, peaches, apricots or grapes. Yet such extravagance was never missed. With a ready abundance of corn and wheat, the bounty of fresh fruit was not missed in the least.

Two principal dishes of the Taosenos were made from corn. The first was *atole*, essentially a thin gruel a woman made by stirring corn flour into boiling milk or water. This hearty, pasty soup was eaten so generally that it had come to be known as *el cafe de los Mexicanos*. Likewise, there were always stacks of tortillas available, made by boiling corn in water mixed with a little lime, then removing the hulls from the cob, and pounding and grinding the soaked kernals into a sodden paste on a *metate*. Next the women rolled the semi-solid mass out flat between their palms, creating a thin crepe with continued patting and then baked the delicious cakes upon a metal sheet called a *comal*, which they placed over a fire. Stacks of the tortillas disappeared with every meal as they became edible spoons that could be used for scooping up *frijoles* or the fiery *chile colorado*.

Scratch marvelled at the bustling, buzzing activity about him, people flitting here and there around the plaza, from shop to shop, from one vendor's stall to another. As poor as they might be, the Taosenos did not seem to regret their lot. Here they were not guarded at all about their meager purchases, not hoarding what little currency they had to barter. Instead, they accepted and moved on, making the best of what little had been dealt them. The old trapper could understand. To keep some of his sanity, a man had to push a lot of his regrets aside, live without them. Regrets could drive him to being touched-by-the-moon.

He smiled, cracking one side of his bearded face, as he leaned against a vendor's stall. The shrill, barking come-ons rang back and forth across the muddied plaza dotted here and there with the steamy droppings of burros, mules, horses, sheep and pigs alike. A blending, raucous chorus of noise that swelled around him. Like Bass, these people looked content with their lot in life. Much happier than many an American back east in the settlements of those United States. Always stretching, always reaching out for something more, that was the American trader's way. Those who carted trade goods into Taos and Santa Fe by the wagonload wanted it all. So it was their kind were often bewildered by the Mexican people.

The traders had always come in their creaking, dried-axle carts and wagons, bowed by trade goods guaranteed to make the foreign eye sparkle and lust. Then they left with their gold specie tied up in rawhide bags and lit out for the settlements to finance another trip. Yet so many of those Americans refused, perhaps were unable, to understand the Mexican people whom they regarded at a lower station in life.

When a man jumped off from the west bank of the great, muddy Missouri River, he crossed into the painful expanse of the great plains country. Then he traveled through a transition zone, a land where he bid farewell to both the best and the worst of civilization, heading for a land where the life lived and those peoples who lived it did not at all belong in the 19th century. A man had to accept that he was leaving the security of his Occidental world and traveling back into those lost ages of the past where Indian and Spanish cultures bubbled and boiled against one another as they had for centuries, the Indian way of life surviving still, despite all attempts to amalgamate it.

Instead, the American trader entered a world which often irritated and befuddled him. He entered a society where the people lived in such squalid conditions, whether Pueblo Indian or Mexican *pelado*. Their very floors were of dirt, they scratched their existence out of the earth, and seemed to do so without complaint. They were generally very ignorant in that manner in which a primitive people remains ignorant during the initial onslaught of a conflicting civilization. And the trader could not reason why the Taosenos remained happy. Still they came to Taos as traders had always come for centuries unknown to lands of foreign, primitive peoples, taking what treasures they could carry on horseback or piled high in their wagons or deep in the holds of their sea-going ships. Traders had always come to visit the unwashed, always offering riches to a poor people.

Riches in Mexico meant there were actually four pesos traded in the New Mexican economy. The standard of exchange began with the *peso de la tierra*, or the "land dollar," sometimes called the "adobe dollar," and worth only about two *reales* or about twenty-five cents. Next came the *peso de antiguo*, or "old dollar," worth about twice as much, fifty cents. The third was the *peso de projecto*, worth about six *reales* or seventy-five cents. Finally came the *peso de plata* or the "silver peso" that Bass always demanded in payment for his trades. It was worth eight *reales* or one American dollar. The Indians, ignorant of the vagaries of exchange, along with the newcomer to Mexico, were often bilked since they knew nothing of the differences in the four *pesos*. To most new traders, a peso was a peso. Not so in Mexico.

Bass turned away from the vendor's stall and stuffed his small bag of currency deep into his shooting pouch. The little bag felt good in his hand as he flushed with the feeling of being a little boy sent off to market by his mother—in his hands a few coins with which to purchase some household necessity along with a treasured piece of hard candy.

He had just traded off some of his poorer beaver pelts so that he would have some hard money to buy some food for Rosa and Mateo, to help replace what his small party had eaten since their arrival in Taos. He also wanted to buy each of his friends and his wife a small bauble for Christmas.

144

The young, nervous Mexican-Indian vendor had been minding the store for his employer when Bass had slogged up with his two small bundles of pelts. There had been some stifled, self-conscious dickering, but essentially the clerk had told the white trapper that his American boss was away on business to Santa Fe and would not be returning for several days after Christmas. If the trapper wished to haggle for a better price on the furs, he might want to wait until his boss had returned from Santa Fe.

Bass had quickly refused that offer, accepting the low price for the poor grade pelts. He did not want to bother with waiting right now. The clerk had seemed greatly relieved as he had stuffed the pelts in hiding below the counter. Time enough to sit down and haggle with this American shopkeeper later when he wanted to trade in his better grade plews. Right now all Bass wanted was a little spending money for the victuals he needed, and what little gifts he wanted to buy for the others.

With all the official concern over American trappers and their beaver, Bass thought it understandable that this young fellow was nervous. He acted a little rigid trading furs here in the plaza, under the glare of a midday sun where all could see. Scratch glanced back at the nervous clerk. "You tell that boss man of your'n, I'll be back to chew a long stick with him. Tell him to be ready to haggle like he's never done afore."

Bass winked and smiled at the young clerk before he stepped off into the crowds milling through the frosty, steamy plaza.

The boy had said his boss man's name was Mr. Hiram, and knew him as nothing more. He was American and had been here in Taos, after some work in Santa Fe, for many years.

How many?

The boy was not sure, but it seemed as if the boss man Hiram had been in Taos now for some seven or eight years. Why, the clerk had asked.

Bass fingered the coins in the small leather pouch once more.

"Why? Oh, I knew a man once by the name of Hiram as I can remember it. But, he was a trapper—not a trader."

And he would be an old man by now. Ten years' worth of aging.

The boy's eyes had stared intently, measuring Titus. He said no more to the American trapper.

It couldn't be. Scratch had gone on once his business was concluded. The Hiram he remembered was a trapper, not a trader. And he weren't all that good at being a trapper neither. Probably wouldn't make a go of it as a trader. Maybeso.

With a final reminder for the youth to inform his employer that an American trapper would return for some hard trading, Scratch had plodded off across the wintry square.

Time enough for the serious trading later. What he wanted to do right now was to spend money—frivolously, gloriously, exuberantly. Spend it on those he loved. That was the joy in this late morning excursion. He drank deeply of the joy in it, the early winter air's chilling bite at his lungs, the frost accumulating on his

145

moustache, the eye-startling brightness of snow and whitewashed adobe buildings alike; for the ears a rainbow of sounds through which a man had difficulty
picking out but one noise. Time enough later for hard business.

Bass stopped near the middle of the plaza, admiring the hard boned mules
hitched to a wagon. Sturdy, peak-eared, the mules reminded him of his dear
Hannah. He and his mule had been together so long, he doubted he could ever
replace her memory with another. It was only lately that the old trapper had
been able to remember the mule without some hurt gnawing at him.

With a deep sigh, Bass moved on to purchase trinkets for his friends.

"FIFTY. And not a peso more," Kinkead told the *hacienda* owner.

The rich land owner shifted his gaze to his foreman, then back again to Mateo.
His eyes closed, then reopened, his way of saying he had refused Kinkead's offer.

"Give him the sixty." Paddock's English sounded foreign in the midst of the
stalls in the Mexican barn. The wealthy land owner had not taken much interest
in the bargaining, choosing instead to counter every offer for the animal Josiah
wanted.

"Excuse us, Don Armijo," Kinkead said. "We're going to think this over." He
grabbed Paddock's arm and guided him outside the big barn.

"No, you're not going to give him sixty for that mule," said Mateo in a loud
whisper. "You'd ruin my reputation."

"What?" replied Paddock.

"I got a reputation around these parts for being a tough, hard-nosed trader,"
Kinkead said. "I couldn't let it get around I gave in to Don Armijo's price. I'd
never live it down."

"I'm gonna get that mule, one price or another," Josiah said. "I just wanted to
find out what the old man's bottom dollar was."

"We should have done our bargaining the way the Don wanted us to."

Paddock chewed on the piece of straw he'd picked up in the barn. He had
wanted to dicker for the animal here in the morning chill of the barn, rather than
accept the Don's offer of negotiating over brandy and pipes in the library of the
big house.

"I'm not going to bargain with him on his ground," Josiah replied firmly.

"I'm saying Don Armijo has taken grave offense that you did not accept his
offer to talk over the sale in his house, after he'd offered you his hospitality. He's
being hard-nosed now."

Paddock chuckled. "He sounds just like some Injun chief who's offered to
have me sit down to dinner and I'm supposed to be glad he's offered me his
ugly, fat daughter in marriage because he gave me some greasy puppy dog
to eat."

"You're right," Kinkead said, "but we're not payin' that much."

"But I'll gladly pay the price," Josiah objected.

"Let me handle it," Mateo countered, as the two men strolled back into the
barn. "Thank you for your time, Don Armijo, but we've decided to look elsewhere. C'mon, son." He tossed a quick wave of farewell to Don Armijo and the

tall, graying ranch foreman, then headed for the huge doors at the east end of the barn where the yellow light of morning spread across the ground.

"Senores!"

"Keep walking, Josiah," Mateo whispered, pressing the words out from between clenched teeth.

"SENORES! Por favor." The Don's voice cut across the cool shadows.

"You don't wanna hear what he's got to say?" Josiah asked.

"Shuddup and keep walking." Kinkead stepped into the yellow light at the barn doors.

"Sixty pesos, senores! Sixty pesos."

The two Americans stopped and turned back to face Don Armijo.

"Sixty," Kinkead said matter of factly.

"Sixty, senor," Armijo replied with a nod.

Mateo sucked on a bad tooth for a long moment, then shrugged his shoulders as if resigned to leave. He knew he'd won. He looked across the sun-streaked barn at the Don.

"Fifty—and the saddle and spurs," he offered.

"Fifty buys you the animal alone," Armijo eventually replied.

"Then we are not buying." Again Mateo turned into the light.

"Fifty, Senor Mateo!" Armijo said.

"And the old saddle and the spurs?" Mateo watched Armijo suck at the air. He knew the Don didn't need the American's fifty pesos any more than any other wealthy land owner did. But he knew Armijo didn't want the fifty pesos going into any other pocket but his own. That was the secret to negotiating with Don Armijo. A little envy, a little greed, and the trade could be consummated. "Well?"

"Si. Si," the land owner replied in resignation. "The animal for fifty—and—the saddle with the old spurs."

Kinkead slapped Paddock on the back as the two of them strode back into the interior of the large barn. "My reputation is still in one piece," he grinned.

"Damn your reputation," Josiah grumbled. "I almost lost that animal because of your damned reputation."

Paddock shook hands with Armijo. It was agreed that the mule, saddle and spurs, would remain at Don Armijo's for the few days left until the New Year. Josiah would come to fetch her on the day of New Year's Eve. And then he planned to hide the mule down in the cottonwoods by the stream close to Mateo's house until it was time to present the birthday gift to his friend, Titus Bass.

It would be something to see the look in the old man's eyes. Something really special for the man's fortieth birthday. Not many a man out here could count that high, much less boast he had that many rings.

Paddock ran his hand once more over the high pommeled saddle hung with live oak stirrups and inlaid with a modest display of silver. The matching spurs were tied to latigo saddle thongs, themselves of silver with engraved rowels five inches in diameter. The gift would make the old trapper speechless. And that took some doing.

A band of American traders had returned to St. Louis in October of 1823 with some 400 "jacks, jennies and mules." This first band or cavvyyard of the four-legged treasure proved to be the beginning of the famous Missouri Mule. The animal was already abundant all across New Mexico, but not so in the east. It was for this reason that most traders' caravans departed Missouri pulled by teams of oxen, making their return trip under the power of mules. This switch in animals had first occurred under the mother of necessity because the oxen which had just completed their journey southwest over the Santa Fe Trail were in no condition for a return trip. The American businessmen at first believed they were having to settle for something less when they accepted strings of mules known as *muladas* to pull the wagons back home. After all, weren't oxen bigger, definitely stronger than a mule?

It took but a single return trip for traders to accept and welcome the mule for its advantages. The oxen were not as adaptable to the realities of trail conditions as were mules, the former refusing to eat either the tall buffalo grass or grama grass which was the only forage of any sort along the extent of the Arkansas River. While the mule may not have exactly relished the favorite grass of the plains buffalo, they could and did survive on it. Another major problem with oxen remained their hoofs. The huge oxen developed tender, split hoofs at times on the long, dry trek, on which occasions the traders would have to wrap those bleeding hoofs in raw buffalo hide.

Paddock turned from admiring the saddle and matching spurs. He nodded once more to Don Armijo and pulled out the pouch of silver pesos from the woven sash at his waist.

One at a time, Paddock plopped the coins into Don Armijo's outstretched palm, each singular coin clinked off with the Don's count in Spanish, Josiah's echo in English. Paddock stuffed the nearly emptied pouch in his sash, then stuck out his hand to the foreman.

"Josiah Paddock, sir."

"Jesus Sylvestre Cordero." The Mexican shook the offered hand with a quick, snappy bow. "Pleased to meet." He spoke in good English.

Paddock looked over at Mateo, surprised. "Thought you said these fellas don't speak any English."

Kinkead was baffled. "Armijo doesn't know any English." He shugged.

"That is correct, sirs," Cordero offered politely. "I, however, have learned quite a bit of your American speech."

"So—you knew all the time what we was saying to each other?" Josiah inquired.

"Most of what you say, yes," he answered.

"I'll be damned!" Kinkead muttered. "And you still let Don Armijo here go on with the trade?"

"Si—ah, yes," he nodded with a quick look at his employer who could not understand English. "Of course I would not have allowed him to be hurt in the matter."

"Of course," Mateo nodded, baffled by the surprise.

"However," Cordero continued, "the Don wants your money as badly as you wish to give it to him. That always makes for a fair and just trade."

They all laughed, even joined by Don Armijo himself.

Jesus leaned back against the boards enclosing the mule's stall and removed from his vest pocket a corn shuck already cut to its proper length for a cigarillo and popularly known as a *hoja*. From the opposite vest pocket he took out his *guagito*, a small tobacco flask, from which he removed pinches of the already crumbled *ponche*, his dried tobacco leaf. The foreman deftly rolled it into shape, then offered it first to his guests who both refused. Don Armijo accepted the offered cigarillo while Cordero quickly made another for himself. From his somewhat baggy pantaloons pocket he took a packet containing flint and steel with which he expertly lit both cigarillos. The Mexicans' smoke curled away to the ceiling of the huge barn as Josiah entered the mule's stall.

The dun mule slowly raised her head from a pile of shucks and dried corn to look the American trapper over with eyes bigger than silver dollars. It was an intimidating stare.

Kinkead came to the stall railing and handed Paddock the rawhide hackamore.

"You know mules?" Mateo asked doubtfully. "Know where to put this?"

"I know mules enough to know right where I'd like to put it!"

They both had their laugh before Josiah added, "I spent enough time around Scratch's old Hannah before—before she was killed—enough time to figure I know enough to get the damned critter for Scratch. From there on out it's his Jenny. He can do with her what he likes."

"You know this critter ain't gonna lead with a hackamore around the neck like a pony, don't you?" Kinkead propped a foot up on the bottom railing and leaned down against the top bar.

Josiah nodded. "Found that out real quick. First time I was wrangling the horses for Bass, not but a few days after I met up with him—that ol' nigger sat there and watched me fight with Hannah like it was the funniest thing he'd ever get to be witness to again in his life. Yep, Mateo—I learned a lot from that old renegade."

Paddock slipped a running noose over the mule's nose, secured it and turned to leave the barn. The gray colored dun Jenny stepped lively from the stall as if more than ready to be on her way with the young trapper. They were in the center of the huge adobe barn when the stall door slapped shut with a loud crack.

"Ohhh, you should not have done that," Cordero declared.

The mule stopped immediately, hoofs kicking up little clouds of dust from the hardened dirt floor.

"Shouldn't have done what?" Josiah turned to give a yank on the rawhide hackamore lashed about the mule's nose.

"The loud noise," Cordero smiled.

"T-this is great." the young trapper gritted as he leaned back against the hackamore. The mule leaned back against him. "Now you choose to tell me I just bought the old man a mule that don't like loud noises."

"You did not ask." Cordero laughed along with Kinkead and Armijo.

149

"Just beautiful!"

The mule held her neck as stiff as possible against the trapper who was elongating it with every tug and pull. He dug in his feet to yank against her brutish strength. She answered by planting her feet in front of her and pushing backwards against his every move. Even though her wide eyeballs owled and popped with the strain, she still stood patient through it all. Much more patient than Paddock ever hoped to be.

Josiah eased up on the rope. The mule straightened. He gave a quick tug to set her in forward motion. The Jenny stiffened against him. He relaxed again.

"W-we ain't going anyplace like this," Josiah husked in an exhausted whisper.

"What's the answer?" Kinkead turned toward Cordero and Armijo.

"A bullet would be a fitting reward, no?" Paddock grinned.

"As much as you might wish it," Cordero said as he approached Josiah and the mule, "that would be a shameful thing. This animal will reward you many times over with her grace and willingness to serve."

"It would be reward enough if she'd show me what she's made of, all this grace and—and her willingness to serve."

"Senor." Cordero stepped up to take the rawhide hackamore from Josiah.

The Mexican foreman stepped up to the mule, face on, and spoke to her with soft, gently whispered words. As he spoke he also soothed by rubbing her forehead between her eyes and ears. It was but moments before the animal responded, her eyes drooping to show she was becoming relaxed, her ears twitching contentedly to show she enjoyed the attention. After a few moments of his stroking, Cordero gently tugged on the halter and set off with the mule. He walked with her to the huge doors where the sunlight splashed in waves of winter brilliance. Cordero turned and wheeled, then returned to stand before the Americans.

"Senores," he indicated the animal with an outstretched arm, "there you have the little angel. With a little love and care from her master to be, she will be a faithful servant."

Paddock shook his head warily. "I don't know. Don't know if I can trust a mule. The one he had before was a real lady. This one still got a lot of fire in her, maybe more than a match for the old man."

"She is young yet," Cordero coaxed.

"I'm still not sure." Paddock shook his head and studied the Jenny.

"We both wish to be fair with you." Jesus indicated Don Armijo with a simple gesture. "It is not our wish that you would have an animal you do not want."

He waited for Josiah to nod in agreement. Then the foreman continued. "We will work with the mule until it comes time for you to pick her up at New Year's. Then, if this old man does not like his gift after a few days, be assured the Don will return your money for the mule, saddle and spurs. Nothing could be more fair than that, *si?*"

"Nothing more fair than that," Josiah nodded along with Kinkead. "Get my money back if the old renegade doesn't take to her?"

Jesus nodded once more in answer.

"I feel a whole lot better about the whole thing now." Paddock stuck out his hand toward Cordero, then again to Don Armijo.

Paddock and Mateo turned to walk away, bidding farewell.

"We'll be coming back on the day of New Year's Eve," Mateo reminded in Mexican, then repeated himself in self-conscious English.

"Will you both be coming to the fandango set for that evening? To welcome in the New Year?" Cordero inquired with a wide smile.

"We have heard it will be here in your boss's *sala*," Mateo declared.

"*Si*, Don Armijo's," Cordero nodded once toward his employer. "It is our honor to welcome in the New Year with friends celebrating in this house." He indicated with a gesture back toward the main *hacienda*.

Mateo glanced at Paddock. "We were planning on attending. After all, it is old man Bass's birthday. New Year's."

"A good reason for twice the celebration!" Cordero was enthused.

"One fandango is quite enough for the likes of an old *vaquero* like me." Kinkead offered. "Twice the fun just might kill me."

"All will be there." Jesus commented with excitement. "From the poorest of field help," he indicated the Indian slaves resting on their rakes behind him, "including the richest of land grant holders and, of course, every American trader and shop owner in town. All the Americans will be coming!"

"Looks like it wouldn't be complete if we didn't show," Paddock nodded.

"*Si*," Jesus nodded.

"It's already in our plans," Mateo replied. "We're going to see in the old man's birthday in real Taos style. The other Americano gringos there will help us show that old man Bass a real hurraw he won't soon forget. A man turns forty, he's got to have one whopper of a shindig."

"We will be sure to all turn out, as you say," the foreman reaffirmed.

"On the afternoon of the big *baile*, the dance?" Kinkead reminded.

"She will be ready for your old man, this Bass." Jesus patted the sleek, beautiful mule on her neck.

"I think we will be, too." Josiah remarked as he wheeled to leave with another wave. "Really ready for a hurraw to see the old man through to his next forty!"

"Think he'll last that long?" Mateo inquired outside the barn with a smile.

"He always tells me he's got no other choice," Paddock chuckled softly. "The Lord, he says, won't take him because he's been too bad. And the Devil himself doesn't want him. Bass himself says the Devil doesn't want the competition. Scratch says he's got no other choice but to go on living."

"He does it with some style," Kinkead commented as they slid atop their ponies.

"He does that," echoed Josiah.

"The man is rich with friends." Kinkead nudged his animal forward at a walk out of the *hacienda* yard.

"You are a good friend yourself." Paddock looked over at Mateo. "We both are blessed with your friendship, Don Kinkead. Both Scratch and I have quite some blessing in you."

"You are too kind." Mateo felt embarrassed with the warm compliment.

"I have enjoyed your hospitality, and Rosa's kindness toward my family," Josiah smiled. "I wish sometimes that spring would never come. This winter is such a beautiful time, spending it as your guests. I wish sometimes—" His voice dropped off—distant, wistful.

"The Taos valley is working her magic on you, Senor Paddock," Mateo replied. "It is said you drink once from the waters flowing down from the Sangre de Cristos," Kinkead pointed out the snow-drenched, sun-dappled peaks, "you will carry this valley in your heart, returning again and again and again."

Josiah nodded easily, slowly. "I believe it, Mateo." His eyes gazed off toward the white and purple majesty of the brooding winter mountains. "I think I really do believe you."

"OUCH!" Bass hollered. "Be careful with me, you lop-eared dawg."

He rubbed the knee he'd just banged against the small table, then stood erect once more. Covering his eyes was a cotton strip, recently torn from one of Rosa's old aprons. A smattering of light came through the cloth, but little else. Paddock held onto one of his arms, Looks Far, the other, as they guided him out of their little house behind Mateo's bigger house. Waits-by-the-Water walked in front of them, little Joshua cradled in her arms. Mateo and Rosa followed them outside.

It had snowed for better than a day, but the sun had finally broken through that morning. Scratch's curiosity had been aroused earlier that morning when Josiah and Mateo had ridden off without him. When his two friends insisted that he stay home, Bass had gotten an inkling that their trip had something to do with his birthday. And when the two men had returned late in the morning, Rosa had brought down the sweet, hard biscuits and coffee.

And now they were leading him outside for his birthday surprise, a fact that he had prodded out of the two men.

The two Indian women giggled as they escorted the blindfolded man outside. Bass felt the cold air suddenly brush his face, splash across his lips and neck. He heard the new snow whine under his moccasins as he stepped from the door.

"Damn, it's cold," Bass said, wishing he had lashed up the elkhide coat he'd slipped into before they left the adobe hut.

"You're the one who was in so much of a hurry," Paddock said as he guided the old trapper around a snow drift.

"I just been—it's only that I'm dyin' to see what my present is," he replied through chattering teeth.

"You're raring to see it, huh?" Paddock teased.

"Yep. That I am, son," Bass said with the enthusiasm of a small child. "Where we goin'? Up to Mateo's house? Is that where you put my present when you two rolled back?"

"Nope," Paddock answered. He paused a moment as he tugged Bass to a halt. "It's right in front of you. Take the rag off your eyes and see for yourself."

The old trapper put his nose in the air to sniff as he heard the others whispering around him. He could not quite make out the new odor here in the crisp, dry air. His hands shot to the folded cloth strip over his eyes and tore it from his face. The intense, high light hurt his eyes, although they had been closed but a few minutes. He squinted and blinked, trying to get them to focus on the dark object in front of him.

Titus heard the animal blow before he actually saw her. His head cocked to the side, listening just the way a dog would pitch an ear a certain way to capture a foreign sound. Bass saw movement, a leg pawing at the snow. He stared at the blurred movement for a moment, waiting for his left eye to help the right. The shooting stars were back in the bad eye.

"Aren't you going to introduce yourself?" Kinkead suggested.

"I cain't see—" Bass said. Then his eyes, squinting against the dazzling light bouncing off the snow, came in focus. His heart skipped a beat when he saw the mule.

"You like it?" Josiah said quietly.

"I'll be damned!" Bass exclaimed. Dumbstruck, he took a step forward, then stopped again. He turned first to Paddock, then to Kinkead, finally over to the three women. He tried to speak, but the words wouldn't come. He looked back at the beautiful mule, then turned to Paddock with a sheepish grin.

"Happy birthday, old man." Josiah was one big ear-to-ear grin.

"You—you done this?"

"Me, and Mateo," Paddock admitted proudly.

"I just showed him where he could get an honery ol' mule for an honery ol' cuss. That's all my part was in this." Mateo handed Scratch the hemp rope halter tied around the mule's nose.

Bass eagerly accepted the lead rope and embraced Mateo all in one motion. Next he turned to Paddock and threw himself against his younger partner with a fierce hug.

"You picked her out special for me?"

Paddock nodded. "I think you'll like her. She's been working on paying heed to her manners. Now you can take over and teach her like—like—"

When Scratch heard Josiah's voice drop off, he realized how remorseful Paddock was that he had been a part of the cause for the old mule getting shot by Asa McAfferty.

"Hannah. Like Hannah, son," he said. "It's awright now, Josiah. The hurt's all gone away."

"I wanted—wanted to get you another mule, ever since Hannah was ki— killed," Josiah continued haltingly. "Now I got you a real special birthday present, too."

"You sure did that," Scratch said as he walked down the side of the Jenny, his bare hand stroking the animal's young flanks. "Damn, but this looks to be one fine animal."

"She comes from one of the finest ranchos in the northern provinces," Kinkead said as he stepped up beside Bass. "Don Miguel Armijo's place is well known for good stock in these parts. And Josiah got the best of the bunch. I tried to talk him into getting a Jack for you—thought you might like a male better."

"Nawww," Scratch said. "I always had ladies. S'pose I always will. Just like the way they act better."

"I figured right for you, then," Paddock said.

"She'll do me well." Waits-by-the-Water slipped up beside him to take a place beneath the old man's arm. "Now I got me two fine ladies," he smiled.

"I believe I'm goin' in and get myself warm," Mateo said. "I don't want to catch my death out here and have to miss the New Year's fandango." He swept Rosa up beside him and they padded through the deep snow toward the little hut.

Paddock motioned for Looks Far Woman to start toward the hut with him. "You coming, Scratch?"

"I'll be along, straight-away," he chirped, not taking his eyes off the new mule. "I'll get this lady somethin' to eat first off when I put her up with the horses."

"You got a whole winter left to work with her before you head back up to beaver country," Paddock commented.

"What you mean before I head back up to beaver country?" he said, twisting to look back at Josiah. "Don't you mean—we?"

"Ah, yeah," Josiah said, dropping his chin. "I meant we." He wasn't sure what to say or how he felt about going back to beaver country, but no matter what happened between them in the days and weeks to come, he was damned pleased to have made the old man this happy with his birthday gift.

"I'll be along straight-away," Bass said as he stroked the neck of the mule.

Waits-by-the-Water crawled from beneath his arm and walked along the side of the animal. "She is strong," she said.

"I believe she will be what we need," he answered in Sparrowhawk. The Crow language seemed so foreign to him this far south.

"You are happy?" She looked up at him and smiled.

"Yes, very happy. It is a fine, fine present."

"When someone gives another something that is long desired, it is always a happy gift."

He turned to her slowly, then reached out to encircle her in his arms. Bass felt his heart suddenly swell, the perfume of her hair filling his nostrils. He wanted to crush her against him here in the snow. Instead, he held her as gently as he could, stroking her long black hair burnished with copper highlights.

"Like you, my woman," he finally said, with a sob caught in his throat. "I long waited for you. When we finally were together for the rest of our lives, it was the happiest gift anyone had ever given this old, old man."

12

EVENING LIGHT SLID blue into the west, skittering off for warmth the way a man would hurry home on a winter evening, eager for family and hearth. For better than an hour the sky hung in purple shrouds while the first stars twittered their introductory light. A special night beneath an extraordinary sky. An evening to celebrate. The coming of the New Year. The advent of his fortieth birthday.

The way the Indians figured time it was the last days of the *Moon of Deer Shedding Horns*. Soon would come this *Moon of the Seven Cold Nights*. December right now to a white man. January tomorrow. Would people of his race call him white, call him Indian, half-breed? What was he anyway—but a man in between? Hell, he'd even asked Mateo what day of the week it was. Tuesday, December 31st. Imagine it had come down to that—Titus Bass wondering what day of the week it was!

It all fit nicely. Bass figured he was the only one crazy enough to be standing here, watching the sky. But, it really didn't seem reasonable to him that others should be shuddering in this bone chilling, rapidly falling temperature just to watch the first stars come out. No one else would be as crazy. He had always heard that when a man hit his middle years, there came a time when no one could count on what that fella would do—almost like he'd gone crazy for awhile. Yet, here he was. All the rest of the folks had gone back inside to continue their preparations for the grand party at Don Armijo's hacienda. They had told him he could stand out here in the yard between the hut and Kinkead's house if he wanted to, but they all had scurried back inside their dwellings after a few minutes of the evening's bitter temperature.

If they wanted to go back inside, so be it. He wanted to stay out here until the night got black as the bottom of a ten year kettle.

Ten years now. Damn! But he could still smile. A lot of water gone under that bridge. Some of it he couldn't even remember himself. But that was exactly why he was here right now. Shivering in the cold, stomping his bone cold feet from time to time, hands tucked under his armpits and coyote cap snugged down as much as possible around his face. Titus wanted to watch this final sunset and moonrise of his thirty-ninth year. The others instantly thought him silly, perhaps even touched-by-the-moon. The others looked at him almost sympathetically before they dove back inside for warmth, leaving Scratch by himself to watch the sun go down, to witness the moon's arrival at the eastern edge of the earth.

Ten years now and there weren't many of these moonrises he could remember missing. Spring or fall, summer or winter—perhaps there were merely enough to count on the fingers of one hand, only that number to show he had not watched the moonrise those few evenings. Through all the seasons, there weren't that many of these evening rituals he had missed. Over ten years, wherever he had been, whatever he had been doing. A routine rarely insulted. This was the last, the final moonrise of his thirty-ninth year. At midnight he would turn forty.

Wagh!

Bass wheeled slowly and gave a little how-do wave to the huge golden globe stretching over the mountains before he put his weight against the wooden door and stepped out of the cold.

Waits-by-the-Water rushed up to him with a warm embrace. She smelled of sweet mountain flowers and rich, dark earth. Here it was winter with a couple of feet of snow covering the ground—and this woman smelled of spring. It never ceased to amaze him. Her freshly washed black hair had been brushed glossy with a porcupine tail comb. She had anointed her body with natural perfumes of wildflowers, herbs, grasses and pine needles. There were spots of vermilion daubed across both her coppery cheeks and the part of her hair was decorated with the purple-red dye. Having put on a dress she rarely wore, the Crow woman was resplendent in her ceremonial outfit. The supple deerskin dress had been beaten thin, then whitened with clay dyes until it reminded one of white velvet—so thin, so supple it clung to her shoulders, trickling around the small, firm breasts and falling away over rounded hips to sprinkle fringe at her ankles. Down the side of the white garment were tied little hawks' bells and tiny strings of red ribbon for decoration. A young squaw in the prime of her life—what a sight she was to behold.

He spun her around and around, admiring his wife, then pulled her into his embrace once more. God, but he was glad she was his woman. It felt as if she had put on a little meat here and there. Especially over the hips. Filling out at last. After all, he thought, she was only yet becoming a full woman. Putting more meat on her bones. No one could fault her for the past few weeks, all of them eating so well here in Taos at the Kinkead's table. With Rosa as chief cook, no one went hungry at all. Perhaps the Crow woman had put on a little weight. He had, too.

Bass stepped back to admire his wife one more time. Then he smoothed out his own calico shirt beneath the heavy elkhide coat. Around his waist there was the faintest hint of his belly slipping. Getting a wee bit of a roll there. He sucked in a quick breath of air and puffed out his chest. Best way to make that belly go away. It happened on cue every winter now. A man couldn't help it. Winter was a time when he got a little more lazy, a little less active, put on a little more lard. This past year it had taken a little longer to get rid of his winter belly.

"You about ready, birthday boy?" Paddock asked cheerfully as he entered the front room of the small hut.

Josiah strutted up in a pair of fancy leggings and a new, Spanish style, short waisted leather jacket worn over his calico shirt. His long curly hair had been brushed to a gleaming luster and slicked back behind his ears. Even his moustache and beard had been trimmed. Bass shook his head and grinned.

"Not near as ready as you," Bass scoffed as he looked Paddock up and down. "You are one fine-lookin' nigger tonight, Josiah. Why—I might even ask you for a dance myself."

Bass swept low with an outstretched arm in a graceful, genteel bow.

"Sorry, old man," he said as he held up an arm to let Looks Far slip beneath it, "but my dance card's all filled up."

"Ahhhh," Bass pouted. "An' here it's gonna be my birthday."

"Well—maybe just one dance," Paddock relented, holding up an index finger. "Just one for the birthday boy."

They laughed as the Flathead woman wrapped the child into a warm bundle, then put her woolen capote over her fanciest outfit. Waits-by-the-Water fussed with the other woman's hair, straightening it out over the shoulders of the capote.

"Ho! The house."

It was Kinkead's voice booming from the yard.

"Let's be getting along now. A fandango is getting ready to kick off and we aren't even there yet."

Bass opened the wooden door to find Kinkead sitting at the front of the small wagon which was hitched to a pair of fine horses. On the plank seat beside Mateo huddled Rosa, bundled in her coat, an Indian blanket about her legs and her favorite *rebozo* pulled tightly about her head. There were two oil lamps fastened to the front of the wagon near their feet where a pair of light halos glowed over a yard now deep in snow.

"We just a-waitin' on this livery ride," Bass shouted as he motioned for the others to scurry out the door he held open for them.

He and Paddock helped the women into the back of the wagon where lay numerous Navajo rugs on which to sit and several thick blankets to pull about them for their ride north past town and up the valley stretching toward Taos Mountain. It was on that great expanse of family property that Don Miguel Nunez de Armijo would hold this special New Year's Eve fandango.

They rode through the frosty night air, past candlelit windows and oil lamps in homes and huts spread across the valley. By the time they had passed over the snow-beaten streets of Taos, the road north was becoming clogged with other revelers heading for the Armijo party. It became quite festive joining the other wagons and carriages, some folks on horseback, everyone hallooing those they rode near with Nativity greetings and wishes for the New Year. Somewhere up ahead a man strummed a guitar and a voice took up the happy strains of a festive Mexican song. A few pedestrians were plodding along the side of the muddied, snowy road out of town—families too poor to afford horses or burros, not to mention wagons. In the happy spirit of the season, others more fortunate would stop and give those walking a ride in their wagons.

Kinkead pulled up rein beside a group of men and women. A young man helped his mother and sisters board, then gave a shove to help his aging father climb aboard. Finally he leapt into the back of the wagon. Mateo snapped the reins that sent the two horses off once again. The young man looked from face to face with a happy grin.

"Senor?"

"Yeah, we met." Bass smiled back and stuck out a hand.

The youth took it. "You sold me your beaver."

"Right again. Where'd you learn to speak such good English?"

"I learn from my boss."

"Yes, I remember now. He was off to Santy Fee when we did our business together." Scratch watched the young man nod. "Is he back yet?"

"He came back two days ago for just this fandango," the youth answered.

"Good," Scratch smiled and nodded himself. "I wanna sell some more of my plews."

"He must be careful so that he will not have the furs taken by the officials, or be arrested himself."

"What?"

"The boy is right," Mateo called over his shoulder.

"But—I just sold him a few plews back the other day."

"A few of 'em is a lot different than all them you got in that shed back to my place," Kinkead went on. "Mexican authorities are allowing only Mexican citizens to trade in furs."

"You mean I cain't sell my furs down to Taos no more?" Titus squeaked in disbelief.

"You can't," Kinkead stated, "but *I* can."

"So, you're saying we sell our pelts through you?" Paddock asked.

"That's right, Josiah," Mateo answered. "Me being a Mexican citizen now allows me to sell 'em with no problem. We'll get the best price in town for 'em."

"Let me get this straight." Scratch stared off at nothing at all. "If I try to sell my plews to this here young'un's boss, the government officials are likely to take my pelts, arrest me and the boy's boss, too?"

"Could very well happen just like that." Mateo's head bobbed.

"Things sure got 'em a way of changin' on a fella," Bass groaned, shaking his head. "Weren't always this way."

"Mexican officials got the notion Americans are trapping on Mexican soil. Got the idea those pelts you have would naturally be Mexican property."

"Shit!" Bass exploded, then caught himself and clapped a hand over his mouth. "Sorry, ladies. Didn't mean to spew off like that. It's—it's just crazy. Them are *our* plews! Trapped in the free mountains of the west. No man gonna take my plews an' say they're his, or his government's."

"If you want the money from all that labor you've invested in those plews already," Mateo advised, "you best let me sell them for you."

"I'll see that this boy's boss gets a crack at them pelts," Bass nodded at the young Mexican.

"What's his price?"

"Other day I sold some to him an' I got me three dollar the pound," Scratch replied.

"That ain't a bad number on 'em at all," Mateo said. "What's the name of your employer, son?"

"Hiram," the youth answered. "I work for Senor Hiram."

Again Bass felt the thick worms crawl through the pit of his belly. There was something about that name which just didn't hang right where it was supposed to in his mind. It was like there was an empty peg where something should be.

"Won't take us long to find out if that's the best number on plew, Titus," he nodded again.

"Yeah," Bass said quietly. Waits-by-the-Water snuggled beneath his arm.

"Looks like we're here, folks," Kinkead announced a few minutes later.

All along the road came a parade of wagons and carts, burros and horses, all slipping into the great yard outside the high walls of the Armijo hacienda. Draped all around the huge iron gates were large tallow candles fluttering in the chilling breeze. The pale light of each candle surrounding the carriage wide gate combined with those along the top of the wide adobe wall to paint the yard in gentle lemon light. There was the constant hum of voices as visitors climbed down from their wagons and carriages or hitched their horses off to iron rings in the wall. Greetings were exchanged while guests passed beneath the portals into the interior of the Armijo home. Each wall was hung with a garland of pinon branches tied every few feet with a wide red ribbon. Several fires glowed brightly in the main courtyard. Around them were gathered those men who had already deposited their ladies inside the grand ballroom and retreated to the camaraderie of their fellows as they smoked their thick cigars and sipped at their strong drink. Even without music at this point in the evening, the party already had a gay air about it.

As they were shown into the huge home by a servant, Bass could tell each Taoseno had cleaned and shined for this extravagant party. Both men and women had gone to great lengths in preparing themselves for the festivities. Immediately evident was the change in the complexions of the women they had passed in the courtyard, the entry hall and now in the grand sala. Every woman had scrubbed her face clean of both dirt and the *alegria*, that red juice of a plant they daily used as a cosmetic to protect their faces from the sun. Now instead, the *alegria* was used solely on the lips, making them redder, fuller, more sensually attractive.

As they entered the grand hallway, practically every woman who could be seen was wearing her most delicate *rebozo* or a *mantilla*. Whereas women in the United States would surely not be caught at such a formal affair without a fine hat, New Mexican women had long worn this more practical item of apparel. It was nothing more than a scarf of some beautiful color, cotton or silk, depending upon one's station in life, ranging from five to six feet in length, by two or more feet in width. With it, a woman would not only cover her head but also wrap her shoulders and upper body. She could shield her face from the sun and storm alike, or hide from a too curious admirer. The *mantilla* was a more delicate version of the *rebozo*, usually made of a fine lace and kept over the head upon a special occasion. Beneath the *mantilla* or *rebozo* each woman's hair was washed and brushed to a deep, gleaming luster before it was braided and plaited into a

159

long queue which hung down her back. Some of the more wealthy ladies in the crowd even had solid silver conchos braided into their lustrous hair as it fell in rippled waves from their shoulders.

Kinkead introduced all his guests to Don Armijo as the host himself was making the social rounds of the huge sala. With him were his wife and a young daughter. Both women were strapped into tight-bodiced silk gowns imported from Spain and wore tiny, buttoned shoes called *zapatitos* that barely peeked out from beneath yards of petticoats and ruffled lace.

Dona Armijo stepped immediately to Rosa's side so that she could speak with the Indian women. The Mexican mistress of this huge hacienda fingered the fringe on the doeskin dresses and touched the quillwork, caressing the skin's velvetlike softness, inquiring about the beads and tin cones sewn to the white hides. Rosa explained all, interpreting the Indian women's simple English.

While the women chatted quietly to the side, Kinkead introduced Armijo to Bass.

"This is the gentleman who sold Josiah your birthday present, Scratch," he said. "He raises some damned fine mules."

"I'll say he does!" Scratch stuck out his hand again. "Just wanna thank you for that prize critter. Along with that fancy saddle an' them silver spurs."

Mateo translated some of what Titus was saying, enough for the host to understand just what the white trapper meant. He then inquired as to Bass's occupation.

"I'm a trapper," Bass said proudly. "Have been for a goodly share of my growed-up life."

He waited for Mateo to translate, watching both Armijo's eyes and Kinkead's lips during the translation.

"Do you ever trade in Mexican furs?" Armijo asked.

Bass noticed the wry smiles on both Armijo's and Kinkead's faces as Mateo translated.

"I s'pose at times I am just like them flat-tailed critters," Bass said. "I don't figger them beaver rightly know when they've crossed on over to Mexican territory—an' neither do I."

When Mateo had translated, Armijo broke out laughing. He presented his hand to shake Scratch's once more, then leaned in to whisper something to both Bass and Kinkead with a wink of one eye.

"He says if both you and the beaver are not smart enough to know which side of the line you are on, then neither of you should feel badly about getting caught."

"Senor," Bass leaned back in to square his eyes with Armijo's, "Titus Bass don't ever get caught in nobody's trap."

They all had another laugh before Don Armijo gave his apologies, stating that he must continue to make the social rounds at the party. He stepped between his wife and daughter, scooped up an arm apiece and swirled them on across the floor toward some newly arrived guests.

"These Meskin fellas tryin' to tell me somethin'?" Scratch asked Mateo.

"What do you mean?"

"I mean—twice now tonight I been told that *my* furs just may not be my furs," Bass explained. "First that boy who works for his American boss, a gringo from the States—"

"Let's not worry about that now," Kinkead said as he looked around the room to nod in greeting to others. "It seems as if the government officials are real skittish lately about American trappers. So we'll have to work right around that for the time being. I'm a Mexican citizen. I've told you how we'll get the furs sold. You know, sometimes you get just like an old woman. Worrying about things that don't need fussing over."

"Ol' woman, eh?" Bass snorted. "I'm only gonna be forty years an' here you are callin' me an ol' woman."

"You just worry too much, my friend," Mateo said. "About things that we can work out. No one will take your furs."

"If *you* say that's the way it is, I'll buy the stump," Scratch smiled. "But I don't agree with you 'bout gettin' old. You're only as old as you can drink. An' I'm thirsty—dry as the belly of a sidewinder right 'bout now."

"Let's get us something for the ladies and then find the whiskey," Mateo said.

"I'm ready to mosey when you are," Scratch agreed. "Josiah? Josiah?"

"Uh, what?"

"Ahhh, you have been watching the comely senoritas? Mateo teased.

"Uh, I never thought I'd see so much ankle and, uh—the neck, down the front—as I'm seeing here."

"Yes." Kinkead patted Josiah's shoulder. "Many an American has come to New Mexico and been quite taken by the high skirts and the low blousas." He gave a quick wink to Scratch.

"They don't catch cold? On a night like this?" Paddock asked innocently.

"Not with enough whiskey in 'em," Bass joked.

"And not with all the warm attention they're getting from the young dandies," Kinkead smiled.

The dresses known as *enaguas* might be made of cotton, silk or satin, worn much shorter than was the fashion in the United States, well above the ankle to mid-calf. Bright colors were worn for festive celebrations such as this, red being predominant. Very few full length dresses were present, and those adorned only the wealthier guests. Most of the shorter *enaguas* were snugged with a wide belt richly ornamented with silver or shiny tin emblems.

Above the belted skirt was the chemise or *camisita* sewn of a fine linen. This low necked, short sleeved blouse amply displayed each maiden's charms. That soft skin of young, fleshy breasts met in an inviting cleavage visible for all the young men to admire. Indeed, these sensual women were not at all bashful about showing what they had to offer their suitors.

All of the women, from the poorest peasant to the wife of the wealthiest land owner, wore precious jewelry: gold and silver necklaces, bracelets, earrings and rings. Around almost every neck hung a large, resplendent cross suspended between the breasts. Combs or bows or ribbons, sometimes colorful silk handkerchiefs, were tied in the women's hair. From bare ankles and legs, all the way past the fleshy expanse of exposed breasts, which tantalizingly shuddered with

161

every seductive sigh, each woman was intent upon making the best use of her hair style, her makeup and her clothing, either to attract a suitor, or to show all the guests at the fandango just how she'd landed her husband. Anyone who had any wealth wore a good deal of that wealth draped about them. Even the poorest of peasants were quick to spend what little money they had on clothing, even before some necessities of life were secured.

The men were equally extravagant in dress as they stood alongside their wives or gathered around young objects of attention. Each wore boots of embossed leather, sharp in the toe with a tall heel for control of a stirrup. Some even had heavy, silver spurs strapped at their boots. Their trousers, or pantaloons known as *calzoneras*, flared open at the outside seam and were laced with gold sash and filigree buttons. Beneath the *calzoneras*, exposed to view, were the white underdrawers each man wore. Around the male waists were wide, colorful sashes that fluttered with the slightest movement. Tucked into the sash was a bright, bold shirt and possibly a vest, over which the short-waisted jacket or *chaqueta* was worn. Those who could not afford the black dyed outfit of the caballero might wear the *sarape* or Indian blanket with a hole for the head cut in its middle. Those men who could afford jewelry most certainly displayed it. If not around their necks, then perhaps laced along the seams of the embroidered, barrel-buttoned *chaqueta*.

Yet tonight, as at every fandango, each man's dark eyes brooded over that tiny knot of buckskinned mountaineers who gathered in the corner around the table where the *aguardiente* was being served.

"You know any of them young pups?" Scratch asked of Kinkead and Rowland, who had just joined them.

"The tall, square one," John said, pointing. "He's the leader. Cleetus Aubrey."

"Is this the bunch that's got the government boys down in Santa Fe all in a uproar?" Kinkead asked Rowland.

"Yep," John smiled. "The very same, Mateo. They've been raising hell ever since they brought their Mexican furs into Mexican territory."

"Where they cache their pelts?" Kinkead asked.

"Can't be over to Robidoux's place," John answered, then licked at his own dry lips. "Antoine's down to Santa Fe for the winter."

"Who's this Robidoux?" Josiah took a sudden interest in the conversation and stepped forward to join the three men. "I knew a Robidoux back to St. Louis."

"Might likely be some of the same big family," Kinkead began to explain. "Antoine came out to Taos in 1824, stayed around and got hitched up to a nice Mexican gal. Just like Beubien there." He pointed to a heavy-set man moving into the midst of the buckskinned mountaineers. They laughed and jostled with the Frenchman.

"Charles came out at the same time as Robidoux," Mateo continued. "And three years later got himself hitched to Maria Lobato. He's got quite a lot to show for his years as a trader here in Taos."

"From the looks of his clothes, he's gone full Meskin," Scratch surmised from the traditional outfit Beubien wore. "Cain't tell him from any other *pelado*, 'cept that his hide ain't as browned."

162

"French boys have been making out quite well down here to Taos for years."
Kinkead nodded to some other light-skinned men who were chatting together.
"Some of the wealthiest purses in the valley are right over there, and some of
that wealth is simply Frenchies marrying smart. They get hitched to the right
gals and fall right into the money."

They all watched Charles Beubien raise his glass of brandy to a group of
wealthy land owners.

"Besides Beubien there," Mateo continued, "there is Ledoux and Leroux.
Antoine Leroux there just got married this past November after his eleven years
in these mountains. The man's moved into the home of his wife's family, on their
huge spread up on the Rio de los Luceros."

"Sounds to me like these Frenchies have slid right on in purty slick," Bass
clucked.

"They feel comfortable right alongside rich Mexicans, like the Armijos, the
Martinez family, the Romeros, and you can't forget the Vigils," Mateo grinned.
"Them Vigils got more than half a million acres of land spread clean across the
valley."

Scratch let out a long, low whistle. "I s'pose that's a lot of land for a man to have
to care for—worryin' 'bout it if someone's takin' a piece of it away from him."

"That's what he pays his hired help for," John Rowland smiled.

"He pays 'em to worry?" Bass inquired.

"No," Kinkead answered. "Vigil and any other wealthy man still got to worry
about their hired help."

"Yeah," Scratch answered. "It's up to the hired help to keep the riff-raff like
me off the place, right?"

"Yep." Mateo eyeballed Scratch in swift appraisal. "You and me, we're not so
lucky. We have to worry about what's ours. We have to worry about what other
folks take from us, perhaps steal with word or gun. We have to worry about those
kinds of things all on our own. Them rich fellas don't worry themselves. They pay
their hired help to worry."

"That's always been the difference between the rich, fat-ass folks in the world
an' the rest of us." Bass grinned.

The knot of young mountainmen eyeballed the room, continually searching
the sala over for likely young women once the music began. They owled over the
brims of their gourd cups as their gazes swept over the older American trappers.
Some of the young men's eyes halted on the three Indian women with Paddock,
Bass and Rowland, but their gazes moved on quickly once they figured it out that
the women were with the new arrivals. Courting a young caballero's girlfriend
was one thing—but to openly woo the wife of another American trapper was
begging for trouble of the worst color. There was almost a national pride involved
that would not allow such a thing to happen. Some of the young trappers smiled
in greeting to Kinkead's party.

"Evening," Mateo called out cheerfully and nodded his head to the young
buckskinned dandies.

Most had taken off their capotes and buckskin hunting frocks. It appeared
most of them had splurged on new shirts for this fancy occasion. Some wore new

calico drop-sleeve shirts in the fashion that was such a rage back in the States, and others wore lacy ruffled shirts so prized by elegant young caballeros beneath their *chaquetas*. Leggings and moccasins were cleaned for the occasion, everything ornamented with beads if not porcupine quillwork. Colorful necklaces of claws and beads dripped from every neck to rival the silver and gold hanging below wealthy Spanish chins. Then there were the gaudy sashes around each waist, most holding a knife or two, perhaps a pistol stuffed down in its folds.

"Upon a time, that was me." Scratch had been studying the young American trappers, all strutting about their corner of the *sala* as if it belonged solely to them.

"You and me, both," Kinkead agreed.

"Just what are you two old fellas jabbering about now?" Paddock stepped up beside them.

"I—I just see myself over there." Bass nodded toward the young Americans. "Years an' years an' many miles ago. That was me."

"They're chomping at the bit for a real hurraw, just the way we were in our day, Titus." Kinkead gently slapped Scratch on the back.

"Put enough of that corn whiskey down 'em," John Rowland mentioned, "them young bucks feel as frisky as a bull in spring."

"Leave it to those boys to find some likely gals no matter what season it is," Mateo said.

"Just like a young bull who's a lil' heavy in the horn, they'll have to shake loose some muscle to get the lady," Bass grinned. "There'll be trouble here afore the night is old."

"No safer bet than that, my friend," Kinkead agreed.

"I'd take some side on that," Rowland nodded.

"I haven't got the least notion what you all are talking about." Josiah wagged his head.

"Let's just say that you'll see soon enough the way we all are figuring it." Mateo smiled broadly at Paddock. "But for right now, I think I'll buy you gentlemen a drink. Anyone thirsty?"

"I don't wanna get in the habit of refusin' a free drink," roared Titus.

Kinkead led the other three off toward a table where huge earthenware containers littered the crowded top. Ladles and mugs were provided for everyone at the party, and a choice of a fine wine, a cupful of the famous Pass Brandy, or stout, heady *aguardiente*.

"What are you drinking this evening?" the old mountaineer inquired of Paddock after he had served both Rowland and Bass.

"I'll take some of what they got."

"I see you choose to live dangerously also," Kinkead grinned. "It's a mighty heady brew, son. Give a man one hell of a hangover. You sure you want to gamble some?"

"At least I'll try it," Paddock answered. "I've had traders' whiskey at rendezvous. I figure this ain't much different."

"You might just be right there." Kinkead handed Paddock a cup. "Only difference might be the traders water theirs down more and more as the hurraw rolls on at rendezvous. While this stuff—why, the last drink will take off the top of your head, same as the first."

They all watched Josiah sip at the potent liquid. He screwed up his face a little as he swallowed, then gasped slightly when the liquor robbed him of breath.

"W-whoooo!" he exclaimed.

"I gave you fair warning," Mateo chimed.

"You did," Josiah rasped.

"This some of Workman's brew?" Bass inquired. "Is William Workman still around, makin' whiskey?"

"He's still kicking—probably even here tonight," Mateo said. "Been a lotta years—gonna be going on eight soon—since he's been making whiskey out to his place, west of town. I imagine this is his brew. Anyone who throws a fandango like this on New Year's Eve, they would certainly have to serve William Workman's whiskey."

"There ain't any better," Rowland admitted and raised his cup in salute.

Kinkead led them over to the band of young American trappers and introduced everyone all around. He found out they had just smuggled their fall catch into Taos, storing the plews in Workman's subterranean crypts where the ex-trapper brewed his strong corn whiskey. Over the weeks of winter they would sell all their furs through Workman to an American trader everyone knew simply as Hiram. The name once again caught Scratch's attention.

"Any of you know much 'bout this fella Hiram?" he asked of the young trappers.

Most shook their heads.

"All we know is that he's just about the last trader in Taos that'll give a man a good dollar on fur," Aubrey advised.

"He's been around these parts for some time now, I take it." Rowland turned to Bass. "A few years as far as his boy tells it. Why you ask?"

"Ain't nothin'," he answered. "I first heard his name the other day from that young clerk he's got workin' for him. Just tryin' to place the name. I knew someone a long time ago by the same handle."

He could not shake the feeling. It rose from the pit of his stomach and raced along his spine, suddenly raising the hackles along the back of his neck.

The room began filling up. At the opposite end of the sala several musicians were tuning up their instruments. Two violins, two guitars of that kind Mexicans called a *heaca*, a mandolin, and a large Indian drum called a *tombe* to keep the rhythm. Bass watched the musicians while the rest of the men chatted.

The room was already getting oppressive from the Mexicans' free use of tobacco, their native brand being a mild, bland and fragrant variety. Here in Taos it seemed everyone smoked. Men and women alike carried the makings for cigarillos: corn shucks and powdered tobacco. They also carried small tins, which contained the cotton, flint and steel needed to light their cigarillos. Some of the women used silver or gold pincers to hold their cigarillos so their fingers wouldn't be soiled with nicotine stains.

Joined again by their women, the four Americans stood in the midst of the huge, oblong room. Groups walked about, now and then stopping to talk to another group of the opposite sex for a few moments, then each group moved on after the men gave a very formal bow. Most women were not daring enough to socialize visibly so they sat in chairs gathered along the length of two walls beneath a great number of large portraits painted of both family and religious characters. And always, as in every room, hung the ever-present crucifix peering down on the festive proceedings.

The room was growing noisier and noisier. Paddock wondered if anyone would be able to hear the music once it began. It seemed as if everyone was expectant of the dancing, anxious until they could sweep the floor clear and whirl the night away in a grand fashion. Here were gathered rich and poor alike, both peon and hacienda owner. Though from different backgrounds, leading very different lives, all were one tonight.

Josiah studied it all, caught up in the excitement of the evening. Men and women openly flirted with one another. Frightened women hid demurely behind fans, which they kept fluttering before their faces. Unsure men scrunched up against a wall talking with male friends, afraid to chance conversing with a certain senorita. And when the young American trappers were present, so were the young caballeros, who felt the gringos did not belong at their Mexican fandango. The young dandies scowled from beneath their heavy eyebrows and wide brimmed sombreros as they entered the warm sala. Instantly they saw the Americans as their competitors. All would vie for the attentions of those young, single senoritas here to dance and be courted.

"Senor Kinkead!"

They all turned to watch the Mexican gentleman approach, his black hair greased back, patches of gray plastered at the temples. He was alone as he strode through the crowd that parted for him as he made his way toward the Americans.

"Senor Cordero. How good it is that you are here this evening." Kinkead spoke in Spanish, then self-consciously repeated himself in English. "I have forgotten that you know my language almost as good as I do."

They greeted each other in the Mexican mode of familiar salutation. The left arm was thrown up to embrace the other's shoulder while they shook hands.

"Como le va?" Kinkead asked.

"I am very well. Thank you, my friend," Jesus replied. "How did your friend enjoy his birthday gift?"

"He seemed to take a shine to the animal right off." Mateo turned and motioned for Bass to come forward. "Jesus Cordero, this is my old friend—Titus Bass. It is his birthday we are celebrating with the gift of that mule you sold us."

"It was this fella's mule?" Scratch inquired.

"Not exactly, senor." He shook the old trapper's hand. "It belonged to my jefe—my boss, Don Armijo."

"Jesus is Don Armijo's foreman on this rancho," Mateo explained.

"You raised one fine animal there, Senor Cordero," Scratch grinned widely. "One fine animal that is."

"Thank you, Senor Bass. I trust you will come visit our rancho again when it is not quite so crowded." The music had just begun and there was a sudden

166

bustling explosion across the floor as people darted around for the start of the dance. "Sometime when it is not so noisy."

Scratch liked the man, liked Cordero's sincere smile, warm with friendship. He shook the foreman's hand once again and saw him move off into the crowd jostling across the floor as several couples began dancing.

"Let's take the women on over there." Kinkead motioned to a bare patch of wall that had opened up near the refreshment table. "We'll all get tromped on standing out here, I'd reckon."

"No differ'nt than a buffler stampede," Scratch said. He motioned for the Indian women to go before them through the crowd.

Looks Far held tightly to Joshua, whose wide eyes were seeking to take everything in at once. He had not uttered a peep since they had entered the bustling sala. Waits-by-the-Water was constantly at the Flathead woman's side, and Rosa was watching over them both. The Mexican woman had been introducing the two women to everyone she knew, and always kept a maternal eye on Rowland's young Ute wife.

Suddenly there was happy laughter and a gay rustle and flurry snaking through the crowd like a wave surging across the shore. A young man and woman were passing through the gathering, handing out party gifts for all the young dancers. These favors were egg shells which initially had been pricked with a pin and the contents blown out of the shell. Then through the same hole the shell had been filled with various perfumes and those holes eventually sealed with a dollop of tree sap. With these fandango party favors the young at heart could announce his or her amorous intentions. An egg filled with fragrant perfume was broken over the head of the person a suitor wished to court. The room was suddenly filled not only with the fragrances of those many, heady perfumes, but also surged with gay laughter as the eggs were broken along with the social ice of the evening.

Now everyone joined in the dancing.

Many young men had crossed the floor and presented themselves to the partner of their choice. They bowed gracefully before that object of their attentions and led the young lady onto the floor where, with a slow step, they paced out the formal patterns of the *contradanza*. Through the first hours of the winter evening the floor was crowded with both the genteel gyrations of Frenchmen and the studied grace of the Spaniard. They danced it all. First a slow version of the ordinary waltz, which was sometimes referred to as the "cradle dance." Next was a variation of the tango. Finally the *bastonero* or master of ceremonies for the evening called for the *cuna*, a beautifully romantic dance wherein man and partner held each other with arms outstretched and locked, their heads thrown back as they spun across the floor. Here were the well-dressed *senoras* fitted in silks and lace whirling beside cotton-draped harlots and whores from town, while the church padre and pickpockets alike took a turn at the floor and the twirling dance steps. Peons and half-breeds from the Pueblo, all joined in the fun, everyone watched over by both the scowling caballeros and wide-eyed young mountaineers hungry for a real spree.

Against the walls fluttered the warm light, flames from all the candles prancing with the movement of air bustled up by hundreds of wide skirts and gyrating bodies. Although windows were open, the room grew warm with the candlelight, with the musky heat of many bodies.

"Let's go trip the light fantastic toe." Kinkead swept Rosa's cup to the table and with a hand at her waist led his wife to the floor to join the other slowly waltzing partners.

Looks Far and Waits-by-the-Water stared in rapt attention. This was something altogether new. Now there were people they both knew out there on the dance floor of this grand palace, actually touching while they were dancing. There was no comparable Indian version where partners made contact during the dance.

Scratch stood swaying slightly with the merry tempo, one arm that held his cup slowly wagging back and forth in the rhythm of each dance. A bigger smile had never been painted across his face. It seemed frozen there, getting wider and wider with every new song.

Josiah divided his attentions between the dancing Mexicans swirling on the floor and those watching near the walls. It was a marvelous sight to witness such a thing for the first time in his life. The only guests who did not appear to be enjoying themselves for the time being were the young Mexican gentlemen and the American mountaineers as they nervously hawk-eyed each other. Both groups were perhaps aware that they would soon be vying for the attentions of the same female partners. And there was a limited supply of those young, fleshy Mexican beauties.

Josiah studied dancers and drinkers alike, watching as both groups of young men continued to consume more and more of the wine, brandy and strong whiskey. The dim light from the homemade tallow candles and the hundreds of hand rolled cigarillos combined for a smokey, romantic atmosphere that could hypnotize a man as he watched the couples sway back and forth across the floor, each man holding his partner gently while her hips swung languidly beneath her short skirt so that much of her legs could be seen.

The long, slow waltz ended to applause. Some men returned their partners to the chairs along the walls while others went back to the tables for liquid refreshment. A few stood on the floor awaiting the next dance.

Suddenly a loud voice slashed across the low murmuring of voices and retuning of some instruments.

"Hey, you durn *pelados*. This here music just don't shine! Let's hit the trail with something a lil' more lively now. A lil' more spunk to it."

Everyone stopped dead in his tracks when the tall, buckskinned mountaineer began to yell at the small group of musicians. He was joined by the rest of his companions near that end of the room where sat the startled Mexicans clutching their instruments.

The American trapper looked about him at his fellow trappers for support, then addressed the musicians once more. "Didn't you understand what I just said to you? We want something with a lil' more life to 'er. Give us something to make us think we're having a real hoe-down, a durn spree."

With the last word Cleetus Aubrey began to stomp one leg onto the wood floor. Along with the leg he set his bent arms flapping like a bird attempting to take off into the skies. He pranced around for a moment in front of the shocked musicians, trying to communicate his desire for a merry song. Whiskey had flowed long enough. Now it was time for the wolf to howl.

At last a few musicians mumbled something between themselves, looking first at one, then at another of their group until they all understood what they should do. Quickly instruments were brought into position and an upbeat, lively tempo was set by the Indian drum. It was next taken up by the guitars, mandolin and fiddles. Almost like a jig, the tune got the other mountain men to stomping their feet and clapping their hands. Some of them spread out across the floor to invite other folks to join them. Some other buckskinned Americans wheeled round and round with each other for a moment before Aubrey shouted again.

"Hell with that, boys. You've danced all year with each other." He stood in the middle of the floor with his fists balled on his hips. "There's real skirts a-waiting hereabouts."

"GRAB YOUR PARTNERS, GENTS!"

The trappers immediately stopped twirling with one another and swung away across the floor to select young female partners. They had all been tantalized by the dark-skinned senoritas long enough. They had watched just so much of the bared brown legs and swirling skirts and rivulets of midnight hair surrounding come-hither smiles. The mountaineers were ready for *women.*

Cleetus sashayed up to a sultry-eyed young lady, full of his own bluff and bravado as only a brash, young mountain man could be. He gave her young caballero escort a quick shove as he grabbed the young beauty by the elbow and started for the floor with her.

"Wagh!" roared another of the Americans.

"They're well lubricated by now." Kinkead shouted at his three friends above the noisy din of both the crowd and the sprightly music.

"You remember us like that—as young as all that?" Scratch asked Mateo.

"Yes, my friend. How well I remember those days."

"You both acted like them?" Josiah shouted above the noise.

"Nawww," Scratch smiled. "We was probably *worse.*"

They all laughed uproariously before turning their attention back to the dance floor. It was there the mountain men had each chosen a partner they seized about the waist with a grizzly hug. Out on the cleared floor they twirled and swirled, jigged, jumped and stomped in time to the lively music. Some pranced and shuffled the ragged steps of an Indian war dance. Occasionally the music was punctuated with a loud war cry as the buckskinned trappers bellowed out their supreme excitement in the dance. One foot up in the air, the other down, the boisterous, loud, profane backwoodsmen pitched around their partners and against each other, the entire dance floor all to themselves.

The older members of the audience gathered back against the walls, enjoying the spectacle and the excitement of the mountaineers' show. Some laughed, most clapped their hands in time to this new rhythm and jaunty sound produced by the Mexican musicians. Some of the young caballeros had started to object to the mountain men dominating their young ladies. The scowling Mexican males were swept aside, back against the wall to sulk in private. Some gathered in dark conference at the whiskey table.

The trapper leader, Cleetus Aubrey, squared the dancers and set them to pacing his tune.

"Allemande left. And—allemande right," he shouted in a nasal strain above the twanging music, the clapping, laughter, and shouts.

"Swing your pardners—an' a doe-see-doe."

The older Taosenos were enjoying the show as the mountain men followed the patterns the leader was calling out. The Americans swung their partners mightily and deposited the ladies on the floor, only to sweep them up again to take a place in line and prance around their small square. In and out, the giggling young senoritas were led by the brash young men.

"Cain-tuck reel."

As the call was given by Aubrey, he stepped into line and deposited his partner opposite him. The others snapped to and lined up beside him, their fair partners facing them.

"First four forward—now back."

They pranced through the old-fashioned, back country reel, getting their partners to step forward when they did. Then Cleetus started down the line with his lady, prancing and high stepping between the gantlet of mountain men and senoritas like some strutting, bluegrass thoroughbred.

Bass pulled Waits-by-the-Water against him so that she nestled beneath his arm. There he patted her hip in time with the thumping of the Indian drum. Her hips were full, padded, sensual in their swelling. She felt good beside him. He loved the feel of her presence so close to him, the smell of her hair, the musk of her body strong in his nostrils. He was suddenly flushed with his desire for her. Like a fever, it washed over him.

Waits-by-the-Water turned her face up toward his and smiled that seductive, half-lidded way she always did to show him she understood what he was thinking, what he was wanting.

"My husband wants his birthday present right now?" she said loud enough for him to hear her over the loud music.

"I will wait until my birthday," he grinned. "But that isn't far from now, lil' one. I'll be forty years old in just a lil' bit."

From time to time one of the braver caballeros would attempt stepping forward to rescue his young maiden from the clutches of that American who had swept away with her. For his trouble the Mexican was summarily given a hearty shove or a mighty thump across the chest to send him sailing back into his crowd of scowling young men.

"Getaway, you damned greaser," one mountaineer shouted, as he shoved a caballero away from the dance floor.

"None of you *pelados* can shine in this here crowd," hooted a second as he thumped a large fist against another protesting Mexican.

"Don't none of you try nothin' cute to ruin our fun with these here purty ladies!"

170

Kinkead caught Bass's eye momentarily and he nodded at his old friend. Mateo brought Rowland and their two wives over by Bass and Paddock. Josiah paid little attention, so caught up was he in what was occurring on the dance floor. He did not notice that the three older men had gathered close around the women and placed them within a loose corral of their bodies.

"You expectin' trouble, Mateo?" Rowland shouted.

"Not for us, Johnnie boy. Not for us. The rest of them *pelados* all know Kinkead too well to cut shines around me and Rosa. They won't try nothing here with us. We just stay tight in case something does break loose."

Suddenly there was movement from the young caballeros. A lone, tall male leaped forward onto the dance floor, his friends failing to restrain him.

"*Carajo!*" he bellowed as he dashed forward into the midst of the trappers. "You scoundrel!"

One of the trappers turned at the movement beside him. His mighty fist swung, catching the Mexican square in the face. The caballero stopped dead in his tracks, stunned. Then he began to slowly corkscrew to the floor, suddenly underfoot in the melee.

"*Chacal! Chacal!*" another caballero shouted and rushed forward to help his compatriot. "Jackal! Jackal!"

Maddened by strong whiskey, driven insane with jealousy, the green-eyed monster was freed. Passion immediately took sway over the rest of the Mexican males in the brash caballero's group—they charged out in force, spilling onto the dance floor.

There was a glint of steel, the flash of candlelight off a knife.

"*Valgame Dios!*"

With passions aflame, the Mexicans surged into the sweating, drunken band of Americans.

One of the trappers was slashed in the first assault. Some of his friends saw the blood gush across the front of his shirt and shouted a war cry.

"Ai-e-e-e-e!"

Knives broke out from sashes and belts. The trappers quickly circled, their backs to one another, all facing outward just as buffalo bulls when confronted by an attack of gaunt, winter-hungry wolves. The young senoritas dashed back to the safety of the shrieking crowd pushing itself against the walls, away from the dance floor, far from the battle. The room was flush with widespread pandemonium as women began screaming and men were hollering to one another, uncertain if they should stay to help the brash young caballeros or if they should seek escape with their wives and daughters.

Fists and knives swung. Loud grunts and groans rumbled through the room as outraged Mexican swains descended upon the small band of mountaineers. There were quick, glinting thrusts in the candlelight as combatants parried knives. The war was on as the Mexicans surged over the trappers. For a moment all seemed to be lost for the Americans. The mountaineers were badly outnumbered some four to one by the young Mexican dandies. Armijo's sala resounded with profane cries in both Spanish and Kentuck. Suddenly the bold charge halted. There exploded sharp cracks as fist impacted against bone, quick grunts of pain as knees slammed up into groins or shoved into a random belly. One tall mountaineer seized a Mexican and swung him overhead, hurtling the body back into some other caballeros. In the wild scrambling one of the young trappers grabbed a rickety chair and smashed it against the floor, sending splinters in all directions. He tore the chair apart to hand out the legs and pieces of the chair back to his comrades for use as weapons. These stout warclubs were put into service swinging through the air, answered by yelps of pain as they smacked bone and muscle.

There was a wholesale wrestling match as most of the combatants refused to use their knives as weapons, preferring instead to keep this brawl on barroom terms. However, a second trapper was suddenly sliced with a knife. Terrified, he screamed for his partners. Blood dripped across his shirt onto the floor as he clutched his torn chest.

Immediately a loud, ringing voice shouted for everyone's attention from the center of the room. The tall, graying ranch foreman held aloft a torch that had been taken down from the wall and extinguished for use as a club. Cordero pulled first one Mexican off the tangled swarm of bodies, then another, this time an American, off and out of the fray.

"Please! Please, *senores!*" he shouted.

Then Kinkead rushed up, his stout, bull-like body yanking and twisting bodies out of the mass of fighters. He planted a knee in the groin of one caballero, a fist slammed into the jaw of an American.

"Heeeyyy! You swine-eatin' hawg!" hollered one of the young gringos. "You're hittin' the wrong fellas, you gawddamned sonuvabitch!"

"My mother hasn't got a damned thing to do with this, you ignernt young fool." Mateo swung and connected.

The young trapper backpeddled, cradling his jaw, and stared back at the wide, old mountaineer. "Why you helpin' them gawddamned greasers, ol' man?"

"I ain't helping no one but the host, you stupid chunk of wolf bait."

Bass and Rowland were in the thick of it by then, flinging bodies, clubbing the fighters. Josiah had been told to stay with the women, to keep them behind his outstretched arms in a corner of the room.

A pistol blast boomed across the sala.

Immediately the screaming women fell silent. The hollering and swearing mountaineers dropped their voices. Impassioned caballeros no longer uttered any profane curses. Don Armijo stood near the group with a smoking pistol in his hand, having just shot a ball into the rough-hewn timbers overhead. He quickly stuffed the weapon into his bright red sash and brought up the graceful, smooth-bored fowler. He was speaking his native language in a taut, controlled voice.

"*Senores!*" Jesus Cordero announced in English for the benefit of the Americans in the room. "Your host, Don Miguel Nunez de Armijo, wants this activity stopped at once. You are asked to leave the hacienda and its hospitality immediately."

Trappers and Mexicans alike moaned at the orders.

"Your sort of fun is over for now, boys," Kinkead shouted. "You fellas seem a

172

mite too heavy in the horn for your own good. And don't think we won't throw your asses out on the road. You come and try us."

The young, wooly trappers glared hard at the caballeros who were slinking out of the way, back into the crowd to disappear out the doors. Then the gringos eyed the four men standing in a knot. Kinkead stood near Cordero, his balled fists on his hips, daring any of the young trappers to try him. Rowland was not far away, on the other side of Jesus, a chair leg in one hand, slapping rhythmically against the palm of his hand to punctuate the silence in the room. Bass stood with arms crossed, glaring hard at the two young, burly trappers.

"You stupid young niggers can behave yourselves an' get your asses on down the road," Bass threatened, "or we can doe-see-doe right now."

There was some mumbling between the trappers as they pushed against each other, feeling boxed in, confined by only the four older men.

"We was thinking on having us a spree—running us some squaw meat," one of the young trappers shouted.

"Yeah. We come to hurraw," said another.

"You had your hurraw," Kinkead hollered back in answer.

"Shit, we ain't gonna let you ruin the party for everyone else," Rowland shouted.

"You best get for now," Mateo suggested in a calmer voice. "You've flat worn out your welcome. Best you all think dry and hard on this."

"What if we don't fix on leaving?" the tall leader of the group said as he took a step forward, standing a good head taller than Kinkead.

Bass smiled. "Then I'd say you got about as much sense as a frog's got hair."

Mateo smiled quickly at Bass before he took a step toward Aubrey. He held his clenched fist up. "Then, boys, we gotta finish the job them *pelados* started."

"You feel like grainin' a skin, fella?" Bass said, his voice like deep water over a sandy riverbed.

"See that fella over there?" Mateo nodded in Cordero's direction. "He didn't get to be foreman of this huge spread by taking any shit off any young pig-sucking caballeros, did he now?"

"That's right," said Rowland.

"And these other two hivernants ain't new to fighting," Kinkead continued. "Atween 'em there's more than twenty years in the mountains. And you all know if a man lasts that long out here, he's got the hair of the bear in him. You fix on tangling with either one of them two, you better go round up some help. There simply ain't enough of you niggers to take on the likes of Johnnie Rowland and Titus Bass."

A long silence followed the disgruntled muttering. Aubrey glared at each of the old trappers. "This damned hurraw's gone dull and flat," he said as he turned toward his comrades. "Fellas, let's go on into town straight-away and do us our celebrating in Diablo's Cantina."

The young trappers began to shuffle past the whiskey table, still shoving some of the party guests aside as they drifted off toward the doors, two men bearing the wounded along.

"We just come to drink an' dance," one fellow muttered as he walked toward the door.

"You had your drinks," Mateo said, "and you danced awhile. It's time for you to push on down the road. I think you all come with damp powder this go 'round."

And then they were gone. The room remained quiet for a long moment as the older trappers looked at one another. Jesus broke into a wide smile, then they all started laughing.

"I thought we were going to have to wade right on into that bunch," Kinkead sighed.

"I'm glad we didn't have to take them on," Cordero said. "We are too old, gentlemen. Too old to be fighting with young men."

They picked up the remnants of the broken chair, threw them in the fireplace at the end of the room, then made their way over to the whiskey table where Josiah had just finished pouring five cups of the heady Taos lightning.

"Mighty happy you got that squashed when you did," Paddock said. "I was getting a mite thirsty. And it's getting on close to your birthday hour, Scratch."

"You been larruping awful close to this here bowl, son," Bass smiled. "Gettin' to like the lightnin', eh?"

Scratch took his knife from the back of his belt and used it to dish up some brown sugar from a large crock. A clump on the tip of his blade dropped into each cup. He stirred the drinks before he wiped the blade and returned it to its sheath.

"Here's to your health, boys!" He held up his cup in toast to the four others.

"Luck to you all for the coming year," Rowland answered.

"Luck to us all," Josiah replied.

"I'll drink to that," Kinkead joined in.

"May we all get what it is we need most," Scratch said.

"Amen, my friend," Mateo added.

13 THE HUGE SALA roared with excitement as the monstrous old clock struck midnight. The huge black hands lay stacked atop one another as the twelve chimes boomed across the suddenly silent ballroom. Then, as the last echo of the final count rolled off the wall, everyone shouted and hollered their joy at the new day, the new year. The musicians made a futile effort to play over the screaming voices. Older women shrieked as they were clutched by various men. The young women enjoyed the grappling too, giggling as they were grabbed, crushed in one embrace, then another, with one kiss planted on their lips, then another and another.

Most Taosenos were making the rounds through the bustling, heated room that seemed charged with its own nervous energy. Each guest wanted to extend his own personal greetings to everyone else. Each person pushed and jostled against every other guest as the room swelled with happy, turbulent tides. Josiah couldn't move. He was cheerfully riveted to the floor. Every young woman in the room had come by to plant a kiss on the lips of each one of the visiting Americans. Undaunted, Mexican males rushed by, planting a buss on the cheeks of the Indian women and Rosa Kinkead.

Only Josiah was numbed by it all. Both older and younger women had been rushing up to him since midnight to clutch his face between their palms and plant a kiss on his lips. Some of them strongly reeked of *alegria*, most of their own cheap perfumes or toilet waters, while a few others carried the fragrance of wine, brandy or the stout *aguardiente*. Each time one of the older women grabbed Josiah, Looks Far trickled her own vivacious giggle, amused at her husband's consternation. He could not remember when he had ever been kissed so much. Never before in his entire life had women been so forward in their affections.

"Happy birthday, Scratch!" Paddock cheered, as he finally turned to his partner, his face smeared with red lip dyes and powdered makeup.

"You look a holy sight, you do." Bass laughed.

"Damn, but I'm glad to see this birthday in with you, old friend."

"Me, too." Kinkead slapped Bass on the back, then wrapped his huge arms around the old trapper in a bear hug. "Uggghhhh," Titus hollered, his arms pinned to his sides.

Rowland came up and squeezed the old trapper. Their cups sloshed and spilled over their clothes and moccasins. The floor ran slick and wet with the spilled whiskey so that when Scratch tried to free himself from their grip, he went tumbling to the floor with all of them collapsing around him.

The gringos lay in a happy, drunken heap, their women standing around them in a small circle, all laughing loudly and slapping Bass to extend their birthday wishes.

"Best to you, my friend. For your next forty to come!"

"You—you all keep beatin' on me like this an' I won't have to worry 'bout havin' another forty years!" Bass roared. "I won't live long enough to worry 'bout it."

Kinkead and Paddock got to their feet. Rowland stood up beside them as they all pulled Bass up on shaky legs. The whole bunch weaved and stumbled against each other.

"Best we let some of this likker set awhile," Kinkead suggested.

"They ain't got any water here," Bass sputtered. "A fella gets purty damned thirsty when he goes to stompin' an' dancin'. Gives a man no other choice but to drink this here awful, pepper-belly stuff."

"Have it your way, my friend." Mateo smiled widely and waved his hand. "I, however, am off to wish others the best of the New Year. For you, my old friend, it is enough that I see you here, that I see you healthy—and I see you just might outlast us all!"

"I'll always drink to that," Scratch replied.

Mateo and Rosa swirled through the room, shaking hands in Taos fashion, giving old friends and family hugs and kisses for luck in the coming year.

"Senor!"

Kinkead turned at the sound of the youth's voice.

"Senor Kinkead!"

The young clerk pushed his way through the throngs of well-wishers, waving his arm at Mateo and Rosa. He had an older man in tow.

"Senor Mateo Kinkead," the young Indian clerk announced as he stopped in front of the old mountaineer. "I am pleased to present my boss, Mr. Hiram."

"We've met, son." Kinkead confessed. "Your name is Tuttle, right?"

"That's right," the older man agreed. "Iglesia, Mr. Kinkead and I have met, some time ago as I remember it."

"I never knew you as anything other than Tuttle," Kinkead continued, "so I never put it together when your boy here mentioned that his boss was Mr. Hiram. Never knew your first name." He smiled and stuck out his hand.

"I suppose you never had any need of my services," Hiram inquired, "though I hear you trap from time to time."

"Not as much as I used to," Kinkead chuckled.

"Neither do I, Senor Kinkead," said Hiram.

"What brought you to Taos originally? The trapping?"

"No, I first came as a trader to Santa Fe back to '24. It was one of the first big trains to come down here, so we were told at that time. Mostly yard goods, some trinkets—just like men would stock themselves for the Indian trade. A few knives, axes and such. But mostly bartered in lightweight dry goods."

"You must have done well," Kinkead said.

"I divide my time now between Santa Fe and my interest here. Ah, there have been better years, that's for certain."

"May things be better for you in '34," Kinkead offered.

"The market is strong, as it has been for the past couple of years," Hiram began. "I expect things to continue this way for a while at least. Why is it that you have never trusted me to buy your furs?"

"Don't know," Kinkead answered honestly. "Suppose I never really thought about it. I knew there were a few of you fellas in town dealing in pelts—but I always sold my own. Since I didn't trap all that much, I really didn't need a place to sell them. But, I do know someone who is in need of your help. In fact, he sold your boy here some of his pelts about a week ago. He's got a passel of fine fur left to dicker over with you."

Mateo looked the trader over, sizing the man up as a negotiator, a cagey buyer and businessman. Tuttle stood as tall as Paddock, yet without as much muscle. Kinkead judged the man to be in his mid-fifties, from all the gray hair and long, gray sideburns. Then, too, there was the paunch that hung over the man's wide belt. Even though there was a youthful appearance to the man, his face was well wrinkled with its years of exposure to the elements of the western frontier.

"I got a look at those pelts Iglesia took in from this friend of yours," Hiram said. "If those were his poor pelts, I'd like to get my hands on his prime fur! I spent long enough as a trapper to know poor bull from fat cow. This friend of yours not only knows how to trap, but also how to skin the critters right the first time. And he knows how to take proper care of the hides after they've been cured."

"Say, c'mon," Kinkead suggested. "We'll let you meet this old feller you'll be dickering with on those pelts."

"I'd enjoy that, Mr. Kinkead."

"Please, call me Mateo, or Matt, whichever you prefer."

"If you wish, but you must first introduce me to your lovely wife here."

"I am truly sorry, sir. I have forgotten my manners, haven't I? This beauty is my wife of many years, Rosalita. We all call her Rosa. I'm proud to say she still puts up with this forgetful ol' hoss."

"Madam," Hiram said as he scooped up Rosa's hand and gave it a gentle peck with his lips. "A pleasure to meet you," he said in good Spanish.

"Senor, gracias," Rosa answered politely, tingling from the gentleman's kiss.

"Now, let us meet this master trapper friend of yours," Hiram indicated with a sweep of his arm. "Where has he come from of late?"

"Following last summer's rendezvous on the Green River, he trapped on down the western slope, over across the Little Snake and the Little Bear River. Says he climbed over to Park Kyack, down through Middle Park and spent the fall trapping plew in the Bayou. Right where he plans to return come the spring hunt, so he tells me."

"All foreign country to me," Tuttle admitted.

"When you were trapping, did you work farther north of there?"

"Yes, indeed. Colder—cold as any place I've ever been. Far up the upper Green, Yellowstone, Wind River—Three Forks if we dared," Hiram chuckled.

177

"You trapped country well known to us ol' beaver niggers."

"You trapped that country yourself?" Hiram asked.

"Most of us did," Mateo replied. "I take it you worked for one of the companies, a big outfit?"

"No, never did, Mr. Kinkead." He shook his head as they wound their way through the crowd. "Lucky, I suppose, that me and my friends never had to hook up with any of them big outfits like most fellas have to. No, instead there was just three or four of us at times, making it as we could, on our own hook."

"That's the way to do it," Mateo responded. "Any of those fellas you worked with back then around Santa Fe or Taos now?"

"No." Hiram wagged his head, pursed his lips. "None of 'em ever came out to these parts with me. I left two back in St. Lou—another—well, none—none of us ever knew what come of him."

"The mountains take their toll, don't they, Mr. Tuttle?"

"That they do, Mateo. There is never any accounting for who makes his fortune, or who goes under. Never any rhyme or reason for it."

"Amen, my friend," Kinkead replied as they reached the group of trappers and their Indian wives. He put his hand on Bass's shoulder to turn him around for introductions.

"Mr. Tuttle, I'd like to introduce you to this master trapper we spoke—"

"B-B-Bass?"

Scratch studied the face that had just uttered his name.

"Titus Bass—yes," Mateo finished his introduction.

Scratch squinted and peered at the man's face, his memory jogged by something about the man's eyes. The face was too fleshy, too full at the whiskered jowels. The hair was gray, too. Titus couldn't recognize the face for sure—but there certainly was something about the man's eyes.

"You two know each other?" Kinkead asked.

"You're—Titus Bass, aren't you?" Hiram took a step backwards. "Arrrhh!" His hands went up in front of him.

"Bud? Bud Tuttle?" Bass lunged like a cat at the trader with both hands.

The two men fell in a heap on the floor, tumbling into dancers' feet and legs. Women guests shrieked in surprise, shocked as the two Americans rolled across the floor. Men cursed in Spanish as they were bumped and jostled aside.

"Dammit, Tuttle!" Kinkead dove after Hiram.

"What the hell is going on?" Paddock watched the two men fight on the floor.

"Scratch!" Rowland joined Paddock as they yanked at the older man's arms to pull him off the American trader. "C'mon, Josiah. Help me pull this feisty ol' nigger off!"

"I am trying to help, dammit!" Josiah said.

Mateo was in the middle of the fight by then, grunting between the two fighters, trying to pull them apart, trying to dodge their wild, haymaker blows.

Bass delivered club-like fists against Tuttle's face and head. Hiram Tuttle had all he could do to defend himself against the shorter, smaller man who was intent upon pummeling him. Bass wouldn't give up. He broke loose from Paddock and Rowland, knocked Kinkead aside, and grabbed Hiram again.

At last Scratch crashed down on the trader's body and got his hands around Tuttle's neck. He began squeezing as if his very life depended upon his choking the man.

Hiram's hands grappled with Scratch's wrists, trying to pull them away from his throat. The trader's eyes bulged as the old trapper's thumbs dug and cut into the windpipe. He tried to yell something at his attacker.

Paddock and Rowland each struggled with an arm but Titus battled them off, too.

"Pull the man off, dammit all!" Mateo ordered as he was trying to force himself down between the two combatants.

Paddock slipped an arm around his partner's neck to secure a tight headlock. Then he pulled the old man off the trader.

Scratch kicked and thrashed against the younger, stronger man as Rowland fought to help Josiah hold Bass up and away from Tuttle, who sprawled on the floor, gasping for breath. Mateo stood hunched over the trader, one arm outstretched to push Bass away, the other hand pushing against Tuttle. The trader coughed in choking spasms as he fought for breath.

"Get 'way from me you stupid sonuvabitch!" Bass gritted out between his teeth.

"Stop it now!" Paddock yelled, lifting the older man off his feet in the struggle.

Mateo watched the old trapper struggling to pull Josiah's arm away from his neck. He glanced down and saw Tuttle slide away from the fray, scramble to his feet, then push off through the crowd. Kinkead was on him in an instant.

"No you don't, Mr. Tuttle!" he roared as he locked an arm up behind the trader's back. "Now what's this all about?" he demanded.

"I—I've got to—can't stay. He's a madman!" Hiram sputtered.

"You're gonna stay 'til we get this all sorted out." Mateo pushed the taller man back over to Bass.

"The man will kill me! You saw it. Lemme go!"

"Not 'til we see what's going on here," Mateo grumped.

"He stole my goddamned furs!" Bass shrieked.

"I don't understand," Paddock said.

"You just sold him a few of yours, Bass, some poor ones," Kinkead scoffed.

"I didn't steal any of Titus' pelts! Not a damned one of them." Tuttle screeched as he tried to break away from Mateo. "Him an' the others," Bass said. "They run off with 'em. Every last one of 'em."

"You gave those pelts to us to trade for you!" Hiram yelled.

"An' you never give me my money for a bloody one of 'em!" Bass hollered back.

They sounded like a couple of schoolboys arguing in a back alley fight. Paddock tightened his grip around Bass's neck and Mateo held Tuttle's arm clamped behind the trader's back.

"I'm gonna kill me a goddamned thief. Lemme go."

"I'll sooner kill you first, you young whelp. I've lived with it long enough. No more will I carry this around. No more!" Hiram hollered back just as loudly.

"Lemme at him, Josiah."

Paddock slowly pieced it together in his mind. "This is—this is—one of

179

them—the three that took off with all your furs? Never came back? You never saw them again?"

"That's right!" Bass lashed out with his legs, trying to break free of Josiah's grip. "Dammit. Now you know, so lemme get at him."

"You figure you're gonna even the score by killing him?" Rowland asked.

"Somethin' like that."

"I knew early on Bass's old partners run out on him," Rowland turned to explain to Paddock. "He told me when we joined up to trap Green River that next year after he was left behind. Told me all about them three running off with his pelts. Told me about losing his hair in the bargain, too."

"This thievin' nigger's gonna lose more'n pelts and hair!" Bass shouted. "I'm gonna eat your liver, you hawg-swillin' bastard."

"I never saw a dollar of your money."

"You stole my goddamn pelts. You got my money. an' now I'm gonna cut your gizzard out!"

"Hold it! Hold it!" Kinkead screamed in Hiram's ear. "You never saw a dollar of Bass's money?"

"That's right," Hiram nodded. "Never got a dollar of it. Didn't want none of it." He returned Bass's steady gaze. "Wasn't right."

"What wasn't right? What are you talking about?" Paddock demanded.

"What wasn't right?" Hiram repeated. "The other two— they kept his money. You was just a young kid then, Titus. Didn't know any better what was happening to you. Just didn't know any different and them other two took off with the plews."

"You was in on it with 'em?" Rowland asked Tuttle.

"Damned sure he was!" Bass hollered.

"I—the mistake I made—I had a choice," Hiram muttered. "I could be left behind with a greenhorn who'd spent his one winter in the mountains with us— one goddamned winter. Or—I could hightail it back to the settlements with the other two and all those furs."

"So," Kinkead declared, "you admit taking off with another man's pelts?"

"Damn. I never laid a hand on the pelts," Tuttle whined, trying to twist away from Mateo.

"Left him in the mountains with nothing wetter'n your promise to bring his money back to him, eh?" Paddock accused.

"I wasn't much of a trapper myself," Hiram moaned. "I'd never lasted long by myself—or along with him. We'd been killed most likely."

"You're wolf bait now, Bud. Damned mangy-assed polecat—steal my pelts, will you!"

"The man's saying he never touched your plews," Rowland said. He turned to Kinkead. "You believe him, Mateo?"

"I—I don't know what to believe."

"Tell 'em how you stole my pelts!" Bass roared.

Kinkead looked around at the gathering knot of Mexican guests. "Get it out, Hiram. We'll sort this matter out right here."

"I never stole Titus's fur," Tuttle offered. "Sure, I was with them other two—

180

but I never took one dollar from his money. The other two poked fun at him. Mostly Silas Cooper—he was the mean one. Cooper never let up a minute on Bass. He's the one laid the name of Scratch on him back then. He never cut Titus no slack. It was Cooper's idea to take the young fella's furs and never come back to the mountains like we told Titus we would. He got Billy to go along with him and then it was up to me—my choice by then. Too late." Hiram seemed close to sobbing.

"Come to think on it—" Bass admitted when he heard the catch in Tuttle's voice, "Tuttle never really did give me a hard way to go. Of the three, he was the best of that bunch that come along to help teach me that first winter."

"You're thinking this makes some sense now?" Paddock whispered in Scratch's ear.

"I think so," Bass replied, staring intently into Tuttle's eyes. "He may just be tellin' me—tellin' us the truth of it."

Kinkead felt Hiram's body sag with relief. "Go on," he prodded, his grip on the trader a little looser. "Tell us the rest of it."

"Let go, son," Bass demanded. He no longer struggled against Paddock. "Just let me go."

Josiah dropped his arm away from Scratch's neck. "We'll hear the story out together."

Hiram shook his gray head. "Ain't all that much else to tell."

"Come on, out with it," Bass ordered. "What'd you do with my damned money?"

"I told you. I didn't take any of the money."

"What did them other two do with my pelts?"

"They sold 'em," Hiram sighed. "Between that powerful catch we all made up there and those pelts and robes traded off the Indians on the way back to St. Louis, we did—we did well enough."

"But you didn't take none of his money?" Rowland asked.

"No, I tell you," Tuttle confessed softly. "The others, Billy and Silas, used it."

"How much?"

"Close to three thousand it was in the trade."

Josiah whistled low.

"What'd they do with my goddamned money?" Bass said, his anger flaring again.

"They spent it," Hiram said. "First on a keelboat to go upriver to the Omaha, Pawnee maybe, possible they were even going to try the Sioux."

"What'd you all do?" Rowland asked.

"I told you," Hiram grumped, "I wasn't a partner with them two any longer by then. I just knew they took the keelboat upriver and tried trading. They didn't make much of a go of it."

"How come?" John Rowland asked.

"They hired them some fellas out of the watering holes in St. Louis to help them. But their kind simply ran off with most of the trade goods. Them as weren't killed right off, that is. The rest deserted when things went sour."

"Their plan for a quick fortune fell apart, huh?" Bass squinted one eye.

181

"What'd they do then? They have any money left over from the poke they stole off me?"

Hiram gulped. "They figured that since the drunks from the watering holes took all their trade goods, heading back to St. Lou to buy bad whiskey—And they figured that since the Indians liked whiskey better than any other trade item, they should open up a tavern in St. Louis."

"Which one, Tuttle?" Paddock demanded. "The Green Tree?"

"No," Hiram answered. "Not near as nice a place as that one. The Rocky Mountain House. They wanted to cater to the fur trade. Traders—Injuns coming in to the big city. Get 'em all drunk fast—roll 'em for what money they had on them."

"Looks like them two niggers didn't ever change their colors," Bass muttered. "Once a thievin' nigger, always a thievin' nigger."

"They still run the Rocky Mountain House?" Paddock asked as he moved around from behind Bass to face Tuttle.

"They didn't have it but a few years, as I heard it," Tuttle admitted. "They lost the place—bad debts. Gambling, as I heard the tale of it from Missouri traders coming down the trail."

"Are they still around St. Louie?" Bass asked. He had a way of boring into a man's soul with one eye squinted, the other like a piercing light shining right on through to a fellow's core.

"Far as I know of it, yes—they still are in St. Louis."

"It's them two I want," Bass growled as he turned to Paddock.

"Right. The two of them were the ones who spent your poke," Rowland agreed.

"My first year and a half in the mountains, an' them two run off an' spent my money. There'll be hell on a big stick to pay now." He brought both cold, green eyes to bear on Hiram.

"We're clean now?" Tuttle asked.

"Looks like we are. I reckon your story holds water," Bass nodded. "We're clean."

"Always have been clean with you—"

"Not really," Scratch protested. "You went off with them two, an' I'll always hold you on account for that."

"How can I make it up to you?" Hiram pleaded, wagging his head. "I want to repay you for—for them plews they took. I wasn't party to it—but I was. I didn't know what to do. Silas talked us into it." He looked up at Bass. "Scratch, how can I ever repay you for what you lost just because I didn't take a stand on it?"

"I don't want you to feel beholdin' to me," Bass muttered.

"I—I could have cost you your life."

"But you didn't," Bass cheered, tapping at the ever present blue bandanna holding the Arapaho scalp to the back of his head. "I learn't, an' I survived to learn some more. I lasted more'n ten years now in these free mountains—in spite of what was done to me. Not just by you, but by a lot of others. Man wants to

182

live where he wants to live, do what he wants to do to provide for him an' his own. Folks won't let 'im, will they?" He glanced around the small ring of Americans who were surrounded by the other party guests.

"But—" Tuttle sighed.

"Nawww, I just wanna be left alone," Bass continued. "If it ain't some damned Injuns, or maybe some Meskin fatass official wantin' taxes on my plews—why it's some white nigger takin' from me what I earned for myself."

"I want to make it up to you some way. I don't know how."

Scratch gazed off into the distance, not really hearing. "You say they're back in St. Louis? Billy an' Silas?"

Hiram heard the determined will, the power behind the soft spoken question, the tone of the words nonetheless like a razor sharp knife as they cut through the heavy, smoke-filled air about them. Bass had uttered the second man's name with something close to a curse. And Hiram Tuttle didn't know whom he pitied more right at this moment. Silas Cooper, because Titus Bass finally knew where he was after all these years. Or, perhaps he should pity Titus Bass when all was said and done. Hiram shook his head sadly. Perhaps he should feel sorrier for Scratch. Silas was a mean, cruel man. Always had been. There never had been an ounce of mercy in his body, never a bright flicker of charity. He truly took some pleasure in hurting. Scratch had maybe some ten years on Cooper, but that was about all. The rest of the odds went to Silas. Add Billy, who was never far from the bigger man's side, never moved without Silas saying it was all right to jump— well, those two old hivernants would be a match for any two, young, frisky-bull mountain men. And Bass was only one, tired, sundown trapper.

"There ain't no use in it," Tuttle said as he looked at Scratch. "No use in it, trying to get your money back."

"It's all gone, Scratch," Kinkead agreed.

"He's right, old friend," Paddock joined in.

"Looks like it's something you'll just have to put behind you and move on," Rowland said.

Scratch's eyes moved from man to man to man, studying each face before he finally answered.

"Maybe none of you lasted as long as this child's done in these here free mountains," he began, words clipped and terse. "I think I know why now. Kinkead, you got it purty easy here in Taos with a damned good life and a fine woman to help you with it. You see no sense in settlin' an old score like mine. An' you, John Rowland," he nodded as he threw up a hand to quiet Mateo's protest, "you say your luck's been down like your dauber lately. I know why, old friend. Looks to be you just give up an' cain't see no sense in keepin' on with it any more, can you?"

Bass turned to Paddock. "Now for you, Josiah Paddock. Maybe you never really was cut out for these here mountains, son. You come out here to get away from something."

"We already talked about this, Scratch."

"An' best you remember what I gotta say," Bass declared. "These mountains won't take you in unless you're here runnin' toward 'em. If'n you're here to get away from somethin', your dream just won't work."

"What dream you speaking of?"

"My dream, son," Bass answered as he stared down at his toes a moment. "It simply ain't the same dream as you got." Josiah stood there in stunned silence.

Bass looked around the crowd clustered behind him. When he saw Waits-by-the-Water, he motioned for her to join him. She swept in beside him and wiped a trickle of blood from his nose. Bass nodded to each of the Americans in turn.

"Tell Senor Armijo I was much pleased with the party," he said. "An' with my birthday present. Pleased to been a guest here in this fine house." He turned to leave.

"Where are you going?" Kinkead inquired as he stepped in front of Bass.

"This is your birthday party, Scratch." Paddock stepped up beside Kinkead to block his friend's way. "You can't go off and leave just like that."

"My birthday party, huh?" Bass shook his head. "Forty years old an' I get a surprise gift, don't I?"

"I—I don't understand," Paddock said.

"Ten long years now an' I can finally put somethin' to rest, finally bury it good an' deep the way it's always s'posed to've been." Bass shouldered the two men aside as he knifed between them, his wife sweeping along right behind him.

"Where are you going?" Paddock called. The Mexican guests moved back in a wave on either side of the old trapper as Bass and his wife made their way across the room toward the huge double doors that led out to the courtyard. "I'm goin' to St. Louie at first light."

"St. Louis?" Josiah echoed. "At first light?"

"Why you going to St. Louis, Scratch?" Mateo called out.

Scratch's answer was snatched away by the cold, bitter, winter wind that swept into the silent room through those huge, oak double doors.

THE BLOODIED line across the east was like a buffalo cow which had not licked herself clean following the birth of her calf. It gave notice of the crimson dawn to come. This first gray light gave the old man just enough reflection off the snow to work at saddling the horse and pack animals. He readied the buffalo runner with the spotted rump. The gelding stood off to the side of the corral where Bass had tied him, munching on cornhusks. The young mule, his birthday present of less than twenty-four hours, was next. Bass was placing the young girl into service a lot sooner than he would have liked. He wished he'd had time to work with her before this frantic trip east.

Two other ponies, a pair of those taken from the Arapahos, had been chosen to carry some of his light trail goods: blankets, pemmican, an extra change of clothes, one small iron kettle, fire makings, a couple of robes, spare moccasins, and the extra weapons. He figured Waits-by-the-Water wouldn't need all the rifles and pistols. Kinkead could let her keep a pistol back in the hut until he returned in the spring. Bass just might need the firepower before then.

Spring.

Damn, but it'd be a long time before he got back here. Scratch turned and gazed sadly at the snowy yard. Here were clustered the three little adobe huts out behind Mateo's larger house. A comfortable life it had been for all of them so far. First stood the tack house, where they'd stored the rewards of their sweat and labor of the last season. Then there was the little house where John Rowland and his Ute woman were staying this second winter. And finally that little hut where he'd found it impossible to sleep after they'd come home from the New Year's Eve fandango. He and Waits-by-the-Water had been given a speedy ride home in a carriage driven by one of Armijo's servants.

Bass turned away from the house and looked at the horizon. That bloody gash was widening along the eastern bowels of the earth. Soon it would be time to go. A ripping, a tearing apart. He would have to bid farewell to her, and this place, until late spring.

His plans for now meant there would be no spring hunt to speak of before it would be time for rendezvous up to Ham's Fork and the Green. Only when he finished this job at hand could he head on back to pick up where his life had left off. She'd be all right here without him. There was the safety of Taos, the security of having other friendly folks close around—the Kinkeads, the Paddocks, and the Rowlands. She would have companionship at least. Someone to talk to.

The bitter cold chewed at his knuckles so that from time to time he had to stuff his numbed hands under his armpits to warm them. After a few moments, Scratch could again work at tying the final knots on the last pony.

He was crazy, after all, he had to admit. Who else but a lunatic would take off in the middle of winter, head out some thousand miles across the trackless desert wastes to St. Louis, just to settle some ten year old score? Who else but a lunatic crazy man?

Or, Titus Bass.

Leaving the warmth, the security, the sanity of this place—it was all without any sense. But, he had his reasons. And they were enough. For him, they were enough.

Scratch felt sorriest for Waits-by-the-Water. He knew she would miss him as much as he would miss her—if not more. Because, after all, he had this search, this quest to occupy his mind. She would have nothing but memories, those thoughts of him.

They had lain cuddled through those late night hours of darkness, with but one solitary candle fluttering on the chilly breezes of the hut. Its feeble light had silhouetted him on the wall through hours of sleepless tossing and turning. Bass could tell by her rhythmic breathing that his wife was asleep when he had slowly pulled himself away from their bed to begin his packing. The hut's outer room was lonely where he busied himself wrapping and binding up things for the trip. Josiah and Looks Far had yet to make it home from the party. Must have turned into some explosive fandango to last until sunup. But, then, that was the way Taos was. Any excuse for a party, and everyone would last as long as the music and food and wine held out. Everyone—except for a tired, old man heading out to settle a score a thousand miles away in the middle of goddamned winter. It made him cold just thinking about what stared him in the face.

185

It always seemed that way. The side of his cheek felt like cold, charred rawhide as it crinkled in a smile. It was always winter when he was fixing to take off on one of these trips. Always one quest or another, in the snow. It was always cold. It was always winter. Going after Asa McAfferty, after his murder of Rotten Belly's wife. Then next to put Asa's ghost to rest at Fort Vancouver. And now he could finally bury ten long years of the past and claim what was his at last. Bass would get his money.

Or he would claim mountain justice. Scratch turned at the sound of the door whiskering against the packed earth. He heard her steps whine across the snow as she came around the corner of the hut toward the big corral. She was bundled against this coldest hour of the day. It was right here in these pre-dawn moments when a lot of things seemed hung in the balance.

Waits-by-the-Water had the hood pulled over her head so that her face was in purple shadow. When she got to his side, mittened hands pulled the hood back. Her black, glossy hair shone oiled and rifle-bright from a recent brushing. Her face had been scoured clean but he could still tell she had been crying. The pooling eyes glowed as sad and red as the new horizon. Scratch wrapped her in his arms.

"St. Louis." She spoke in English, then laid her head against his chest.

Something distant, almost mystical for her as the Indian had learned the words. Bass tried to explain where he was going, why he was going, all through the long night, but he didn't know if she understood that St. Louis was more for him than a physical place. St. Louis was more a state of mind, perhaps an emotion. Something too raw and itchy to be left alone. He finally had to scratch all those places that had tortured him for so long.

This was something strangely difficult and repetitive to try to explain the why of St. Louis to someone who had never been to a city before. To explain his need to go, to explain that need to someone who had grown up in a transient village moving among the mountains and plains of the far west.

What was it about this St. Louis that took him away from her? Why was it, she asked, that he needed to go to a city or town after they had only recently arrived here? After being here, why did he have to go to this St. Louis?

Was this Taos not city enough for him?

Each time Bass had hoped all the more she would understand. Each time he knew from her questions that she had not.

Scratch watched her back away from him and turn to run a gentle hand down the side of the mule. Then the woman flashed a melancholy smile his way, her slant eyes glittering in her bright, redstone face.

Sure as tarnal sin he was going to miss her. Watching her now among their animals, he knew he was definitely one of those few, fortunate ones in life's pairings. Damn if he weren't. He knew she always asked questions of him, like those she had plagued him with about St. Louis. But the woman never complained.

Waits-by-the-Water accepted what came her way, accepting without complaint. It seemed she always accepted tomorrow and what came with the new day, for good or bad, without the illusion that the new day would bring her some bright and wondrous change. The brightest part of her life was whatever was happening right at that moment. Damn if that weren't just like an Injun—and a woman to boot. But she accepted what was right here and now. She lived her life to its fullest without a discouraging word. When the nights had been cold crossing the passes and no one could sleep because of the sub-freezing temperatures, Waits-by-the-Water hummed and sang around their feeble little fires each bitter night in traversing the snowy mountains. Yet she hummed and sang the same happy songs seated beneath a shady tree when the air was warm and their bellies were full. The woman was a pure marvel to him. It made Bass smile to think on it, watching her now. He could recall her smiling face as she would have grease from juicy hump ribs sliding down her chin. And he could recall her beautiful smile when all they might have for a meal was some roasted bones from which she sucked the warm marrow. She was happy with whom and what and where she was at that moment, every moment. Whether her self was put into her tongue swirling around a piece of juicy buffalo hump or her very self was put into the tip of her tongue as it swept deep to scoop marrow out of bones. She remained a marvel for him—and a blessing.

Many times this trip Bass knew he would remember her just like this, standing in the cold, dim, early morning light. He would surely think on her back here in Taos, and his heart would break like the dry, parched earth crumbling beneath a pony's insistent hoofs. Yes. He was one of the few, one of the fortunate men in life to feel this way about a woman. And he was glad to feel the hurt already, that hurt in leaving her.

"Waits-by-the-Water," he whispered softly, then paused for her to face him once more. "I want—" he chose the words as best he could in Sparrowhawk since it was far easier for her to understand his bad Crow than his bad English. "I want to be the end of your rainbow on every stormy day."

He reached out for her and brought the woman to him, crushing her bulk gently within the circle of his arms. "I want to be all those stars that will fill your every night while I am gone from you."

"I will remember," she whispered, seized by a tearful sob caught in her throat. She stared up at his face intently, as if she were trying to memorize his features so she could recall them during their long separation.

"How long, my husband?"

"Two moons for the journey to St. Louis. Some time to find the men I want. Then two more moons in coming back to you."

"Four moons?"

"Maybe it will be closer to five," he answered.

"That is—a long time in my life, husband." She smiled feebly.

"Come hold me again," he begged. "We have been apart before."

"I remember those days of worry—those days of sadness."

"Just hold me again."

This time he spread her capote and pulled open the flaps of his elkhide coat so that he could capture as much of her warmth as possible. He clutched the

187

woman desperately. She clung to him just as ferociously. Bass ran his hands down across her hips. They felt full, warm. He rubbed a palm sensually across her lower belly, then stepped back to look down at her.

Her belly was plump.

"You getting fat on me, woman?"

"No," she answered in a husky whisper, flashing her husband a smile that could warm him every time like the break of morning. "I will be heavy in the moons to come. Perhaps by the time you come back, I will be light again."

He shook his head a moment. It was like a riddle he didn't understand at first. "Heavy—like a c-cow is heavy?"

"Yes, my husband. Four moons now and already it kicks in my belly."

"You—you—are?"

"I am to have your child, *Pote Ani.*"

She so rarely used his Sparrowhawk name. Now she spoke it formally, almost reverently. A Crow woman respected her man for the gift of new life he gave her.

"You will be—light when I return?" he asked, dumbfounded, not knowing what to say.

"Perhaps." She gazed down at her puffy belly. "The little one begins to move already."

"A child. Think o' that. Me! Havin' a child. At my age. I'm gonna be a pappy. Wagh!"

She pressed against him once more, clinging to him within that protective circle of his arms for this last time. Bass felt her body quaking gently within his embrace, yet she said nothing of her sadness at this terrible moment of parting.

Now his eyes brimmed with tears of happiness.

"I will hurry," he promised as he rested his chin atop her head and spoke in Sparrowhawk. "I will hurry on my journey so that I may return to you and the new child we will have."

At last the sun slipped its bright yellow lip over the range to the east. The purple shadows in the valley lengthened but would soon begin their retreat. Scratch gathered her in his arm, then led his woman along the pack train of the animals he had chosen for the trip. His small caballada was ready. The sun was just coming up. There was no reason to tarry any longer.

He wheeled and brought his lips down to hers, pressing his cold lips against hers, so warm and soft. Then he cupped her head in one palm and pressed it against his shoulder with a fierce embrace. Finally Bass stepped back across the trampled snow and untied the buffalo runner.

"You fixing to leave without me, old man?"

Bass turned at the sound of the voice. Around the corner of Mateo's house strode Josiah, pulling a pair of ponies along behind him.

"Well—I—" Bass stuttered. "Where you get them—" He glanced over at the corral and saw a couple of the Nez Perce ponies were missing. Josiah Paddock had them, packed and ready.

The back door of the Kinkead's house suddenly opened and Looks Far stood braced in the doorway with Joshua cradled within the folds of her blanket capote. She stepped into the dim, ice blue light of the yard as Rosa and Mateo filled the doorway behind her.

"Mateo was the one to get 'em ready for me right when we came back from the fandango," Paddock admitted, a hand brought up to his aching hangover.

"You're settin' to go with me?"

"Kinkead and Rosa didn't pour all that black coffee down me just so somewhere down the trail this morning I could take a nice, long pee."

Scratch shook his head. "This ain't none of your fight, son. I got me some old debts to settle up. I really do appreciate it—but this ain't none of your affair."

Paddock grinned, fighting that pain clawing its way across his forehead. The severe cold of the morning air did his hangover no good.

"You know, Scratch," Paddock declared as he stood toe-up with the older trapper, "I made me one big discovery this morning. It seems going to sleep is very bad for a man's health. Even a young one like me. You see, I was feeling just great last night after you left. Whiskey got to tasting better and better every drink of it. Hell, I was feeling purely good after a little bit. But, Mateo here brings me home and puts my ass to bed up to his place."

Bass chuckled when he saw his younger partner clamp a palm against his forehead.

Kinkead stepped off the porch when Rosa walked up beside Looks Far Woman and put a blanketed arm over the Flathead mother's shoulder.

"I thank you, Josiah," Scratch said. "Thank you for gettin' up to head out with me. But there just ain't no sense to it. I got me an old debt to settle up in St. Louis. It's my affair. You best stay here with your family an' help watch over the women. You take care of Waits-by-the-Water for me."

"Bass," Josiah pleaded as he grabbed hold of the sleeve of Scratch's elkhide coat. "I—I ain't the kind to watch you go off on this by yourself."

"I don't need your help, son."

"Dammit—no one is saying you do. If you don't want my help, so be it." Josiah waited for Scratch to reply.

"Then I best be leavin' now." Bass moved past his woman to the buffalo runner's side.

"But I'm still going with you, Scratch." Josiah stuck a foot in a stirrup and rose atop his pony. "I got a ghost or two I need to settle back there myself."

Titus didn't answer right away. He and Josiah stared at one another for a long, cold moment. Finally he reached in his pouch and pulled out a twist of tobacco. He chewed loose a small chunk that he tongued to the side of his cheek. Now he began to feel some of the cold seeping out of him.

"LeClerc?" Bass asked around the moist chaw.

Paddock nodded. "Yeah," he answered quietly. "I've—I found me some real happiness, Scratch. So it looks like I gotta go back and get things settled with that family before I'll be able to get on with my life."

"I know what you mean, son," Bass sighed as he slipped a moccasin into his own wide stirrup. "A man's gotta say farewell to what's left behind before he can welcome in the rest of his life."

"Then—I'm riding with you?"

Scratch brought his tired gaze down from the cold blue mist hanging like a collar over the Sangre de Cristo Mountains. His breath had already gathered in icicles dripping from his mustache. He swiped a mittened hand across his lower face, then smiled over at his young partner.

"Glad to have the company, Josiah."

His eyes slid across the yard to the tight knot of those left behind. The three women and old Kinkead. Little Joshua bundled up within his mother's arms. Behind the older trapper, the pack horses were fresh and frisky, skittish in the cold, winter morning air. The sun rested on the top of the peaks as he gazed back at Mateo Kinkead.

"Old man, you take care of these here women for us. I ain't never been nothin' big up on a stick, Mateo," Bass called, "but I'll make it worth your while to watch over them women proper. You hear now? All them pelts you got of mine stored in there," he said as he pointed to the tack house, "any of 'em is yours. All of 'em if need be. You just keep them women cared for in the best way."

"Like they was my very own, Scratch," Mateo replied. "I'll take care of everything here, my friend. You—you just watch your own topknot."

Titus stared off into the distance, his eyes watering with the bitter cold, his left eye fogging more than usual. But, he no longer needed that eye to see what his mind was visualizing in St. Louis.

"I'm gonna be comin' back clean, Mateo," he finally uttered.

"I know, I know," Kinkead answered. "Every man has to do for himself—the ones he loves."

"I ain't never been a nigger what plants his nose under a robe all winter, you know. I ain't never been one to lay 'round camp all through a robe season—never was a durned corncracker, a damned Ned."

"I know that, old friend," Mateo soothed again with a crack in his voice.

"I gotta go back where they raise seam squirrels as big as rats," Bass chuckled. "I'm gonna miss these here mountains—all these free mountains, you know."

"I figure they'll miss you too, my friend." Kinkead threw an arm east. "Now, you two get along. Sooner you leave—sooner you'll get back to us."

Scratch leaned over the side of his saddle with his left arm outstretched. Waits-by-the-Water dashed back to his side The old trapper leaned over and hugged her. She put a foot atop his in the stirrup and pulled herself up to give him a kiss. After he lowered her gently to the ground, Bass gazed over at the others to see that Looks Far was backing away from Paddock after giving him a farewell embrace.

"Take care of this plump one, Mateo," Bass reminded. "Rosa will be happy to know she's heavy with my child right now."

"You ain't plucking any of my feathers now, are you?" Mateo said.

"You're gonna be a pappy?" Josiah asked, stunned.

"It's the pure-dee truth," Bass beamed. "She's some four moons along now by her count. I—I wanna make it back by the time my child is born."

Kinkead stomped up and encased the young Crow woman's shoulders beneath his huge arm and pulled her back a step from Bass's pony. "I'll take care of her as if this were my own grandbaby she's having."

" 'Til I see these hills again." Bass choked on the words as he tugged the pack animals into motion.

Paddock blew his woman a final kiss with his mittened hand, then waved farewell. He yanked his solitary pack animal across the yard.

Bass turned his face east for the first time in over ten years. He knew there was no looking back now.

14 OVER THE FIRST range of winter-smitten mountains, the pair of trappers climbed without too much difficulty. It took them four long days to push over the second and tougher range, fighting those remnants left behind by the same storm that had recently dropped its frigid surprise on the Taos Valley. The sun came out for the short daylight hours it allowed the men for travel. They didn't have to worry about hunting at first. The two men had packed trail food to last them until they were far down the east slope. It was then they decided they'd better hunt and save the pemmican.

The wide, white plains yawned before them as they descended the foothills on the eastern slope. The vast expanse of the prairie flatlands could give a man serious second thoughts about travel. Horizon to horizon, the land stretched out before the travelers under the endless, blue domed heavens. Almost nothing else to hit the eye but blue and white, and these tiny, black, insectlike specks moving east, lost in the frightening immensity of the land.

The trappers pushed across Rock Creek, Rabbit Ear and McNee's Creeks, all the time bearing northeast. By the time they had completed the sixty-odd miles on to Cold Spring the men had set their daily routine and trail ritual. They arose some time before sunup and packed the animals for the day's travel. By mid-morning the pair stopped and let the horses and mules take a short rest. It was here that the men ate broiled meat left over the previous night's supper. Again in the mid-afternoon, they halted for a brief rest. Then came another long pull through the shank of the day while the sun raced to its bed in the west.

It was along a creek or stream where they would find some cottonwoods. Down in the ragged vegetation they could build a fire, dispersing the smoke through the leafless branches of the trees so as not to be spotted by any searching eyes. Here they would halt briefly to cook their supper, then hurry on a few more miles before finding a place to rest for the night. With completion of the daily ritual, their scanty baggage would be dropped from the animals' backs and the horses picketed for the deep, long hours of darkness. Without any warmth of a fire to fight the frosty air already making icicles of their mustaches, Bass and Paddock crawled wearily into their rock hard, frozen robes.

Here at Cold Spring on the great Santa Fe Trail the pair picked up the Cimarron River. From the winter-parched riverbed they were able to drink their fill of the murky water that oozed up to fill the little pockets their fingers scratched out of the wet sand. First the men drank, then their animals. They had to pass the Upper Spring, Willow Bar, then Middle Spring before the pair finally reached the Lower Spring of the Cimarron.

The pale winter sun hung feebly near mid-sky when they stopped to water and rest the animals. Domed overhead, the sky squalled a tarnished pewter—low, cold, and ominous.

"Looks to be this is where we'll have to leave the river now." Scratch had been studying the direction the river took as it rolled its flow away from them, dipping to the southeast now.

"North by east, huh?"

"Yep, Josiah. We just keep usin' the sun each day to track where it is we're headin'."

"Doesn't look like a whole hell of a lot out that way," Paddock said as he stuffed a foot back in a stirrup.

"You're right there, son," Bass answered. "Some call all that nothing out there the Cimarron Desert. Others—well, to them it's known in Spanish as the *Jornada del Muerte.*"

"Are you gonna tell me what that means in English?" Josiah smiled as he settled down atop the old Santa Fe saddle.

"Journey of Death."

"Glory be. That's prime." Josiah's pony pranced around and he brought it back around. "We're heading off through something called the Journey of Death and here you are acting like all we're doing is heading down to the sutler's for supplies and a goddamned picnic."

Bass chuckled. "Ain't gonna be all that bad for us, Josiah. I heard tell it's only 'bout fifty mile or so of the Jornada."

"Just what makes it all so hard then? What makes this stretch of trail a journey of death?"

"No water," Bass answered.

"No water?" Paddock squeaked in reply. "You mean we had us our last drink for better than fifty miles?"

"Yep. Probably the way it'll turn out. Except for this." He patted the two large gourd canteens lashed at the back of his saddle.

"That's all there'll be for us to drink for better than two days, huh?"

"Not 'sactly, son." Bass shook his head. "We might have to make do without any ourselves. Might have to give these here ponies a taste of water along 'bout the second day. We just cain't plan on what will happen when we go to cross a long stretch of water scrape like this. Best you always hold onto as much of that water as possible."

"You're positively beautiful, old man." Josiah smiled, showing all his teeth as he tapped heels to his pony once more. "You're leading me across a Journey of Death where we got only two little Mexican gourds filled with about as much muddy water as we could piss and you're planning on giving that water to the horses."

"Jumpin' Jehoshaphat! I do believe you've got it." Bass heeled his pony into motion and snapped the rope to the new mule, pulling along the rest of the ponies.

Beneath his grin, Bass hid a private concern. The dry heat of summer was worst of all on a water scrape. No arguing that. But the dry cold of winter could suck up a man's juices just about as quickly. Any traveler crossing the prairie in winter learned that reality all too soon. Eating snow was no answer either, only a temporary relief. The cold flakes took more heat from a man's body than they were worth in moisture.

For the next hour the small party wormed like black beetles scurrying across the snow. The sky dripped heavy with gray, afternoon light as the men pushed on at an animal-saving lope. A monotonous blanket made the country they viewed over each hill look the same. Endless snow smeared the land from horizon to horizon beneath a leaden dome almost close enough to touch. Beneath that ground layer of white, each pony's hoofs pounded against earth baked to a forged iron hardness.

Bass finally spoke after more than an hour of silence. "Josiah, you ain't fought you many Injuns, have you?"

"Only those back in Bayou Salade," Paddock replied as he glanced over at his partner. "Them in Pierre's Hole, those Bannocks, too, is all."

"Then, it looks like we're fixin' to teach you some more 'bout red niggers."

"W—what?" Josiah's head jerked around. His eyes followed Scratch's arm to the north and west.

Some two miles off, atop another low rise in the swelling white landscape, dark figures stippled the horizon. A line of horsemen came to a halt on top of the rise, looking like so many pickets in a fence seen from afar.

"What are they?"

"Don't rightly know, Josiah," the older man answered. "Out this way they could be Kiowa. Hell, they could be some Comanche wanderin' up, some southern Cheyenne. This is the southern part of Arapaho country, come to think of it."

"They've seen us, huh? Whoever they are?"

"They ain't standin' there drawin' our picture, son."

"They want the ponies?" Paddock asked.

"Most likely." Bass studied the warriors on horseback. "Might be we just run onto a winter huntin' party out for grits. But there ain't one of them that don't have his mouth waterin' right now, seein' two solitary white men. Every one of 'em thinkin' how big their bark'd be to hang our hair from his lodgepole tonight."

Paddock breathed deeply before he spoke again. "How you gonna have this go?"

"We're gonna slide off up there." Bass motioned. "Top of that hill yonder. Let's ride flat out on the withers, boy!"

Josiah followed Bass's lead and kicked his pony hard toward the hill a half mile off. Scratch circled his buffalo runner so that he could race along the pack train, whipping the animals into action. At the same time, the trappers saw the Indians peeling off the horizon, heading across the white swales in their direction at a ground-gorging gallop.

Snow cascaded from each pack animal's hoofs as it came sliding to a halt at the top of the sharp rise. White rooster tails billowed about the old trapper as he plunked to the ground.

"Tie 'em off nose to nose. Two by two," Bass shouted as Paddock dismounted.

The men used each animal's halter rope or rawhide reins to tie the six animals into three pairs. Feverishly each trapper worked at the knots with numbed fingers yanked out of warm mittens. Their eyes fretted back and forth from the work at hand to the onrushing, triple handful of warriors. Paddock counted them quickly as he yanked the last knot tight.

"Looks to be there's fourteen, maybe fifteen of 'em coming!" Josiah shouted under the low, cold dome of a winter-hard sky.

Scratch squirmed on his last knot and slapped his new mule's haunch. "Ain't even given a thought to namin' her yet," he said as he wheeled to pull free one of the rifles. "A shame. Should call her Peach Pits."

Josiah's mustache crinkled in the cold. "Why Peach Pits?" he asked.

"'Cause that's what a man shits when he sees a passel of blood-crazed Injuns screamin' after his hair," Bass announced with a crooked grin.

Paddock laughed to choke down his first flush of fear. He slipped his rifle over the saddle of his pony as the Indians closed on the rise. Beneath the veil of humor, Josiah actually felt his innards pucker at the sight of the onrushing warriors. It was an altogether different thing going after an Indian—something entirely different. Now the warriors were charging in on him and the old man. Suddenly he felt boxed in, almost helpless in a suffocating way here within the tiny corral of horses. Nose to nose, tail to tail atop the small hill. Bass was right, Josiah decided. Just watching the Indians skimming across the snow toward them was sight enough to set a man's asshole to puckering.

"Tighter than an old redbone hound passing a peach pit," he muttered as he glared downhill across the gray snow.

By then the onrushing band of Indians was little more than a hundred yards from the tiny knot of trappers and ponies—effective range for the big-bored mountain rifles.

"Don't you do nothin' with your gun, Josiah!"

"We'll keep it for backup while you load?"

"Somethin' like that, yeah," Bass hollered above the growing cacophony of the yells and screams and taunts of the Indians. "Watch this, young'un."

Scratch slipped the rifle over the saddle and brought it into his shoulder as if ready to fire at the bobbing cavalcade of snorting ponies and screaming Indians. Unexpectedly it was as if the old trapper had become a wizard and the rifle his wand. With that singular gesture Bass watched the onrushing band split itself into two groups, one team of horsemen moving to the left, the second team of warriors galloping to the right, both streaming around the brow of the small hill. Atop that rise both trappers watched in amazement as the warriors seemed to disappear from the backs of their ponies. They rode hidden behind their horses in that manner for a short distance until they had pulled their animals back out of rifle range where they slid upright once more and swung their war ponies in a graceful arc onto the rolling plain.

"I see what you mean," Josiah hollered up close to Bass's ear.

"They're 'fraid of the big guns. Looks to be they know 'bout white man's rifles," Bass said without taking his eyes off the regrouping warrior band. "Maybe so, they've seen that the big guns reach out there a ways, huh?"

"Probably so."

"Just don't fire less'n it gets to be there's no other choice." Scratch turned and gave Paddock a flash with his eyes. "We're in better shape if we each got us loaded weapons, 'stead of empty guns."

"Only one of us fires at a time," Paddock said.

"An' you do that only when I tell you to. Got it?"

"Yep," Josiah responded. "Think I do."

"They're just a bunch of poor niggers." Bass chewed off a hunk of tobacco and put the twist back in his shooting pouch where it always remained handy. "Goddamned Arapahos!"

"Them Arapaho?" Paddock turned to face him.

"Appears to be for certain, son."

"I thought so. Something familiar about the way they're dressed."

"Just a poor-digger, rag-tag bunch of 'Rapahos. Thievin' bandits that they be. Damn all your hides!" Bass shouted.

"You think they understand your language, old man?" Paddock asked with an icy grin.

"They only know I'm tauntin' 'em, tellin' 'em all to bring the fight on into me, Josiah. Very same thing they do to an enemy." He swept the snow beneath his feet nervously, a toe digging into the white, wind crusted surface. "All that really matters is that they know I'm brave enough to shout my medicine back at them."

"They're coming in again." Paddock said suddenly.

Titus turned his head. The Indians peeled off to begin another ground-eating charge up the rise toward the trappers.

"You young niggers wanna steal my ponies? Do you now, huh?" Scratch screamed at the top of his lungs.

"That ain't all they want, we both know that."

"Damned sure, it ain't. They'd love to raise our hair." Bass spurted tobacco juice across the snow at his feet. "One of them young niggers'd love to have your purty, curly topknot hangin' from his scalp pole."

"God's blood but I aim to do everything I can to see that none of them red sons of bitches get their damned hands on these locks of mine!" Josiah roared lustily.

"Tell you what, son. I'll make you a deal. If one of them niggers gets your hair—I'll cut off his bean pole for you. We'll make a present of it to his squaw."

They both laughed until Bass had to slide the rifle over the saddle again to threaten the fast approaching parade of copper-skinned riders.

Scratch tapped the barrel of McAfferty's well-used rifle. "This ol' tool, she works on them Injuns just like it were powerful magic, don't she?"

Both trappers marvelled as the band of warriors again split into two ribbons circling around the knoll.

"Howg—howg—owg—owg—owg," the Indians screamed up the rise at the white men.

Feathers in ebony hair flitted brightly against the dull, pewter light. Fringe and fur and blankets streamed back in the wind as the warriors raced around the low hill. Long braids, horses' manes and tails alike fluttered on the icy breezes. Then the warriors swept away again in their grand arc to regroup on the plain.

"Most of 'em look to be brassy young'uns." Bass spit and a brown spurt of tobacco juice sank into the snow. "Most of them brownskins only got one, maybe two feathers tied up to their topknot. Ain't done all that much in the way of gainin' man sized coups, I'd reckon."

"How about that one?" Paddock nodded toward the warriors. "The one those younger ones are all gathering around. He ain't wearing no feathers at all."

"Ummm, most likely he's the leader," Scratch pronounced. "He's either earned enough feathers that he don't wanna wear 'em anymore, or he's just cocky enough that he don't have to brag no more."

"He's older than the rest, eh?"

"Believe so, son. Probably so," Scratch answered. "He's what the Crow call *Basuk-ose*. That first part if it, *basuk*, means somethin' on the order of 'in front.'" Bass snugged his rifle into his shoulder as the leader wheeled and sped back toward the trappers. "Then, the *ose* means the number 'one' or 'first' in Sparrowhawk. 'He's the bravest' it means in Crow, because he's the one who 'goes first.'"

Josiah examined the leader of the war party closely as the Indians approached the white men's stand atop the hill. That warrior was definitely older than the rest of the bunch. And because he did not wear any of the feathers signifying his coups, this leader drew all the more singular attention to the symbolic dressing of his hair. Two long braids were tightly wrapped in strips of red trade cloth and left to swing in the breeze at the sides of his head. What hair remained loose on the top of his head was swept forward in a grand manner and thickly greased until it stood nearly straight from the top of his skull. It served as a silent, yet daring, affront to all his enemies. A bold challenge to any man's scalp knife.

The Indians' charge came like the rush of a strong wind against them. The warriors pushed up the hill before sliding around the trappers and disappearing. This time the cavalcade of warriors came even more tantalizingly close. Close enough to be tempting. Close enough to dare. Close enough to put a man's bowels to puckering.

"Josiah!" Bass glanced at his friend, sensing Paddock's temptation. "Don't you dare pull that trigger. Just act like you'll pull it should them niggers get too cocky."

"They're gaming with us?" Paddock inquired.

"Sure they are, sassy young niggers." the old man answered.

The bold leader was one of the last ones through the gantlet and finally swerved off around the brow of the hill. Unlike the others, however, this older rider did not drop off to the side of his horse now. He taunted the white men. Waving a bow strung taut, with an arrow nocked, the leader screamed out his challenge.

"Seems like that'un don't believe we'll pop him—he comes any closer," Bass spit as he watched the rider circle the back side of the hill.

The leader made as if to fire his arrow, then tapped his knees against the pony's side to swerve away from the trappers' horses. He returned to the noisy acclaim of the other warriors.

"Look at that, will you?" Paddock said. "He's cock of the walk with them other younger niggers."

"Yeah," Bass said. "What he's doin' is whippin' them youngsters into a bit of a fightin' fittle right 'bout now. Hold your fire this time."

Scratch watched the warriors heading back for another charge at the hill.

He was intent upon how the warriors aligned themselves. The dozen or so younger men were coming directly up the hill while the leader placed himself last in line. He rode almost alone as the others split this way or that around the top of the rise only a few daring yards away from the white men's horses. The leader came on, racing up the hill, seeming to stare at young Josiah as he charged toward the small circle of ponies.

Dark eyes burned fiercely in the old warrior's scowling face. The Indian looked hideous, monstrous at this close range, his cheeks and chin painted oxblood and shiny with bear grease. He held on his course, the bowstring drawn back as if he would let his arrow fly.

Paddock pushed the rifle back into his shoulder a little harder, snugged his cheek down onto the stock a little more firmly. The sound of the pony's hoofs pounding, pounding, pounding ever closer echoed in his ears.

The trappers' horses and the young mule began to dance and stamp and whinny with the closeness of the Indian's animal. They jostled and pulled against each other, yanking against the reins and halters and hobbles used to keep them in a tight, defensive circle. On came the lone warrior, bow drawn. His pony's nostrils flared, snorting steamy gauze into the freezing, winter air.

"You just hold your aim on him, son," Bass said. "Don't shoot 'im. Don't shoot that nigger just yet."

Scratch let his rifle slip from the back of his pony and struggled with the prancing, frightened animals.

The war party leader rushed past that point where the attacking warriors had always turned away. Still he charged on up the sharp rise. The other, younger warriors shouted and screamed their encouragement of his bravery, urging him on closer to the trappers. The feathers on the shaft of his arrow were brought back to the warrior's cheek. Then he suddenly slipped down the side of his pony.

Paddock eased out the breath he'd been holding in the vise of his chest for those long moments of torment. Relief washed over him as the warrior scampered away. The Indian had come dangerously close, almost as if he had wanted to plunge right on into the midst of the white men's horses.

In that next instant, the warrior popped upright on his racing pony. He yanked the arrow back to his cheek again as he quartered his pony broadside to the trappers. He sent the shaft flying, almost at random, seemingly with no real target.

"Uuuhhhhhnnnn!" The sound of Bass's voice barely carried over the screams of the younger warriors, above the brays and whinnies of their own pack animals frightened by the smell of the Indian horses.

Paddock grinned tightly, knowing the arrow was only shot out of defiance, perhaps more so out of a ridicule of the white men for not firing at the warriors.

"Pop that nigger!" Scratch barked with a cold wheezing strain to his words.

Josiah didn't raise his cheek from the rifle stock. His response was automatic. There was no question in his mind about the sudden change in orders. Now he was to fire at the older warrior whereas before he was to hold in the face of the charges. Yet just as he started to pull the trigger on the big gun, his target disappeared behind the racing pony once more. Paddock did what he figured was the next best thing. He drew a bead on the head of the warrior's horse and squeezed the trigger.

Over the flash of the pan and the gray muzzle explosion, Josiah watched the leader fly off the back of his mount. The painted pony pitched headfirst after spilling its rider across the snow covered ground in a neck wrenching fall.

"Attaboy, son!" Scratch roared with delight, his voice crackling electric with excitement.

"I get him?"

"Lookee for yourself." Scratch watched the other warriors as they milled about down on the flat. He knew they had seen their leader toppled from his horse, the pony rolling over on top of him. They would try something immediately.

"Best you reload real quick, Josiah. Real quick for the sake of us both."

Josiah set to pouring powder and driving home a patchless ball. He held the wiping stick alongside the barrel as he sprinkled priming powder down into the pan and snapped the frizzen over it. His glance shot back toward the warriors.

"They're comin' in again," Scratch warned.

"I'm set now."

"Then I'll keep my load," Scratch grunted. "You take another."

Paddock watched the young warriors speed up the sharp rise. Two of the Indians pulled to the side while the others drew the white men's fire. They had begun their sweep by their fallen comrade, hoping to scoop him up from horseback. Immediately, Josiah knew what his target would be. After he squeezed the trigger and began to let the rifle slip down from his shoulder, the weapon was yanked away from him. He found the older trapper taking the empty rifle from him and shoving another loaded weapon in its place.

"Have—have you do—all the shootin'." Scratch twisted to the side to put the rifle in the young man's hands. He peered over the saddle of the runner. "Looks to be you got one, boy. Whoooeee! Sonuvabitch. That's prime shootin'. Center, she is. Do 'er again for me, son. Make 'em come!"

Paddock studied the scene through the disappearing gray smoke that hung like a dirty sash across the frosty air. He had spilled one of the two riders coming to pick up the daring leader of the war party. And near him lay the body of his dead rescuer.

"Take 'nother before they drop back outta range," the old man barked in his ear. "Get that young shit!"

Paddock responded immediately, automatically leveling the rifle at the second retreating rescuer. He eased back on the trigger of Bass's heavy rifle, for an instant hopeful that its sights were held the same as his on a target, The weapon's kick still surprised him when it bit his shoulder.

"Looorrrdeee! You got that nigger too!" Scratch slipped the wiping stick back down the thimbles along the underside of the barrel and shoved the loaded weapon into Paddock's hands.

Josiah took his rifle back and turned to a pack saddle to yank free another of the weapons Bass had brought along. He freed the rawhide straps and pulled the old smoothbore free of the baggage.

"I'll load for you, son. You're shootin' center today," Titus barked, frost dripping from every word. "You pop 'em if they come in again. That way we'll keep at least two of these guns here ready to use."

Bass coughed heavily, wracking with the sound of fluid in the winter-dry, crackling air.

"How come you changed your mind of a sudden?" Paddock slid his rifle up top of the pack animal's back so that it pointed toward the warriors.

"That one nigger." Scratch turned his head slowly, eyes crimped tight with something like blue pain, so that Josiah couldn't see the flash of it cross his face. "That nigger leadin' the bunch got too damned froggy for his own good, I s'pose."

"Looks like it might have worked."

"How's that?" Bass turned his attention back to the rolling flats that sloped away from their little rise of land.

"Seems to be they're deciding just what to do now," Paddock ventured.

"That could be. Maybe so," the old man answered.

The remaining warriors milled around, gesturing wildly and arguing amongst themselves. The two trappers could hear those loud voices as the young men hollered back and forth at one another.

"Lookee there what you done, boy." Scratch patted Josiah's arm as he turned slightly.

"We done it, old man." There was a grin buried deep in Josiah's brown whiskers. "We done it together."

The remaining warriors began to trickle off from the scene. With three dead companions, the rest of the Indians seemed to have lost much of their nerve. Some of them began to ride away, north and west.

Several warriors hung back for a few minutes, taunting the white men, hurling their oaths of revenge up the slope. Finally they, too, rode off.

Paddock slipped the rifle completely off the back of the pack animal.

"Here, Scratch." He pushed the weapon toward the older man. "You hold this and I'll get started loosing these ponies. I think we best get the flying hell out of here."

"Cain't hold 'em all," Bass growled, painfully testy.

Josiah noticed that the old trapper already had two weapons tucked under his right arm and was attempting to reach for this third with his right hand.

"You got two good paws, don't you?"

The pain was almost too much for Bass to grit against any longer. The danger had passed. The adrenalin was seeping out of his blood. There was left only the fiery torment in his chest. The old man turned ever so slightly so that Paddock could see why his left arm hung useless.

"My—sweet Jesus Keeerist!" Paddock exclaimed breathlessly. He stared, transfixed, at the shaft protruding from the front of Bass's shoulder. Blood had soaked right around the arrow, darkening the shaft's hole in the elkhide coat.

"You gonna—stand there like some goddamned Ned struck dumb? Has some poor digger run off with your tongue, boy?" Bass rasped nastily. "Son, you best help me get this right sleeve off." He fought for breath, woozy with the loss of blood, the press of cold, and the letdown after their short skirmish.

"Here, I'll take these." Paddock slipped the weapons out of the old man's hands and stuck them atop baggage where they would be handy.

Josiah tugged gently at the right sleeve of the elkhide coat, pulling it off the rotating shoulder as Bass fought his way out of the heavy garment. The older man held the coat so that its weight wouldn't bear down on the arrow.

"What do I do now?" Paddock's voice showed his exasperation, his panic.

"You never had to mend me up afore, did you now?" Bass sank slowly to the snow, his legs buckling under him.

Josiah eased the older man to the ground, then quickly unlashed some robes. He stacked two of them behind the trapper, threw a third over Scratch's legs.

"That's—that's fine, son."

"All right. All right."

"Let's get this damned thing outta my shoulder, huh? Whaddaya say?"

"Yeah," Paddock squeaked nervously. "All right. What—whaddaya want me to do first?" He couldn't take his eyes off the feathers on the shaft as he watched the fletching bob and sway with every ragged breath the old man yanked in.

"First," Bass swallowed hard against the dry, wracking pain. "First you take both hands an' put 'em round the shaft. No, one right up close to the chest—like that. Right."

He watched Josiah put his left hand around the shaft right against his shirt. Then Bass took Paddock's right hand in his and placed it right next to the other hand, right around the shaft.

"Now," he groaned, feeling like spitting. The chaw of tobacco had wedged itself dryly in his cheek so the old trapper ended up coughing instead. "B—break the goddamned sonuvabitch!"

Paddock studied the old eyes a moment, then did as he was told. Bracing the left hand as securely as he could, he snapped the right hand down, sensing the crack of the shaft. He watched Bass open his eyes after a moment of grimacing against the pain torn through him.

"You all right with—with—"

"Yeah. Yeah, I'll live," Bass moaned. "Now, let's get this damned coat off my arm so you can go to work."

Josiah leaned the older man forward a ways, then slipped the left sleeve off Bass's arm. He eased Scratch back against the coat and buffalo robes.

"Actin' like I was pure gut shot, ain't I?" Bass rasped.

201

"Nawww, old man," Josiah reassured. "You're doing just fine for a fella who's got an arrow sticking in him. It's—it's me that's in trouble here. I'm afraid I don't know what to do to be of help to you. Never before—"

"We wanna—gotta see where the head of it is," Bass rasped, the pain high in his chest spreading in a burning circle from his shoulder. "Feels like it's a might stuck in there, son. 'Fraid it's hung in some bone."

"You're breathing all right?"

"It didn't tickle my lights, near as I can tell." Bass cracked a phlegmy cough as he eyeballed the stump of the shaft.

Paddock leaned over to peer at the old man's back. No blood darkened the back of the shirt. He ran his fingers over a lumpy area near the top of the left shoulder blade.

"Oooouuch! Goddammit!"

"I thought so," Paddock grinned as he leaned back on his haunches to look Bass in the face again.

"What you mean by that?"

"The head of the arrow is right below the skin. Almost made it through your tough old hide. Almost—but not quite. Came in low down here—going out higher up here on the back of your shoulder. Like this." Josiah showed the direction of the arrow's path through the old trapper's body.

"Right below my hide, you say, huh?" Bass asked, then spit out the chunk of tobacco.

"Yep," Josiah nodded. "What to do now?"

"First, you're gonna cut a long slice in the back of my shirt there. That way you can get your hands on the head when it comes popping through."

"You're fixing to have me push it right on through your back?" Paddock squeaked in disbelief.

"Dammit!" Bass gritted his teeth a moment and clenched his eyes shut before continuing. "Dammit, Josiah. I just don't see no other way to butcher the thing outta my hide. You're just gonna have to cut the shirt a bit—so you can—can rip my hide open back there."

Paddock looked away from the old man. He knelt behind the wounded trapper and removed his knife. With the tip of the blade, he pricked the leather shirt, then opened a slice in the deerskin some six inches long over the head of the arrow. For a long moment he stared at the lump caused by the protruding tip pushing up against the surface of the skin near the top of the shoulder blade.

"Got your knife, son?"

"Right here."

"How 'bout your pistol?" Bass cranked his head over his shoulder, attempting to stare down at the arrow's head pushing up beneath the surface of the skin. "You get that pistol out."

"All right." Josiah came around to kneel at the older man's side. "I'm ready. How about you?"

"Let's be done with it, Josiah Paddock. Let's be done with it." Bass swallowed hard. "Take the flat of the knifeblade there. Set it against the end of the shaft you broke off. That's it, flat against it. Don't push none now. Just leave it be. Leave it be on the end of it. Like that. Good. I don't want you wigglin' it around none. Hurts just like you're pushin' a hot poker right through my chest, up there to my shoulder."

"I don't want to hurt you none—"

"Just be done with it!"

"Don't want to cause you no pain—"

"You're just gonna tap the knifeblade there with the butt handle of your big pistol. You see? Easy as that."

"Then what?"

"Dammit! Them Injuns out there just might up an' come ridin' back on in here. So let's just get this cut outta my hump. You're gonna push the nigger's damned arrow on through my shoulder there. Push the head on through, then grab it on the other side with your fingers and pull the sonuvabitch straight outta me."

"You're gonna tell me what to do every step of the way, right?"

"Yeah, yeah," Bass answered. "Here. Gimme that—that piece of the arrow you broke off. There."

Paddock retrieved the broken arrow from the snow and handed the fletched portion of the shaft to Bass. "This?"

"Yep." Grimacing against the burning river in his chest, Bass put the shaft between his teeth and bit down on it securely enough to hold it while he spoke. "G'won," he mumbled. "Dewit!"

Josiah gazed at the old man's eyes a moment more. He positioned the pistol butt out from the chest a few inches.

"More'n dat," Titus mumbled around the arrow shaft. He watched Josiah pull the pistol back farther from the knifeblade, measuring the strength of the blow it would take to send the arrow point out of his back, through the muscle and tissue and skin.

"Ride dere. Dewit!" he snapped.

Paddock studied the knife blade an instant more, then drove the pistol butt down against the knife with a loud, metallic clunk.

The pain burst through him like a liquid ribbon of fire boiling over and pouring through his chest. The pain dripped red and orange, hot beyond relief. Then he felt the cool purple and blue pour over him, and finally shadow black.

"Uhhnnn!"

Paddock's eyes darted to the old man's face and he saw that Bass had slipped into unconsciousness. Merciful, blessed unconsciousness.

He peered over the slumped trapper's shoulder. Sure enough, the arrowhead had pierced on through the old man's hide. It dripped red as it poked fully out of the ragged hole in Scratch's back. The black, ragged line of lacerated tissue pulsed bright with blood that already began to coagulate and freeze.

Josiah placed two fingers behind the arrowhead, using the other hand flattened around the shaft in the hole. Then he yanked quickly with everything he had. The old man's body twitched. The fletched piece of broken arrow tumbled from Scratch's lips.

The shaft was free. Paddock stared at it a moment before he finally flung the arrow aside in the snow.

Josiah rose to retrieve a small chunk of buffalo hide he cut free from a sleeping robe. He sliced it in two and placed the pieces over both sides of the wound. The blood oozing from the two holes was enough to make the fur cling to the older man's skin. Quickly Paddock found one of the wool blankets Bass had packed and cut a long bandage from it. With that blue blanket strip, he bound the two fur compresses tightly against the bleeding holes. Then he pulled the bottom of the trapper's shirt down and laid the heavy elkhide coat over Bass.

Paddock rose, suddenly apprehensive. He stared off in the general direction the warriors had taken in their retreat from the battle scene. He wasn't sure, but he thought he saw some dark objects moving away from them, some distance across the whitened landscape. At least it didn't seem as if any of the warriors were going to hang around long enough to attempt another attack right off.

But he knew he had to get them moving. He glanced down at the unconscious trapper, and wondered if he should make camp right there. No, he decided. That spot on the hill was too open and the wind would be too damned cold. And those warriors knew right where they were. He would have to get them moving.

Squinting into the pewter light hanging over the rolling, snowy plains, Josiah mulled over where he should go. He figured he knew what direction the old man had been heading in, pretty much north by east. Up ahead there might be some shelter. Perhaps some trees along a stream or creek. Some place, he'd have to find a spot where there'd be some cover for a fire.

The animals were skittish now, nervously pulling against one another since they had been tied nose to nose. He went to the first pair and released them. Knotting the ends of their tethers together so that they remained paired, Paddock nose-hobbled the ponies. It was after he had done the same with the second pair of pack horses that he heard the old trapper's groan.

"You're coming around, eh?" Paddock cheered as he knelt beside the wounded man.

Bass coughed, then swallowed dryly. "Got anything to drink?"

"I might be able to dig something up for you, old man."

"Wish you would," Bass nodded. "Make it strong, too."

"Planning on it."

After he had located the flask of whiskey and worried the cork out of the top, the younger man watched Bass sip at the strong liquid. Scratch tapped the fingers of his right hand along the bandaging job, then looked up at Josiah with pain-glazed eyes.

"We gotta be moving, you know, Scratch."

Bass nodded again. "Yeah." He brought his trembling legs up under him, sloshing the whiskey flask. "Here, help this poor child up on his feet, will you?"

Josiah stuck his hands under the older man's arms and pulled Bass up. "You're looking a trifle better than you were a few minutes ago."

"How long I go out on you?"

"Long enough."

"How long, I asked?"

"Not long, Scratch," Josiah answered. "Long enough for me to pull that arrow out of you." His toe indicated the bloodied shaft he'd tossed on the snow. "Long enough for me to bandage you up and figure out we had to be leaving."

"Help me with the coat." Bass struggled with the heavy elkhide coat. "Maybeso, it won't be all so bad, huh?"

"You'll be fit real soon, Scratch. A little hole like that won't keep you down, will it?"

Bass gazed out on the plain near the bottom of the rise. "Let's get on down there an' take a good look-see at them young niggers who was hungry for our hair so damned bad." He helped untie the knots on the remaining ponies with his right hand and got the animals sorted into line.

"You want the hair?"

"It's your'n, son." Bass looked at Josiah. "You was the one to pop 'em, make 'em come."

"And you were the one who caught an arrow for all your trouble, right?"

"Yeah."

"Well, I don't want the damned hair."

"Then I do," Scratch declared.

"Let's get down there. We gotta get the man his damned scalps."

When they got down the hill, Bass slid off the buffalo runner awkwardly, cradling the left arm protectively so that the shoulder would move as little as possible. He stumbled a moment on the slick snow before he regained his balance. He toed over the first warrior so that he could examine the face. Already the body was stiffening, both in death and from the freezing temperature.

"Just a young, frisky one, this'un," Scratch advised as Paddock slid from his pony.

Josiah remained at the head of the horses to hold onto reins as Bass ripped free the first scalp and hobbled over to the second warrior. There the older trapper circled the knife blade around the warrior's head and yanked the scalp off the cranium. With the bloody trophy stuck beside the first under his wide belt, Titus scrambled off a few yards across the frozen snow to the final warrior. He kicked the leader over with his toe. He stared at the Indian's dead horse before looking off at the horizon for a long moment.

"Josiah."

"Yeah?"

"C'mon over here, son."

"What is it now?" Paddock shivered with the cold as he dragged the reluctant animals behind him.

"You see anything special 'bout this here nigger?"

"He's got those three same puncture scar marks across one side of his chest, just like those others that came through the Bayou Salade—the marks you told me says he's Arapaho. That it?"

"They all are here," Bass snorted against his dripping nose. "All three of them Arapaho."

"What the hell is that?" Paddock's head jerked down, then he knelt beside the leader's body for a closer examination.

"You see it, huh?" Bass hobbled over to the opposite side of the body.

"The scars—it, they— " He stared at Bass briefly. "It spells—spells T."

"An' a B—for Bass," Scratch finished. "I cain't believe it my own self, Josiah."

"This—this is the one who took—" Josiah looked up to the top of Scratch's head that was now covered with the coyote cap. "He took your scalp-lock?"

"Nawww, not 'sactly," Bass answered. "I killed that one down to South Park some time ago."

"That's right. That's right," Paddock gushed. "I remember it now. This is the other one. You just wounded this nigger after you'd blown the other one's face in. You said you decided to let this one live. There, that's the bullet scar in his shoulder where you hit him all them years back. So then, you cut your initials in his chest and left him to make his own way back to his village. My, my, my."

"The world travels in some mighty small circles, don't it?" Bass sighed.

"I can't believe it." Josiah shook his head.

"I cain't either, son. After—all these years—to run onto this particular nigger. Here in the free west. Some small, small circle at times."

"You gonna take his hair, ain't you?" Paddock asked. "Then we can be going, Scratch. Let's get on outta here."

He didn't want to let the older man know, but Josiah was feeling more than a mite spooked running onto this Arapaho. First the Snake warrior, Slays in the Night. Then all so innocently they had bumped into Hiram Tuttle back to Taos. It made him shiver with a deep cold to look down on what the years had brought Scratch's way, to look down on the Arapaho warrior with a broken neck, the old trapper's initials scarred in the copper chest. Josiah wondered if he felt a cold that no amount of travel would warm.

Bass looked around in three directions across the rolling plains. He saw nothing but white, lumpy hills butting up against the lead gray horizon.

"Won't take long for the light to slide off this sky, Josiah," he commented.

"You're right. Let's be done here an' on our way while I can move."

Bass knelt awkwardly by the hardening body. "Been a long time that we've both been waitin' on this meetin', nigger. Your medicine turned sour. You just wasn't lucky as all that, I s'pose. First off, you was unlucky ridin' with the bastard what stole my topknot so you got my letters carved in you for good measure all those years ago. Then—to cap it off, our trails was meant to cross right here." He made a grand sweep of the landscape with his right arm. "Out in the middle of all of this, with Ol' Winter Man bearin' down on us. This was a damned unlucky draw at the cards, son. Damned unlucky."

Scratch inscribed a circle around the top of the man's head, wiped the knife blade off on his leggings, then stuffed the weapon in its sheath. With a foot braced on the Indian's neck, the trapper pulled the scalp loose with a moist, sucking pop. Scratch rose and slung the bloody prize around in the air a few times. The bitter air did most of the work in freezing the blood and gore on the scalp.

"It's been all these years," he whispered to the corpse. "I let you keep your scalp all these years an' looks like you finally got tired of wearin' it."

Bass squinted with the cold bite of the wind on his rawhided cheeks.

Bass squinted with the cold bite of the wind on his rawhided cheeks.

"C'mon, let's go," Paddock prodded as he climbed aboard his pony.

Scratch looked back at the impatient young man.

"You're right, son," He began to turn away from the body. Then he stopped and gazed at the dead warrior.

"Maybe, just maybe," he said as he nodded at the corpse. "I just might be a lucky child myself by the time I get to St. Louie. Looks to be another circle will be comin' back around on itself there, too, my friend. Another circle in my life comin' back around to heal itself."

He dragged himself over to the buffalo runner Josiah held for him and pushed his tired, chattering body into the saddle. Once he was settled atop leather, Bass gave a last, parting, farewell nod to the older warrior that was being left to the wolves and coyotes.

Scratch tapped his heels against the pony's sides and let Josiah lead them north by east across the rolling snow, Paddock muttering something about Bass wanting scalps when all he wanted was some trees so they could find firewood before dark. Josiah kept on complaining quietly, mumbling almost under his breath about finding a decent, warm camp for the night, some shelter against the wind and the cold, maybe the Indians. He was jabbering a bit so the older man decided not to pay any attention to him. Not really.

Instead of replying, he turned in the saddle and looked back one last time across the graying snow dull under a charcoal sky. The bitter wind came up and whipped the snow in a swirling ballet across the hills. He could no longer see the carcasses they had left behind. His own face was stretched cold across the cheeks and nose. No matter, his left shoulder was already hot. No matter about the cold. He was warm enough.

Bass eased back around to face forward into the wind blustering out of the north. All the way down from Winter Man's home. It did not matter much, really. There would soon be more carcasses for Winter Man to claim. Soon enough there would be more bodies.

It was about time the circle came back around for him, he decided. About damned time. He could feel the warmth of it spreading through his chest. It was about time the great circle of things decided to include him in on something. Make him a part of something. It was about time the great circle blessed him at last. About damned time.

15

THE FOG PARTED for a brief, fleeting moment before it rolled back over the landscape. He thought he could see the dim, faint lights of a town before they disappeared in the roiling gray mist.

Bass heard the water splashing over rocks and stumbled through the thick forest in the direction of its gurgling sound. He fell over something, a downed tree, a large stone—it was difficult to know what it was in the fog. As he struck the ground, he yelped in pain. But the sound caught in his throat. The old trapper rolled over on his back and stared a moment up through the boiling banks of mist. Then he tried to speak again, to shout, to cry out with one sound or another. But it was futile. Nothing passed his lips but the breath he pushed from his lungs.

Then he heard her voice.

"Papa!"

He blinked, trying to clear his vision against the gauzy mist.

"Papa. Come dance with me." Bass turned his head to see the little girl coming toward him. He was not sure how old she was, maybe four, perhaps five. But, from her size she looked to be about three years old. Yes, she was but three years old. Beckoning to him from that edge of the bright light, she smiled and waved.

Her glossy black hair hung past her shoulders, combed straight from the crown. There was a brilliant radiance emanating from it as the white light flared behind her. She beckoned again and took another step toward him.

"Papa! I want to dance. Come on, Papa."

The old trapper felt himself shake his head, almost in disbelief, almost in reluctance to move. It had been so many years since he'd danced. Too, he wasn't sure if he should trust his rusty legs. Mostly, Bass wasn't sure if he truly believed he was the young girl's papa.

It was almost as if meteoric light billowed around her with each step she took closer to him. Then her movement showed him that she wore something white, lacy, almost a gauze in texture. Layer upon layer, it swam around her body like waves licking at the shoreline of a lazy river, swirling around her tiny body like clouds nestling among the high mountain peaks. His eyes moved down her tiny frame to the pointed boots peeking out from beneath the billowing petticoats and bloomers. The boots too were white and as the folds of cloth swam and swirled up her legs, the boots appeared to reach over her ankles, boots studded with tiny mother of pearl buttons. What damned contraps to make a lil' girl wear, he remembered thinking.

As she came spinning up to him the little girl gave a low curtsy. She kept her body bent low at the waist, but her face lifted and shone into his with its pipestone radiance. She looked Indian. The cheekbones were higher than a white child's. Her black cherry eyes sparkled with amusement. The young girl's smile broadened across the dark, coppery skin. He wanted so much to reach out, to touch her face. To feel its childhood softness, to assure himself it truly was Indian skin.

Just as he was about to touch her cheek with his gnarled old fingers, she took his hand in her soft, little hand.

"Come, Papa. I want to dance."

She pulled him along beside her toward the light until he finally saw its brilliance change to a softer warmth radiated by many, many candles and oil lamps. Then there appeared a huge ballroom full of faceless people, each one applauding and nodding happily, showing their approval that Bass should dance with the little girl. As the guests gathered on the dance floor slowly moved out of his way, the color changed from white radiance to a burnished sepia tone.

Brown, he thought. Like the crumbled earth spilling through spread fingers.

Those shades of brown darkened as a shadow fell across the old trapper and the young girl. Bass looked up to see a tall, faceless man suddenly reach out for the little girl. "Papa?"

She began to cry as her hand slipped from his, taking first one step then another toward the faceless man with hairy arms and chest billowing out of his shirt opened at the neck. He reminded Scratch of a faceless brown bear. The creature took the little girl's tiny hand in his huge, hairy paw and led her away.

Bass could not move. He seemed planted on the spot. Only an observer now. Powerless to act, to defend. He could only watch the little girl weep.

From her tiny lips came no words, only sound. Mournful screams, howls, whimpers of despair. Nothing he could make any sense of—only sound. Yet he knew she called to him and him alone. Her arms thrust out to him, imploring Bass to help her.

His feet could not move.

She sobbed piteously, with something almost like a scream caught in the back of her throat. Seeking his help still, the little girl was pulled away by the huge, hairy, brown bear of a man.

It was as if her whimpers echoed Bass's own sadness in not helping, a reflection of his own impotence in the face of the bear man. He wanted to scream out himself, to yell at the others in the grand ballroom, someone, anyone—to help the little girl who was being dragged away from the old trapper.

The crowd suddenly surged and swirled around him. Only their lower faces appeared. No eyes. Only gaping, brightly painted lips, spread wide in laughter and smeared across their white splotched faces. Roaring at him with their cacophony of hideous ridicule, they taunted and teased him, shamed him. Bass wagged his head, filled with a black remorse. He could not move. Helplessly, he could but watch.

At that very moment two huge oak doors, some twelve feet tall, swung open as the bear man dragged the little girl out through the massive portal. Instead of that brightness wherein the dance floor had been illuminated with many bright candles and warm, glowing oil lamps, now there was nothing but a dull, pewter gray mist hungrily swallowing up all the white light spilling out the tall doors. The snow smeared across the ground was the color of lead, buried beneath an ominous, charcoal sky upon which roiling black clouds scudded out of the west.

Screaming in fright, the little girl turned and turned again, pleading with someone to rescue her from the sudden, bitter cold. Huge hairy hands clawed at the spinning, billowing yards of lacy white cloth and tore the dress from the young girl's body. Shred after shred was ripped from her shoulders, off her legs.

She was terrified, not knowing why any of this was happening to her, not knowing why her pretty dress was being ripped from her, not knowing why she was being victimized by the bear man. Why no one came to help. All she wanted was to go to the merry party. All she had wanted was to dance with her Papa.

Layer after layer was wrenched from her body. First the dress, then the layers of petticoats and finally the bloomers covering her shivering legs. As the last act of cruelty, those high button boots were ripped from the little girl's feet so that she stood barefoot in the gray snow, shuddering, totally naked.

She stood naked—except for that tiny doeskin pouch with an amulet of porcupine quills sewn on it hanging from her neck. The bear man tossed the clothing up into the swirling, frigid breezes. All her shredded garments sailed away on a wind whipping the snow across the ground. The crowd of laughing, jeering mouths with their hideous, haunting screeches disappeared behind the huge doorway. It was quiet beneath the joyless wail of the wind.

Bass began to cry. He could not move. Not a participant, the old trapper could only watch. He was only a spectator. Tears froze to his ruddy cheeks.

Footsteps whined across the snow. As he turned, the woman appeared from his left, out of the west. Bass could not see her face, shadowed as it was beneath the hood of her capote. Yet, something was familiar about the woman. Something tore at him in the way she trudged wearily across the snow toward the naked child. Her earthy fragrance burned keen in his nostrils, a smell of land and sky borne to him across the dry, cold air.

Bass shuddered, already sobbing for the little child who cried out to the woman. Snow billowed up around the young girl's bare ankles. Immediately the woman was aswirl with a heavy, woolen blanket. She wrapped it around the girl, then helped the child to sit. Upon the frozen, bluish feet she drew some doeskin moccasins. The woman rubbed and kneaded the child's cold feet until she knew there were tingles and pricks of feeling returning to the numbed flesh. Next, she slipped a second pair of moccasins onto the girl's feet, heavier still and laced their tops securely around the ankles. This outer pair was lined with the shaggy fur of the great buffalo. The young child's whimpering began to slow and she grew calm as some of the cold drained from her feet.

He watched the woman draw a soft, doeskin dress from the folds of her capote and quickly tug the garment over the head of the young girl. The animal hide was smoothed over her tiny body. Then long, skin leggings were brought up each limb and tied to a narrow belt wrapped around the waist beneath the dress. The child stood, braver now, and pulled the thick blanket about herself once more as protection against the wolf-wail wind and blowing snow. There was a smile across her face at last. Symbolizing something close to a small victory, although the wild laughter still continued to roll out from the huge double doors.

Voices screeched out that here was not her place—that the little girl belonged out in the snow, out in the cold. The voices laughed and yelled that the child did not belong with them, there inside, in their warmth.

The woman struggled to her feet. Bass wanted to reach out for her, but he felt without form. He had no arms with which to enfold her. He was just an eye, watching, merely a spectator.

The woman attempted to accompany the child slowly toward the light and warmth of the ballroom, but at the door they were stopped by the tall bear man. He said nothing, merely pointed off across the snow. More hideous laughter erupted from within the ballroom. The woman tucked the child beneath her arm maternally and stumbled across that gray snow billowing wildly in a violent ground blizzard. The streamers of flakes whipped around the pair as they plodded away into the dimming light.

While Bass swiped at the frozen tears across his cheeks, the woman pulled the blanket up about the child's black, storm-ravaged hair. Both of them shuddered with the sudden, gray cold settling in with the violence of the new storm. Both figures disappeared from the trapper, lost in the white gauze mist.

He yearned to know who they were—both this child and the woman. A child who called him Papa. The woman who had smelled so familiar, who moved as if she were a part of him. In some way he was suddenly sure they were tied to him. And their travail made him shudder as he could not tear his eyes from that particular spot where the two had disappeared into the storm. Perhaps they truly did belong to him. There was a grief, a remorse—a deep mourning because of the tearing away that he felt. A sadness for his loss. Perhaps even a terror that he felt for them as they had to wander away into that unknown, trackless, winter desert—a land that was swallowed up by the howling blizzard. Terror. He knew they felt terror out there in that wasteland, smothered in the bowels of this storm. A blizzard where a man could not tell up from down, left from right, front from back, and in from out.

He felt connected to their agony. And the old trapper was overwhelmed with the shame of having in some way caused their terror. For some reason he had caused this to happen to the two of them. He had caused them to be turned away and refused the light and its warmth.

His vision moved from the dancing, swirling tides of white washing over the landscape, finally to rest on the huge oak doors. He turned back to the roaring, laughing, ridiculing voice of the bear man. That sound became almost maniacal as that faceless head turned in the direction of the old trapper. His laughter slowed, then ceased as the tall man motioned, indicating that Bass was to follow.

Scratch plodded painfully up the wide staircase, frozen, his cold joints protesting their years in the mountains and icy streams. Both feet were like lead by the time he reached the top landing.

The bear man pushed open the cracked doors. Instead of entering the grand ballroom where the party had taken place, the tall man led the old trapper through those huge doors where a dark forest appeared. Thick and overgrown. The bare branches of the trees bore no green leaves, yet their dark limbs were thick, gnarled fingers hanging like tendrils to block out almost all the light from reaching the forest floor. What feeble sunlight could slip through the dark, charcoal and dusky tree branches was itself gray—barely enough to allow the old man to stumble along over the thick undergrowth. It clawed at him, snagging at his clothing. Branches snapped into him, cutting his flesh, tearing at his face, ripping at his skin. Deeper and deeper he wandered into the darkening forest, following the sounds of the bear man crashing through the dense vegetation ahead of him.

Bass did not know why he was following this creature into the forest. Why shouldn't he be going to help the woman and the child? That's where he should be heading if . . . if only his feet could take him in that direction. This was not right, heading off on some damned tromp through these godforsaken woods.

So he turned slowly and looked back toward the doors he had left behind to enter this dark, primeval forest. The old trapper stopped. Behind him through the dark tendrils and gray branches of the overgrown vegetation, there were no doors. They had simply vanished. If the doors had ever been there to begin with. So now there was no way out for him.

Ahead the cruel bear man continued to stomp through the forest. Bass sighed, then reluctantly turned back toward the thrashing sounds. He would have to see this through now. There wasn't a solitary thing he could see to do about getting back to help the woman and little child. Nothing at all, with no way out of this that he could find.

No way back at least.

Once more, he considered in his own melancholy way, that he was trapped in something that he must plunge on through. No way back and no left nor right. In cases such as these throughout his life there always seemed to be no way but forward, get right on ahead, forge straight on through. He could not figure out why his options were always so limited, why most of the time there seemed to be no options at all. Didn't seem fair, not fair at all.

Hell, Bass decided, whoever told him things had to be fair? No one he could remember. A branch slapped him in the face and he stopped momentarily so he could rub the laceration across his cheek where the bloodied line beaded, then began to ooze. All he wanted was a chance. That's all Titus Bass had ever asked for—a chance.

That clumsy, crashing noise from the bear man was fading. He decided he had better plunge on after the creature, see this matter through to its end. Find out what connection the man had to that woman and child. Lord, he even had to find out what the woman and child had to do with himself. Why the girl had called him Papa. Why the woman had smelled so familiar. And he had to find out why that monstrous creature had turned the two of them away before bringing him here.

Why here?

Why the same dense, rank forest where he had been led by—Emile Sharpe? That was it!

He ducked a snapping branch and remembered it more clearly now. This was the exact place that the half-breed, Metis giant had brought him last year. That huge killer with one eye scarred shut, sent from St. Louis to kill his friend Josiah. He was like a bear, too. A tall, monstrous grizzly bear rearing on its hind legs, the hideous white worm of a scar running from its brow down across the eye to seal it shut forever before the white line ended on the creature's snout.

Damn!

But that creature had been defeated before, and he could defeat this one. All he wanted was the chance.

A man could really ask for little else. Just a chance to try.

"DAMN!"

He looked up and blinked, watching Paddock's lips move."I didn't think you were going to give me the chance to talk with you ever again, old man," Josiah grinned, a look of relief on his face. He brought the cup close to Scratch's lips and gave the older trapper a sip of water. "I was beginning to wonder if you were going to babble on through another night."

"Wha-a-a—whadda—mean?" The older trapper's lips and tongue crackled dryly.

"The fever, Scratch." Josiah set the tin cup aside. "Something on the arrow. It must have been—when it went through your hide—it must've had something on the shaft."

"Mo'ah."

"What?"

"W-wadder. Mo' wadder."

"Oh, yeah." The young trapper retrieved the cup and let some more of the melted snow spill across Bass's fever parched lips.

"Chance?" the old trapper wheezed like a dry bellows.

"Yeah, a chance. That's what I said to you. I wanted to have the chance to pay you back, Scratch." Josiah smiled again.

"My chance. Mine."

"You might say that, old man. I wanted to pay you back for saving my life. All this time while you been down in your fever and out of your head, I've been thinking about bringing my account flush with you. I just hoped you were going to make it so I could feel like I saved your life and then we'd be square. But then, I remembered you saved my life more than once. I might save your life this time—and we'd still not be even, old man."

"I ain't the one keepin' count."

Paddock nodded and said nothing.

"Why, son?"

"Why what?"

"Why you keepin' count?"

"Guess—I'm just that way."

"Water?"

Josiah spilled some more drops across the old trapper's lips and set the cup aside. "Maybe too it's what I been thinking about while you've been busy mumbling your gibberish. I figured there was only one, solitary way either one of us was going to make it round to St. Louis and back again to Taos. That was together. The two of us. I figured that'd be the only way. We need each other right now. Maybe more than we ever have before. Even though we each have our own private matters to bury, we still need the other one to see us through this. Since we've gotten each other through so damned much already."

"How long, son?" Bass asked after a long silence.

"How long 'til we make it to St. Louis?"

"How long I been outta my skull?"

"Better than a day now." Josiah looked up at the charcoal sky. "Evening now. It'll be night soon. You fell off your pony yesterday, in the early afternoon. Hot as a cheap stove. God's teeth but you were burning up with some fever. It scared the shit out of me. I lost my mother from a fever a few years back. Didn't—didn't want to lose you, too."

"No, won't lose me."

"You had me wondering for a while there. I had to lash you into the saddle, feet and hands. We finally came on this dry creekbed and I made camp last night. You started babbling about that time. Wouldn't take no food, none of what I fixed for you. Wouldn't take none of this gourd water neither. Your eyes stayed popped wide open and you jabbered away like a Sunday circuit preacher about some dance and the snow. All the time I was damned well worried about some Injuns hearing you and coming down here to find us in the bottom of this wash. You talked about the cold, then about a little girl. And you were muttering about the forest and the bears. I wasn't able to make much track out of it all."

"Little girl and bears in the forest?" Bass snorted weakly.

"That's right. Some mighty strange things you were babbling about."

"S'more water, son."

Paddock held the cup to Bass' dry lips and let him sip at the cool, melted snow. There was no problem having enough snow. The moon lay half-lidded beneath those low clouds rolling in waves across the prairie sky.

"No fire."

"I know," Paddock said. "Couldn't find a stick to start a fire for you."

"I mean, no fire is good."

"Yeah." Paddock raised his head and looked about the camp. Weary animals were picketed nearby down the wash. The sides of the old creekbed were mottled in luminous snow and dark shadows beneath the pale moonlight.

"I figured we might just be all right to spend the time down here. That way we wasn't up there on the prairie where we'd be too easy to spot."

"You're learnin'."

"I had a good teacher, old man." Josiah gently eased Scratch's head back down to the robes.

"Who was that?"

"Hell," Josiah grinned. "Just some old fart who really didn't know what he was

214

doing most of the time. He stumbled around into things. Fortunate that way. He was just the lucky sort, I figure."

"How's that?"

"Lucky he ain't been et up by a bear yet, that's what," he chortled quietly. "Lucky he ain't got an arrow still stuck in his roast. Lucky—lucky to have a friend along."

Bass wheezed. "That just ain't luck, son."

"I know, I know," Josiah answered and pulled the robe up to the old man's chin after he had stretched out beside Scratch. "Seems for some folks it is blind luck," he whispered into the old man's ear. "For some they just naturally run through spells of good fortune. Then there's the rest of us. With our kind, it's just a struggle to make our luck. Bad or good, we gotta do it all on our own."

"A man can go on—or he can go back," Titus husked behind the robe curled at his cheek.

"I think we've already decided what we're about to do, haven't we?" Paddock asked quietly. He watched the first few slowflakes curl down upon the robes.

"Ain't nothin' wrong in goin' back, Josiah. If a man figures that's the only way, an' he ain't runnin' away from somethin'—he can't be faulted for goin' back."

"Sure—sure feels strange."

"What does?"

"To hear you talking that way about a fella giving up."

"I ain't talkin' 'bout givin' up, Josiah. It's not the same thing. Goin' back is always a choice for a man. Just as much a choice as goin' on."

It was a long time before either one made a sound. Each man listened as the winter night settled around them. Only the ponies snuffled with the bitter cold. At last Paddock heard the old man's breathing become rhythmic, regular, with that familiarity born of all their time together.

Josiah finally closed his eyes, thinking that the old man probably knew already. Perhaps he was trying to say he understood, too. Perhaps Bass already understood the decision Josiah had made. Maybe Scratch was trying to tell him in his own convoluted fashion that it was all right, what he had decided.

The snow came down a little heavier, the wind picking up and whisking the flakes in swirls gusting down the dry wash. It wasn't shaping up to be much of a storm, Paddock figured.

It was about time their luck changed. After all, they really were two of a kind in that respect. He and the old man. They made their own luck. They had up to this point, and they would continue to forge their own weapons against the tides of fate as they always had done before. It gave the young man some small comfort there beneath the buffalo robes and blankets, listening to the night winds howling harmlessly above them on the winter scarred prairie.

With the wind, this snow would never lie deep.

16

IN THE HOUR before dawn the prairie was like a bell jar of excruciating silence. Bass was not sure if he was alive or dead. He could not hear a thing. Beside him, the younger man slept perfectly still. Down the dry wash, the ponies and mule did not twitch an ear.

He moved the robe off his cheek and peered out at the night. Some of the new snow that had landed on the buffalo hide fell against his neck. Those cold flakes felt good. He could faintly remember being so damned hot there for a while. The snow soothed him with its icy touch. Above them the moon rode low, having become a chalky disk glowing dim but true behind a wide bank of charcoal clouds roiling out of the west. That near-full moon reminded him of the puckered, white bullet scar on that old Arapaho's chest.

The silence here was almost absolute. Scratch felt totally alone for a moment. He knew better—but he could not escape the feeling of lying here the day after God had made this big, yawning stretch of nothing. Each new day seemed as if man would never leave a mark on this lonely, white creation. Lying here bathed in what dim moonlight dripped from the slate gray clouds, his loneliness brought a sudden agony. He turned to look at the body beside him, to be reassured.

He had fought the weight of his eyelids long enough, along with the bitter cold across his cheeks. Titus pulled the robe over his head once more. Back in the cocoon, his breath warming, the old trapper wriggled against the taut ribbon of fire that laced through his shoulder until he found a comfortable position. How many days since the arrow had been removed? Seemed like this would be number three with the coming of dawn.

Neither of them had been making the best of time across the Jornada since bumping into the Arapahos. Titus would be able to ride for only so long, then he would have to slip from the saddle and rest the shoulder. Here it was, the worst part of the whole trip and he couldn't travel across it fast, light, lean—the way he was used to scurrying across a water scrape. This was the worst part of being wounded on the trip—he couldn't travel across the desert fast.

Sometime tomorrow they would reach the river he heard tell of, bordering the northern boundry of this wilderness. Maybe age was telling him something. Forty years old now. He could no longer expect to travel like a colt. Those days were past him. All that was left was living up to what he could do.

Yesterday they had run down to the bottom of the pemmican sack. Both of them had even scraped at the bottom with their fingernails before giving up on it. Now things were simplified—hunt or go without.

They were both getting gut shrunk, no doubt about that. Without one decent meal in better than two weeks, there had been no fresh meat to lay firm and juicy in either man's gut. Hell, it was the price he supposed a man paid in sacrifice to reach what he was striving toward. At least, he kept saying that to himself while he'd chuckle and tell Josiah a crow would have to pack vittles across such godforsaken country as this.

The poor animals had the look of suffering the worst. Yesterday had taken the most out of them. Throughout that long dawn to dusk torture the men had to frequently halt while they carefully doled out the diminishing water supplies to their gaunt ponies—their hides shrunk to look like nothing more than wispy skins stretched over bony skeletons. Hour after hour those animals had plunged through snow drifts in agonizing lunges. Between the monstrous hills of snow the horses would rest and blow before driving into the next drift. It was an act of faith that kept Bass going, faith they would all make it out of the dizzying white alive. It hurt him to see those obedient, faithful creatures, their ribby sides heaving like a forge bellows, their frosty breath like wispy gauze around flaring, icy nostrils, suffering so. From time to time the winter wind had swept clear a brief stretch here or there where they found evidence of someone's passing. Wagon tracks. Neither buffalo nor Comanche, not snow, ice, rain, sleet nor wind would ever wipe the face of the land clean to erase those tracks. It had been better than nine years already for this trail. Now it seemed nothing would ever obliterate the sign of man's passing.

Somewhere along this trail he had heard tell of rivers that sank away to oblivion in shining sands glistening under a torturous summer sun. Veterans of the trail always regaled others in dark, cool Taos watering holes and cantinas with their stories of men's tongues hanging black, swollen, and sticky in thirst from their cracked and bleeding lips, having to stare longingly at the conjured mirages of mountains stretched silver-bright across the edge of the earth, until those Rocky Mountains really did appear on the horizon at last, glistening beneath an inviting bank of fluffy clouds.

The trail was organic. It changed and wandered from time to time as did those life forms which wandered over it. The trail beat with a life of its own. Although its rhythms were different in winter, it was a tune nonetheless dictated by that wilderness, played for all who entered there.

His cheeks and nose were gnawed raw by the cold. Enough of it for now. Bass put his head beneath the robe once more. Here his breath rewarmed his face. One of the animals blew. It sounded like the mule. The horses would be in their deepest sleep at this time, in the hours preceding dawn. Bass let go, wanting this day to be their last on the winter desert. He welcomed sleep again, huddling beneath the robes and blankets remaining between him and freezing. He let it all go.

"LOOKEE THERE, son." Bass pointed to the trees.

"What of 'em?"

"I think we made it, boy. Think we made it."

"Yeah. Trees. That mean we come across the desert?"

"Ain't you seen at all how the land's been changin'?" Bass turned in the saddle, the two wounds tight and nipping in protest, "an' them two big ol' cottonwoods say there's a water course nearby. Somethin' as big as them silver cottonwoods don't mean no pittle-ass stream. We're talkin' a river, Josiah."

"I do hope you're right, old man."

"Why, you ought to feel right proud of what you've done," Bass beamed in spite of his frozen eyelashes and whiskers. The hoarfrost stiffened every exposed hair on his face and lashed his skin until it felt like burnished rawhide.

"You helped pull this old man across the Jornada," Scratch said as he gazed at low gray clouds scudding close to the ground, a strong west wind lancing flakes in their direction.

Little more than a mile from the cottonwoods first sighted they came upon the Arkansas River. Off in the distance they could hear the mournful notes of coyotes, howling like so many agonized souls' voices echoing out of hell. Even some of the landscape appeared just like it might belong to the Devil. Here was a sand belt in that valley of the Arkansas, a strip some seven miles wide and composed of bright hues of red earth that made the area appear to be burning. To this land in the spring would return the buffalo and antelope. Sign of elk and deer had already dotted their trail. Down farther in the Cross Timbers the curious prairie dogs poked their tiny rodent heads out of their burrows and yipped at the travelers.

"Leastways, you won't be havin' to go hungry," Bass chortled.

"It's gonna be good to sink my teeth into something other than that crumbled-up moccasin-sole leather you call pemmican trail food."

By the time they reached the Arkansas, the scattering of snow flakes had changed into a knifing of icy sleet. Bass turned to his partner.

"You plant it here for a bit. I best hunt us down a crossing."

Without another word the old trapper disappeared down the river bank. Just as unceremoniously, the man reappeared out of the blowing snow some twenty minutes later. He took up the lead rope to the pack animals from Josiah.

"You found something? Somewhere to cross?"

"Bet I have, son," he answered and nodded. "Heard it said a man's got to watch out an' tread soft. Lots of fellas say this river's nasty with bogs and sand sinks."

"Quick sands?"

"Call 'em what you will," Bass replied and waved it off, nudging his pony east. "Found us a buffalo crossing. A man cain't hardly go wrong if he lays his nose along a buffalo trail."

The heavy, sharp drops lanced at man and animal alike as the two men plodded through the freezing rain toward a small stand of trees on the north bank of the Arkansas. If it had not been for that vegetation growing in among the bordering trees, the river crossing would have been lifeless and spare. Both banks were nothing better than sandy buttes standing sentinel over a water course barely two feet deep. Sand and sleet drove at them from every angle by the wind before the travelers made it into the stand of trees.

As Bass pulled the pack animals into the sparse vegetation something caught the corner of his eye. Instinctively he brought the rifle out of the crook of his arm and fired, in one fluid motion.

"What the hell?" Josiah exclaimed, sliding from his wet saddle when the old man fired.

"Supper, boy."

"Supper?"

"Right over yonder." Bass nodded into a thicket of bramble.

Bass tore off a twist of tobacco and stuffed it between his teeth and cheek. He pulled the stopper out of his powderhorn and began reloading. "Go on over there an' find out what we got. Seems only right. I done the shootin', you do the butcherin'."

"Shit. This won't take me long." Paddock slid his rifle across the crook of his arm and wiped his wet face with the back of his mitten. "Ain't nothing to skinning out some skinny varmint you're likely to plug."

"You wanted supper—I got you supper."

Bass watched Paddock stride off toward the underbrush. Driving home the patched ball, he was just pulling his ramrod when Josiah yelled out.

"I'll be damned! Venison tonight," Paddock shouted. "Dee-licious deer meat. I didn't really believe you, old man. But here you got what appears to be a buck, maybe a couple of years old."

"I wasn't all that sure what it was, or how old it was," Bass snorted. "I just saw meat. I'll get the fire started, then we'll pull our truck an' plunder off these critters here. They're likely as not soaked clear through with rain an' ice as bad as we are."

Bass stuffed his hands back inside their mittens for a moment. "Only thing we gotta worry about here is wolves. They'll likely smell blood on the winter wind. They're bound to come on down here to see what it is. Cold weather—them critters get bold an' downright sassy as can be. Walk right on into a winter camp an' eat your saddle gear, hobbles an' knife scabbards if they cain't find no fresh meat to suck up. Eat anythin' rawhide they can swaller, they will."

Turning slowly, he listened to the joyless cry of the wind as it whipped those ghostly tree branches above them with its driving force of icy rain. Here in their little grove the men and horses escaped most of the storm's fury and icy blast. Overhead the branches creaked eerily beneath the wind's incessant force.

Bass snapped off some kindling from the dry, dead branches he could reach from the ground. "We're lucky we don't have to start a fire out there on the prairie. Damned hard to find buffler chips in the snow."

As their little fire crackled and spit in protest of the driving sleet coming through the stand of trees, both men set about quickly pulling the spare baggage off the animals and picketing them close by in the surrounding trees for the night. To the east the sky shone a pale yellow in fading twilight. Soon the sputter of sleet in the fire was drowned out by the spit and crackle of juicy meat raining grease on the flames.

Overhead the sky sank dark and gravelike around their tiny camp as the trappers finished supper and sat back to huddle in their robes against the cold and coming night. Bass tied most of the butchered venison in a pouch made from the buck's own hide, and strung the satchel high in a tree.

He came back to the fire leading his pony, slipping the runner's lead into the belt of his coat. "We'll take every scrap of that critter's meat when we pull out of here later on, but that'll keep it safe from camp robbers for now," he said as he scooted into the fire's cheery corona of warmth.

"You mean when we set off in the morning," Paddock corrected. He stretched his legs near the fire and rubbed bare hands over the flames.

"No. I meant just what I said." Bass settled wearily down upon his own robes and a Navajo blanket that would repel any water from his bedding. "It wouldn't be fair of me to come tap you awake for the surprise. Best you know what we've got planned. We'll sleep out this here storm an' soon as it's passed over, we'll repack to light out an' cover some ground."

Josiah stared at the runner a moment. "You trying to make up for some lost time? Two days ain't all that much."

"It ain't lost time at all that I'm worried about, son," Bass answered with a wave of his hand. "Pawnee."

"That's why you brought the pony into camp, right?"

"If we get hit by niggers tonight, I figger on havin' least one horse I can use to track the rest of 'em down. This won't get very far." He tapped the rawhide lead he had knotted to his belt. "Pawnee."

Paddock watched the older man let his head settle back into his robes before he spoke. "You plan on having me shoot some more Injuns for you while you catch arrows, eh?"

"Hope to sweet hell things don't go that way, Josiah. Close enough to dyin' for this nigger. I don't plan on that happenin' at all if we travel at night through this next stretch of country. Them niggers love to burn a man at a stake. Maybeso, they'll spit him over a fire. So ol' Glass tol't us all."

"Glass? The one who got himself killed by Rees last year up on the Yellow-stone?" Paddock rolled on his side to face the fire and the old man.

"One and the same. Hugh Glass. Got hisself mauled by a grizz long time back. Never was really right for it ever since the time he bumped into that sow grizzly an' her cubs. Yeah, Josiah. The same fellas the Crow huntin' party found murdered an' brought into Rotten Belly's camp where we was stayin' the robe season last winter."

"How does he know—and live to tell the tale?"

"He was Pawnee hisself for a while. They took him in as a son," he nodded. "Like you, like me."

"Adopted him, eh?"

"'Dopted is right. He an' another fella had been took off a tradin' ship an' forced to be pirates or take 'em a one way swim. But they both managed to

220

escape with their hides all in one place. Headed out walkin' north, right across those deserts way south of here and nary a critter to carry a load or an idea as to where they were bound for. Lordee, but did they run smack dab into a big war party of them Pawnee."

"Yeah? So how come they took such a shine to this Glass fella?"

"Well, now, Josiah, they didn't take a real shine to him right off, you understand. They was set to roast him an' his partner for somethin' real special, you see."

Scratch paused as Paddock feigned sleep.

"You ain't goin' off to sleep on me, are you?" Scratch howled indignantly.

"No," Josiah moaned, opening his weary eyelids to half mast.

"Well some. Like I was sayin', them Pawnee were fixin' to have a big bonfire to roast ol' Hugh an' his buddy. As lucky as it turned out, Hugh's swabby friend was the first to go, an' a awwwful way it was to be burned. Why, them red niggers tied a man up an' stuck tiny splinters of wood all over his body. Then they put a bunch of kindlin' wood 'round his feet. With that all ready they started settin' fire to the splinters so that his flesh would roast slow an' real painful. Broils a man somethin' fierce. Ol' Hugh used to get a mite ghosty when he'd talk 'bout how the fella screeched an' screamed an' yowled somethin' pitiful."

Josiah gulped. "Yeah, go on."

Bass leaned back and pulled the robes about his shoulders. "Not much else to tell, really."

"Not much else? Dammit, old man! You got this Hugh Glass in the damned Pawnee camp and his friend was just cooked to a burnt cinder like some bad cut of cow meat. Now the old pirate is next to burn—and you're saying there isn't that much else to tell."

"All right, all right, Josiah. Lordee. Let a man tell his story, will you?"

"Go 'head."

"Next it was Glass's turn at the stake. They tied the ol' boy to a pole buried in the ground just special for him. They was fixin' to come on with the splinters, you see."

"Yeah?" Paddock raised up on one elbow.

"The smell of flesh cookin' on a man's bones must've just 'bout drove ol' Hugh crazy. Probably ain't no other smell like it in the whole known world—just like there ain't no other taste like it anywhere I knows of."

"Them Pawnees eat their prisoners, eh?" Josiah asked.

"Not near as I've heard anyone tell, Josiah." Bass tossed a limb on the reddening coals. "Then again, no one I ever heard of ever come back alive from Pawnee country to tell the tale of it."

"Why, you old bastard. I'm onto you now. You only wanna scare the living shit outta me, don't you?"

"Might not hurt, seein' where we're headin'."

"You just go ahead with your story, Scratch. Tell me how Hugh Glass got himself outta that scrape, will you?"

"Seems they brung ol' Hugh on up to his special burnin' post an' was fixin' to

221

lash him to it. Afore they did, they had to strip off his shirt an' britches so they could jab them splinters into his skin. That's when the ol' boy's medicine got strong."

"What medicine?" Josiah prodded.

"Well, them red niggers were rippin' his shirt off an' what dropped out but some packets of vermilion ol' Hugh forgot he had. Some he stole from the pirate ship, see. An' you know there ain't much else that'll make a red nigger's eyes sparkle like Chinee vermilion."

"Just how did that make his medicine strong?"

"The vermilion didn't make his medicine strong, son. The vermilion was there 'cause his medicine was strong. You see, that ol' pirate bent over calm as he could be an' picked up all them packets of vermilion off the ground. He stuck his hand right on out, open as could be toward that terrible Pawnee chief. Hugh was givin' that murderin' red bastard that valuable present."

Titus coughed and looked into the dying blue licks of flames that danced back and forth along the dry limbs in the fire. "That whole camp had been yowlin' real blood thirsty, ready for ol' Hugh's blood they were—but now of a sudden they all got as quiet as a foggy graveyard 'round about midnight. This was some big, big magic. This very feller they was fixin' to set on fire an' roast just made that vermilion appear like magic an' then give it to their head man for a present. That was some now."

"What's so magical about vermilion?" Josiah lowered his head to prop it on his elbow.

"It ain't the vermilion that's got the magic, it's how it appeared an' what Hugh did that had the magic in it. To them redskins it was some powerful medicine to have a man who's about ready to die give a very special present to a man who was 'bout to kill him. All of a sudden, Josiah, Hugh Glass weren't just your ordinary fella no more."

"Takes a brave man to do what he did, don't it?"

"Man faces death just like any other foe he's got to fight—he can do it bravely, or some lesser way. An' in this situation, it worked for Ol' Hugh. That Pawnee chief thought it was such powerful medicine for this white man to give him a magical gift he'd just made come right out of nowhere, why—he give Glass his life back. They took him into their tribe as one of their own. Ol' Hugh had him at least one Pawnee wife that he spoke of in the later years. An' all his months with them Pawnee he was waitin' for the right time, the safe time to escape—all them moons when Hugh Glass learnt 'bout survivin' in the wilderness. And critters. An' livin' off the land all on his own. All that came in mighty handy when it come time that he was chewed up by that sow grizzly he'd riled up, left for dead by his friends an' he had to crawl back to a fort on hands an' knees over hundreds of miles of wilderness. Maggots eatin' on his bloody wounds most of the way in to Fort Kiowa."

Bass clucked and watched the last blue flame lick itself out along a burnt limb. Nothing was left now but dark red coals as the gray sky finally fell to black velvet outside their shelter of trees. The wind rose and fell, creaking through the protesting branches of the dried-up trees.

222

"We ain't never had it near as bad, Josiah. Ain't gonna, neither. We'll just sneak right on through Pawnee country, easy as you please. Way to do it is lay low whil'st it's them short, winter hours of daylight. We'll travel on the long hours of nighttime. That way we'll be a luckier sort than ol' Hugh Glass. We won't get ourselves et for dinner. Pawnee or grizzly—we won't get et."

"Good night, Scratch."

The older trapper heard Paddock sigh and adjust himself down in his robes. He waited a moment to see if Josiah would comment on his story any further.

"You don't appreciate my bedtime stories, huh?"

"Story was fine."

Bass smiled, satisfied in a small way. "But you didn't like me tryin' to scare you, huh?"

"No, I didn't." Josiah's voice was muffled beneath the warm robes and blankets. "I'm not the kid you met a year and a half ago."

"I—I know you're not, son. S'pose—I was just havin' some fun with you."

"I don't know why you're always trying to joke with me, especially when we're about to get ourselves in some new lick of trouble or having to get ourselves out of a stupid fix. Don't understand why you always have to do that."

Scratch stared intently overhead at the gnarled, gray branches and limbs of those old trees outlined against the storm clouds. Looking at the sky this way made it seem as if he were looking through a piece of shattered glass. Sleet splattered into the firepit and spewed up wisps of steam into the frigid night air.

"It helps me, son. I ain't so old that I don't get scared at times. Tough to own up to. For a man, that's often a hard thing for him to admit to others. Maybe it's hardest for himself to own up to. Sometimes, no matter how old he gets, no matter how many rings he's got around the middle, he gets scared of somethin'. That's the time when Titus Bass is at his best to make a joke of what that somethin' is, or make some fun out of what he's afraid of—that's all, Josiah."

The eerie silence of their camp was punctuated from time to time with the ghostly, climbing wail of the winds galloping by. Snow and sleet continued to pound into the grove of trees.

"Thanks—thanks for telling me that." Paddock spoke softly, with a gentleness born of friendship with the old man. "Never knew that about you."

"Each man faces his worst fears in the way he knows best, I s'pose."

"Your way is probably one of the best," the younger man answered. "What say we get some sleep. You're wanting to pack up and pull out pretty soon here— soon as this storm rolls over us. We'll need the sleep if we're going to ride all night."

"It's always worked for me, son," Bass replied. "Laughin' in the face of it has always worked for me."

His eyelids fell heavy and he felt some of the trail drain from his tired, wounded body. Bass listened for a while to the pawing and stamping of the animals nearby. Then he asked, "How many days has it been by your count, Josiah?"

"Days for what?"

"Since we left Taos? Since we left the gals?"

"It's been better than three weeks now," Paddock answered, suddenly reminded of his wife and family and Taos.

"By travelin' at night, we can pick up the pace some."

"I don't mind that," Josiah said.

"Sooner we get there to St. Louis, sooner we can get back. Just like ol' Mateo said it."

"I'd like that—getting back, Scratch."

"You're happy there," Bass stated. It seemed without question.

"I was, yes. I want my family around me. I miss 'em."

"Know what you mean, son. There's a emptiness inside that cain't be filled with nothin' else. Not even a big mess of hate. I cain't fill that big empty spot inside me with all this hate I feel for them two fellas who owe me so much. Not even with all the hate, that special spot will stay empty 'til I get back to her."

"Then you know how I feel?"

"I believe so, Josiah. I think I know just how you feel. A man finds somethin' special after all the years, after all the pain, after all that searchin'—it's hard for him to let go of that."

"I never want to let go of what I've found, Scratch."

Bass picked up what sounded almost like a plea in the younger man's voice. Finally he responded. "I haven't heard a solitary soul tell you that Josiah Paddock had to give up what you found. Not a soul."

"Good night, my old friend."

"Good night, son."

17 MURKY STREAKS OF gray smudged the dawn sky. The sun was just beginning to paint the clouds with hues of orange and red when Bass decided to make camp for the day. The bright orb was little more than a hand's width over the horizon in the east when at last they settled down into their stiff robes and sank into exhausted sleep.

The night before they had covered quite a bit of ground. Twenty miles beyond their ford of the Arkansas River the trappers had come upon a place known to Santa Fe Trail traders as The Caches. Emptied holes in the ground were still visible after some twelve years of relentless work by Mother Nature. Back in the fall of 1822 William Becknell's party had been caught by early snow storms and forced to construct what they could of improvised winter quarters on an island in the Arkansas River, for security against Indian attack. Throughout the winter most of the pack animals wandered off and were presumed dead or captured by wandering warriors. When the warmth of spring finally arrived and the snows abated, the men forged ahead to Taos where they purchased mules. With those new animals the trading party marched back to that site of their winter camp where they dug up their cached goods and plodded back to Mexican territory for a profitable completion of their trading ventures.

Some thirty-six miles past that marshy area pocked with the old cache pits, the trappers crossed Coon Creek and tramped on to Pawnee Fork, sometimes called Painted Rock or Rocky Point. It was there the trappers found that many of those who had passed this way before had carved their names, initials, perhaps even a date, upon a sandstone column rising out of the prairie to the left of the trail. Some thirty-five to forty feet in height, its flat front surface had been used for a decade now by travelers to record their passing. In the soft sandstone surface of the rock Scratch had Josiah inscribe their passing.

Titus Bass, Josiah Paddock, 1834.

They left the refreshing waters of Pawnee Fork and began to drift out of the short grass country at about the same time the waters of the Arkansas became too alkaline to drink. It was in this general area that the spring caravans headed for Taos would leave the tall, abundant grasses of Missouri and plunge into that region of the shorter, tougher buffalo and grama grasses. Deer could be scarce at times, but buffalo, elk and antelope were all known to thrive west of here.

After crossing Ash Creek and pushing through half another night, the pair arrived at Walnut Creek. Here they left the Arkansas River behind as it tumbled away to the south. Now the travelers had to use the stars to hold their bearings. Few landmarks existed for them to use in navigating the plains at night. A dozen miles farther on the trappers reached Cow Creek, a scant 250 miles from Independence, feeling as if they were finally cutting both winter and the trail down to size.

Past the Little Arkansas River and Turkey Creek, some sixty-two miles later, the pair was confronted with the slippery ford of Cottonwood Fork, a small stream so named for the great number of cottonwood trees lining its steep banks. It was here the horses stumbled and slid down one icy, muddy bank and clawed their way up the other. For the rest of the night both man and beast alike rode along, miserably soaked, muddied, chilled to the core from their plunge down the slick banks and into the freezing, ice-laden waters of Cottonwood Fork. They had to pass Lost Springs before they made the long haul up to Diamond Spring, close by the renowned Council Grove where massive stands of hardwoods grew.

Many a hardened trader of the Santa Fe Trail considered this the best camping spot on the whole journey. Well known as being the last spot along the trip south where the traders could obtain wood varieties hard enough for spare axle trees and wheel spokes, here a man could cut oak and maple, hickory and ash. This beautiful spot would ring with the crack of an axe or the whine of a saw as the traders felled one species or another, slinging those rough-hewn logs beneath their wagons before they pressed on to Taos or Santa Fe. Here the travelers heading to Mexico had to leave behind the many varieties of oak and butternut, along with the great number of shrubs clothed in the rich, fragrant foliage of spring. Coursing through the grove, a beautiful little stream burbled along a gravel-bottomed bed, accompanying the song of robin or warbler or thrush. Here the southbound hunter had to leave behind those dense forests populated by large, piping turkeys which lived off the rich, verdant growth.

After countless days of winter storms and low hung clouds graying the land, the sun began to make a more regular appearance each morning as the trappers bedded down their weary stock. After leaving Council Grove they had crossed Rock Creek, then pushed on to Big John Spring and over Bridge Creek. They passed 110-Mile Creek, tramped by The Narrows and Round Grove, making good time each night with clear, cold weather until one dusk the western horizon again lay like a slash of burnished gold beneath a purple thunderhead.

"We'll lope along as best we can tonight, son," Bass commented after he had torn his gaze away from the dome overhead.

"That sky tell you bad weather's coming in?" Paddock yanked down the pack saddle cinch, satisfied that the load was secure atop the pony.

"Very well could be, Josiah," Bass answered. "I mean to make good time while we can."

"You know you haven't really given that shoulder of yours a chance to heal, old man."

226

"Ain't a damned thing wrong with healin' on down the trail." Bass's lip curled in a lopsided grin.

"I suppose I should have known you'd say that before I even wasted my breath." Josiah smiled, despite the cold battering his face. His gaze rose to the slash of falling light to the west. "At least in this country we can find cover just about anywhere now. This is beginning to look a lot like where I grew up as a boy."

"It ain't been all that long for you."

"Since I was a boy?"

"Nawww," Bass responded with a grin. "Not all that long since you were back here, in this kind of country. Not quite three years now. Right?"

"Right," Josiah answered wistfully. "But, in so many other ways, it has been a long, long time, Scratch. So much has happened to me, for me—I ain't the same as that kid was just three years ago who ran off from St. Louis, away from LeClerc."

Bass slid a foot through a stirrup and pushed into the saddle. He adjusted the rawhide rein. "That's maybe the hardest thing some folks got to learn, Josiah. Man sets himself up for a lotta misery if he cain't accept that things around him don't always stay the same. Change'll come—whether he's ready for it or not."

"Are you ready for what you're gonna see changed in St. Louis?" Josiah asked.

"In a way, I s'pose I am. Get 'long now," he clucked to his pony as he snapped the lead running back to the mule. "Yeah, that sort of change don't really bother me all that much. That's just buildin's, stores an' more streets—all whatnot. Just things. Such as that always changes around a man because of other men. They're always wantin' things to look just the way they want 'em to look. But, out to the free mountains, Josiah—why, the country don't change its face on a man. He can count on it stayin' the same. Year in an' year out. That's somethin' good an' clean he can count on. Somethin' rock solid an' hard. Somethin' honest he can trust in. Maybe that's why I'm one to prefer the mountains an' the far west to the settlements an' man's towns. God his own self made that country where I choose to live. God his own self. Man has made the other places where he can stay jammed up agin his neighbors. Man made those places where he's got no other choice but to smell the stink of his fellow man, an' pigs an' cows. He made it so he's scrunched right up agin all them others who don't mind bein' pushed around."

"For some folks, it's—it's what they want," Josiah offered. "It's what they—feel right in."

"For some, Josiah, it's all right." Bass turned to let his eyes rest on the younger man. "I ain't one to be pickin' where to lay the blame. For those who need a lotta folks around to make 'em feel alive, Josiah, it's all right."

He nodded and gave the rump-spotted buffalo runner a little nudge with his knees to pick up the pace.

Throughout the long, winter night, the stars whirled slowly overhead. A pale, milky slice of moon slipped over them as the hours crawled by. It snuggled close to the western rim of the earth by the time the east was draining black. Bands of red and orange, then bars of gold shot up into the sky as the travelers emerged from a long stand of thick timber. Bass threw his hand up into the air, signalling a stop. The ponies sagged to a weary halt as Josiah reined up beside the old trapper.

"You hear that?" Bass whispered as he let his arm drop.

Josiah strained to hear across the open, rolling meadows, his ears separating the thundering roll of woodpeckers and the busybody chattering of squirrels. He thought he heard it.

"A dog?"

"Right, son. That's just what I heard."

"What do you think it is? A village?"

"Don't rightly think so." Bass twisted in the saddle and had a look around to satisfy himself. "I do believe we've tramped ourselves right on outta Pawnee country. I'm thinkin' that particular hound belongs to a white man. It don't sound like no Injun dog what's half civil, half coyote. That there's a man's huntin' dog—his hound. Listen again."

They both set their ears straining to pick up the distant yip and bark of the canine on the faint, chilly breezes. There it came again. Bass nodded along with Paddock, then motioned with his head that they should push on.

He steered the party back into the thick stands of hardwoods. Somewhere deep inside, Bass felt the stirrings of a bittersweet lament for his childhood home. Out in the far mountain west for the past ten years, he had suffered no reason for regret, suffered no painful memories. But here in these forests that rose around him, the old trapper was stabbed with the first pangs for what had been. Such a warm yearning a man felt at times, that deep need to let someone else care for him. Across his tongue now ran that remembered taste of breakfast hominy, hoe or johnny cakes smeared with butter and dripping with Ma's preserves. He swallowed with the tang of his salivating memories, recalling evenings spent astraddle the top rail of the snakelike fence his father had long before thrown up around their fields. There he would watch the western fall of the sun while he munched on crackling, earth-tasty parched corn. His ears echoed with the mournful toodle of the whippoorwill calling out to its sweetheart, followed by the abusive call of a catbird. Memories, well worn and homespun, recollections of a time that was, or never had been. He recalled the pain in leaving that Ohio River country, youthful and sure that the wilderness to the west offered the only life that would suit him. A farmer he was dead certain he could never be.

Ahead darted the bright, white flag of a young doe as she bounded away across their trail, disappearing in three leaps among the thick stands of oak and hickory. His eyes strained after her, remembering his first whitetail and how it had filled him with pride to provide his family of brothers and sisters with meat for their oft-bare table after his father had been injured in a tree felling accident.

Bass searched the darker shadows of the forest for those places where, come spring, there would burst blood-red clusters of maple flowers, bright yellow daisies, and burnished Indian apple blossoms pink against the many soft shades of green. Woodsmoke drifted past his nostrils as they neared the edge of a dense thicket and stopped to peer out on the clearing. There stood three small, low cabins. Thin wisps of gray tendrils curled from one stone chimney.

A door scraped open. A short, stocky man took two steps into the yard and whistled loudly as he tugged suspenders up over both shoulders, stretching the waist of the pants around his ample midsection. The bony blue tick hound galloped around the edge of the far cabin and loped up to its master. As the squat settler was scratching the dog's ears, both kneeling near the snow covered stump where firewood was split, Bass and Paddock stepped from the dawn shadows of treeline.

The settler rose slowly as his dog caught scent and turned. His gaze never left the two buckskinned trappers as the travelers came to a halt out in the growing, gray light of the clearing around the squat cabins. Growling, the hound snarled with a sinister, harsh gurgle deep in its throat. Heavy jowls quivered back to show some yellowed teeth.

"Buck!" the square farmer snapped quietly at the dog. "You just's well hush up. These fellas appear to be visitors." He smiled as he studied the bearded, bedraggled newcomers.

"Howdy, friend." Bass's voice carried a happy tone across the clearing. "We truly mean you no harm. Didn't mean to surprise you." He let the old rifle slip from the crook of his arm and stood it beside him. Nodding for Josiah to do the same, Scratch smiled once more at the settler.

"Y-you, ah—you are a bit of a surprise to a man, I've got to admit." The square man flashed a quick, wide smile. He nervously rubbed at the day old stubble on his chin. "You're somethin' new hereabouts. I'd figured to see a army hunter maybe, if not one of the Kansaw Indians coming in to beg, maybe steal what he could lay his hands on. We gotta watch them somethin' awful. But you fellas, you ain't like no Indians I ever see'd before. You speak good English, too."

"We ain't Injuns, friend," Bass replied with a smile, stepping into the light where he might be seen a little better.

"Dressed just like 'em. But, I see the beards good—at last. You ain't Indians, you say?"

"Never have been, least as I know. Neither one of us." Scratch brought up an empty hand to indicate his partner. "This is—"

"Just where I want you both to freeze!"

Bass jerked his head around and looked in the direction of the new voice that had sliced through the clearing. He was instantly angry with himself for not having paid better attention to his surroundings. Framed in the door of another cabin stood a taller, but no less square, settler, his nervous hands filled with a double-barreled fowler.

"As I was 'bout to say, this here's my partner, Josiah Paddock." Scratch raised his left hand in the air, showing a sign of peace. "I be Titus Bass." He spoke clearly, slowly, so that each man could understand and not read a lick of apprehension in his voice.

From the third cabin came the scraping noise of a door opening. There stood what appeared to be the youngest of the three men, not much more than a teen, holding an ancient smoothbore in his hands.

"We didn't mean to startle none of you," Josiah Paddock said.

"May be that you best tell us *what* you are," directed the second settler with a growl.

Scratch stared a moment at the huge double yawns of those shotgun muzzles. "Maybeso, we two best just be on our way, son."

"You'll stand your ground and answer my question!"

" 'Lias," the first man said. "They're just hunters in from the prairie. You can see that plain as day, brother."

"Here to scalp us raw and rape the women before they steal whatever they find to be valuable and then be on their way."

"P-p-pshawww!" the first man responded. "If they wanted to do that, they would have killed us in our beds and be done with it. Not waited until fair light like it is."

"I go 'long with Renfro there," said the third and youngest member of the trio, the thinnest, too. "I believe you just might be jumping the gun a bit here."

Stepping out into the light, he let the old musket point at the ground. The hound skipped over to him playfully, expecting to have its ears scratched. Instead, the settler kept on walking toward the two visitors. He wasn't much more than a boy, gangly, perhaps eighteen or nineteen, his face still splotched with the final ravages of adolescence. Yet the peach fuzz smile surrounding his yellowed teeth shone true. A wide gap between two front teeth gave him a boyish look. He was everything his older brother was not—open and friendly, while his elder brother was hard and suspicious.

Bass stepped out to meet the youngster, his empty hand offered in friendship. "Titus Bass, son."

"Augie is the name. Ketcham. August Ketcham. Most calls me Augie." He licked his lips, continued to smile as he turned and nodded toward the other two men. "That far one is my oldest brother, Renfro Ketcham. And that there big one is my next oldest, Elias."

"This here's Josiah Paddock, like I started to tell you." Bass took a couple of steps toward Renfro when he noticed the squat settler ambling his way.

"Mr. Bass." The oldest brother nodded and shook hands, his smile fuller than Augie's. " 'Lias is a bit—suspicious."

"Cautious is a better word, brother," the middle brother corrected.

"We don't have much to offer you fellas."

"So it's probably best that you move along," Elias added.

"Pshaw," Renfro scoffed. "These men might require some breakfast, brother. And I think it our Christian duty to feed those in need. Come. Come," he said. "It will not be long before my wife has a meal prepared. Johnny cakes and cured ham. It is the best we can offer two weary travelers."

It was the first time Bass had looked up at the squat cabin planted behind Renfro. There in the dim light of the doorway stood a woman every bit as round as she was tall. Peering from the single window in the front wall were six shining, rosy, cherubic faces intent upon the proceedings.

"I—I'm afraid I don't eat Ned—ah, I don't eat pork," Scratch stammered. "Wouldn't want to take nothin' outta the mouths of your young'uns there neither.

But, I would truly love to have just a small taste of them hoe cakes you offered. That would be right friendly of your woman, sir."

"We have plenty of ham to share, Mr. Bass."

"What would you all say to venison for breakfast?" Paddock asked. He stepped back toward one of the pack animals. "We have plenty of that. And it won't tap your larder none." Bass watched Elias and saw that the big man's look was not altogether suspicious any more.

"Just like the boy says," Titus continued, "we have plenty and would gladly share our meat with you in exchange for a hoe cake or two."

"Fair trade, it sounds to me," Augie offered.

"I should say it is," Renfro agreed. "What say you, brother? Are you game for a venison breakfast?"

"I—could be," Elias admitted.

"We ain't the best of hunters, you see, Mr. Bass," Renfro explained. "Live mostly on what stock we could manage to keep alive since last spring. That, along with what game is stupid enough to let us shoot it."

A tall woman, thin as a fencerail, stepped from Elias' cabin with a huge coat in her hand. "You men are likely to catch an ill out here without your coats on," she exclaimed. "I declare, Elias. Your mother never warned me you'd need raising when she gave us her blessing. My, oh, my. Come in out of the cold right now."

Paddock watched the thin woman slip back through the door into the darkened cabin.

Renfro, the eldest brother, took Scratch by the arm. "Come, come now. We'll eat to my place. You, too, Augie and Elias, and bring your woman, Elias. Best to have your own table fixings, brothers. We have guests to entertain and not much service to go the rounds." Renfro stopped at the door to his cabin, shooing away the children from the entryway. "I do have two things to ask of you, Mr. Bass. Ah, Titus—may I call you Titus?"

Bass nodded and watched the other three adults scurrying across the yard.

"Titus, there are but two things I ask of you. First, I wish to have my belly filled with a fat, juicy steak from that deer meat you have with you," Renfro continued. "And, next, I wish to have my ears filled to overflowing on your tales of the vast prairies yonder."

"I can satisfy you with the first, Mr. Ketcham."

"Renfro, please."

"Renfro," Bass corrected. "Howsoever, we don't live out on the prairie, sir."

"Then, you are not hunters for the army?" Augie asked as he came up.

"No, we ain't," Titus answered.

"Well? Where—out there—why'd you?" Renfro stammered as bad as a weak buggy spring.

"We just come across all that out there, up from Taos," Paddock explained.

"Taos?" Augie said, a wistful look on his face.

"What the hell is it that you do with them Mexicans and dirty red Injuns down there?" Elias asked with a carbolic tone, his deep voice demanding an answer.

"Don't do nothin' with the Meskins, 'cept drink their fine whiskey an' sell 'em my pelts," Bass said. "As for them dirty Injuns, I'm married to one." He glared at the tall brother. "Anythin' else'd be my business, Elias Ketcham."

"You're a mite too old and a mite too small to be speaking up to me that way," Elias declared acidly. He straightened himself within his heavy mackinaw coat and took a step backwards.

"It appears that you an' me simply got off on the wrong foot," Bass sighed. "I don't cotton much to a man gettin' piggish when it comes to speakin' of another man's wife." He slipped loose the knot in the sash about his waist so that he could open the flaps of his coat. "But, I feel like givin' a fella a fair chance to show me his intentions—show just what he's made up of inside." Scratch grinned as he stepped back away from the door. Paddock moved back, too. He had seen that look on the old trapper's face before.

"If you've a notion to cause me trouble, then be about it and quick." As Bass backed away from the doorway and the press of bodies, the flaps of his coat flailed open to show the two knife scabbards at his waist, the handles of both knives pointing inward toward each other.

"We can't—we ain't—don't aim to cause no man harm, Mr. Bass," August pleaded. He stepped in front of his brother so that he stood between the two antagonists.

Elias reached out with a big paw and yanked him back to the side. "Don't get in my way, brother!" he snapped savagely.

"This is all so absurd," Renfro prattled as he stepped between the two men. "Here are our guests, and we are about to sit ourselves down to the table to share Christian charity. Yet, you two grown men aim to spill each other's blood?"

"I decided I don't want him on my land," Elias growled.

"This is land you share commonly with your brothers," Renfro reminded. "It is not your decision to make alone."

"Force of might took this land from the wilderness and force of might will hold this land," Elias said. "There is no welcome for their kind here."

"We'd best be moving on, Josiah," Bass surrendered. "Augie—Renfro, appreciate the offer of your sit-down hospitality an' them johnny cakes. But, we'll push on down the trail just a bit afore we set in for breakfast on our own." He mounted his pony and Paddock climbed aboard his own horse.

Renfro followed into the snowy clearing where the trappers and horses raised a mist like tissue in the dawn air. "I had so hoped it would not end like this, Mr. Bass, Mr. Paddock. My brother—well, he is the reason we have moved this far away from the settlement. So quick to anger," he whispered.

"My 'pologies, if'n we done somethin' to set him off," Bass sighed as he sawed his reins and pushed the animals out of the clearing, heading east.

Barely a couple miles from the settlers' cabins, Scratch decided to make their camp for the day. In a grove of blackjack oak and old hickory they cleared the ground of snow so their camp would not be muddy once the fire started warming the earth. Paddock cut branches and limbs of shrub and brush until there were enough to soften two beds near the firepit. The animals stomped, snorted and chewed, some twenty yards off, at times snorting and nipping at each other.

"Seems Elias ain't the only one touchy this morning," Paddock remarked as the strips of venison steak popped and spit juice into the flames.

"You know, I feel real sorry now that I had any part of that poor affair," Bass admitted. "S'pose it's that I haven't been around all that many civil folks lately. Not so tolerant as I once was, I'd reckon. Maybe I've gotten too old an' it gets too durn easy to let a stupid man rile me up like he did."

"Glad nothing came of it." Paddock leaned over the flames to tap at a lean strip of meat with his knife. The grease spilled into the yellow flames, each heavy drop sending up red and blue flares spitting and crackling around the meat.

"Nothin' more fearsome than fightin' a big, smart man—unless it's fightin' a big, *stupid* man. Nothin' worse," Bass chuckled. Then he fell silent and listened.

He brought a finger to his lips signalling Josiah to silence. Leaning to the side, both men brought their rifles across their laps. Paddock pulled out his pistol as soon as he heard the crunch of steps on the snow. He glanced at Bass. The old trapper nodded, indicating the direction Paddock was to take.

Bass heard the sounds of more than one set of feet on the snow. He was pretty sure it was not Elias Ketcham. The strides just weren't long enough for the big man. The steps kept coming—crunching, padding, across the old, icy, wind-scoured snow.

Scratch nodded to his young partner. Now was the time for them to disappear. Josiah melted into the brush while Bass placed himself back in the shadows of two tall oak. And he waited.

"Well, I'll be damned." the old trapper boomed cheerily.

Renfro wheeled, frightened. His round wife twirled, bumping into her husband and nearly spilling the basket she carried slung from one arm.

"You—startled me." Renfro put a hand to his chest.

"And you scared us a mite, Mr. Ketcham." Paddock stepped into the camp clearing.

"Land o' Goshen!" Mrs. Ketcham exclaimed as she dabbed at the beads of sweat across her upper lip. "If we had been savage Indians here to put a knife in your breasts and take your scalps, we wouldn't have stood a chance."

"I've never had no one near as pretty as you try to scalp me, ma'am." Bass set his rifle down atop the robes before he plopped down again at the fire. "Please, sit."

The Ketchams dropped their ample bodies down on the offered logs and stared for a long moment at the juicy venison cooking over the flames. "Where the young'uns?" Bass asked with the hint of a grin.

"They've been fed their breakfast, Mr. Bass," Renfro said. "We've come with a peace offering and didn't want to get bogged down by them. Louisa?"

The squat woman stood uneasily, tugging her heavy blanket coat about her before she held out the basket with a yellow gingham napkin draped over it.

"Mr. Paddock? Mr. Bass?" She beamed as Josiah took the basket from her. "I do so hope you like these johnny cakes we promised you."

"My, oh, my," Scratch exclaimed as he smacked his lips. "Ain't that some, Josiah?" He smiled and saw the woman's eyes flick to the venison.

Renfro cleared his throat. "I am in hopes that my brother did not lead you to believe that all the Ketchams are rude hosts."

"Not in the least, sir." Bass smiled warmly as he pulled back the bright gingham napkin to peer into the basket. "My Lord. You've grilled enough cakes here for a small brigade, woman."

Mrs. Ketcham giggled and bowed her head slightly.

"They smell just like—why, as heavenly as the mountains at moonrise, ma'am," Bass chirped as he sniffed the basket.

"Mr. Bass, you are a kind one, indeed," Renfro remarked.

"Would you folks care to join us?" Paddock pointed to the venison with his knife. "I'm afraid, like you, I've fixed a bit too much here for the two of us to eat by ourselves."

"Only—only if you have enough," Louisa smiled shyly.

"Surely, surely," Bass piped as he knelt to pull out tin plates for all.

Between the two ravenous, trail-weary travelers and the two portly, game-starved settlers, the entire basket of johnny cakes was soon devoured along with the entire venison roast Josiah had cut into thin broiling strips. At last they each leaned back against their logs.

"I'm afeared I won't be worth a tinker's damn today," Ketcham chuckled. He patted his rounded belly.

"That was—quite pleasant, Mr. Bass," Louisa complimented. "Thank you, Mr. Paddock. I have missed wild meat, I must admit. It was just about all my father raised his children on. That—and teaching us all to have kindness and charity in our hearts."

"I can see his lessons took well with you, ma'am," Paddock smiled. "You have been very kind to us poor wayfarers."

"I hope we've been able to repay you?" Bass inquired.

"Make no mistake about that, sir," Renfro said. "I am only sorry that August did not see fit to join us here for breakfast."

"You asked the boy to come 'long with you?" Scratch raised his eyebrows.

"I did. He said he might try to slip away later and follow us. He is so afraid of brother Elias—a bully that big one can be at times."

"It's strange that such differ'nt folks can sprout up in the same family," Scratch explained. "You folks bein' so kind an' givin' in so many ways. Your brother Elias has got a mean, stingy streak as wide as the Yellowstone in him."

"The Y-Yellowstone?"

"Yeah, Mr. Ketcham," Bass answered with a smile. "It's a beautiful river, up to the northern Rockies. It runs right through the heart of Crow country. Ah, Absorkee land—home of the Sparrowhawk people." He glanced over when he heard Mrs. Ketcham sigh and saw that both she and her husband were beaming with delight.

"We are in hopes you will choose to tell us more," Renfro pleaded.

"Yes, please! Please, Mr. Bass." Louisa clapped her hands merrily.

"Well, now—" Bass glanced at Paddock.

Josiah just rolled his eyes back in his head, knowing how much Bass loved an audience. He, however, wanted to sleep.

234

"I—I don't rightly know where to begin," Bass claimed.

"How about when you lost your—your ponies and all to them Arapahos down on the Little Bear River, Scratch," Paddock suggested. He winked and rubbed the crown of his head.

"Ah, yes," Bass cheered. "Good place to start. Seein' how I was such a sull young'un then." He pulled his shooting pouch around and retrieved a twist of tobacco. He bit a small chunk and snugged it inside his cheek. With this yarn lubricant in place, Titus Bass began to weave his spell over his captivated audience here in the little grove.

"I'd spent me but one winter in them awful, turrible mountains, you see. Barely hangin' on—why, I looked somethin' close to a skiliton by the time spring come an' the first hunt of the year was done."

Paddock collapsed back into his robes, jammed his otter cap down over his eyes and stuffed both hands beneath his armpits. Here he could peacefully snooze while the old man wove his magic over the adventure starved settlers.

". . . a mess of them ponies I had with me. An' there's only one thing a Injun likes better than a white man's ponies—why, that's a white man's scalp!"

Titus Bass ended up burning the whole day with the Ketcham family. Unabashed, the man simply loved an audience. He would never in his whole life be able to walk away from anyone who would listen to his stories.

Paddock had first grabbed about an hour's sleep while the Ketchams returned home to fetch their children. The couple wanted their young ones to hear the windies and tall tales of those far, blue mountains they'd never seen. The camp in the little grove was quiet for little better than an hour before an ancient, rickety wagon rumbled back into the hardwood grove, brimming over with the stout Ketchams, a half-dozen children, and Augie Ketcham, who was grinning ear to ear and waving an arm off at the socket.

Throughout the remainder of the day Scratch regaled Renfro's family with the best he had to offer. Late in the shank of the afternoon, Scratch announced to Paddock that they would not be traveling that night.

Paddock drifted off to sleep, despite the drone of Scratch's voice and the punctuation of excited laughter and shrieks of delight and screams of terror from the Ketcham clan.

When next he awoke, Bass was just stirring from the robes. Light was only beginning to rip a thin, red gash across the eastern edge of the horizon.

"No telling how long I'd have slept if I hadn't had some ugly jackass making a lot of noise," Paddock grumbled from his warm bed.

"Jackass yourself, young'un. Let's just be doin' it." Bass climbed to his feet and shuddered in the frosty, dawn air.

"Why are you in such a hurry today, when yesterday there was time aplenty to waste while you spread your crap on pretty thick?"

"Them folks was extra special kind to us," Bass said. "Been a long, long time since last I ate such good johnny cakes—hell, any johnny cakes at all. Besides, I just figured it only neighborly to entertain 'em, if'n that's what they wanted in return for their kindness."

Josiah kicked off the blankets and robes. "I figure at this rate, Scratch, we ought to make it back to Taos, say—come next fall."

"Bullshit!" Bass snapped. "As big a crock of it as I've ever heard."

Paddock shivered in the heavy, cold fog, laughing with a deep down belly-shaker. "I'll be damned. If that don't take the circle, I don't know what does, Scratch. I ain't lived all the years you have, and I don't claim to have gone all the places you've been, but the biggest crock this child's heard was right here—all day yesterday."

"Now just a goddamned minute there." Bass stomped up closer to the young trapper. "All them stories are true."

"I don't recall doubting that you'd spoken the truth."

"Then—what's all this about yesterday bein' a crock?"

"Those stories all didn't happen exactly the way you told 'em—did they?"

"Well—now—not 'sactly, son."

"How much truth was there in 'em?"

"Uhhh, there—were some."

"Yeah, just as I was saying, Scratch. You took a kernal of the truth and you blew it all up to make those folks' heads spin with your amazing yarns."

"Well—I s'pose—"

"Then you borrowed tales from other fellas, too, didn't you? Like a couple of yarns I remember from Jack Hatcher. Mad Jack."

"Why—I just figured—yeah, I did take a tale of two from ol' Jack. I'm sure he wouldn't mind me keepin' the stories goin'. Not Mad Jack Hatcher. God rest his mortal soul!"

With that, Josiah turned away. Horses and mules loaded, the trappers mounted and rode east.

Yesterday had not been totally lost on Scratch's yarns. He and Bass had learned a few things about the trail on east from their grove. Renfro Ketcham had informed the pair that there were but ten miles until they reached the new village of Westport Landing. The new community had been established the previous year after the steamboat landing at the nearby town of Independence had washed away. The Missouri was off like a lady, changeable in her mind, direction and mood.

Independence had been established in 1827 as frontier settlements fingered farther west to expand with the growing mountain and Santa Fe Trail trade. Wharves were installed at a modest landing almost before other construction on the town had begun. There the steamboats on the muddy Missouri would tie up, taking on supplies, letting off furs and robes from the upcountry. It wasn't long before the little settlement became the main jumping off point for both the mountain and plains trail trades. In Independence, a man could get himself outfitted for whatever direction he chose to take. So too, the town's saloons came replete with gamblers and the sporting women who followed men wherever men gathered with enough money to spend and strong appetites to satisfy.

When the town's landing washed away a mere six years after its founding, the river pilots needed a new and more permanent bank to tie up to and conduct their business. Upriver a ways they chose a spot soon christened Westport

Landing, so named as it was the embarkation point furthest west on the prairies. It and Independence long continued to thrive in their strategic locations to the trade since it was nearby that the mighty Missouri took a turn and headed north to the Platte, Yellowstone, Musselshell, and the Three Forks.

The pair of trappers loped across the rolling, undulating prairie, passing through skirts of black oak and dense thickets that come spring would be budding with plums and apples. They gave wide berth to the villages and towns, preferring to travel as far away as possible from the beaten track. What few wagon borne or horseback riders they met along the way, they greeted with a smile and a quick "how-do" as they trekked on through the chilling daylight hours.

At the tiny settlement of Booneville the trappers rode square through the middle of town. The old man had decided on that route right after Paddock had read aloud the road sign crudely inscribed with the town's name. Titus had nodded, cocksure, declaring that any place named for the honorable Dan'l Boone was good enough to ride straight through. So, he had led them down the main, muddy thoroughfare bisecting the village.

Across the river on the northern bank lay a larger town that Bass was glad they wouldn't have to travel through. New Franklin. The older settlement of Franklin had been built in 1817 as a place far out on the prairie for the plains trade. At that time, the only communication with St. Louis was by horseback. But, by 1820 a stage road serviced the line which plied an irregular schedule up and down the southern bank of the Missouri. And in 1821 the era of the steamboat churned its way to town.

Bass had known of this place during his work as a blacksmith along the wharves and levees in the big, thriving Mississippi River metropolis of St. Louis. But long after Titus had turned his face west toward the mountains, the fickle Missouri River had once again reclaimed the land on that north bank as her own, and man be damned if he had put buildings in the way. In 1828 the town fathers had to begin anew, this time constructing New Franklin some two miles back from the capricious river's flow. There in a bend of the Missouri beneath thickly wooded hills, the hardy citizens erected their stores, taverns, billiard rooms, a post office and jail, along with a weekly newspaper office, and better than one hundred fifty log houses and a few brick buildings. Two large steam mills joined the rest to supply timber not only for New Franklin's construction, but also for the expanding settlements farther to the west. The town's log prison soon proved to be far too small and a two-story addition was added. Four blacksmiths were kept busy full time, sweating in two forges across town from one another. All citizens promptly had renewed faith that the whimsical river could not come this far to lay claim to her alluvial bottomland.

The trappers camped one evening not far east of the new settlement of Jefferson City near the mouth of the Osage River. The next day they crossed the Gasconade River near the mouth where it emptied into the Missouri. Here they stared across the muddy river at the lights of the village of Portland. Another hundred miles or so they were told was all they had left of their journey, perhaps even less if they did not follow the Missouri as it coursed northeast toward St.

Charles before it mated with the Father of Waters, the Mississippi. The land rolled on as they loped due east toward the rising sun, cross-country through massive hardwood forests and meadows and fields of winter cured grass grown full and stiff and yellow.

They knew they were getting close. The farms and houses, wagons and horses and people all grew too numerous for them to count. They had both waited long for this day, a part inside each man hoping that this day never would come. Yearning and dreading at the same time, the moths drew closer to the flame.

The sky at their backs had grown rusty brown early in the afternoon, that dome overhead seeming to fall farther and farther, ever closer to the ground as the weary pilgrims plodded through snow and mud and those icy puddles of dirty, standing water. By late that afternoon the corroded sky had finally grown old and gray, black and ominous around the edges. As they pulled up and sat hunkered against the sleety blasts of icy wind at their backs, the two wayfarers turned and gazed a moment into one another's eyes. Drenched to the core, with their cold, soaked animals' heads drooped behind them, the men watched the day's light slide headlong from the winter sky before they finally pushed on down the hill.

Below them lay the Mississippi River town that in some way had spawned them both, the city that had given each man his own most private dreams of the far west and what that wilderness would bring him.

Below them waited St. Louis.

18

THE STREETS WERE splotched with smeared coronas of pale light spilling from oil lamps as the two brought their small caravan down into the outskirts of town, where Barn Street was but a muddy ribbon in the storm. In the time Paddock had been gone from St. Louis, the city had grown up around this area of town and pushed on past the livery where in 1831 he had purchased the fine sorrel Morgan mare that had carried him west to the Rocky Mountains.

A modest wooden sign swung on hooks and eyes above them as the sleety gusts battered the clapboard siding of the huge barn.

Livery—Amos Tharp, Prop.

The icy rain blustered hard and cold, right at a man, causing even the strongest to walk hunched over until he found shelter. With the animals tied off, Paddock struggled with the huge wooden handle and pulled open the door just far enough for both men to slip through. Inside, the huge old barn breathed warm and sensually alive with fragrances of steamy animals and their earthy dung. Here and there an animal pawed at the packed dirt floor of the barn; another could be heard chewing on its hay or feed. At last Paddock's eyes adjusted to what dim light was thrown out from two oil lamps, one hung at either end of the long barn.

"Mr. Tharp?" Paddock called. "Mr. Tharp? You here?" He turned quickly to Bass and shrugged his shoulders before he yelled out again. "Anybody here?"

"Don't let your bowels get puckered!"

Out of a far stall emerged the old man, pitchfork staked in one hand, the other held atop a stall door. He gave the two trappers a quick appraisal.

"We were in need of—"

"I'm closed for the day." Tharp cut the young man off. "You'll have to come back tomorrow."

"What?"

"Just what I said, lad. I'm closed. Now, be off with you."

The crotchety old livery owner began to turn back into the stall he had been mucking out.

"Well, why would a man who's been in this business for so many years not want to cater to an old customer—a customer who will be paying gold for his keep?"

239

Paddock took two steps forward so that he could stand beneath a halo of lamplight.

"Gold?" Bass whispered as he slid up next to Josiah.

"Gold, you say?" Tharp retraced a step away from the stall door.

"Yes, that's what I said, Mr. Tharp." Paddock shoveled a hand down into his shooting bag and came up with a leather pouch plump with coins.

Scratch's eyes bulged momentarily at the surprising sight. "Didn't know we'd pay nothin' of the kind in gold," he whispered.

"You interested in putting these animals I have outside up for the night, perhaps two or three nights?" Josiah bounced the leather pouch lightly in his palm.

"Just how many horses you say?" Amos Tharp's attention had been snagged but good.

"We've six animals," Paddock replied. "Five ponies and a mule." He watched Amos Tharp limp toward them.

"Male or female?" Tharp prodded.

"What?" Paddock was confused by the question.

"The mule. Male, or be it female?"

"Female," Josiah disclosed. "It's a young female."

"Lad, I'd be one that's interested in looking her over." Tharp moseyed up to Paddock. "If she's got the makings of a good 'figuration, I just might be willing to buy her from you."

"Don't recall no one sayin' she was for sale," Bass growled, suddenly entering the conversation.

Tharp twisted to eye Bass hard for a fleeting moment. "I'd like to have me a good, young girl. But, if you say she's not for sale—then there 'pears to be I ain't got room for them horses of yours."

"The hell!" Paddock pressed forward a step. "Just a minute ago you were ready to take our money."

"She was a birthday present to me," Scratch announced. "From my trappin' partner here." He wagged his head at Josiah. "I turned forty on the last one an' I'm a real sentimental, soft hearted soul, Mr. Tharp. Couldn't think of partin' company with either one of 'em. The boy here—or my mule."

Bass watched the livery owner's gaze crawl down his frame, then up again, finally darting back and forth between his eyes.

"So, you wouldn't be one to sell 'er, eh?"

"Not somethin' special my partner here gave me for my birthday. No, Mr. Tharp, I wouldn't."

The old businessman's posture suddenly relaxed.

"My usual charge for keeping an animal such as yours is a dollar on the week. Oats is extra, you know. That'd be two bits. For the lot of 'em—six, you say?" Tharp watched both trappers nod in agreement. "Six, hmmm—five dollars for the week—six with oats if you'd like, fellas."

"That sounds mighty fair to me." Paddock grinned over at Bass.

"Then you boys bring them animals in here out of the foul weather. Been a nasty winter so far," Tharp muttered with a wag of his head. He gestured toward the livery door before he wheeled to hobble back toward his stall. He stopped and called out to the trappers. "Just how far you two come in, fellas?"

"How's that?" Bass inquired.

"You come in from the mountains?"

"Taos, this time," Bass said.

"You've been there awhile." Tharp nodded once, in his matter of fact way. "It's been some time since you last were back here to St. Louis. I see that."

"Lil' better'n ten years, Mr. Tharp." Scratch's face crackled with a slight grin. "An' I ain't never once been back here yet."

"You'll find that much has changed, friend," Tharp proclaimed with a wry smile.

"I seen already how much the town's been spreadin' her arms out, up an' down the river."

Tharp spit into the fragrant, heady dirt on the floor of the huge barn. "I see why you wouldn't let that mule go," he declared thoughtfully.

"I'm glad you understand why she ain't for sale," Bass replied.

"Well, now, you both come ahead and just bring them poor animals on in here where they can warm themselves and have a good meal. No telling what they've had to feed on since you've been on your way here. No telling."

Titus watched Amos Tharp step back into the splotchy darkness between the two oil lamps. He turned to Josiah and led the way out the door. A gust of cold wind drove icy sleet at them outside. This sort of weather made a man hunker down and yearn for a place in that cozy barn warmed and fragrant from the horses' breath, all heady and appealing.

Minutes later Tharp hobbled along the stalls, appraising each animal.

"By the sweet love of the Virgin Mary, but yours looks like the sort of rag-tag outfit that the good Lord stays up nights and days-off looking after."

Both trappers chuckled, busy with cinches and bridles, halters and robes.

"We for sure ain't got much tallow left, Mr. Tharp," said Bass. "A trip like we had tends to lean a man and his critters down to the spare side."

"Looks like there ain't all that much spare left to go around, gents."

"Hardly enough lard left on any of 'em to make a flea fat an' sassy," Scratch agreed.

"I'll be locking up soon as you fellas are gone."

"Why—I was figuring on spendin' the night right here," Bass commented.

"I—I wouldn't think you'd want to—after you've come all the way to St. Louis. Why, there are three fine hotels and several inns—"

"We'll be just fine here, Mr. Tharp," Josiah added.

"I wouldn't know how to feel in a—hotel," Bass admitted. "Wouldn't know what to do not sleepin' at night near my critters."

"That's just not—the usual way it happens here," Tharp explained. "We get men in from the mountains, maybe down from way upriver. They're ready to shuck it all for the citified life. Ready to get as far away from the animals as they can, to sleep on a bed and a mattress, curl their legs under a table with a cloth spread on it, maybe eat with a fork. I just thought—"

"Your place here suits us just fine," Bass reassured.

"Why, of course." Tharp gestured with a wide sweep of his arm. "Make yourselves comfortable as you can. Plenty of hay. Pitch some fresh over there to stretch out on. I can't 'llow no fires though. Can't set with no guest doing that." He watched the two trappers shake their heads. "I'll be back come sunup to open the blacksmith shop."

Amos stepped past the mountaineers and set the pitchfork alongside others leaning against the west wall.

"Mr. Tharp?"

The old man stopped at the door, one hand held ready to push his way into that icy blast of the winter storm.

"Yes? What is it, lad?"

"What day would it be?" Paddock asked.

"Why, Friday, young man."

"What date is it today?"

"I—I believe it to be the twenty-first of February, lad. Must be right 'cause the twenty-fourth is Monday. That day I'm selling a pair of Morgans to a fellow from St. Charles."

Josiah turned to his partner. "The twenty-first of February, Scratch."

"You calc'late how long it took us then?" Titus asked.

"That's some fifty-two days."

"Wagh! An' we lost two on the trail as it was with this old shoulder gettin' a hole in it."

Tharp hobbled closer. "I'm to understand you two just made it in here to St. Louis in fifty-two days?"

"We pulled out of Taos on January first. By my count, that's a tally of fifty-two, right?"

"By God's blood." Tharp chuckled. "Fastest anyone's done the trail in good weather on horseback's been forty-nine days. You loony fellas done it smack in the pee-wad of winter in fifty-two. Just how long you gents calc'late on staying here in St. Louis?"

"We don't know just yet, Mr. Tharp," Paddock declared.

"Two—three days, you said before."

"Mayhaps," Bass remarked. "Only long as it takes us."

"To finish up your business here?" Tharp asked. "Strange that a man would come all the way in to St. Louis from the mountains, in the blue-blinding pee-wad of winter and not hunker himself down until spring at least."

"Ain't the first time I'd be called the strange sort, Mr. Tharp," Bass chortled. "Probably won't be the last, neither."

"Head on back when your business is wrapped up?"

"When our—business here is done, Mr. Tharp. Only when we see it's done."

"Goodnight, boys." Tharp gave a quick nod and slipped out through the creaking door. The door hung open a moment before Tharp shoved it closed. In that instant the cold, sleety mist knifed its way into the warm barn. It sent a slice of mournful darkness down the aisle running through the middle of the stalls.

Bass shuddered involuntarily. Wasn't that just the way of things? he thought.

A man's all set and warm, feeling safe and secure in the light when the slash of something dark and evil comes to pay a call. Just what always happened.

ST. LOUIS had long occupied a preeminent position in the American fur trade. Here she sat near the junction of the Missouri and Mississippi Rivers, two great waterways that led a man either to the northern or western fur territories. Here, too, she sprawled along a course that would take trade goods from farther up eastern rivers all the way down to New Orleans on the Gulf of Mexico, from there on to distant ports around the world. This little village under the hill had grown immeasurably since last Bass had stalked her streets. Yet, St. Louis still remained the raw, crass and crude, adventurous and cocky metropolis she had always been right from her earliest days following her American acquisition from the French.

Stone towers and bastions, along with fortified blockhouses, stood up the hill from the village in the early days of the French, an ideal position from which the army could command control of the river. No longer did the hub of the American fur trade require such archaic protection from invaders. The only danger lay within her own teeming streets and crowded, shadowy back alleys.

By now there were better than thirty physicians in St. Louis. Twice that many barristers practiced law in crowded courts where better than half the cases involved civil litigation and suits demanding sums of money rather than crimes of passion or greed. Four print houses were kept busy as were two gristmills and three sawmills. The population had grown from some 4,600 in 1820, when many thought the city could hold no more, to its present ten thousand plus.

Fifteen schools taught the children of folks wealthy enough to pay for an education, helped along with endowments necessary to support such a venture in the classical separation of the classes. Yet in this city, itself as gangly as any fence rail backwoodsman, all classes rubbed elbows together, if not by design then at least by necessity. One could always hear a babbling mixture of tongues and languages: the foreign sound of Indian dialects from those coming to visit the home of the famous red-haired William Clark; the Spanish and Caribbean dialects which had come upriver; the sing-song of Canadian French alongside the phlegmy-toned local French, and the nasal twangs of American backwoods-men and southern mountaineers come west to see this bustling, thriving city. All these sounds contrasted greatly when opposed to the richer, fuller baritones of mountaineers returned east who were so long accustomed to the bass, rumbling tones of a summer storm rolling off the mountains onto the prairie or the low roar of tons of water tumbling over a cataract to fall hundreds of feet below. Such a man who had long been out west within the bosom of nature's voice had come to sound so different from his eastern brethren.

"Fella in there behind the bar looked at me awful strange." Josiah slid up beside Bass beneath the leafless trees some doors down the muddied avenue from the Rocky Mountain House.

"What fella? You find either one of them two, that what you mean?"

243

"I got news to peel your eardrums like a prairie onion, old man."

"You saw 'em, right?"

"Neither one of the two there right now, Scratch. What I could learn before they closed up and wouldn't talk, looks like there's some good news for you and there's some not all that fine."

"Give it to me quick, son. Give it all."

"Bad news is they say that Silas Cooper ain't worked for them better than two years now. They ain't seen him in almost that long. Rumor has it he was a hunter for an army post upriver. But that shut down. One fella let that word slip out right before they all got real quiet about Cooper."

Bass appeared to gaze off into the distance. "Silas gone from St. Louis, huh? Upriver they say?" He looked back to Josiah. "What 'bout Billy? You hear anything about Billy?"

"That's your good news, Scratch."

"He was there, right?"

"You weren't that lucky, old man. I told you neither of 'em were there when I went in."

"C'mon now. Tell me! Tell me!"

"Billy works there at times, they say. At times they have him doing other work for the new owners. He's gone for a while."

"How long is he gonna be gone for?"

"They expect him to come down from upriver this afternoon. The way I figure it, best we go back there to that watering hole come—"

"Evenin'," Bass finished, that distant look clouding his eyes again.

"That's what I'm thinking, too."

"Where's the livery from here, son?"

"Why, it's back across town from here."

"Good. I wanna go on down by the river on the way back. That's near where I used to work." He put a hand on Paddock's arm and pulled Josiah off toward town. "I want to see some more of St. Louie."

Fittingly, the Rocky Mountain House on First Avenue squatted in one of the older parts of the city, a section with the roughest reputation, a squalid, poorer section that befitted the tavern's clientele. In the old days, much of this neighborhood had been where the poor French had squeezed out a living. There were many more of those peasants than there were wealthy, powerful French families who controlled much of the American fur trade and the social life of St. Louis.

In this part of the city, the avenues were extremely narrow and crooked, seeming to follow the sporadic way some of the first French settlers had thrown up their homes, very much at random. While those houses appeared quaint and picturesque, all built of wood from the nearby forests, in reality they were now tumbledown affairs falling into disrepair. Most of the galleries or porches were not safe enough to walk upon. Almost all of these shanties had to be approached by ladders or stairs from the streets. There was an odd mixture of little shops and drinking houses sprinkled in amongst the dwellings which all sported the high, garret-style gable windows perking up into the steep hip roofs.

Bass and Paddock passed Olive, St. Charles, Mulberry, and Lombard on their return toward the core of the city. In a more Protestant section of town than old St. Louis, the Unitarian Church sat at Fourth and Pine while the Presbyterian Church held its services at Fourth and St. Charles. The trappers walked on past the Berthold house at Fifth and Pine. Until the time of his death in 1831, this was the home of one of those made most wealthy and powerful in the fur trade. Bass and Paddock burned through two hours swapping windies with other mountaineers and frontiersmen in the Hawken Brothers' rifle shop at 37 Washington, then ambled over past the Robidoux Bakery near First and Walnut. With a sweet pastry treat in the hand of each man, the trappers headed south once more.

At Noah Ludlow's theater on Second Street the huge sign outside the establishment advertised the current offering as The Gambler's Fate. Paddock had quite a time attempting to explain to Bass just what a play was. The fact that grown men would get up and act out a story appeared to be utter foolishness to the old trapper. Until, that is, Josiah reminded Scratch how he acted out some of his very own stories for enthralled audiences.

Down on Main Street a man had the feeling he had dropped into the commercial heart of St. Louis—the last thoroughfare before the hulking warehouses and brick buildings all shoved against the ancient levee of the Mississippi River. Main Street was narrow, barely able to accommodate two passing freight wagons. Every other corner sported either a dram shop, where some of the finer liquors could be purchased, or a popular billiard parlor.

Outside 10 Main, the pair stopped to gaze in the windows at the colorful display. Across the glass were painted the words:

THE SIGN OF THE GOLDEN HAT, J. CHRISTMAN
Prices within the reach of all persons in need of tiles,
fur caps, waterproof hats, plugs and beaver.

Here the mountaineers could see what became of their beaver after the mountain traders had returned to St. Louis. Christman was one of the most respected hatters in the entire country, who turned the beaver felt into shiny, stiff top-hats called *tiles* or jaunty, sporty bowlers, all impervious to water.

Next door they passed the Chouteau Berthold warehouse, one of the largest fur holding facilities in the city. Farther down the avenue were the two grand old hotels of the city, the Union and the Missouri. Since St. Louis was just that sort of crossroads where money came and went, it was only fitting that one of the chief counting houses of the town stood between the two hotels. The Benoit Counting House was perhaps the largest and most prestigious banking facility of its time.

The trappers finally turned east along Second Street, also known as Church Street or La Rue De l'Eglise, and passed beneath the shadow of the Catholic Cathedral. Nearby sat the Green Tree Tavern with a large swinging sign of a huge spreading oak tree advertising its location. At the mouth of the street, the view opened up to the majesty of the old river.

Here at the levee were tied the mighty, pumpkin shell paddle wheelers being loaded for destinations north or south. Upriver steamed others which whistled their grand salute of arrival. The names painted in four- to six-foot letters along

245

the decks were the likes of: *Belle of the West*, *Ben Franklin* and *Svetlana*. Rugged, muscular stevedores sweated in the frosty weather as they splashed through mud and slush, pushing their loads aboard the vessels or pulling shipments off. Bales of cotton and hemp stood two men high on the docks. Barrels of sugar and molasses awaited storage in the bulging warehouses. Back in shadows cast down by the huge, puffing smokestacks atop the river boats, were endless bales of buffalo robes and beaver pelts. The world awaited the commerce of the plains and the distant mountains.

Here, joining the stevedores, both black and white were French *engages*, dark and swarthy in their coloring, vibrant in their language and dress. Riverboatmen and the operators of the keelboats strode about in their tall leather boots directing the loading or unloading of their small craft which had the appearance of so many squat insects bobbing alongside the larger steamboats. Untold numbers of clerks and accountants checked off shipments and bills of lading as they tediously kept the wheels of commerce grinding smoothly. Their kind was easy to spot, papers spilling about them and ruffling in the stiff breezes, their garb somber and unadorned as befitted a monotonous life of countless numbers with no end.

A few plainsmen strode back and forth waiting to board keelboat or paddle wheel steamer, having booked passage for some upriver destination. Their kind found some satisfaction in waiting, leaning on their rifles, eyes slewing over the noisy hubbub while they themselves remained patient and aloof, distant and taciturn. Every now and then above the ear-crushing noise of commerce would rise the sharp crack of a whip or the cry of the bullwhackers in charge of the gigantic Pittsburg freight wagons rumbling back and forth along the wharves. The drivers dared any man to step in the path of their teams of monstrous draft horses.

His hat tilted to a jaunty angle, the stump of a smoldering cheroot clamped between what he had left of teeth, one such driver cried out a warning for the two buckskinned trappers to move their asses aside or lose them.

Bass tipped his coyote cap in a genteel manner to the man. The driver gave the old trapper a second look as he passed on down the levee.

From time to time expensive carriages rolled past them, bearing passengers to or from the steamers. The wealthy men wore tall stovepipes, while beneath their dark blue or green wool coats they sported light colored pantaloons and ruffled shirts. Their female companions pulled at wide, floating crinoline dresses with yards of petticoats billowing underneath.

Bass put his nose into the chilly breezes, eyes half closed, and sniffed downwind at the toilet waters and expensive perfumes worn by the loading passengers.

"You sniffing those dandies?" Paddock smiled when he noticed his friend.

"Them ladies," Bass replied. "You gotta remember I ain't seen a white skinned gal in some ten years now!"

Paddock slapped Bass on the shoulder. "You know what we ought to do is get you a whore."

Scratch turned slowly to look at Josiah. "It has been a long, dry ride at that,

246

Josiah Paddock. I do believe you have some idea there. Mighty fine idea at that."

"But—just a minute here," Paddock sputtered. "I—I didn't really—I don't think—"

"Don't think what, boy? That I'd want a woman after all them weeks on the trail? What do you think I am, son? This child might be forty years old, but he ain't been gelded. Not by a long chalk."

"You're the crazy one, I'll say." Paddock grinned when he looked down and saw Bass miming with a fist full of his breechclout in hand.

"An' you're the one to know this St. Louie, Josiah Paddock," Bass whispered. "You ought to know right where we can find us a likely sportin' house, with one strong sportin' lady in it for me to—" he inhaled deeply, "—smell."

"Serious?"

"Dead certain of it, son. We ain't got nothin' else to do but sleep an' eat, maybe brush down them critters back to Tharp's livery for the rest of the whole day. What say you take me to one of the better sportin' places in town an' we'll see what we can do to spend some more of that gold we brung with us. What say?"

Paddock looked at Bass. What did it really matter if he took the old man over to some place like The Diamond Supper Club? Wouldn't hurt, he supposed. Waits-by-the-Water would never know Titus had sported while he was in St. Louis. The Supper Club was known to have some of the prettiest whores in town, with fees to match the needs of most visitors to St. Louis. It had been ten years since last the old man had been with a white woman, so what the hell?

"Yeah," Paddock grinned at Bass. "I know a place you ought to like. Let's go get you one of those white women to—to—smell."

19

"NOW AS I remember it, this house here was one of the better that offered ladies for those fellas who were in need of a woman," Josiah declared.

Titus and Josiah climbed up the steps to the front gallery, a wide porch stretching around the front part of the two story house. Much of the front lawn here at Fourth and Mulberry was taken over with a sweeping drive filled with hitching rails for horses and carriages. At this time of day, the yard was empty.

"Don't look all that busy," Bass commented sourly. "You sure this is a good place?"

"We're just lucky you've come here this time of day," Paddock laughed, stomping his muddy feet on the porch. "You come on back here in a few hours, toward evening, we'd have to wait in line just to talk to someone pretty."

"How do I know I can take your word on this, son? You sampled the wares here your own self, huh?"

"A time or two," Josiah confessed as he opened the door. "In my younger days."

Bass closed the door behind him and stood frozen in awe of the grand entryway. He was immediately enveloped in a warmth that reminded him just how cold it was outside. Very little furniture lined the foyer. There was a long brocade rug, some paintings on the walls, and two overstuffed chairs. Beneath his feet lay a huge horsehair mat. Paddock brushed his moccasins back and forth over the mat, nodding for Scratch to do likewise.

Bass stepped into the fragrant foyer, neck craning, curious as to where the other doors led.

He whirled around at the sound of the bell.

Paddock let go of the long, gilded bell cord. "We'll find out if any of the ladies are awake this early in the day."

"Early in the day?" Bass squealed.

"For them, it's early. For these gals here, their day doesn't start till after sundown."

Paddock's attention was drawn to the young woman who came to the second floor landing and stared down at them. She wore a long, heavy housecoat which hung open at the neck. Her strawberry blonde hair was yet to be combed that day. A second woman, red-haired, joined her at the railing. They stared down at the grimy, bearded frontiersmen.

248

"Yes?" the redhead asked.

Paddock swallowed hard. "Well, we—we was wondering—are you ladies open for business?"

"You—gentlemen, wait right there." The blonde turned and disappeared.

The red-haired woman appeared to be in her early twenties. Her ample white breasts pressed against her houserobe as she leaned over the banister. Her unabashed flirting caused both men to grow uncomfortable.

"Damn, but she's bold," Bass whispered as he turned to walk along the length of the foyer. He glanced into one of the sitting rooms. The room was crowded with overstuffed chairs covered in velvet or brocades. In the center of the outer wall was a large fireplace.

"Good day."

Bass wheeled around to find a face to match the cheerful music in the voice. She was older than the first two women, but gave nothing to them in the way of beauty. She was a little plump, but the woman carried it well. Her silk housecoat was cinched tightly around a narrow waist and full, rounded breasts. Her dark hair was piled atop her head with a series of combs. He could see that she had just scrubbed her face of last night's makeup. She wore no lip coloring or rouge, yet her cheeks radiated a natural, healthy glow. Her smile was what captivated him most—until she began to descend the stairs and the housecoat parted to exhibit a fine pair of delicate ankles ascending into well-turned calves and rounded thighs.

"What can we do for you gentlemen today?" She continued to grace them with her bright, warm smile as she floated down the staircase. "It's not often we have visitors so early in the day."

Bass and Paddock looked at one another, then glanced back at the pretty woman. "G-good afternoon," Paddock finally stammered the words loose.

"Yes, it is a good afternoon," the woman answered. "But, how can we make it a better one for you fellas?"

Josiah felt foolish, but then remembered that they were paying customers. They weren't there as beggars.

"It's been some time since I was in St. Louis."

"I can see that," the woman agreed as she studied him with her dark brown eyes. "So you were wanting a lady, for your pleasure?"

She seemed to caress him with her smile and her eyes, and the way her words washed over him with their sing-song lilt, Josiah knew he could easily succumb to the siren's song.

Bass's mouth went dry and he felt a warmth in his groin. But, he knew if he didn't wrest control of things, Josiah would likely put them both in trouble.

He stepped up beside Paddock and put his arm around the younger man's shoulder. "My partner here, well, he was telling me just a bit ago about how nice you ladies are here."

The madam glanced over at him as if he were an intrusion, but then she softened.

"Go on," she coaxed musically.

Scratch shrugged his shoulders. "So, he brung me here. But, I'm the one who wants to be entertained, proper." He grinned widely, his age-yellowed teeth shimmering in the dim afternoon light.

"So, how is it we can—entertain you?"

"I ain't all that sure yet, ma'am," he answered as he remembered to pull his coyote skin cap off his head. "Maybe you'd help me make that choice."

"I think we could, my good man," she said with a slight drawl. "If you fellas wouldn't mind waiting in the parlor there." A white arm poured out of her sleeve to point the way.

Bass nodded. "Thank you, ma'am. We'll be right in there till you get back."

"Oh, gentlemen," the woman called after she had climbed a few steps. "Just how long has it been since you were in St. Louis?"

"My friend here," Bass said as he patted Josiah on the shoulder, "it ain't been quite three years now. With me, I'm proud to say it's been better'n ten years, ma'am."

"My, my, my!" she chimed. "A man of your stature and rugged good looks couldn't have gone for ten years without—some entertainment, could he now?"

"Nawww, not someone like me, ma'am."

"A man like you wouldn't have—any illnesses to worry him, would he?"

"Nary a one in them ten years. Not a one, ma'am."

"I ask only because a fella could catch—such an illness from an Indian squaw, couldn't he?"

"Well, now." Bass cleared his throat and twirled the coyote cap around on his index finger. "I s'pose a fella could catch somethin' like a dose of ills from a squaw. Surely could. You'd be right the first whack on that, ma'am. But, we all know that squaw had to catch her ills from some white fella first, wouldn't she now?"

She hesitated, then smiled. "I suppose you are right, Mr.?"

"Bass."

"Mr. Bass," she nodded. "So if a man has been fussy about who entertains him, he has no reason to worry about catching a cold."

"I think that's pretty much my way of thinkin'."

"My, my. You are a cute one too," she bubbled.

The woman turned and continued up the stairs, holding up the silk robe to show that she had little on beneath it. Milky legs flashed in and out of the folds of dark, shimmering cloth. At the second floor landing, she whirled and disappeared.

"C'mon, son," Bass said as he pulled Paddock back from the doorway near the foot of the stairs. "You cain't spend your afternoon starin' at that banister up there."

He loosened the knot in his sash and pulled his coat open as he strode over to the fireplace. He found the ashes still warm so he placed some split wood atop the coals and blew until the red nuggets glowed hot enough to catch at the dry firewood. Almost immediately the room took on a warm glow. He threw his elkhide coat over the back of a nearby chair and sank down with his legs stretched out before him. "You was right, Josiah."

"Right about what?"

"This is one fine place, son," Scratch claimed as he glanced around the room that was full of couches and chairs and cozy loveseats. There were several tables scattered about the room which held crystal glasses and decanters of liquor. "You care for somethin' to drink, Josiah?" he asked as he ambled over to one of the tables.

"Me? Oh, no. Thanks anyway, Scratch. Not right now." The young trapper wagged his head and continued to stare at the doorway, expecting some pretty gal to glide through it at any moment.

"Well, I wasn't raised such a foolish child," Bass grumbled as he poured whiskey into one of the glasses. "When a man pays the price for spendin' time with a handsome woman in such a foofaraw place as this, he should sip at their liquor."

"I'm not so sure you should be doing that—without the lady here." Paddock glanced around at Titus.

"We'll be payin' for whatever I drink. Don't worry 'bout that, Josiah Paddock. Fact is, we'll probably be payin' for whatever it is I don't drink, too."

"How you figure that?"

"They spend a lil' on the watered down liquor like this." He brought the glass away from his lips, smacking them loudly. "Just as I thought. They softened it down a bit. An' the better they make their customers feel through the whole evenin', why—the more them customers will loosen up their purses. Right?"

"I don't need any of that whiskey," Josiah uttered, gesturing with his hand. "I'm just fine."

Bass chuckled. "I'm sure them gals wouldn't need to force no liquor down you, Josiah Paddock. Why, it truly does appear you got drunk enough just by lookin' at all their wares!"

Scratch strode across the sitting room floor, goblet in hand. Gliding down the stairs slipped an assortment of young beauties. Most of the girls wore flowing housecoats and slippers. A few wore simple dresses. Fourteen of them descended the walnut staircase singly or in giggling pairs, their eyes flashing at the two bearded trappers. With their hair brushed to a sheen and their faces scrubbed until their cheeks glowed like wild roses on a spring prairie, the women slinked into the room. The madam swept through the doorway as the last of the young women found seats to their liking.

"You have you quite a—a fine remuda here, ma'am," Bass offered with a salute of his half empty goblet.

"Remuda?" the madam asked.

"Like a—hand-picked herd of fine thoroughbred fillies, ma'am."

"Thank you, Mr. Bass. This is a sampling only. There are more." She swept up beside him and laced an arm through his, guided him over toward the warm radiance of the fireplace. "But, it takes a—special talent at entertaining a man with your ten-year-old appetite. Not everybody can satisfy that sort of hunger, you understand."

"I believe I know just what you mean, ma'am." He smiled down at her, drinking in her perfumes as he looked at the shimmering ringlets of her black hair gathered around her head with mother of pearl combs.

The old trapper glanced at Paddock who was wedged between a pair of young

251

women. On Josiah's left sat a honey brown blonde who repeatedly raked her fingers through his beard while on his other side was a brunette with hair the color of polished oak. She fiddled with the fringe on Josiah's legging.

"We don't see that many—frontiersmen like yourselves," the madam announced. She took the goblet out of Scratch's hand and sipped from it.

"Why's that, dear missy?"

"I would suppose their tastes run to something—perhaps a little less expensive."

"Yes'm. Most of them other frontiersmen wouldn't care a damn for your watered down whiskey, leastways," he growled as he took the goblet back and took a healthy swallow.

Titus slipped free of her grip and sauntered to the center of the room, appraising each woman as he went.

"These what you got to offer a man that's been ten years away from seein' a white woman, huh?"

The young girls in the room went silent and stared at the old trapper, then glanced nervously at each other. "Yes, Mr. Bass," the madam replied, her voice soft. "I told you—I selected these girls for someone of your—experience, your particular appetites."

Bass stopped beside the red-haired woman who had been at the second floor landing when they had come calling out of the cold. He took another swig of the pale whiskey and dallied with the flaming curls nestled atop her shoulders.

"Just what is the fare for the ride, ma'am?"

"If you'd care to tell me what you have in mind, Mr. Bass?"

"We was talkin' about bein'—properly entertained, wasn't we?"

"Twenty dollars is our usual price, but that doesn't cover—unusual circumstances." The madam had yet to move from her spot near the crackling fireplace. "However, since you might have need of some special services, we'll just say thirty dollars, Mr. Bass."

"Thirty?" Bass snorted. "Hell, even twenty would buy a man a decent horse here in St. Louis. We ain't talkin' mountain prices here, missy. We're talkin' St. Louis prices—at the trailhead."

Scratch brought a lock of the young woman's hair to his nostrils and drank deeply of it. "You know, young lady," he whispered huskily, "I ain't see'd a woman with red hair in better than ten years now." He saw the nervous look in the girl's eyes as he let the curl fall back on her shoulder. He stepped behind the woman, running his hand down her spine as if appraising her structure, just as he would assess a pony he was bartering for.

He looked across the room at the madam. "Is she really a red-headed gal?" he asked. "She got red hair—all over?"

"Why do you ask?"

"I ain't never been with a red-haired woman before." As he walked around and stood in front of the young prostitute, Bass let two fingers glide down her white neck and into the soft cleavage between her full breasts. "I'd just like to know if she's got red hair all over."

The madam of the house swayed up beside him. She removed his hand from the young woman's breasts, kissed his fingers and let the hand drop. "Well, then, Mr. Bass— you'll just have to pay the going rate to find that out, won't you?"

"Nawww." He turned away from the young woman and grinned. "I won't pay a toll of thirty dollars for her. Fact is, I won't pay nothin' for her. Simply don't want her."

"Which one will it be, then?" the madam asked with a sweeping gesture of her arm, watching the young redhead sag in relief.

"Why—" Bass looked from one nervous girl to the other, all around the parlor. "I think I'll pick—" he said as his gaze returned to the madam. "You."

"Me?" Her hand flew to her neck in surprise. "Why me? I haven't sported in— a long time now."

"C'mon now, missy," he chuckled. "What with all them rich purses fat with money out there in St. Louie, purses just waitin' to be picked by the likes of a handsome woman like yourself? You tell me you ain't sported in a long time? What about the likes of all them rich, stuffed shirt dandified fur traders an' army gen'rals? How 'bout them businessmen with all their money an'—an' them bankers?"

"Well—I haven't—really, Mr. Bass," she protested as she took the goblet from his hand and swallowed long and hard, stalling. "I began to leave the—entertaining up to the girls some time back. Really, I have."

Bass didn't believe it, especially when out of the corner of his eye he noticed a few of the younger women roll their eyes back in common disbelief.

"I'd've expected a lie from the lips of these others, ma'am, but not from the likes of a spunky gal like you."

Bass threw his head back and drained what remained of the pale whiskey in the goblet before he handed it to the red-haired woman. "Get me some more of that whorehouse whiskey, will you, sweetheart?"

"You know I'll cost you dearly?" The madam squared her shoulders as she stared at him.

"Why's that, missy? Why should you cost any more than the others?"

"Because—I'm worth it," she smiled.

"Just how much are you—worth, lady?"

"Forty dollars."

"Forty dollars?" His voice rose an octave as he glanced over at Paddock.

"Yes. If it's me you choose, forty is what it will be, Mr. Bass."

"I don't know if any woman is worth that kind of money," he grinned. "No tellin' what-all forty dollars will buy here in St. Louis. The worse part of it is that none of you gals got the least idea how long it takes a man to make him forty dollars wadin' streams an' skinnin' beaver—watchin' over his shoulder for them hair-stealin' red niggers that wanna put an arrow or hawk atwixt your shoulder blades."

He watched her gulp.

"I—I'd just thought you were—an upriver man—hunter for the army. I had no idea you—you'd been out to the mountains for ten years."

Scratch glanced at Josiah. "We got us enough in that poke of yours for forty dollars on this?"

"I'd have no problem coming up with—with forty for the lady." Paddock was chin deep in his own concerns at the moment.

"Ma'am, I think I got me a plan that'll work for us both—get this dickerin' done so me an' my partner here can get on down the road to business." He gulped again at the watered down whiskey.

"I'd be interested in hearing what it is you have to offer, Mr. Bass."

"Good money, ma'am. It's good money I'm offerin'. Fifty dollars for you—not none of these others here. Just for you."

"Why—I don't understand."

"The fifty dollars is for me—an' Mr. Paddock here." He placed his hand on Josiah.

"Wha-a-a?" Paddock's head jerked up.

"You can't be serious." The madam minced a step backwards, her gaze flitting between the two bearded trappers.

"Serious as Blackfeet, ma'am." He put the goblet to his lips and drank long at it.

"This is outrageous! Completely out of the question, Mr. Bass." She turned toward the fireplace.

"Why, ma'am—you was just sayin' how much you was worth the price, ten dollars more than these other gals get for entertainin'. That's 'bout twenty dollars more than any of these young'uns is worth, if'n you'd want my honest feelin' on it. So, here I am, offerin' you five times as much as I'd ever wanna pay for a woman, an' all you gotta do is entertain us both for a short time."

"W-why both of you?" Her hand was at the base of her neck again, fingers spread and trembling slightly.

Bass eyed her carefully over the lip of his goblet. She hadn't led all that hard a life. The years appeared to have been kind to her. The woman had taken good care of herself, or at least someone else's money had been good to her. She appeared to still be solid, even though her life had been easy. Most women in the cities and towns didn't have it all that rugged, he mulled. Nowhere near as hard as someone like his mother would have suffered. That type of unrelenting labor and child rearing exacted its toll on a woman, an awful toll.

This one here before him was fleshy and full, not skinny and bony and worn out like most women who reached their middle years. Even most Indian gals would be fat as a full tick by their middling years, but this one wasn't all that plump for her age. A narrow waist and she didn't appear to have a stranglehold whalebone corset lashed around her either. He figured she couldn't be anything past forty-five.

"Just how old are you, ma'am?"

"Why—I certainly don't think that's any of your business," she snapped back at him, her dark eyes quickly filling with flares.

"Mayhaps you're right, missy. Just was wonderin', that's all. You see, I cain't figure this out. I took you to be a smart lady. One that had a lot of life sorted out for herself. That's what I mean by it. An', I savvy that calc'lates that you'd be least as old as me."

254

He felt not only her eyes but the appraisals of the others in the room. All right, he'd asked for it.

"I don't think so," she stated cautiously. "I don't believe I am as old as—as you appear to be."

"An' these others," Bass nodded here, there, "why—they could be a daughter to someone my age, you see."

"We have many—older customers for the girls here. Much older than you, I would imagine. It makes little difference what a man's age is."

"But we wasn't really talkin' 'bout my age, missy," he said with a smile, bringing the goblet down from his lips and handing it to the redhead for another refill. "Please, miss." He brought his eyes back to the madam. "We was talkin' on you an' your years. I was merely thinkin' how surprised I was to find that someone who looked like she'd be a wise ol' gal just wasn't actin' anything but like a stupid kid. Passin' up fifty dollars like that," and he snapped his fingers. "Here, I thought you was least smart enough to be forty-five—"

"I'm thirty-eight and not a day older!" she flushed, the words pouring out of her mouth before she realized she had sputtered them.

Her eyes instantly shot about the room, flitting here, there, looking into each surprised face, each young woman shocked to suddenly find out just how old the house madam actually was. She had been bested by the old mountaineer, and knew it. But—it wasn't all that bad a feeling, really. Not near as bad as she had feared. Most of her adult life had been spent scurrying along, trying to stay one step ahead of men in what was very much a man's world. Hers was a tough profession for a woman whose place it was to please a man without giving sway to him. But now this dirty, hairy, smelly old mountain trapper was cagey enough that he'd gotten the best of her, after all these years.

And, it appeared he was getting the better of her on the dollars, too. But, it didn't feel bad. Strangely enough, it didn't feel all that bad.

"That's all right, ma'am. I'll believe you." His eyes moved from the madam to the redhead as he took back the refilled goblet. "Thank you, young lady."

Then he sipped and continued. "I turned forty back to January. Ain't nothin' to it. You got some mighty good years left in you. Why, look at you, ma'am. Just look. These here others ain't got a thing on you. You still look some seal fat an' sleek, you do. Prime you are an' I'll bet you just keep gettin' all the better to boot."

He watched her beam a little in spite of herself, self-consciously tugging at a curl that hung near her cheek.

"I got fifty dollars here, for me an' my partner, ma'am. We'd both be much obliged should you take me up on my offer."

Bass backed off a few steps, sipping at the goblet, allowing the woman some space around her, allowing her some time to consider the weighty proposition.

'Why—why b-both of you?"

"Ma'am, we're partners—have been for some time. Been through a lot with each other. Fact is, we saved each other's life a time or two. Partners like that, we don't get separated now, do we, ma'am?" He offered her his glass.

255

She nodded slowly, then took a healthy slug of her own from the crystal goblet. "Then, partners you shall stay."

Bass turned to wink at Paddock who appeared dumbstruck by the turn of events. Josiah's cheeks brightened crimson as tradecloth.

"You ready, ma'am?" he asked as he took back the glass.

"I—I believe I am ready." The madam floated across the sitting room, almost regally, her chin held high, through the double doors and began her climb up the stairs. About midway she stopped to cast her eyes back down into the parlor where she caught and held the old man's attention.

"Are you coming—Mr. Bass?"

"Yes'm," he said as he leaned over with a free arm and pulled Josiah off his comfortable perch, taking the young man from his two young admirers. "We're comin' along, right quick."

"I—I—I don't know about this," Paddock stammered.

Bass jerked him into motion. "You come 'long with me. We said we'd get me a woman to smell, Josiah."

The older trapper nodded at some of the young women nearby who giggled at the remark. He smiled at them before he went back to whispering into Josiah's ear.

"You said you'd find this place for me, well—I'm returning the favor doin' this for you, son. Fifty dollars is fifty dollars! An' we'll get our money's worth, now."

"I ain't all that sure I wanna go up there with you." Josiah was almost begging as they began their climb up the stairs.

"Now, why would you not wanna go up an' be entertained by that handsome lady?"

"J-just don't feel right about it. Not right about it at all."

"Why? You bein' a married man, huh?"

They reached the second floor where he stopped to look about, to find where the woman had gone.

"Say, missy? Where'd you go off to?"

"In here, Mr. Bass!"

The soft voice floated to them from down at the end of the hall. He pushed Josiah onto the long, brocade rug that ran the length of the narrow hall.

"Huh? What with you bein' a married man?"

"I think t-that's it."

"An' you don't wanna do Looks Far wrong, do you?" With that, Bass stopped square in the middle of the hall.

"I suppose that's what I feel I'd be doing—doing this to her."

"Josiah, when a man gets into a woman's hoop, he's as helpless as a one-legged bullfrog."

"I-I can't help it. I'm just ass over kettle in love with the gal."

"Boy. Am I ever glad to hear you say that!" Bass slapped Paddock soundly on the back. "I was beginnin' to wonder 'bout you downstairs. You was lookin' like you was a hawg in slop there, enjoyin' them young gals just a mite too much. S'pose it weren't fair at all for me to do this to you, was it?"

"D-do what? I—I don't understand!" Josiah was genuinely baffled.

"I really figured you wanted to slip your poker betwixt a gal's legs, least from what I was seein' of you down there in the parlor."

"No, no I wasn't. We—we come here for you—'cause you said you wanted to smell a white woman after all these—ten years. It just got too big on us too fast. I just thought you wanted to smell—"

"I do."

"Then why the hell you dragging me in? Makin' me do this?"

"Say now, if you don't wanna come, you don't have to. I just figgered wrong when I was dickerin' with the woman. An' I'm one child that's purely happy to find out he is wrong, too. I was tryin' to make a deal for you to get your poke an' me to get my smell of her fancy perfumes."

"You could have smelled any one of them, or all of 'em downstairs. What the hell we gonna do up here now?"

"I ain't leavin' till I see me that woman skinned, Josiah. An', you're comin' along with me."

He began to tug on Paddock's arm.

"For what? Thought we got that settled! I don't want a poke in her."

"Then you come an' watch."

"I ain't gonna watch you poke her!"

"Nawww. I ain't 'bout to do that to Waits-by-the-Water. She's my woman. I'm her man. Crow women ain't known to be the most faithful critters in the world. Lord knows that. But, I'm gonna be true to her an' let her know I ain't gonna bed down no other gal long as she's my wife."

"Then—what do you want me to watch?"

"I want you to watch me get my fifty dollars' worth, son."

"You ain't gonna poke that good-looking woman, and you're still gonna give her our fifty dollars?"

"Mr. Ba-a-ass?" The madam's voice sailed down the hall musically.

"We're comin'. Just keep your clothes on."

"My clothes on?" she hollered in surprise.

"That's right, ma'am. Keep your clothes on."

"I-I already disrobed for you."

"Well, dammit. Put your goddamned clothes back on."

"Ah—all right."

"Yes, Josiah," Bass whispered. "I'm gonna get my fifty dollars' worth."

Paddock shook his head. "You'll spend fifty dollars an' not get your pecker wet? I can't figure this one out. What the hell else could be worth fifty dollars?"

"Not much, Josiah. Not a whole hell of a lot." He pursed his lips. "But, the way I figure it, I've been in the mountains for ten years. So, how much is that a year?"

"What do you mean?"

"The fifty dollars and the ten years. How much a year?"

"Why, that's five dollars a year."

"See. It ain't all so bad a price then, is it, Josiah Paddock?" He rared back and slapped his partner square on the shoulders. "I just calc'lated that I've been spendin' five dollars a year savin' up for a real good smell on a white woman. You understand?"

Josiah shook his head. "Sometimes, old man, I don't think you yourself understand the things you're teaching me. But that don't matter. Let's go get you your smell."

The older trapper stepped into the room with Paddock at his heels. She lounged seductively on a small, blue velvet loveseat. These private quarters were richly decorated, crowded with furnishings and three cedar wardrobes stuffed with all manner of expensive clothing. Shaded oil lamps sat on every table draped with crocheted lace coverlets. He gazed about the room, finally settling on the madam.

"Why did you have me put my clothes back on?" she asked demurely.

" 'Cause I wanna take 'em off you."

"You what?" She bolted upright on the loveseat.

"For fifty dollars, I figure I got the right to skin you, ma'am."

"Skin me?"

"Take your clothes off. Don't you figure fifty dollars gives a man that right, Josiah?"

Josiah sat down, nodded.

"See, there? My partner and I are in agreement. For fifty dollars there's gotta be a lil' more to this than me climbin' on your bones, ruttin' an' then climbin' off."

She inhaled deeply and let it out slowly before she finally rose from the loveseat. "Where do you—you want me?"

Bass came close to her, watching her face intently for some clue to her thoughts. Carefully he worked at the knotted sash of her housecoat. It spilled open to reveal a thin, cotton garment that barely reached to the middle of her thighs. It fell loose everywhere but over her ample breasts. Bass slid the silk robe from her shoulders with both hands, letting the garment flow down her arms, off her hands and into a crumpled heap to the floor. He heard Paddock gulp as he looked back into the woman's eyes.

"You ain't scared, are you?" he asked quietly.

'No, I'm not scared," she said as she squared her shoulders. "It's just—just I haven't smelled so—so many foreign odors before."

He watched her nostrils flare slightly.

"Ma'am, you're foreign to me, too. Leastways your smell is. Don't any men sweat around here?"

"Oh, men sweat a lot around St. Louis, Mr. Bass. Especially when they get around me." She grinned impishly.

"I don't doubt a word of that, missy. Just lookin' at you might put a man to sweatin' somethin' serious."

"I'll take that as a compliment."

"It were meant to be, ma'am. You're some fine looker." He walked around her slowly, appraising every inch, only his eyes reaching out to caress her.

"Just what was it you had in mind?"

"This."

"This?" There was a slight tremor in her voice.

Bass tugged at the straps of the cotton chemise she wore, pulling them over her shoulders. First one arm, then the other was pulled through the straps. Then ever so gently he tugged the garment down to free her breasts, exposing them. He could tell she was chilly in the cool room by all the goosebumps instantly prickling her skin. Before he disrobed her farther, Scratch glanced about.

At the small fireplace he threw some pieces of dry wood atop a few feeble flames, then blew on the red coals until the hearth radiated some cozy warmth.

"C'mon over here, missy. It's a mite warmer."

The madam quickly kicked her bare feet out of the silk robe and hopped over to the warmth of her fireplace.

"This—is very kind of you."

"Cain't ever let a woman freeze, now can I?"

Bass winked at Josiah who sat frozen, eyes transfixed on the woman. Paddock wasn't even aware Bass had looked over at him.

"We're just about grained, ma'am."

The old trapper gently pulled the garment down over her waist, across her full hips and slid it down her rounded thighs. He let the chemise fall about her ankles on the brick hearth in front of the fireplace. She shuddered and he hoped it was because of the chilly air in the room.

"Wh-what now, Mr. Bass?"

"I'm gonna smell you."

"You're what?"

"Said, simple enough—I'm gonna smell you."

He raised one of her arms and stuck his nose along her skin, from wrist to the hair of her armpit, drinking in the fragrance of her skin and perfumes both, all along the way. Next his fingers danced up across her freckled shoulders as his nose went down to smell the curve of her neck.

"Wish't I could count, Josiah."

"How's that?" The younger man gulped, staring at the older woman's full body.

"I'd count all these freckles on her shoulders, here on her back, too. They're pretty freckles, missy. I ain't seen such a thing as a freckle that I can remember in over ten years—you gotta remember that."

Bass knelt behind her, his two hands on either side of her right leg. Slowly he rose, letting his fingertips glide up the softness of the leg's dark hair and powdered skin. Finally at her hips his hands stopped and softly squeezed at her waist. He dipped his head to smell of the madam's belly.

Next the trapper stepped around the woman slowly, examining her hair. Bass pulled one of the mother of pearl combs from her dark tresses, freeing some curls to fall at the side of her face, spilling against her neck and down over her shoulder. He darted to her left side and did the same with another comb. More of the dark, glossy tresses tumbled across her white, freckled shoulders. Standing behind her, the old man pulled loose the last of the combs, watching the cascade of fragrant hair tumble across her back.

Bass fingered up a delicate ringlet and brought it to his nose. Eyes half-closed, he sucked in the heady fragrance of her hair. "That's really some, ma'am."

Circling her again so that he stood before the madam, Titus brought up a gnarled forefinger and thumb. Between them he gently rolled a nipple on one breast. She twitched.

"I hurt you?"

"N-no, Mr. Bass. You didn't hurt me at all. I-I'm very sensitive on my breasts."

He took a gentle squeeze on the second nipple, amazed to watch it respond to his touch, becoming firm and hardened like the first. Then he placed his nose right between her breasts and drank in the fragrance of her cleavage. Eventually he brought his face away from her breasts and sighed with a huge smile across his mouth.

"I'm done, ma'am."

"What?" she squeaked.

"How 'bout you, Josiah? Your turn."

"Not me, Scratch." Josiah raised a palm in denial. "I just come to watch, remember?"

"Yeah. But she smells real good, for a white gal. You oughta come on over here an' take a good sniff, son."

"Thanks. But, no, Scratch. I can smell fine from right here. Everything looks just fine from right where I'm sitting."

"Wha-a-a—I don't understand at all what you gentlemen are doing here," the madam said.

"Simple, ma'am," Bass replied as he bent over to pick up her silk robe. He handed it to her. "I got me a fifty dollar smell off a white gal."

"You what! That's all you're doing?"

"Right, missy."

"Smelling me? Feeling my breasts? That's all?"

"Yep." Bass went over to a small table and retrieved his goblet.

"For fifty dollars?"

"Why, missy. Weren't it worth fifty to you?"

"I—I don't know quite what to say. Fifty dollars and all you did was touch me a little, smelled me a lot."

"Fifty dollars is quite a bit to spend smellin' a white woman, don't you think, Josiah?" Bass said.

"Yep," Josiah nodded from his chair.

"Fifty dollars surely ought to buy us both a bath, too. Don't you think, Josiah?"

"Yep."

"Oh, of course. Of course," the madam answered happily, relieved. "For both of you."

"Hmmm, not just a bath, though." Bass plodded around the room, touching this object, examining something else. "Maybeso it oughta buy me a nap after one of them young gals scrubs my back. What do you think 'bout that, missy?"

"A nap? Here? In my bed?"

"Just what I was thinking, ma'am. Thank you. Where can my partner have a nap?"

The woman looked bewildered.

"What you got planned for supper, ma'am?" Bass rubbed his hands together before the fire.

"Uh—"

"How long till y'all eat supper anyway? I'm sure getting hungry, old man." Josiah chuckled.

"Huh?" The woman looked from one trapper to the other.

"We both wanna know when we're havin' supper—an' what it be that you're feedin' us."

"Supper?"

"Yeah. What's on the bill of fare this evenin'?"

"I—I didn't know it would involve all this when I agreed to the fifty dollars."

"Wait just a minute, missy. Ain't neither one of us crawled on top of you, have we?"

"No."

"That's right. An' Josiah got the fifty dollars right here. Give her the gold, son. Fifty dollars' worth."

Bass watched as Paddock counted it out into the woman's palm. Her other hand continued to clutch the silk robe tightly about her.

"I just think you're bein' a bit stingy if you don't allow a couple fellas a chance to take a real bath, catch up some sleep in a nice soft featherbed, an' then eat supper with all you fine lookin' fillies."

"Sounds to me like she's definitely coming out on the better end of this stick," Josiah offered.

"Me, too," Bass said, setting down the goblet. "But, if you don't wanna let us do that—well, you got your money, ma'am. I misjudged you. My fault, not your'n. I just figured you wouldn't mind havin' us around for a bit longer, till evenin' time. I gotta go see me an old—old friend. I don't know if him or me will walk away from it. But, then, you don't understand none about that sort of thing, do you? Not in your fancy world. Gal like you just sits up here with all the purty smellin' young gals makin' all that money for you. So, you ain't gotta get any dirt under your fingernails. You just turn your mind off an' take a man's money, don't you? An' the problem with things right now is that I want your mind to be workin' proper. I ain't askin' you for nothin' you ain't already got. Problem is, missy—I'm askin' you for somethin' you ain't never give to no man before. Right? Ain't that right?"

"I—I—"

"Right. You give a man your body, but you never give any of 'em the time of day, a lil' kindness—"

"They all got what they paid for!" The fire was back. "Each and every one."

"Bed ain't the only jury a woman has." He let the words sink in. "Ma'am, I wanna pay for some of your time, an' your kindness. But," he announced as he swilled down the last of the watered-down whiskey, "if you cain't see your way clear to do that—why, Josiah an' me'll be on our way back to Tharp's livery."

They were just about to the door when she suddenly spoke.

"Wait."

The men turned and looked back at the woman, huddled in her silk robe at the fireplace, suddenly looking very small in the crowded room.

"I suppose I was a bit hasty—but, I never did say no, did I?"

Bass looked over to Josiah. "No, not as I recollect."

"Would you fellas want to spend the rest of the afternoon and evening here with us, in the house where it's warm? Until it's time for you to—to go find this old friend of yours?"

"Why, yes, missy. I believe we would. Truly would enjoy that."

"You know something, Mr. Bass?" She swiped at her nose and smiled. "I really believe I would, too. I believe I'd enjoy having you here, too."

20

THE DAY DISAPPEARED in the time it took them to cross Fifth Street. Iron light drained from the threatening clouds overhead as the trappers were jostled back and forth by passersby scurrying off to home or another equally warm destination. Josiah led the way.

The lamplighters were out, torching the streetlamps. Bass stared intently at each lamp as he passed under it, cursing man's frail attempts to light the black of night.

Soon enough Scratch recognized the street where earlier that day they had come to find the tavern. City or mountain valley, a darkened street or sharp-toothed ridge on a moonless night—they were all the same to him. Titus Bass paid attention to the lay of the land. He knew they were near the Rocky Mountain House.

Billy would be there. Before Billy would die he would spill where the old trapper could find Silas Cooper. Billy Hooks would tell him where to find the man responsible for stealing his beaver money.

Halfway down the muddy street they were able to hear shouting, laughing, profane joking, along with vicious snarls of dogs each trapper assumed could only be coming from the infamous watering hole. The place had never been known as a drinking establishment, even so much as a saloon or tavern. No such kind words had ever been used so loosely to describe the Rocky Mountain House. This was a place the respectable classes of St. Louis steered clear of, including the newly formed municipal police force. Constables would come only in the day to this neighborhood, and only then with a strength found in numbers. Life was as cheap right here as it was on the upriver, or out in that big nothing of the prairie, even in that terrible vastness of the mountains for which the tavern was named. Life just wasn't worth all that much here on this street.

A sizable crowd of men, of mixed shapes and sizes, all pushing and shoving against one another, gathered in a circle. They jostled back and forth as the center of the circle flowed across the huge, muddied lot that served as the front yard of the place. From within the midst of the agitated crowd arose the snarls, yips, howls, and barks of fighting dogs.

"I gotta see what's goin' on here," Bass nodded to Josiah. "I'll be right back. Don't you go nowhere."

He was gone. Through a crushing sea of bodies bundled in coats of wool or animal hides to ward off the cold, frosty night air, Bass disappeared. Even before

Josiah could say a word, the old man dove into the midst of the carousing drunks. Paddock recognized one, then a second, of the stevedores who had been on the docks that morning when the trappers had been down to the levee.

Josiah shouldered through the shoving crowd until he stood three rows back from the center of the ring. Still, he could not see Bass anywhere in the yellow, glimmering light of the crude torches several men held overhead.

The animals tumbled toward the building and the crowd shifted. It was just a dog fight, Paddock mulled. All this excitement just to watch two dogs fighting. Then he knew why. Here in front of him stood one of the bookmakers, taking bets on one cur or the other. Across the center ring hurriedly stepping out of the way of the two roiling animals was another, his hands also full of currency, scratching down on paper what type of coinage he had received and from whom. Pistoles, guineas, dollars—it did not matter. Any currency at all was of value in St. Louis.

One animal clearly appeared to be getting the better of the other. A large, black and brown cur showed he was clearly the aggressor, pinning the other animal down a good portion of the time. For its part the smaller dog was trying to hold its own against the stronger, larger mongrel. Every now and then it would break free and dive for the larger mutt's neck, holding on for its life until it would be flung off. It was plain the gray dog with its wide forehead could not last much longer. Betting was shifting against the dog. Blood oozed from the animal's numerous wounds to smear the canine's muddy coat, but none as serious as the gash torn open on its rear haunch. The noisy crowd shouted back and forth, most of them beginning to roar with laughter at the owner of the gray dog, heckling his loss. It was readily apparent he would lose his shirt to the crowd, as many of the bettors were shifting their bets to the black and brown mongrel. The larger, dark animal was a hometown favorite anyway, one of the crowd shouted to Josiah. The stranger explained the dark animal belonged to one of the old stevedores who worked and lived down on the levee. Over the past two years folks had always come from up or down the river to pit their dogs against his. The gray dog belonged to a mate on the *Belle of the West,* one of the steamboats plying the Mississippi and Missouri Rivers. He had brought it along to the Rocky Mountain House in hopes of finding out just how tough the stevedore's animal was. The boatman simply hadn't believed all the wild stories he had heard told about the black dog. He had found it hard to believe that few dogs had been known to walk away from a fight with the black cur.

Suddenly a short, stocky man jumped into the open ring and whistled loudly. He called again for the dark animal which hesitated, then obeyed. The old stevedore knelt in the mud and held his animal around the neck until the fighting juices cooled in the dog, all the time cooing to the strong animal in his broken English.

Just as quickly there was another man in the ring—younger, taller, screeching in his thick Irish brogue. He cursed and tried to throw his pot belly against this man and that in his anger. The spectators did nothing but laugh at his tantrum. Then he leapt to stand over the gray animal at the center of the ring.

Its sides heaving painfully, blood oozing from all its wounds, a rear leg chewed to jerky, the smaller animal looked all but dead. Flecked with blood, the dog's tongue lolled out of its mouth as the animal gasped for air. An ear that had been nearly torn off hung across one eye.

The Irishman began waving his hands and screaming at his dog. He kicked the dog savagely in the ribs with his round-toed boot. The gray mutt whimpered and tried in vain to crawl away from its master. Cruelly, the crowd laughed at the dog's predicament and the futile anger of the boatman. They egged him on and on, ridiculing him for his dog losing the fight. They drove him madder and madder while he kicked the animal more and more savagely until it no longer tried to move.

Bass smashed his fist into the side of the muscular Irishman's face and watched the boatman stumble back several steps, holding his jaw, before he caught his balance.

The crowd quieted a moment. This was something novel. They had come for a dog fight and now it appeared there would be a real fight here tonight. At least twice a week you could count on someone getting killed at the Rocky Mountain House and this looked like it could be the start of something bloody. Spurred by the prospect of gore and excitement, the drunks began to roar anew.

"You leave the dog alone!"

The Irishman shook his head, clearing it before he glared at the trapper. He gave the mountaineer a close, hard appraisal.

"My dog. Ain't a soul in hell gonna tell Timothy Sullivan how to treat his dog!"

The boatman handed his betting papers back to a man in the crowd and removed his heavy mackinaw. Suddenly he wheeled around to face Bass. Glinting beneath the bobbing torch lights was a huge steel blade. Titus took a step to the side. The rooting crowd was pressing in at his back. He slid to the left, fighting the thongs holding the elkhide coat about him. If he could get his hands under his coat—he carried two knives.

Grinning, the Irishman feinted as he advanced, circling the trapper. The crowd jeered at Bass, laughing at his sudden predicament as back and forth they passed their pewter mugs or earthen jugs of whiskey.

"My dog!" the boatman roared again as he lashed out at Bass.

Scratch stumbled over the gray animal and nearly went sprawling on his back as he fought to get out of the heavy coat.

"I'll kill you for meddlin' in this just as surely as I'll kill that worthless animal right before your eyes."

Bass tried to rise but his hand slipped in the icy mud and he spilled on his left shoulder. The hot pain exploded through him. Just as he was closing his eyes against the agony of the old wound in his chest, the old trapper saw the stocky Irishman lunging at him, the knife held up and back, ready to plunge into his heart.

Instead, the crowd watched the weapon go sailing, tumbling through the air before it plopped in the mud near the wounded dog.

Dumbfounded, the Irishman turned, clutching his right hand, screeching out about his good hand being broken.

"Did you see that?" one onlooker asked.

"What?"

"What happened?"

"How'd it happen?" asked another.

Bass was up on an elbow. Paddock helped him to his feet as the young trapper held out his own huge blade.

"He kicked the Mick's hand."

"Come sailing outta the crowd from over there."

"Why—I never in all my borned—did I ever figure to see someone do that."

"No man can jump that far and do that."

"He done it. I saw him."

"No he didn't. Couldn't have. You're drunk!"

"Wanna wager he didn't? Tell 'im, Coons. Tell 'im you saw it with your own eyes."

"I saw it with me own two eyes, but I still don't believe none of it."

Scratch knelt at the side of the dog's body, a palm laid against the heaving ribs. He knew the pain the animal suffered. He understood the fear of death, of not comprehending what was happening, yet sinking down so low that you accepted death's own coming. He understood. The gray dog whimpered beneath his touch. Bass glared back at the crowd.

"Nobody else gonna take care of 'im, I want the critter."

"It's my dog." The Irishman had blood trickling down from his busted, swollen lip and a bloody nose where Scratch's fist had smashed into his face.

"Ain't no more, you bastard."

"We'll see about that, my friend."

The Irishman squatted slightly to make a lunge toward Bass but Josiah stood over the older trapper just as quickly. Sliding in the icy mud, the boatman skidded to a halt. Paddock had the blade of his huge knife up and ready. He casually took a step to stand in front of the old man.

"I ain't that ready to spill another man's blood, I want you to know," Paddock said, speaking low, hard. "But, I ain't afraid of it either."

Bass rose to stand over the dog at Josiah's side.

"Young'un here kilt his share of Injuns with me. An' I ain't talkin' about the piddly, beggar Injuns like you got 'round here. He's stared in the face of 'Rapaho, Snakes— even Blackfoots."

Bass hissed the last word at the crowd.

"With that sticker he's a-holdin', the boy's even kilt wolves. I ain't ever seen another man as good with a blade. An' this here child's seen a lot of men go down with a blade stuck in 'em, he has."

"I w-want my d-dog back," the Irishman stammered in his frozen rage.

"He ain't your dog no more."

"Is so!"

"You was ready to kill 'im," Bass hollered back, just as loudly. "You give 'im up for dead—he's mine to take."

"How you figure he yours to take?" the boatman squealed, his body still quaking with unspent rage.

"A nigger throws somethin' away," Bass sighed as he sank to his knees at the animal's side, "I figure it's free for the takin' if I'm the one what comes along to claim it." He stroked the dog's wounded chest.

"That dog mine or his by right?" the stocky Irishman roared at the crowd. He circled the group, eyes angrily darting here and there, still holding his wounded right hand clutched in the vise of his left. "Well, is the damned mutt mine or his?"

"It's the stranger's," one of the crowd asserted.

"That's right!" hollered another.

The boatman could see all support erode from the drunken group. He glared about him a moment, listening as more of the crowd voiced their sentiments for Bass to take the animal as his own. Finally the muscular Irishman stepped between a couple of his boatmates and readied to leave by slipping on his heavy mackinaw.

"I want my knife!"

"You ain't gettin' it back," Bass snarled as he scooped it out of the ice-slicked mud puddle beneath the gray dog.

"You taking my knife, too, you bloody bugger? Eh, that it, my friend?"

"You ain't my friend." Scratch wiped it off across his thigh and examined the weapon quickly in the torchlight. "But, yeah—I'm takin' it—just like the dog's mine now. It appears to me you threw the knife away. Didn't it look that way to you, Josiah?"

"Just like he threw the dog away, Scratch."

"See. We got us a witness. Unless you an' your friends there wanna doe-see-doe with a couple of hard boiled mountain fried hardcases like me an' my friend here."

"Mother of God! May your souls burn in hell!"

The Irishman suddenly whirled and shoved his way through the circle of spectators, followed by his two mates. Laughter and jeering, mocking jokes, trailed after them into the night.

"Now what the hell are you gonna do with a—dog?"

Paddock knelt beside the old man as the crowd began to disperse. Warily the young trapper kept his eyes focused on the bodies that swayed and juggled about them. He did not trust the Irishman and his two friends. In fact, he trusted no one here at the Rocky Mountain House except Titus Bass—and even the old man was capable of surprising him. Like right now. What the hell did he want with this half dead mutt anyway?

"I—I figure I can take him back to the livery. Over to Tharp's place. I'll get out my medicines an' fix up all the places he's been boogered. 'Specially that back leg. I don't think he'll be able to walk on it for a few days. Tharp can care for 'im. Give 'im a good home with the other critters. It's a good place for a dog. Right? Ain't I right, Josiah?"

Paddock saw the imploring look in the old man's eyes. Josiah wanted to reassure the old man that the dog would be all right, that the wounds would heal. But, he wasn't all that sure the animal could survive.

"Good as new, old man," he answered lamely and patted Scratch's shoulder. "You can make him good as new, I'd wager. Why, just look at me. Look at what you done for me when I had a bullet blown through my lights. You'll mend him good."

"Thankee, son." Scratch stuffed both hands into the ice coated mud puddle where the dog lay, scooping his arms beneath the animal as it fought for each ragged breath.

Shakily he rose with the mangy, muddy dog flopped across his two arms. The heavy animal did not protest but only continued to whimper.

"We'll take you somewhere warm. Get these places fixed up where you been boogered."

"You need anything, you let me know?" rumbled a deep voice.

Bass looked around to see the older stevedore whose dog had won the fight standing alongside Josiah.

"I think he'll be just fine now. I thank you kindly for your help in endin' the fight when you did."

"I—just feel somethin' strong agin a man what treats a dog like that," the stevedore replied. "A man with an oily tongue like his—ain't fit to live he treats his own dog like that."

"My friend, I'm mighty glad you stepped in when you did to end it," Bass nodded. "When a man sees his dog's won, ain't no use in keepin' on with the blood lettin'."

"No, there ain't," the stevedore agreed and smiled. "You just tell me if I can help. I'm down at the wharf—most all the time."

"Thank you." Bass nodded again and set off with the dog draped across his arms, the animal semi-conscious and in great pain.

"What about Billy—that fella you was coming here to find and—and kill?"

"That sonuvabitch can wait, Josiah." Bass kept marching right on up the dark street, Josiah striding along at his side. "It's been ten years already. I don't figure another hour will hurt for that—business to wait."

Bass heard Paddock sigh as they crunched along through the snow and icy, frozen mud on the streets.

"Killin' comes next after you take care of the livin', son. We'll see both get done tonight."

"I SUPPOSE I'll never figure out why you're so all-fired set on getting yourself cut up, maybe even killed—all over a mangy dog."

Paddock kept probing at Bass all the way back to the livery. While Bass had carried the wounded animal, Josiah kept an eye on their back trail, suspicious and nervous, positive they would be followed by the three boatmen. That stocky Irishman had not looked at all like the kind to give up and be chased off so easily.

"Sometimes a man's just gotta step in," the old trapper kept repeating. "No matter what the stakes are on the table, he's gotta play his hand."

Titus made the animal as comfortable as possible on some fresh hay Josiah had spread out before he got down to applying his roots and herbs and creams to the wounds. The big gray dog would pick up its head to watch at times, but other than that, gave no sign that it cared in the least for the nursing being given by the

268

old man. It didn't appear the dog was really aware of what Bass was doing. The animal was simply in too much agony.

Before they left the barn, the old trapper found a wooden bowl Tharp used to scoop up oats for the horses. He filled it with fresh water and left it by the big gray's bed.

Josiah chose a completely different route back to the Rocky Mountain House. The black sky drizzled on them steadily, coating everything with a thick layer of ice that made it something less than ideal for a man's winter moccasins. There were stretches where the trappers had to push themselves along the streets using the shops and buildings for support as they slid and skated back to their rendezvous with Billy Hooks.

A couple of times Paddock got himself nigh on to spooked by watching shadows, and the hair crawled at the back of his neck. He was positive they were being followed. It seemed every time he turned around, a dark shape slipped back into the rest of the shadows on the street.

But then the two huge, tarred torches appeared out of the foggy drizzle, spitting and hissing with the freezing rain. The yard in front of the Rocky Mountain House was empty now. Everyone had moved inside to escape the icy sleet. From within came the raucous laughter and shouts, the feeble attempts at music as someone played a squeezebox and a lonely fiddle, and someone else sang painfully off-key. Out rolled the sounds of chairs scraping on wood floors, with mugs clattering on plank tables, the undertones of a dozen noisy conversations.

ROCKY MOUNTAIN HOUSE
25 cents/day keep—25 cents/meal
Best care this side of the Rocky Mountains

Beneath the paint-peeling sign sat a hard-eyed man, leaning back in a chair against the wall of the tavern, his steely gaze assessing all who entered the yard. Bass glanced at the outside of the two story structure and strode in the open door.

Nearly the whole lower floor was devoted to saloon, the exception being what they considered their kitchen where dishes of questionable ingredients and vintage were prepared. Few customers complained. Whatever a man ordered, at least the meal was served piping hot, and the proprietor was not at all stingy with serving huge portions. Every so often a man at a table would claim he knew for a fact that either dog or horse, maybe even scrawny mule or goat, often graced the bubbling stew pots of the Rocky Mountain House. And just as quickly the other men at the rough-hewn, plank tables went back to eating. Most of them had eaten far worse on the upriver, out on the endless prairie, or beyond in that shimmering expanse of shining mountains.

The old trapper shouldered his way through the crowded room, followed by Paddock forcing his way through the surging bodies clustered at the rough plank bar. Scratch hailed one of the two tavern keepers.

"What'll you have, mate?"

"Whiskey. Your better barleycorn, if you've any. Two'll do us for now."

"Water on the side?" The tavern keep's eyes darted between the two trappers. "Barefoot will do for us both, friend."

"Aye."

Bass puckered his eyes in a cold scrutiny over the rough crowd hoping to catch a glimpse of Billy Hooks. His old partner should have been here by now. Through that smoke and haze thick enough for a stew broth, he let his eyes touch here and there around the teeming room. Most of the patrons were sucking hard at a mind-numbing drunk. Some customers sat around what remained of wooden tables, atop rough benches. Most, however, stood or sat on the floor, involved in one game of chance or another.

A large man entered the tavern, instantly recognized by several others. This newcomer was given several sturdy, open-handed blows to the back by his friends before he pulled from his shoulders the half of a buffalo robe he wore for covering. Slinging it free of sleety rain, he draped it on a bare patch of floor where he plopped with a loud belch.

"Who cares to wager a toss with me?" he roared across the noisy room.

Dragging out the carved sticks he would use in his Indian game of bones with one hairy paw, the other hand pulled free from his belt a small bag stuffed with coins. Several men jostled roughly among themselves to be the first to play and soon they all were at it in grand style, contestants and spectators alike hollering and swearing, beating each other's backs and shoulders, singing and shouting, all meant as a noisy distraction for the opponents. Over by the huge rock fireplace the fiddler and squeezebox player worked in pitiful concert at the middle of a merry group of those who danced to the sprightly music. One hairy, rank-smelling riverman spun a succession of male partners around the floor in a loud, stomping display. Here man danced with his fellow man. Only those women hardy enough to work as barmaids were present. A hardcase reputation had quickly spread so that even the street harlots, as sorry a lot as they were, refused to patronize the place. In their absence, men chose dancing partners from likely friends. Whirling and spinning, stomping and stamping, their feet following the primitive beat of a distant Indian camp. Many more just circled the dancers, clapping and singing along, trying to make as much joyful noise as they could for every nickel spent on the watered down whiskey.

The square glass lamps swung from the ceiling spreading their bright oil light upon the damp, sweaty, whiskered and greased crowd below them. Pivoting, the older trapper put his back against the bar and studied the room, his eyes cutting through the thick haze. Paddock joined him in drinking the strong whiskey and looking over the crowd.

"Why, daddammit! I'll tip you back on your saddle sores, nigger."

To their right a good-natured argument broke out. Two greasy boatmen grappled with one another, laughing and roaring in delight as they exchanged blows and cuffed one another.

"Damn. Is ol' Pete Skull dead a'ready?" A small crowd quickly formed around a limp body on the floor to pay a moment's attention to the identified deceased. Men had been stepping over and on him until someone finally gave voice to the question. Now the inquirer himself got down on his own wobbly hands and crackling knees to peer into Pete's face, to feel for breath and listen for a heartbeat.

"Nawww." The inquirer raised his ragged face to gaze up at those circled around him. He smiled with a crooked, toothless mouth. "Skull's just sleepin' out the smooth water."

Passed out, dead drunk, as alive as a sack of rocks—so Skull's friends went back to forgetting about him, concentrating on their own impending oblivion. The whiskey here was bad, so bad it was said to rival what the traders offered up at the annual fur trade summer rendezvous out in the mountains. But that was exactly its very claim to fame. Here a man recently returned from the mountains could buy himself a swallow or two of memories for his tongue. Whereas a sensible man might want to have a taste of something better in the way of grain spirits, it seemed the mountain trapper was not a sensible man at all. He would do with the real taste of those raw, untamed, terror-filled spaces out west. He would drink the bad whiskey that reminded him of an adopted home. After all, no one really had to question the sanity of a man who spent his youth wading up to his ass in icy streams while keeping one eye peeled along the horizon for brown-skinned visitors. No one had ever claimed the whiskey at the Rocky Mountain House was good—just that it was lethal.

Everywhere the strong odors of men who worked hard at life, scratching out a rough living, rolled into one's nostrils. Often someone could not make it out to the yard and would let his stomach lurch right inside where the vomit would be stomped into the floor until the next morning when an attempt would be made to clean the tavern before the next night's go-round. Blood, whiskey, urine, vomit and more blood mingled with the rank smell of sweated bodies huddled together here for a release of one color or another.

"Can I buy you fellas a drink?"

Bass twisted his head to see the old stevedore who owned the winning dog. The man stood by him, dripping of melted sleet.

"Nawww." Scratch smiled and held up his mug. "Got us one. But thanks to you anyway, my friend."

"Any time," the old dockhand replied. "You need help, anything, you just holler."

Although he was shorter than a lot of the men bumping around the bar, the stevedore had no trouble moving through the crowd. It appeared he had the respect of most patrons. Those who did not move out of his way he summarily shoved out of his path using a shoulder as thick as an ox's haunch.

"Let's go on over there," Bass suggested with a nod toward the fireplace, "over by the music."

Josiah followed him to the huge stone fireplace. Their spirits warmed as quickly as did their bones. Despite the crude roughness to the place, filled to overflowing with one hardcase or another, the tavern was by and large a friendly place where congregated happily drunk, hard working men who were the backbone and sinew of commerce along the river.

"You 'bout ready for a refill on that?" Scratch nodded down at Josiah's mug after they had been tapping their feet to the music.

"Nope," Paddock replied. "You go ahead though. I'm fine with what I've got right here."

He had never acquired a real taste for bad whiskey like Bass, and thought he might follow the old trapper up to the counter for an ale. But when Josiah saw that Bass had already disappeared into the well-packed crowd, he decided against trying to force his way back to the bar just for a drink with a foamy head on it. Instead, he'd just sip at the bad corn spirits through the rest of the evening and be done with it. If they could ever be done with Billy Hooks and Silas Cooper. After all, Josiah had come to St. Louis for his own funerals. That was just the way he had come to think about them all those days and weeks gone by on that winter-long trail up from Taos. He was responsible for holding a couple of funerals of his own. Josiah Paddock needed to put a couple of things to rest with some folks, put them to rest forever.

Most important seemed to be old man LeClerc. Paddock didn't know the old Frenchman's first name, but he figured it would not be all that difficult to find the man. After all, the wealthy businessman had sent assassins out after him. The old Frenchman wasn't trying to hide from a young American guilty only of self defense after falling in love with a beautiful Frenchwoman.

So, she would be next after LeClerc. A second ghost to exorcise from his soul. She had lain there within him, without festering, for so long now. No real pain in the thought of her, only a sad memory tainted deep blue. Looking back now he could see for certain that it never would have worked out between them. Even if she had been in love with him.

But the LeClerc family changed a lot of things for him. Young Henri LeClerc had won the right to wed Angelique. Henri forced the issue toward a fateful duel on Bloody Island out in the muddy river. And from that time on the life of Josiah Paddock was tied inexorably to the LeClerc family. No one else could ever free him from that bondage. It was something Josiah had to do for himself. Face it head on, confront the old man and be done with it. He would not be able to go on with his life, never knowing just when the next assassin would come, hired out of St. Louis to track down and kill the young man with a price of gold on his head. What kind of a life would that be anyway, he had asked himself so many, many times. What sort of a life for a man with a young wife and a beautiful boy child—gnawed at by fear and dread, rather than embracing the joy and wonder of each new day. There was but one choice. He would have to put the matter to rest as surely as you bury a body in the ground. Only then could he turn and walk away, to get on with his own life.

Paddock sipped at the strong whiskey, mulling it over sadly. The prospect of confronting old LeClerc was something he dreaded, yet something which was still strangely seductive. It sucked him closer and closer to its finality. It only made sense that he should see it all the way through. The toughest part had been back in Taos—deciding to head out for St. Louis in the first place. That done, each step got a bit easier along the trail. Each step back to St. Louis had brought Josiah Paddock closer and closer and closer to moving forward with his life. Oh, those plans he had made along that trail, remembering Taos and those loved ones he left behind. So many things were beginning to fit together now at last, after all these years of wandering. A sense of place, a sense of belonging, a sense of who he was in the ultimate exchange.

But he had to see the old man before the rest of his own life could go on. See both LeClerc and that young French beauty who had twisted his young, foolish heart and used Paddock's ill-fated attentions to secure a jealous betrothal from dashing, handsome Henri LeClerc. Both ghosts could lie at last in a common grave.

"Who's that you say?" Bass inquired of the barkeep as he came back down to the old trapper's end of the bar.

"Why you asking?" the man snarled suspiciously.

"Just was wonderin'. I had me a trappin' partner once long ago that looked a wee bit like him." Bass plunked down his mug on the wet counter.

The barkeep brought the refilled mug back and set it before the grizzled trapper. He glared at Scratch.

"Trapping partner, you say, eh? That meant you was up there a long time ago, mister. Maybe long enough to know of Silas Cooper, what say?"

Bass's eyes snapped to the barkeep's face.

"Remember him, too, that Silas Cooper. Yep."

"They trapped together, on the upper river, them two." The barkeep nodded toward the newcomer and his friend at the other end of the counter. "Silas Cooper and Billy Hooks. Is he the one you was asking about?"

"Billy Hooks was the man." Bass brought the mug to his lips and pulled hard on the whiskey. "Billy Hooks was one of 'em." He swiped the back of his coatsleeve across the lower half of his face.

The barkeep eyed him as Bass began to shoulder his way down the bar.

"That old man there ain't the same Billy Hooks you remember, mister. I want you to know that," the barkeep hollered after the trapper.

Scratch studied the newcomer a minute. Now he wasn't all that certain. It did not look much like Billy Hooks, at least it didn't look at all like his memory of the man. Instead of a tall, muscular, healthy young man, before him stood a gaunt, thinning shell of what once was. Instead of the coal black hair that had fallen in long waves to his shoulders, Bass was amazed to see what remained on Hooks' head was almost totally gray. The scraggly whiskers around his face were the color of caps on the wind-whipped Missouri River. Beneath his huge, whiskey-veined nose hung an ugly wisp of a mustache. Hands that were once as steady as his ready smile now shook holding a glass of whiskey. Hooks spilled some before he threw his head back and drained his mug.

The three men about Hooks were evidently friends. Plunking coins down on the bar, one of the trio kept a barman busy at that end of the counter. The quartet was working straight at punishing the whiskey hard. They laughed and joked, slapping each other on the back with mighty blows.

Bass wasn't sure now if this was the right Billy Hooks. The man he remembered laughed a lot, never taking too much seriously. To him life had been one episode of fun after another. There wasn't much he wouldn't laugh at—going without food for a week, not finding good water to drink, being snowed in at a pass for days on end before they could fight their way through. Bass remembered the man as taking life in stride, finding humor in almost anything he did.

The man he looked at now appeared to be a stranger, but his laugh ultimately told Bass he had found one of the two men he'd come to see.

"B-Billy Hooks?"

It was one of the three friends who wheeled to look Bass over at first. They each measured him with the residue of their smiles still painted across their faces before the grins slipped away and each one became sullen. Finally the man in the center of the group turned, his still happy face fighting to focus on the stranger who had called out his name.

"Billy Hooks? That's me."

His grin was as wide as it ever had been. The hair was going, so much so that it appeared his forehead sprawled halfway back to the top of his head. His jowls sagged in weathered creases and accentuated the smile of yellowed and rotting teeth. He licked at his lips almost like an old hound would lick its chops. Around the cloudy eyes hung flesh in sad pouches.

"What you want with Billy?"

Scratch looked up at the big man who stood with his arm clamped around Hooks' shoulders.

"We—we're old—friends—partners. We was partners," Bass admitted as he stared at Billy. "It's been a long, long time, howsoever."

"You know this man, Billy?" another of the trio asked of Hooks.

Through the cloudy, watering eyes, Hooks peered intently at the stranger. He looked at Bass slow and without blinking, studying hard on it, attempting to work something over in his mind just like he'd turn it over in his hand. Then his smile grew all the wider for a moment. It fell away just as suddenly.

"No." Hooks wagged his head and turned back to his mug of whiskey.

"You've just had too much a snootful, ol' timer. Now be off with you, man," the first of the trio growled. He dropped a hand on Bass's shoulder, nudging him away gently.

"Billy?" Scratch would not be deterred.

"I told you—"

"Billy, it's me. Titus Bass."

Hooks slid his dulled gaze back at the stranger.

"Bass?" The word sounded flat, as if it had not registered in his mind.

"You're rocking his head-hobbles," a second man snarled as he wedged himself between Hooks and the old trapper. "Best be moving on now, mister."

"Yes, Titus Bass. Scratch! You all called me Scratch."

Billy stared down at the floor for a moment. His eyes slowly climbed back up the trapper's frame. His lips moved as if he tasted his words before giving them sound.

"Scratch," Hooks replied.

"Yes, Scratch! That's me. Where's Silas Cooper? You gotta know where Silas Cooper is. Where do I find him?"

"You worn out your welcome here, Mr. Scratch!" The first man shoved a palm into the old trapper's chest, pushing him back into the crowd along the bar.

Stumbling, Titus slipped on the soppy floor and went down. He fought his way back to his feet and dove straight back at the bigger man.

"Don't you ever lay a hand on me again or they can use you for wolf bait!"

"Wha-a-a?" Another of the trio turned.

"Tell me where my money is, dammit!" Bass stabbed a hand through the bodies and grabbed hold of Hooks' coat collar. Bass was not going to let go. "Where's the blood money you stole from me? Where do I find Cooper? Silas Cooper?"

"I give you fair warning!" the first man howled as he brought a huge hamhock of a fist back and slung it forward.

Bass saw it coming at the last moment and ducked to the side. The monstrous fist glanced off his jaw. He careened backwards into the drunken crowd and wondered if he would have any teeth left on that side of his jaw. Shards of pain lanced up through his head. His eyes misted over with the clear, cold, icy heat of that shrill drum beating inside his skull. Everything became a soft blur above him just as he felt someone's hands yank him back to his feet.

Two of them had him now. They crushed him against the bar right beside Billy Hooks. Bass wanted to roll away to the side and escape the pain, but they wouldn't let him go. They slammed him against the bar a second time. The man with the hamhock fists started pummeling the nosy stranger.

Again and again, the two big fists exploded against Scratch's ribs and into his gut. He fought to stay on his feet. All he could think about was finding out just where Silas Cooper had gone. He'd take the licking if he could find out where Silas was.

His sopping moccasins slipped on the floor. He cursed them and his wobbly legs. He cursed himself for shrieking out in pain each time a fist pounded into his face. His nose felt broken. He wanted to cry and could feel his eyes welling with tears, or blood, as they began to swell. He wanted to scream out but that only made his puffy, swollen lips hurt more. All he wanted to do right now was drift off to sleep—just to back away from the pain.

"Looks like your friend needs your help," the old stevedore said as he slid up beside Paddock at the crowded fireplace.

"Who you say?"

"Your friend. The one who took the gray dog away to care for it at the livery." He nodded toward the bar.

Over the tops of heads, Paddock spotted the commotion at the bar. Both the barkeeps stood their ground, hickory axe handles on their shoulders, ready if the fracas became a general free-for-all. Three men had somebody pinned against the bar. Two of them as big as Paddock held the victim while the third, a larger man, threw his fists at both sides of the victim's head, driving it first this way, then back in the other direction. The crowd was surging around the brawl, hollering one profane cheer after another, everyone wanting someone's blood.

275

"My—friend?" Paddock handed the stevedore his mug and began to push on the shorter man.

"You'll want my help." The stevedore set the mugs on the mantle.

"Thanks. I try not to make a habit of turning down an offer of help." Paddock shoved and clawed through the crowd. Whiskey and ale spilled on him as the drunks weaved and bobbed out of his way.

Josiah dug the fingers of his left hand into the first man's shoulder and spun him around in a vise. He saw the look of surprise as the man winced under the clawlike grip.

"I don't like your idea of odds!" Josiah yelled as he flung his fist into the big man's face, twirling him against the bar.

That was the first time Josiah caught sight of Bass. For an instant, he wasn't all that sure it was Bass. The blue bandanna was there. The greasy, old elkhide coat was draped on the man. The salt and pepper beard sprouted on the face, although it now glistened with blood. But he couldn't recognize the battered face.

Bass slipped from view as the two men who had been holding him lunged for Paddock. They each captured an arm and flung Josiah face down into the bar. The last thing Josiah remembered seeing was a barkeep swinging the axe handle into the air above him as he was smashed against the rough countertop. He knew he'd have to get out of the way quick or he'd be done for good with a busted skull.

Josiah twisted away just as the hickory cracked against the counter. He yanked one arm free and threw a punch at the man holding his other arm. Out of the corner of his eye he caught sight of the old stevedore.

The old dockworker threw one of the trio off to the side and immediately stuck up a hand to catch another falling axe handle. He held it firmly in the grip of his huge hand. With the barkeep on the other end, the stevedore drove the handle back, smashing the man against the shelves of mugs and the row of whiskey kegs behind the counter. The barkeep collapsed to the wet, whiskey-slick floor that was now littered with broken glass and pottery, wincing with the pain of broken ribs and struggling to catch his breath.

Now the first man got back in the thick of things and caught the dockman on the back of his neck with his large fist. The stevedore stumbled forward, crashing against the counter. He was stunned for a moment by the blow to his thick neck, but surprised everyone when he drew himself back up to full height and whirled on his attacker. He ducked his head and dove into the bigger man like a mad bull, jamming his head into the attacker's belly. The pair tumbled in a muddy heap on the floor.

Two of the fighters grabbed for Josiah again, but this time Paddock was quicker. His leg flew up and caught one of the attackers in the groin, doubling the man over as he screwed to the floor in a gasping, agonized heap. Almost in the same movement the younger trapper threw up an arm to ward off a blow from the axe handle. He cried out when the hickory crushed muscle and sinew and flesh. The handle tumbled loose across the wet bar.

A third man scooped up the weapon and flung it overhead as he rushed Paddock. Josiah stumbled backwards to get out of the way, almost falling over

Bass who lay unconscious beneath all the feet and legs. Paddock twisted and launched himself up on top of the bar just as the hickory handle smashed against the counter, sending wet splinters in all directions. He rolled on over behind the bar and slid on the wet wood floor, fighting to keep his footing. He found himself face to face with the barkeep who had swung the hickory at him a moment before. But now the desperate man held a huge butcher knife out in front of him.

The barkeep's feet slipped as he lunged at Paddock. That was all that saved the young man. Josiah caught the barman's hand in both of his, even though his smashed left arm hurt too damn much to have any strength in it. The knife blade twisted in toward him. They struggled, the barkeep jabbing the blade toward Paddock's chest.

Josiah pressed himself against the bar. He saw something drop past his eyes, then was shocked at the sudden pressure on his neck. Someone had yanked something that felt like a belt around his neck and was now set on choking him. With the last vestige of strength in his right arm, fighting for his breath, Paddock ripped the knife down and away from his face. He felt the knife plunge into something soft, then strike a hard resistance and glance off. Paddock let the knife handle go when he realized that the other man's hands had jerked away.

Josiah rolled against the bar and caught a glimpse of his attacker above him pulling on the strap around Paddock's neck from atop the counter. Paddock frantically pushed his fingers between the thick leather strap and his neck, fighting for the next breath that wouldn't come.

He saw a misty vision of Looks Far Woman standing in the New Year's Day snow at Kinkead's place. She was waving goodbye to him as he rode farther and farther and farther away. God, did he want to bring that useless left arm up to help him breathe again—but it hung limp, in pain, suspended at his side.

Josiah caught a vague glimpse of Joshua. His son stood in the snow at his mother's side, waving farewell to his father. Suddenly the little boy began tottering toward his father, still waving, his little hand beating wildly like a tiny sparrow's wing in the cold, winter morning air. His son tottered, unsteady, trying to keep his balance in the deep snow as he set out to close that gap between him and his father. The child cried out for his father, arms raised, tears frozen on his little, ruddy, copper-skinned cheeks.

But Josiah didn't know his son could walk, much less toddle after him. Funny, but he simply didn't know.

Josiah wasn't worrying about getting one more breath any longer. It just didn't matter.

Scratch dug his fingernails into the attacker's throat. The man jerked around, surprised. Bass slammed him to the muddy floor, then plunged right on top of him.

Paddock rolled over as he realized the leather strap had fallen from his throat. He watched Bass descend on the attacker who had been choking him. The old trapper stuffed his fingers in the man's hair, gripping both sides of the head as he smashed it again and again into the muddy slop across the rough floor.

Exhausted at last, Bass shuddered, let go and leaned back. The big man was totally unconscious. A small pool of blood oozed from beneath his head. Titus crawled off him and rose unsteadily to his feet, the fire of adrenalin still hot in his battered body.

The stevedore dragged the first attacker by his collar over to the bar and flung the body beside Scratch's opponent.

"You look to be hurting bad," the dockworker sniffed as he peered into Bass's puffy face. "We'll get some help. A doc—"

"First I gotta find out—" The words came out slurred between swollen, bleeding lips. He turned round to Josiah.

Paddock slipped off the soppy bar and rubbed his hand up and down the aching arm. "I don't think it's broke," he said. "My lucky day." He tried to chuckle, but couldn't.

Josiah watched a couple of men climb right over the counter and kneel by the barkeep. They looked the man over, felt his chest, then shifted their gaze to Paddock. "He dead?" Josiah inquired.

"Never serve another bad dram of whiskey ever again," one of the men admitted with a half grin.

"He shouldn't oughta come at you with the knife like he done, stranger. Man pulls a gun—same thing. Makes things a mite messy in a fight."

"I—I didn't want to kill—kill him."

"Why not, pray tell?" The man behind the counter rose from the barkeep's body. "This sonofabitch sure was tryin' to kill you bad enough."

"I said: I didn't want to kill him!" Paddock growled.

Josiah turned back to Bass, who shoved aside the attacker who had been soundly kicked by Paddock. The old trapper struggled to stay on his feet, using the counter as a crutch. Scratch desperately grabbed hold of Hooks at last.

"Billy. Billy, it's me—Titus Bass. You understand?"

The old trapper bored deeply into Hooks' eyes, trying to read something beyond their twinkling humor.

"Scratch!" Bass shouted the word into the older man's face, studying the watery, cloudy eyes.

"Scratch?" Hooks replied weakly through his tongue-wetted lips.

"Yeah, Billy. Scratch. It's me!" Titus yelled, certain that by hollering at the crazed old man he could make himself understood.

"I come to get my money, Billy. What'd you do with my money?"

"Money?" Billy Hooks burbled again. "I ain't got no money." He stuffed his big hands into his torn britches and pulled out the empty pockets.

"My money. Dammit, my money!"

Filled with sudden rage, Scratch grabbed the lapels of the man's coat and began to shake him. He could do nothing to wipe that silly smirk off Billy's face. The sick, childlike smile seemed cast in granite.

"Money?" One of Hooks' companions turned to Bass. He dabbed at a bloody, split lip with his sleeve. "That's a laugh, ol' timer. Billy ain't got anybody's money. Why, he ain't got no money himself."

Scratch pulled away from Hooks and yanked savagely on the front of the speaker's torn shirt.

"What you mean—he ain't got no money?"

"Simple. The man ain't got any money. For the past couple of years everybody in this town knowed he's needed someone looking after him."

"What—what you mean, lookin' after him?"

"See for yourself," the man explained as he nodded at Hooks. "Does he look right in the head? Does he look right to you? He ain't got a full cord of wood no more, mister."

Bass examined the face of Billy Hooks for only a moment more before he wheeled back to that man at the bar who was still trying to catch his breath from the blow to his groin. "What happened to him?"

"He spent all his money. Billy just didn't have all that much after the keelboat was gone. His partner stole most of it, all about the time Billy was going mad."

"Mad?" Bass glanced at Hooks' sad smile again. "How can he go mad?"

"The syph, man. The syph," the attacker barked the word like the dreaded curse it was. "Somewhere he got him a good, evil dose of it and them bugs is driving him mad in his mind. What's left that them bugs ain't eaten up yet. Look at him now and tell me he ain't mad."

"How? How it—"

"Syph's eating him up from inside out, mister. So, we take care of him. He don't cause nobody no harm, but he ain't got nobody else but the three of us." He gestured to the floor where his two partners lay unconscious. "We feed 'im, wipe up after 'im. Try to care for him best we can. He ain't got nobody else now."

"He used to have someone else he hung with," Bass stated with a quiet edge to his voice. "Name of Silas Cooper. You know where a fella might find Cooper? Someone here yesterday told my partner that Cooper'd gone upriver to be a hunter."

Bass watched the man shake his head and smile through bloodied, swollen lips.

"He ain't upriver, dammit. Whoever that was told you that gotta pull his head outta the jug. Man don't know what he's talking about—"

Bass grabbed the man's shirt front and shook him twice as he gritted his words between clenched teeth. "Dammit! Tell me where he is. Where's Cooper?"

"Last year he took off to the mountains, mister. Got clean away after robbing a family here 'bouts. Killed the man, savagely. Tied the fella's guts to a tree and made the man walk around and around the tree, pulling yard after yard of his slimy guts out—" The man's head wagged sadly as he stared at the floor. "Fella's wife told folks about it when she could come into town. Cooper made the man walk round and round that tree. Then when he couldn't walk no more, he made the man watch as he raped the fella's wife and his daughter. Right before the dying man's eyes—ain't a thing she said her husband could do about it. Woman said Cooper took off. Far as we know, he got clean away—"

"Where'd the black hearted bastard go?"

"The mountains, that's all we heard at first. Ain't a soul bound to track after him out there," the man answered with a sigh. "All we hear is he's gone and hired on to Bents' Fort, out there in the mountains. Working for them traders—"

"Bents' Fort? What the hell is Bents' Fort?"

"Hell if I know. I ain't never been west of St. Charlie myself."

Bass grabbed at the man once more. The attacker offered no resistance.

"I-it's a fort—west to the mountains."

"Where in the mountains, dammit." Bass insisted.

"I hear tell it's on the Arkansas—"

"Arkansas River," Bass whispered, his mind instantly working on just where it was.

"Near the foot of the mountains so we're told," the man explained. "I don't know nothing else. Cooper just took Billy's money and run off, headed west with the supply train setting out for the new fort. That was all we heard of him last year."

Scratch slowly let the man's lapels slip from his fists.

The man straightened up. "If I'd be a man to give advice, mister, I'd tell you not to pay Silas Cooper no never mind. He's nothing but suffering and death, that one is. Might just as well forget about Silas Cooper. Ain't a man I know of man enough to track him down."

"Silas Cooper?" Bass asked absently, his eyes staring out the door at the gray sleet knifing past the spitting torches in the front yard.

"Yeah, that son of the Devil hisself," he nodded once, then swiped at the bloodied front of his torn shirt. "Ain't a man I know of bad enough to wanna catch up with Silas Cooper. They'd sure do a lot of us a favor if any man did track him down and put that sonsabitch out of his misery. Just like a dog gone mad—put him out of his miseries. Do us all a favor and send that man straight to hell. But, there ain't a soul gonna track Silas Cooper and live to tell about it. There's too many dead on his trail already. The man's blood crazy! Ain't no one I've ever known before loves seeing blood much as that man. Blood crazy that one is. Meeting up with Silas Cooper is like waking up to find a cottonmouth's tucked down in your blankets—"

"I'm the one what wants him." The words were spoken quietly enough, as quiet as a razor sliced at the black of night.

"How's that?" The man's face jerked up in surprise to study Bass.

"I said, I was the one what wants him. I'll track him, and I'll find the bastard. He's got a lot that belongs to me."

"You and a lot of folks around here, mister." The man grinned sourly. "Best you see the Priest, or some preacher man, get him to forgive you all your sins first. Tracking after Silas Cooper is like going for a one way walk right into hell."

"Billy Hooks?" Bass hissed as he peered closely at the simple, smiling face. "I want you to know I'm settin' out on Silas Cooper's trace. Seems now he was that evil at the core of it all from the very get-go."

Bass took hold of the man's arms as he spoke softly to Hooks. "Bud told me some about it. I think you always was too simple to mind much of anything, an' a man like Silas Cooper just preyed on that part of you. His kind'll always suck life outta others. What he cain't take—he kills." Bass touched the man's cheek with his bloody fingers. "Pretty durn soon Silas Cooper'll be in the Devil's own paw. Soon enough, Billy Hooks. Titus Bass'll see to it soon enough. Looks to me like you're in God's own hands now."

280

The old trapper limped out the tavern door into the night's icy sleet, favoring one game leg, with one arm held protectively around his midsection. Paddock followed close behind him.

Someone splashed a mug of ale on the two unconscious men sprawled across the floor at the foot of the bar. The stevedore watched Billy Hooks screw his face up, gaze at the doorway long after Bass had gone. Finally the gray headed demented man spoke all on his own. It startled a lot of those gathered around who knew Billy Hooks, scared them because these words were strong and clear. It didn't sound like Billy Hooks had for the past two years. These words were clear and strong. For some of those gathered round the man, it was downright spooky.

"I wanna see Silas Cooper in hell," Billy spewed, his words strong and clear, which startled those in the room. "See him burn in hell. In the Devil's Paw. Titus Bass'sll blow his black hearted soul right on back to hell for us all. Right on back to hell."

21 THE WINTER SKY seemed close and suffocating overhead, a sky made colorful if not bearable here only at sunset. From time to time he would move from where he leaned against the lamppost back into the purple shadows by the shop where he had been patiently waiting out his vigil. The house was right across the street. Old man LeClerc's huge residence encompassing an entire city block had the appearance of a fortress in the falling light, surrounded by a twelve foot high stone wall some two feet thick. An imposing barrier to keep the unwanted and unwelcome without.

Barely a day ago, just last night, he had been forced to kill a man. Another nameless, faceless man intent upon killing him. But this barkeeper had never known just who Josiah Paddock was, much less had cared that the young trapper carried a very expensive price on his head. If more men in St. Louis knew of that rich price, Josiah Paddock's life would be worth only what old man LeClerc was willing to pay them for it.

Across the street stood the massive house and barn and servants' quarters, the building's whitewash dimmed gray in the twilight. He had been studying the house itself, circled on four sides by a fourteen foot wide porch. In the back of the house he could see the porch had been enclosed so that two more rooms were on the ground floor. Plus a basement and an attic.

Perhaps that was the way. Sneak into that cellar and find his way into the house. Still, there were far too many comings and goings through the huge iron gate in the massive wall, with black skinned servants scurrying off on foot or horseback. So much activity for a house where lived but one man.

Paddock had found out as much as he could over the past few hours of winter afternoon light. Store keepers and shop clerks told him what little they knew of the LeClerc family. Wanting nothing more than their privacy, the family had always imprisoned itself behind the high walls after young Henri was murdered in an unfortunate incident involving a duel.

How could he approach those who had visited the house to ask about the floor plan without drawing suspicion? His interrogation of those who had been inside the LeClerc estate was questionable enough in itself. Some way over the wall, into the basement and then he was on his own to find the old man.

Oil lamps were being lit. Behind the lace and damask curtains their light appeared muted and subdued. Shadows flitted back and forth past the windows. A lamp finally went on in the second floor of the house. There, in the tiny window shadowed below the overhanging gables, Josiah watched first one figure, then a second, dart in front of the light, intent on something below them. Preparations for something, he mused. Servants busy preparing for some special occasion. It was, after all, Sunday evening. Perhaps the Catholic French family was holding court at a special supper this night.

He would get over the wall. Slip into the cellar. Maybe it would be warmer down in the bottom of the house than it was here in the snow and ice and mud on the street. Then he would have nothing to do but wait until the regal supper was over and the house made ready for bed. In moccasins he figured he could move about the house silently enough to find the old man's bedroom.

The lamp stayed on in the attic. Then a third head appeared across the tiny window. Three heads bent and concentrated on something in the small attic garret. Perhaps with all the hustle and bustle of those preparations for the evening, it would be a good time to scramble over the wall and into the basement. Find his way into the house while everyone was taken up with the meal and guests.

Paddock slipped past the circle of lamplight and back into the purple of the winter evening as he crossed the muddy cobblestone street. *Walnut,* he said to himself and turned the corner onto Fourth Street. Suddenly he was startled as an ebony skinned houseman slipped from the shadows behind the wall and swung open both halves of the twelve foot high gate. Their iron arms spread across the narrow sidewalk so that Josiah had to step into the street to pass by the gaping entrance in the wall.

Clattering down the street came the chattering beat of iron mounted carriage wheels and the racing rhythm of a horse pounding its hoofs over the cobblestones. He turned and backed out of the way just as the carriage turned off of Main and careened around the corner. The solitary rider snapped the horse's reins and maintained control of the small carriage on the icy street before it shot through the gate and climbed up the winding drive toward that house atop the rise.

That one was in a hurry for supper. Perhaps one of the old man's boys, hurrying home from a hard day at the warehouse, counting and re-counting all their beaver money.

Paddock went on down Fourth and turned the corner at Main to fall once more beneath the security of darkness. Here under the cloak of night-black shadows at the foot of the wall, his hands groped along the stones, feeling, assessing, trying to figure out if he could climb the structure. He tiptoed, one step at a time, fingertips feeling for lips on the rocks, crevices in the masonry, something which would allow him to scale the high wall and drop into the dark yard. Frustration raced through him when he found nothing to hold on to.

What was this?

His hands circled the stout iron bars.

Another gate?

As he quickly scanned the street, Paddock's fingers encircled the iron bar of the small gate, which was just wide enough for a man to walk through. Frantically he felt at the sides of the gate, testing the hinges, determining that it was

283

locked securely to the stone wall. He couldn't open the gate, but he could use it to climb over the wall.

Again he glanced at the street where splotches of yellow light from the oil lamps splattered across the snow. He heard voices, footsteps, the clattering of another carriage racing down Main. He had to do it now.

Paddock slipped a foot into a rung on the gate and raised himself off the ground. His hands clutched at the top of the iron bars. There was room for his other foot some three feet higher, at the top of the gate, but no place to put his hands.

Frightened, as the sounds of voices and footsteps grew louder, the young trapper pushed his weight up on to the second foot. Now he stood on the top of the gate, pressing himself against the stone wall to keep from falling. He clenched his eyes shut and trapped his breath, afraid of being discovered by someone passing along the walk as he hung like some huge spider draped against the stones.

Push. Push!

Eyes still closed, Paddock let his fingertips see for him. Up, up—farther they crawled feeling along the stones for lips, crevices, a place where he could get a fingerhold. He found nothing at all. On and on the fingers climbed until they reached the top.

The top of the wall? How could that be? Finally he opened his eyes and glanced down at the street below him. He realized that he stood on top of the gate, with his tall frame stretched against the stones, his arms extended upward—hands clutched at the top of the wall.

Paddock dug in with his fingernails and pulled. The approaching voices were almost below him. Carriage wheels clattered but half a block away. His toes skittered up, trying to find a hold, something he could brace them against. His knees banged and scraped against the stones as he clawed his way up at last. Josiah dragged his legs up after him and lay along the top of the wall, becoming a part of those dark shadows twelve feet off the ground as the pedestrians scurried along the narrow stone walk below him. He paid little attention to their hushed conversation regarding fortunes and wills and business disputes. He was relieved as they hurried on and turned the corner onto Fourth, their voices drifting off into the blackness beneath the heavy sky that was beginning to spit flakes of snow like leaden puffs of goosedown.

Figuring he could slip down the inside of the wall in the exact same way he had climbed up the outside of the stone barrier, Josiah began to curl himself up to slide off the top when the approaching carriage rumbled past. Frantically the driver attempted to slow his pair of horses clattering along the icy cobblestones. Paddock spread himself along the top of the wall again, trying to blend with the dark shadows.

"Sacre d—"

A terrified voice split the frosty air with a shriek.

Josiah watched the frightened French passenger clutch at the driver as they passed beneath him and careened onto Fourth, both horses and carriage slipping, very nearly colliding with a lamppost at the corner. They were gone as quickly as they had appeared out of the dark.

Paddock let his legs dangle over the side of the wall, his arms bearing the weight of his body. Toes crawled down the stones, searching for the top of the gate. Finally his moccasins found the iron bars and he lowered himself into the snow on the ground. His heart still racing, Josiah pressed himself against the wall a moment, back into the shadows and let his harried breathing slow. Snowflakes began to fall more insistently. He studied the house up the hill for a moment as the carriage rumbled up the long, gravelled drive and clattered to a frantic halt before the front entrance.

Wide double doors opened and light spilled out across the porch and onto the drive where both driver and passenger tumbled out of the carriage. One man wore a long, heavy coat which reached to his knees. The second wore a long cloak—no, he wore a frock, the black robe of a Catholic priest.

Back in his shadows the young trapper smiled. Old man LeClerc was covering all his bets. Inviting the priest from the cathedral to dinner. How fitting on a Sunday evening.

This snowfall would be heavy. He was glad he had made it over the wall before it had begun coming down with so much insistence. Now he just had to push on past the barn and livery, scoot around the other building which appeared to be servants' quarters, dart into the shadow of the large gazebo standing in the middle of the yard, and he would be at the wall of the house. His nose smarted with the odors of damp hay and sweated horses. He figured the stable hands were putting up some carriage animals, brushing them, feeding them. The earthy odors balmed strong in the night air—reassuring to the young trapper who had for years relied upon strong animals. Something close to comfort coursed through him as he slipped out of those shadows of the barn and darted around the low, stubby cabin he figured might be the servant's haven.

Wealthy French were all the same. Angelique Saucier's family or the LeClercs. They all gave their help nothing better than a wind-chinked shanty to live in, nothing more.

He grinned. It would be on their consciences. For the wealthy to explain when at last they were presented to St. Peter at the Gates of Heaven. Just how they had treated their fellow man, treated even those Inks who so faithfully served them in the kitchens, laundries and stables, and—perhaps even the bedchambers. Each man answered the last questions ultimately for himself. No one gave testimony for him at that final hour. It remained between a man alone and his Maker.

God granted life and He was present when life slipped from the mortal being. It was lonely being born a man, later to be filled with that agonized loneliness in dying. Paddock smiled as he reached the wall right below the back porch at the rear of the house. Awful lonely getting born, shoved out into a world you weren't ready for. Probably all the more frightening, scarier, filled with that agony of aloneness being dragged screaming on into death. And in between his birth and his death, a man fought against loneliness by bringing close around him family

285

and friends, sounds and sights to push away his agony—until it was time for him to face the ultimate loneliness and meet his Maker at last.

OLD JAUNE had been the first to discover the master of this house as the purple light slid from the window. He had climbed those narrow, creaking steps to the attic room where old man LeClerc had entombed himself for all these past months. It had long ago become a daily ritual for the white headed Negro house servant, his skin a high yellow from ancestral matings with white slave owners. His own father, it was said, had owned quite a sizable plantation in Georgia. But Old Jaune would never see any of his father's wealth. He simply wasn't in the will. No son of a white man who had sneaked down to the slave cabins two or three times a week ever received an inheritance, unless it was an inheritance of pain, of shame, of never knowing your papa—never having your father call you son.

So long ago Old Jaune had been sold with his mother to a slave trader, and from that man to a family in the Illinois country. After his mother had died, the grown slave was finally brought to St. Louis where he ended up in the house of a long established French family. The LeClercs had renamed the old Negro, referring to the appearance of his skin. Jaune was French for yellow.

Over all his years of faithful service the aging man had become more friend than slave to Josef Gabriel-Rene LeClerc. More a confidant than a man who merely had to keep his mouth shut about family business overheard. The master had in some sentimental moments told Old Jaune that he was the only friend the old fur merchant had truly had in all his life. Beyond his wife and sons, there had been few things for the patriarch to care about. Little more than a wife who died trying to give her husband the sons he had always wanted.

Old Jaune himself had never married. By the time he had been sold into the LeClerc family, he was already getting too old to start a family of his own. Oh, he had lain with women a time here and there through the years. But mostly when the urge grew strong in his loins, Old Jaune would find something else to work his mind or his body on until those urges passed. And over the years, by burying those human needs and hungers, the old Ink had gotten to the point where the needs and hungers came to bother him no more. He had been relieved when he finally grew old enough to look at all women, no matter what age they might be, as daughters and grand-daughters. Family all. Memories of a musky, damp body beneath his rarely came to haunt his muggy, summer night sleep. Those sensual memories were simply too old and worn to be recalled.

The master of the house was his friend, and Old Jaune had borne that friend through the death of a wife and the murder of a son. A favored son, Henri—dead of massive head injuries on Bloody Island. Old Jaune had rowed across the murky waters of the Mississippi that spring of 1831 to the island with Monsieur LeClerc and the others to investigate the crime. There was to have been a duel. Only one pistol had been fired as far as any man knew. It had been found beneath Henri's battered body.

The second weapon had evidently disappeared and although the family and the constables had searched the brambles, the other pistol had not been found. It was finally assumed that the weapon had been thrown in the river, yet unfired.

Henri's brother and a cousin had accompanied Henri to the island. It was they who had identified the killer, stating that Josiah Paddock had been only wounded by Henri's quick bullet—a scalp wound which had merely dazed the American. Then, so they told their story to the constables and Josef LeClerc, instead of Paddock shooting Henri down for his dishonorable early shot, the American had defiled his victim by beating him, kicking him to death. They had attempted to stop the murder of Henri, but had themselves been knocked unconscious by Paddock and an unnamed companion. No one they knew had witnessed the final blows which put a bloodied, gruesome end to young LeClerc's life.

Murder and dishonor. Josef LeClerc had accepted as his own duty to right any affront done to the family and to his son, Henri. From that terrible day on Bloody Island, Old Jaune had watched his master begin to age all too quickly. The burning desire for revenge consumed LeClerc. He wasted away, feeding himself on a feast of his hatred, impassioned beyond reason to find his son's murderer. There was nothing Old Jaune could do to divert his master from his self-consuming suicidal course.

Over these recent years, Josef LeClerc had grown thinner and weaker. Whereas before he had been a robust specimen, now in the winter of 1834 he was little more than a shell of what he had once been. Praying each night at his cot, Old Jaune asked his God to protect his French master, to drag out of him that very hate and bile wasting at his French soul.

Old Jaune could no longer help his master. LeClerc would not allow him to. The old negro knew there was but one source of help for the old man before the Devil himself claimed Josef Gabriel-Rene LeClerc's soul as his own. Only one answer before the old man destroyed himself and let the Devil take him.

The Lord Himself would have to visit this house and touch his master's soul. The Lord Himself who often worked in some mighty mysterious ways. Old Jaune prayed for the Lord Himself to visit this house.

He had entered Josef's small attic room, as he did every evening at dusk, to light the oil lamp which sat on the small table by the narrow bed. Why the wealthy man refused himself so many comforts, Old Jaune would never know. Below the attic in this huge, rambling house was every comfort known to civilized man, including the company of people, the sounds of life, the joy of laughter, the sharing between hearts.

Old Jaune shook his head and lit the lamp on the small table. With the flare of the wick the little room filled with a dull glow. Suddenly a cold fingertip raked down his spine. With tired, yellowed eyes, Old Jaune gazed again at the table. It was gone. The hackles at the back of his neck stirred. The pistol was gone. For so many months it had lain on the table. Now suddenly Old Jaune knew his master had the weapon. Death's hot, foul breath grew rank in his nostrils.

After he adjusted the wick, the servant turned to check on his master. The lamp shed a simple yellow oval of light on the narrow bed and Jaune could not see the thin man for all the quilts and comforters piled on the bed. Old Jaune was continually putting them back over the frail body. The black man picked up the lamp and took it closer to the bed. He did not like what he had just heard. It scared him so. Old Jaune yanked back the covers and peered down into a face he didn't recognize. Cadaverous, with sunken eyes, the skin sallow around the cheeks and jaws, Josef looked more like a skeleton than a living man.

The death rattle crept from his lungs once more as the chest rose weakly and fell, rose weakly and fell again. Each breath was a battle, sucked through a hoarse, phlegmy throat.

Old Jaune began to shake so much he was afraid he would drop the lamp. With it set on the table he went to the door and hollered down for Abner to come up right away. Abner was called because Old Jaune believed the young servant to be the smartest Negra he had ever known in all his life. Surely Abner would be able to help the master.

Out of breath, the young servant put his ear against LeClerc's chest. Slowly he brought his hand up, his eyes sadly telling all he knew to Old Jaune. Master was dying.

"I'll be gettin' the doctor," Abner announced as he tore from the room and shot down the narrow stairs.

Within a few moments Old Jaune was joined by one of Josef's sons in the tiny attic garret. He, too, turned to the old servant and nodded sadly.

"My father is dying."

"Please, Mossa LeClerc—get him a doctor!"

At the door, young Jacques turned for a moment to catch the old Negra's fear-crimped eyes. "I'll bring the priest, too."

Soon the small room filled with the servants of the house. Jacques had rushed out to get the priest and to inform his older brother that their father was dying. Abner had gone to fetch the doctor who had cared for the LeClerc family for all these many years.

They bumped and jostled into each other in the tiny room, each man pacing back and forth beneath the low ceiling, each wondering just what to do until the doctor finished his examination. Old Jaune stoked up the small stove in the room, and with all the people in there, the attic garret was quite warm. Yet for all of it, the old man's body shook and trembled as surely as if he lay beneath an icy waterfall. More than once Jaune dashed to the small window to assure himself it had been closed properly. And each time he looked at the table, he saw the empty place beside the lamp where the pistol should have been.

As the physician leaned back from the frail body, he rose and rolled down his sleeves, tugged at the tails of his satin waistcoat. Turning to the patriarch's two sons, he let his gaze drop to the floor. Finally the physician gazed up at the priest who waited by the door.

"Father, I believe it is now up to you."

The doctor stepped away from the small bed. Unable to do anything more for his long-time friend, he pulled on his checked linen coat. The time when medical science could help had come and gone.

Josef LeClerc rolled his eyes as the man in the black robe knelt alongside the low bed, placing the prayer beads in the old man's bony, wrinkled hand.

Everyone in the room joined in reciting the rosary over LeClerc, everyone except Old Jaune. He just watched, the lamp-brightened tears spilling down his leathered cheeks. Whispered prayers and the hissing of the fire crackling in the stove, snowflakes tapping at the window, accompanied by the sobbing of a faithful old black man—so much filling such a tiny room.

Josef listened to it all. He knew they each had come to his side a little early. It wasn't time for him to go just yet. He had one thing left to do. The murderer of his son must be killed. No one else had been capable of doing that for him.

Josef wanted to tell them all to go away. They were too early for their mournful wake. He was waiting for the murderer and did not want them all to scare the young American away. After all, he had been shown that star sign in the winter sky by God Himself. The Divine Light had told old Josef that God Himself would bring the murderer here to him, to this very room. LeClerc could wait.

He had no strength to move anything but his eyes. Josef watched the physician warming his hands over the stove. He gazed at the priest kneeling by his bedside, reciting the rosary along with Josef's two sons. Then he saw Old Jaune waiting anxiously by the door, standing beside the table. That old servant knew. His ancient, yellowed eyes told Josef that he knew about the pistol.

Old Jaune glanced down at the table where the weapon had rested for all those months. When he looked back up, Josef returned a steady gaze, his tired old eyes saying to the servant that there was purpose in it all.

Old Jaune swiped at his tears and straightened his back as stiff and straight as his years would allow. He licked the salty drops out of his mustache and smiled at LeClerc. If his old master could believe it would happen, then who was he to question it?

Just how that could be, he was bumfuzzled and it hurt to think on it. The killer was supposed to be out west beyond all that vast openness clear to the mountains. He was way out there and gone. How could the Master figure on that man walking right into St. Louis, right down this street and into this very house? How was LeClerc so damned sure that young murderer would climb up these stairs, right into this tiny room where he lay dying?

In some mysterious way LeClerc's own faith invaded Old Jaune, just the way it had so many times before in their years together. It was an overriding faith that the young American was going to be seen climbing those stairs and coming to the old man's bedside.

Old Jaune pulled aside the flap of his coat for a moment, just enough to expose the ivory handle of that knife old man LeClerc had given him for a birthday gift many years before. Ever since, the old Negra had worn it proudly in a sheath at his waist, imagining he would someday need it for protection of his master.

LeClerc felt a sense of peace come over him. Yes, he had seen Old Jaune's knife. And he understood that Old Jaune knew what to do with it should the master of this house fail to kill the murderer with his own hands.

Josef knew that his old friend Jaune would kill the American if he himself grew too weak to pull the trigger. He could count on Old Jaune.

THE DAMP cold of the cellar enveloped Josiah and caused him to shiver almost continually. His clothes wet from plodding through the snowy yard, the young trapper felt frozen to the core.

His nose was assaulted by the dank, musty smell of things old, damp, and dusty. His ears strained for the sounds above him on the main floor of the house, but most of what he heard was the scurrying of rats along the wood frame members or across the dirt floor among the crates and trunks and wine racks. In the dark, the rodents seemed as big as badgers and when he finally saw one of them in the pale moonlight that slanted through a casement window, he knew that the rats here were almost as big as gray squirrels.

All through the next several hours of darkness and waiting and cold, Josiah huddled against his frozen dirt wall. And listened. Straining his ears to make out the faint sounds above him, to make some sense of the footsteps and movement patterns up there, Paddock conjured up a picture of the floorplan of the house above him. This huge cluttered basement seemed to run beneath the kitchen, dining room and the main parlor or sitting room. Perhaps the library. There was quite an expanse of area that had been scoured by hand out of the hard ground.

In faint, mist-laden memories, he remembered his mother working at the soil in her garden, turning the dark, heady earth, chattering about its promise and what it would bring them each new growing season. It had been one of the few things his mother had cared about throughout her life—a tender link with the soil she had shared with his father.

Ezra Paddock had gone off with Manuel Lisa in 1809, following his dream of finding something more to life than walking at the southern end of northbound oxen straining against a plow. Wanting something more, something better for his own family, Ezra Paddock had left his wife, Sarah, and pushed upriver to trap beaver at the Three Forks and Blackfeet country. Two years of back-breaking, dangerous work in the mountains and he just might have a stake to buy a little shop back in the city. In 1809 in the far mountain west American trappers were still pretty ignorant about the Blackfeet and their hatred of white men come to trap their territorial waters. The tribe had always tolerated the British, but the hated Indian confederation had sworn to wipe the country clean of Americans and their allies. At the Three Forks lay Ezra Paddock's body—one of the first casualties in the Blackfeet war. Left behind were his wife and a newborn son Ezra had never seen. To that son yet unborn when he had left St. Louis, Ezra passed on a legacy of something better, something brighter for his family.

For the last half hour or better things had quieted down. Only rarely could he hear the sound of feet scraping across the floors above him. Josiah had gotten to where he believed he could tell the difference between men and women in their walk by the length of stride or the weight pounded on each foot as it stepped across the wooden floors or beat onto those rugs which muffled some of the voices filtering down through the walnut boards.

Things were settling down at last. It seemed as if he would have his chance to make it up the steps and onto the ground floor of the house shortly. If his estimates were right, those steps he could just barely see some twenty feet away led up to the kitchen.

He was cold and miserable, damp and chilled. Scared, too. Josiah Paddock was beginning to doubt this was really the sanest path to follow right now. But, he knew if he confronted LeClerc in any other manner it could mean the old man just might kill him before Josiah had a chance to explain, to get it all out.

He had come up with this plan of sneaking into the old man's bedchamber, there to present himself to LeClerc alone when the old Frenchman was unarmed, perhaps clothed only in his dressing gown for the night. Then Josiah would have only to contend with the old man physically, and to keep him from screaming out to alarm his sons. They were probably just as crazy, just as mad as Henri was three years before—just as crazed as Josef Gabriel-Rene LeClerc must be today.

He climbed the creaky stairs one at a time. When he reached the top step, his cold fingers circled the door knob and turned it gently. The hasping clattered softly as the bolt slid back from the jamb. Cracking the door an inch at first, Paddock felt the rush of warmth. Then the light snaked through to touch his face. Another inch and more warmth. His ear strained to hear voices, laughter, movement, merriment. All he heard was the subdued, muffled sounds of the Negra dialect coming from somewhere off to his right. They must be seated in the kitchen, he thought, if his calculations were correct. But he could not know for sure until he opened the door.

The problem was the door opened to the right and he would have to crack it wide enough to push his head through, then crane his neck around. That just might expose him to the danger of being seen. He wrestled with his fear, then pushed on as Bass had always taught him to do.

Paddock was relieved. Where the stairs came up to the kitchen, the door stood beside a huge pantry area, a place where he couldn't be seen by house servants gathered in the kitchen. At least that was what he figured from all the low voices muttering, and the scooting of chairs across the floor. He heard someone open the door to the stove. He heard the scrape of wood coming out of a box, the clanking of the door latch, then the dull thunk of wood landing in the coals of the stove. Josiah breathed a little easier.

Still, he had to get on into the parlor, then down the front of the house where the bedchambers would surely be located. With the cellar door open only far enough for him to pull his bulky blue capote through, Josiah held his breath. The flames had been allowed to fall low in the sitting room fireplace. The place was chilled, heavy with a musty, unused smell to it. But, perhaps it was only his imagination. After all, he mused, his nose was used to the open spaces of the mountain west, and he had just spent the last few hours down in a dank, musty cellar. The odor might be only a lingering saturation in his nostrils.

His fingers ran over the rich fabric of the chair as he passed by, moving on catlike, moccasined feet to an open doorway leading to the foyer. Nothing else there but the candlelit chandelier, along with the horsehair mats spread on the walnut floor in the front entryway. He crossed the foyer and slipped down the hallway out of the light.

Cold candlelight flickered behind him as he toed along the thick carpet, one foot at a time, pushing his shadow before him. Three rooms and none of them appeared to be the old man's bedchamber. None of them had been slept in for some time. All the furnishings in each room had been draped with muslin sheeting. The chambers squatted cold, deserted, lifeless.

The last room's door stood open. This was his last chance to find the old man's bedchamber. Slowly Josiah pressed his back against the door, expecting at any moment to be heard, or seen—discovered and shot before he could ask. But this room was just as cold as the three others before it. Yet, unlike the other rooms, the furniture here was not covered with sheeting. Someone could indeed be living in this room, but it looked as lifeless as the other chambers he had just seen. But this particular sleeping room sent a chill up his spine and set the hackles at the back of his neck to tingling. This room felt as if it had had its very heart ripped out—a heart still bleeding, still beating.

He was breathing heavily, frightened by the unknown, a stranger trespassing in another man's world in order to save his own life. Josiah felt the growing panic, felt just how ridiculous he was to try to explain everything to the old man. But, he was already here. The choices snapped clear and sharp before him. He could slip back to the cellar and over the wall, escape all the way back to the mountains—there always to wonder, always to dread that next stranger come to darken his doorway or his night fire. Or, he could forge on, find the old man at last, get it said, and be done with it. Then he could return to Taos anew, reborn with a second chance. Redeemed and having forgiven himself.

Josiah knew he didn't have a choice. Even if the old man would not forgive him, he could never forgive himself if he did not go on now. So if LeClerc held steadfast to his lust for retribution, clung to his raging desire for revenge, at least Josiah Paddock would have done everything he could, and in that he could accept whatever would come. He would have forgiven himself at last.

Back at the end of the hall widening into the foyer, Paddock stopped and listened. He heard the voices. They weren't the darky dialect he had heard from the kitchen. And they weren't coming from that part of the house either. French and English—both—spoken in soft, hushed, subdued tones.

Paddock slinked to the bottom of narrow stairs winding their way to the attic. He had no idea why the men were up in the attic rather than in the spacious parlor.

His toes tapped at each step, testing the boards before he put his weight on them. It seemed to him that it took a long time to climb the stairs, his heart jammed up in his throat until he finally reached the landing which formed a crescent around a small, open doorway. From that opening fluttered pieces of hushed, muted conversation slipping out of what must surely be a small room.

Years ago he had known more than a mere smattering of the Gallic tongue, but tonight's whispered French ran by his ears too quickly for him to understand it. Even the English sounded garbled.

Right under his prickling skin, Josiah Paddock was certain that Josef LeClerc was in that room. Probably some sort of private study, a place where only the rich and influential would gather to discuss their power or money. He had never before seen LeClerc, but down beneath his tingling flesh, he was sure he would recognize the Frenchman if he saw him.

Josiah slid the last few steps to the edge of the open doorway, softly, as if there were nothing but the wind beneath his moccasins. He pressed against the wall. Perhaps these men were even plotting another attempt on his life at this very moment.

He understood the word used for death, even that expression he remembered which should mean a slow death. And, as he listened, the young trapper was sure they were speaking of him. Yet, there was something disturbing about the voices. There was no anger, no vile hatred, no cancerous bile built up behind each word. For so long now, Josiah had assumed there would be something close to that dark passion in a man who already had sent three men to kill one simple American shop clerk.

He heard them say Josef LeClerc was a man with a brave, strong heart.

Not when he would send someone else out to murder a man for him!

He heard them declare their sadness that his heart was no longer strong, that there had been one blow too many suffered by the dying man.

Sans vie.

Without life. Dying? Old man LeClerc?

Josiah knew immediately they were talking about the family elder, suddenly certain right down to his marrow that the old man was dying. He prayed he was not too late.

Paddock wheeled, a shoulder held against the doorjamb, turning into the room. Every eye immediatedly whirled his way as he stooped so as not to bump his head against the low-hanging, exposed beams overhead.

"Who are you?" one of the men demanded.

Josiah was a moment in answering. He didn't know who had asked him the question. His own eyes were riveted on the tiny bed and that frail, old man buried within his dampened sheets. Beside him at the doorway, the young trapper sensed a sudden tensing in the old house servant who stood pressed against the wall. A tingle of apprehension rushed through him, yet he refused to look away from the old man's bed. Josiah felt the old Negra's glare boring a searing hole between his shoulder blades as he took two more steps into the room.

"I asked—who are you, sir?" Now the speaker's tone was not merely annoyed. It was fully demanding.

"I—I'm a friend—a friend of Monsieur LeClerc's."

"What's your name?"

"That does not matter—right now."

By the time he arrived at the dying man's bedside, he knew that if anyone in the tiny room remembered how Josiah Paddock had looked back in the spring of 1831, they would not recognize him tonight. He was dressed in greasy, trail-worn buckskins. He wore long, unkempt, curly brown hair and a full beard and mustache that hid most of his face. Three long years of changes hid his identity.

Josiah watched the old man's eyes open, half-lidded at first, as they attempted to focus on him. He knelt closer to Josef, almost close enough to hear the agony of that labored breathing, that same death rattle which had come to rob his mother of her life years before.

He knew LeClerc was dying. All would be safe for him now. LeClerc could not send any more assassins out after him. Oh, his sons could—but they would never share the blind passion which had burned within the old man. No, they had seemed like the kind who would be more interested in their wealth and security and aristocratic society. If LeClerc died here tonight and no one in the room knew it was he who had come, Josiah knew he would finally be free for the first time in three years.

But, as he gazed into the old man's half-lidded eyes, Josiah Paddock knew he was wrong. He knew he could never leave this room unknown to the old Frenchman. When all was said and done, Josef LeClerc would have to do what Paddock could not do for himself. Josef LeClerc had to forgive the young American.

Josiah reached out, slowly, gently, to touch the veined, waxlike hand atop the blankets. He felt the others in the room shuffle up behind him. Right now he wasn't even sure how many there were surrounding him. They had only been faceless people and the only one he remembered looking at as he came through the door was the white-haired old Ink. Although he felt vulnerable and naked as a newborn at the moment, Paddock knew his most private, painful pilgrimage was over.

Those old, veined, gray eyelids twitched open farther at the touch to his hand. They did not flicker in recognition, nor was there a quickening jerk of the hand when they focused on this new visitor kneeling at the side of the small bed. Instead, the tired, watery old eyes stole away from Paddock's and leapt across the room to meet Old Jaune's.

This is the man! the eyes said as surely as if they had spoken aloud. This is the one I have waited to kill.

Old Jaune shuddered violently inside his ill-fitting, threadbare suit, a hand-me-down from the master of the house. The old Ink servant had long wondered just what religion to believe in, his own old voodoo black magic that terrified the superstitious faithful, or—his master's more sedate, quiet, candle-fragrant but nonetheless superstitious Catholicism. Now Old Jaune felt the heebies crawling up his spine to raise the hackles at the base of his neck. Now he was certain. The master's religion was the most powerful one of all. The master had willed this murderer to come all the way from the mountains here to St. Louis, walk right into this house and up to this tiny room. Master had drawn this evil man right to his bedside. Perhaps this wasn't purely Catholicism; perhaps not entirely voodoo. Whatever it was, Old Jaune decided in that instant of understanding in this attic room, whatever it was that had brought the murderer to his master's bedside, it was some mighty powerful magic, mighty powerful.

The Negra's age-yellowed eyes told LeClerc he understood what was wanted of him as he slipped his ebony fingers around the ivory handle. At the time that knife had been presented as a birthday gift it had been explained to Old Jaune that the ivory for its handle had come from the faraway land of his ancestors where huge elephants grew gigantic tusks with which they battled each other or common enemies.

So now Old Jaune understood all the better. Ivory that would come from such a powerful animal, ivory used in battle against a common enemy—what strong magic had brought that ivory all the way to St. Louis. This night it would kill the murderer who was likewise brought here by perhaps the same powerful magic.

Josef LeClerc saw that Old Jaune understood and was ready. Like an oiled, knotted rope, the Negra's black hand was clasped around the knife handle, and ready. Yet, all the old Frenchman had to do at this moment was have the strength to pull the pistol out—but he was so very tired.

"Monsieur LeClerc," Paddock whispered. His words were spoken so quietly the others in the room all leaned in close to overhear.

"I come a long, long way to talk to you." Paddock said. The words his mind had memorized were gone. All that remained were those simple words he held in his heart.

"It was all a mistake," he began. "I've come so far now, after all this time to tell you about me—tell you about Henri."

Paddock heard the hard leather shoe soles scuffing the wood floor behind him, inching closer, to hear better perhaps. Maybe to jab a knife in his back—now that he had mentioned a connection with Henri. Funny, but it didn't seem to matter all that much right now.

"I was a lot younger then, Mr. LeClerc. Me and Henri were both young then. You probably don't remember all that much about being young, how you make mistakes, growing up to be a man. And—and you don't recall how a man's pride can trip him up at times. Well—Mr. LeClerc, it's been three years, almost, and I've come back to see you, to stand up for myself—come back to tell you what it was I did. And, how I know it was the worst thing I've ever done in my life."

He gulped, watching the watery old eyes stare at him.

"Henri was the first man I killed. And I run away because of it. I should've stayed on and tried to explain it to you back then, just taken what come of it— but—I was more than a little crazed by that time. The girl, that—Angelique. The one Henri was fixing to marry—she was the faithless one who played us both for fools, you understand? She caused one man to get killed. And she caused another man to go crazy enough to kill him. All over a damned faithless woman. She used me like a chess pawn to get exactly what she wanted. And she wanted Henri— not me. She wanted him for his money, all his power, his family position. Didn't want me." Salt began to burn at his eyes.

"She's the only one who's won out in all this. I knew I had killed a man. Plain and simple killed him. He'd never walk again, never talk with his family again, never have any children—like I got my own son, Mr. LeClerc. I got my own son and that'd surely cause me pain to know my boy wouldn't ever get to have any children of his own."

The hot coal flared at the back of his throat. Josiah choked on it, swallowed hard and sniffled.

"I think that was one reason I come back now, when I did," he continued. "I'm a father now, too. And I want that little boy of mine to know I love him enough to tell him about killing—"

"Sacre dieu!" the priest exclaimed with a gasp.

"My—" the doctor sputtered.

"Oui! Oui!" one of the LeClerc sons cried out.

Out of the blankets the gray, waxy hand yanked free a pistol and pressed the muzzle against the trapper's temple.

Josiah gulped. The barrel was cold. Stone cold. His eyes blinked with the smarting of tears.

"You can kill me if that's—that's what you figure you've gotta do, Mr. LeClerc. I—I only hope you'll let me get this all finished before—before you pull that trigger. I don't want to go on to meet my Maker till I'm done explaining things to you. Even a condemned man who's gonna hang gets some last words, don't he? I figure to get this all off my chest before you—y-you take my life in exchange for your son's."

Paddock was crying now, the tears quietly spilling down his cheeks. Unashamed, Josiah let the tears fall into his beard and onto the blankets crumpled over the old man's body. They flowed like they hadn't in such a long, long time. "I—I've had me almost three extra years of living, Mr. LeClerc. Simply 'cause I ran away from St. Louis. But, now—my time's up. Oh, I ain't saying I'll not miss a thing, sir. I will. I got me my son. He's just a lil' sprout, just a baby right now—ain't even learned how to walk yet."

Josiah pulled at his nose with the back of his sleeve. He was beginning to weep all the poison free.

"And—and I got that boy's mother. She's a quiet, pretty woman, too. Been something of a real blessing to me, sir. A man, no matter who he is, couldn't ask for anything better than that, I don't believe. Living the life of a free man, you see?"

The young trapper felt the muzzle quiver, tremble against his temple. Damn, but it was cold steel. He never thought death would come this way, so cold. Once before, in Absaroka of the far shining mountains, young Josiah—shot by Asa McAfferty—had lain close to death, trembling with its chilling touch. Funny, but he had always thought death would burn like hell.

He just didn't want the old man's finger to twitch and pull the trigger until—until he got it all out.

"I think I've known all along I wasn't a free man. No, Mr. LeClerc. Josiah Paddock wasn't a free man as long as he had this to deal with back here. I can't bring your son back, although God knows I'd want to if I could. I'm here to take what's coming to me."

Paddock straightened his shoulders, batting back the tears that burned his raw, winter-dried lips. "I—I guess that's all I really gotta say. You've got the money and power to reach clear out to the mountains to kill me, but I decided to make it easier on us both. I can't keep lookin' over my shoulder and I can't let my woman and my boy suffer on my account. Running and waiting—wondering when the next killer will catch up to me."

Josiah took a deep breath and continued. And with the flooding of tears came a cleansing.

"I'm here to right all the wrongs I've done you, sir. I can understand if you don't forgive me. I took something mighty special away from you, and all I've got to give back to you in turn is—is me. Just a poor boy whose own daddy got himself killed trapping beaver upriver to the shining mountains before I was born. A boy whose mamma died while I watched her waste away with that same rotten sound in her chest like you've got. A mamma who finally gave up living and left me on my own. That's all you get in return for Henri. Just this poor boy who's finally tired of running. A poor boy who's so damned tired of running."

Paddock blinked back salty tears so he could see the old man's face. He was surprised to see LeClerc's cheeks glistening with tears and his frail, withered lips quivering. Josiah froze when he heard the click of the lock mechanism on the pistol. He waited for the shot that would blow a bullet through his brain.

Josef let the pistol sag and fall to his chest. He sighed and coughed. He tried to gaze back at the young American through his own tears but saw Old Jaune starting forward, knife poised in his raised hand.

With his last vestige of strength, the old patriarch raised his hand to stay the black man. He let his eyes talk to his old friend, his old companion of so many years. Eyes talking, speaking their own language of forgiveness. Eyes saying yes, the young American had taken something great from the elder LeClerc, but also proclaiming that Josef was now going to do something greater than take life away—he was going to give it back again to this young American. Here was the greatest lesson of all to be learned and he wanted his old black friend to understand. Tonight on his deathbed, he had come to know in this final hour exactly what all men asked of God when their time had come. This evening the very same thing had been asked of him. Perhaps, his tired, gray eyes pleaded with Old Jaune's yellowed ones, perhaps that redemption would be his own salvation, a grace he could share before crossing over the river.

Old Jaune let the knife slip out of his fingers. It tumbled to the blanket next to the fancy dueling pistol. He turned and shuffled away from the bed.

Paddock stood, his aching knees rattling so much it was painful to stand. He tore at the sash about his capote and pulled his own deadly dueling pistol free. The young trapper placed the pistol beside its twin brother on the old man's chest. Together after all these miles, all these years.

He gazed down at LeClerc. The old man looked so vulnerable, withdrawn like a wounded animal ready to die. Paddock reached out to gently touch one of the old man's bloodless, gray hands. In the next moment the young trapper turned and was gone from the room, his moccasins padding silently down the stairs.

Philippe LeClerc's glare flicked between his dying father and the empty doorway where Josiah had disappeared. He wasn't sure it was all over. After all this time, after all the money spent on finding out who the men were who could tell them where Paddock was, after all of that and all the lives gone in the wind— how could it all be over so quickly, so simply?

Rushing from the door, Philippe bounded across the landing and headed down the stairs after the American. Josef LeClerc beckoned the priest to his bedside. With his rosary beads laid over both the pistols and Old Jaune's knife, the black robe began to pray. He was just as quickly interrupted by the dying old man's raspy death rattle.

Paddock heard him coming down behind him. An instant too late he began to turn and was caught as the older brother flew through the air, crashing on top of the trapper. They crumpled in a heap of flying arms and legs across the muddy foyer, rolling and grunting with pain and exertion. Philippe swung again and again at the trapper, connecting each time and pounding the American's head against the wooden planks. Somewhere inside his thoughts, Paddock knew he would have to fight back in a moment more—that, or he might be dead.

"Philippe!"

"Philippe, please!"

Through the blood dripping from a fresh gash over one eye, Josiah could see the black robed priest and the second LeClerc brother pulling at Philippe.

"You musn't! For Papa!" Jacques cried in desperation.

The two finally managed to drag Philippe off Josiah, pulling him back across the entryway where he continued struggling to free himself.

"Papa wants to see him, Philippe."

"Oui, Philippe. Your father wants to see Monsieur Paddock."

"What for?" Philippe spit out the question venomously. "My father should be finished with all the talk. It is time for this one's blood!"

"Philippe. Philippe," the priest coaxed. "For your father, the time for blood is finally over. He wants no more of our prayers. This he tells me. No more prayers over him. He wants only to see Monsieur Paddock."

"Me? He wants to—to see me?" Josiah's suspicions itched. That, and the quick scuffle with Philippe had caused a fiery adrenalin to pump through him.

"Oui. He asks to see you now, Monsieur." The priest nodded up the stairs.

"Go ahead, Monsieur Paddock. I will stay down here with my brother," Jacques added, restraining Philippe.

"Non," the priest replied quickly as he turned toward the younger brother. "Your father asks that you both be present when he speaks with Monsieur Paddock."

Weakly old man LeClerc beckoned with his bony fingers for Paddock to come to his bedside.

"Go ahead, my son." The black robe prodded Paddock forward. "It is very important for Monsieur LeClerc to speak with you immediately. He does not have long for this side."

Paddock nodded dumbly and gazed back at the old man. The dueling pistols and knife lay on the window sill below the small, frosted pane. LeClerc held a set of black beads his knobby fingers worked at and twisted like a strand of oil-blackened rope. Josiah stepped to the side of the bed and knelt, so close he could smell that fragrance of death he had tasted in his nostrils only twice before—when his mother and his partner Mordecai Thayer had died. All the others had met quick, violent ends.

"Young man," Josef began, his English not crudely broken but well practiced, his voice crackling as if it had not been used in such a long time. Yet, his tone had in it a strength his wasted body failed to exhibit.

"Young man," he began once more, stronger still. "It is so beautiful, yet so simple what you have done for me. Such a difficult thing for me to see for these past three years that I was blind to it. So simple what it is that you show me now."

"I—I don't understand, Mr. LeClerc."

"I am dying, young man. Surely you see that my day has come, yet—you have saved me."

"H-how have I saved you?"

"That is truly the gift." His wrinkled lips made an effort to smile. Instead only a little saliva rolled out of the corner of his mouth. "The gift we have given each other. Not long now. Not long do I have. But this gift we have to give to each other. I—" Josef broke off into a coughing spasm.

When the seizure had passed and the physician had let the old patriarch sip at a cup of water, LeClerc cleared his throat and continued.

"You came here to ask—ask something of me, young man. For forgiveness, for your life. For those years yet to come with your wife and your son. Forgiveness and mercy. Through all those weeks and months and years of hating you, wanting your blood on my own hands, I never once saw that you held the key for Josef LeClerc. Never once did I see it at all. When I gave you the gift of your life—that gift of the rest of your life by forgiving you—I received so much more."

"I am—I'm confused."

"Young man, I thank you for the strength it took to come here, to St. Louis, to my house and kneel by my bed, knowing that I would want your blood on my own hands. God gave you that strength, I am sure. It took someone as strong and as young as you to carry the weight of it for both of us."

"The weight for both of us?"

"Oui, Monsieur Paddock. If you had not had the strong heart to come to me here, neither one of us would have been saved."

"Please, tell me."

"I save your life—"

"Yes, I know," Josiah answered.

"You, Monsieur Paddock—you have saved my soul."

"Y-your soul?" Josiah's eyes blinked several times as he tried to comprehend.

"Oui. My soul is at rest, and ready. I have been redeemed at last. The soul of Josef LeClerc would not go tonight to be with his God if you had not come here to allow me to forgive you, and thereby forgive myself for the evil I would have done to you. For that evil I have sought desperately to commit against you."

"You—you are—a—good man." Josiah rose, holding onto LeClerc's hand.

Josef squeezed that young, strong, roughened hand of the American frontiersman.

"Likewise—you too are a good and gentle man, Monsieur Paddock."

"Thank you, Monsieur LeClerc."

"May you raise your son in peace, my friend."

Paddock fought to hold back the tears as he let go of the old man's bony, cold hand.

"Thank you, thank you so, Monsieur LeClerc."

"Non, my son. Thank *you*. I have never before felt this—this quiet peace, this contentment ever before. Thank you."

The last words fell soft as a wind whisper. Paddock felt the wax-like hand slowly loosen as the fingers lost their tension in his. The heavy, tear-glistened eyelids drooped, then closed. Beneath them the wetted lips grew softly radiant with a smile. Josiah gently laid LeClerc's hand on his chest and stood back from the tiny bed.

Instantly the physician was there, his ear pressed against LeClerc's chest. The priest brushed holy water on the dead man's forehead, intoning the ancient ritual. Behind Paddock, Jacques began to cry out, answering his father's death with grief. Beside him, his brother Philippe stood, numbed by the suddenness of his father's final moment.

Josiah turned to leave, his shoulder brushing by the old Ink servant. Old Haune's burnished, ebony cheeks gleamed shiny with tears, but he wore a ragged smile across his face.

Paddock stopped, put a hand on the old man's quaking shoulder.

"We all been blessed by that man," the old Negra sputtered between sobs.

"Yes. We all have been."

"Master ain't here no more. He's gone on to his peace. He ain't here on earth to be troubled no more."

Squeezing the old servant's shoulder, Paddock was gone.

22 DEAD SURE HE had heard a strange sound, Bass woke with a start. His eyes opened into narrow, swollen slits as his mind quickly came up out of inner darkness. His ears pierced the darkness of the barn, a darkness assaulted by the light of but one oil lamp lapping at the black shadows. Dusk had already disappeared and pulled on west. The night around him was as dark as the inside of a Blackfoot's heart.

A horse blew. Others chewed on their feed, stamped their feet in the frosty air. All around him rose sounds he had become accustomed to. Yet, what his ears strained for was something different. Whatever it was that had awakened him it was something foreign.

Beside him in the hay, the wounded dog raised its head and started to growl. Scratch clamped its torn jaws shut with his bruised hand. The mutt fell silent. Now the old trapper was positive. The dog had heard something out of the ordinary, too. They weren't alone in the barn.

Trying to remember, like a dull knife hacking at stiffened rawhide, the old trapper sorted through things quickly, wondering first where Josiah had gone. He couldn't recall. He'd been asleep when his young partner left. The past night and day had been a lot of blurred fragments he could only snatch at, nothing much to hold onto.

Bass felt the aches in his body—from the back of his head where it had been pummelled into the top of the bar, clear down to his moccasined feet that had been stomped with the hard leather heels of men's boots. Not a square inch of him seemed without a cut or bruise or knot of fire. He swore it would never happen again.

That image of Billy Hooks' face, with its dumb smile, had loomed up in his fitful dreams as the old trapper tried to sleep numb through most of the healing that first day after the beating. When he had awakened in a sweat, Josiah had always been there to help calm him, rewrap the wounds with clean bandages and apply more salve or dope from the old man's medicines. But Josiah wasn't there now.

A board creaked behind him. Scratch held his breath.

The other sounds he had heard came from the darkness somewhere in front of him, out toward the back doorway. Now they came from the side door, too. That meant there were at least two of them. Whoever was here in the barn with him knew about those small doors Tharp never kept locked because he said a thief could never slip a horse through them.

Scratch leaned over and pulled the pistol from its resting place atop his old coat. He felt for his knife, then found the second blade. The rifles stood against the stall close beside him. Apprehensive, the old man took one down silently and brought the lock back half way, then to full cock as quietly as he could. The scuff of a boot across the hard packed dirt broke the stillness in front of him. He heard someone catch his breath behind him. Bass decided it was not time to wait any longer.

The roar from his rifle cut through the silence of the livery. He had closed his eyes before he pulled the trigger and now opened them after the bright panflash of the muzzleblast had momentarily lit up the barn's interior. Animals whinnied and hehawwed. Others stamped around and banged into their stalls. Above all the clatter Bass heard the pained grunt of a human.

"Tommy boy!"

The accent sounded somewhat familiar, pricking his memory.

"Alson!" The voice was a little more frantic this time.

"Yeah. I'm here."

"You see Tommy?"

"He was on the other side of you, dammit!"

"Tommy! Tommy. Answer me, boy!"

"I—I'm hit!" The third voice gurgled with pain. It sounded like he was down, somewhere behind the stalls at the back of the barn.

Scratch plunked the rifle down beside him and grabbed for the second. He had started to sweat like a whiskey jug in humid weather. Now there seemed to be three left to worry about. Two in front of him and one behind. Damn, if he didn't feel like he was so far over the barrel that his ass was pointing noon high.

"You just stay put now, you hear me!" the familiar voice cried out.

"I ain't going nowhere. I'm d-dying, Timothy."

"We'll get you to a doctor soon as this is done, Tommy. Soon as we get him gutted and we're on the way."

"I ain't gonna last. You gotta help me now!"

"You gotta last, Tommy. You ain't got no other choice. You hang on there till this is done. Tommy? Tommy?"

There was a long silence, punctuated by the sound of rapid breathing somewhere behind Scratch, back where Tharp kept the tack. The dog whimpered at his side, then growled low in his throat.

"Tommy?"

"He can't hear you no more, Timothy."

"How can you be so sure?"

"I just know it. That trapper blowed a hole in him big enough to stuff a tackle block through. Tommy's dead."

"Then we know what we gotta do."

"He killed Tommy in the dark!" There was fear smothering the shriek.

"The sonuvabitch was lucky, that's all. Just stay out of the light from that lamp."

Bass yanked on the trigger of the second rifle, muzzle pointed at the sounds of a voice, and instantly knew he had not hit either one of the pair. The ball crashed through something of wood. Then the barn went quiet as the blast rolled away from the walls.

"Alson?"

"He—he didn't hit me."

Bass knew he had to save the last ball in his pistol for the one behind him whenever that attacker made his play. He'd have to make do with the third rifle and the two knives.

"Let's take him now. He can't have more than two guns, can he?"

"I—I don't know."

"No, he can't. Now's the time, Alson. C'mon, lad."

First one black streak, then a second rushed out of the darkness at the end of the long, lamplit aisle down the middle of the livery. They hurtled toward Bass with knives drawn. The dog began to growl with a terrible, pained rumble.

Through a splotch of light Bass finally saw his attackers. The dog beater and one of his mates from the steamer. Both stumbled along clumsily as if they had been drinking. They ran toward him, screaming at the top of their lungs, knives held over their heads.

Scratch flung one knife hard. It caught Alson high in the chest. The blade struck the man with enough force not only to stop his headlong rush, but the impact shocked the assailant enough to cause him to hurtle backwards. The surprise of it crimped his face, knowing he was dead where he stood. Alson dropped his own weapon and clutched both hands around the handle protruding from his chest. Blood pumped out of the fatal wound, gushing across the front of his coat.

Timothy Sullivan slid to a halt on the dirt floor and watched his mate crumple to his knees. With eyes full of pain and terror, Alson gazed up at his companion. Just as quickly a blank look slid over his face like autumn ice slicking a high country beaver pond. Then he keeled over to the side.

Two down, two to go.

Sullivan was on top of him with a thud, before Bass could pull his second knife from its scabbard. The only thing Bass could do was to put up his two pained arms to catch the wrist that held the knife poised above him. The weapon hung there a moment, the light-glinted blade piercing the darkness like an evil needle ready to prick his soul. Timothy's eyes glittered in the pale lamplight, filled with jealous pride.

The wounded dog made an attempt to rise in defense. It got up on its three good legs and hobbled toward the men grappling in the dirt between the stalls. Growling with his teeth bared, it went for the Irishman. Timothy merely swatted the injured dog away with a blow from his left fist. The animal skidded across the dusty aisle, yelping in pain.

Scratch's weakened, bruised arms could not compete with the Irishman's heavier strength. He gritted his teeth in one last desperate push against Timothy Sullivan. He knew it was over when he felt his arms collapsing beneath the weight of the Irishman. Sullivan's gritty smile loomed close to his face, breath hot and noxious in his nostrils.

So close to Billy and Silas at last, only to die here after he had learned Billy Hooks had gone mad and Silas Cooper was back near the mountains. Here he was, dying beneath this liquored-up drunk Irishman in a St. Louis barn. He had to laugh at himself. Better that than crying when you die. He had to laugh—until he felt the tip of the knife puncture his torn warshirt and push its way into his skin. He knew it had drawn blood and in an instant more the sharp blade would plunge downward into his heart. His strength was gone and he could not hold back the man's wrists any longer.

Scratch tried to twist away from the knife and go for his pistol. The tip of the blade raked along the old trapper's breast as he rolled. Bass couldn't get the pistol out. It was trapped, pressed between them.

He felt the Irishman's blade prick his skin a second time and he knew it was over. Last play of the night, old man. Last hand you'll ever play.

He expected to feel his own body quake as the weapon slid through his chest wall. Instead, Sullivan's body jerked. Drops of something moist splattered Scratch's face. He thought it was sweat until he looked up at his attacker's face.

A jolt of cold shot down Bass's spine, like a waterspill in a February cold snap. Sullivan wasn't sweating. He was bleeding. The body-hot blood oozed out of four holes in the center of his chest as sharp tines plunged on through the man's body.

Scratch gasped, horrified at the sight of the four steel spikes close to his face, each one dripping blood and gore.

His body jerking uncontrollably in its death throes, the Irishman dropped his knife and gazed down at the four metal prongs that had just put an end to his life. Eyes frozen in horror, Sullivan toppled off the old trapper, dead as a barn rat in a river snake's belly.

Shocked, Scratch slowly looked up from the corpse to the handle of the pitchfork still clutched in the hands of a young woman. Her tiny fingers trembled as she let go of the handle. The pitchfork quivered with the last spastic jerks of the man's body. A foul, steamy stench rose in the frosty air of the barn as the Irishman's bowels voided in death.

The girl turned and began to sob as she stumbled down the aisle, then collapsed some ten feet away where she sat in a crumpled heap.

Bass pulled his own tired legs out from the tangle with the Irishman's. He tore his shirt away from his chest and peered down at the slash across the muscle of his left breast. It was a deep cut, but it hadn't penetrated his lungs. The skin and muscle tissue would mend. Suddenly the wounded dog was at his side, licking his face and whining.

"It's all right, boy," Bass cooed. "I know you tried. That's all that matters."

Bass winced when the big, wolflike dog licked at his chest wound. Just the way of animals. Then the dog lifted his muzzle and dragged a sloppy tongue over

Bass's cheek before it turned away. Hobbling over to the young woman, the animal licked at her hand. She jerked with surprise at the dog's touch.

"He won't hurt you none," Bass offered as he pulled a leg in beneath him. "Critter's just tryin' to tell you he cares."

Scratch was downright curious about her. With his other leg beneath him, he rose and stumbled around the Irishman's body as he made his way over to the young woman. He sat down beside her, slid his palm beneath her chin and lifted her face toward his. Tears stained her painted eyes, causing the dark color to streak her cheeks. Her lips brightened moist with red tint.

If I didn't know better, Bass thought, this young'un looks like one of the gals from the sporting house.

Her face looked hauntingly familiar in the pale light of the oil lamp. Bass stood again and hobbled down the stalls to turn up the wick. When he returned she was daubing at her cheeks, staring at him. It was unsettling to the old trapper to look at her, certain she was one of the girls from the sporting house, yet feeling that he knew her from before. There was something about her face, the cheekbones, the curve of her lips, something that nagged at him from a long time ago.

Surely she was the one with hair like polished oak who sat beside Josiah at the house while he and the madam had bargained. But, why was she here? And, why was she tugging at him from out of the past? He could not have known her all those years ago when he had lived here in St. Louis. She didn't look a day over eighteen. So, why did he feel the way he did in the pit of his stomach?

"I'm not hurt."

Her tiny, frail voice surprised him. For someone who had just killed a man with a pitchfork, her voice sounded small, weak.

"I'm glad you ain't hurt." He reached out and patted the hand clenched in her lap. "You just stay here, missy. I'm gonna tidy up your friends here." He rose slowly, feeling the pain across his cracked ribs.

Scratch grabbed the Irishman by the collar and pulled the body down the aisle, dropped it in a lump near the back of the barn in an empty stall. Next he walked over to the second victim. With one foot on the man's chest, he was able to yank his knife from the victim's body. He picked up the attacker's knife and wiped both blades across his leggings. When he knelt to scoop up the Irishman's knife, he winced at the fire across his chest. Chopped up like a bad cut of meat.

He dropped the second attacker with the Irishman, then walked back to the dark shadows at the rear of the barn where the stench of blood and feces was overpowering. He tapped his toe in the darkness until he touched the corpse. He dragged the body and dumped it with the others. The horses snorted and stamped, their nostrils unfamiliar with the rank smell of death.

"I put all your friends back there, gal." He plopped down into the dirt across the aisle from her and leaned against the stall railing at his back.

"T-they're not my friends, Mr. Bass."

"You know my name, huh?" he asked with the crimp of surprise in his voice.

"Yes, I do," the woman answered as she swiped at her cheeks.

"From the—sportin' house where you work?" Scratch guessed.

She threw her head back and glared at him a moment. Then she nodded and lowered her eyes. "Yes. I heard your name yesterday."

"You say them ain't your friends?"

"No. I don't know them. Never saw them before."

"How come you came here with 'em to kill me, then?"

"I didn't come with them, Mr. Bass." She dragged the back of her hand across her nose, then dabbed at it with a kerchief. "I was already here."

"You was?"

"Yes. I sneaked in a back door of the livery while you were sleeping. I was sitting back there, wondering what to do about you, Mr. Bass. About the time I decided I had to go through with it, I heard the others come in over there. That was when you woke up. At least that's when you raised your head up and the dog started to growl. I might have gotten away with it, too, because you didn't even wake up when I came into the barn."

"Say, you'll just have to slow down a bit here, missy. I'm just a simple man who's spent the last ten years out in the far mountains stayin' alive. I ain't as yet had me no woman tryin' a sneak on me. You say you wasn't with them three back there, yet you say you almost got away with it. I don't s'pose you'd care to tell me what it'd be you're talkin' about."

"You have part of it right, and part of it wrong," she began and dropped her eyes. "The part about not being with them is correct. B-but, I was here to kill you."

Scratch tilted his head back and studied her a moment.

"How were you gonna do it? Shoot me?"

She wagged her head and stuck a hand in her bag where she pulled out a huge knife, one found in a kitchen that would be used for butchering cuts of meat.

"Whoooeee! That'd sure be a messy job for a lil' gal like you." He shook his head and tried out a grin on her. "I'm sittin' here, knowin' you said you come here to kill me. I just wanna know what stopped you."

"I—I'm not sure myself," she answered as she looked into his eyes. "I was ready to push this knife into your heart when those others came in. I froze right there in the corner and waited. It got scary then. I was stunned by all the killing and when the third man jumped on you, I just couldn't let him kill you."

"That's when you found the pitchfork an' used it on my attacker."

"Yes," she sobbed quietly. "I didn't want to trust myself with this knife. If I had stabbed him in the back with it, he could still have killed you. The pitchfork seemed the only sure way of k-killing him. I—I never killed anyone before!"

The young girl shrieked and crumpled over in the dirt, her dress and petticoats billowing out beneath the long, hooded cloak she had tied around her. The girl clutched the kerchief at her eyes and ground her knuckles into the sockets.

Numbed by her display of raw emotion, Bass couldn't do anything but stare at her. After a minute, he crawled across the aisle and brought her shoulders up.

He cradled her head against his chest and leaned against the stall rails, soothing his hand along her hair.

"I know it don't help, missy," he cooed, trying to calm her, "but, killin' don't get a damned bit easier. Sometimes killin' seems like the handiest thing to do, but it don't ever get easy."

He felt her nod before she began to wail again. Bass just held on and rocked her against his chest for the longest time until she grew quiet.

"What's your name?" he asked. "You know mine."

"Amanda."

"Why, that's purty. Real purty name. Never knowed anyone named Amanda before. What's your last name?"

"I don't have one," Amanda answered as she brought her head away from his chest.

"Nawww, cut that out. Everybody's got 'em a last name, Amanda. Everybody." He looked down at her tear-streaked face. Lord, she was young. Maybe too young to be working in the kind of place the Supper Club was.

"Just how old are you, girl—Amanda?"

"I turned eighteen last June," she answered.

"Lord, your folks—they know you—" he stammered. "They know what you do for a livin', Amanda?"

"I ran away from my ma better than a year ago."

"Where's she live?"

"Not that far away." The answer sounded distant.

"You ain't seen her since you started—started to entertain men?"

"No, and I'm not likely to again either."

"Why's that, Amanda? Why you don't wanna see her again?"

Bass didn't know why he was asking her the questions. He just wanted her to talk, to take her mind away from the killings she had witnessed, and the killing she had committed. Besides, Titus Bass knew exactly why he himself had left home when he was sixteen. And he knew over those first years of independence he had thought many times about going back to see his folks. In the end, he felt all the worse for never having gone back to see them. They might both be dead now, for all he knew. Both dead and it would be too late.

"She lied to me about my father. Said he had died. All those years while I was growing up she never told me the truth. That's a terrible sin to lie to your own child, isn't it, Mr. Bass?"

"I—I don't rightly know, Amanda. I ain't never had a child yet myself. I wouldn't wanna answer for your ma anyway. It's just that, sometimes folks tell the ones they love somethin' that might be a lie just so they don't cause that loved one a big hurt—"

"And what happens when I find out the truth?" The young woman suddenly pulled herself away from the old trapper and stared squarely up into his leathered face. Her green eyes flashed defiance of his rationalization.

"I don't know what to tell you, Amanda. Did your ma tell you why she lied? Did she do it to protect you from somethin', maybe protect you from bein' hurt?"

"She gave me the same nonsense you just did. All that stuff about trying not to hurt me. It was all just a bunch of horse dung." Amanda clenched her eyes shut against the tears.

"Why'd she wanna keep somethin' about your pa such a secret from you for so long?"

"She lied to me about having a father! I never had a pa."

"C'mon now, missy. Everybody's got a father."

"A young woman gets herself with child, Mr. Bass," she said as she squared herself, "and the man leaves, probably knowing she's going to have his child. Isn't that child without a last name? She hasn't got a father because he won't own up to his very own child."

"Hold on here. Why are you throwin' all these here questions at me, Amanda? I'm just a trapper. Ain't been nothin' more than that for the past ten years. I just worked the levee in St. Louis afore that. Worked on a farm once afore comin' to St. Louie. Was a smith—blacksmith, when I come to this town the first time. So, I don't know how you get soundin' me out 'bout all this stuff. It makes a man's head hurt somethin' fierce just tryin' to figure all this out for you, child. Why ask me?"

She lowered her head, then gazed up at him with a familiar look in her haunting green eyes.

"I'm asking you—because you're that man."

"What man? What man are you talkin' about?"

"You're my father, Mr. Bass."

"N-now—now w-wait a minute here!"

Her words shot through him as surely as that arrow had pierced him. Only this felt worse. The arrow had cut only some muscle and skin, mere flesh at the most. But this young woman's words had just penetrated to his core with the fire of a lead ball.

"It's the truth! That's why I came here tonight to kill you," she said as she looked down at the knife in her lap. "And that's why I couldn't kill you."

"How you so dad-blamed sure about this?" Bass shook his head, not at all sure he even wanted to talk about it.

"I'm sure, Mr. Bass. I'm as sure as any of us can be after some nineteen years."

"You said you was only eighteen. I cain't be your pa."

"You are. After all this time, you are still my father."

"None of this fits, missy. You ain't told me a thing to make me believe this half-baked story 'bout me bein' your—your kin."

"My Gran'pa was the one who let it slip one day when I was sixteen and courting a fella whose folks owned the place down the road. Me and Ma lived with Gran'pa ever since I was a little girl. Gran'ma took sick and died and me and my ma stayed with him and helped him on the farm."

"Go on. I don't see what any of this—"

"Gran'pa wanted to tell me about my ma, see? His heart was right, because he wanted to warn me about men and the trouble they could cause a young girl."

308

"Just what happened to your ma?"

"She got herself with child, Mr. Bass. The young fella who did it worked for my Gran'pa for a while."

"What was your Grandpa's name, Amanda?"

"Guthrie. His name was Guthrie."

The breath snagged in Scratch's throat. He swallowed hard on the huge egg of fire choking him. Could this really be? The young woman sitting two feet from him—was she his daughter? Surely he would have known about it if he had had a child. Surely someone would have come to St. Louis and told him. He had been in St. Louis all that time after leaving the farm. The Guthrie girl had been seventeen? Eighteen? He saw her face come more clearly into focus across the years.

"M-Marissa Guthrie?"

She nodded. "Yes. That's my mother's name."

"Lord!"

Suddenly the old trapper sprung to his feet and fell back against the stall railing. He pushed himself off and stumbled away, pacing back and forth past the young woman sitting on the ground.

"Now—now just a shake here. We can put this all together an' sort out who your rightful pa is here," Bass began, trying to convince himself more than the girl. "I left home when I was sixteen years old, close on to seventeen," he recalled aloud. "Spring? No, fall, as I recollect. Went down the Ohio River to Owensboro. Kentucky. Worked there till I was twenty."

He turned and looked over at the young woman. "I was twenty when I left Owensboro on the Ohio River."

Bass turned away, uncomfortable with the way she looked at him with those imploring eyes. He continued to pace, accounting for the years.

"On down the Ohio to where it fell into the Mississippi. Must have been spring when I left Owensboro an'—an' run onto the big river where I went north an' lived with the Guthries for a spell. Spring on to the fall. Maybe November, huh? Most likely November when I left the Guthrie place."

He stole a furtive glance at the girl and walked on by her. Lord, it was like looking at Marissa's ghost. The girl had his eyes—and Lord knows the child was cursed with his nose. Nawww, it couldn't be. She was so close to being a mirror image of her mother, Marissa Guthrie. He shook his head.

"I heard Mr. Guthrie an' some of them others palaverin' an' talkin' about this big town called St. Louis. That's right where I headed when I come upriver a ways to see those things every young man wants to see when he turns a man." He gulped. "But, a purty young gal like yourself wouldn't know about that, would she?"

"I would, Mr. Bass," she answered and lowered her head to stare into her lap. "I'm one of those things a young man wants to see when he comes to St. Louis. Young men always want to meet some—accommodating ladies, don't they?"

Her words cut at him as surely as if she had taken that knife off her lap and slashed at his wounded breast.

309

"It—it's just that a young man's gotta find his—his own way out there in the world. I was twenty-one as I recall, gettin' to St. Louie an' startin' out in the blacksmith trade. Ol' man Guthrie had showed me a bit of what he could do at a forge an' I liked the work. So, I kept on learnin' when I come to town. Nine—nine years I spent here. That's a long time, Amanda. Nine years before I turned thirty an' come out to the mountains."

"You were in St. Louis all that time and never once came back to visit my mother?" she demanded.

"I—I had no idea 'bout you. No idea 'bout her wantin' to see me."

"Most likely you're right. She probably didn't want to have a thing to do with you, Mr. Bass. I don't blame her a bit, frankly. After all, you're the one who left without a word, only a note saying goodbye. Why should she come traipsing after you?"

It was a moment before he replied.

"I ain't got no answer for you, Amanda. I didn't know I was somethin' all that special to your ma."

"Nine years and not once did you come downriver to see what became of the girl you left with your baby?"

"H-how was I to know she was with child? An' just how the hell do I really know you—you're really my child?"

"My mother admitted that my father's name was Titus Bass before I ran away from home." Amanda put a hand out to pull herself up on the stall railing. "She'd lied to me all those years and finally she wanted to tell me everything she could to keep me home. Titus Bass was his name, she said. It was 1814 and the war was winding down when Titus Bass stumbled onto her pa's farm down the Mississippi. Marissa Guthrie. Titus Bass. Just how many of either one of them folks do you figure there are along the Mississippi River?"

"I ain't got no answer to that'un, miss."

"I was born in June of 1815, a few months after you left my Gran'pa's farm."

"I don't know what to say," Bass sighed as the tears welled up in his eyes. "I ain't no good at apologizin'. Never did all that much of it. I—I never knowed. I never knowed I had me a—child."

"You didn't just have a child," she said, beginning to sob again. "You've got a daughter. Me."

"I'm your p-pa, Amanda." He reached out and brought her fiercely into the circle of his arms. "You have—a—pa."

The old man clung desperately to the girl as the years of foolishness and selfishness washed over him. A daughter, he thought. He had a daughter.

As if she would fall—frantically the young woman clutched at him. Amanda dove into his comforting embrace, letting the arms swallow her as no arms had ever swallowed her before. Men had held her while dancing, had swept her into their arms gallantly, even romantically—they had wanted to sweep her off her feet and take the beautiful young woman away from that life she led at the house. But she had let little come through to her, allowing so little to seep into that private place where she kept herself protected. She had long believed herself betrayed by a man she had yet to meet, a father she had never known. So it was

310

easy to hate all men for what the one had done to her mother, to hate all mankind for what Titus Bass had committed against Amanda alone. So very easy to run away from her mother's arms and love, escape to St. Louis and be swept up into a life where men used her body, and each time they used her for their own pleasure she got even a little more with Titus Bass for leaving. For better than a year now, Amanda had been getting even with her unknown father, slowly giving away a little piece of that sunshine in her soul each time a man shadowed her in that second story Supper Club room so richly decorated in silk and satin and sin.

23 NEITHER OF THE house servants knew exactly what to do, nor did they know just what to make of the American stranger who came to the door and boldly asked to come in, stating his intention of seeing their young mistress. The younger maid who answered the door and let him into the main hallway was immediately flustered by his strange garb and babbled about the rest of the family being gone to New Orleans for the month. She told him to wait while she went to inquire.

The older maid who returned with her looked Paddock over closely, almost in an accusing sort of way, startled at his crude frontier garb. He faintly recalled her face. She was the same maid who had answered the door the last time he had visited this house years ago. That recognition on his part made him a little nervous, especially under her silent, piercing scrutiny. He thought it peculiar that Angelique had stayed home while her family rode the river steamer south to visit family or friends in New Orleans. Stranger still, that the beautiful young woman had not taken another suitor and wed. He remembered how masterful she had been in her plan to snare Henri LeClerc. Duped grandly into believing the young French beauty really wanted him, Josiah had willingly played the pawn who had caused the handsome French dandy to propose marriage to Angelique.

He saw now that he had not only taken Henri LeClerc's life, but Angelique Saucier's future happiness from her as well. Yet, at the same time, both of them had ruined his life in the bargain. Now he had come back to St. Louis to put her ghost behind him. As painful as it might be to gaze upon her dark beauty again, Josiah was prepared to see it through and wipe the slate clean.

Only then could he return to Taos. Only then would he allow himself to live free.

Many of the rooms were darkened. Cautiously, Paddock toed down the long entryway and peered into one of the parlors. It could have been the very same sitting room where she had told him the bitter-tasting truth and he had first gagged on the bile of love lost. The room was tall; a huge chandelier with dozens of dead candles hung overhead from the vaulted ceiling. Across the black walnut floor the fading afternoon light glowed lustrous and bold. The same way her dark hair had held the shimmer of sun or candle, he remembered. The mahogany furnishings, covered in their varied hues of rich velvets, looked almost unused, undisturbed. Lace draped all tables and those arms of chairs and cozy settees alike. It appeared no one had graced this room with warmth in some time. The family had indeed been gone for weeks.

Outside the cold snow rattled and spat against wide double veranda doors leading out to a wide porch which extended clear around the house. The glass-paned doors rattled with the insistence of the wind. He felt a forceful gust snake itself into the room and he shuddered. Paddock turned at the sound of feet padding in his direction.

The older maid failed to recognize him at first. Back at the livery Paddock had cleaned up as much as he could with cold water and a bar of lye soap Tharp had provided, using a scrap of old sacking to scrub with. He tied his long, curly brown hair back in a queue, using a whang from his legging fringe. He had cleaned his leather shirt and leggings, then used a curry comb to brush the mud and thorns and trail filth from his light blue capote.

Paddock stood bravely under the assault of the older maid's stern scrutiny. He had watched her eyes flash at the long-forgotten sound of his name. She remembered the name at least, even though he didn't look to be anybody she recognized at first. For much of a fall and winter, into the warm promise of a new spring, Josiah Paddock had courted the devastatingly beautiful Angelique Saucier. Not once had he allowed himself to believe their love could end in any other way but marriage.

The maid told him that Mademoiselle Saucier was ill. Still, Paddock persisted, telling her that he would only be a few minutes with Angelique, that what he had to say would not take all that long. The maid spoke mostly French and it had been so long since Josiah had used the language, it was difficult for him to keep up with her primping words.

Vautour he knew was vulture. Why the older maid shook her head sadly and stared at the hardwood floor as she spoke of vultures, he could not answer. *Chien loup* was wolfhound as far as he could remember. The maid tried to explain Angelique's illness as *la tristeusse, mania a potee.* All that meant to the young trapper was that Angelique had a great sadness about her, a great depression at her illness. The maid continued to mumble something about *mauvais pourceau,* an evil, wicked pig of a man who had caused her mistress to be this way.

Josiah wanted to ask if the wicked swine she spoke of was Angelique's new suitor, but he asked nothing more. Instead, he watched the two maids mutter between themselves and wag their heads. The expression in the older maid's eyes softened when she turned to look at Josiah again and said something he didn't understand.

The two women turned and started up the steps. The young maid wheeled around after she'd take a few steps and saw that the American stood motionless in the foyer.

"Ici!" she cried, pointing upstairs, motioning for him to follow.

Paddock bounded up the mahogany steps two at a time, holding his otter cap primly with both hands. At the top of the stairs, the trio turned down a hall. They stopped at a door and the older maid took a large key from an apron pocket and inserted it into the lock. Odd that Angelique's door would be locked.

Before she turned the key in the lock, the maid instructed him in broken

English and painful French how she wanted him to slip into the room quickly. She would lock the door after he entered. Paddock began to speak but she tapped a finger against his lips. She told him he would have only to knock on the door, or call out, and she would come to see him from the house.

Surprised by the mystery of it all, Josiah wanted to ask more questions, but he heard the door creak on its hinges as the maid opened it. He shoved a shoulder into the tiny opening, feeling someone or something on the other side trying to push against the door. He wedged himself into a foul pit of darkness as the door clunkered back against its jamb behind him.

He caught his breath and tried to hold it against the stench of urine and excrement, his mind stinging with confusion.

Gradually his eyes adjusted to the dim afternoon light slanting feebly through the narrow slats of the shutters nailed outside the windows. Then he heard someone breathing and assumed it must be Angelique, somewhere in the room, perhaps lying on her sick bed. So ill she must be, he thought, that she had dirtied herself, unable to use the chamberpot.

For a civilized, sophisticated, society bred nose, the odor would have been overpowering. Besides the rank stench of urine and feces were the acrid odors of vomit and human sweat, wasting flesh and musty, airless quarters. Added to the nauseating odors was the underlying smell of strong lye soap, which he figured the servants used to clean the room.

That hard, raspy breathing from across the room crept back into his consciousness. He remembered how it had been hot at his neck when he had squeezed past the door into the darkened room. Perhaps the sense of heat had only been in his imagination.

His eyes swept over the room slowly, allowing time for his breathing to become more regular, acclimating himself to the stench in this dark cell. What little light stole through the slats in the shutters spilled across the wooden floor leaving little trails of gray smudge that reminded him of late afternoon sunbeams streaking through the picked-over ribs of a buffalo carcass long dead and varmint-cleaned on the plains. Ribs, stark and naked in the failing light, and everywhere rose the stench of dead and dying.

There was a light scratching on the floor. He was startled by the flight of something dark and birdlike that streaked across the smudges of light. Suddenly, he felt the hands at his throat. Stunned so that he couldn't respond. There was someone's breath in his face—hot, acrid, heavy with the sour smell of old vomit.

With fingers digging into his throat, clawing at his face, the young trapper finally grabbed the hands away from his cheeks. He felt the captured claws, wondering at the suddenness of the attack, thinking at first it might be a cat or dog, some feral animal. Then he realized that what he held were human hands. They were moist, mostly around the fingernails, as if the person had been scratching at something damp. The nails were battered, torn, and sharp fragments of wood stuck beneath what was left of them.

Just what was this? Who was this?

He brought the grotesque hands down away from his face and in the meager light, tried to focus on the object in front of him. A glimpse of the face was all

314

Josiah got before the person's chin tilted up and the creature broke into a hideous, cackling laugh. The young woman danced away, spinning across the shadows to the opposite side of the room.

Swallowing hard, Paddock looked down at his own empty hands, his eyes finally focusing dimly in the scant light. The moistness from the woman's hands had been something dark, maybe blood. Perhaps his own. His fingers scoured his neck and cheeks. Only some superficial scratches and none of them deep enough to cause the amount of blood she had on her fingertips.

She spun around and around before she rushed to a windowsill where she began to claw at the dirt-crusted pane with her fingers. She scratched desperately for a few seconds, then, as if she caught herself, the young woman began to laugh. She cackled hysterically as she went spinning about the room. Her soiled, torn dress, without benefit of numerous petticoats, gathered and fluttered about her legs as she stumbled across the floor.

Completely stunned by what he was seeing, Josiah swallowed hard again, trying as much as possible to breathe through his mouth. As she pranced around the room, he finally saw the dark splotches that stained her bare legs and feet. Blackened spots smudged her dress both front and back where he supposed this mystery creature had dirtied herself.

Horrified, the young trapper watched her spin and spin and spin across the room as if she would never tire. She danced right up to him and whirled to a stop. She peered up into his eyes, touched his beard. He was afraid she would try to claw him again. Instead, she caressed the thick, brown beard.

Finally Josiah let his gaze climb to her battered head where she had done so much damage to herself. Where once her black hair was kept so lustrous with nightly brushings, always piled high atop her head with pearl or ivory combs, now the ringlets fell limp and dirty and matted with her own body's fouling smeared in it. What hadn't been defiled by her feces had been yanked out by the roots, leaving raw patches here and there where her hair had been sacrificed to her frequent rages.

Oh my God. Angelique.

Frantically, he drank in a breath of air and fought to hold down his bile as the odors stung the back of his throat. He wanted to reach out and touch her and yet, he felt as if he had suddenly been given an injured animal to comfort, or to put out of its misery.

Josiah brought a hand up to caress her cheek. Suddenly she began to cry, softly. Huge teardrops bubbled out from the brim of her eyes and rolled down the coat of dirt already smudging her cheeks, creating dark trails in the filth.

"Angelique."

Instantly she tore herself away from him and darted like a frightened hummingbird across the room, her long dress slurring along the floor. Angelique flung herself into a dark corner and collapsed. Her laughter had become a fit of hysterical crying. She drew her legs up, rocked back and forth, arms clenched across her belly, clutching her stomach tightly as if in severe agony from something caught deep in her bowels.

That memory of her had long ago become a pastel color in his mind. But now the vision came rushing back in sharp, vivid colors, no longer muted by time and distance. He found it hard to believe that this was really her.

"Angelique," he whispered softly, although the sound of her name filled the room.

She stopped sobbing and clutched childlike at one of the damp, wool blankets surrounding her in the corner.

Paddock took a couple of steps toward her, then stopped, not knowing what to do or say. He wondered if he should stay and try to explain who he was, what he had been to her. Or should he leave now while she was quietly cowering in the corner, while he could escape from this room and from this ugly image of Angelique—like a caged, desperate animal?

Struggling with the decision made him even more weary than he already was. Last night he had been unable to sleep after visiting Josef LeClerc, being at the old man's side when death came as a welcome release from torment. Instead of going directly to the barn, Josiah had wandered the streets and levee, returning to the livery only as the first rays of orange burst up from the eastern edge of the world. He had stayed up to drink hot, thick coffee with the old trapper as Bass related every detail of his attack by the three boatmen.

Now Josiah felt all the more sapped for the loss of sleep. He settled to the dusty floor, struck by the fact that the vile stench was even stronger this close to the dirty wooden planks. He sat for hours on the floor, studying the sad animal he had once loved. The light slanting through the wooden slats on the window shutters turned golden, then rust brown as it crawled across the floor, then finally disappeared into the gray of early evening. All that time he did not move. And all that time she remained rolled in a ball, staring at him like a wounded, frightened animal.

There was no look of accusation as fear drained from her gaze. Strange that he should see some hint of faint light behind her dark, demented eyes. That light reminded him of an inner hope, and peace. That light was all that had kept him here this long.

Finally Paddock rose and took a step toward the sad creature cowering in the corner. A second and a third. She had jerked into a tight protective ball when he had stood, but now she allowed him to approach her without a sound crossing her bloodied, cracked lips.

"Angelique, I suppose this is gonna be goodbye," he said, putting a palm out to lightly touch her ravaged hair.

She reached out and let her fingers play with the fringe along the outer seam of one legging.

"I ain't sure you'll hear me at all," he continued, "but I got this faith that somewhere inside you, there's someone listening to me, someone who hears what I'm saying."

Paddock dropped and knelt before her to stare into those once lustrous eyes, now blackened and bruised, stained from her fits of crying.

"All this time I thought I just might be the weaker one," he said and shook his head. "Time was I really thought you had it all: the beauty, the powerful family, the money. I thought you would survive, Angelique. Especially during those

316

first few months while I grew hungry and cold and afraid of all that I had done. Back then I thought you would last and I'd be the first to blow away with the wind. I was about at the end of my string when I bumped into the best friend I ever had in all my days."

The hot, stinging tears began to well at the edge of his eyes, spilling over the lids and down his cheeks.

"He took care of me, taught me, filled my soul where you had wounded it so badly. That man taught me to live all over again—and to dare to love again. Starting to love all over again, by loving him—my friend, good and true. Then I found Looks Far woman—and came close to losing her. Almost like I'd lost you all over again, it seemed, Angelique."

She stared blankly at him and he wondered if she understood any of it.

"Through a whole painful year I wandered without that woman, your vision all that time like a dark cloud, a piece of you mixed up with the memory of her. Then finally my old partner brought Looks Far to me. We've had us a boy, Angelique. Through that whole time while I was thinking she was lost to me forever, my child had been growing inside her, exactly like my love for her had been growing inside me. I was just about completely healed except for that aching thorn you had always been in my side."

Paddock gulped against the lump in his throat.

"I nearly died out there, Angelique. Got shot by a madman's rifle. But it didn't take me nowhere near as long to heal from that lead ball as it took to heal from the pain of loving you and being cast aside. I'm different now. Grown up—and ready to take your thorn right outta my side where you've been festering me with all the evil my loving you has caused me."

His fingers pulled apart the folds of his wool capote and reached down inside the neckline of the deerskin shirt. There he tugged at the leather thong that held the small doeskin pouch so he could look down at it. His tears splattered on its leather, causing dark splotches to stain the smoked animal hide. From around the top of the pouch Josiah unwrapped the faded silk ribbon he had carried there for so many miles over all those years since he escaped St. Louis.

"This ain't yours, I know, Angelique. And I don't even know the gal's name it came from. It's just that I know the two of you are tied up together some way in my leaving this city and heading off to the far mountains. The gal who I took this from was there for me the night you scorned me. You took your heart away from me, and she gave me her body that same night. That's why you two are tied together in my last memories of St. Louis. And this was hers."

Paddock reached out to touch a lock of her hair. She flinched at first, then relaxed. He tied the faded ribbon around a large matted curl at the side of her head.

"It's time I leave St. Louis, Angelique. Most likely for good now. All this is behind me at last. I'm leaving you and the memories behind where they belong, those memories that almost destroyed me twice. I've got so much waiting for me back there, out there. So much that you'll never be able to know in your life now. Even though you almost destroyed me twice, I want that part inside of you that's listening to me to know—know that I'm shet of it all, all that hate. I want that part of you that knows what I'm saying to hear me—to understand that I truly wish you well. The only harm you'll ever be caused is the harm you'll do to yourself."

After planting a gentle kiss on her dirty forehead, he walked to the door and knocked. After the maid came and unlocked the door for him, Josiah stood in the doorway, gazing back at that pitiful creature huddled in the corner of the dark room. A great sadness flooded over him as he realized she bore little resemblance to the beautiful woman he once loved.

"I-I'm sorry for all of this that's happened on account of me, on account of you, too. So damned sorry for my part in it, Angelique. See, no one of us has the right to judge what might have been—not a one of us. For so long now I judged myself on that score and it made me unfit for anything but pain. I hope you can hear me. I don't want you judging yourself too harshly on what might have been. No person should be allowed to do that to themselves. Can't judge what might have been."

Nudging the door open the young trapper slipped out into the hall. The warmer, clean air rushed over him in swells like electricity in a bolt of lightning. He almost swooned at the sweet fragrance in the hallway, those smells of woodwork and fabrics, the smell of fresh wash and delicate toilet water that swirled around the young maid who stood beside him to relock the door. Her hair had been freshly shampooed, sending through him a sudden remembrance of Taos and Looks Far with her fragrant, radiant hair, shining black with flecks of burnished rust under that high light of the far mountains.

"Will you be coming back to visit, Monsieur?" the maid asked at the front door.

"No, M'amselle. I have no need of coming back here again."

"Monsieur Paddock?" she said as he started out the door.

"Yes?"

"Angelique has only been like this for less than a year. Since last spring when he came and did this to her."

Paddock's eyes widened.

"W-who came? What do you mean?"

"Angelique told it was a big man who called himself Emile. He raped her twice—here in this house—while everyone else was gone."

"Emile? Emile Sharpe?"

"She said his name was Emile, Monsieur Paddock. That is all I know except that he raped her twice and told her in French that he was being paid handsomely to go to the mountains to kill a man. He said he wanted to see what made her so special that Henri had been killed because of her and that he was being paid to kill another."

"It was Emile Sharpe," Josiah whispered, his dark eyes staring into the distance. "I was the one he was sent to kill."

"You?" She clapped a hand to her mouth, astonished.

"Yes," he sighed. "And I killed Emile Sharpe. He will never bother her again."

She gazed now at the cold, lancing snow through the frost-brushed windowpanes on the door. "I am glad that you came to see her, Monsieur Paddock. Glad it was you who came to see how she is now. What is left of her is not the same woman you knew years ago. He killed her, that man. As surely as he had stabbed a knife into her heart, he killed her. He should have murdered her that day instead of leaving her like this. Nothing lives, tst-tst, inside her nothing lives any longer. It is a stinking, rotting shell of a person he left behind. But, so! It is good! You have killed the big one who took so much from her. I am glad you have killed him. Glad it was you who came to see her."

The maid reached out and quickly patted one of his arms.

"To know he is dead, Monsieur—after he left her an empty, rotting shell."

"No. No, M'amselle," he replied taking that last step toward the door. "That isn't just a—thing up those stairs. There's a person still alive, somewhere down inside her. I talked with her and know she heard me. Seems she just couldn't cope with the pain of it any more and drew back inside herself. Maybe she'll never come out. Maybe that's the way it was meant to turn out now. All I know is, there's a person alive in that room up there. That person is still the someone I knew a long, long time ago."

"Oui, Monsieur," she nodded. "Oui, merci."

As quickly as she had said it he was out on the wide porch, standing, staring at the cold, icy flakes knifing out of the sky like flat, cold darts. He tugged on his mittens and breathed deep of the purifying cold. He could have explained it differently to the maid, but it really did not matter now. After all was said and done, he had explained it the best he could to the one who mattered. He had told Angelique exactly what he had come so far to tell her. His sigh filled the air like a gauze tissue before his eyes.

He was done with pain for pain, hurt for hurt. His ghosts were buried and life awaited him anew. No matter what it held, he awaited it with a ravenous hunger.

At the wide porch steps the young trapper held a moment before plunging into the failing, gray light. Paddock turned to look at the house behind him one last time.

"Not a one of us can be a judge on what could have been, Angelique. I'm just gonna see to what will be."

Josiah Paddock stepped off the porch and slogged into the twilight as the snow turned to a cold, sad rain.

24 "YOU RECKON YOU'D ever head back here, son?"

Scratch had twisted in the saddle, his eyes brushing by Josiah as he gazed down the hill at the city nestled below them along the banks of the somber Mississippi.

Paddock sighed. "I can't really think of a thing that'd ever bring me back here, old man. I—I truly believe I can leave it all behind me now." He looked up at Bass. "Time was, back some three years ago, I ran away from that city down there, thinking I really was leaving it all behind. Now—" He paused. "Now, I think I can leave it all where it belongs—behind me. Exactly what I haven't been able to do since leaving St. Louis the first time."

Josiah raised his eyes from the gray, cottony smudge of morning fires lifting out of hundreds of chimneys as the town below them stirred for the day. His gaze shot west. Everything he had ever wanted awaited him out there.

"No, Scratch. I don't think I've got a single reason to come back here ever again. Everything's done that needed doing. Memories are all that's left here—everything else is dead. And, as for the living, that's waiting for me out west of here."

The young trapper turned to look again at his old partner. "You finally find Cooper, get that business settled with him after all these years—you think you'll wander back east this way again?"

"I reckon as I might, son," he nodded and smiled in the heavy, cold morning mist. "It ain't that I gotta come back—just that I might be wantin' to come back. Sometime."

"Your daughter?"

"Time will be that I'll come back to see her an' the family she's bound to have. Bounce some grandkids on my knee."

Suddenly the old trapper chuckled. "Will you listen to me. Here I am, I got Waits-by-the-Water back there to Taos, 'bout ready to shed herself of a pup, an' I'm already talkin' 'bout grand-pups around my knee."

"Ain't all that different, I suppose, Scratch."

"Maybeso you're right," he sighed. "Out there to the west, is where I gotta finish it all, or let it finish me. Ten years of waitin' to get paid for my first season in the far mountains. Ten years of waitin' for my beaver money. There's a nigger out there who's been owin' me for a long time. I'll find him for Bud an' Billy both.

320

Track Cooper down so I can finish it—that or leave my bones to bleach under the high sun."

"You think you won't come out on top when you run into this Cooper fella?"

"Sometimes, Josiah," he wagged his head, "it just don't matter all that much to me. Other times it matters so much I can taste it. Dyin' ain't so bad if you can die like a man out there under that big blue belt. But this ol' boy's got somethin' really special waitin' for him out there."

"Then why the hell're you talking this way about dying?"

"It ain't that I want to die, son," Bass answered with a sad grin. "It's just that I'm ready for whatever comes my way. If it's my day to die, so be it."

Paddock felt the cold chill shudder down his spine. At last he ripped his gaze from Scratch's milky-pale left eye, battered in the tavern brawl. He never liked it when Bass got spooky this way. "I'm still not so sure you oughta go on through with this, Scratch. From everything I heard down there in that town about this Cooper, I ain't at all positive you should go picking a ruckus with him. He ain't got a good bone in his body."

"Wanna break every one of 'em—be they bad or good," the old man scowled.

"Why you so all-fired—"

Josiah stopped suddenly. The look on the old man's face told him to shut up right then. He'd asked the question before, and for sure Josiah knew the answer why Bass had to see this through with Cooper. Most of the time, it didn't make much sense at all to Paddock, why a man would walk right into a nest of rattlers on purpose, armed only with a little stick to stir the damned things up. But every now and then, down inside the pit of his stomach, Josiah Paddock had the feeling he was beginning to understand the old man. Maybe because Josiah had begun to understand himself.

"I believe I'm ready to get on to this place they call Bents' Fort," Josiah grinned, trying to soften Scratch's stern look.

"Let's skedaddle, boy," Bass said with a nod. He put jabbing heels to his buffalo runner's ribs. Turning in the saddle to look behind him at the braying mule and their other three ponies, the old trapper whistled loud.

"C'mon, Zeke!"

"I still ain't figured out why you'd want to choose—"

"Sometimes, boy, you ask too damned many questions of this old man. Here, Zeke!"

The big gray dog came loping up, still favoring the hind leg that had been chewed up in the dog fight.

"Just don't figure you sometimes, old man," Josiah chuckled. "Here you are, barely able to travel your damned self, taking haul of a critter that ain't fit itself to travel out west. *Ezekiel*. My, my. What a handle to lay on some poor critter."

"Zeke's his name."

"I stand corrected. Zeke it shall be." Josiah watched Scratch tug on the lead stretching back to the young mule. "I just don't know about you, old man. Sometimes you pick up the damndest strays."

Scratch turned to gaze at his young partner. "How you think I run onto you a couple robe seasons back? Why, I was out lookin' for strays. And, son, you're the biggest dang one this nigger's ever took under his wing. You and that dog are just alike."

Paddock laughed. "Maybe you're right, old man. We've both found someone to mend us when we needed it most."

"That dog's gonna be happy when we get him out to the far mountains. A man needs a companion, son. Zeke an' Samantha will be awful good compañeros an' friends to me."

"What about me?" Josiah asked. "I'm your friend, your companion."

"You never know what might happen, Josiah Paddock," the old trapper finally answered, his words soft and sad. "Might come a day when you're not around any longer, son. Child like me needs companionship."

Josiah studied the eyes of his old friend, those eyes of his best friend. What he read in Scratch's face was that the old man knew about the choices Josiah Paddock had made. It appeared the old trapper knew just what the young man was going to do, and he had come to accept it, sad as it was— he had to accept it. Suddenly, Paddock understood just what Titus Bass was trying to tell him, in that peculiar way the old man tried to touch a thing first before really grabbing hold of it, rub a finger or two across a subject before really stirring it up. It was almost as if the old trapper tested things a time or two, exactly like a man would stick his toe in the water, testing the temperature before he would dive on in. Paddock had always thought it a strange quirk in the old man, just a crazy trait. But, right now as he saw the sad eyes drooping and wrinkled above his fortified attempt at a smile, Josiah knew there was no other way for the older trapper. Titus Bass had come to know, and in knowing, had come to understand and accept. He was trying in his own peculiar way to tell Josiah Paddock all was well in his decision.

Josiah knew right then that Scratch was telling him it just might be time to let him go. Sad as it was, there always comes a time to let go of what was and can no longer be. He knew the old man was teaching him that very thing: a most special gift, this lesson about life. Scratch was saying to Josiah that it was finally time for the young man to move on. Scratch was saying he had come to know, and had come to accept that this young partner no longer needed him.

Paddock swiped at a tear with his dirty wool mitten. Scratch sniffled and turned away to face the chill wind bearing out of the northwest.

"Cold, break-of-the-mornin' air out here sets a man's nose to run, don't it, son?"

"Yeah." Josiah's voice quivered. "Making my eyes water a bit." He looked ahead to the west. "Let's get on to Bents' Fort."

"When we get there, I'm doin' this on my own, you know."

"Nawww, I can't let you do that."

"You'd damned well better let me do just that, Mr. Paddock. I'm bound to do it on my own hook."

"Well, I'm riding along with you back to the mountains 'cause it's a long, lonely trail. You don't mind me needing your company, do you?"

Bass finally cracked a begrudging smile. "Nope, I don't think I mind at all, Josiah."

"Let's go to Bents' Fort, then." Josiah turned his head and looked into the brush. He whistled. "Here, Zeke! C'mon boy! We're heading back to the far, blue mountains."

OLD MAN THARP had played host to the pair of mountaineers for three more days while Bass nursed both the dog and himself back into some sort of health. Every morning the sprightly old livery owner would show up before first light at the barn, a canvas satchel slung at his side bulging full with foodstuffs Tharp claimed the Missus was only going to throw out to the pigs since it all was leftovers anyway. Bass had known right from the start just how much a transparent phony the old livery owner was. Hell, each day there was more food there in that oiled satchel than an old man and woman would eat in a week of Sundays. And every morning, every damned morning, it was embarrassing to see the spread Tharp laid out before the two buckskinned frontiersmen. That wasn't all, what with the way Emily Truesdale had come fluttering in with her basket of baked goods and treats the next morning after Scratch had delivered Amanda back to Miss Truesdale's house. The young girl had told her former employer all about the three boatmen who had come to take Titus Bass's life, and this after he already had been soundly railed the night before in a bloody fracas at the Rocky Mountain House. Emily had torn open the livery door and fluttered right in, yards of silk and layers of crinoline petticoats aswirl, stammering that she simply would not take "no" for an answer—the two mountaineers were coming with her back to her Supper Club straight-away, right where Titus Bass would finish his convalescence.

His what?

Emily had explained she wanted him to finish his healing in her house, where she could feed him, change the bandages, watch over the knots and bruises herself. With both Josiah and Tharp standing close by, all she would explain openly to the old trapper was that she wanted to repay Titus Bass for helping a young girl named Amanda, for helping that young girl get her life straightened out and on a different track.

No need to thank him, he had told Miss Truesdale.

Surely a man would do nothing less for his own kin, wouldn't he, he had asked.

Titus Bass remained steadfast in his desire to stay at the livery. Nowhere else did he wish to go while his wounds and pride healed, preparing himself for that trail back to the mountains. At last Emily accepted the fact she could not change his mind and gave up using her wiles. Scratch and Zeke would stay here with Samantha and his ponies. Finally Miss Truesdale admitted she understood his wanting to remain near the animals—that was simply the way of things with Titus Bass.

Over the next few days both Tharp and the pretty sporting house queen brought food and tended to the needs of the old mountaineer while Josiah paid his respects around St. Louis. Primary was a visit to his mother's grave. At the base of the carved marble stone he placed a lock of his own hair he hacked off with a knife and tied with a whang cut from legging fringe. There were no flowers he could leave her in this season. Besides, he reckoned leaving a piece of himself, the man he had become, was best of all.

The following day Josiah spent searching out Mordecai Thayer's family. Having located them at last south of town, Josiah gave most of the afternoon over to soothing their grief and pain at finally knowing of their son's death. Both of Mordecai's parents had in some way already come to accept their son's fate in the mountains. It had been three years since last they had heard from him. A part of each had admitted they would never see their boy again.

Paddock relayed every detail of their trail out west and how the two of them had survived into the winter before Mordecai had died. Every lasting detail he could recall—all but his friend's death—everything he could add to those already cherished memories the Thayers held close, until the sun finally nestled in the western quadrant and the sky was draining to purple.

That next morning broke clear and cold and ringing with sparkling winter hoarfrost. Josiah had scurried back to the chilly barn from his visit to the outhouse, surprised to find Adler and Old Jaune waiting politely, hats in hands, talking with the old mountaineer as Bass reclined on his straw pallet by the stalls.

Josef LeClerc's funeral was set for that afternoon, Paddock was informed. Old Jaune told the young trapper he thought it only fitting that Josiah should attend the burial. Even without asking for Jacques' or Philippe's permission, the old Negra had come to beg for Paddock's attendance. Old Jaune was sure the brothers would not truly mind. Hat crumpled in a sweating hand, feet shuffling in his nervousness and new at this sort of thing, the old thick lips trembling with his own private grief, the black servant told Josiah Paddock that most surely Josef LeClerc would have wanted it that way. Since the young American had been right there at the old man's side when LeClerc had passed on to everlasting life, Old Jaune was certain Josef would have wanted Josiah there when the old patriarch was laid to his final rest.

What had begun as a bright, cold, frosty morning later settled to a dreary, drizzly, freezing afternoon. Under a heavy, raw lead sky, the curtain-draped carriages pulled into the large, walled cemetery. Crows hunkered overhead in the bare skeleton fingers of tree branches as the black draped hearse creaked to a stop beside the LeClerc family plot.

Out of other gloomy carriages and traps emerged the wealthy and powerful French of St. Louis, all looking like so many tiny, black-backed beetles scurrying across the white snow beneath the ominous, unforgiving gray skies of late winter. Women with their black cloaked hoods pulled protectively round their white-powdered faces were accompanied by men wearing tall, beaver felt top hats shiny in the murky light, each and every face cut grave with grief and cold. Not a bereaving soul knew of that young American hidden back in the dark trees, watching from a distance, listening to the French priest's faraway incantations, his distant words nothing more than a confusing, faint babble.

That is, no one knew of Josiah Paddock except Old Jaune.

Josef LeClerc's personal servant stood stiff and uncomfortable beside the LeClerc sons, his eyes raking over the crowd from time to time, old eyes attempting to catch and hold Josiah Paddock's gaze some fifty yards away among the sleet-crusted oak and elm and hickory, trees which come spring would at last spread their leafy shade over this final resting spot for the French patriarch. Already there were five graves filled in the family plot, here surrounded with a four foot high iron fence. A wife, three stillborn, and Henri. This cold day's freshly turned soil would welcome Josef within its dark, rich bosom.

The black-cloaked beetles had skittered back to their shroud-draped, darkened carriages and promptly rumbled away on the gravel cemetery drive before Jacques and Philippe finally turned from the gravesite to leave in company with the priest. At last Abner and Old Jaune were the only mourners left, alone at the side of the grave with the squat undertaker and his grave diggers, all three of them leaning casually on their shovels some ten yards away, waiting to cast that dark soil down upon the polished wood box, waiting as patiently as if there were nothing better for a man to do on a freezing, sleety, winter's day.

After he had thrown a handful of the dark soil atop the mahogany box, Old Jaune arose again as erect as his stooped, aged frame would allow. When he turned back toward the trees where Josiah Paddock had been standing, the Negra was surprised to find that spot empty, the young American gone from the shelter of shadows and sleet. The old servant wheeled at the sudden sound of soft, sodden footsteps close at hand on the frozen ground. Abner's breath caught in his throat. Josiah pulled back the hood of his blue capote and stuck out his hand to the elder servant.

For a moment Old Jaune did not know what to do, nor at all what to say. No white man had ever before offered his white flesh freely to the old Negra. Only Josef Gabriel-Rene LeClerc had ever shaken his hand. And that act had always been in private, when they were no longer master and servant; when they were just what they had truly become at last—friends. Now this young American stranger was offering his hand. He stared down at Paddock's offer of reddening skin.

Josiah glanced a moment at his weathered, roughened hand growing raw in the freezing drizzle. "John," he sniffled. "John, I want to thank you deeply for asking me to come here this afternoon. Want to thank you personal."

Old Jaune was amazed. He had never been called a real name up to now. Always before it had been "nigger," or "boy" or some other term universally applied to every other slave he had known. He was already growing old when he had been given the name Jaune. But, never before had anyone called him a real name, even though it was the wrong name. Evidently, this American had heard Jaune and believed the Negra's name was John. The old servant smiled widely with his aged, yellowed teeth shining, that smile widening warmly as he finally took the offered hand.

"Thank ye, Mossa Paddock."

"No, John," Josiah replied. "Never have been a high-falutin' white man. Ain't likely to, neither. Don't go and call me Mr. Paddock. Please, just call me Josiah. I'd really like it if you'd call me Josiah."

"Josiah." The old Negra drew out the word, forming the syllables with his cold cracked lips and testing the word like it definitely was some new flavor across his old tongue.

"That's right. Josiah." He clamped the servant's hand a little harder before pulling his away. "Just Josiah."

Paddock next presented his raw hand to Abner. The young servant readily shook it and smiled in the failing light, nodding his head once in recognition before Josiah took his hand away and gazed back into Old Jaune's eyes.

"Sometimes," Josiah began, then cleared his charred throat in the frosty, winter-heavy air, "sometimes things ought'n been different somehow. I think that's why I feel so bad about Mr. LeClerc. Can't help but think if I'd done something different, things wouldn't've turned out the way they did. Keep telling myself not to reckon on the things that might have been, not to judge what should have been—"

"Things been differ'nt, J-Josiah," Old Jaune finally spoke again to fill that vacuum left open by the young American trapper, "you'd been kilt by them the Master hired on to do it. Things been differ'nt at all."

Josiah felt a cold shudder rise, then pass within him. "You're right. Had things been all that different, I'd be a dead man and not able to stand here right now talking with you the way I am, beside his grave. Maybe, most likely, I'd had myself no grave at all."

"Can't feel no sorrow 'bout it now."

"I—I do feel some, no matter what my head tells me—I do feel some sorrow," Paddock admitted. "Maybe if I'd gotten to know the man. Maybe if I'd come to him after killing Henri, I'd gotten to know who the man was."

"He's g-gone now, J-Josiah. Ain't gonna be troubled no more."

"I know, John. Trouble for me is, I was the one who caused him all his pain for the past three years. Me. I was the one."

"He forgive you."

"I k-know he did, there at the—the end."

"You forgive yourself. What you need to do, for full sure. Forgive yourself."

"I think that's just why I came here today. It—it's like the final healing of a deep wound that's been bleeding for all these years. I came here to see it finally healed over proper."

"Then it is over for you." Old Jaune showed some of his teeth at the corner of his gentle smile. "It's over and life go on. Master over with it too and he at rest. You be at rest with it now."

Black crows hulked against the gray light within the branches of the bare trees, watching the trio of men below them. The grave diggers shifted foot to foot impatiently a few yards away. Abner's eyes bounced up and down the tall American's frame.

At last, Josiah felt some welcome warmth wash over his face. "I believe I can be at rest with it now, at last."

Quickly he knelt and bare-handed scooped up some of that hard, dark soil clumped at the side of the yawning hole. It felt so cold in his hand, almost as cold as Josef LeClerc's hand had felt in his own that last night of the Frenchman's life. A hand so cold, so brittle, so tenuous— just like the soil that had opened up its arms to draw the old man in welcome to its bosom.

Josiah let the dirt tumble from his loose fingers, spilling it on the top of the carved mahogany box along with the brittle wreaths tossed there by family and wealthy friends.

Better this heady soil for a blanket. Keep a man warmer for all eternity. Much, much warmer for all of God's eternity.

And in tossing that soil on the box, Josiah felt all the closer to his belief in something to come when his own short life was through. He had wondered at his mother's funeral just what might lay beyond the grave. At last the trapper finally felt he could truly believe old man LeClerc had gone on to his peace and his rest. Just like Old Jaune had declared. Josef had gone on to be troubled no more. And Josiah felt the peace within himself that came in knowing.

This was not the end. Paddock took another handful of dirt and tossed it down onto the box. The graves, the boxes, the tearful services, they were all for the living, those who were left behind to cope with things, the day to day of life. Such ceremonies were only for those left behind, those to go on living, he decided. LeClerc was not really here. He had gone ahead, on into peace. And I can be at rest now.

I can be at rest. "Abner." Josiah turned and shook the young servant's hand a last time.

After he had shaken the older man's hand, Paddock nodded once. "I wish you well, John. I wish you both God's speed."

Paddock turned back into the failing, winter light, crunching away across the snow until his moccasined steps could be heard no longer. Both black men left standing at the graveside watched after him as the freezing laborers trudged through the gate in that iron fence raised round the family plot. They waited politely for Old Jaune to nod before their shovels lacerated the frozen pile of dark soil beside the hole. The dirt splashed across the mahogany box like water spilling on a floor, Old Jaune thought. Come full spring cleaning, we'll be down again on the floors, scrubbing at them, like nothing had changed.

The Negra smiled and looked back into the gray light, staring after the American disappearing among the stone markers and winter-gray trees at the far end of the cemetery.

Life went on. How many years had he been alive?

The old Negra could not reckon on it. That would take too much remembering now. If his old master and this young American had taught him anything that snowy night, up in a tiny, attic garret room, it was that life always rolls on. Often against our will—still life goes on. Josef LeClerc had wanted life to continue after he had passed over. Old Jaune understood. He smiled and wished the young man well. Life would go on, and above all, he wished the young American well.

"SURE would like to be heading out with you boys," old man Tharp said as he leaned against the livery door when the mountaineers had been preparing to leave in the blackness of pre-dawn.

"Just why don'cha?" Bass inquired with a wide grin, pulling hard at the rawhide straps lashing some possibles to the mule's pack saddle.

"Believe I could, boys. Believe I could at that."

"Nawww." Scratch turned and dusted his cold hands together. "You really couldn't, Amos. You got—got—"

"Responsibilities," Josiah filled in.

"Yep, you got a passel of responsibilities right here, ol' friend." He patted a hand on the old man's shoulder before pulling on a wool mitten.

"I've thought many a time about going out there to them spaces, out to all of that where you two are heading. Many a time," and with that he spat a big, brown glob onto the old snow at their feet.

"If'n you went with us now, just who would we have to come back to see when we come visitin' St. Lou?" Scratch waited a moment while Tharp mulled that one over. " 'Fraid we wouldn't have us no one to count on hereabouts. Nawww, Amos Tharp. We need to have you here, take care of us when next we ride on back here for a spell."

"When you figure on that—when it might be?" the livery owner scowled.

"Never know for sure," Scratch replied. "Man can never be certain on such a thing. Leastways a man such as me. Never know just what I'll be doin' from season to season, year to year."

"You've done us well while we were here." Paddock came up to stand with the two older men.

" 'Tain't a thing I done I wouldn't do for any of my friends." Tharp's frown would not go away, etching furrows on his brow.

"I'm glad to count you as one of mine," Josiah admitted with a wide smile. "Man finds out just how much he's worth when he goes to tallying up his friends. Real friends, that is. Not just the folks he knows, them as will step on by when times get lean. No, a man knows who his friends are when things really aren't all that good. And when a man wants to know just what he's worth, he can tally up his true friends—like you."

Paddock pushed a hand out of the end of his capote sleeve and shook with Tharp.

"We owe you anything more, ol' fella?" Scratch stepped up to present his bare hand.

"Nary a thing."

"Not for all that food you and your Missus couldn't eat while I was mendin' here in the barn?" Scratch grinned.

Tharp suddenly snapped his fingers and winked at the older trapper. "That reminds me, son."

He disappeared into the livery stable for a few minutes before returning with a canvas pouch about the size of a potato sack and stuffed full to the flap.

He presented it to the older trapper. "Here. The Missus says this is for your trip."

Bass took the satchel, feeling its heft. "Whoooeee! You tell the Missus, Missus Tharp, we do appreciate this kindness out of her hands. An' yours too. What all she put in here?" He sniffed deeply at the top of the sack gathered and tied with a piece of brown baling twine.

"Mess of ribs, a roast, some cakes and parched corn. A sweet or two, I imagine, if Martha packed this satchel," Amos replied, patting his own ample belly.

"Ribs?" Bass squinted. "You sayin' pork ribs?"

"My heavens, no." Tharp chuckled. "We know better than that by now, Mr. Bass. Martha wouldn't dare feed you on no pig."

"She understands I don't eat me no Ned."

"Those ribs'd be beef cow. We butcher least two a year. Feed off them two all year."

"I just cain't cotton to eatin' no Ned. Not a ham nor bacon, neither."

"Scratch. The man said it ain't pork." Josiah slapped him soundly between the shoulder blades. "Now, can we be going? I got a family waiting for me back to Taos."

"Here, son. You tie this on the lil' lady, Samantha there." Bass nodded toward the mule as he tossed the bulky satchel over to the young trapper.

"Well, my friend. Cain't begin to tell you what all I could say to a man what helped take such good care of me whilst I was mendin' up from my beatin'. You got me back on my feet. Oh, I'm still off my feed a mite, but I'm glad to say I'm patched up an' on my feet again." Scratch put a hand on Tharp's shoulder. "A farewell to you, friend."

"God's speed to you both, my good man. God's speed to you both out there."

Tharp watched Josiah, then Bass swing onto their cold leather saddles and snug their heavy coats about their legs.

"You'll both watch your hair in all that out there?"

"What ain't fallin' out—why, the rest's turnin' gray on me," Bass chuckled.

"I'm serious now," Tharp reprimanded. "I want to lay eyes on your face again here one day soon."

"You might come to see that very thing, Tharp." Bass grinned widely in the pale lamplight.

"So, now—you watch your hair out there in them mountains I heard so much about. Out there in them mountains."

"I've pertected my hair for better'n ten years now," Scratch nodded in reply. "I savvy I can watch over it for another ten years if need be."

"Part of me is going with you boys," Tharp admitted. Bass could hear the sentiment tugging at the old man's voicebox.

"An' I'll be proud to watch over that chunk of you what's going with us too."
Bass sawed the pony's reins and wheeled right.

"So long, friend!" Paddock yelled back as he kicked heels into the pony's flanks and burst ahead of the old trapper. He was anxious to get this return trip over and on with his life. Back to his family and that heady freedom at last, to begin all over again with a second chance at life and happiness.

"Take care of that old one, won't you, Josiah?"

"I'll do that for the cantankerous ol' bastard!"

"Now who you callin' a cantankerous ol' bastard?"

"Why, I ain't got the slightest notion what the hell business it is of yours —"

Tharp listened to those two deep voices cutting through the black and blue of pre-dawn light, the trappers wending their way down the frozen road and through the sleepy outskirts of town. They were fussing with one another, arguing over nothing at all, just the way friends would. Good friends. The best of friends. He was glad to have known them both. Titus Bass and Josiah Paddock.

Two mountaineers tramping back to those far, blue mountains of his dreams. Tharp yearned to go with them, but his bones told him no. He turned to look back at the light spreading from the two lanterns he had hung outside the livery while the frontiersmen readied their animals. Right here was where he belonged. Not all could fortify themselves for the far mountains. Amos Tharp merely did his small part to fortify those heading out. His own part to play, Amos decided. Though he yearned for those high and far places, Amos Tharp knew he would never be like Titus Bass or Josiah Paddock. Theirs was a special breed cut for a special place where few survived. Fire-hardened on the anvil of blistering heat and soul-numbing cold. Beaten and pounded under relentless watchfulness, forged by adversity and quenched in that joy of truly relying on no man— theirs was a breed of its own.

Hell, who really was to say Amos Tharp's role in the grand scheme of things wasn't all that important after all?

He spit into the snow once more and pulled down one of the lanterns. Amos snuffed it. After all, how many of them mountaineers had he outfitted and seen take off to the far places? Wasn't Amos Tharp always one to be counted on with a fresh wick for such men? He had truly helped many a man on his way west and the land of their far dreams.

He grabbed the second lantern and held it a moment, then turned to gaze in that direction where the sounds of horses' hoofs were faint and fading off in the heavy morning frost. These two trappers were something different than those others gone before them. There would be few like them two in those mountains out there. In fifty-two days they had crossed the great expanse of prairie in from Taos. And they had done that run right in the maw of winter to boot.

Amos Tharp wagged his head. No wonder young Josiah Paddock had wanted to know what day it would be with this rising of the sun. He was just the kind of fella to tally their days on the trail back. See if they couldn't set a faster pace for the return side of things. They'd hurry to get back home to them mountains,

Tharp figured. They'd hurry to get back home. After all, the weather should cooperate all the more now. They should have better conditions than they'd had coming east.

Those two homesick, hardened mountaineers would hurry back to the hearth of the Rockies.

25 THE MOURNING DOVE called out its three lonesome, blue-sky-clear notes from the snow-drenched hillside. *Oowheee- oooo-oooo.* In less than two full puffings of the moon these rolling timberlands would be alive with colorful buds that announced the coming of grapes, plums, persimmons, mulberries, pecans, and hackberries. Wildflowers would burst into spring bloom. A bewildering array of wildflowers—verbena, larkspur, lupine, indigo, and morning glories would carpet the ground, while down in the washes would sprout the fragrant hazel and wild roses. Soon enough all the patches of last year's grass would grow boggy and mossy with this year's new growth pushing up through last season's spongy carpet.

The wind sang its lilt across ruffled ponds where prairie chickens, grouse and ducks stirred and dreamt of spring warmth to come. As Bass and Paddock rode past with their pack of animals, the mallards rose with a familiar whir, then settled once more on the ruffled surface among little waves with ivory caps looking like so many tiny boats bobbing across the surface of these new prairie ponds. Golden plover began to stick its bright head through the receding snow here and there across the prairie, nourished rich by snowmelt and warm early spring sun, hearty enough to stay the cold late-winter nights. The eye danced with the choreography of it all on the open, awakening prairie, danced with a song of a rebeginning, now accompanied by the singing wind, rising and falling, a chorus full in their faces.

The two men had pushed beyond the Missouri River as it bent its way toward the frozen north. From there they headed west by southwest, retracing their inbound trail across familiar creeks and landmarks. The land was being reborn while man and animal scurried across its youthful face moistened by recent winter snows and heavy, early spring rains. Sweet yet hearty spring flowers dotted and colored the spreading green sward beneath the horses' hoofs. Still here in the long grass country, the frontiersmen camped beside lively brooks just freed from winter's icy hold and bubbling cheerfully once again over pebble-strewn beds. Around each night's camp rose the groves of blackjack and other varieties of oak, elm, hackberry, ash, and raspberry bushes. This eastern prairie land was country full in the promise of itself renewed.

"This mornin' I want you to get out your knife, Josiah." Bass spit a stream of brown juice into the snow-whipped grass. "Have to help me slice this venison as thin as your blade will let you."

"I've already had enough, old man." Paddock patted his belly and let out a sigh of contentment.

Scratch chuckled and waved the tip of his blade across the small fire they had built in the gray darkness of pre-dawn on the late winter prairie. "I ain't worried none 'bout your damned meat bag this mornin'. I'm worried 'bout our bellies come tonight an' the next night, an' the night after that."

"Just what are you fixing on doing?" Josiah sat upright from his old saddle and peered through the thin wisps of gray smoke rising out of the fire.

"We're back here smack-dab in Pawnee country, son," he growled as he laid out the venison on a section of the deer's green hide. "We'll stop awhile this evenin' for it to get full dark afore we push on through the night. This is the day we change time, Josiah. Go to travelin' in the night an' catchin' sleep hunkered down in a hollow place for the day time."

"Shit," Josiah muttered with a grin. "Just when I was beginning to believe we weren't going to be doing none of that nonsense this trip."

"Pawnee land. Ain't no nonsense to that fact." Bass set his knife to work paring thin slices of the lean, red meat which he hung on a framework of green willow branches over the cottony puffs rising from the fires.

"How much of this you gonna smoke?" Paddock inquired.

"We'll do it all. No tellin' when we'll get us 'nother chance to hunt over this next stretch of country, nor to have us a fire. Comin' east out to St. Louis weren't all so bad. What with it right into winter an' them Pawnee sonsabitches hunkered in close to their villages. Now with the prairies bloomin' we got to be extree careful. I don't figure on bein' guests for them niggers' dinner."

"Awright." Josiah chuckled. "I'll ride in the black of night with you and sleep under the bright sun every day if that'll make you happy, old man."

"Won't just make me happy, boy. I'd hate to think 'bout seein' that curly hair of your'n draped from some bald Pawnee's scalp pole."

"Bald? You mean they haven't got any hair?"

"Right, son." Bass slipped another thin slice of red meat onto the willow wand framework. "Most of them young bucks shave their heads. If they keep a little hair, it's a roach right on top, maybe a long tail comin' outta the back of their head."

"Old man, I believe I'd like to keep my hair so Looks Far can run her fingers through it, and lil' Joshua can tug on it at my shoulder—thank you."

The prairie sighed gently beneath a rich, purple sky shrugging itself with birds' songs and morning wind whispers in new leafed branches, rippling along a bubbly brook beside their camp. Radiant with rebirth, the first lip of the red sun crept above the eastern edge of the new world. Soon its saffron light would warm the land and their bones while they sliced and smoked, smoked and sliced some more through the long morning hours. Red to orange, orange to yellow, yellow on to late winter white, the sun climbed higher and higher until full at noon on its sky path by the time the travelers were finished in their jerking of trail meat.

Buffalo robe bedrolls, blankets, and Navajo rugs were lashed to pack animals and each man slid his weary, trail-hardened rump into a saddle. They turned their ponies' noses west for the last daytime ride they would have for a few weeks to come.

Bass and Paddock were leaving the land of the thick stands of trees and timber ringed meadows. Into the land of the uninterrupted prairie they forged, crossing the Little Arkansas and on to Cold Water Creek. They were entering a land where the rich, verdant growth sprouted only along the fringe of streams and river courses. That tall grass country left behind to the east, beneath the horses' hoofs now grew the hearty grama grass, a wiry species which seldom sprouted any taller than a couple of inches, yet bristled as thick in places as the hair on a blue tick hound's back.

Walnut Creek was reached near onto dusk and but half an hour later the Arkansas itself flowed beneath them. Given birth in streams fed by southern mountain snows, the Arkansas would take them almost due west toward the Rockies.

"We follow this river's trace now, Josiah," Bass announced. "It'll take us right on up to Bents' Fort."

"You gonna stop to eat now?"

"Hungry, son?" Bass grinned in the falling light. "We'll stop for a bit of supper when we reach them trees up yonder."

Here in the valley of the Arkansas River a traveler could look down from the heights above the river on an imposing yet picturesque landscape. Rippled and wavelike, the undulating yellow, sandy ridges bordered the water course and yawned away into the rolling hills of prairie beyond. Here the river itself could reach a width of a quarter mile, its lazy flow uninterrupted by the verdant islands dotted with cottonwood, their thick growth speckling the Arkansas on its lazy tumble to the sea. In some places the banks were low and monotonously barren except for an occasional stand of timber, mostly stunted trees which hid behind the sand hills of stretches of boggy swamp.

"We'll sit here in the hollow to wait till slap-dark comes over the land," Bass mumbled later as he chewed a piece of smoked venison. "Then we move on for the night travel. We'll keep the river to our left, just close enough to follow its course."

After the new, filling moon stuck its head above the eastern horizon, bathing the prairie in silver shine, the trappers nudged the ponies out of their cover of trees and penetrated the yawning loneliness of the night prairie.

"This child's glad Andy Jackson got hisself put back to the President for 'nother four years," Bass commented as they rode along.

Josiah snorted. "Never would've thought you was much a one for politics."

"I ain't, the clear truth be known. Leastways, I don't believe one man should be governin' over me, son." Scratch tugged at the coyote cap, snugging it down over his ears. His swollen, broken nose reddened with a raw, mean wind whipping face on. "That's one thing I enjoy 'bout this country out here where we're headin'. It ain't yet been spoilt by laws and sad, joyless politicians. It will be someday though, you mind my words, Josiah."

"I will, old friend," Josiah chuckled. "I'll remember you said that."

Four nights later the pair drew up on the Pawnee Fork, better than a quarter mile above where the stream emptied into the Arkansas River. Clumps of vegetation at the water's edge whirred with tiny, busy birds out gathering breakfast in the freezing dawn air. A small covey of quail burst up, exploding beneath the ponies' hoofs as the trappers led their weary animals within the circle of an oak-shaded depression near the stream's bed.

"This'll have to do," Bass declared wearily as he slid from his saddle.

"You damn betcha it'll have to do." Josiah plopped to the frozen ground. "I can't go another mile right now. Gotta get some sleep."

"Loose them cinches first, young'un." Bass threw his stirrup atop his saddle and unbuckled the wide, coarse-woven cinch before he pulled the saddle to the ground. "This here ground's stayin' harder. Must be gettin' colder the farther west we go."

"We're climbing, too," Paddock replied as he pulled his Santa Fe saddle from his pony and dragged it beneath some low branches where he would sleep out the day.

"More an' more sign ever' day, too." Bass chattered from the side of his mule. "Deer an' elk an' antelope, too. Grass's greenin' up for 'em early this year. Them critters know spring's right around the corner for 'em. They can feel it in their blood."

"And what I feel in my bones," Josiah sighed as he stretched out and pulled the robes over his aching body, "is my need for some sleep, old man."

"I'll be right there with you, son."

The moon gave out with a low yawn and slid beyond the long, yellow hills as the sun rose red in the eastern sky. Above them, blackbirds and crows squawked from the trees. A stiff, freezing wind cut through the budding brush and hacked at their bedding.

Keeeer-eer-eer-rr-r!

A hawk cried out as it circled above their hidden camp in search of food. Nearby, the ponies snuffled and whickered low, pawing at the earth. Bass fell asleep surrounded by the familiar sounds of the prairie wilderness awakening for the day.

Out of his dreams, a pony snorted. Bass came half awake and started to doze again. There was another sound that tugged at him and brought him out of the black pit of sleep. Eyes still closed, his pulse quickened as he tapped his fingers on his pistol, the rifles at his side.

Feigning sleep, the old trapper rolled over casually so that the robe and Navajo rug fell from his face, his ears uncovered. He waited long moments for the sound to stretch around him again and when it did, it came from a different direction.

For some reason, Bass didn't believe it was Pawnee. In fact, he didn't think it was Indians at all. Whoever was out there crawling around in the morning cold was not very good at keeping himself quiet. He listened hard and heard a whispered voice mumbling as it came closer.

Scratch sat up with a rifle in one hand, the pistol clamped in the other, as his robe and blankets slipped from his shoulders.

335

"You niggers best stay put!" he yelled.

Beside him, Josiah wrestled from the robes, a rifle filling each hand as he fought to untangle himself from the bedding.

"Stay put an' you won't get your arse shot!" the old trapper repeated.

Josiah glanced over at Bass, his eyes gummy with sleep and a puzzled frown on his face. Scratch nodded in the direction of the nearby bushes. Josiah looked that way, then turned slowly and scanned the area behind them. "I'd sure hate to let blood!" Bass hollered into the snowy bushes. "Less'n you come on out now, you give me no other choice."

He suddenly remembered the dog. He quickly turned his head from side to side, looking for the big gray animal.

"You seen the dog?" he whispered.

At the same moment he heard the animal growl and snarl, its throaty sounds coming from the bushes where Bass had heard the movement. The birds hard by stopped cawing and burst into the sky with a rush of air beneath their frightened flight.

Bass and Paddock ripped the robes off their legs and pressed their backs together so they could cover each other's flanks. The dog snarled and yipped, a muffled sound, as if he had a good grip on something.

Bass was suddenly afraid for Zeke's safety. He whistled to the animal. Still, it growled and snarled with the unknown enemy.

"Get 'im offa me!" someone cried from the bushes. "Pleeez, get him offa me! Lemme go, you devil critter!"

Bass saw the flash of movement in the bushes as snow fell from crashing branches. He sprang to his feet and advanced on the thrashing scene.

"Please, mister. Pull this critter offa me!"

Scratch parted the bramble branches with the muzzle of his rifle. Josiah was right behind him, facing the other direction, but glancing over his shoulder to see just what Bass had found in the bushes.

"Zeke, back off!" Bass ordered when he saw the dark-skinned man struggling to tug his torn shirt from the dog's jaws.

The big dog let go of the torn shirt, ripped across the shoulder near the wearer's ebony neck.

"I'll say—it's a Niggra," Paddock exclaimed with surprise.

Skin the color of polished black walnut, wide, white eyes shimmering in fear, rage, exasperation, the black man's yellowed teeth glittered every time his tongue would nervously dart in and out to lick his dry, winter-cracked lips. This newcomer shuddered in the heavy cold. That nappy stubble on his head was dirt crusted and flecked with dried leaves, broken twigs and bird down. It was plain to see his head had been shaved recently. Evident was the fact the young man had not cleaned himself in many long weeks. Already the tears were coursing down the dirt caked on his dark cheeks, causing muddy rivulets.

"Please don't k-kill me, mister," he sobbed and put his palms together. His gaze darted to the big gray dog, over to the muzzle of Scratch's gun, then to the old trapper's face. "I ain't d-done you no harm."

"J-just what the hell's a Negra like you doin' out here in this country?" Bass stammered.

"Damn, but if we didn't think you was a war party of Injuns." Josiah felt the tension drain out of his shoulders.

"Where you come from?" Bass got down on one knee to stare into the black man's face. "How you get here? Where's your—folks?"

"I ain't g-got no folks." The man licked his dry, thick lips. "You got anything to eat, mister? Been so long since last I et, tapeworm's hollerin' for feed."

"I asked you where you come from," Bass repeated.

"Awww, give 'im somethin' to eat now." Paddock reached inside his shooting pouch, then held out a small piece of smoked meat. "Here."

As quick as a crow would chase its shadow across the ground, the black hand swept across Josiah's and clutched at the piece of meat. It disappeared into his mouth just as quickly.

"Man appears to be genuine hungry," Josiah commented, staring at his empty hand.

"I wanna know where he comes from," Scratch pressed on. "Could be more of 'em."

"You want some more to eat?" Josiah urged.

"Y-yes, yes I do. Please." The black man licked at his fingers.

"You come along with us." Paddock wheeled and headed back toward their camp. "You tell my partner here all he wants to know—I'll get you all you want to eat."

The black man rose to his feet, dusted himself off as he kept a suspicious eye riveted on the big dog and the old trapper. "There ain't but me here-'bouts."

"You're alone out here, boy?" Bass squeaked in disbelief.

"Tha's right, mister. I alone. All alone—an' real hungry, too." With that he marched past the old trapper and the gray dog and followed Paddock.

The two trappers watched their visitor greedily devour a good store of their smoked venison and a gourd of creek water. All the while, Bass sat with his rifle at his side, Zeke's scabby, gray head in his lap. The stranger took a final gulp of water and set the gourd aside.

"You finished, eh?"

The newcomer looked up at Josiah and nodded with a toothy smile. "I do thank you—both of yous. I ain't et in so many days, I can't tell you to count."

"Where you hail from, son?" Titus asked as he scratched the dog's ears.

"Was in New Ahleans with the family, last real home I had."

"How come you got yourself in a fix way out here then?"

"No easy trick, that wuz'n." His yellowed teeth shone bright beneath the winter sun.

"I'm dyin' to hear the story, boy." Bass let his slitted gaze emphasize his demand. "What's your name?"

"Esau," he answered as he stared at the ground. "Esau's my name."

"Who you belong to, son?" The old man's tone was softer.

"Nobody now, mister. They all gone now." "Where'd they go, Esau?" Paddock inquired.

"The In-dee-yuns got 'em—c-cut 'em up an' b-burned 'em somethin' frightful," the black man blurted it out.

"Injuns? What Injuns?" Bass felt the shudder flash up his spine.

"I d-don't know one In-dee-yun from the next. I don't." His hands fluttered anxiously before him.

"Awright, awright." Bass cleared his throat and stared into the black man's eyes. "How your people get themselves outta New Orleans an' in such a fix with them Injuns?"

"New Ahleans where my master was set for tradin' up the Ark-saw." Esau bowed his head, pausing before he went on. "Him an' many other'n goin' up to trade an' meet the In-dee-yuns."

"You sure as sin met them, didn't you?" Josiah grumped.

"Of a rainy day they filled up both sides of the river, on the sandy banks. We had us no where to turn an' run. Then all them white fellas was beggin' to trade away they goods for they lives."

"But them Injuns just took both, didn't they?" Scratch asked.

"Both them goods an' the white folks' lives," Esau repeated.

"How come they didn't kill you, too?" Josiah asked.

"They took a shine to him, I'd imagine, son. His black skin an' all," Bass speculated. "They kept you around the village to diddle their squaws, didn't they?"

"I—I don't know—"

Scratch tapped a gnarled finger into Esau's chest. "They wanted you to bed down with their womenfolk, didn't they?" he smiled. "Bet they wanted your black blood in their tribal lines."

"Bed down with they women, yes," Esau nodded cautiously. "They kept me like a b-breeding stud, moving me from one place to 'nother place each day to be with another one until I finished all of them."

"When did you and the white folks get captured by the Injuns?" Paddock asked.

"It were back to late May when we started up the mouth of the Ark-saw, and they killed my master an' them white folks before the leaves turned in the trees."

Esau took another sip of water from the gourd. "That's when they took all my hair off'n my body."

"How'd they do that, boy? Esau?"

The black man turned to look at Bass. "They held me down an' pulled it right outta me—like you'd pluck a dead chicken for the fry pot. My head, too, sir."

"Name's Bass. Titus Bass. An' I think I know what Injuns you been diddlin' with since last summer."

"Who are they?" Paddock asked as he studied his partner's face.

"Who're we tryin' to stay hid from, boy?"

"Pawnee?" Josiah asked.

"P-Pawnee In-dee-yuns?" Esau's eyes owled wide in fear again.

"They wear hair in a strip right down the middle of their head, all hogged up

338

an' greased like this here?" Bass raked some fingers over the top of his skull to show his meaning.

"Y-yes, sir."

"Maybeso they wear a long black scalplock what might be the only thing hangin' from the back of their head here?" Bass patted the crown of his head.

"Yes, sir," the black man nodded once more.

"Pawnee, Josiah. It' gotta make some sense to you now, us travelin' at night through this stretch of country."

"Sleepin' out the day," Josiah added with a yawn. "What do you think, old man?"

"Where you goin', sors?" Esau asked.

Bass ignored the visitor. "I think a fella oughta get his sleep without somebody wakin' him up, eatin' his food, drinkin' up all his water. That's what I think, Josiah."

"Best we pile on back into them robes." Josiah dropped to his hands and knees and crawled over to his rumpled bedding.

Bass smacked the big dog on its rump and sent it scooting off toward his bedroll.

Within moments both men were tucked in. Esau sat alone, a bewildered look on his face. Finally he crabbed across the snow into the bullberry bushes on his hands and knees.

Scratch kept track of him, watching the intruder through squinted eyes until he spied Esau returning, still groping on hands and knees. This time Esau dragged beside him the tattered remnants of two blankets, both strong with the Indian odors of rancid grease and old fires. One appeared to be the remaining shred of a thick, Hudson's Bay Company blanket, now reduced to less than half its original size. The other was a tattered, coarse Navajo rug, muddied and pocked with several threadbare holes worn in it, each of its four sides unraveling. Both sorry remnants the middle-aged black man clutched against him as he came crawling through the thicket. At last he plopped himself down right between the two trappers, spreading the Navajo rug on the cold ground beside the dog. Zeke momentarily raised his head to study the black visitor, then once again dropped his chin on Scratch's shoulder.

Esau figured this would be the warmest place to sleep. Right here between the two white men, beside the big dog. Even if he didn't have much in the way of covering, at least the others' animal heat would surround him.

He pulled the wool blanket over him, tucking his long legs up against his abdomen so the old, thinning shroud would reach to cover his feet and shanks. Finally he let his head plop to the hard ground where he gave out a long, wearied sigh.

"How long since't you run away from the Pawnee camp?" Bass inquired.

"Four, no—five days now it's been."

"You sleep much since then?" Josiah asked.

"No, sor."

"Josiah's my name, Esau."

"No, J-Josiah. I ain't recollect that I have sleeped much since then. Just

339

runnin' an' walkin'. A bunch of hidin', too. I know they gonna be comin' after me."

"Not a bit of doubt about that, Esau," Scratch lamented.

"You've been awful lucky, Esau," Paddock added from the other side.

"I knows that, Josiah. I knows."

"Them blood-lovin' Pawnee don't count on luck to find you," Bass warned. "They don't stop lookin' till they get their bloody hands on you. Won't be a pretty sight when they catch up with you."

"I know, Mr. Bass."

"Call me Titus, please."

"Mr. Titus. I see'd what they do, so you ain't tellin' me nothin' new, Mr. Titus."

"I s'pose it won't be a pretty sight when they get a hold of us here in Pawnee country, will it now, Josiah?"

"I believe not, Scratch. But that's the chance a man takes to get on back to the mountains."

"Tha's just where I figured you two was lightin' out for," the black man grinned. "I was really hopin' you two was headin' back east where a man don't have to worry none 'bout no savage In-dee-yuns roastin' me for dinner."

"Just how you so sure we're headin' west?" Bass twisted around and propped himself up on one elbow.

"First I catched sight of you was yesterday evenin', when you set out from you day's sleep," Esau answered. "You was goin' toward the place the sun sinks down—an' that's always been west in this man's learnin'."

"You're pretty damned smart, ain't you?" Bass owned up.

"You don't talk like no field hand, neither," Paddock commented.

"Never licked or spit any field work after I turned twenty-four."

"How old you now, son?"

Esau glanced at Bass, running a tongue over his thick lips. "Seems to be I'm thirty-two now, Mr. Titus."

"You know books, reading, Esau?" Paddock asked.

"I know some book learnin'. My master had me teached some cipherin' after his Missus died in the cholera of '32 an' '33. Made Master come to depend on me all the more."

Bass cleared his throat. "So now you want to go out west, huh?"

"No, I don't, Mr. Titus. But, I s'pose it's as good a place as any. Ain't likely to make it back to the Mississippi River on my own."

Bass snorted. "I don't reckon you would, Esau."

"This poor soul," the slave commented, "he don't know what's a-waitin' for him out in all that open space out beyond—but, I'm bound to try. Onliest thing I can do is head that way with you two kind gent'mens."

"Now, who says you can—"

"I won't be no bother at all, Mr. Titus," Esau pleaded.

"Didn't ever figure on carryin' along no extra baggage this trip."

"I'll walk if you don't want me to ride one of them horses," Esau begged. "I keeped up close 'nough with you two yesterday night. On these tired ol' feet, too." He held up the tattered remains of ankle-high boots he had lashed around his feet with rawhide strips. Through some of the holes in the boots, Bass could see the swollen, bloodied feet.

"You figure to keep up with us all the way to the mountains on those?"

"I g-got to keep up with you, Mr. Titus," Esau whispered. "Or you two'll run off an' I be alone again with them savages after me. Don't ever wanna be that alone again. I ain't got much choice."

"Well, your feet ain't in no shape to walk much," Bass sighed, staring at the tattered feet at the end of the threadbare blanket.

"You can ride one of them pack animals, Esau." Paddock watched a smile spread across the black man's face.

"Looks like your feet'll fit into some spare moccasins of mine, boy," Bass added.

"I—I don't know how to thank you kind folks."

"What direction's that Pawnee camp you come out of, Esau?" Bass asked.

"Why, j-just north of here a ways."

"See, Josiah?" Scratch cheered as he turned to his young partner. "Esau's already payin' for his keep."

"I do believe he is, Scratch. I do believe he is at that." Paddock grinned in the frosty air.

"S-say I'm proud I'm help to you two fine men." Esau's teeth still chattered as he spoke.

"Yep, Esau," Bass began. "You keep with us, an' we'll all three see this through to the mountains."

"Y-yes, sir."

"You scared of somethin', Esau? Say—you ain't scared of Titus an' Josiah, are you now?"

"N-no, sir—Mr. Titus."

"You're cold, ain't you?" Paddock rose up on one elbow to ask. "You're just plain cold."

"N-no, Josiah. I'll be j-just fine here. Got me two blankets I stole't, k-keep me warm since I run out from the village. Two blank—"

"They won't keep you warm on that frozen ground." Josiah yanked off the huge Navajo rug from atop his robes. "Lay this down under you. Keep the ground cold from coming up into your bones. There. No—fold it over once so you got two layers. That's right—like that."

"You'll be wantin' this too, son." Bass had propped himself up and pulled at one of his full-size, thick wool blankets. "You roll yourself up like a caterpillar weavin' his fair cocoon. You'll get warm 'nough to get you some decent sleep."

Esau had himself bundled within the blankets and wrapped atop the rug in no time. Bass and Paddock winked at each other before letting their own heads plop back down into their warm buffalo robes. Even before the old trapper had himself snuggled down and comfortable once more, he heard unfamiliar snoring. He twisted around again to look over at Paddock. But Josiah wasn't wheezing. He was staring back at Bass.

"Esau ain't gonna have a bit of trouble gettin' himself to sleep, is he?" Bass whispered with a soft chuckle.

"Looks like the man's tired, Scratch."

"He ain't the only one, Josiah. He ain't the only one."

"Pretty plain that good fortune's smiling its sunshine on Esau too."

"How's that, son?"

"Him running onto us, out of all the prairie like that," Josiah yawned, exhausted. "What's maybe more important—Esau ran onto you, Titus Bass. That's his special good fortune."

"That's nothin' but pure-dee luck now."

"Not the way I figure it, Scratch. And you gotta remember, I oughta know 'cause I'm one of those lucky ones to run onto you, too."

"That's the way you savvy it, eh?"

"Exactly."

"Seems you like partin' with tall tales, wagged with a forked tongue, boy."

"Esau's got good fortune smiling on him now for a change."

"Way I see it, the man's already made a fair start on his own good luck, Josiah. I just might be one to say good fortune smiles on a man what goes out an' makes his own luck happen."

"I've seen it happen many times with you, old man. Titus Bass has forced Lady Luck to open her hand and deal square with him."

"Goodnight, Josiah."

"Esau's good luck just may rub off on you yet, Scratch."

"I said, goodnight."

"His good luck may rub off on you."

"I make my own luck, son. I make my own."

26 "HOW MANY OF them Pawnee are back there?" Josiah whispered as the old trapper crabbed back to the pair of men waiting in the brush-choked draw.

"Seems to be some half-dozen of 'em." Scratch settled down beside Esau with a grunt. "I savvy they was just out lookin' for Esau here—so they didn't send out a big war party."

"T-there's six of 'em after me?" Esau stammered.

"That's right," Josiah answered.

"Merciful Lord." Esau shuddered. "I know what them murderin' In-dee-yuns would do to me for runnin' away."

"Think what they'll do to us, they catch us with one of their prisoners." Scratch cocked back his coyote cap, turned his head and winked at Josiah.

Paddock saw the twinkle in the old man's eyes.

"You suppose, Scratch, them Pawnees would be willing to trade us for our lives?"

"Them blood-lovin' runagates?" Bass spit a brown splat into the snow. "Trade us for somethin' they want fearful bad? Nawww."

"You mean they wouldn't let the two of us go free, even if we gave 'em what they were looking for?"

"Well now, son," Scratch chewed on that, watching Esau from the corner of his eye. "You just might have you a real fine notion there."

"W-wait a minute—" Esau whined.

"Don't you think they'd appreciate having their property back?" Josiah fought the grin that threatened to spread across his face as he watched Esau's discomfort.

"You two aren't gonna turn me over to them Pawnees, are you?" Esau started to get up. "No, you can't!"

Scratch put a hand on the black man's shoulder and sat him back down. "You stay put. We ain't yet decided what to do with you, Esau."

"But you can't give me up to them murderers." Esau pleaded.

"Don't you think he'd fetch a pretty price from the Pawnee, Josiah?"

"I'm certain as rain, Scratch. The man's a fine specimen. Make those red niggers a good roast."

"If you two men won't he'p me, I gotta do on my own." Esau started to bolt, but the two trappers wrestled him back down to the snow covered ground in the bullberry bushes.

Bass smiled at Josiah. "You know, son, on second thought, Esau ain't the kind to make no man a good slave. Hell, I doubt he'd even make a good servant. He ain't got no manners, wantin' to leave this party right before it's fixin' to get started."

"Yeah," Paddock agreed. "I don't believe Esau's worth them Pawnees' trouble to take him back to their village to roast."

"W-what you two talkin' about?" Esau croaked.

"Think we owe it to them Pawnee to see they don't catch Esau?" Bass licked his tongue across his chapped lower lip, delighting in watching Esau squirm.

"I think so," Josiah agreed with a straight face. "You suppose he's anything of a shot with a gun?"

"Esau? Nawww," Bass replied. "I don't believe a man like him has ever been 'llowed to handle a gun, Josiah."

"I c-can shoot a g-gun," Esau stammered, his face full of hope.

"He says he can shoot, Titus. You think we oughta give him a try at it? Let him kill one of them red niggers who's fixing to kill him?"

"A perfect idea, Mr. Paddock. But, does he know how to reload a gun?"

"I learn't once, from my master," Esau beamed. "I s'pose I can remember."

"Supposing ain't good enough," Josiah said. "We need to know if you can reload for yourself."

"That's right, Esau," Bass nodded. "The boy here an' me — we'll ride on our own hook. That means you have to reload on your own."

"Tell us what you remember about reloading a gun, Esau," Paddock suggested. Esau explained the sequence of reloading a rifle as best as he remembered it. He got some of it wrong and had to be corrected, but soon enough he pantomimed with Josiah's powder horn and wiping stick.

"Where'll the Pawnee be?" Paddock asked as they rambled back to the ponies.

Bass gave Zeke a final scratch behind his torn ear and crawled atop leather. "I lost 'em a ways back when I cut down the draw. They'll be back on our trail soon enough, but I cain't say where them red niggers'll be when we come bustin' outta this wash."

"You gonna just ride right on up to 'em and ask for a dance?" Paddock took up his pony's reins.

Bass nodded. "Leg up, fellas. This bunch is fixin' to lay flat along the withers for a hard run."

"That the way you reckon to get through this?" Paddock scowled. His breath was like fine mist rising in the early morning air. Already the new day's crimson sun gave their words a pink glow like frosted sun.

"Half dozen of them Pawnee. They never was the best horse fighters." Bass spit brown juice into the old snow along the dry wash. "Best we go for a barehanded, straight up, ride through, son."

Josiah nodded reluctantly, then turned to the black man. "Esau, you just hang onto that horse for your life as we come busting outta this draw." "You don't want me to shoot the rifle?"

"Ever you shoot from horseback afore?" Scratch asked as he wheeled up beside him.

"No, I ain't."

"Then just hang onto them reins an' ride on through with us," Scratch demanded. "Josiah an' me—we'll do some shootin' if need be. You just suck in your guts an' gather your wind for a long run at 'em."

The old trapper looked down at his gray hound, tongue lolling happily. Zeke looked as if he was ready for this next spurt of activity. Bass gazed back at the former slave.

"Oh, Esau?"

"Yes, Titus?" Esau's hands clutched the reins so tightly his knuckles went pale around the cold rawhide.

"Can you yell, son?"

"I c-can yell," Esau nodded.

"Then I want you to holler as loud as you can when I tell you to—just like the Devil hisself was reachin' out of hell's acre to nab you."

Bass kicked his pony's flanks and the buffalo runner burst down the brush-choked wash. Behind him, Bass heard the pounding hoofs of their other horses. He figured Esau would be near the tail end of the pack string with Josiah. All the better. That way both of them could keep the pack animals tight and bunched when the time came for cutting through the Pawnee. All the better that way— Esau would not get separated from them. Tears were wind-whipped from the corners of his eyes by the stiff, cold daybreak breeze. As yet, the land had not had its chance to warm under the late winter sun, much less the air take on that high plains spring feel to it. The black man behind him along the packstring did have some grit. He might not rightly remember how to load a rifle, maybe he wasn't all that much of a shot even for a Negra— but, by God's blood, Esau did have him a lot of grit. The stupid son of a bitch was ready to take his chances tackling the winter prairie all over again on his own rather than become the main course for a Pawnee barbecue. Bass admired the black man for that very thing. Esau might have been a slave at one time, nothing more than some man's lowly piece of property—but now he was riding tall, square and clear-eyed into the jaws of death on a cold, Injun winter ride-through.

Scratch smiled as he made the last lunge up the side of the wash to break over the lip and onto the rolling prairie less than a mile from the Arkansas. It didn't really matter the color of a man's skin. Lots of white fellas out here in the west get themselves ring tailed into being just as much a slave to a fur company as Esau ever was a slave back in the settlements. Thing was, Esau was breaking free of all that. And most of them company trappers didn't have a solitary idea what else to do than slave away for and spend all their wages with the almighty company traders. Seemed their kind simply enjoyed getting honey-fuggled by the company booshways. Esau, whatever kind of man he turned out to be, was already a head up toward being a free man in every sense of the word.

Scratch saw the Pawnee about a quarter of a mile off to his left, down by the river and riding obliquely away from his small band. Again the old trapper was thankful to have Esau along on this cold-ass, bluster and bellow ride-through.

About the time Scratch had turned back to look ahead after seeing Josiah and their packstring clear the rim of the draw, he saw one of the Pawnee twist around. Frantically the warrior pointed and his mouth *o-ed* black and puckered as he hollered warning to his companions. Immediately the hunting party drew to a halt and all attention was riveted on the white men boiling across the prairie in their direction.

Scratch checked behind him one last time. Good. Esau was in the middle of the packstring, his pony rushed along with the speed of the others. Josiah was at the tail of the group, keeping the horses in a tight bunch. Perhaps the Pawnee would believe there were actually more than three men tearing their way. If Bass's group were lucky, the Pawnee would think the trappers' group had more than two cold white men and a frightened black slave in it.

Round and round the warriors milled for those long moments while Bass's party closed the gap on them. He had not figured on what the Indians would do for certain—just that he saw a chest-puffed ride-through as the only way to cut down the odds, and cause the Pawnee some confusion and a scare while they raced to narrow things down a bit. This was a better idea than making a run for it and being hounded by the warriors. The trapper animals might last longer than the Indian ponies, but he seriously doubted it. None of his horses had really regained a summer strength after that big pull east followed by a mere handful of days under Tharp's oats and care. No, he decided. A run to save their scalps was not the way. There'd be no guarantee at all with a run.

Laying in secret, hiding out—none of that appealed to him either. No telling how long they would have to wait until certain of escaping with their hair. Nothing guaranteed they'd hit plumb center on that, either. His group just might wait it out, then be discovered for all their trouble when they finally stuck their noses above ground. And they'd have to fight it out in the last account anyway.

No, this was better, he thought as the wind scoured the startled tears across his rawhide cheeks. His plan for a ride-through didn't waste any time at all. Take care of these brownskins who were out hunting for a black nigger, finish them off, then he could cock his tail high while skedaddling on outta Pawnee country. Besides, Titus Bass had an important errand to complete. Something crucial was waiting for him up the Arkansas River at Bents' Fort. Scratch had never been the kind of man to put off doing what had to be done.

One of the warriors raised an arm which held what appeared to be a rifle at the end of it. He could see the whole bunch of them tear off now, heading straight for the trappers. Scratch watched their mouths pucker and "*o-o-o-o*" as they hollered out their own death songs, perhaps their war songs for personal bravery. He'd had them confused and bewildered for a moment there, he had. These Pawnee had probably never seen a white man attack them before. Maybeso, these Injuns never before had a white man run face on into them for a knock down fight.

"Well, here's your first, you young bucks. Eat my Galena lead!"

The two groups were less than a hundred yards apart now. Bass twisted and craned to look behind him. Paddock still had the ponies bunched tight so that over the rolling prairie the bobbing horses and three men in the early sunrise shadows might give the illusion of being more like a half dozen horsemen on the charge. However, the Pawnee came at the trappers in their own tight bunch. Their feathers and fringe fluttered on the frosty dawn breeze. Cries of challenge and prayers for a proud warrior's death first tickled his ears now. He could hear their shouts and admonishments to one another.

At about the same moment a voice behind him began to holler. It was Josiah, no mistaking that, yelling and screaming at the top of his lungs. Just as quickly a second voice burst past him, hurtled toward the Pawnee warriors. This was a high-pitched wail, eerie and haunting—almost as if the black slave was echoing the Indians' own ululating battle cries. That spooky sound sent an involuntary shudder right up the old trapper's spine. He shivered with its icy touch at his back.

Sounded just like Esau was being chased by the old boy from hell his own self. Those huge red jaws snapping, bloodied claws scraping after his black hide. Esau could yell—that was certain. What a bone-chilling whoop the man could deliver. Its eerie cry would probably turn an enemy's blood cold.

Twenty yards and closing. Bass was glad the warriors were still bunched. Most of them wore feathers in their hair—proud young bucks that they were—the brown-splotched war eagle plumes fluttering out from the short, greased roaches splitting down the middle of their heads like the hogged mane of a mule, plastered erect and arrogant. What naked scalp remained on either side of the roach was smeared mosaic with paint like their faces. Some wore blankets, a couple had capotes and one warrior sported a heavy warshirt over which he had pulled a vest made of buffalo fur. From the looks of things most of them carried a bow and quiver strapped over one shoulder. The hunting party looked ready to tackle most anything they might encounter in tracking down a runaway black prisoner. Almost anything—but not a pack of wild wolf, winter-crazed, hell demons screaming at the top of their lungs as they rode smack into the hardened warriors.

Several of the young Pawnee tried to level and fire their old smoothbores across the closing gap. Scratch could hear the loud pops explode in the dry winter air, then watched the gray smoke blossom in the new light. Warriors never were all that accurate with the old weapons anyways. They just weren't consistent with the powder charges, not even patching those lead balls they drove down fouled barrels.

Most Injuns never learned to clean their weapons. Damned things seemed more a danger to them red niggers than they were a threat to a white man.

Just as quickly Bass was in the midst of the Pawnee. Behind him, he could hear the brass-lunged, high-pitched "screeehaw!" of his young mule as Samantha smacked into all the confusion. Around him swirled those painted, panic-tight faces, the eyes full of fear and hatred both. Scratch swung his muzzle down on the first warrior he approached and fired. The red blossom exploded across the Indian's chest, spilling life on his buffalo vest. The old trapper dropped the rawhide rein to give the Nez Perce runner its head through the thick of the battle. Bass whirled the huge rifle about in his hands, grasping the muzzle in two tight fists. Swung overhead, the sturdy weapon cracked into a second warrior as Bass shot through the Indian ranks.

347

That impact sent a shudder through the rifle, up his arms into his tired shoulders. Bass sped on across the prairie some twenty yards before he tapped the buffalo runner with his knees to slow up and cut back to its left. As he wheeled about for a second ride-through, the old trapper watched the rest of his pack string reach the painted warriors. Now the Pawnee were spread out, busted apart after the first white man had ridden point blank into their midst.

Josiah dropped one. Spilling backwards off the warrior's pony, the body tumbled heels over head into a skiff of old snow.

Bass couldn't see Esau. Maybe he had fallen, perhaps wounded, hit with a Pawnee ball. Right now Scratch wasn't sure of a damned thing as he tapped frantic heels against the pony's ribs to catapult him back into the fray. There was a mad surge of motion, a blur of activity swirling around the warriors. Pandemonium, the whinny cries of frightened ponies, shouts of pain and surprise from the lips of men, the skiffs of snow dust kicked up by the hoofs while gray-white blooms of burnt powder hung like death's twilight over the dawn battlefield.

The packstring burst through the Pawnee line, clattering dead straight for the old trapper, led snorting and nostrils flaring by the owl-eyed, young gray mule. Josiah had no time to reload. It was foolish, dangerous for a man to even consider wasting his effort on it. Whirling with his rifle in hand like a club, Paddock flailed away at two warriors on either side of him. One of the Pawnee brought his own smoothbore crashing down on the young trapper, smacking the iron barrel across Josiah's shoulder and the back of his neck. Things went gray for him and the sky filled with a dirty meteor shower of light fragments.

Bass remembered seeing Josiah jerk in pain before slumping sideways in his saddle, just about the time the gray dog flew out of the snow mist being stirred up. Suddenly Titus was yanked back into the thick of it with his pistol drawn. The warrior who had clubbed Josiah saw the old man coming. He opened his mouth to scream out his death song and put a brave look on his painted face. But it was too late. His black-splotched, grease-painted mask disappeared in a blazing corona of red as he tumbled to the ground. By then the second warrior attacking Josiah had jerked up a heavy, spiked warclub and was raising it over Josiah's head. Bass twirled in a tight circle and kicked his pony back to help his young partner. And just as quickly, Bass knew he would not get there in time to save Paddock's life. He was simply too far away to help.

Then as suddenly he saw that blur of shadow loom behind the tall Pawnee warrior. Esau's horse tore straight into the Indian's pony, ramming that warrior's animal on into Josiah's pony. The jolt caught the warrior by surprise. It was all he could do to say on top of his pony. Frantically he clutched at his animal's mane as the huge warclub spun from his grasp. In desperation Esau had clamped both arms around his own pony's neck, hanging on for his precious black life while he had spurred the animal right into the warrior.

Paddock waggled his head, trying it out. Everything was a crimson blur, ears maddened by the screeching and warcries ringing all about him. The young

348

trapper bolted upright and whirled just as a round bullet passed by, cutting through the arm and shoulder of his heavy wool coat. He felt the ball tear through the fabric and graze along the flesh across his back at the same time he heard a grunt from someone to his rear. His skin already on fire, Josiah kicked his pony savagely to set it in motion, driving straight toward the warrior who clutched a rifle still belching gray smoke from its muzzle.

In one liquid motion the huge blade was wrenched from the rawhide scabbard at his back and flung forward at the Pawnee as Josiah closed on the warrior. The massive blade struck the young Indian high in the ribs, right beneath his outstretched arm.

As if it had been nothing more than a wasp sting, the Indian glanced down at the blade for an instant, Paddock's knife protruding from his left side, gushing rose petals across his white capote. He looked up at the young trapper with huge, questioning eyes muling out of his yellow-painted face before slipping from the pony's back. Dead before he hit the snow.

Just as quickly the air was punched out of Paddock's lungs as he crumbled against the ground. Someone was on top of him as he rolled across the grass and snow. There flashed a glint of orange light streaking off the knife as he twirled and struggled to get himself on his knees. Pawnee hands tore at his long hair and lunged with the knife. Paddock jerked to the side as the knife slashed through his heavy blanket coat.

That was all the time he needed.

Josiah brought his leg up and sent a crashing blow into the warrior's groin. With a grunt of air rushing from the Pawnee's lungs, the Indian spilled forward, then collapsed to his knees. Both hands clutched at his breechclout in agony. Out of that snow at his feet the young trapper scooped up the Indian's blade. With one quick twist the sharp edge was heading in the right direction, behind it all Paddock's strength. The tip of the iron blade started on its path just as the warrior raised his face up to glare at the white man. It struck the Pawnee's collarbone and continued upward at an angle across the windpipe and jugular on the other side of his neck. Paddock watched the green and black painted face lose its sick glare, then twist in death panic. Crimson splashed from the raw fountain of his throat. The warrior fell backwards, that stench from his voiding bowels steaming free in the sub-zero air.

Across Paddock's right hand the Indian's warm blood was already thickening. Still the ooze seemed slick, making it difficult to hold onto the warrior's blade. Out of the corner of his eye, Josiah caught a flutter of mirrorlike motion as he watched a Pawnee rushing up behind him on foot, a huge tomahawk swung overhead.

A blur of shadow ripped out of the curtain of stirred-up snow, a gray shadow driving the warrior off balance and rolling him across the ground. The Pawnee came to his knees with Zeke clamped around his left forearm. The frantic warrior swung and swung and swung again with his arm, attempting to get free of the dog's grip. He found he could not shed himself of the wolflike dog, so the young Indian brought his other arm up above his head. In it flashed the tomahawk he would first use to kill the pugnacious dog, then he could split the young white man's skull. The wide, rusty blade began its descent toward the animal's head.

Paddock watched the warrior twitch spastically, then straighten. The Pawnee's hand fell open and the tomahawk spilled to the snow. The warrior swirled around slowly, his chest blown open with the exit of a huge lead ball fired at close range. His greased, black and red face stared almost impassively at Bass before the warrior collapsed open-eyed and nose down into the white-powdered grass. The young trapper's gaze climbed to focus on his old partner. Bass's rifle was still held at his hip where the muzzle curled lazy smoke into the freezing air.

Only then did Josiah finally scan to his left, then to his right. All about them the snowy, winter-cured grass was trampled and scuffed with hoofprints and those moccasin steps of battling humans. Dead bodies were strewn across the site, body heat escaping in that steam rising from their gaping wounds and their foul smelling bowel release. Death got uglier and uglier and uglier the more of it Paddock witnessed.

Suddenly the bile gathered at the back of his throat and gagged him as he collapsed over to his hands and knees. He was afraid his stomach was coming up so the young trapper drew in long, deep breaths of the shocking, cold air. Within moments his belly grew quieter. Then he remembered Esau.

Paddock gazed about him again and struggled to his feet. "W-where's Esau?"

Bass slid the rifle's butt to the snow and searched the blood-slicked scene. Hearing a groan behind him, near a clump of gray-backed bullberry, the old trapper tore off in that direction, Paddock shaky but close at his heels. The slave was just propping himself up on an elbow when the two trappers rounded some brush and spotted their fallen companion.

"He looks alive at least." Josiah was relieved. He sank to his knees beside the former slave.

"A mite lucky, too, it appears," Scratch added as he squatted down beside Esau.

"I see what you mean." Paddock saw the blood through the black man's thin coat sleeve.

Esau had watched the white trapper's eyes. He pulled aside the threadbare wool blanket he had cut a slit in so it could be worn like a Mexican poncho draped over his shoulders. Then he spotted the dark blood on his upper arm and immediately froze in terror.

"Dear Lord a'mighty! I'm a-dyin' right here," he screeched.

"Esau," Paddock shouted above the Negra's horrified wail. "It ain't a bullet hole. And you ain't dying. Just a little hide scraped off."

"W-wha's that you say?"

"He said you just got winged a bit. Nothin' to worry 'bout at all, son," Bass cooed. "We can get you all fixed up with some of my medicines an' a strip of this here blanket you're wearin'. Couple days go by, I dare say you won't even remember bein' plugged there 'cross your arm."

"You say I ain't gonna—die from it?" Esau's eyes widened as he looked from trapper to trapper.

"No, I don't believe you got a chance of passing on, Esau," Paddock grinned.

"What 'bout all the b-blood I'm losing?" The black man still screeched like a scalded cat.

"Shit." Bass rocked back on his heels and smiled. "That's no blood to worry 'bout, Esau. 'Sides, that booger'll freeze up quicker'n you can take a piss in a snowstorm."

"You sure 'bout that?"

"Certain as sun, my friend. Lookahere at Josiah." Scratch tugged at the bottom of Paddock's wool capote and exposed the small of the young trapper's back.

The black man craned his neck around to peer under the raised coat and buckskin warshirt. Paddock knew the raw flesh was terribly tender, remembering he had come so close to a painful gut wound—if the circumstances had been any different. If he had not been turning at that exact moment the warrior was firing his weapon—

Esau looked down at Josiah's bloodied, raw and torn flesh, all white and pink and laced crimson, oozing red free from its lower border in dribbles and drips. But he did not study Paddock's wound for long.

All the while Scratch watched Esau's wide eyes flicker, then roll backwards as his lids fluttered just like aspen leaves caught in a bracing autumn wind. Esau passed out cold as night.

Josiah leaned over him. "He all right?"

"Just sleepin' out this rough part of the trail, I s'pose," Bass grinned.

"You shouldn't have showed him that oozy wound of mine."

"Damn, Josiah. How am I ever gonna make a mountain man outta him if he takes a lil' nap ever' time I go to show him a piddly-ass bit of blood? Huh? Now you tell me how I'm gonna scrub all the green off the nigger here if he goes passing smooth away on me?"

"Y-you really think Titus Bass is gonna make a trapper outta Esau—Esau here?" Paddock could not believe it.

"Why—why sure, Josiah." He sounded convinced. "Lookahere what I made outta you, son."

"Outta me?"

"That's right. Made a mountain man outta you, didn't I?"

"Damn if that don't take the circle, old man. Just go get your medicines and you can have at us both here. I'm waiting right on this spot, Scratch. Ain't moving an inch while I wait for you. Besides, I gotta look after ol' Esau here since he's fainted dead away on us."

Paddock shook his head and grinned at his partner. "Sometimes, I'll swear there ain't another like you in all the known world, Titus Bass. M-make a mountain man outta Esau here? If that ain't a cork, I don't know what is. I do declare you got a real sense of humor."

"I mean it, son." Bass rose on his cold, cramped knees. "Esau's got the basic makin's of a fine trapper."

Josiah watched the old man hobble off a few steps. "Come to think of it, he did do exactly what you wanted him to do, didn't the boy?"

351

Scratch stopped and turned. "He did, that," and Bass nodded once.

"And he wasn't afraid of riding right down the throats of them red Injuns, was he?"

"Didn't look to be all that scared to have him a go at a bare-handed ride-through like we give them Pawnee."

"Esau screamed just like the Devil was on his tail, didn't he, Scratch?"

"He did so—an' a right scary hoo-doo holler it was to hear. Made the hairs on the back of my neck stand up an' quiver."

"M-maybe you're right after all, old man," Paddock finally admitted. "Maybe Titus Bass can make Esau into a mountain man."

"At least I know he's got a head start on Josiah Paddock." Scratch started to turn away once more.

"Now just how in hell you figure that?" the young trapper snapped with a scowl, supporting the slave's upper body against his own.

"Esau's got a head start on you for one reason alone, son. Simply 'cause he pays attention to the old man here. An', he does what he's told to do. Seems I remember Josiah Paddock being real contrariwise most all the time an' doin' whatever it was struck him to do—no matter what this old man here tried to teach him to do for the sake of savin' his very own hair."

Paddock glared at his partner for a moment, then got through with that first flush of anger. He pursed his lips and screwed up his face, contorting it with deep thought. Finally his wound began to hurt more than his pride now that the flush of battle-ready adrenalin was wearing off.

"Esau here has got a good head start on Josiah Paddock," the young trapper admitted. "And, he's gonna be all the better than me, or you, Scratch."

"Whoa! J-just how you savvy that, boy?"

"Simple enough, old man. Like adding one and one to make two, if you care to cipher it." Josiah grinned up at his partner.

"One an' one to make—"

"Esau's got both of us to teach him. That oughta mean he'll turn out twice as good as either one of us."

"T-that boy there?"

"Don't it make sense to a square thinkin' ol' coon such as yourself?"

"I-I-I cain't rightly think he or anybody ever gonna be as good as Titus Bass."

"Why not? You taught me, and you'll teach him. Right?"

"Wrong, son. That's where I gotcha. When it comes to learnin' how to be a mountain man, Titus Bass teaches you an' Esau ever'thing the both of you will ever know."

"See? Just like I told you." Paddock nodded quick in a self-assured way.

"Ho-hold on, son. I did say I'd teach the both of you ever'thing you two will ever know 'bout bein' a mountain man." He paused a moment before going on, wearing a smile growing wide and toothy across his winter-burned face. "But—I never said I'd ever teach either one of you ever'thing what I know."

Josiah watched the older man casually turn on his heel and disappear around the bullberry bushes. Damned if that old trapper weren't exasperating when he won an argument.

Paddock shook his head. Two men lucky now to have met up with Titus Bass. What with all that man knows about life in the far yonder and those big blue western mountains, it had to be Lady Luck smiling down on Josiah and Esau both that meant they had run on to Titus Bass.

"About damned time Lady Luck stopped being such a whore and acted like an angel. Right?"

27 A GREAT FLOCK of redwing blackbirds rose in a dark cloud from the trees a few yards ahead of them. Rust tinted females with cream colored undersides generously mixed in with the darker males showing off by fluffing up their red shoulders.

Over the next rise a cardinal sang out merrily, *With-with-with cheer.* Down the brush-lined draw a mourning dove answered a call of its own kind with the familiar *ooooah-koooo-kooo-koo,* then fluttered off as the riders marched past over the tossing, kneaded land. In wind and water-cut ravines, back in sun warmed pockets of delicate shade were sprouting blue flax and sour dock, firewheels and windflower along with the pretty buds of beardtongue and scarlet gilia, and the first yellow-green shoots of saxifrage.

The trio had passed the lower crossing of the Arkansas River, leaving behind country made familiar to Josiah on the journey east. From here on out it was territory new to Bass and Paddock both. Wide-eyed Esau owled at everything the land displayed as it fell away beneath the travelers, as here and there they scared up little bands of sand colored antelope, all heads cocked in one single direction only a fleeting moment before their white tails flagged and the herd set off over the knolls like so many small boats adrift in the swells of those waves cresting upon this inland sea.

Dawn and the sun oozed up red like a huge blood clot from a lung-shot bull elk. At the horizon low clouds gathered their billowy down in pink swales around the distant peaks like some fluffy comforter. Bass rose on an elbow and began hawking up great balls of night phlegm to clear his throat.

"You sure are noisy," the muffled voice of his young partner puffed out of its robe. "What the hell time is it, old man? Time for getting up already?"

"I figure so, Josiah," he answered and spit once more toward their firepit. "It's 'bout a half-dozen winks shy of bein' full sunup. Time to rouse Esau an' get on to them mountains."

Paddock rose to a sitting position, swiping at both weary eyes gummy with old sleep. There was a heavy dew beading their blankets, thick rugs and sleeping robes. Atop the black, nappy hair in the blankets beside him, hundreds of tiny drops sparkled in the newborn pink light, looking just like so many diamonds encrusted on the slave's head.

"We're getting close, ain't we, Scratch?"

Bass watched the younger man kick his way out of the blankets, then stand to pull aside his breechclout, aiming for the surrounding bushes.

"Yep. You saw 'em your own self yesterday. They looked 'sactly like nothin' more'n some tiny hills way out on the edge of the world off yonder." His arm and a finger bee-lined west. "Them little, teeny, blue mole hills out a'yonder."

"Kiowa country, you said?"

"Come through that a'ready. Arapaho an' Cheyenne now."

"Don't much matter does it?"

"Matter 'bout what?"

"Us sleepin' like normal folks again." His toe nudged the lifeless form sprawled at his feet. "Riding in the daytime and sleeping like real folks when the sun goes down." He tapped the black man a second urging.

"Uh-uhhh?"

"That's right, Esau. Time to get your ass outta them blankets—now." Paddock gave the ex-slave one last tap with his moccasined toe.

The slave sat bolt upright. "I'm ready. Let's get on today. Can't wait to get on to the Bented place you two keep jabberin' about."

"That's Bents' Fort, I keep tellin' you." Bass stuffed a brown chaw inside his cheek. "How many more times I gotta remind you, Esau?"

"That Bents' post sound like some fine place to me for us to be headin'. Let's get on with the gettin' for this mornin'."

Bass looked up at Josiah and shook his head with a grin. Paddock shrugged his shoulders and went back to rolling up his robes and blankets.

"He's a prime one, this Esau," Bass chuckled.

"How's that, Mr. Titus?"

"I was fixin' to tell Mr. Paddock here just how you was prime, Esau. You gonna let me have the chance to?"

"I will."

He eyed the black man rolling his blanket and two rugs so they could be thrown across the back of a pack animal. "You're just like me in a lotta ways, Mr. Esau." Then Bass watched Paddock turn from his packing with rapt attention. "Life is just a simple joy for you, ain't it?"

"That it is, Mr. Titus."

"I think you found a secret there, Esau. Once you accept the whole of things, life becomes simple, so full of joy."

Josiah turned to look square at the older trapper.

"That's right, son," Scratch answered and cracked a soft grin that told Paddock volumes. "I think you finally got it, too. I savvy that my young partner's finally got the secret to it all."

"T-took some time, that it did." Paddock nodded. "Figuring out that you just accept life on the whole, on its own terms—and then everything else just seems to fall into place after that."

"I don't have an idea what you two is talking about." The black man's head snapped from side to side as he followed the conversation bouncing from one trapper to the other.

"Esau," Scratch began, "let's just say you got things figured out long afore either of us had it sorted through. Seems like it'd be better for a man to let go of a lot holdin' him back just like you have. Let go an' let life roll on around him. If he works at takin' care of the small things—life'll just take care of the bigger things for him."

"I s'pose for a fact I ain't worried a bit about where to sleep or eat." Esau nodded his black head as he licked a chapped lower lip. "There'll always be somethin' to eat come my way. An' whenever I want to sleep, all I gotta do is lay down my head."

"Right on the mark. Seems you do enough of that, Esau." Paddock came up to slap the black man's shoulder.

"Boy here's got him no problem findin' a place to sleep, does he, Josiah?"

Paddock chuckled amiably. "No doubt about that."

"Life is purely simple, sors," Esau responded. "Eat when you wanna eat, sleep when you tired."

"See, Josiah?" Bass spit once into the dirty, melting snow at their feet. "I told you Esau had the makin's of a mountain man."

"Mountain man? Great life that is, eh? You eat only what you can find to eat," Josiah smiled broadly, his teeth gleaming in the early light, "and sleep where and when you're told to sleep. Some life of a mountain man, Scratch. Some life you'll train Esau to."

"W-why don't you just shut your yap an' plop your ass on leather, boy?" Bass scowled at his young partner. "This is the goddamndest thanks I get for watchin' over your purty hair for Looks Far an' Joshua."

Paddock couldn't help it. He had to grin. The old man looked so, so darn wounded. Josiah settled down onto the old Santa Fe saddle. "Damn, but you really get a mite testy when you don't get all your sleep, don't you?"

Scatch merely "hrruuumphed" and wheeled his buffalo runner toward the western light, pulling the young mule and a pony behind him. Dancing a frantic jig around his horse, Esau attempted to leap aboard twice before he finally made it to scamper off behind the graying trapper. Paddock merely shook his head and grinned before he tapped heels to his anxious pony's ribs.

"Maybe some folks just wasn't cut out for this mountain trapper's way of life," Paddock grumbled as he caught up with the older man later on. "Maybe me, maybe Esau. You ever think about that? You think Esau's not made for the life you are?"

Scratch turned and studied the young man beside him through long moments before his chiseled scowl softened and a corner of his mouth turned into a grin once more. "True fact, some folks ain't cut out for the life," he admitted. "Mayhaps I'm here to take care of them that's not made for it."

"Maybe I am cut for it." Josiah puffed out his chest a bit in false pride before he let the air out of his lungs. He knew better. "But, maybe Esau's not."

"By Jehoshaphat's blood!" Bass snorted. "What 'bout the way that boy lit into them Pawnee back yonder? How 'bout that? Esau's got him good makin's."

"T-that?" Josiah stammered in answer and question both. "Esau was just plain scared, Scratch. That's all. He rode right down into them 'cause he didn't have any better idea what to do. He couldn't say no to you—'cause you're his only way outta this bad stretch of territory and on to some settlement, someplace like Bents' Fort. He ain't about to turn you down on a thing you've already figured out and settled on for the three of us to do."

Bass dropped his eyes to the horizon in the west, the mountains showing off pink and purple with fluffy pompadours. He chewed and chewed and chewed on the words—still they tasted no better. "Y-you really think that's why he done it? 'Cause he was more scared of bein' alone out here in all this wilderness than he was of them Injuns?"

Josiah nodded twice, quickly. "I really think Esau was a lot more scared of you than he was of them Pawnee."

"Is that somethin' I should be proud of, son?"

"Most folks might not say so," Josiah smiled. "But, to me—to have someone more scared of you than a half-dozen Pawnee warriors, that's gotta be a mighty fine compliment."

"Man's gotta do what he's gotta do, Josiah. It's up to other folks to accept that, an' to understand the best they can. This ol' child just does his best, what he thinks is right."

"That old child's helped me keep my hair locked on this long," Paddock grinned, beaming at the older man.

"Red niggers an' white," Scratch replied with a nod of his own. "Most of the time the red ones ain't all that bothersome. It's them white ones I truly cain't savvy at times. Red ones you know for what they are. With a white man, why it's a shame you gotta wait to figure what he's about. Mayhaps by then you've got his knife stuck in your gullet."

"We got to watch out for Injuns around here, worry anymore?"

"Nawww." Scratch shook his head. "Look up there, son."

Bass pointed ahead of them to the west. In the shimmering, cornflower blue sky of late winter hung hundreds of tiny specks of black flotsam. The old man watched Josiah focus on the distance, then nod once before Scratch went on.

"Them is cow swallows, Josiah," he answered. "An' that's the surest sign there ain't no red niggers runnin' these parts. You savvy that? Them birds follow the buffalo herds, an' if the herd gets spooked 'cause some Injun is huntin' buffalo, the cow swallows don't act a bit like that at all. See them hangin' lazy up there, driftin' on the breezes just like a chunk of wood floatin' on the Yellowstone's current. Them birds is more scared of red niggers than Esau back there. Swallows'd be long gone from here if there was some brown-skinned hunters around."

"You mean to tell me in your roundabout way there's buffalo up there?" His voice rose a pitch with excitement.

"That's the short of it, Josiah."

"W-why I ain't had buffalo to eat since we left South Park last fall, old man." Paddock licked at his cold-cracked lips. "I do believe I could stuff some juicy buffalo down my paunch, Scratch."

"Your meat bag's hollerin' for some proper fodder, huh?"

357

Josiah chuckled in agreement. "Hump steaks'd make this boy's belly feel pretty damned good about now."

"I'm a-gonna fix me some boudins, Josiah. Some boudins for me an' Esau here."

"You wanna drop it—or can I?"

"Be my guest, son. You got the honor. Just, don't make it no bull. I want a cow."

"You won't catch me disagreeing with you on that, Scratch. Fat cow it is for camp."

"We'll get on up there, that rise over yonder—take us a look around an' see how the land lays for us. Figure out where the wind's from, then you can go on down to pick out a cow for us. I'll keep Esau with me and the stock up the rise in case the bunch of 'em busts loose after your shot, an' they start a run."

Overhead gray clouds with dark underbellies scudded past, racing across the sky faster than a man on horseback riding at full run to save his white hide from a war party of screeching, blood-crazed, scalp-hungry Indians. Damn, if it weren't just his luck to come upon some buffalo and need the meat, then here rumbles up a big prairie storm. Bass pressed his group to the top of the rise and peered down upon the blackened waves below them. The herd was in the middle of its casual migration north once again. Year after year the buffalo ate their way south for the hard prairie winter, then gobbled an ages-old path back to the north, dropping their young, strawberry brown calves as they moseyed across the disappearing chinook-eaten snows.

It was good. The wind was square in their faces. Most of the ponies pawed at the earth or stamped at the cold ground. And Zeke—young pup that he was— raced right around the horses yipping and howling in his excitement at seeing and sniffing the big dogs below them. Eyes wide with wonder, Esau's mouth was already drawn up in a pucker of astonishment.

"That down there's a sight a man will always carry with him—right to his grave, Esau." Bass took his eyes away from the black man to gaze at the herd once more. "A man cain't help but remember his first sight of a blood-wild buffler herd."

"Where's it end?" innocently he inquired in awe.

"Nowhere I can see right now." Paddock chimed in.

"There's no tellin' just how far that stretches to the north of here." Scratch threw an arm in that direction. His eyes scoured west over the tossing land. "Appears we got here about the right time, fellas. We come any sooner, there'd be but two choices for the three of us. We'd either have to head way south to get around the ass end of the herd—or, we could sit right down an' wait 'em out. But, now it seems we can get Josiah's huntin' done an' move right on around them hills over yonder, then cut back over west to scoot along the river again."

"Pray tell. What's the unlordly stink?" Esau's nose wrinkled up as he tested the air.

"You finally end up smellin' your own greasy hide?"

"No, Mr. Titus," the Negra guffawed quickly with the joke on him and flashed his teeth. "I thinks I know what that smells like. Them down there is some dirty, dirty, dirty creatures."

"A heap big stink, they call it." Scratch nodded once, staring into the midst of the roiling brown sea below them. "Them buffler are truly a dirty, dirty beast—that's for sure. An' he can be a dumb bastard, too. Most times a buffler don't know stink from catch'um."

That much was true, all of it—just what he was telling Esau about how dirty and stupid the buffalo was as a creature of God's free prairie. But, perhaps there was reason for the animal to be filthy and stupid both. With the coming spring these huge animals, male and female all, would tremble, their skin boiling beneath the annual itch. Against tree trunks and limbs, against huge rocks or down in self-made wallows scoured out of the prairie, the buffalo scratched and rubbed their coats, all the while attempting to shed their matted, scraggly hangings of dead hair. Off those mattings of hide and hair would come, all of it crawling with the beasts' insect vermin, caked over with layers of pale prairie mud and the ever-present scabs from previous brutal rubbings. A year's worth of the animal's sweat, cemented with the hair and hide in layers, also fell away in huge patches, which left the creature's skin almost naked and bleeding. They hardly looked like a creature any man in his right mind would desire to eat—what with their mange-eaten, shaggy hide ruffling in the strong, storm's-a-coming breezes.

"You picked some cow yet, Josiah?"

"I'll wander on down there a ways," he answered as he handed the pack string rope over to Esau. "Have me a look-see to decide what's for supper."

"Just find a cow down near the bottom of the hill, son," Bass advised paternally and let his nose rise into that strong wind blowing the clouds out of the northwest. "It don't appear we got all the time in the world right now."

"You never was afraid of a little rain before," Paddock commented before he turned back to watch the buffalo rambling below him. Then he nudged his pony forward into a walk.

"I've made my mistakes, Josiah," Scratch answered behind him. "This time I wanna have us a dry camp down to the river yonder. You hear this ol' man?"

"What's that?" Josiah hollered from down the hill.

"Let's fort up afore the danged storm rolls in, boy."

"I don't think he heard you, Mr. Titus," Esau finally admitted.

"I don't think so neither, son. Zeke! You pay attention to me!" Then he whistled to the dog. "You stay here!" And with that Bass shook his head, watching the young trapper mosey down toward the outer fringe of the black-brown herd. Zeke plopped down near Bass's buffalo runner, his own wet snout cocked into the air, testing it, tasting its excitement, tongue lolling, his muling eyes flicking from time to time up to his master in hopes Titus would recant and let him race down the hill with Josiah toward the buffalo.

Those bare and bleeding areas on the buffalo's hide would become a delicious magnet for the animals' vicious and blood-thirsty enemies. Small, terrifying, black clouds of them would descend over the herd. Santa Fe trail traders,

359

frontiersmen and mountain trappers alike, anyone who had crossed that great expanse of the plains had come to call this particular fly the "bulldog," simply because it would not easily give up its quest for blood until killed. Exactly like a huge tick, the bulldog was not done until it had drunk its fill of buffalo's blood, then finally fly off for a rest, gut filled red and drunk with its own satisfaction. When the biting flies took to the wing, only the huge, torpid ticks were left behind to feed on the poor prairie beasts. Ticks by the hundreds clung on one animal alone, all hanging with their heads buried deep in the hide. There they drank their fill and were borne about, drank some more and rode along north with the herd and their host. Ticks were gluttons, by the hundreds of them—so ravenous that a buffalo would be seen bleeding from tiny wounds punctured in the hide by the huge, spongy-soft prairie leeches. As if the bulldog and tick were not curse enough, still the poor bison would have to contend with mosquitoes, horseflies, fleas, and wood lice, all tormentors of the monstrous four-legged creatures navigating these inland seas.

Bass long ago had seen a poor old bull, quite like himself, standing draped by a cloud of insects hovering around him, his eyes and forelocks matted with the black specks, their tiny bodies crusted at the rims of the old bull's eyes where they had come to drink. Scratch's own skin of a sudden crawled with the thought of it—that dreadful itching. Thank goodness for the cow swallows. The old trapper's eyes studied those birds rising and falling over the herd. They would ride along on a buffalo's back, picking at the flies and ticks and vermin, their own appetite satisfaction assured only by staying with the herd. Here they could daily eat their fill of the host buffalos' enemies.

At times even a man needed his own cow swallow or magpie or crow to keep tormentors off his back. Even a man needed some help a'times.

He watched as Paddock grew smaller and smaller, his blue capote dipping in and out of the black brown mud of the shaggy beasts. Scratch had no idea why Josiah had wandered down into the midst of the grazing herd, except that it was a stupid choice for the young trapper to get in the smack-dab of them critters the way he was right now. A mite dangerous, too.

"What's he doin' now?" Esau inquired quietly.

"He's fixin' to get hisself turned to hoofjam, looks to me, Esau. Damn his stupid hide!"

"H-how's that?"

"Josiah's fixin' on gettin' hisself killed down there, an' there ain't a thing I can do but let him get on with it—damn him anyway!"

"He really gonna d-die, Mr. Titus?" There was a serious edge of apprehension registering in the voice. "Mr. Paddock gonna kill hisself?"

"I—I hope not." He flicked his eyes back over to Esau. "He's gotta watch just what he does now that he's down in the middle of the critters."

The cold, damp wind swept round the brow of the hill and raced through them. Bass shuddered with its foreboding. There was something faint and intangible, something more telling than the scents of rain and ozone carried on the breezes. He had never liked that tingle of apprehension being aggravated by the chill of a prophesying wind.

360

Beside him on the snowy hill, Zeke began to whimper, a mournful sound fraught with a primitive, animal fear.

If those buffalo down there begin to stampede, he thought, no telling what would happen, where they would end up. Herd this size gets its tail up and its head down, they'll run clear through to next week.

The freshening wind brought to his ears a rumble of thunder creeping out of the west. Bass turned his head just in time to catch a glimpse of the last streaks of lightning webbed off the dark horizon. A moment later and there roared another low blat of drums rolling toward them following a second shower of streaking light in the black purple sky. He wished all the more the young man would get his ass right on out of the herd and back to safety before the storm trampled over them—before there was a chance of the weather stampeding the animals all by itself, without any help from Josiah Paddock and his rifle.

Bass had watched the tribes in the northern mountains stampede the creatures, whooping and hollering all the way, into a river where the buffalo would drown themselves by the thousands in the frothy, muddied waters. Those in front were shoved forward and under the muddy waves by the snorting, frightened, bellowing masses plowing up from the prairie behind them. Most of the crazed creatures would attempt crossing on the floating bodies of those dead creatures gone before, only to succumb themselves and go under, never surfacing again until drowned, their own bodies now footing for those yet to come along. Still the tribesmen and their women brought up the rear of the bug-eyed, snorting herd, yelling and waving their blankets, driving the pitiful creatures to suicide at the river. Great gouts of water spouted up as the lungs of the buffalo exploded and filled with the muddy, spraying froth. Over and over the explosions sent fountains high into the air, spraying from bank to bank until the whole channel was eventually choked with their writhing bodies, the frothy brown river made black with their bobbing death. Even the children gave no quarter— pushing, yelling, scaring until the last frightened creature attempted crossing the spring-swollen river to safety and finally collapsed, down, down, his terrified bellow all but drowned in the boiling waters.

And then there was terror no more. Only joy at the river's edge while the Indians dove into the mounds of floating corpses, butchering away tongues and livers and intestines, some eaten raw on the spot with the relish of a successful hunt. Such a scene could be painted only by a madman: the black-brown bodies mingling together at the bank, black hulks beaching on the sand, perhaps still kicking in something only resembling a faint flicker of life and descended upon by the blood-lusted, yelling, shoving brown bodies of the tribespeople, hacking at their prey, blood dripping from hands and arms, down chests and out of mouths onto chattering chins until they too were at last satisfied it had been a good hunt. There in the cold, early spring air, with steam drifting free from thousands of sundered guts, opened and misting on frigid breezes, the primitve, hungry peoples warmed their hands over the butchering before slashing away once more at the monstrous piles of beached carcasses.

Could this land ever truly be his? Bass wondered on it as a huge drop of rain splatted against his cheek, then another atop his thigh, each about the size of a tobacco glob spit from his lips. Would he ever feel this land was truly his? Or, would it for all time belong to those copper-skinned creatures who followed the massive herds, who lived in an ancient harmony with their land and the creatures who wandered above? No, he shook his head. The Indian had already been forced out of things back east when elbow room got tight there many a year ago. White men would come to do the very same thing out here eventually, maybe another hundred years or so. Perhaps longer. Hell, it'd taken white folks least that long to crawl from the eastern seacoast to that eastern edge of the great plains. So it should take them every bit as long now to push on out here, cross over the mountains, on to the great western sea.

He still had time. That's all that really mattered. Him and his kind still had some time left to live out their dream—a free trapper's vision.

His was a dream of a time that would never be again.

Scratch swiped at the salty tear and flicked his eyes over at the black man. Esau remained intent upon the herd and Josiah. Worried about the youngster, no doubt.

A puff of smoke rose stiffly around that blue splotch almost lost amongst the black and brown of shaggy beasts. Then the roar of a muzzleloader reached their ears. Tails shot up and heads went down, snorting and screams filling the depressions and bouncing off the rolling hills. Another surprising crack of thunder, then a blinding flash burst up from the ground in a wide vee. The herd was off as if the ground itself had shrugged them loose.

"Damn you, Josiah Paddock!"

Scratch found himself yelling, standing up ramrod straight in the stirrups, shaking his tight fist at that carpet of black rumbling by his feet near the foot of the hill.

Zeke jerked up, his chin thrown back a-howl, with a wail of challenge sent at the leaden underbellies of the clouds. Down the slope he galloped toward the thundering bodies. It was only when Bass whistled a second time the dog turned and heeled back to the buffalo runner's side.

Esau's eyes muled wide in fear and question, twitching back and forth between Bass's fist-shaking, lip-foaming curses to that herd below them tearing off to the northeast.

"Can't we he'p 'im?" the Negra screamed his question above Scratch's frantic hollering.

"Not a thing we can do now, dammit!"

"He d-dead?"

Bass bit his lips, bit so hard he was sure he had drawn blood. He knew he had watched it with his own eyes.

"Damn," he choked the word out. "Most l-likely, son." Scratch shook his head, turning his face away with that sting of tears just freshening at his lids. "Ain't many a man gonna live to ride out of somethin' like that down there." His words whimpered away on the brutal wind.

Thunder cried out its own rolling chorus, blatting across the white prairie. Rain drops grew in size, pelting the two men and their animals on that low rise above the surging sea of black and brown bellowing below them. There was nowhere to go now, nowhere for the pair to escape the storm as it rumbled on over them. Bass tugged the sopping coyote cap more snugly on his head, pulled his elkhide coat about him and clung tightly to the mule's leadrope. The air was alive with water raging around them, swirling monstrous drops at man and beast like heavy, painful buckshot.

They'd just have to sit it out right here, on top of this endless prairie, watching the herd race north and east, watching all those hoofs pound what once was Josiah Paddock into nothing more than a greasy smudge on the snow-frosted plains.

He heard the black man sniffle beside him. And Bass turned away, almost shy and self-conscious for the man. It wasn't up to him to interrupt a man's sorrow. Even if it was a shared sorrow.

The storm passed quickly, yet with a sodden fury that bowled into them, blowing and raging, throwing water sideways at man and beast until they were left fairly soaked and shivering. Some twenty minutes later the black capped clouds finally scurried past, leaving behind only gray bellied thunderheads far, far overhead and with little prospect of more rain. The horses snorted and shuddered, shaking their drenched coats. Below the old trapper the last black stragglers were washing wavelike to the north, clearing the plain below them to make possible a search for Josiah's remains.

He had a sudden vision of Looks Far and Joshua. Bass wanted to take back to them something of Josiah Paddock's. There seemed to be no other choice but to find what was left of his young partner and take back a special memento to Taos. Simple enough—it seemed he'd have to settle his score alone with Cooper now for certain; that, and get back to Taos so he could explain Josiah's unnecessary death on the prairie to the young man's little family.

Yet, as far as his old eye could see across the kneaded, rolling swales of inland sea, Titus Bass could not spot a thing but that one dark lump of a fallen buffalo. Most likely the herd had pounded man and horse right into the ground, leaving nothing but an oily, crimson spot on the snowy mud. Or, perhaps, just maybe, there might still be a chance the young man would be alive. Could he afford to hope once more? Could he now, after all that hope he had already exhausted?

It took no prodding at all to have Esau move out behind him, pulling with him Josiah's pack horse. The black man urged his pony to bring him alongside the old trapper, mouth shut in unspoken agreement to Bass's own unspoken request for silence. Esau figured there really wasn't any need for frail words being uttered between them just yet. Not for a while anyway.

Scratch drew up beside the monstrous, jostled body of the young cow. Zeke sniffed and scampered around the corpse. Not too much the worse for wear considering a herd of buffalo had stampeded around her. By and large the other animals had given her huge, black body wide berth and not trampled her corpse.

If the herd had swerved around the bulk of the cow—perhaps they had steered clear of the young trapper's body. Could he hope against hope?

Tapping his heels along his pony's ribs, Titus loped off again at a fast walk behind the big gray dog, heading in the direction the herd had taken. From time to time he rose tall in the stirrups, eyes raking the prairie swells and waves for some sign of the retreating buffalo, for any sign of a man and his horse alone out there in all that emptiness ahead of him, an emptiness left all too silent in the herd's wake. Not a damned thing blotting the horizon or the snowy swales but an occasional scrubby plant, some scrawny bushes along a thready little stream. Nothing to give Bass a single, solitary clue as to what happened to Josiah Paddock. On he rode.

Suddenly he saw the animal—coming over the rise, off to his left and trotting toward him at any easy lope. Only the heartbreak was the pony carried no rider. Like a whimper gone quickly in the wind, Bass's hope was snuffed all the more swiftly.

With its spotted rump flagging across the darkening prairie, Josiah's pony trotted right up to their horses, with Zeke in tandem, and whinnied in greeting, knowing it was finally back among old friends. Reluctantly the aging trapper dropped from his saddle and hobbled across the rain-sodden ground to tie Paddock's lathered horse in line with the other one in Esau's charge. After spending a few mourning moments stroking the weary animal's neck and withers, Scratch loosened the cinch, straightened out the saddle on the pony's back and recinched it.

Back atop his own leather, Scratch allowed the animals to ease over the next series of low hills, his eyes squinting in that dull pain left behind and weeping now inside him, eyes scouring the prairie for some sign of Josiah's body. It seemed almost a certainty now. Finding a man's horse meant one thing and one thing only: its rider had been thrown. And he savvied the riderless horse meant Josiah was thrown during the stampede. Somewhere up ahead they would find that broken, splattered, trampled body of the young trapper—a foolish, stupid young man thrown from his pony in a buffalo stampede. Another chapter finished.

For better than an hour they had been slowly backtracking to the northeast now. Behind him the sun had but two hand widths before it fell beyond the earth's western rim. Then it would grow slap-dark, black as the inside of a Digger Indian's empty gut and they'd have to suspend their search until morning. Only a couple hours left to find the remains.

The old man's eyes squinted as he tried to blink away the stinging tears. Off to his left the horizon shimmered all white and gold with the burnished grass as the sun began to slip out of the dun colored underbellies of the clouds, spraying the landscape with fractured rays of gentle light. The glittering prairie colors made it hard for a man of his years to see clearly with the one eye left him, that left eye damaged and milky, not worth a tinker's damn any more. He cursed the barroom brawl beneath his breath—then choked on those words as the horizon fluttered before him.

Out of the shimmer of gold and saffron and blinding white flares rose something dark and wavy, indistinct and almost formless at first.

He was sure it would turn out to be the young man's pummelled body. Bass yawed the buffalo runner's reins to his left and cut hard for the object.

The shadow form's own blackness shuddered and wavered, the way an object would dance on the horizon with heat ripples shimmering around it. Nothing at

364

all now like a mirage. The black form seemed to grow, sprouting itself out of the bushes, taller—then taller still. Finally, it was waving to him, signalling. With the arm of a man. And, not just any man. *Damn!*

God, but it—damn! If that didn't look like Josiah Paddock!

The gray hound twisted his head round to flick eyes up at the old trapper, as if asking permission, as if expressing its own hope. Scratch threw his arm across the prairie and the dog burst off with a howl at a ground-eating gallop, hard and straight toward the shadow on the hill.

Waving with both arms to beat hell, his rifle held high in one, his mouth o'ed up and hollering back at Bass and Esau, Josiah screamed with joy and relief. He was dancing atop his little knoll, whirling a delirious jig, full of frantic happiness in being found.

He'd be damned, but Scratch couldn't hear Josiah's voice from this far off across the prairie, he could only watch the young man's mouth open and close, open and close. Then again, maybe he couldn't hear young Josiah because Esau was hollering, even louder than he had yelled while riding into the bloody maw of those hate-painted Pawnee warriors. Damn, but if that black man wasn't yelling louder than he had facing the hoary, copper-skinned countenance of death.

Maybe Bass couldn't hear Josiah Paddock simply because he was hollering so damned loudly himself. There he was.

Josiah Paddock.

And he was alive! Damn, but he was alive.

Simple enough, Bass couldn't hear the young trapper's voice because he was hollering so damned loudly himself right back at Josiah Paddock. Tears streaming and whipping. There he was! Standing in one piece, looking like he'd just sprouted up right out of the prairie, old gray Zeke whirling and leaping around him like it was the happiest discovery the dog had ever made.

Damn, but if it weren't him. Josiah Paddock. And he was alive. Glory, but he was alive!

28

IT WAS JUST like forever.

Bass had felt as if it took an eternity to find his young partner. And when Josiah had been found alive and none the worse for wear, the long hours of dread and waiting suddenly became all the more crushing to his soul. The old trapper had wondered if he should care for any man, care for any friend, the way he cared for Josiah Paddock. He had wondered there for a moment if any other man had ever felt for a friend what he felt for his young partner.

Without a word Titus dropped out of the saddle on a dead run, his pony's hoofs kicking up snow in a cascading shower around the men as it haunch-slid for a stop. He dashed the last few yards on foot, crunching into Paddock, locking his arms about the young man, crushing him with a grizzly hug. Tears streamed down his old, leathery cheeks, sun-burnished beneath the intense winter sky that at times in spring could be just like a mirror over the gleaming, hard white landscape.

Josiah drew back, startled and bewildered with the old man's tears, dismayed by that sobbing as Titus clung to him desperately. Scratch never said a word; he only stared and blubbered and embraced, finally letting Josiah go when Esau drew near to shake Paddock's hand and welcome him back to the fold. Somewhere near the base of his spine Josiah could not shake the feeling that he had been away on a long, long journey—and now his old friend was welcoming him back home again. Strange to feel that way, having been gone but a couple of hours at the most, only a spatter of time spent wandering south and west across the open prairie, knowing he would eventually catch up with Esau and the old man.

Like coming home again.

Silent still, Scratch crawled back atop his buffalo runner and headed out, backtracking to the south again. From time to time he turned round in the saddle to peer at Paddock, and then crack a quick smile for him.

At last the horizon spat up the carcass of the buffalo cow. In circling the body, it appeared the animal had pitched head first after Josiah had shot her. As she had gone down, the cow vaulted heels over head several times across the hoof-beaten snow until she finally landed on her side, head akilter atop a broken neck and tongue lolling out of her mouth. Oozy blood had frozen in a crimson icicle dripping off her lower lip. Esau shook his head and refused at first to dismount—simply scared out of his life's wits once again.

"C'mon down now," Josiah coaxed, tapping the big cow with the toe of a moccasin.

"It cain't hurt you none, Esau."

His wide eyes muled back at Scratch, full of fear and disbelief.

"I ain't all that certain about that, Mr. T-titus," his voice quivered. From where he sat, the buffalo looked all the more monstrous than he had ever imagined they could be. This close, smelling the damp, musky wool, the odors of death and blood all hanging about them, Esau remained totally transfixed as the white men began their incisions.

"I think this Negra man got as close to it as he wanna get," the slave replied a bit later as blood seeped before it eventually oozed and froze solid.

Esau watched in fascination at the process. Always before the hunters had taken smaller game—perhaps a deer, maybe an elk, occasionally antelope. Nothing ever this massive. He had never before been so close to an animal so huge, its monstrous head appearing to take up a full third of its body.

Nothing short of pure amazement was registered on his ebony face, studying the process beginning with slicing a transverse cut in front of the shoulder right at the nape of the creature's neck. Scratch next gathered the hair of the boss or hump and gradually pulled back as he sliced down along the backbone. Exposed at first was the buffalo's hump itself, replete with the rich ribs so highly regarded by the plains traveler. Continuing his incision down the backbone, the old trapper cut free half the hide and stretched it flat on the ground as it was skinned all the way down to the brisket. On it he began to place the choice portions they would take with them. His knife held along his index finger, Scratch removed long hunks of the white fleece lying tucked just beneath the skin, the fleece the cow's inner, winter insulation. Next the humpribs were separated from the carcass, using a tomahawk, and tossed onto the green hide beside him. Then chosen were some roasts and steaks, along with the animal's monstrous liver and a long section of intestine. Josiah finally dropped the tongue into the pile of their choicest pieces after he threw Zeke another meaty rib to worry at while they were butchering the cow.

After that the old trapper took his bloodied hands and pushed up his sleeves before kneeling beside the carcass a last time. He hacked and he sliced and cursed, his hunkered form obscuring just what it was he was intent upon. But at last he moved back and yanked on something, moved back a bit more and yanked again. Over and over he grabbed hold of some object and dragged it inches by inches away from the cow's carcass.

"You ain't thirsty, are you, boy?" At last Scratch scowled a bloody look Esau's way.

"W-why now, Mr. Titus." Esau glared down at the slimy object lying by the old trapper's feet. "I-I ain't t-thirsty at all."

Bass knelt beside the organ, its huge, oozy mass almost two feet in diameter. He pricked it with the tip of his knife, making a small incision that allowed the flesh to open up only slightly, revealing the contents.

"It ain't all that bad, Esau. For any man what's truly thirsty."

"W-what is that?" he asked dolefully, his nose wrinkled.

"This critter's paunch, son."

"The stomach, Esau," Paddock explained as he slapped him on the shoulder. "Its stomach?" He rubbed his own in mime. "Where the food go it eats?"

"That's right, Esau!" Scratch complimented. " 'Sactly."

With a bare forearm the old trapper plunged his bloody hand into the stomach, swishing around in its contents, his fingers feeling around inside that paunch, his face staring off with only a disconcerted look into the distance. Finally Titus discovered just what he'd been looking for. That thick fluid dripping from his arm began to freeze just as quickly as his skin was removed from the stomach. In his hand was held that object of his search—a crude ball of hair almost big enough to fill his palm.

"Now what the hell is that, old man?" Paddock leaned over the gut-smelly hair ball and studied it a moment.

"Just what it looks to be, son," he answered.

"Looks hairy."

"Right. 'Cause that's what it is. A buffler hair ball."

"What'd you want with such a thing?"

"Keep it."

"Why would a fella want to keep such an awful, slimy mess?"

"Medicine."

"Ahhh, yes. Medicine." Paddock nodded, as if the word explained everything, although he knew little more than when their conversation began.

"You still don't really understand, do you, Josiah?" Bass watched his young partner shake his head.

Esau finally slipped down from his horse's back and cautiously approached the butchering.

"What you think of that critter, Esau?"

The black man peered deliberately at the hair ball in Bass's dripping, freezing, slimy hand. "Whatever it be, it shore do smell somethin' fierce."

"I'll agree with you there, Esau," Josiah chuckled and gazed at Bass. "Why the hell do you want such a thing, really now?"

Bass looked away from Paddock and stared at the hair ball in his right palm. "Medicine. Simple as that. Injuns say it's a help to any aches an' pains of an old man's joints. Been some time since last I had one all this big. Most of 'em just tiny lil' balls. You can find 'em in deer, elk too. But, I kept lookin' for a big one like this. It'll work wonders on my tired joints an' bones. You just wait to see."

This buffalo cow had spent her few years on earth licking her coarse tongue across her coat, cleaning not only her own hide, but also those young calves she had given birth to each and every spring. What hair had not worked itself on through the digestive process had been caught and trapped, gradually working itself into something resembling a ball as it was tumbled around in the cow's belly. Among the tribes of the plains and mountains, such a hair ball from the stomach of a buffalo was considered to carry great medicinal value.

"You'll keep it to cure all your aches, huh?" Josiah asked doubtfully.

He gazed up at Paddock and smiled. "That, an' anybody else what needs it too."

"I'm ready to pack this meat and find us a place to make camp for the night." Josiah at last gazed to the west where the sun was quickly slipping down the westerly quadrant. "I'm tired."

"What you got to be tired for?"

"Say, old man—don't you remember who did all that walking today?"

"Josiah, you just oughta be a mite more thankful you had all that walkin' to do. Things been differ'nt for you, there'd be no more walkin' at all."

"I catch your drift the first pass," Josiah snorted and cracked half a grin. "Let's pack up to move toward camp."

"First—" Bass knelt by the cow one last time, slicing a square piece of hide loose. "I need me somethin' to keep the hair ball in for a while." After a thin, green string had been sliced from the soft skin, Scratch wrapped the ball within the square of green hide. The top was secured with the narrow thong and the small pouch was finally suspended from the back of his saddle by a strip of latigo.

Back to the fringe of trees and brush along the Arkansas he took his friends to set up camp. The sun had tilted off on a slide into the west and already a pale rind of moon was crawling over the silver land by the time the trio had a fire cheerfully popping in their little circle, strips of lean, red flesh sliding past greasy lips and down hungry gullets. The heady fragrances of rich, juicy meat mingled with the comforting crackle of limbs snapping with the odors of buffalo fat and fleece in a cozy, warm corona amid the cold prairie twilight. Soon the frosty stars popped their heads out like so many prairie dogs peeking out of their holes across the flat tableland of the plains.

Esau was working hard on the ribs, his teeth ripping strip after strip of the rich meat from the huge bones. Meanwhile Bass had sampled a little of everything and had settled back to top his own meal off by lapping up chunks of buffalo gut. The old trapper cut off sections of the raw intestine, then drew each section between his clamped fingers to squeeze out as much of the undigested grass as possible before searing the gut over a kiss of flame and stuffing the dripping chunk in his mouth, swallowing without much mastication at all.

Zeke sat at Esau's side, right where the gray dog was assured of getting the pink ribs after they were picked over and set aside for him. Time was, Esau would have fought the animal tooth and nail for just such a discarded treat. But now he felt rich enough to share all his meaty wealth with Zeke. Right at this moment the dog knew just who his best friend was in the whole world. Tonight the black man and the mongrel cur feasted together as they had but few times in their lives.

Behind Esau in the purple light rose the cry of a coyote. Soon another took up the chorus out on the rolling prairieland. Those mournful bays brought the black cold of night a bit closer to their little campfire.

For long minutes Esau's attention was riveted on the open plains beyond their little halo of light. He seemed to stare off at almost nothing at all—until he set his unfinished ribs aside and appeared to want no more.

"What month is this, Mr. Titus?" His wide eyes glowed a dull yellow in the dancing light of their small fire.

"Why, I reckon its near the end of the *Sore-Eye Moon*."

"What's that mean—this *Sore-Eye Moon?*"

"Injuns keep track of time with the moon only. They ain't got 'em any clocks, or wrote down calendars, Esau. So that's why each and every month has its own name and has it something special that'll happen while the moon grows to full before getting old and fading away."

"No, not that, Mr. Titus." The black man shook his head seriously. "What's this Sore-Eye mean?"

"Ahhh, that's what you're after is it? I see now," Scratch nodded, wiping his greasy fingers on his beard. "You see, this time of year in the west, here on the prairie an' in them blue mountains not all too far off, the sun burns real bright down across the snow. Frightful it can be, sun's so bright. What it does to a man, an' his beasts too, is make 'em blind from all that bright, glory light. If it don't make 'em blind—an' they keep their eyes squinted up like this here," he uttered as he demonstrated for Esau with tight, slitted eyelids, "then the poor devil might only get sore eyes. So snowblind he'll be after a few days of that bright light bouncin' off the snow."

"Just what month is this *Sore-Eye Moon* to you white folks?"

"D-don't ask me, son." Scratch up and waved a palm in protest. "I ain't a white man—not a true white man—any more. You best ask Josiah. He's been keepin' track of all our days."

Paddock grinned. "Them white folks Bass talks about would call it the last days of March. In just a few more days it will be the next month of April. What—ah, what moon will that make it, old man?"

"Next one to come by will be called *Moon of Ducks Coming Back,*" he answered. "Some of them red niggers call it *Moon of New Grass.*"

"I'll never figure those moons out," Paddock replied with a wag of his head. "Seems like we've already been seeing both those things happening already, here in the *Sore-Eye Moon.*"

"Yep, that's for sure." Bass let another piece of the fire-roasted gut slide down his throat. "I've seen both ducks an' geese comin' back north. An' we all seen lots of new grass peekin' up all over the prairie, ain't we?"

"What's so danged special about the In-dee-yuns' way to call the months?"

"It ain't just the names, Esau," Scratch began to explain. "They tell what happens in a certain month's time. Not just a name, but some part of their life what happens 'round that time in all those years of any man livin' loose out here in all this free west."

"It makes sense to me, Mr. Titus."

"Lookahere, Josiah. Esau savvies it."

"I was afraid it'd make sense to him." Paddock sliced off another strip of buffalo roast, letting more grease and fat and juice drop and splatter into the low flames.

"The sun get named somethin' ever' month, too?" Esau slid his words around that chunk of meat he was chewing.

"Not that I know of," Paddock answered, then gazed over at Bass. "You know of it?"

"Don't savvy as I do, son. No, Esau. Each month, the sun doesn't get a new name the way the moon does. I s'pose it's 'cause the sun stays round like that hair ball I dug outta the cow's paunch. You can track time passin' on the moon 'cause it changes from full, down to just a wee sliver, then grows to full again over a whole moon-time, you see?"

"Say, Mr. Titus—there ain't anythin special like a In-dee-yun story of what happens to the sun?"

"You just had to ask, didn't you, Esau?" Josiah flashed a bright grin.

"Oh," Bass chuckled, ignoring his young partner, "now there's stories 'bout the sun, but not like—"

"Will you tell me one, huh?" The black man bolted up and shivered in excitement, almost childlike for a moment, giddy with the prospect of a brand-spanking-new nighttime story.

"Well, now." Bass cleared his throat with a rapid smile for Josiah, cogitating on exactly what tale to use on Esau.

"This here's a true Injun legend of the sun. Case you don't understand, the neither of you—that means somethin' the Injuns believe happened to their people from long, long time ago—so long ago our grandpappys' grandpappys weren't around at all."

Bass licked his fingers clean of the grease, then finished wiping them across his old shirt before plopping back against his saddle. "That country out there to the west, clear on over them big mountains, past the big salt, farther an' farther, an' farther away than this child's ever been is the country they say where the sun goes to its bed each night."

"It goes to sleep too? Just like us, just like a man does?"

"Yep, Esau. Or, so the Injuns say. You see, the sun is the big chief, the booshway of it all. The moon up there," he declared as he stuck his knife up in gesture before sliding the clean blade back into its sheath, "why, she's the sun's squaw. An' all them stars—" His open palm brushed the sky from horizon to horizon in a long, casual sweep. "All of them stars are their young'uns. All of them children to look after—my, my, my!"

The trio stared up at the stars for long moments, the blackening heavens a heavy canopy overhead until Esau interrupted the peace of their communal tranquility.

"That's it?" he asked. "That's the end of your story?"

"God's teeth, no." Scratch replied with a weary grin. "Them children up there, all them stars, they're dead-afeared of their pappy."

"Why they so afraid of their pappy?"

" 'Cause the Injuns say the sun eats his children."

"H-he eats his children?" Esau squeaked.

"That's right, Esau. Just like Zeke here, gnawin' on his bones." Bass gave the gray dog a loving pat on its wide head. "But the sun's got a bad, nasty habit of eatin' his own children right up. They're all so afraid of the sun they hide from him when he gets up in the mornin'."

"So we don't see any stars in the day, right?" Josiah had that look of total disbelief written on his face.

"That's right," Scratch winked. "When he gets up in the mornin', all the sun's children run away from him so he won't gobble them up. They stay hidin' till he goes to bed at night when they can come back out again to play."

"What about their mama? The moon? They scared of her, too?"

"Oh, them children ain't afraid of her. She's real good to 'em, in fact. They come on out only when she's out to watch 'em like a good mama does. Watches over her children when they're out playin'. But, once every month, the Mama Moon starts grievin' for all them children the sun has already et, so she paints her face just as black as Esau's here. That's why you cain't see too much of her a'times of a month. She's grievin' for all the children what got eaten by the sun. When her face is black, that's when the sun gets his chance an' gobbles up more stars to keep his belly goin' for a while longer."

"My, oh my, he eats his own chirrun—" Esau's voice was full of wonder and awe as he stared transfixed into the sky overhead.

"See, them Injuns savvy the sun's really shaped like a snake. All we see is just his head 'cause he's so bright all the time through the whole day long. You cain't see his tail or the rest of him 'cause he's so damned bright. When he goes to his bed in the west, way far out yonder in the west, he has to crawl through a thin tunnel to get to his robes an' goes in head first. After he sleeps the night a bit, the sun has to keep on crawling through that bed 'cause it's so small, to fit right around him. Then he can only come out the other end of that tunnel. Now, that's how them Injuns think the sun goes to bed each night in the west an' then gets up in the east every mornin'."

"Glory gracious!" Esau smacked his lips, then licked the grease from them. "What a story. Almost like my mama tol't us chirrun when we was little. Almost like that. Sometimes a In-dee-yun story can purely bumfuzzle a man's mind, sorely bumfuzzle it."

"You like good stories, eh?"

Esau turned round to Josiah. "I surely does."

"Almost as much as you love the women?" Bass grinned.

"Surely do, Mr. Titus. Esau surely do."

Paddock leaned to the side and tore away at some of his baggage, finally coming up with a small, rawhide parcel. Loosening the thongs, the young trapper removed two parchment-wrapped volumes. Both books were thick, their cloth-covered hardboards appearing brand new, without wear or stain.

"Where'd you get them?" Scratch leaned around the fire to peer more closely at Paddock's surprise.

"Back to St. Louis. Where'd you think I'd get them?"

"I mean to say, just where in St. Louis? I already knowed you didn't have 'em when we pulled out of Taos."

"There was a little shop down on Second. They had a lot of books in their window, so I went on in. Seems the proprietor took an interest in me of a sudden—he said because of my clothes, these here trappings of the mountains. So, he told me about a new writer on the scene back east. A fella by the name of—" Josiah opened the front cover of the first book, wrapped in a rich, oxblood cloth. "Here it is, writer by the name of James Fenimore Cooper."

"What's he write about? Stories like that Shakespeare fella you read to me last year? A tale like ol' *Mack Beth?*"

"I don't think he writes at all like Shakespeare, Scratch," he answered with a wag of his head. "Man at the shop said Cooper writes about the old frontier, and the new."

"Old frontier, an' the n-new?"

"Yeah. That's what the man said. Back to 1826 Cooper published this one. It's called *The Last of the Mohicans.*"

"Who're they? Some family's name—the Moreheecans?"

"I'd take a guess and suppose they're Indians from the looks of things here on this drawing."

Josiah flipped the book around so Esau and Bass could study the engraving opposite the title page. In it were pictured many fringed, feathered, and roached warriors skulking out of the shadows of a woodlands forest.

"The last of 'em, huh?" Bass pursed his lips and leaned back into his saddle to cogitate on that. "Cain't rightly believe there'd ever be the last of any Injuns. Just too damned many brownskins. Back of a time there got to be too damned many white men in the east, so the Injuns just moved a lil' farther west. Nawww." He shook his head decisively with a considerable frown. "I cain't believe there'd ever be the last of any tribe. East or west, Josiah."

"Looks like it might be a pretty good tale from the sounds of it." He had turned to the first page and now began to read:

> Mine ear is open, and my heart prepared;
> The worst is wordly loss thou canst unfold;
> Say, is my kingdom lost?"
>
> —SHAKESPEARE

"Why, I'll be damned! Josiah, I asked you if this fella wrote like Shakespeare. An', here he is, usin' the Shakespeare words."

"Naw, Scratch. He's just quoting from Shakespeare, that's all."

"What do you mean, quotin' from Shakespeare? Sounds to me like he's stealin' from Shakespeare, stealin' Shakespeare's words."

"When you quote, you tell what another man said, maybe because what he said fits right where you need it to fit. Anyway, it ain't stealing at all. He's just telling you what another writer said. Now, can I go on reading?"

Bass raised his knitted eyebrows sheepishly and said, "Any time you're ready, son."

It was a feature peculiar to the colonial wars of North America that the toils and dangers of the wilderness were to be encountered before the adverse hosts could meet. A wide and apparently an impervious boundary of forests severed the possessions of the hostile provinces of France and England. The hardy colonist, and the trained European who fought at his side, frequently expended months in struggling against the rapids of the streams, or in effecting the rugged passes of the mountains, in quest of an opportunity to exhibit their courage in a more martial conflict. But, emu-

373

*lating the patience and self-denial of the practised native warriors, they
learned to overcome every difficulty; and it would seem that, in time, there
was no recess of the woods so dark, nor any secret place so lovely, that it
might claim exemption from the inroads of those who had pledged their
blood to satiate their vengeance, or to uphold the cold and selfish policy of
the distant monarchs of Europe.*

Josiah looked up past the flames into the old man's face. "Sounds like they're
talking about a time back east when it was wilderness like this mountain west is
now."

"What else you think all that said?"

"Just that they roamed and wandered through it all, until there wasn't a place
they hadn't roamed."

"And when there wasn't a place they hadn't wandered through, the land
weren't the same ever again, was it, Josiah?"

"How's that, Scratch?"

"The land ain't ever the same when you run out of new country to lay your
eyes on. Just ain't the same no more." Bass sighed softly, his eyes falling back
to the yellow and blue licks of flame at his feet. "So, what's that other'n sittin' there
in your lap?" He crouched closer to his young partner.

"It's called *The Prairie*."

"And this same Cooper fella wrote it too?"

"That's right." Scratch opened its light tan cover. "Got this one out in 1827.
Just a year after this first book, about the Mohicans."

"Wonder if he's any kin to Silas Cooper." Scratch chewed on his lower lip and
reclined against his saddle blanket.

"That ain't very likely, old friend," Paddock assured. "A man who can write
books to give something really special of himself to folks, why, I don't believe he's
likely to have any kin like this hard case Silas Cooper who's only set on killing and
ruining peoples' lives."

"Seems to make sense," Esau injected to everyone's surprise. "Man what
spends his life makin' other folks better by his words wouldn't have any no-count
kin what spends his whole life causin' *e-e-evil* to all folks he meets."

"Maybeso you're both right," Scratch nodded and stared into the flames. "Just
wondered, is all. What with them two havin' the same name."

"Sometimes, we simply born to wonder, Mr. Titus."

"Esau, I'll declare!" Josiah beamed. "At times, you come up with the most—
most sensible things, putting something into words when I can't."

"W-what'd I say so special?" He was purely baffled by the sudden compliment.

"At times we are made to wonder on the why of things, Esau. Aren't we?" Bass
turned to inquire of the slave.

"Yes, Mr. Titus. Like I said. Some things are better left for us to wonder about.
That's all I said. Didn't know I come up with somethin' so—so special an' proper,
so tailormade."

"Maybe it's simply the company you're keepin' these days, huh?" Bass
grinned.

374

"You mean he's getting so smart with his words because he's keeping company with us?" Josiah prodded.

"Well—I was really meanin' me—keepin' company with me." Bass pursed his lips and widened his self-important grin.

"Oh, just you, eh? You're the only one to rub off any good on Esau? You're the only one?"

"That's the way I figure it, son. Don't think you've got any reason to reckon you've been any help to him. Why, if you hadn't been so damned lucky yourself today, it'd be just Esau an' me here, all alone now. So, you tell me just how smart you think you are, gettin' yourself pitched off your pony in the middle of a stamp—"

"It wasn't the middle!" Josiah protested. "I told you. I worked my horse over to the edge of that herd. Slow, real slow, just like you taught me. Them buffalo were snorting all around but they moved out of my way if I didn't push 'em too fast. Then I got to the edge of the herd just about the time I was getting plumb tired of holding onto the reins and my rifle both so damned tight. All about the time the herd started across a prairie dog town—"

"Don't make any differ'nce, any of that," Bass injected. "Not a bit of it. You still done somethin' real stupid gettin' right in the middle of them critters that way. Been differ'nt — you'd be hoofjam for the magpies an' coyotes to pick over right now."

"But I ain't hoofjam." Josiah replied. "Scratch, I'm not dead. See?" And he slapped his chest. "I'm right here with you still."

"I can see that. I ain't blind yet!" Bass spat with a scowl. "You was almost killed though, for certain."

"Maybe I was close to getting tromped," Paddock finally admitted with a nod. "But, I wasn't rubbed out."

"An' that there was a pure-dee miracle, son."

"No, it wasn't a miracle at all." Josiah shook his head. "Not any of your medicine either."

"Oh?" The old trapper cocked his head a little in question. "Just how you account for gettin' outta that herd all in one piece? It 'cause you're such a damned good buffler hunter?"

"No," Josiah grinned. "It ain't because I'm such a good buffalo hunter, or a good horseman either. Only way I see it that I got myself outta that herd is because Titus Bass taught me how."

"Wagh!" Scratch snorted with the growl of a grizzly bear rising to battle. "I didn't ever teach you such a thing, Josiah Paddock. Never did I."

The younger trapper stirred the edge of the dying fire's coals with a small stick. "What you've taught me is even better, Scratch. You didn't exactly teach me how to ride out of a buffalo stampede. But, what you've taught Josiah Paddock is how to get out of the messes he gets himself into. That's the greatest gift I suppose you could give to me. Not teaching me everything you know—but teaching me enough so that I can go on teaching myself, old friend."

"I done all that?" Scratch's eyes were suddenly wide and muling across the licks of blue flame.

"I never had thought on it all that much until now. And that's the best way—maybe the only way—to put it. Man like you'd spend the rest of your life teaching me everything you know. And that just wouldn't make a lick of sense for either of us, would it now?"

Josiah watched for Scratch to wag his head in reply before he went on. "Thing is, in the end, after you'd spent the whole of your life teaching me everything you know, I'd have no idea what I'd use from all that you'd taught me. No, old friend, I still think the best way is the way you've done it. You took me under your wing just long enough to teach me how to go on teaching myself."

"Lord, but that's a headful to ponder on." Esau suddenly blurted after a few moments of silence between the two white men. He had studied them back and forth across their little fire, knowing something very special and rare existed between his two friends of the wilderness. "If I didn't know better, I'd say you both made Esau's head hurt so bad he gonna hafta sleep now."

"You'll find any reason to put your head down in them blankets, won't you?" Paddock tossed the twig in the black man's direction.

Esau ducked the charred stick, deflecting it with his forearm. In the light-sapping darkness his skin glowed ebony and his eyes a bright, yellowed hue. "You bet on that, Mr. Josiah. If we ain't movin', ol' Esau's bones here gonna be sleepin'." With that he plopped his head back into his blankets.

"Goodnight, Esau," Scratch said.

"Goodnight, Mr. Titus. Goodnight to you both. See you in the mornin'. A day to make them mountains come a lil' closer to us."

"Amen, Esau." Paddock watched Scratch stare at the flames before he kicked his legs around and stuffed them down into his buffalo robes.

The old trapper continued to gaze mesmerized into those dancing licks of yellow and blue racing up and down the limbs in their firepit. It seemed he was in another world for now. Beside Scratch lay his gray dog, snuggled right next to the fire ring, its muzzle serenely plopped between his front paws and already snoring soundly, a full belly assured and happily dreaming of tomorrow's chase of rabbits and prairie dogs.

Paddock ground his hips down into those boughs he was using to soften his bedroll. He believed the old man must surely find some peace and contentment there by the dying fire, staring at the flames, perhaps warming his soul the way those licks of blue and yellow would warm his tough old hide. Yes, hypnotized and warming his soul.

Amen, my old friend. Amen.

THE AIR seemed busy with the questing hawks circling over the tossing land along with those blackbirds and white and black scissor-tailed magpies stirring up from a tiny carcass here or some rotting carrion there. Occasionally there came a grand sweep of sandhill cranes passing wide-winged over the land on their annual flight north, following the hungry chinooks which blew across the face of the land, eating spring snows with a voracious appetite.

Moon of New Grass. April now, Josiah had told him. Already it was the beginning of spring in the mountains. Turbulent times when a man might expect seasonal rain then get a surprise blizzard of white three to four feet deep across the land. Or, he might expect only a spring thundershower and be deluged for a day and a night on end without a single dry spot to be found from horizon clear to horizon. Spring in the far west. A time for that last mighty flexing of Old Winter Man's muscles, the first days of rebirth for the prairies and mountains.

Rebirth. *Moon of First Eggs*—come the next month of May. And that moon when Waits-by-the-Water's own egg would burst. He had to make it home to her by then. He just had to.

Buffalo grass sprouted beneath their horses' hoofs and the willow speckled along the streambeds already puffed in its reddish brown pride with rising sap beneath the warming spring breezes. Balsam root and rabbit brush and sulphur flowers filled the cool air with sweet perfumes offered to a man nowhere else in the world. There simply was country like this nowhere else in the world: an open, breathing land where often the loudest sound a man could hear was a hawk's shadow gliding over the turkeyfoot grass in pursuit of its breakfast.

Off to their left a great flock of white cranes rose majestically. As tall as a man on foot, the gangly birds were so heavy, most had to trot a few steps before they could vault themselves into the sky to become airborne. Always there were the service berry birds, fluttering their white-flashed stern feathers, each one fluffy as milkweed down, hunkered in the matted bullberry ahead, screeching out their high-pitched banter.

Times such as these made the old man feel so very small in such a big, big land. Yet, Bass knew and understood why he was all the bigger for living in this gigantic land. Strange in the way of the Indian, it was. Strange in the powerful medicine laid on him. That power to be both big and small at the same time.

A reek of smoke slapped him in the face even before Scratch brought them to the top of the bushy rise. Down along the river's course were thick stands of cottonwood, in open places the trees giving over to lodges looking like so many browned Indian breasts nippling up against the hard jay blue sky. Here and there through the clearings roamed scatterings of slat-ribbed ponies gnawing on what little new grass stuck up through the spring-hardened snow.

On through the cottonwoods sprawling along the northern bank of the Arkansas River, fourteen miles above the mouth of the Picketwire River, shimmered pumpkin gold walls of mud. Late afternoon sunlight painted vivid colors on the adobe fortress, the mountains hulking purple and looming cold in the background. With the luster of a dirty gold coin, this new fur post welcomed a man to the southern Rocky Mountains.

Eyes slit, staring ahead at the monstrous structure and the clearings surrounding it where the stock grazed for the coming night, Bass let out a long breath. He really had expected something far different. Nothing quite this huge, this monolithic. He had been all the way to Fort Vancouver on the grand sweep of the mighty Columbia River: a huge imposing log structure carved out of the thick northwestern forests. Yet, this adobe, mud-gobbed, two-story fortress shone now at sunset like the reddish center of a daisylike mountain firewheel. All

377

shone now at sunset like the reddish center of a daisylike mountain firewheel. All the prettier for its earthy color, all the more massive for the human effort taken to daub those massive walls with mud.

"By the blood of Jehoshaphat!" he swore under his breath.

"It truly is something to behold, ain't it?" Paddock answered as he edged his pony beside the old man and pulled to a halt.

Esau came up on the offhand side of the old trapper. "Is this the Bented place?"

Scratch turned, ready to scowl. Yet, he let it drain away to a grin. At last he was close. He could finally afford to be loose. Bass slapped the black man on the shoulder, sending up a tiny puff of dust from his rug poncho.

"This is where I promised I'd bring you, to a settlement Esau. I done exactly what I set out to do for you, friend."

Esau smiled like there was no end to teeth. Then his happy eyes flicked past the old man's and snagged on Paddock's. Right then and there, his happy eyes flitting back and forth between the two white men, the ex-slave was not all that sure he really wanted their journey to draw to an end at long last. Not so sure he wanted this place more than he wanted to remain by the trappers' sides.

"I t-thank you both," he nodded, his nappy head still covered with a scrap of wool blanket cut from his bedroll and tied beneath his chin with leather fringe from Scratch's legging. It had kept most of the cold winds out of his ears and away from his scraggly scalp.

Esau pulled free the Pawnee knife Bass had awarded him after their scrap with the warriors and tugged at the bottom of his poncho, pushing it aside so he could get to his britches. With the knife blade, the black man sliced carefully at the inside of the waistband on his pants until his left hand came up with a round, gold coin.

"I'll be go to—" Paddock muttered.

"What the peewaddle is that?" Bass was just as stunned, watching the Negra's grinning face for an answer as Esau held the coin up to the bright spring light.

"Where'd you get that?" Paddock asked.

"My master. It was his. When them Pawnee In-dee-yuns fixin' to roast them white folks, they found the gold pieces on 'em. Not much gold left now, 'cause them Pawnee each took a piece to wear round they necks. I got my hands on the rest of it when the savages didn't know, an' sewed it up in my britches here." He patted at his waist. "Figured to have it come in handy some a'day. To get me home to New Ahleans again."

"Well, I didn't get you home to New Orleans, Esau." Bass looked a little stern suddenly. "An' I ain't gonna let you pay me for the trip I did give you neither. You got that, son? You don't pay Titus Bass for his help. Understand, Esau?"

"I-I unnerstan, Mr. Titus." Esau stared at his gold coin for a long moment, fully befuddled now until a glow spread its charm across his face. His eyes flicked over to Scratch.

"Seein' as I got this'un out now," he grinned, "I don't s'pose you'd let a fella buy you two gent'mens a drink of somethin' strong down there to the fur post—

just in the way of sayin' how happy I am you brung me all the way here? Can I do that for you?"

Bass let his eyes crawl around to Paddock's where the young man's smile was already plastered wide and solid as the walls of Bents' Fort.

"I reckon we shouldn't take the chance Esau might lose that coin, should we, Josiah? Good chance he just might lose it afore we could waste it on bad whiskey."

"Let's go get us a drink and then we'll find Cooper for you," Josiah declared flatly and businesslike as he nudged his pony into the cottonwoods.

"Whiskey does sound good, son."

"Whiskey for white men, an' a ol' Negra boy to boot." Esau was grinning all the way to his cold ears.

"Certain as rain, Josiah," Bass agreed. "Whiskey first, then we'll settle with Silas Cooper what's been waitin' ten years to be done with."

"That's a long time to wait, Scratch." Josiah's eyes held the old man's. "I never said this to you before, but I know ten years is a damned awful long time to carry inside such as what you had to."

"A lil' sip or two of barleycorn whiskey an' then I'll be ready—"

Scratch's words trailed behind him as he pushed on down the hill.

29 ZEKE FINALLY LOPED up after he had dallied behind to wrestle some dogs that had bolted out of the Indian camps to give him a sniff and a going over. He was bigger than all of them and so had himself quite a romp.

Esau sat slack-jawed on his pony, staring up at the fort's huge nine foot high by seven foot wide entry tunnel. No less in awe at the sight, Bass and Paddock waited out Zeke's return, gazing along the adobe walls of what the nearby Indians had come to call the "big lodge," here at sunset painted a pumpkin orange. Dusk lay languid like a rusty, crimson strap of burnished gold against the dark hills to the west.

Scratch had circled the entire perimeter after tramping up from the marsh at the river's edge, drawing his party around the fourteen foot high walls as he let the buffalo runner plod casually along the foot of the western wall. Because it was a little longer than the eastern wall, the whole of the fortress had the immediate appearance of an out-of-kilter rectangle. The main entrance to Bents' Fort faced a little east of true north, not quite square on the compass, looking out on a broad plain where some young men were driving in the horse herd for the coming night.

With his dog now in tow, the old trapper tapped heels and brought the Nez Perce pony to the north wall where he wearily slid from the saddle. Tingles of apprehension shot up his spine from time to time along with a sense of relief and nearing completion calming his nervous, rawhide-tight gut. Bass ground hobbled the buffalo runner and knelt to tell Zeke that he was expected to stay put and guard the ponies and Samantha. With a lick of his huge tongue across Scratch's hand, the dog told its master he understood.

Into the tunnellike gate thick with evening shadows, the trio plunged past outer doors cottonwood-stout and sheathed in iron so they would not easily burn. At a window to their left stood two old warriors, now reduced to trading with a clerk of the Bent, St. Vrain & Company. By closing the inner gates, the fort's occupants could trade with Indians at a service window without allowing the Indians access to the fort's interior.

Lamps and torches were only now being lit as the trio stepped into the fort's quadrangle. Bass halted and drew it all in, soaking up the imposing feel of its massive bulk around him, a fort grown up from the prairie right here at the foot of the mountains, thrust from the bowels of the earth to stand at a crossroads of plains Indian trade. The walls were three adobe bricks thick, making the outer walls at least thirty inches wide. At the northeast and southwest corners of the outer walls stood the vaulted round towers four to five feet higher than the tops of the walls and about seventeen feet in diameter. Sabers and lances joined small field pieces in the unlikely event the fortress was ever subjected to a wall scaling siege and hand to hand combat.

His old eye surveyed the twenty-five rooms skirting the huge quadrangle, all facing inward, their floors nothing more than beaten mud and clay, each plaster walled apartment averaging fifteen by twenty feet in size. The larger storage and trading rooms stretched along the western wall, along with a massive dining room, blacksmith shop, cooperage, council room, kitchen, and attached pantry.

Bass stepped across the open, bustling quadrangle, past a group of men who occupied themselves in constructing a tall fur press near the center of the square. At this busy season of the year more than a hundred men were needed to operate the fort. The rest of the time only sixty men sufficed to handle company duties.

Beneath his feet lay stream washed gravel, placed there to hold down the choking yellow brown dust in dry times, then limit the gumbolike, foot-sucking mud in the wet seasons. As the trio of two white trappers and a poor black slave strolled by, most heads turned and studied the newcomers with silent, sneering appraisal.

At the south end of the structure by the livery sprawled a huge corral attached to the outer wall of the fort. Bass shook his head in quiet awe and turned, plodding back to the sunset orange mud of the quadrangle.

"This is purely some marvel," he gushed at last, his gaze scaling the lower rooms to second floor apartments along the west wall.

Above the huge entryway stood a squat watchtower, windowed on all sides, topped with both a flagpole bearing the stars and stripes and a belfry with an iron bell for use in emergency or to call company workers to their meals. At the southwest corner rose a type of blockhouse near the well and latrine, along with an office used by company clerks. Just west of there ran a long, rectangular room where the owners and honored guests often retired with their cigars and port after meals, there to discuss matters of trade and Indian affairs. From the second-story catwalks, a man could peer far to the southwest to the high, cloud-draped *Las Cumbres Espanolas,* the Spanish Peaks, *Wah-to-Yah* to the neighboring Indians—their "Breasts of the World." Far to the northwest reared the massive head of Zebulon Pike's mountain, jutting up here at the edge of these great plains.

At last Bass leaned against an upright on the veranda stretching out from the rooms along the eastern wall of the fort's interior. It, like all beams and posts here, was peeled cottonwood, readily found nearby. Everything else was adobe.

"Whyn't you go on up there." Scratch's casual gesture indicated for Josiah to try the trading room along the eastern wall where several men came and went in succession. "See if them traders got any whiskey so we can spend Esau's gold, an' glean us some news of Cooper to boot."

Paddock nodded and turned on his heel without a word. Amid the noisy confusion of the fort compound, the black man stepped a little closer to the old trapper. With a blizzard of cold, hard looks cast in his direction, Esau did not feel the least bit welcome here under the Bents' roof. He decided he'd just lean against that same cottonwood timber Scratch was content to hold up, just stay close to the crusty old trapper.

"This is nothin' less than a pure-dee wonderment, Esau," Bass commented under his breath. Never had he imagined seeing anything of the kind rise out of the ground here along the Arkansas River, the headwaters of which rushed out of the Bayou Salade itself on the first leg of its journey to the sea.

"Why, I ain't see'd nothin' quite such a wonderment since't last I was to New Ahleans." Esau bobbed his head in agreement. "This is quite the place, Mr. Titus. Quite the place."

"Looks to be quite the spot for some, Esau," Bass commented, his eyes carefully surveying all who passed by beneath both the glowing torchlight and the full, spring-swollen moonglow. Every hard look cast Esau's way was regarded with just as stiff a rawhide glare from the old trapper. He tapped fingers on both knife handle and pistol butt, at ready should Silas Cooper show up to march across the quadrangle. There had been a time early on in his life when Titus Bass could be caught by surprise, but not after he'd spent ten long years gleaning the lay of the land.

Here he stood within an amazing place created by traders, this fortress where gathered a breed of men who wanted to bring their civilization along with them into this far mountain west. Theirs was a species he had never understood, although he had been dealing with them reluctantly for better than ten years now at rendezvous in the mountains. Those who carried civility and eastern society into the wilderness, there to protect their chunk of it behind thick, high walls, wrenching from the land forcefully what the land would not yield up willingly—this new breed of trader he came instantly to despise. Always before, entrepreneurs from the east had come to barter at rendezvous, seduce the natives, and rape the trappers with their overpriced goods—then left when business was complete and every hard-won beaver pelt filled their packs, running back to the settlements. They always left the mountains behind. On the other hand, this new species of trader was altogether a different animal—they had come to stay, and in their staying were intent upon changing the face of the far west in their own civilized image. The old man knew this quiet, open land would never again be the same.

Three Bent brothers, George, William, and Charles, had joined with the two St. Vrains, Ceran and Marcelin, to plunge their dreams of empire into the very heart of the plains Indian. From here they would command much of the southern Rocky Mountain beaver market and hope to garner the bulk of the Indian robe trade. Back to 1829 the St. Vrains and Bents had chosen a site on some northern benchland of the Arkansas River simply because the sandy southern bank belonged to Mexico. The traders saw to it that some hundred and fifty peon laborers, along with wagons straining under loads of cheap, coarse Mexican wool, were brought over Raton Pass to the bottomland they had selected to raise their fortress. That wool would be used in addition to the abundant marsh grasses nearby to bind up the mud intended for adobe bricks.

The peons freighted up from Taos had been paid some seven to eight American dollars per month for their excruciating labor, depending upon just what skill they were called upon to use. Those wages were primarily paid out in trade goods, mostly calicoes, or coarse cloth, some powder and lead, coffee, too, as it was a much desired commodity of trade. Every item the Bents and St. Vrains used in place of wages was horrendously marked up, yet the citizens of Taos clamored after the construction jobs. Even though the weary dawn to dusk labor paid only a few dollars per month, the wages were nearly twice what the peons would have received for work in the San Fernando de Taos.

Gangs of laborers would haul barrels of river water up from the Arkansas in wagons, dumping it in huge pits which had been scoured out of the prairie near the construction site. In these pits the earthen clay was mixed with the water to a proper consistency by yokes of powerful oxen circling, circling on end, as the beasts tromped round and round through the endless workday. Into molds some ten inches wide, six inches thick by a foot long, the mortar they had created was daubed. The molds were quickly dumped on the ground and removed, leaving the adobe bricks to dry beneath a relentless sun. First hundreds, then thousands, were hauled up rickety cottonwood ladders as the workers clambered along scaffolds ascending the walls ever higher as the fourteen foot high enclosure shrugged itself up from the bowels of the Arkansas floodplain.

All roofs were first constructed with a gentle slope to the interior quadrangle for proper drainage. At the outset a ribbing network of cottonwood poles was intially covered with brush and grass from the nearby river and streams. Atop that cottonwood lattice was placed a layer of the thick clay from the oxen pits. When it had dried, gravel from the streambeds was poured over the clay to cut down both dust and the chance of foot-soaking mud. Almost flat, laying some five feet below the top of the walls, these roofs offered good footing for defenders while still allowing for proper drainage during the spring and fall rainy seasons.

For three years the painstaking seasonal construction continued, the adobe brick walls rising ever upward until at last they could be smeared with a final coating of protective mud. By the fall of 1833, the Bent and St. Vrain brothers were finally ready to commence formal trading with the surrounding tribes. Here at last stood their mud fist arrogantly jammed down the throat of the southern plains Indian.

Bass wheeled at the sound of Josiah's voice calling out his name. Paddock beckoned Bass and Esau to the trading room. Inside these large quarters the air was a bit warmer, hung heavy and fragrant with pipe smoke and the stench of old chewed tobacco spit and splattered across the earthen floor. The place teemed with men bustling about in the lamp-bright twilight, many of them Canadian Frenchmen. His old eye shot over the lot of them quickly, looking for a tall man, black headed and strap-jawed, shoulders wide enough to carry the span of a hickory axe handle with room to spare.

"He ain't here." Paddock had watched the old man's roving eye.

"What you mean, he ain't—"

"Right now—he ain't here right now," Josiah confirmed. "I already asked about Cooper. He truly is a hunter for the Bents, that much is certain. Fella there told it all." His nod indicated one of the two clerks busy behind the rough hewn counter. "Told me that near as he knows the group Cooper's with is bound to roll back in here the next day or two. They've been out trading and hunting with some Utes. Not too far away, but far enough away for you to think twice about going after him. A few days' ride, they say. Looks like you'll have to wait for him to come to you now."

"He'll be comin' back here, you say, Josiah?" Bass's parched throat scratched at the sudden dryness the news caused him.

"Simply gotta wait for him. Let's have us a drink and we'll go make camp," Paddock suggested.

Esau read those lines deeply etched across the old man's forehead below the blue bandanna. "I got me my coin to drink on. C'mon now, Mr. Titus. Let's cure your thirst."

"Ahhh, yeah." Bass shook his head, as if coming to, realizing just where he was again. "Let's us do that—get some whiskey down our gullets an' make camp."

Bass turned as the curly headed clerk stepped up to the counter, the older of that pair who sought to serve the milling group of smelly, gaudily-clad fort workers.

"What's it to be, gents?"

"You've whiskey?"

"Aye, I do," the man answered. "Whiskey bad enough to put a blister on your moccasins should you spill any. You boys ain't together, are you?" he asked as he eyed Josiah and Esau.

"We are that. Together." Bass spoke a little more loudly than he might have had to, to be heard. "These here're my compañeros. Josiah here," he beamed as he slapped a hand on Paddock's shoulder, then one of the black man's, "an' this is my new partner, Esau."

"Ain't never served no Negras before," the clerk replied, looking a little sheepish. "I suppose I really—"

"You got a Negra cook here, don't you?" Bass blurted out.

"Yeah, but Charlotte's a-working here for the Company — just like me."

"She drink your whiskey?"

"Not that I know of," the clerk snapped.

"Good," Scratch replied. "Give her share to my friend Esau here."

"He's your slave, right?" The clerk shifted his glare back to Bass.

"You cuddle-headed fool! A free man, this one. Nothin' short of bein' a free man." Scratch answered, then from the corner of his eye watched Esau draw himself a wee bit taller.

"Why, then, what have you in trade?" The clerk squinted narrowly at the old trapper.

"We've this, friend." Esau confidently pushed against the bar and slapped the gold coin down on the wood plank with a resounding thunk.

"This, eh?"

384

The older clerk promptly scooped the coin from the bar and jammed it between his teeth where he bit and chewed to test its integrity.

"Just where a Negra boy like you come up with a gold piece like this?" he inquired suspiciously.

"Why, Mister, I got me more—"

"He got more than he bargained for out to Pawnee land, is what he's tryin' to say, mister," Bass quickly interrupted Esau. There were men present in the trading room, men with loose tongues and dull, liquored minds, men who might not suffer a sore conscience about slitting a black man's throat for some easy gold if they knew he had more on him.

"The rest of it," Bass went on when he was sure he had the attention of all those close by, "why, it's now hung round them blood-suckin' Pawnee necks. My friend here escaped with this one piece, you see. He had promised it to me for pay should I get him to a civilized spot." His eyes slewed around the room as if to say he wasn't all that convinced the place would pass for civilization.

Bass leaned over and snagged the clerk's hand in the tight vice of his own fist. He began to squeeze, bringing the man's face right up to his across the counter.

"That's my money you hold, Mister—Mister who?"

"Gilstrap. My name's Cyrus Gilstrap."

"Want you to know that's my money, Cyrus Gilstrap," Scratch growled. "My friend here give it to me for gettin' him here to your fort, safe he be. An' I aim to do a little drinkin' on that gold piece there."

With his fingers Bass spread open the clerk's palm. Behind him, the whole room had gone quiet and drained of sound. "How much whiskey this gold buy me?" He tapped one fingertip on that gold coin in the open palm.

"You might get one of the kicker-kegs here." The clerk pointed with his free hand to some small wooden containers.

"One of them little'uns for this? That all?"

"Y-yes, stranger. Going fare that be."

"Wagh! Mountain prices for certain. A keg, then, Mr. Gilstrap." Bass dropped the clerk's hand and leaned back from the counter. "Along with some information."

"What kind of information you want?" The clerk plunked the keg atop the plank counter, rubbing his sore hand and flashing an apprehensive eye in Esau's direction.

"What's the matter, Mr. Gilstrap? You let Injuns get drunk, don't you? Huh?" Scratch waited for a reply but got nothing more than a nervous look from the clerk. "You let Injuns get drunk on your trader's whiskey—why don't you let a Negra get a bellyful, too?" He slapped Esau square across the back. "Anything wrong with my friend here getting him a snootful of this saddle varnish?"

"I suppose not, Mister—"

"The name is Bass. That's Titus Bass." He turned round to pronounce it plainly to the room. "You all should know who I am now. An', you should know I come here to find a river rat, runagate blackguard by the name of Silas Cooper."

Immediately the clerk's eyes shot to Paddock. Aroung them erupted a hushed, furtive conversation bubbling about the old trapper's disclosure.

"I told him, Cooper ain't due back for another day or two." The clerk glared at Paddock accusingly. "Won't make us no never-mind—but, what's the why of you looking the man up?"

Bass pulled the cork out of the keg and held it under one arm to pour the amber liquid into a large tin cup. He held it up before his eyes and saluted the clerk with a quick toast.

"I aim to kill an' scalp the sonuvabitch." Scratch tossed back the fiery liquid in a single gulp.

"S-silas Cooper?" Gilstrap guffawed as he looked Bass up and down. Laughter rippled through the room. "Mister, you got to be joking! That, or you simply gotta have the wrong Silas Cooper."

Just as quickly as his words were spilled, his face was yanked across the counter and down into Scratch's. The place fell quiet as several men scurried out the heavy door, leaving in their wake cold, night-black air rushing into the traderoom.

"This Cooper you know come from St. Louis?" Bass held the clerk's collar prisoner in his gnarled fist.

"Y-yes, he did," Gilstrap replied with a faint squeak, breath crimped in his throat.

"He tall, this Cooper you know? Black of hair?" Bass asked. "Wide of shoulder an' meaner'n a pit of cottonmouths?"

"Most his hair's turned to gray now, but that sure does sound like the Silas Cooper I know, mister," the clerk gulped.

"Then, they're one and the same who I'm hopin' to get my hands on after these ten long years." Scratch released the man's coat, smoothing out the lapels.

"Mister, I gotta tell you—"

"Name's Bass."

"I gotta tell you, Mr. Bass, you might as well whistle a jig to a milestone as try that monster on."

"Just how is it you figure I shouldn't look hard an' long for Silas Cooper?"

"Friend, that man ain't been here all that long working for the Bents, but he sure is a hard keeper and they'd as soon he get his scalp lifted by the likes of them Utes up there in the hills as they would he drown crossing the Arkansas River."

"I heard tell he's got a reputation smellier'n a Kiowa breechclout." The second, younger clerk ambled up to the knot of trappers while the others in the room talked about Silas Cooper in hushed tones.

"He is for a fact an eagle-eyed demon wind, that Cooper," another faceless man commented before he buried his eyes behind an upturned whiskey mug.

"He's gotta be better'n f-fifty years old now," Bass commented, bewildered by everyone's appraisal of Cooper.

"He for certain might have a load of years on him by now, mister," the younger clerk agreed, "but that ain't slowed the man down none. He's still as hard a case and a no-count reeky villain as I'd ever want to let in my walls here."

"You just might be doing everyone a favor should you put that one out of his misery, Mr. Bass." Gilstrap showed a hint of a sour grin.

"How's that?" Scratch cocked his head.

"Told you, simple enough. The boss wouldn't mind how Cooper buys himself a little plot of some private land in a graveyard. Whatever or whoever does it. Methinks Cooper's getting to cost too much—more'n his keep is worth."

"How's he doin' that?" Bass took the tin cup back from Josiah and passed it over to Esau.

"Injuns. He's hard on the friendlies. Stirring up some shit here, adding fuel to a fire over there. Biggest problem the Bent boys got hereabouts is Cooper. Man is a bit too greedy for the bosses."

"Greedy?"

"Yep, Mister. Silas Cooper wants it all for himself. Greedy from the husk straight on in to the smack-center of the cob. Whether it be robes and furs—or women."

Titus studied on it a moment before he spoke. "How come your face just went sour as clabber and looked to be twice't as old?"

"Mr. Bass," Gilstrap replied sadly, staring into the plank counter, "it'll fair put up a good man's hackles to see what that man Cooper does to a woman—why, even her being an Injun squaw."

Scratch's brow creased as his eyelids fell to slits. "You care to tell me?"

"He's just a hard user," the younger clerk piped up. "Takes a woman out there in the Indian camp when and where he wants, though he's got his own woman and her lodge pitched right outside the walls. Cooper killed a buck who tried to stop him from yanking the man's wife right outta her lodge."

The older clerk nodded vigorously. "Why his own woman stays on with him, I'll never know. What she has to put up with from that bastard is enough to curdle a man's blood to gnat pepper."

"Sounds like this Cooper is the same one they described to me back in St. Louis," Josiah offered.

"How's that, son?"

"A bad case of the cards, all the way." Paddock took the tin cup back from Esau and pulled long at its bite.

"Nothin' any of these fellas said, or you, has made Titus Bass's backbone turn yellow." Scratch pulled the cup from Josiah and swilled down the last of the whiskey.

"M-maybe you ain't heard all of this right," the younger clerk declared. "If you're set on picking some trouble with Silas Cooper, Mister, you got about as much sense as a turtle's got hair."

"He's right." A man sidled to the bar and nodded his agreement in their assessment of Cooper. "Best idea'd be for you to pull in your horns and move right along like you never come here."

"When a boar hawg sprouts milk teats!" Bass wagged his head and smiled as wide as he could, showing off his age-yellowed teeth. "I ain't believin' none of this. Josiah, you hearin' all this about Silas Cooper? Seems all these niggers're full of tea. I'd say Cooper's got the bejabbers scared right out of the lot of them."

"Maybe it ain't just because they've been working hard at the popskull, Scratch. Maybe they've got 'em a good reason to be scared of the man."

"You best listen to your young partner there," Gilstrap nodded.

"You go looking to pick a fight with Cooper, you best understand you won't kill a man like that in a straight-up, push-ahead go at him. Nawww, suh," the younger clerk advised. "The only way you'd kill Silas Cooper is through some serious underhanded jigger-pokey."

"That bastard fair chews up a man's bones and spits them out when he's done toying with 'em," the first clerk agreed.

"It's all enough to make me at least a bit nervous about Cooper coming back in the next couple of days." Paddock slapped Bass on the shoulder and stuffed the cork in the top of the keg.

"You best be scared, young man," voiced another spectator.

"Best bet is to move on, is what I'd say," offered another.

Bass swallowed hard against the dryness that charred his throat into roughened rawhide. He looked slowly around the room and saw the frowning faces, the smiling faces, those faces registering concern and the faces that showed that their owners didn't give a damn what happened when Titus Bass confronted Silas Cooper. He took their warnings with a grain of salt, simply because most of them had been burning their goozles raw on the potent traders' brand of whiskey.

Yet, there still nagged that underlying uneasiness that was just now beginning to prick at his insides. These western men of the mountains and plains would know something of the true measure of a man, whether that man be Silas Cooper or Titus Bass. Here around him were those frontiersmen tough enough perhaps to last a season or two out west—all rowdy, dirty and loud, roiling and rum swilling, whiskey swaggling—but all of them coming down into this far western river valley with laughter, all smiling, happy, and self-reliant, riding down into this far western valley of the shadow of death.

A queer mix, these French Canadians. Whether it was snowing and below zero, or the sun was baking their brains to johnnycakes, they remained the same carefree fellows. It seemed they would allow no dark cloud to overshadow them for long at all. They loved their simple squeezebox music and their ready laughter. At last, most of them turned round to resume their chattering amongst themselves, apparently forgetting about the crazy American trapper who was wanting to commit suicide by calling Silas Cooper out.

"Let's go find us a camp." Scratch scooped up the small keg and tucked it under his arm, resigned at last to taking his leave.

"Down to the dining hall, you might find Marcelin St. Vrain," Gilstrap suggested. "You might ask him about putting you three up in the fort for the night. Appears to be some weather sneaking over the hills."

Paddock wheeled and peered out at the cloudy night sky as he held the door open for the older trapper. "We thank you gentlemen for your help this evening. Appreciate your offer of hospitality, along with the news."

"And the whiskey," Esau added as he ducked out the door into the full moon night.

388

"Man's born to do more than exercise nothing but his own good sense." Scratch halted at the door, his back growing cold from the frosty night breezes pushing past him into the trader's room. "Comes a time when that man's just gotta do something that don't make a lick of good sense at all. He's simply gotta do what's right."

30 "ALL MEN ARE borned like that." Esau spoke wistfully as he stared across the snowy compound at the kitchen. Every now and then he caught a glimpse of the cooks, one of which was black and fleshy and, to him, all the more sensuous for it. Charlotte, whose nappy hair stuck out in unkempt sprigs, had clearly caught his eye.

"Will you just come away from the door?" Josiah demanded with a scowl. "Hard enough keeping warm in here without you standing there with the door pulled wide open on and off, all day long, while you eyeball them women over there."

"Can't help it." Esau turned, his face flooded with a wide smile. "I loves the womens an' there's one about the fort for Esau to love. She makes the best pies an' hoe cakes this lover man ever put cross't his lips. I bet she makes the best lovin', too."

"That what makes your clock tick?" Paddock inquired as he threw some more greasewood on the flames.

"Is the way all men are borned, like I said." Esau scraped the door shut. "Is the way men are, Mr. Josiah. Right from the get-go of life, a man gets a woman to open up her legs for him. An', he never stops tryin' to get them womens to open up they legs for him."

"Man starts his life the same way he'll spend most of it, eh?" the younger trapper chuckled, amused.

"Tha's right." He still had a toothy smile on as he plopped down beside the tiny corner fireplace in the small room. The greasewood crackled on the fire—so named for the popping, eager flame it created, much like a cut of meat spewing grease on a fire. Though the wood burned quickly, it did provide a hot, sparkling fire to any southern plains traveler who used it for fuel.

Outside the small adobe cloister where they'd slept the night before, big, heavy flakes of a spring snowstorm covered the ground. Smokey fires burned inside the compound and out along the misty river where the Indians camped, raising wisps of gray into the sow belly sky of early afternoon.

In the compound, work continued on the huge fur press. Other fort employees beat robes free of dust and vermin before bundling them for shipment east. Protected from the snowfall beneath the verandas, buckskin and wool clad hunters and plainsmen sat around in small knots—one group intent upon a game of hand, another noisy clan hard at the bones. Others lost their hard-won

390

pelts or wages gambling at euchre or seven-up. A hunter, his pack animals burdened with game, headed for the fort kitchen. Copper-skinned native girls, ajingle with their hawk bells, strolled by the gamblers, trying to entice the white men with the heady musky scents of willing bodies beneath their blankets.

Josiah turned to glance at Bass.

The old trapper reclined on his bedroll, huddled in a heavy wool blanket, staring hypnotically into the fire. His eyes still a mean red from the whiskey he had punished so hard the night before, Scratch had continued to work at the amber liquid since early morning, taking his juice slow for the present, inside his belly a warm, summerlike glow spreading to ward off the damp chill brought on by this sudden spring snowstorm that had blown out of the hills. It had been hours since last he'd uttered a word to his companions. He had preferred to stare at the mesmerizing yellow blue flames and nurse his hangover in his own fashion, while Josiah and Esau talked to each other across the room.

"Josiah?" The crackling whisper filled the room.

"Yes, old friend?" Paddock replied just as softly, surprised by the old trapper's sudden speech after hours of silence.

"Josiah, what's it like to—to die?"

"W-why," the young trapper stammered, dumbfounded, "I—I don't know what you mean, Scratch."

Both of the old man's companions waited for him to speak again. Never did his eyes leave that ballet of fire spinning across the greasewood. The limbs crackled and popped. Outside, just occasionally, a voice could be heard struggling with something or someone, hollering out an order or cheering a good turn of the cards, then all fell quiet once more. Outside their tiny room it grew almost quiet enough to hear the heavy snowflakes sloughing around their little mud world.

"You gotta know what it's like to die, Josiah. I reckon you come as close to dyin' as any man—twice now, son."

"Twice?" Josiah said, a puzzled look on his face. "When McAfferty blew a hole in my chest, but I can't recollect any other time."

"Just a few days back." Bass glanced over at his young partner for an instant before staring at the fire again. "When you came out of the buffler stampede alive. Walked away from it like few men'd ever do."

"You know I got over to the side of the herd—"

"You was sure as dead, son. There's gotta be a reason you wasn't killed—twice now. Man gets thrown from his horse in such a shitteree of buffler hoofs, he can count on bein' just 'bout as dead as grease on a Blackfoot's braids."

Bass had sure enough thought the young man was dead—twice already. So something stuck right down in the craw of him told the old man that Josiah just might have an answer or two about those black, nagging clouds kicking around inside him—things hung on this matter of confronting Silas Cooper.

Win, draw, or lose—Titus Bass wanted to be ready for whatever came his way. So far down through his life he had been ready. It was just his way. Always had been. And now that those ten years were nearing their confrontation with the present, he owed it to that decade to be as ready as he could be. Everything that had gone before readied him for what was yet to come. Ten years of preparation for this one moment. If the moment dictated Titus Bass was meant to—die— then Titus Bass would do it the best way he knew how. He would be ready for that hoary-hooded countenance of death. He'd be ready where many men had not been, each one dragged kicking and screaming down into the bowels of hell. No two ways about it. Titus Bass'd plain be ready.

Josiah patiently explained to Scratch how he'd felt when he'd been suspended in the icy limbo coming back to Absaroka from that cold winter manhunt trail for Asa McAfferty. He told his old friend about the pain of leaving far too many things undone and unsaid to those he loved, and he told of leaving that love unspoken for far too long. Then Paddock told of the agony his selfishness had caused him, how putting his own needs above the needs of those he loved had brought him to be flat on his back, slowly mending over the long months of winter in Rotten Belly's Crow camp, into that spring of promise and reunion. Sometimes, a man somehow owes others much more than what he owes himself.

"Maybe—" Paddock stared at the flames in their little fireplace along with the old trapper. "Just maybe because what we owe those others is bigger than ourselves, Scratch."

Josiah let his partner be, shuffling away across the tiny room to join Esau where he sat among their bedrolls and robes and saddles. There they sipped at the thick coffee and chewed on the leftovers of last night's buffalo roast. It wasn't long before both began to sense the need in cheering up the gloomy mood in their small quarters, to sense the need of bringing the old man out of his dark reverie and contemplation of death. Paddock began his banter with Esau and within a moment the black man realized just what his role would be.

"Ain't much better than this here buffalo that old man over there by the fire got for us all to eat," Esau pronounced around a huge chaw of hump roast.

"W-what you mean by the 'old man got it for us'?" Paddock grumbled. "I was the one who shot it, by damned!"

"I suppose you're right, Mr. Josiah." Esau bobbed his head up and down, smiling widely. "But, it were Mr. Titus who led us to them critters natural as you please in the first place."

"Dang it all, you black assed, bull-headed mule. Titus Bass didn't get this meat for us. I did!"

"Just tellin' you the way I see'd it." Esau bobbed his head again matter of factly. "You just pulled the trigger is all."

"Well now, Esau—Mr. So-High-And-Mighty," Paddock snapped, his tone indignant. "I'd like to see you do the same. Why, come to think of it, we ain't even seen you pull a trigger on this little trip since we ran onto you and saved your black hide. Not once have we seen you bring any food down and into camp for our hungry bellies, have we?"

"So? From the looks of it, ain't a thing to shootin' a buffalo, Mr. Josiah," Esau stated, his face knotted up in a grin. "Critter half as big as this room, why, you just point your rifle gun out there at it an' pull back on the trigger. That buffalo bound to drop an' you're done."

"Just like that?"

"Just like that, what I said," Esau replied.

Paddock guffawed, bursting out in a gusty laugh. "You chuckle-headed Negra. I don't think you could hit a critter even as big as a buffalo—even if you were sitting smack-square on top of the damned thing!"

"Well, I ain't never heard of such a thing near so dumb as to try to hit somethin' I was sittin' on. That'd be damned foolish now for a man to be sittin' on the critter he's 'bout to shoot. You're bein' purely simple now, Mr. Josiah. Tryin' to poke some fun at me."

"Esau, y-you just ain't worth a red piss, are you?" Josiah was almost doubled over in laughter.

"I is so!" the black man snapped with a grin. "I'm worth every inch a red piss!"

They both fell to laughing in wild fits, seized by that sudden joy of laughter after all they'd come through together. Esau nearly choked on a piece of the buffalo roast, finally getting it out of his throat and spitting it out across the room while Josiah pounded him on the back. The chunk of meat went sailing across the tiny cell and its crazy flight sent them both into another seizure of hysterics and back slapping, tear weeping, belly aching laughter.

"Why, just look at the two of you, will you?"

The old trapper's words slowed their wild guffaws. Both of them suddenly turned quiet, gazing at Scratch. After tossing a couple more sticks of firewood on the flames, Bass glared back at the two for a moment before his face finally cracked a wry smile.

"The two of you tryin' real hard right now to make a man believe you both just come up with the idea of grinnin' an' gums all on your own."

"Glad to see you still got a grin all of your very own, Scratch." Paddock tossed him a healthy piece of hump roast.

"I ain't really hungry, son."

"Best you eat," Paddock coaxed. "You ain't eaten a thing since last night when we pulled in here. All you done is painted your tonsils steady with that coal oil they call whiskey."

Reluctantly, Scratch began to rip small bites out of the juicy meat, gazing back into the licks of blue yellow flame darting back and forth across that shimmering horizon of warmth in the tiny fireplace. He felt cold, so cold, as if he might never be warm again. He wondered if what he felt was the first fingertip touch of Old Man Death himself. Yet, with that milky left eye, Scratch thought he saw the sudden flash of something bright and hopeful in his self-inflicted gloom. Only his whiskey weary mind playing tricks on him? Nothing tangible, nothing he could get a grip on. But, perhaps something warm enough to fight off that chill specter of death itself in the end.

"Snow appears to be letting up." Josiah stood in the doorway and watched several men plow through the half foot of new snow. He listened to the voices that rose in the compound.

"What's goin' on out there?" Scratch asked.

Josiah turned and looked at his friend, his eyes touching Bass in a gentle yet resolved way. "They're saying the watch just spotted some wagons coming in from the northwest, Scratch."

Bass jerked up, suddenly sobered by the thought that Silas Cooper was back. He got to his knees, not yet trusting himself to stand.

"You say they spotted the wagons?"

Paddock walked across the room. "The day watch on the north wall glassed 'em. They're coming in now."

Bass stood and yanked on the elkhide coat he'd worn for two winters now. He stared down at his rifles, the knives and the pistol he usually cinched about his waist. He shook his head suddenly.

"Time enough to get them later." He turned on his heel and bolted through the open door.

Esau scrambled for his blanket poncho while Josiah swept up his blue capote. They both dashed out the door after the older trapper. Zeke set up a howl after Bass, straining against the ten feet of rawhide rope that tied him to the cottonwood rail in front of the trappers' quarters.

Nearly the whole parapet along the northern wall was already jammed with bodies as fort workers and visitors all gazed into the swirling remnants of the passing storm for sign of the returning wagons. A few held long glasses in their hands, straining to catch a glimpse of something dark appearing out of the receding parade of white. At last there were some shapes—indistinct at first, then the shadows took form. Huge draft wagons could be discerned through the lifting, swirling snow, crawling along out of the northwest like a many-jointed centipede struggling across the gray grasses and frost-stiffened marsh rushes. Over each wagon hung a delicate, misted cloud, issuing from the nostrils of man and mules alike. The harnessed animals strained at the deep snow, some of it carved in wind-iced drifts, their heads down and bobbing with each cold step, frosty breath circling their heads like halos. Drivers and riders all huddled in soggy lumps aboard their wagon seats, indistinguishable from their hump-robe loads—their heads hunkered down into warm collars or capote hoods. A man moved only when he absolutely had to, only when absolutely necessary to direct the animals home.

Now that the wagons were plain to see through the swirling, dancing remnants of the spring storm, someone began to toll the iron bell in the watchtower right next to the old trapper. He nearly jumped out of his skin with the first startling peal clanging out across the countryside to announce a 'welcome home', that bell as much like a beacon for weary plains travelers as a lighthouse that might reach out through the darkness to lodestone a sailor's way home. From the Indian camps scattered down by the river raised a few voices, loud and shrill, surely the excitement of women knowing their men had finally returned. Out of those nearby lodges scurried cloaked figures plowing through wind-scoured drifts and across ice to meet the traders and laborers who had been gone little better than a week now—wives to some of those company employees who lived down in the buffalo skin villages.

There arose more shouting behind them in the quadrangle as a short, swarthy man, dressed head to toe in brain tanned buckskin leggings and wool chaqueta, stepped from his office, ordering the gates swung open for the approaching wagons. He plodded across the snowy roof of his second-level quarters and kicked white plumes of snow down the cottonwood planks with each step as he descended to the bustling compound, pulling a wool greatcoat around his shoulders, shuddering still at the sub-freezing temperatures here at the middle of the day.

Below Bass the huge wood and iron reinforced gates swung open painfully, complaining like rusty buggy springs, a creaking torture to his ears. The old trapper grew intent upon each man riding in those huge draft wagons, intent upon each and every company worker as the procession crawled up to the fort. Just as the first wagons began to pass into the entry portal, Scratch wheeled and flew down the cottonwood steps, two at a time, slipping and unsteady on those icy flakes smearing everything. A plowed arc had been etched across the snow as workers swung open both sections of the inner gate just before the first wagon creaked into the quadrangle. After completing its full circle of the compound, the wagon drew to a halt, facing the north entrance once more. Driver after driver performed the same ritual, plodding slowly around the compound until they came to rest on the eastern side of the fort, nearest the trading room, blacksmith's forge, and cooperage. Not one of the riders or drivers budged until all the wagons were in the fort and brought to a halt.

Mule heads hung in cold fatigue and hunger. Each dark-shrouded rider hunkered against the icy temperature, reluctant to move from what little warmth he had created for himself. The short, dark-skinned man stepped forward.

"Gentlemen!" he shouted. "Welcome upon your return to Fort William. Appears the Utes' hump hunting went well. Get down! Get down!"

Drivers and laborers alike shook the crusted snow from their coats and hats as they crawled to one side of their humped wagons and dropped to the ground. Scratch could smell them all, every one strong on that breeze shuttling round the post. He did not like their odors, that reek of buffalo men so new to him. While a warrior or Injun gal might stink of some rancid bear grease smeared on black braids or coppery skin, these hide hunters stank of rotting hump fat smeared on their clothes, or old, crusty blood and black rotted teeth, long ignored anuses and stiffened urine stains on their britches. Theirs was a breed proud to steer far abreast of soap and water for so long.

Bass mentally checked off each man he saw, eliminating the thin ones, the short ones, those of middling height and frame.

A sudden quake of familiarity coursed through him as his whiskey-reddened eyes focused on one particular, black-coated hulk of a man who was sliding off a creaky seat plank. Bass remembered that hard-jawed face from across all those years. His eyes narrowed as he watched the man dust ice and snow off his shoulders. The stranger ripped his broad brimmed, flat crowned hat from his head and used it to beat icicles from his blood-blackened coat. Scratch had never really forgotten those wide, sloping shoulders which gave the man the appearance of having no neck at all.

"Silas Cooper," he spat, the hushed whisper like a curse not fit for speaking aloud.

Like a shot, Bass wheeled around and headed for the tiny room where he'd left his weapons. He heard Paddock and Esau plodding close at his heels as he brushed by Zeke and stormed into the room, leaving the wooden door open behind him. Their moccasins came to a sliding halt on the beaten clay floor as he yanked on the belt with his two huge butcher knives sheathed at the back. Bass whirled round to face Josiah.

"Just what the hell're you doin', son?" he demanded.

"I ain't gonna let you go on your own, Scratch. I saw that fella Cooper. If you set out alone on this, by damn, you're bent on a fool's errand!" Paddock strapped his belt around his waist, knife over his right hip.

"Told you once, Josiah," Bass grumbled, "this ain't none of your affair. You don't back off now, I'm afraid I'll have to hobble you."

"Why, you stupid scut! Just like McAfferty weren't none of my business either, eh?"

"Yeah," Bass agreed quietly, "just like that hunt for McAfferty. Another cold winter's day, Josiah. Just like today." He waited for Paddock to turn toward the wall to scoop up his pistol.

Esau whipped around at the strange sound, a loud thunk like someone had whacked a chunk of wood against the adobe wall. Josiah slinked to the floor, unconscious. Bass stood over him, stuffing a pistol back into his wide leather belt.

"Y-y-you—" Esau's eyes widened with fear.

"Yeah, I did, Esau." He nodded and whirled to march past the black man. "For his own good. Josiah's got a family waitin' for him in Taos. Now outta my way!" He shoved Esau aside. The black man stumbled over a saddle and banged his head against a wall as he fell.

"SILAS COOPER!"

His loud, croaking voice brutally slapped and silenced everyone in the compound. Cooper was the last to turn around, his black eyes squinting to focus across the snowy quadrangle.

"Yeah. I'm Silas Cooper. Who the hell cares to know?" The deep bass of his voice rang off the cottonwood timbers.

"You remember Bud? Hiram Tuttle?" Scratch began to pace slowly across the snowy, gravel compound. "I'm here 'cause of him. How 'bout Billy Hooks? You remember Billy Hooks, don't you, Silas?"

"Billy Hooks? Yeah, I remember Billy Hooks, my friend. What's this all about? If it makes any difference to you, old Billy's probably back in St. Louis wearing out the ladies of the evening right now."

"Wrong, Silas Cooper! Billy's got a broken mind now, you bastard son of the devil. Don't you remember how you left him?"

Bass waited and got no answer, only the grim, dark eyes glaring back at him, full of wonder, full of hate.

"Silas Cooper, how 'bout you rememberin' the man you killed back to Missouri. And his wife an' little girl you raped afore you come out here to Bents' place. You recall any of them?"

The other drivers and laborers around Cooper backed away a step at a time,

396

giving the big man wide berth. His marble-dark eyes darted here and there among the gathering crowd, accusing them at the same time as questioning.

"I know them, all and one, friend." Cooper shouted as he glared at Bass again. "Tuttle and Hooks both. Yeah. And that little family in St. Louis. They just got in the way of a little fun, that's all."

"Like me, huh? Like me, Silas Cooper?"

There was some twenty feet between them now. The big man pulled open his black mackinaw coat and yanked his pistol free.

"Just who the hell are you, stranger?" His voice rang like a whipcracked command from the walls of the compound.

"Titus Bass!" the old trapper hollered, snagging the pistol out of his belt. The sound of his name joined the dying echo of Cooper's words bounding off the mud walls. "Scratch!"

The last word was drowned out by a low blat of muzzleblast as Cooper brought his pistol up and out and at the end of his long arm, then pulled the trigger.

Scratch ducked as he jerked his own pistol clear of his belt. Not quick enough. The ball smacked against his side, low under his left arm. His gut instantly burned like the fires of hell as he was blown backwards, already twisting out of the line of fire when the shot struck him. He felt the pistol tumble from his grip and didn't know where it landed as he slid to a crumpled stop on the snow-covered gravel.

"Titus Bass." The dark shadow loomed over him. "My, my. Never knowed you lived, Titus Bass."

God, did his side ever hurt—but nowhere near as bad as when he looked up at the small feral eyes that narrowed and glittered crimson like a timber wolf's when it was closing in on downed elk calf. They glowed red and raw, not all of it from the wind and cold. Red and raw, like Cooper'd been punishing the jug hard and steady. Bass smelled the whiskey-sodden breath as Cooper hauled him to his feet.

"Damn, I missed you, Titus. Sorry I bungled my shot, old friend. Meant to get you clean on one ball—put a blow hole in your lights big enough to catch rain water. Now, I'll have to do this slow."

There was something in Silas' face, something Bass hadn't seen all that often in his life, something you only see in reckoning the face of a fella who's been working at the whiskey something serious for several days straight—and what you do see is a strange thing barely hidden behind that face, a strange, walled-off thing. Something so shut off Bass wasn't sure if it was human anymore. He could not figure it for being a human look staring back at him from Cooper's face. And that made the old trapper more than uneasy.

"I apologize, old friend," Silas grumbled as he stared down at the blood soaking through the side of Scratch's shirt and down his legging. "Appears now I'll have to wade on into your young liver."

Scratch drove his knee up and smashed it into Cooper's groin. Silas grunted and clutched himself just as Scratch crunched a gnarled fist into his face. Cooper reeled backwards three steps before he caught himself. He stood motionless in the snow, then touched his fingertips to his bleeding nose.

Scratch eyed a second pistol and a knife stuffed in the buffalo man's belt. He ducked his head and drove with bull fury into Cooper's gut. Silas buckled backwards with an *ooofff* and began hammering on the old trapper's back with his balled, hamhock fists—until he spied the two knife handles. He hauled one out from the back of Scratch's belt and pulled it up, ready for deadly work.

The snow beneath Titus' buffalo moccasins was wet enough to cause them to slip. As the old trapper fell face down in the snow, he felt the blade slash along the back of his thick, elkhide coat. Bass rolled to his side and lashed out with both legs, tripping the big man. Silas crashed to the ground, knife still in his hand.

Although the pain in his left side demanded his attention, Scratch rolled over and over, through the thick snow, escaping from the big man until he could crawl to his knees. He yanked the last knife on his belt, clambered to his feet.

Bass felt woozy from the loss of blood, the shock of the bullet wound.

Cooper struggled to his knees, dusted himself off, and grinned at Bass. "Say, old friend, that was slick as paw-paw pulp. Danged good slip-through you pulled."

Shrill voices rang out about the two men as fort workers yelled for blood, some hollering for the stranger, most screaming their begrudging support for Cooper. Bass paused and caught his breath and watched Silas do the same. They weren't young pups any longer. Just two tired old men, suddenly intent on killing each other.

Bass sucked hard at the dry, cold air, drawing it down deep into his aching lungs. With each expansion of his chest came a lick of unbearable fire branding his lower ribs. All around him swam the faceless spectators, faceless except for Esau's wide eyes beaming out of his fearful ebony mask, and beside Esau, Josiah's face which showed only acceptance of what had to be.

Bass turned to glare at Cooper.

There he saw a reflection of his own face, mirrored from the eons of but a decade ago. Both of them were looking into eternity now, looking at that very great possibility they would join each other in a dance at the gates of Hell before this day was out.

"You learned yourself a few tricks over the last double handful of years, haven't you son?"

Strange to have someone call him son. For so long now everyone else had always been young enough to pay him the deference of age.

"I survived, Silas Cooper," Bass husked. "Now I'm here to do what I should've done a long time ago. I want my money, what you owe me."

Cooper laughed loud, head thrown back with a guffaw that sang off the adobe. "You want what, Titus? Your money? Ha! I spent it all, you weasel-stoned pup! Took every last bit of it. I spent it on bad whiskey and on women who were worse than the whiskey. I used it for a boat, Titus Bass. Then I spent the last of it on more bad whiskey and more bad women, the two most important things in this man's life." Cooper slapped his chest.

"I want my money," Bass demanded again. "You owe me."

"Even if I did have any of your damned money left, Titus Bass, I seriously doubt I'd let you have any of it now. Ten years and you're just now coming to claim it? Shame on you, you little weasel-stoned pup! Why'd you wait so long to come get your money? Huh? You waited too long and now your stones have all shrivelled up."

Bass saw that same ugly, taunting, vicious man he'd once known. And he recognized an evil in Silas Cooper that made the animal in his own being rear right up on its haunches, readied and set to do bloody work without so much as a thought to the outcome. There was no longer any thought. Only will, a will born of action.

"Is it that, my old friend?" Cooper roared with a sick, punishing smile. "Is it that you've no balls left now that the green's wored off?"

"Nawww." Scratch shook his head, gritting against the hot pain in his left side. "Not that at all, old friend. The way I see it, I never had a problem with my stones."

Bass shifted his icy feet and glanced around at the spectators who gathered on both levels of the fort's snowy quadrangle to watch the fight. It seemed everyone connected with Bent, St. Vrain & Company had box seats for the main event of the day, perhaps the main event of the fort's first year.

"Cooper, the way I've come to savvy it, you was the one what had problems with your stones! You run on outta the mountains, didn't you? Run clear back to St. Lou an' left me out here to die. But, I didn't run away—as all can plainly see. Nawww, Silas Cooper—you're the one without the stones of a prairie cock. You still want to kill Titus Bass? Then, you best be about it now, for this is to be your last chance, Silas Cooper. You'll have no others. Dig in your toes for a fast shuffle, Silas Cooper. No more can you run from me!"

He watched Cooper take the tongue-lashing at first, thinking the big man was momentarily dulled from the cold trip, or perhaps numbed by all that whiskey he'd punished to combat the freezing journey home. Then, ever so quietly, the big man took a step. And a second. Now a third before he crossed the distance between them. Cooper's face twisted up to look like a cross between an enraged badger and a wounded boar grizzly. Bass didn't like that look at all.

"I ain't running from you now, Titus Bass. Not now. You've found me. So now, just set yourself on dying slow, for I aim to cause you some grief and pain before you're done in, my old friend. I aim to be hard about it with you. I want to hear you beg, listen to you cry out your prayers that you wish you'd never found me."

Some three more steps and Cooper would be upon him. Three more of those long-shadowed strides and he would be square atop Scratch.

"Silas Cooper," Bass roared with a bull's bellow born deep within him, "if Titus Bass is to die here today, then by all the gods there'll be a new face in hell right beside mine afore the sun sinks to black in the west! By damned, you'll for certain join me in hell tonight!"

The crack of their collision rang off the mud walls, grunts of exertion and the whine of combat quickly smothered once more by the pain-hungry shouts and profane cheers of spectators gratified to see more blood.

All four arms rose over the fighters' heads. Two knives, four arms, every ounce of strength bolted against those locked, straining wrists. Scratch dug his finger-nails into Cooper's right wrist, but Silas switched the knife over to his left hand.

Bass quickly began to dig the fingers into the other wrist, again trying to get the big man to loosen his grip on the huge skinning knife. Instead, the old trapper watched Cooper stare back into his face and grin a black-toothed smile, his breath heavy with whiskey and red peppers.

Then he understood why Cooper had switched hands. The big man's fist was suddenly free and immediately put to work just as Scratch knew he'd made a big mistake, knew as certain as if he had just stomped slap-smack in a pile of fresh mule dab.

Silas swung the hamhock of a fist into the bullet wound. Again and again he pummeled the huge mallet into that bloody trace left by the lead ball along Bass's left side. Scratch grunted and groaned, holding his tiring arms against the knife with everything left in him. Already he knew what he had was not going to be enough to last. His mind told him more than just blood was draining out the holes in his side. His strength was ebbing, and with it oozed away his life. With each succeeding blow driven soundly into the bloody wounds, he felt himself being ripped open by Cooper. Bass knew with the coming of each pounding fist, it would be the last and he would surely fall.

His legs buckled and at last he had to let go of the big man's left wrist holding the knife. He crumbled to the side on his hands and knees, shaking from side to side his swimming head wearily slung between his shoulders. His eye struggled to focus. There Zeke was, straining at his rope, with Esau kneeling beside the gray animal. Both of them good companions. And Josiah stood with them, crying too.

Damn, but he didn't want to see the boy blubber over him. He flat didn't want to see Josiah Paddock cry over a used-up, old mountain trapper. Right then, the bright, hot sparks shot across his vision.

Cooper's moccasined hoof crashed into Bass's ribs, sending Scratch wheeling through the snow and gravel with a yelp of agony and searing pain. Silas stood his ground, laughing, catching his breath. He tossed the skinning knife from side to side, hand to hand, playing with it, laughing crazily, taunting his unarmed, vanquished enemy.

"I'm gonna cut you up just like the Kiowa do it, old friend," Silas growled. "A piece at a time till this compound runs red with your blood. We'll let the Injun dogs gnaw on your bones this night, while you're still breathing. Them Kiowa know a mean trick or two. Just like their cousins, the Comanch'. Thing is, old friend Bass—with them Kiowa, the women do the torture and the blood-letting. Not the men. Too bad, Titus. Too bad. 'Cause here I'm about to do everything I learned from 'em right on you—while everybody including my Kiowa wife watches."

Scratch swallowed hard against the dry air, watching Cooper's hawk eyes dart over to the edge of the crowd to a huddled form of middling height. He supposed it was Cooper's woman, but he could not tell for sure. Her hood was pulled down to shadow her face. At least she wore woman's leggings, and he could see she held both arms crossed beneath her pendulous breasts. Older gal, he thought, as his weary head plopped into the snow.

It was so damned cold, it startled him. He blinked and felt something roar out within him at its icy touch along the hell-hot side. That cheek below his wounded eye grew numb, then his fingers finally tingled with the snow's icy bite.

Amazingly there no longer burned the licks of flame through his side. Their fire had been put out by the icy, numbing cold of the snow. Ready once more, he watched Cooper approach, reach down to snag his collar and drag him over to the site of the unfinished fur press. As Silas flung the old trapper's limp body onto the wide base of the robe press, Bass whirled and lashed out with everything he had left in his tired legs. Both feet exploded dead center into Cooper's chest, knocking the wind right out of him with a loud, grinding grunt, and driving the big man backwards several stumbling steps.

Scratch was on him like a crazed, wounded wolverine before Cooper could recover. The pain in his side gone somewhere else, the old trapper grabbed Silas' hair in his left hand and commenced to pound the big man's face with his right fist. His hand was numb so he didn't know how many times he smashed his fist into that black-bearded, rotten-toothed, marble-eyed grinning face—but now it didn't look at all like Cooper anymore. Both eyes spit blood each time he punched their puffy lids. The busted nose sprayed gouts of crimson over him and dribbled across swollen lips. He worked hard at punishing the big man. Ten years of fury stored up and unleashed at last.

Over and over the old trapper drove his knee into Cooper's groin with savage fury, holding the big man's frame up with both hands. Then he would let go with his right fist to send it careening into Cooper's head. Once more gripping the man's shirt, Titus brought another smashing blow into his groin. Back and forth he worked Silas over like a rabid badger at work on a silvertip, unrelenting, first here, then there, before the big animal could react and defend himself. Tearing, smashing, clutching to bash again and again and again until Cooper lost consciousness and his own rubbery legs could hold him up no longer. Bass had used up all the strength he had left to continue the beating. Bass had used it all up.

He let Cooper go. With a rush of air, Silas grunted to the snow, out as dark and cold as any night. At last the old trapper sagged beside him, his weary eye raking up and down the big man's frame. From Silas' belt he slowly pulled a large skinning knife, well-used over the years, honed and sharpened to mountain readiness. As he took Cooper's hair in his left hand and yanked the big man's head back from his shoulders, Bass put the feather-fine knife edge to the throat.

His ears crowded with the jeers and taunts of those spectators gathered round him in the compound. Scratch held the knife a moment instead of yanking it along the leathery skin over the thick trachea. For his delay, the crowd jeered at him all the louder, taunting what they saw as cowardice. Bass raised his eye and slewed it over the group jostled shoulder to shoulder to watch Cooper's death.

From every open mouth puffed white breath, crying out for him to finish the job at hand. As his eye peeled around the quadrangle slowly, his gaze stopping here and there, Bass began to feel sorry for every one of them. Who were they to taunt him? There truly was not a man among them, a man who could match the likes of Silas Cooper. None of them had ever faced what the glory mountains of the west had to pit against a man—not a one of them. They were but common men, lazy clerks, shirkers at best because they had not come to live and die on the land's terms. No, he decided. Their kind had come to change the rules in the mountain west. Here were the cheaters—these fort builders, the company hands, these little men who dragged civilization along behind them. Who were they to taunt him?

Silas Cooper was more than any ten of them, he roared back at the crowd suddenly. Silas Cooper was bigger and braver than any twenty of them. Bass struggled to his knees, then to his feet.

"Ain't a man among you know what Silas Cooper's shadow crossed ten years ago in these here shinin' mountains. Ain't a man among you could stand to live in his shadow ten years ago! What he saw would cause the likes of you to tremble an' quake an' run back to your mama's skirts!"

He heard himself bellowing, not really knowing where those brave words were coming from. Yet, it was his voice for sure. And the words gushed like warm blood from a slain buffalo's heart in celebration of life, giving life, giving life all over again in that great circle of mystery. The words spilled from him.

For a moment there, Josiah Paddock had watched his old friend, his best friend, and knew it was right for Bass to slit the big man's throat. Just or not, no matter how he felt about killing anymore, Josiah knew it was right for Cooper's life to be given over to Bass. Mountain justice. He had come to understand it. If not to believe in this brand of justice, he had at least come to understand it.

The young trapper had watched Titus Bass's lone eye flitting like a candle, from man to man to man around the quadrangle, the light in that eye unsure and unsteady at first, like the dancing flame of a candle or the flickering lick of fire along a limb. Of a sudden Josiah had been awed to see the fiery light in that one good eye change as the old man creaked to his feet. Its radiance grew strong and steady, sure and bright. And he knew the old man was resolved to what he was to do from here on out. The light from that one eye told Josiah Paddock the old man's courage had never really wavered. A brilliance shone from Bass's face just like a lampwick, unfettered by the winds of change. Steady and sure. Josiah Paddock saw more courage in that gleam than he had ever seen before in Titus Bass.

The old man's eye finally touched each and every man gathered hard and close by to study the blood and the pain and the torture one being can cause another. Always the pain they came to see. His eye leaped out to tell them just how sorry he felt for the lot of them, every damned one. His sorrow was not ridicule, just a realization that said he knew they still had a long way to go down that trail he had already traveled. He truly felt sorry for them—for their wanting to witness his cruelty commited against Silas Cooper. They had gathered close to watch one man kill another and not a single one of them was worth the time it'd take to spit. Scratch leaned over and snagged the back of Cooper's coat collar in one hand, dragging him over to the hide wagons. The muttering crowd surged back out of his way, their whispers wondering what he was about and when he would finish the job. Bass raked the group with his eye one more time, looking for Gilstrap.

"Where's this man's boss?" Scratch hollered, not all that loudly at first. "Where's the trader?" This time his roar demanded an answer.

From the corner of his eye he watched the crowd jostle against itself. The squat, swarthy man presented himself before the old trapper.

"I am St. Vrain. What do you wish of me?"

"Savary, eh? Heard tell of you down to Taos." Bass spit some blood from his lower lip.

"I was there since '25."

"Silas Cooper works for you?" God, but the hole in his side kicked up a hell of an angry fuss.

"He is in the employ of Bent, St. Vrain & Company."

"Cooper works for you, that we know, friend." Scratch spit more blood and licked at the swollen lip. "I wanna know what the man's wages are, simple as that."

"I am afraid that is none—"

"This bastard owes me money, a lot of it. Ten years worth of it now!"

"Still, it would be none—"

He had a hold of Cooper with his left hand, the big man's body slung at the end of Scratch's arm, and suddenly he had a grip on St. Vrain with his right, crushing the short Frenchman's gold-trimmed Mexican chaqueta.

Several of the crowd moved to reach for Bass as he yanked St. Vrain forward, but they fell back from the old trapper and the trader just as quickly. Right behind Scratch stood Esau and Josiah, a pistol and rifle apiece in hand.

"I don't aim to kill you, lil' trader." Bass tried not to snarl. "Want you to know that. But, less'n you tell me just what this nigger's owed for his wages, I aim to take a few dollars of it out of your hide an' anybody else's what's gonna try to stop me from gettin' what's mine."

"Y-you can't come in to my post and proceed to threaten me—"

"I ain't threatenin', Senor," he mimicked St Vrain's French-Mexican accent. "Titus Bass is tellin' you simple. Now, you can pay me, or you can pay Silas Cooper. What'll it be, Savary? You owe the man money, don't you?"

"Well, now. Yes—"

"You can pay me or you can pay him." Bass shook his left arm, at the end of which hung Cooper. "What do you owe the man?"

St. Vrain glared at the old trapper for a moment before his gaze relented and he finally turned his eyes into the crowd. "Hobbs!"

The capote-wrapped wagonmaster stepped forward, rifle still slung across his arm. "You want us to throw the lot of 'em and the goddamned darkie out, boss?"

"Just tell me what Cooper's owed, Hobbs."

"Awww, Cap'n Savary. We throw 'em all out and be done with it. You don't owe Cooper nothing."

"You best tell your cap'n what Cooper's owed, sonny!" Bass dropped Silas' body and loosed his grip on St. Vrain's jacket. He took a step toward Hobbs, a step forward as the wagonmaster slid two steps back.

"Cipher it, Hobbs—and tell me, dammit!" St. Vrain snapped suddenly, his face gone white and tight as rawhide. "Just tell me what Cooper's got coming these last two trips."

"Awww, C-Cap'n—"

"Tell him!" Bass spit the words into Hobbs' face.

"H-he's got some four hundred eighty dollars coming with this trip," the wagonmaster growled in resignation.

"And what's his back pay now?" St. Vrain asked of Hobbs without his eyes leaving Bass's face.

"That amounts to but a few dollars—"

"How much, Hobbs?"

"Forty-six, nearabouts."

"Five hundred twenty-six," St. Vrain nodded with the sum. "Gilstrap! Get me my pay satchel."

Bass never saw the clerk leave. All he heard was that sound of leather boot-soles scraping across the wood and clay, both going and coming back. Gilstrap slung a leather case into St. Vrain's arms and stepped out of the way once more. The bag sure enough looked heavy to the old trapper. St. Vrain counted out the pieces of gold and dropped them one by one into a small, skin pouch which he slapped dramatically into Bass's outstretched palm.

Scratch turned quarter round, his reddened eye slewing the crowd until he found the woman, her hood still cowling her face.

"You Cooper's woman?"

Finally she answered. "Yes. His woman. Coooo-per."

Bass hobbled straight up to her and pushed back the blanket capote hood. Behind him came Esau's gasp of astonishment and Josiah's gulp. Cooper was indeed a cruel, hard, punishing man.

With pity the old trapper gazed into the face of a middle-aged Kiowa woman, cursed with both a hard life and a cruel man to live it with. He thought for a moment how pretty she must have been in those younger years gone by. At one time perhaps the wife of a warrior, then cast out by her own people when that warrior was killed in battle and she was husbandless, without a man wanting her old, sagging, used body.

"You do not live with your people?" he asked of the woman quietly, with his fingers and hands dancing in the language of the plains Indian as he spoke the words aloud.

"They have cast me out," she whispered in reply, her eyes flitting to his. "He took you in?" Scratch indicated Cooper, still sprawled unconscious on the snow near St. Vrain.

"He bought me," she sneered out of the corner of her mouth suddenly, the first real emotion to cross her face. "I—had been used by Comanches who found me, captured me after I was cast out. They had used me up so they sold me for a drink of the white man's whiskey. Coooo-per paid his Kiowa and Cheyenne customers more for a single buffalo robe than he paid for me."

"He fed you, didn't he?"

"He kept me like a dog is fed—and shadowed with his lusts."

404

"How is it you got your—" His voice dropped off and a single finger slashed at his nose to show her what he meant.

The woman's nose had been nearly chopped off, leaving only an ugly, gaping scar where once had been a prominent feature on her face. Two small holes quietly whistled their breath in the dry air. The woman cast her eyes down a moment to the frozen ground.

"I did not want to be his dog anymore," she sobbed. "No longer did I want him to climb on me as the dogs crawl on each other. I met a Cheyenne cousin who wanted to take me away from Coooo-per. We ran to get far away."

"Cooper found you, didn't he?"

Her eyes eventually crawled back to his. Tears glistened on the hideous scars. "My cousin was killed before we could get back to the safety of his people." The woman gazed back down at Cooper and spat on him. "This man is very cruel in how he kills another. Following his disgrace of me, he brought me back to this place with him. Coooo-per called everyone from far around to watch as he lashed me to the front gate. And he used his knife on me, the same bloody knife he killed my cousin with."

"He—Cooper cut off your nose?"

"To mark me as an unfaithful wife—so no other man would want me ever again." The bitter tears had begun to flood down her copper cheeks, welling from the cherry-black eyes. "He laughed each time I tried to escape and each time he cut me more." She pulled aside her dirty, matted black hair to show where an ear had been hacked off and another purple scar wormed down her cheek, disappearing beneath the neck of her dirty capote.

"You do not need to cry anymore, woman. Go, and leave."

"No!" She shook her head violently, the tears pouring. "He will follow me! As he did before!"

"No, woman. He will not." Bass grabbed up one of her hands. "Here." He counted out a palmful of coins as her wondering gaze darted between his eyes and her hand.

"Go back to your people, woman. Forget this man. Forget what he did to you—and to your soul."

"M-my nose! They will never take me back—"

"No, woman. They will welcome you back." Bass gently closed her fingers on the pieces of gold. "Buy them presents. Go back to your people with gifts. They will be glad to have their daughter return home."

Scratch turned and wearily shouldered his way into the smelly crowd, heading for his two friends and Zeke. Spectators washed back in the wake behind him as he pressed through the throng. Suddenly a shriek flew across the compound and screams echoed back at the wagons.

He whirled, apprehensively, positive Cooper was rushing at him. Hot juices of danger squirted through his veins again. The old trapper stood crouched and frozen, paralyzed by what his eye fell upon.

Silas stood on wobbly legs in the middle of the snowy compound, his knees shaking. At the end of his arm hung a huge horse pistol that had been pointed at

405

the old trapper's back. Slowly, the huge, yawning muzzle was dropping to aim at the snow. Across his leathery face no fear crimped the features. Instead, Silas Cooper wore only a look of bewilderment, a look of astonishment and total surprise.

Behind Silas stood the Kiowa woman, her capote hood and head thrown back wildly, her right arm flailing away with a small camp axe she must have had concealed beneath her coat. Already she had cleaved off the side of her man's head and continued to savagely hack at his shoulders, his neck, the back of his head, spraying blood and gore on everyone crowded close by as they frantically scrambled to get out of the way of her attack. She shrieked like a banshee with every blow, every sickening thunk slicing into Cooper's body as it refused to go down. Blood gushed over what was left of his bewildered, wondering face as she crushed his skull with her axe.

Nearby, the wagon mules "scree-hawed" at the stench of fresh blood on the dry breeze. Finally Cooper collapsed and she with him, squatting on the big man's body, screeching out her Kiowa curses on the soul of Silas Cooper. Around her, not a single person moved to stop the woman from her bloody task. No one uttered a word. The compound rang heavy with their stunned silence. After all, she was due.

Blood weeps slower, harder at times. And blood always weeps longer.

31

BASS TURNED AWAY from the grisly scene and motioned for Josiah and Esau to be off and readying their animals for departure. Before he plodded two more steps, the old trapper crumpled to the snow.

Paddock was at the old man's side in that next moment, for the first time realizing just how much blood Scratch had lost. Crimson spread its icy film over most of the left side of the Scratch's shirt and down the legging. With so much blood soaking everything, it amazed the young trapper to find a faint heartbeat ticking in Bass's chest, his quaking ribs rising and falling in short, labored gasps. He scooped his old friend from the trampled snow and threaded through the silenced crowd that parted before him like a wake spreading out from a beaver's nose as it skimmed across the glasslike surface of a timberline pond.

By the time he got Bass inside their little room, Esau was already there, spreading the robes and blankets out for the old man's comfort. Although his ebony cheeks glistened, Esau uttered not a word, stifling his quiet sobs and for the moment, fighting to keep his grief to himself.

Most carefully Josiah pulled up the bottom of the old man's warshirt to inspect the wound in his side. Both entrance and exit wounds oozed the crimson fluid unchecked over skin as white as a fish belly. He would first have to stop the bleeding or his old friend would surely die.

"I will send for someone who can help."

Paddock turned, surprised to find St. Vrain hunched over him, peering down at the old trapper's wounds. As soon as Josiah nodded, the trader wheeled and sped from the tiny cell. At the narrow doorway a thick knot of onlookers stepped aside for him, momentarily allowing a smattering more light into the room as St. Vrain disappeared into the crowd. Paddock cut two small hunks of buffalo robe and clamped them over the wounds, holding the fur against the bleeding as tightly as he could, all the while biting his lower lip, bitter tears sliding silently down his cheeks, one lonely drop after another.

Both hands were cramped and hard to free by the time someone tapped a finger on his shoulder. It was St. Vrain, and with him stood a short, wrinkled, old Cheyenne wizard. The Indian was painted and feathered, his sagging, ribby chest bare and streaked with grease and pigment and blood to visualize his most potent symbols.

A quick inspection beneath the chunks of buffalo fur and the medicine man flicked his eyes up at Josiah. Then he rambled off some foreign, toothless words.

"He says the bullet passed on through," St. Vrain translated from Cheyenne.

"I know the goddamned ball went on through him." Josiah shook his head in exasperation. "I can see where it came out, dammit! Doesn't he have anything better to tell us about the old man? What can he do to help him? Will he keep him alive? Dammit, is Titus going to die?"

Josiah turned away, almost collapsing himself and fell against Esau who steadied the young trapper. Now they had to be content to watch, each with his own private faith that the old man could be brought back from death's door.

The old Cheyenne began by blowing some powder into the two holes through an eagle wingbone. Whatever it was, that powder started the wounds bleeding all over again, harder still. As the old man put two small gourd cups beneath the holes to catch the crimson fluid, Paddock leapt to his feet, angrily lunging for the medicine man.

St. Vrain and Esau caught him short, yanking him back from Bass's pallet.

"You must calm yourself," St. Vrain soothed. "There isn't a damned thing you or I can do now. Perhaps this old Cheyenne is your friend's only chance."

"S-so many times," Josiah began to sob, no longer fighting the arms that restrained him, "Scratch told me to have f-faith in how things would always turn out for the best if a man just tried to make his own luck every once in a while. B-but, dammit—all I can remember now is him asking me this morning what it felt like to—die."

He sank of his own accord to the clay floor and pushed himself back to the saddles and studied the Cheyenne's ministrations in strained silence.

With the blood collected in the tiny gourd cups, the medicine man smeared nondescript animal and celestial symbols alike across the old trapper's chest, face and groin. Next, he struggled to his feet and took pinches of some type of dust or ashes, tossing them into the air over the body until the room was filled by the starry particles dancing on the muted sunbeams faintly streaming into the room over the heads of the curious spectators clustered at the door. With a buffalo bladder rattle he pulled from his belt, the old wizard then began to chant and stomp his arthritic dance around Scratch's pallet. Over and over the sing-song of his chant echoed off the mud walls.

For a little more than two hours, the old Indian wearily mumbled his prayers until he finally collapsed from exhaustion and thirst. By now his own painted symbols and figures were smeared with sweat and rubbing. The old wizard gasped for breath, his left hand fluttering to Bass's right shoulder as delicately as a lilypad would float upon the quiet surface of a summer pond.

Low in the southern horizon, the late winter sun at last dipped out of the lifting snowclouds. Gold waves splashed into the compound, streaming over the heads of those fort workers who kept a silent vigil at the door. The particles of dust and ash danced all the more vividly as the sunlight broke into the tiny room.

Painfully groggy, the old trapper's head slowly creaked to the left as the warmth of the sunbeam brushed his cheek.

Paddock's breath caught in his throat. He began to rise, then caught himself. With a hand he quietly tapped Esau to watch. Together they heard the old medicine man gulp without twitching a muscle.

For long minutes Bass let the yellow sunbeams wash over his face as they streamed into the tiny room, aimed directly at his pallet. Only now did he finally raise his eyelid, the left one, that wrinkled, leather lid over the milky, useless eye. With it he stared at the sun for such a long, long time, a look of peace gradually softening the crimp of pain and fear that had been chiseled across his weather-etched face. It was not until the sun finally dipped into pink below the southern wall of the fort that the old trapper bid farewell to the warming light and closed his milky eye. He was so tired, so damned tired, as the sun sank in fire and loneliness, like an ache of ages, spread upon this great land.

When the trapper's head turned back to the right and both eyes were closed again, the ancient medicine man waited until the breathing was regular and deep once more before he struggled to his creaky knees. He crabbed his withered, wrinkled form around the foot of Titus' pallet to check the wounds. With a bright, toothless grin, he peered over at Josiah through the falling darkness of twilight. A few gummy words were mumbled as he put the buffalo fur back on the holes.

St. Vrain knelt beside the young trapper. "The old man says the bleeding has stopped and your friend is back from the Land of Darkness where souls cry."

"Oh, Lord!" Paddock whispered in a gushing sob as the tears began to creep down his cheeks again.

In relief Esau put his arm around the young trapper as St. Vrain rose and stepped from the room, throwing a blanket over the old Cheyenne's shoulders. Black slave and white trapper huddled together long after the door was closed and the crowd shut out from the tight circle of their little world. The darkness brought with it that cold of a winter long in leaving the land.

With the disappearance of the sun, their tiny cell quickly grew chilled. Esau threw some more greasewood on the coals, their only light now through that long night as each man shared his turn at watch over the old trapper.

Those first streaks of gray light were creeping like a thief to steal the black of night away when Josiah awoke with a start. Something intangible had awakened him, nudged him up and out of that private place where the mind goes when a man has had too much to ponder.

Immediately he sensed there was something wrong with the old man and kicked free of his blankets, burning with shame that he had fallen asleep during his watch. On hands and knees he crawled and slid to Scratch's side, fearing he would find the old man dead. Such a cold, bitter knot rose in his throat, rank with the taste of bile.

Instead, he found that look of peace still gracing the old man's face. But now, clutched in his right hand, Bass had that medicine pouch he always carried around his neck. Just barely visible through the wrinkled fingers in the newborn gray light of dawn, Josiah could begin to make out a quillwork pattern Waits-by-the-Water had sewn on the pouch. A bright wheel of light, rays of greasy yellow and oxblood red radiating out from the magical power circle of the sun.

Josiah peered down as his own teardrops began to spot Scratch's buckskin warshirt, already stitched and bloodstained along that line where the Irishman had tried to plunge a knife into the old trapper's heart. Teardrops making dark splotches on the smoked-brown shirt; dark circles, each and every one, like the blood of life itself. Circles with no beginning and no end. Just like all the old ones had tried to teach him.

The awesome power and unspeakable mystery of that greatest circle of all—life.

IT WAS not until that second day following the fight with Cooper that Bass had at last grown conscious of his surroundings and well enough to be held up to sip at a stew broth Esau brewed up with Charlotte's help. Of her own accord, she had helped the ex-slave prepare poison-drawing poltices for the two wounds at the trapper's side—huge, gaping, oozing holes that crusted and bled, crusted and bled, until at last the old man himself had awakened and begged for something to eat.

Esau and Josiah cried in joy at that moment, and bustled about their tiny cell to stir up a fire and put something on to boil. It wasn't until after Bass had wolfed down two bowls of thick, meaty broth that they finally told him just how long he had been gone from them. With a faint smile Titus leaned his head back into the blankets, signalling that he had had enough soup and wished to sleep again.

"J-just like I told you both." His whispered words were raw and raspy. "Neither of you get rid of Titus Bass that easy." His smile led him into the land of peaceful sleep.

Five more days came and went before Bass was strong enough to ride in a travois slung behind his buffalo runner. On the seventh day after Scratch had been shot, the impatient trio waited while the fort's huge gates creaked open just as dawn seeped over the spring prairie to the east. They pointed their noses south toward Raton, beyond the rim to Taos and the little family waiting for them in Mexico.

Air so fresh and new and blossoming full of life that it stung their nostrils and lungs like sweet ether going down. A yellow-breasted meadowlark cried out, *Kuk, kuk, br-r-r-r*, as it fluttered its nervous white tail feathers in the pinon ahead of them. On they plodded through the *Moon of New Grass* across the wide white plains under the bright blue dome of the heavens. Spring was roaring up the slopes of the mountains once more, set on wiping away the effects of the storm that had blanketed itself upon the land. The hard-crusted snow whimpered every time a man stepped on it, or creaked beneath the lodgepole travois bouncing across the prairie—ever closer, closer still to those mountains where she waited for his return.

Their route up the Raton followed a well-worn path strung along a steep valley. On either side they were shouldered in by sharp, abrupt hills dotted with pine and pinon and sprinkled with gray rock. Most of the way the trio climbed beside a creek that tumbled behind them on its way to the *La Purgatoire* of the Mexicans, the Picketwire of the southern plainsman.

It was their last night out, coming down from the icy mountains into the first ridges of foothills surrounding the beautiful San Fernando valley. Bass was anxious at first to hurry on to Taos and Mateo Kinkead's homestead. But just as quickly he decided instead he wanted to rest the night and go down fresh in the morning. Their little fire popped and crackled, each man very much in his own thoughts of homecoming as sunset spread itself over the western edge of the world.

"Sometimes, seein' such a pretty sight as that out yonder just somehow makes up for a lot of hard doin's a man goes through." Bass lay easy on the lukewarm edge of consciousness.

"I don't think I ever see'd anything quite so pretty as that sun goin' down out there." Esau was mesmerized by the sight. "Nothin' quite so pretty."

"So how come you stayed on with us, Esau?" Bass inquired as he sipped on brutally cold water from a stream flowing beside their camp. "Here I take pains gettin' you to Bents' place, then you up an' take off into the wilderness again on me."

"M-Mr. Titus, I done promised myself, an'—I promised you that first night— you was down, Esau wasn't 'bout to take off on you like that. Not the way you was. No, Mr. Titus. Esau ain't that kind. You didn't give up on Josiah that time he got hisself tossed off his pony in the buffalo stampede. You kept on lookin' till you knew he was gonna be all right. Esau ain't gonna let you down an' give up on you."

The black man's eyes darted back to the fire like dark hummingbirds, then nervously to the brilliant star-dusted sky overhead when he saw the old trapper quietly begin to cry, tears creasing down his leathery cheeks. Esau knew Bass would be embarrassed if anyone saw him cry. Paddock had turned away and plodded into the trees outside the bright circle of their firelight to gather more deadfall, along with a swipe at his own nose to free it of those sniffles threatening to embarrass him.

It was some time before anyone spoke again. But at last the old trapper cleared his throat of clogging emotion and gazed at Esau with that one good eye gleaming clear in the firelight.

"I thank you for carin' the way you do, son. I don't think I'd made it if I didn't have good friends to watch over me. More an' more an' more every day, Titus Bass comes to know that no matter how hard the winters of my life—spring is always sure to come along."

THE NEXT cold dawn Scratch asked his young partner to bind up his wounds especially tight. With bandages repaired and finally in place, Josiah watched in amazement as Bass hobbled off toward the buffalo runner all by himself.

"W-wait, goddammit!" he yelled, trotting after Bass. "We haven't got your travois strapped on yet, Scratch."

"Today, I'm gonna ride in like a man, Josiah."

Paddock stopped dead in his tracks, speechless for a minute, rubbing at his nose, deep in thought. "You—you sure you're fit enough? Certain you don't want to ride more comfortable in the travois?"

"By God, I'm a man as spry as a spring rooster what's spent enough goddamn time in that contraption already. I ain't gonna go ridin' into Taos an' up to Kinkead's place laid out in no gandy-bed like this here!"

The old trapper wheeled slowly. "Esau! You pull them robes and blankets of mine off that travois an' roll 'em up proper-like—the way I taught you things're done in the mountains. You hear me?"

Esau finally nodded as a huge smile sprouted ear to ear across his mahogany face. "You bet, Mr. T-Titus. G-glad to have you feelin' better. 'Tis good you're back with us again, friend."

Scratch stopped his clumsy hobble, startled a bit. He slowly turned back to stare at the slave, then scrambled three steps to Esau and flung his arms around the black man.

"I'm truly glad to be back with you, my friend."

Just as quickly, the old trapper whirled round and busied himself with the cinch of his buffalo runner, his head tucked down and away from judging eyes.

Josiah understood and nodded for Esau to be about what Bass had asked him to do. Then he himself went about saddling the other two riding animals with his own Santa Fe and the pack saddle Esau rode upon. The horses stood rump-tucked and hide-shaking beneath a cruel spring morning wind.

"Esau's learning, Scratch. He truly is."

The old trapper turned round, his eyes reddened and raw with the cold air. "He'll be one to go on doin' just that, Josiah."

A gentle smile began to spread its warmth across his face as Bass stuffed his right foot in the stirrup. By hauling himself up on the horn, Scratch finally got his rump into the saddle. The buffalo runner turned its head around to cast a quick, appraising glance at its old master.

Bass stroked the animal's neck a moment, then gazed over at Paddock. "That man will go on learnin' for you, Josiah. He's got a heart in his brisket as big as that scroungy old horseblanket he dragged into our camp that first mornin' we met up. Esau'll do you proud."

Paddock opened his mouth to speak but before any words could cross his lips, Scratch threw up a hand for silence. "Don't you argue with me on this, Josiah Paddock. There's a damned lot of wrinkles on my horns an' I've come to know that for some, a change of grass sure can make the calf seal fat an' sleek. So don't you dare go hunchy on me now, young'un—'cause I finally got things all sorted out. There was a time there at Bents' Fort I figured everything had turned sour an' gone to clabber—wouldn't ever see my woman an' that baby she's 'bout ready to get shet of. Makes—makes a man think twice, it does. About those dependin' on him. Trust is a real soft—fragile thing, Josiah. Almost like a tiny, little flower you can hold softly in your hand without breaking. Trust like that is hard to come by, son. There's four folks countin' on you, trustin' in you to do what is right by them, Josiah."

"Four of them? I-I don't understand four." Josiah gazed at the ground for a moment, wagging his head. "Looks Far and Joshua."

"That's two of 'em, son," Bass agreed and nodded, wrapping his left arm around his wounded side at a sudden twinge of pain. "Esau's the third."

"E-Esau?"

"That's right. He's countin' on you now more'n he's ever counted on anybody before. You can see it a'times in the man's face."

Josiah gazed at the black man as Esau finished lashing the robes and blankets to the pack animals. "If—if you say so, Scratch. But, who's the fourth one?"

"Young'un, back there at Bents' Fort I was a foolish ol' man. I'd been hopeful there for a lil' bit, hopeful but foolish to believe Cooper'd never go after his Kiowa woman to bring her back an' cut her some more, maybe even kill her. I was a hopin' but foolhardy to think such a thing there. It took me awhile to realize that gal was lookin' at things in a whole lot more real way than I was when she went ahead an' killed him. The woman, pure an' simple, had seen to it Cooper would no more threaten to cut her, no more would he ever stab her soul and make it bleed."

"I don't understand what any of this has got to do with me and those folks depending and trusting in me."

"I-I make mistakes a'times, Josiah," Bass answered suddenly, blurting it out. "An' now I'm trustin' in you to do what's right by all the rest of them folks who count on you."

"I see. You're the fourth one?"

"That's right, son. An' I'm countin' on you to make me proud I knowed Josiah Paddock once upon a time."

Scratch tapped heels into his pony's ribs and set the animal off through the trees. Behind him, Josiah and Esau scrambled to get aboard their horses and pulled the pack animals along down the hill, following after the old trapper. Each and every step southward brought Bass closer, ever closer to her. That thought, that nearness was a pain-drawing balm of itself—easing that agony brought to him by so many hours in the saddle. His heart was going home at last, after a grueling, agonizing journey. She was his home—wherever she was. The woman was the only home he could remember ever having, that home for his restless heart he had been searching for across half a lonely wilderness and that forever span of forty years. She was his home.

Down through the pine and aspen and cedar, flowers starring the foothill meadows they crossed, stirring up the perfumes of bluestem, shootingstars and scarlet globemallow before they dropped to the valley floor and the bright crimson show of Indian paintbrush.

A goldfinch sang out from a nearby pinon. *See-see-ee! Baby-babeee!* Even the air had a mellow, spring luster to it, decked out with fleecy clouds colored a rosy, newborn hue. The round stemmed prickly pear cactus dotted the plain, its sharp spines bedecking every pancakelike leaf. Here and there the pamilla, with its bayonet arms, joined the ocotillo and barrel cactus. A green fan of the soap plants spread among the aromatic silver sage, harsh and stiff in savory rebirth. The scents of chokecherries and wild plum and sweet rose lay heavy and seductive on the breezes that bent the rich grasses before them. Everywhere around the horsemen this silent prairie uttered the supreme joy of new life.

It was a high, clean country he was destined to live in, country as wild as any animal that roamed its far reaches, country pretty as paint and still more seductive to boot. And it was country as lonesome as time itself.

The little group had pushed on through the icy, cluttered streets of Taos, attracting no special attention, and headed south along the road to Kinkead's little ranch. They rode past a new American-owned grist mill going up alongside a burbling stream. Here and there gringos were establishing themselves all the more in Taos as blacksmiths and gunsmiths and businessmen. With happy waves the trio was greeted by a group of farm children pulling away from the new mill in a carreta rolling atop a dry axle, squealing as noisy as a stuck pig.

Mateo must have spotted the horsemen coming down the spring-muddied ruts and announced it to all. His yard filled quickly as the main house and Rowland's hut belched free those who stood watching the three riders approach.

Zeke loped alongside the old trapper's mount, and finally looked up at the old trapper with expectant eyes. Bass nodded to the dog, in that secret language only they understood.

"Yep, ol' boy," he whispered down to the dog, "this is a good place. You go on ahead. I'll be along shortly."

The dog shot off at a brisk, happy gallop, tearing through the grass and around the brush lining the muddy road. Scratch had to chuckle. Damn, but that was a good feeling. He hadn't laughed in such a long time.

"I don't see a cradleboard, old man." Josiah was beside him a moment later. "Just a fat woman down there."

Titus stared into the distance and could not make out anything but the shapes of shadowy forms willowing like a mirage by the front door. The hot tears did not help things at all.

"Y-you see all that plain from here, son?"

"Yeah," Josiah smiled back at Bass. "And what I can make out is that you aren't too late to see that baby of yours get born, my friend. It looks like you made it here in time."

A single tear spilled from his milky eye as the old trapper turned ahead once more to gaze at the group gathered to welcome the travelers home. Now he saw her arm raise high in the air and wave to him. She was trying to run, but she looked more like a clumsy, fat buffalo cow than the thin, willowy girl he had left behind so long ago in the cold of Winter Man's breath bearing down on the plains. She waddled to a stop at the adobe gate, catching her wind, a hand to her swollen belly, another hand clasped at her mouth in wonder and awe and joy.

As if the horsemen had only been gone to town for an hour, the scarred, gray dog loped right on up to Waits-by-the-Water and plopped his chin in her hand like he had known her all his life, his tail wagging so hard it was bound to fall off any moment. Just as quickly, Waits-by-the-Water knew this animal belonged to her man, as surely as she too belonged to his life. Zeke wheeled and sat beside the young woman, tail still wagging happily on his homecoming, his tongue lolling, looking back and forth between Waits-by-the-Water and the oncoming riders cresting the last little knoll up the road.

At the gate the old trapper slid painfully from his buffalo runner and slapped its rump. The pony would remember where to go. It had been here before.

He stood for a moment only, testing his wobbly knees, before he lunged for her desperately. First he clutched the woman to him as if he would never let her go. Here was life itself to him, the very breath he pulled into his nostrils, the food that fed his soul its strength. At last both of them were soaked with each other's tears and he backed off a step.

"By God an' Jehoshaphat's back teeth, if you ain't a balm for these sore eyes!"

Now he gave her a long once-over, the first time he had had to study the woman in many months. The old trapper put his hands around her belly, marvelling at its size where she carried it low on her hips.

"You look awful close to calf time, woman." Then he knelt and put an ear to the roundness at her belly button.

"This is my baby," he whispered. "Your papa is talkin' to you, lil' one. I'm your papa."

"It is the first time this little life has heard your voice in such a long, long time, my husband." From eyes suddenly bright and birdlike, tears streamed down her cheeks.

"My heart was strong to get here before your time."

"W-we waited for you, the little life and I. For so long a stone lay upon my heart in waiting. N-now with the excitement of your return, we both can wait no longer."

She slowly pulled up the side of her capote and dress to show him, exposing the brain-tanned doeskin leggings both soaked with fluid.

"Rosa!" he turned to holler.

Mateo and his wife trotted up from welcoming Josiah and greeting Esau to their home.

"Rosa! Help me. Help me, please. I'm gonna have a b-baby!"

EARLY by dawn's light the next morning a brand new baby girl had come into the world, wailing away with such a powerful set of lungs, she could be but one man's daughter.

Rosa had brought the tiny child to the bedroom doorway and presented her to Bass, who wore a smile full of joy and wonder.

"Ain't ever held my own—baby afore."

The little pinkish cheeks flushed as her tiny fingers opened and closed, opened and closed around one of his thick gnarled thumbs. Scratch stepped into the birthing room and plopped down on the pallet beside his wife. For the longest time he was simply without words, content to gaze back and forth between Waits-by-the-Water and his newborn daughter's face.

"Y-you are happy, my husband?"

"Oh, yes, dear one," he replied in Sparrowhawk, his eyes darting anxiously to the doorway where a small crowd of his friends had gathered. He was nervous although he knew the others understood little of the Crow tongue. "I am so proud of you, I can't begin to tell you all my heart has to say. My woman has given us a daughter. And a beautiful gift she is to behold."

"T-then—you are not disappointed?" She dropped her eyelids to the bright comforter Rosa had wrapped around her after the long, arduous labor process.

"Wha-a-a?" he blurted out in English before remembering. "No, I am not

415

disappointed at all, dear one. You think I would be saddened because you did not give me a son?"

Her only answer was a quick nod of her head. Still her eyes did not rise from the comforter.

"Woman—" He took his free hand and placed his fingers beneath her soft chin, gently raising it so he could gaze into her eyes, and she into his. "Woman of my heart, I look down at this beautiful face you have given our child, those tiny fingers and toes, her eyes like ripe chokecherries, skin the color of the sky in the west at sunset. How could I possibly be disappointed with what we have done here with Grandfather's blessing? He is truly the one who decides what child to grant us. With this little one," Scratch smiled as he chucked a finger beneath the baby's chubby chin, "I am well pleased and would take no other. Boy or girl."

Waits-by-the-Water bolted upright to fling her arms around the both of them, hugging her man and newborn child frantically. She had been so frightened he would not want the girl child, since most Indian males wanted only boy children. Tears bubbled and welled in her eyes, her heart filled almost to bursting with that joy she felt once more that he was home with her again and the long wait for this little life was over.

"You will not worry that she is a little girl, my husband?"

"No, dear woman. I will not worry—until she reaches the age when the boys start lusting after her and want to drag her into the bushes with them."

"You—you are such a devil man at times! That is so many years from now, it is a long time before you have to watch after your daughter every minute."

"Just as your father had to watch you, pretty one?"

She nodded and lidded her eyes again. "Yes. Just as my own father had to keep his stern eyes watching out for me."

"I'll bet you drove all the little boys wild, didn't you?"

"But, I had eyes only for one in those growing years."

"Ah, and did he not want you? That is it? That is why you never married?"

"No, he did not marry anyone else."

"Was the one you had eyes for, was he killed? A warrior taken in battle?"

"I thanked Grandfather every time the one I wanted came back to our camp at those winter times. But, no—he was not an Absaroka warrior."

"Waits-by-the-Water, you are confusing me. The one you wanted was not a Sparrowhawk warrior?" He watched her nod her head in answer. "When you were growing into a woman, who was this man you had your eyes set on?"

"My heart was already set on you, *Pote Ani*."

"B-but—"

"You have been coming to visit my people for many winters now. More than the fingers of one hand and three on the other. I grew to be a woman, knowing I wanted to be the wife of that man with the snow sprinkled in his face hair, wife to the *masta-sheela* whose green eyes twinkled merrily whenever he looked at the little children playing in our winter camps. I ached to be the lover to that man who cared for his animals each day as if they were part of his own family. That is the man I came to love and wished to marry."

416

"M-me?"

"Among the white man who has no tribe to protect and sustain him, a man and a woman need each other all the more I think. It is this way with us now. We have each other, my husband. And we have our daughter to bring us the joy only a child can bring to its parents. I will give you sons, many sons—"

"Whoaaa! Hold on there, woman. Let's just take it one pup at a time. I would like a son, someday—a son to teach in all those ways the mountains of this great land have taught me. But, we do not need to hurry. There are many years left to us, you and I. Many years, dear one. So, someday, I will tell you all about my trip to that city by the great river. A river so much bigger than anything you have ever seen here in the mountains. Too, I will tell my wife about the people I met while I was in that great city of the *masta-sheela*. And, if my woman so wants, I will take her and our daughter to visit that wondrous place someday. There are people there who wish to meet you, dear woman."

"They wish to meet m-me?"

Bass cracked a wide smile. "And they will learn to love you as I have. We will take our daughter and show her this place where the white man crowds together thicker than the buffalo herds cover the prairies."

"This would truly be a marvelous place. Bigger than this Ta-house?"

"Much, so much bigger, with as many white men as there are stars in the eastern sky at night."

She shook her head in wonder at his words and swiped at her teary eyes. "Then, someday soon you will also tell me about how it was you came to spill your blood on the shirt I made for you." The woman ran a fingertip first along the ragged seam he had repaired over his heart where dark crimson stained the leather beneath those crude sinew stitches. Next she tapped lightly along his left side where practically the whole shirt was blotted dark, the garment now no longer hidden from view beneath his elkhide coat.

"S-someday," she choked somewhat on her words, "soon, you will tell me how it was you came to wager your life to come back to my side."

"I am here with you at long last," Bass sighed, staring down at his daughter's sleeping face. "Not much else matters but you, and this little one we made with the Grandfather's blessing. It does not matter what I had to do to get back to you both. I am here, and will never have to leave your side again. I promise my heart to you on that, dear woman."

"I—I want to go home now," she stammered a little, the tears beginning to flow once again down her coppery cheeks. "Go home to our mountains. I have been long enough in this town where so many want to live. I want us to go home again, husband."

"I will take you as soon as you are ready to travel."

"We will leave tomorrow—"

"When you are ready to travel, woman."

"I want to go back to my place in the world, *Pote Ani*. My place, the mountains up there that all know who I am. I have grown up with them, and they know my name."

"Your husband did not grow up with the mountains, my woman." He looked into the welling pools of her dark eyes. "But, I have grown old with them. They too are my home. They too know my name."

"I want to rest now, my husband."

"You both must rest." He laid the child within the crook of her arm, placing the comforter over the babe. "Both of you worked hard to see this morning's sun. Rest now while I prepare for our trip back home."

Waits-by-the-Water turned her head on the goosedown pillow and closed her eyes, a smile painted in gentle pastel across her face.

"Yes, my husband," she whispered softly. "Take us back where they know our names."

32 OVER THE NEXT two days it was hard for Bass or Looks Far, even for Rosa to keep the Crow woman confined to her bed. She simply had not been raised that way. Waits-by-the-Water was constantly getting up, being discovered, and being taken back to her room. She was happy only in being busy, mixing this in the kitchen or fussing with that in the main salon where everyone gathered between the big meals Rosa always prepared. The young mother was quick to regain her strength after the delivery and was anxious to begin her trip north.

Her husband had been no less anxious to prepare for that journey. In the shed where his pelts had been stored for the winter, Bass found Kinkead had set aside none for himself to pay for the women's keep while the two trappers had been gone. Mateo had only laughed and claimed that the Indian girls had eaten so very little, he and Rosa had hardly missed it. Kinkead remained adamant that Bass owed him nothing in the way of pay or plews.

So the old trapper had busied himself sorting through the pelts, grading them once more, going over their respective values with Josiah to be sure the young man knew just what they were worth. Later, in private, Bass had rummaged through their store of powder, lead, beads, axes, knives, wiping sticks, flints, finger rings and bracelets, and the leftover tradecloth the two women had used for new dresses at last summer's rendezvous along the Green River.

Bass stuffed a large handful of flints into a rawhide satchel, setting aside a few wiping sticks he lashed together with whangs. A little powder and even less of the bulky lead he packed away for their journey north into the mountains. Most everything he set aside, laying it all out for Josiah's inspection on the darkest, richest, most luxurious beaver pelts the two of them had trapped last fall up to the Bayou Salade. It all filled the tiny storeroom, spread across the floor as it was—quite a display if a man should decide to open up a shop for the Mexican trade.

The final task proved to be the animals out in the large corral they had built with Kinkead at the beginning of last winter just after their arrival in Taos to spend a cold robe season in the warm bosom of friendship. He gazed longingly at those horses now, thinking back on how often a man gets his plans changed for him. At times, things seem to unravel right before his eyes—just how instead he had spent his winter fighting off the cold of hatred, evil, and death. Beneath the spring skies pranced the beautiful ponies they had traded from the Nez Perce,

419

what seemed now like so damned long ago. Their spotted rumps flagged in among the paints and piebalds and duns of the Arapaho warriors come to count coup on white trappers and from the Pawnee chasing down an escaped prisoner.

That final night, Bass cut out Waits-by-the-Water's favorite Absaroka pony, his own buffalo runner, Samantha, and two other ponies for packing. These he pulled out of the large corral after darkness had inked itself across the valley and placed those animals in the smaller corral near the shed. Beneath the stars of spring the old trapper slung bags filled with corn over the animals ears. They would need that strength the grain would give them for the coming journey north.

Scratch stepped from the kitchen door of Mateo's squat adobe building into the cold, spring air of pre-dawn darkness. Looks Far, Joshua, and Josiah had spent the night in their little hut behind Kinkead's, but Rosa continued to insist Waits-by-the-Water and Bass should sleep in the big house.

He sucked in the chill air, feeling it sing through him. *Moon of First Eggs.* May, to these folks here. His mind wandered a moment as he tugged the old coat about him a little more tightly. Titus knew he would shed it before noon, but for now it felt damned good to have the warmth and familiarity of the elkhide around his tired, old shoulders. The right shoulder joint had begun to ache a little more than usual in the last few days. Ah, what the hell, he thought. He would soon be on the way and would not have time to worry about it. His first cold duty was to cut out the little Arapaho pony Esau had grown so accustomed to on their ride west to the mountains. Throwing a rawhide hackamore over its nose, Bass walked the animal out of the big corral, right over to the little shed. After he had cinched that Spanish saddle Don Armijo had thrown in with Samantha atop the piebald pony, Scratch draped the fancy silver-roweled spurs over the cantle and brought the horse to the hitching post at the side of the adobe house where it was soon joined by those animals Bass and his woman would push north.

What little they were taking with them was already packed atop the restless ponies, themselves eager to be gone from the corral and on their way once more. Waits-by-the-Water saw him motion to her from the window where she had been watching, waiting, eager for this tearful moment to be over and they could be gone. He beckoned to her again and she slid from the wooden door into the front yard to stand among their animals. Man's and beasts' breath alike hung in halos like thick tissue over their heads.

Scratch heard the back door scrape across the hard clay ground, the footsteps slurring across the morning-damp soil and then two dark forms leapt out of the indigo background. The squat Kinkead and his Rosa, his arm slung around her shoulders in tandem, both scuffled up to Scratch's little group of horses.

"Here, now. Give me your hand, me hearty. You weren't really going to leave without a word of farewell, were you, friend?"

"I-I couldn't do that, Mateo." His eyes wandered over to Rosa and the Crow woman, exchanging hugs and teary kisses on the cheeks, hurried, whispered words flying back and forth between them, cooings given the baby girl wrapped tightly in Waits-by-the-Water's cradleboard. "Neither of us could leave without

420

saying just how much we owe you for all you done for the both of us—the three of us."

"You don't owe us a thing, Scratch." Mateo shook his head and slapped Bass atop the shoulder before he hauled the old trapper into a fierce embrace. "You have given Rosa and me so much joy, I will never be able to repay you."

When he pulled away, Bass could see Mateo was crying unashamedly. Now Scratch did not feel so bad for weeping himself.

"What's the end, old friend?" Mateo inquired at last, his voice crackling with emotion. "Is a fella to be chased down by Injuns all his natural days? Wagh! I'm one getting old, Scratch. Getting old and feeling more and more how fortunate I am to have a pretty woman's face around my lodge for the backside of my days."

Scratch nodded, and swiped at his nose. "Ahhh, them were the times we shared, old man. Them were the times when we first come to these here mountains on the top of the world, an' beaver were better'n six dollars the plew—be it old cow or just a kit. Them times is past, I know, Mateo. But, I ain't never been big up on a stick—never been nothin' but a mountain trapper. That's what I am, who I am. I'll be trappin' the big rats on the day I die—an' not by chance. I'll be doin' it by choice."

"Yes, old friend," Mateo nodded wistfully, looking back across the years. "We did all the waters clear from the Red River of the North, buggered by them durn Britishers, all the way south to the warm waters of the Heeley, down to this Spanish country for sure. Our kind gloried to see the old days on the Arkansas and the Platte and the Yellowstone and the Musselshell. We seen it all, old friend. We seen all the sights there was to see in them days gone by, Scratch."

"Lots of them what we shared a fire with are gone now, Mateo. It sure does this ol' nigger's heart good to see your face is pink with life just like a newborn buffler calf's behind. Too, too many's scattered their bones upon the prairie, got their flints fixed one way or t'other, but very few done in by the hand of murderin' Injuns. Most probably rubbed out 'cause they didn't get out of the mountains when they should've got."

"Y-you ever think of coming down here to this country to settle in, Scratch—you and the whole family—you know you've always got a place to be with friends here."

"Mateo, I truly thank you, old friend. Cain't thank you both enough." His gaze went east while that narrow strip of gray at the mountains was turning a vivid red streaked with flakes of orange as the sun came rising up out of the eastern bowels of the earth. "Offhand, I cain't really think of a thing right now short of the Judgement Day itself what'd make this child come down out of the mountains an' live with a passel of whitefolks who look at a old trapper like me with their wide muling eyes an' their disgusted looks. I appreciate your offer, but I just ain't fit to spend out the rest of my days at a table eatin' Meskin brownberries for food. Not while there's buffler still in the mountains. Plumb again' nature to leave hump an' go feed on hog. Lord help me, Mateo—but I gotta go on tastin' the free life."

"I understand the way you feel, friend," Mateo nodded knowingly, years ago having made the sad decision to give up the wandering life himself and settle down in Taos. "You're just a homeless spirit who's all too much at home in the wilderness awandering."

Bass knew he was indeed like a fleck of iron ore, drawn without any control, pulled with no hope of holding back by the force of some powerful magnetism to the lodestone of those high and lonesome places of the far western mountains. Too long ago to remember, the old trapper had learned to accept who he was, what he was inside. Some things would never be explained to a man, mere mortal that he be. That much he had learned. Some things could not be explained. Some things were only left for a man to accept.

There was no other choice for a man of his cloth to make. There was nothing else like that special feel of the vast distances and those high, sky places his eye could soar across in the upcountry. There simply was nothing to compare with that singular feeling he had course through his veins every now and then over the past ten years as he would amble his way across some brand spanking new country. Deep inside him each time burned that raw, born fresh feeling that told him it was just like he was plopping his foot down here the very next day after the Lord His Own Self had created that very place for Titus Bass and his kind alone. As far as his eye could see, there would be no sign of man to mar the view.

He stared at the mountains for a long moment, these Sangre de Cristos brooding under the new light of day in an unfolding vision of a million years long ago.

"Sometimes, Mateo," he mused as he ran a hand under his drippy nose, "sometimes up there in those high, lonesome places, it's almost like I'm nothin' more'n a clean wisp of air—an' no one can lay a hand on me. Almost like the years don't matter any more. Like I ain't so damned old any longer."

"I know the feeling, Scratch. I know."

"Just what is it you two know, Mateo?"

Bass and Kinkead wheeled at the sound of Josiah's voice. He was pulling on his blue capote at the same time he was hobbling along in untied moccasins and swiping away at eyes still gummy with last night's sleep.

"Do you know you were going to let this old bastard take off this morning without me—without us?" Josiah's arm circled Looks Far Woman's shoulders, as she held an armful of sleepy Joshua Paddock. She went immediately to huddle and whisper with Rosa and Waits-by-the-Water.

"W-why—"

"You was fixing to take off on me again, old man?"

"This time I was, Josiah," his voice cracked and he swallowed around the hard lump choking him.

"Run off and leave me behind, eh?"

"It's where you belong, son."

"Oh, so you just up and decided that yourself, did you now?"

"No, Josiah." Bass shook his head and felt the bitter sting of salty tears at his eyes once more. "You decided that some time ago. Even before we left here to skedaddle back east for a visit."

"Y-you knowed that long ago I was thinking about staying on in Taos?"

The old trapper nodded and forced a brave smile. Paddock rushed into him and crushed the old man with a frantic hug, ended by beating Titus on the back.

"I figured you were trying to tell me you knew—in your own peculiar way. Y-you know you could always stay here with us, we'll all do just—"

"I could do this! I could do that! Jumpin' Jehoshaphat! Everyone's got enough to worry about—what without worryin' about Titus Bass! By the Devil's backside, with all the 'coulds' you folks think up for me, my poor mind gets sorely bumfuzzled. Hell, with all the 'coulds' you all bring up for me to try—I might as well sprout wings an' try to fly, young'un."

He scooped up Josiah's hand and clamped it between his two old, gnarled, mountain-scarred ones. The gesture was one of an aged, gentle embrace.

"But, let's just forget me stayin' on here, son. Mateo's tried his best to talk me into it for certain. Yet, it appears you've finally found yourself a home." His eyes danced around Kinkead's tidy spread. "I'm proud of you. Truly I am. Glad as can be, the truth of it be known. A home right here. Mayhaps somewhere on down the trail that's exactly what we're all huntin' for, Josiah. I just reckon you've run onto your home sooner'n this old child has. Mayhaps for the time bein', my home simply ain't in one place."

Bass turned slightly, still clutching the young man's hand in a combination of something between a grizzly's grip and a loving embrace. "There's too much country left to see up there at the top of the world, son. An' I gotta see as much of it as I can to fill the rest of my days before all them owl-eyed white women an' the Bible squawkers get their muley hands on that country an' lay down laws about 'Thou Shalt Nots.' Up there, son, things is all so much more simple than their kind will ever come to appreciate. In the mountains, only a few things are forbidden. Only a few things a man shan't do. Everything else, why—you can do it, free as you please. But, down here in the settlements, there's only a few things you can do. Everything else is again' the law. An' that fact makes it again' my nature, Josiah."

Paddock finally wrenched his hand free so he could bring Bass's face back round to look into his eyes. "Scratch, I know what you are—who you have been all along, since—since that first day you began to save me. It—it—"

"Just ain't for you, I know."

"There's a fickle, fickle bitch called fate out there in that world, old friend." Paddock shook his head. "And, I can't escape the nagging feeling that I've tempted her all I trust to tempt."

"Mayhaps, Josiah Paddock is dead center on the truth of it this time."

"I haven't ever been one to get down on my prayer bones and sashay up to the Lord a lot, Scratch. You know that for a fact. So, I'm wanting to quit my pulling on a trigger and give my family all I can give them now."

"I—I'm glad you're tired of the killin', Josiah. Takin' another man's life don't ever make for a soft pillow at night. All too often the price of my own life's been takin' some other man's life. But, I still gotta take that bit of sour clabber along with all the good that's still waitin' for me up there in the hills. I don't know for certain, but common sense tells me that a bird put in a cage will soon forget how to sing. Son, Titus Bass ain't ready to forget how to sing just yet."

"I don't know as yet what I'm gonna do here, Scratch."

"So, I got that figured out for you, Josiah Paddock." Bass slapped a hand atop the young man's shoulder, swallowing hard at the hot coal in his throat. Some of the words were damned hard to get around it. "You have Mateo find you a lil' shop where you can go to work makin' a livin' off these Meskins an' whatever mountain wanderer rides down into Taos."

"H-how—"

"You hush, I'll tell you." Scratch's head bobbed forward. "Over in the shed yonder, there's a whole rendezvous supply of lead an' powder an' beads an' shinies—foofaraw every pound of it. It's all your'n to sell an' trade so to put food on your family's table, Josiah Paddock. This too."

The old trapper pulled from his sash the pouch of coins he plopped into Josiah's palm. In it was Cooper's money, for so long owed Titus Bass.

"W-what about you?" Josiah was beginning to have trouble talking, sobs choking the words in the back of his throat.

"I'll fare well, son. Always have. The three of us don't need all that much. Got a rendezvous to be goin' to in a couple of moons. 'Bout enough time to make it— see some old faces I ain't seen in a long time now. Show off this new lil' girl of ours to Frye Teeter an' Jarrell Thornburgh. Show 'em what a pretty girl child this ugly old man made for himself."

"You—you tell them two fellas—"

"Josiah, time was you an' me tramped down some hard trails together. Ain't nothin' ever gonna change the fact you come with me on the hardest trace I've ever made—to settle a ten-year-old score. You chose to ride beside me on that trail. So, nothin' ever gonna change that fact, or how I feel for you, son. Nothin' in the world gonna change my feelin' for you. Understand?"

He waited until Josiah wiped at his eyes and nodded his head. "Good. 'Cause friendship sometimes is just like havin' one mind in two bodies. We had that for a time, Josiah Paddock. One mind in our two bodies. But, when them two friends ain't of the like mind no more, it don't make all that much sense in keepin' the bodies together. Ain't no shame at all in any of that. We're both growed men an' gotta come to accept what must be."

"What about your plews, Scratch? Why aren't you taking them to rendezvous with you?"

"I'm leavin' 'em here for you to sell."

"They ain't all mine. Better than half are yours."

"Sell 'em to Tuttle. You tell him they're mine, an' he'll give you a good dollar on 'em, Josiah. He's bound to. Then you'll have plenty of hard cash to buy a heap more trade goods when the traders come in from Missouri with their plunder. I figure I taught you how to be a shrewd trader, workin' on them clerks up to rendezvous. Ahhh, you'll do just fine as a shopkeeper. You was one once a'time after all."

"J-just a clerk," Josiah stammered, unsure about it all. "Never had my own place before."

"So it's time you did somethin' on your own hook, Josiah Paddock. Quit hangin' onto me an' get out on your own." It sounded a wee bit more brusque than he had wanted it to, but there—his words were already spilled, out and said for the boy's sake.

"I don't—"

"Dammit, son! You know sign. I know you do 'cause I taught you my own self. Now, Josiah, you just gotta realize offhand or on a rest, Ezra Paddock's son will make 'em come. You will fare well an' prosper here, my friend. You'll fare well."

"Maybe—ahhh, damn. I haven't ever been all that much Ezra Paddock's son, Scratch. Maybe, just maybe it was Ezra Paddock who sired the boy. B-but, it was Titus Bass who sired the man Josiah Paddock became."

He pushed himself into the old trapper again, crushing Bass within his huge, muscular arms before drawing back a step from Scratch.

"N-never knowed you f-felt that strong for me, son."

"I did—always did. Just never had the guts to tell you before, old man. You were like the pappy I never had, down deep inside of me where lives what I am. You were the first one to really care about me, about me making mistakes and growing up. It's all because of you that I finally grew up. And Josiah Paddock the man can't let you ride off without some of those prime plews we trapped together. You'll need some of all this money you're giving—"

"What the hell do I need with money, Josiah? Got all what I need to get me through to rendezvous an' then on to Absorkee land where I'll hunker down for my fall hunt with Rotten Belly's folks. This child don't need all that much, really. I just got me the Indian fault of seein' happy in most everything. Way I reckon it, I don't need me much from down here. Everything else is right on the land, son. The trail I take through this life is a one way ride. Ain't no round trip for any of us that I've heard tell of in life. An' Titus Bass is certain as sun there ain't gonna be no pockets on my funeral shroud. Ain't takin' no money with me when I go to meet my Maker."

Something inside Mateo suddenly twitched. He knew just how superstitious some men of the western mountains could be, and how uncannily accurate some were at calling their own fate. "You—you aren't ready to meet that Maker—soon—are you, Scratch?"

"Wagh!" Bass snorted loudly with derision into the new pink air of dawn. "God's blood no. I ain't the least bit ready. Just look at them two." He flung an arm out at his woman and their daughter in the midst of Rosa and Looks Far, all hugging and kissing and whispering in excited woman chatter. "Why, I got me so damned much to live for, I can't wait to get back home into our mountains again."

"Just the way you was talking there, I thought—"

"When I die, it won't be down in no town, Mateo. Just like my old brother man Rotten Belly has told me many a time: it's best to be killed out in the open, right smack-dab under the biggest sky you can find. Only that a-way, says he, the ones-with-wings can eat on your dryin' flesh an' the winds can sigh over your bones an' blow through 'em to make them ol' bones pure for all that time left to come on earth. Yes," he nodded and scuffled a moccasin toe across the new grass in the yard beneath his feet. "Here is this new green to blanket the earth of those open spaces under the big skies. The old Earth Mother covers everythin', an' one day she will cover me, too."

"So, you're leaving me to take this gamble on my own now. Is that it, Scratch?"

Bass turned to face Josiah again. "This ain't a gamble, son. You'll fare well at it. You got the makin's of a success right inside you—I seen that from the start, right off. Most men are losers. Fewer still are winners like you're gonna be, Josiah Paddock."

"And—what are you, Scratch?"

"Me?" he chuckled. "Why, my friends—I ain't all that worried about bein' a winner or a loser. I'm just content about bein' a part of what is each day. I only know I'll probably run out of days long before I'll run out of wild mountains to roam."

"I'm comin'! I'm comin' 'long straight-away, Mr. Titus!" They all wheeled to watch the black man shuffle along the side of the huge house, holding up his britches as he attempted to tie the drawstring around his waist. Beneath his arm were his moccasins, stuffed there in his hurry. He was barefoot in the dew-fresh spring grass, its dampness cold beneath his feet.

"Don'cha forget me now!"

"Ain't a need in skedaddlin', Esau. I'm leavin' you right here." The words were brisk, but not sharp. Nevertheless, they brought the ex-slave up short.

"Y-you leavin' me here? Wh-wha' I'm gonna—"

"I'm leavin' you here, Esau—with your friend Josiah. He's gonna need someone to give him a hand." Bass watched Mateo and Paddock turn round to stare at him. "Someone he can count on with his new shop he'll be busy openin' up soon."

"Sh-shop? I—I don't know nothin', Mr. Titus—Mr. Josiah—I don't know nothin' about workin' in no shop."

Bass chuckled softly at first, then stepped up to slap a broad hand on the black man's shoulder before yanking the ex-slave into a tight, surprising embrace.

"Esau," Scratch finally relented and stepped back, both hands still on the man's shoulders, "you'll do just fine. You're that same man what rode straight up an' go ahead at them Pawnee warriors back a couple of moons ago, ain't you?"

Bass watched the black man nod.

"An' you're the same one who said you'd rather have a go at all that prairie in winter by your own damned self rather than be handed over to the Pawnee?"

"Y-yes, I was, truly."

"Then, a man such as you ain't nobody's boy any longer, Esau. You ain't a slave to no man. You an' Josiah here, you'll make do like you was partners. I'm givin' you both the fixin's to make a start at a good life for yourselves here in Taos. It's up to the two of you to make a go of it from here on out."

"Why—I don't know what all to say—" Esau's eyes dropped shyly to the ground.

"What's the matter, son? Got you a mouthful of hornets an' you cain't spit 'em out? C'mon, friend—man's got to get his words out an' said." Bass flicked a look back to Josiah for a moment. "Time comes when a colt needs a chance to kick up some sweet earth an' taste him some fresh, spring grass. When I first met you, Esau—you plain didn't know your ass from your earhole. But you learn't, an' you learn't fast. Both of you are gonna do well. You got the makin's for it—for whatever you both wanna do with your lives here on out."

Almost simultaneously, Josiah and Esau dove into the old trapper, almost bowling him over. The three of them were quickly joined by Mateo, all four men blubbering and crying at this moment in their time together. At last, Bass drew away a step and pointed out that horse he had saddled with the special gift Josiah had given him for his fortieth birthday.

"Someday, have Josiah tell you what he an' Mateo had to put up with just to get that saddle for me, Esau." He nudged the black man toward the horse. "But, for now, I want you to get used to ridin' with a saddle an' I don't ever wanna hear of you usin' them spurs on this lil' gal you rode halfway cross't the flat prairie world with me to get you down here to Taos. You hear me, Esau? No spurs on her."

"Y-you givin' me your horse an'—an' your saddle, too, Mr. Titus?"

"Yes, son—I am. They're yours now. I ain't got a need for either one as you can see. An', frankly, you'll be needin' somethin' to ride back an' forth into town to that lil' shop you fellas is gonna make a go at."

"I don't know what I can he'p Mr. Josiah out w—"

"Esau," Bass instructed, "a fella doesn't get a chance to win many big pots at the card table unless he hangs his bare ass over the fire once't in a while. So, I'm countin' on you two — Josiah an' you both—to stay in that game until the last raise of the night has been plopped down on the table an' the last call has been made. Only way you two will make it here on out in life is to go on out an' make it happen."

"I won't ever forget what you said about him back to Bents' Fort, old man." Josiah sniffled and put up a brave smile as he looped an arm over the black man's shoulders.

"What was that, son?" Bass trudged over to his pony and stuffed a left foot in the stirrup to raise himself onto leather.

"You told that clerk up at Bents' that Esau was a free man. By God, he was a free man."

Bass stared down at the shining, ebony face, tears glistening in pink tracks down his cheeks as the new sun broke over the purple mountains to the east with a thin lip of brilliant yellow. "Esau ain't ever been a slave to my way of thinkin', Josiah. The man pulled himself up an' did what he had to do in gettin' away from them Pawnee. No slave would ever do that. A big, big man got away from that killers' camp."

"I—I just thought of somethin', Mr. Josiah." Esau brought his eyes down from the old trapper to meet Paddock's. "A free man's always got him a Christian name an' a last name."

"What's yours, Esau?" Josiah requested. "I've never known."

" 'Cause I've never had me no last name before." He flicked his eyes up toward the old man in the saddle. "But, if you don't mind, I wanna take one that's real special to me, one I'll keep for the rest of my natural-borned life. I want folks here 'bouts now to call me Esau Bass."

"I—I'd be plenty proud." Titus barely got the words out around the hard knot choking him. He stuck his hand down to the black man, crushing Esau's fingers in the powerful grip of his own roughened paw. The moment of leaving this place, of drawing away from his friends and those who had truly become his family — leaving all of that behind suddenly swelled fat with thoughts he could not put to words.

The hot coal burned in his throat as he took up Samantha's lead rope and nudged her toward the adobe gate that would lead his little family up the road and beyond.

"Man's got to have him a dream all his own. Maybeso for others, it's down here—an' that's all right for them. I ain't makin' no judgment on it. But, as for Titus Bass, his dream's still up there in all the high places, waitin' for me, somewhere up there in all that lonesome wanderin' I've still left to do. Out there, somewhere."

Suddenly he drew up and reined full round so he could shout back to those friends, that family he was leaving behind.

"It ain't the last you've heard tell of me."

His tear-stung eye roamed over the mountains flecked with sunlight as a bright beam suddenly broke over the peaks and hit him square in the face. In his voice rose the haunting echo of a wilderness never to be tamed.

"This ain't the last you've heard of Titus Bass!"

Taos and the Fur Trade

THE SPANISH RECORDED visits by at least four parties of French trappers entering New Mexico between 1749 and 1752. Government officials confiscated their merchandise and made it as difficult as possible for the traders to return to Louisiana. Many were the fantastic tales of those Spanish settlements in the southwest. Cloaked in the ages-old formula of a quest, a sojourn to those New Mexican provinces involved a waterless journey across burning deserts before reaching the beauty of those valleys where Santa Fe and Taos citizens awaited the traders' arrival. The reports of confiscation of trade goods, physical abuse, imprisonment in rat-infested cells before being abandoned to their own devices at the Mexican frontier with instructions never to return to Spanish lands—none of it deterred the hearty entrepreneurs who would venture a substantial capital gain. The possibility of riches was always accompanied by some risk. And in the settlements of Santa Fe and Taos lay the prospect of great riches and wealth.

Louisiana became part of the United States and President Jefferson dispatched Lewis and Clark to explore the unknown west of the northern mountains. Meanwhile, private enterprise had already heard of the fertile prospects that lay in the lands of New Spain to the southwest. Independent entrepreneurs began to finger out into the great expanse of the southern mountains that belonged to Spain. Jacques Clamorgan and three other Frenchmen, along with a slave, completed the unthinkable. They had actually made it to Santa Fe by way of the Pawnee villages along the Platte River. It was there they were placed under arrest in December of 1807 and sent to Chihuahua, the Spanish capital, for imprisonment. For some strange reason, Clamorgan and his group were mysteriously allowed to sell their attractive wares. With those New World trade goods sold to an eager market, the prisoners were allowed to return to St. Louis following the route they had come out by.

From St. Louis next came three Americans to make their first attempt at trade with the foreign land. Joseph McLanahan, Reuben Smith and James Patterson headed into Comanche country with packs brimming full of trade goods. Along with a Spanish guide picked up along the way, Emanuel Blanco, and two Negro servants escaping the monotony of St. Louis, the party was discovered by a Spanish patrol near the Red River in 1810. They were arrested, removed to Santa Fe and eventually taken on to Chihuahua where they languished in prison until late in 1812. Finally the Americans were allowed to go free on promise never to return to Mexico.

Word traveled fast even across that painful expanse of the early far west. From mouth to mouth the tales were recited over and over again around the barroom tables in St. Louis watering holes. The possibility of Santa Fe and Taos trade caught the imaginations of those fur traders who heretofore had as their main objective the trapping of beaver along the upper rivers. Manuel Lisa, never one to put all his eggs in one basket, decided to test the Spanish waters. A Spaniard by birth himself, Lisa dispatched Jean Baptiste Champlain on a trading expedition to the Arapahos, who were probably on the Arkansas in that year of 1811. The waters of commerce proved warm, and as yet, undisturbed.

The next year Lisa dispatched a second party to penetrate farther into New Spain. This trading group, led by a man named Lafarge, made it all the way to Santa Fe in the early summer of 1812, about the time a small group of enterprising Americans showed up. Robert McKnight, James Baird and Samuel Chambers were taken prisoner by Spanish officials at the same time Lisa's men were captured, all confined in one Mexican city, then another until 1820.

The Spanish government of Mexico was gravely concerned with stemming this onrushing tide of American traders. It would do everything it could to keep the foreigners out of the far flung provinces of Santa Fe and Taos.

If the Spanish trade could not be tapped at the moment, at least the southern mountains could be. The wealthy traders of St. Louis soon realized there was more than one way into the mountains. The Missouri River was not the only route to fur wealth. Many of Lisa's men had ranged far to the south already, after initially ascending the muddy Missouri.

That large party of Lisa men under Champlain had already spent the fall and winter of 1811–1812 trapping the waters far up the Arkansas River. Under constant harassment from Indians interested in giving the Americans a less-than-hearty welcome to the southern mountains, the brigade returned to the Platte River by June, 1812, and there disbanded. They had already heard from Indian sources that Lisa's fort had "broke up," the Spaniard and his men having headed back to St. Louis. Lisa had, in fact, abandoned the post built at the Three Forks and the news of that retreat from the upper river had spread like prairie fire among the inhabitants of the Rocky Mountains.

Champlain, along with nine others, including the American, Ezekiel Williams, chose to head back for the upper Arkansas, perhaps still in hopes of tapping something of the Spanish trade. During the fall of 1812, the small party was continually harassed by Indians until only three survived. Champlain, a "Porteau," and Williams wintered with friendly Arapahos on the upper Arkansas. By early spring, it seemed Ezekiel was ready to quit his companions. In March, 1813, he cached his wealth in furs, and put a small dugout into the waters of the Arkansas, setting out alone for civilization, his companions apparently dead by that time.

Back in Missouri country, Williams quickly interested two men in a partnership with his stories of his cache of furs. In May, 1814, Braxton Cooper and Morris May left the Booneslick area of Missouri with Williams to recover that beaver fur left behind. Tagging along, under the direction of the veteran Williams was a party of eighteen Frenchmen under Joseph Philibert. Ezekiel retrieved his cache of beaver and with it returned to the settlements of Missouri. The Frenchmen continued on to the upper reaches of the Arkansas River.

News had already spread quickly that another band of foreigners was invading Spanish territory. Reacting just as quickly, the Governor of New Mexico dispatched 250 army regulars to capture what remained of Philibert's brigade.

Their merchandise and the beaver they had already trapped were seized, the men allowed to leave Spanish land unharmed.

Undaunted, Philibert decided to have another go at those riches of the southern mountains. In September of that same year, 1814, he joined forces with powerful St. Louis money and started west once more. Auguste P. Chouteau and Jules de Mun augmented Philibert's own trapping party as they ascended the upper Arkansas. With the tall, blue mountains of the front range in sight, they chanced upon an independent group of four American trappers who had left St. Louis just three days before the Chouteau-de Mun party had embarked. Caleb Greenwood, a former Lisa man himself, led those American trappers, working their way into the southern mountains. Into those foothills of the front range, Chouteau and de Mun laid plans to penetrate the mountains to the north in order to secure trade with the Crows at a time that tribe was believed to be at the headwaters of the Columbia River. Had Spanish soldiers not found the Chouteau-de Mun brigade, confiscated their beaver pelts and trade goods, sending the party back east, these intrepid Frenchmen from St. Louis just might have crossed on over to the Colorado River basin many years before General William H. Ashley led the American parade to that part of the country in 1824.

Two who would later become Taos residents, Etienne Provost and Francois LeClerc, acquired their first view of New Mexican lands along with the Chouteau-de Mun party. These two French trappers would become some of the first fur hunters to work out of New Mexico when Spain gave up that realm in 1821. Provost led many an expedition across the Colorado River drainage, on one early journey running all the way into the Wasatch Mountains where he bumped into Peter Skene Ogden and a large brigade of Hudson's Bay Company trappers working out of Fort Vancouver.

News that New Mexico had fallen from Spanish hands in 1821 reached young American ears up and down the Mississippi and Missouri Rivers. Hoping now the new government would more readily welcome foreign trade and trapping, many Americans set out for the northern provinces of the new country. William Becknell took a large group with him from Missouri, trapped a small fortune in pelts, then set out for home in the fall of 1822. He left behind better than twenty men who had decided to remain in the southern Rockies to trap. Two of those who stayed in New Mexico would later help form the vanguard of American influence in the fledgling country. The gangly young carpenter from Tennessee, Ewing Young, and the Kentucky-born marksman William Wolfskill would later lead their own notable invasions of the Colorado River basin.

It was two years after the 1822 Issac Slover party had penetrated the southern Rockies that the first grand assault on those mountains began in earnest. The year 1824 represented a watershed of American efforts in the northern area of this foreign land. One such brigade was led by Thomas L. Smith, then only 23 years old and not yet wearing his famous pegleg.

By October of 1824, Etienne Provost and Francois LeClerc had pushed into the Wasatch region at the head of a significant expedition to tap the riches of Mexican territory. By the waters of what later became the Mormons' Jordon River, the brigade bumped into a large band of Shoshone under chief "Bad Gocha." The Snake headman invited Provost and his trappers to lay down their arms and smoke the pipe of peace. It was the last thing eight of the party would ever do. Only Etienne and one other trapper survived the slaughter. Provost would later blame the Hudson's Bay Company for inflaming the Indians to butcher the American trappers pushing into territory hitherto roamed solely by the British interests. In fact, Peter Skene Ogden later reported to his superiors in the HBC that the Snakes had blindly retaliated against the Americans because a Hudson's Bay man had killed a Shoshone chieftain in an unfortunate squabble. To the Snakes, white skin was white skin. No matter what nationality, a white man's hair would look good on a Shoshone scalp pole. Animosity flared again between British and American trappers as they parried and thrust across the western drainages of the central and southern Rocky Mountains.

In April, 1828, the Mexican National Congress meeting in Mexico City finally legislated tough, specific conditions under which a foreigner could become a Mexican citizen, and thereby lawfully trap Mexican territory. Replacing a vague and unworkable governmental decree that allowed American trappers free run of Mexican waters since 1823, the new law took special notice of those Americans moving in and out through northern New Mexico. The legislation stated that now a foreigner had to reside in Mexico two years prior to applying for citizenship. In addition, the foreigner must become a Roman Catholic, be employed in gainful industry and be "well-behaved."

Watching one's manners had always been an insurmountable task for American frontiersmen. They came to Santa Fe, more often to Taos, for the same diversions they sought at rendezvous. Whiskey and women drew the southern mountain trappers like bees to honey. Taos beckoned. In fact, by 1833 one Santa Fe official had bitterly complained about two American trappers who had been ordered to leave New Mexico immediately due to their "bad behavior." The Santa Fe official informed his own superiors in Chihuahua that the two trappers had instead taken off for a nearby Taos where, it was commonly known, gathered " . . . various foreigners who do not conduct themselves very well."

Wine, whiskey and dark-skinned women were the honey. Taos was the hive.

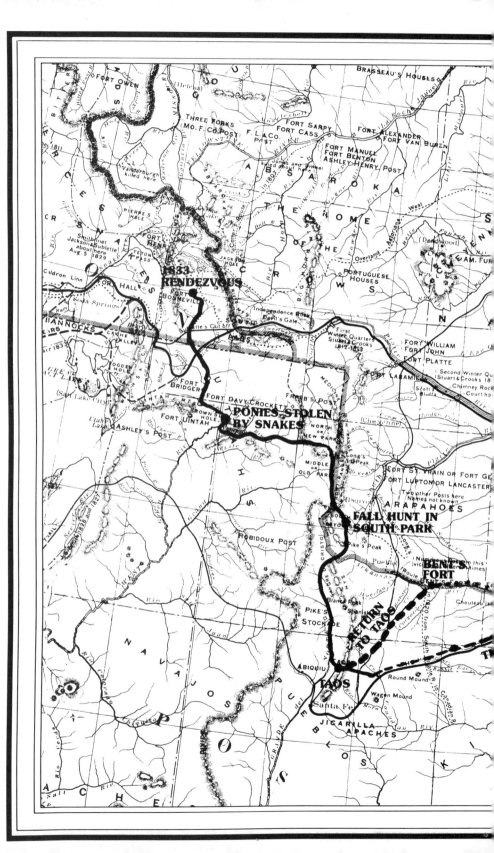